CRISIS FOUR

Also by Andy McNab

Non-fiction
BRAVO TWO ZERO
IMMEDIATE ACTION

Fiction
REMOTE CONTROL

CRISIS FOUR

ANDY McNAB

BANTAM PRESS

LONDON · NEW YORK · TORONTO · SYDNEY · AUCKLAND

TRANSWORLD PUBLISHERS
61–63 Uxbridge Road, London W5 5SA
a division of The Random House Group Ltd

RANDOM HOUSE AUSTRALIA PTY LTD
20 Alfred Street, Milsons Point, NSW 2061, Australia

RANDOM HOUSE NEW ZEALAND
18 Poland Road, Glenfield, Auckland, New Zealand

RANDOM HOUSE SOUTH AFRICA (PTY) LTD
Endulini, 5a Jubilee Road, Parktown 2193, South Africa

Published 1999 by Bantam Press
a division of Transworld Publishers
Copyright © Andy McNab 1999

A catalogue record for this book is available from the British Library

ISBN 0593 042379 (cased)
ISBN 0593 045513 (tpb)

Typeset in 11/13pt Palatino by Falcon Oast Graphic Art
Printed in Great Britain
by Clays Ltd, St Ives plc.

1 3 5 7 9 10 8 6 4 2

In memory of Edward C.S. Hooper
30 October 1979–15 April 1999

CRISIS FOUR

OCTOBER 1995

Monday 16 October 1995

The Syrians don't fuck around if they think you're invading their air space. Within minutes of crossing the border, your aircraft will be greeted by a three-ship intercept, flying so close you can wave at the pilots. They won't wave back; they've come to get a visual ID on you, and if they don't like what they see they'll hose you down with their air-to-air missiles.

The same rule doesn't apply, of course, when friendly commercial aircraft blip onto their radar screens, and that was why our team of four had opted for this particular method of infiltration. If Damascus had had the slightest clue about what was about to happen aboard our British Airways flight from Delhi to London, their fighters would have been scrambled the moment the Boeing 747 left Saudi Arabian territory.

I was twisting and turning, trying to get comfortable, feeling jealous of all the people sitting upstairs behind the driver, probably on their fifth gin and tonic since take off, watching their second movie and tucking into their third helping of *boeuf en croute*.

Reg 1 was in front of me. Six feet two, and built like a brick shithouse, he was probably having an even worse time in the cramped conditions. His curly black hair, going a bit grey at the sides, was all over the place. Like me, before I left in '93, he had been selected to do work for the intelligence and security services, including the sort of job for the US that Congress would never sanction. I had done similar jobs myself while in the Regiment, but this was the first I'd been on since becoming a K. Given who we were going in against, none of us was giving odds on whether we'd get to do another.

I glanced across at Sarah, to my right in the semi-darkness. Her eyes were closed, but even in the dim light I could see she wasn't looking her happiest. Maybe she just didn't like flying without complimentary champagne and slippers.

It had been a while since I'd last seen her, and the only thing about her that had changed was her hair. It was still very straight, almost South-East Asian, though dark brown, not black. It had always been short, but she'd prepared for this operation by having it cut into a bob with a fringe. She had strong, well-defined features, with large brown eyes above high cheekbones, a nose that was slightly too large, and a mouth that nearly always looked too serious. Sarah would not be troubled in her old age by laughter lines. When it was genuine, her smile was warm and friendly, but more often it appeared to be only going through the motions. And yet, just when you were thinking this, she'd find the oddest thing amusing and her nose would twitch, and her whole face would crease into a radiant, almost childlike, grin. At times like that she looked even more beautiful than usual – maybe too beautiful. That was sometimes a danger in our line of work, as men could never resist a second glance, but at thirty-five years of age she had learned to use her looks to her advantage within the service. It made her even more of a bitch than most people thought she was.

It was no good, I couldn't get comfortable. We'd been on the aircraft for nearly fifteen hours and my body was starting to ache. I turned and tried the left side. I couldn't see Reg 2, but I knew he was to my left in the gloom somewhere. He was easy to distinguish from Reg 1, being the best part of a foot shorter and with hair that looked like a fistful of dark-blond wire wool. The only thing I knew about them apart from their zap numbers was that, like me, they had both been circumcised within the last three weeks and that, like mine, their underwear came from Tel Aviv. And that was all I wanted to know about them, or about Regs 3 to 6 who were already in-country, waiting for us – even though one of them, Glen, was an old friend.

I found myself facing Sarah again. She was rubbing her eyes with her fists, like a sleepy child. I tried to doze off; thirty minutes later I was still kidding myself I was asleep when I got a kick on the back of my legs. It was Sarah.

I sat up in my sleeping bag and peered into the semi-darkness. Three loadies (load masters) were moving around with orienteering torches attached to their heads, glowing a dim red so as not to destroy our night vision. Each of them had an umbilical cord trailing from his face mask, and their hands moved instinctively to make sure it didn't get snagged or detached from the aircraft's oxygen supply.

I unzipped the bag and, even through my all-weather sniper suit, immediately felt the freezing cold in the unpressurized 747 cargo hold. None of the passengers or cabin crew would have known there were people down here, tucked away in the belly of the aircraft. Nor would our names have appeared anywhere on a manifest.

I folded the bag in half, leaving inside the two 'aircrew bags' I'd filled during the flight – plastic bags with a one-way valve which you insert yourself into and piss away to your heart's content. I wondered how Sarah had been getting on. It was bad enough for me because my cock was still extremely sore, but it must be hard being female aircrew on a long flight with a device designed only for males – or the female commander of a deniable op. I put a Post-It on my mental bulletin board, reminding myself to ask her how she got round the problem. That was if we survived, of course, and were still on speaking terms.

I could never remember which was starboard or port; all I knew was that, as you looked at the aircraft from the front, we were in the small hold at the rear and the door was on the left-hand side. I clutched my oxygen tube as a loadie crossed over it,

13

and adjusted my mask as his leg caught it, pulling it slightly from my face. The inside was wet, clammy and cold now the seal had been broken.

I picked up my Car 15, a version of the M16 Armalite 5.56mm with a telescopic butt and a shorter barrel, cocked it and applied the safety. The Car had a length of green paracord tied to it like a sling; I strapped it over my left shoulder so the barrel faced down and it ran along the rear of my body. The rig (parachute) would go over that.

I pushed my hand under the sniper suit to get hold of the Beretta 9mm that was on a leg holster against my right thigh. I cocked that, too, and pulled back the topslide a few millimetres to check chamber. Turning the weapon so it caught one of the loadies' red glows, I saw the glint of a correctly fed round, ready to go.

This was my first 'false flag' job posing as a member of Israeli special forces, and as I adjusted my leg straps I wished I'd had a little more time to recover from the circumcision. It hadn't healed as quickly as we'd been told. I looked around me as we got our kit on, hoping the others were in as much pain.

We were about to carry out a 'lift' to find out what the West's new bogeyman, Osama Bin Laden, a Saudi multimillionaire turned terrorist, was getting up to in Syria. Satellite photography had shown earthmoving and other heavy equipment from Bin Laden's construction company near the source of the river Jordan. Downstream lay Israel, and if its main source of water was about to be dammed, diverted or otherwise tampered with, the West needed to know. They feared a repeat of the 1967 war, and with Bin Laden around it was never going to be a good day out. He hadn't been dubbed America's 'public enemy number one' by Clinton for nothing.

Our task was to lift Osama's right-hand man – known to us only as the 'Source' for op sec (operational security) reasons – from on site. His private jet had been spotted at a nearby airfield. The US needed to know what was happening in Syria, and, more to the point, maybe learn how to lay their hands on Osama. As the briefing guy had said, 'Bin Laden represents a completely new phenomenon: non-state-supported terrorism backed by an extremely rich and religiously motivated leader with an intense hatred of the West, mainly America, as well as Israel and the secular Arab world. He must be stopped.'

Once ready and checked by the loadies, it was just a question of holding on to the airframe and waiting. There was nothing to do for the next few minutes but daydream or get scared. Each of us was in his or her own little world now. Before any operation some people are frightened, some are excited. Now and again I could see reflections from the red torches in people's eyes; they were staring at their boots or at some other fixed point, maybe thinking about their wives, or girlfriends, or kids, or what they were going to do after this, or maybe even wondering what the fuck they were doing here in the first place.

Me, I didn't know what to think really. I'd never been able to get sparked up about the thought of dying and not seeing anyone else again. Not even my wife, when I was married. I always felt I was a gambler with nothing to lose. Most people who gamble do so with the things that are important to them; I gambled knowing that if I lost I wouldn't break the bank.

I watched the glowing redheads pack our kit away into the large aluminium Lacon boxes. Once we'd been thrown out and the door had closed again, they'd stow all other evidence that we had been there in the boxes and just sit it out until they were taken care of in London.

Two of the loadies started a sweep with their torch lights to make sure there was nothing loose which could be sucked out as soon as the door opened. Nothing must compromise this job.

We got the order to turn on our own oxygen, disconnect from the aircraft supply and stand by. Sarah was standing in front of Reg 1, who was to tandem jump with her. She had never failed to amaze me. She was an IG (Intelligence Group), the very top of the intelligence-service food chain, people who usually spend their lives in embassies, posing as diplomats. Their lives should be one long round of receptions and recruiting sources through the cocktail circuit, not running around, weapon strong. Then again, Sarah had always made a point of finishing the jobs herself.

She was masked and goggled up, looking for all the world as if she'd done this a thousand times. She hadn't; her first jump ever had been three weeks before, but she took her job so seriously that she'd probably read ten books on freefall and knew more facts and figures than all of us lot put together.

She turned and looked for me. We got eye-to-eye and I gave her an everything-is-OK nod. After all, that was part of this job, to look after her.

The loadie motioned us towards the door. Our bergens, each containing forty pounds of equipment, were hanging from our rigs and down the back of our legs. We waddled forward like a gaggle of geese, putting weight on each foot in turn. Thankfully the bergens hadn't needed to be fully laden. If everything went to plan, we'd only be on the ground for a few hours.

There was a pause of about five seconds as the loadie by the door spoke into his mike to the British Airways navigator, then he nodded to himself and swung into action. The door was about half the size of an average up-and-over garage door. Pulling out all the levers, he swung them anticlockwise, then pulled the handles towards him. Even though I had a helmet on, I heard the massive rush of air, and then a gale was thrashing at my sniper suit. Where the door had been there was now just a black hole. The tags on the aircraft's luggage containers fluttered frantically. The freezing cold wind whipped at the parts of my face that weren't covered by my mask. I pulled my jockey's goggles over my eyes, fighting against the blast, gripping hard on to the airframe.

Seven miles below us lay Syria – enemy territory. We did our final checks. I wanted to get this jump out of the way, get the job done and be in Cyprus for tea and toast tomorrow morning.

We rammed up close to each other at the exit, the roar of the wind and the jet engines so loud I could hardly think. At last came a handheld red light from the loadie. We all joined in with a loud scream: '*Red on, red on!*' I didn't know why, no-one could hear anything; it was just something we always did.

The loadie's light changed to green and he shouted, '*Green on!*'

He moved back as we all shouted to ourselves, '*Ready!*'

16

We rocked forward, trying to scream above the roar: '*Set!*'

Then we rocked back. '*Go!*'

Out and out we spilled, four people on three rigs, tumbling towards Syria. Being the last man, I was pushed by the loadie to make sure there wasn't too much of a gap between us in the sky.

You can now freefall from an aircraft flying at high altitude and miles from the target area and land with pinpoint accuracy. The HAHO (high altitude, high opening) technique calls for extreme weather clothing and oxygen equipment to survive temperatures as low as minus 40°C, especially when a fifty-mile cross-country descent can take nearly two hours. It has now largely replaced the old HALO (high altitude, low opening) approach, for the simple reason that, instead of hurtling towards the ground at warp speed, with no real idea of where you're going to land or where the rest of the team are once you're on the ground, you can glide gently onto the target sitting in a comfortable rig. Unless, of course, a man in a white coat has recently clipped a bit off the end of your cock.

I felt the jet stream pick me up and take me with it. As the aircraft thunders over you at 500 miles an hour you think you're going to collide with the tailplane, but in fact you're falling and never hit it.

Once I was out of the jet stream it was time to sort myself out. I could tell by the wind force, and the fact that I could see the aircraft lights flashing three or four hundred feet above me, that I was upside down. I spread my arms and legs and arched my back, banging myself over into a stable position.

I looked around – moving your head during freefall is about the only thing that doesn't have an effect on your stability – trying to see where everyone else was. I could just about see a figure over on my right-hand side; I didn't know who it was, and it didn't matter. As I looked up I saw the tail-lights of the 747 disappearing way above us, and downstairs, on the floor, there was nothing, I couldn't see a single light.

All I could hear was the rush of air; it was like sticking your head out of a car travelling at 120 mph. What I had to do now was

17

keep stable and wait for the AOD (automatic opening device) to do its bit. The drill is just to assume that it's going to work, but to get in the pull position just in case. I thought, Fuck that. I knew my pull height – 30,000 feet, an 8,000-foot drop. I moved my left hand up, just above my head, and my right hand down to the pull handle. There has to be symmetry with everything. If you're in freefall and just put one hand out, that will hit the air and you're going to tumble.

I could see the needle on my wrist alti. I was past 34,000. Instead of waiting to feel the pull of the AOD on the pin, I kept on looking at the alti, and bang on 30,000 feet I pulled the handle and pushed my hands up above my head, which made me backslide, which meant the air would catch the drogue chute to bring the main pack out. I felt it move and rock me slightly from side to side. Then bang – it's like running into a brick wall. You feel like one of those cartoon characters that's just been crushed with a rock.

I still wasn't particularly worried where everybody else was in the sky, I just wanted to sort myself out. I could hear another canopy cracking open, and I knew that it was near. I looked up to make sure I had a canopy rather than a big bag of washing above me. The middle three or four cells of the big mattress were full of air. I grabbed hold of the brake lines, the two handles attached to paracord on each side of the canopy, and ripped them from the velcro that held them in position on the webbing straps just above my shoulder and started pulling. There are seven cells to the canopy; by pumping you expose the end cells to air to quicken the process.

I had a look around me now, trying to find out where I was in relation to the others. Fuck, my cock hurt! The leg straps had worked their way further up my leg and it felt like someone was giving my dick a squeeze with a pair of pliers.

Above me I could see Sarah and Reg 1. I must have had a slow opening of the end cells, as they should have been below me. They were now spiralling past me, his right arm pulling the brake line down to get into his correct position in the stack. Sarah just hung there like a small child as he slotted in between me and

Reg 2, who was below me somewhere.

Being the last man in the stack, it was a piece of piss for me; I was just bringing up the rear. As long as I was directly above and just touching the rear of the canopy below me, I wasn't going to get lost, unless Reg 1 got lost with Sarah. Reg 1 would be doing the same to Reg 2, who was at the bottom; he'd be doing all the navigating and we'd just be checking. And if the worst came to the worst, we could actually shout to each other once we'd got off oxygen.

Reg 2 would be looking at the display on his sat nav (global positioning device, via satellite). All he wanted was one bar in the centre of the display. Technology is wonderful. We were travelling at about thirty-five knots; the canopy gives you twenty knots, and we were running with the wind, which was fifteen.

I checked my height – just over twenty-eight grand – good. Checked the sat nav, good. That was it. Everything was done: the oxygen was working, we were stacked. Time to get comfy. I got hold of the risers which attached the canopy to the rig, and pulled myself up and wiggled my legs to move the leg straps halfway down my thighs.

For the next thirty minutes we minced along the sky, controlling the rig, checking height and the sat nav. I started to see lights now. Small towns and villages with street lights following the roads out of the built-up areas for about half a mile, then darkness, only car lights giving away the road.

I looked at my altl. I was about 16,200 feet. I thought, I'll just go for a few more minutes and I'll take my oxygen mask off. The fucking thing was a pain in the arse. If I started feeling the effects of hypoxia, dizziness, I'd bring the mask back to my face and take a couple of deep breaths. By now I was just under 16 grand; my mouth was full of saliva and it felt all clammy. I got hold of the clip with my right hand and pulled the press stud off, and the thing just fell down and dangled by the left-hand side of my face.

I could feel the cold around my mouth where all the moisture from the mask had been. I was freezing, but it was nice; I could

19

stretch my mouth and chew my jaw around a bit.

After about ten minutes I checked my alti again: 6,500 feet, time to start working. I put on my NVG (night viewing goggles), which had been hanging round my neck on paracord, and started looking for the flash on an IR Firefly (infra-red detecting system). It was the same flashing light that you would expect to see on the top of a tall tower to warn aircraft, but these are just little hand-held things that throw out a brilliant quick flash of light, through an IR filter. No-one would see it apart from us – or anyone else with NVG, of course. I kept looking in the darkness. It would be easy to pick out. Bang – there it was to my half right.

We were coming in on finals. I was concentrating on keeping myself positioned right on top and to the rear of Reg 1's canopy, which was larger than mine as he had the extra weight to jump with. I heard him below me sounding like an infant-school teacher. 'Right, any minute now, keep your legs bent and under your hips. Are your legs bent?'

She must have acknowledged. I pulled the NVGs off my face and let them hang.

'OK, put your hands up by me.' I imagined her with her hands up, holding Reg 1's wrists on the brake lines to keep them out of the way so she didn't damage herself if they took a bad landing.

I couldn't see any ground yet – it was far too dark – but I heard: 'Standby, standby. Flaring soon . . . flaring . . . flaring . . .'

Then the sound of his bergen thumping into the ground, and his command to Sarah: 'Now!'

His canopy started to collapse below me as I flew past. My bergen was dangling by the straps from my feet; I kicked it off and it fell beneath me on a three-metre line. As soon as I heard it land, I flared too. Hitting the deck, I ran along for three or four steps, turned quickly and pulled my lines to collapse the canopy.

A body appeared behind me. Regs 3 to 6 had been on the ground for five days preparing the job and were manning the DZ (drop zone). Fuck knows how they'd inserted in-country, and I didn't care.

'You all right, mate?' I recognized his voice. Glen, the only one whose name I knew, was the ground commander. He looked as if you'd hear steely Clint Eastwood when he opened his mouth, but in fact what you got was softly spoken David Essex.

'Yeah. Fine, mate, fine.'

'Let's get all this shit off.'

Within minutes our rigs, sniper suits and oxygen kit had been stowed in large bin liners and we were aboard two Toyota Previas, the drivers wearing NVGs, bouncing along the desert floor, heading for a light industrial estate on the outskirts of a town less than a mile from the Golan Heights and the border with Israel. All of us were dressed the same, in green jump suits, with civilian clothes underneath as part of the E&E (escape and evasion) plan, plus belt kit and our own choice of boots. Mine were a pair of Nike hiking boots, which we'd checked were available in any Tel Aviv high street.

Glen and I went way back. We had done Selection together in the early Eighties, and had got to know each other later while chatting up the same woman, who was now his wife. He was the same age as me – late-thirties – had a swarthy Mediterranean look and a few moles on his face which were sprouting hair, and he always needed a shave. Constantly smiling, he was one of life's good guys – in love with his wife and two kids, in love with his job, probably even in love with his car and the cat. For the last five days they'd been preparing and placing an explosive attack on an electricity substation, which was going to close down the town while we hit the target, and I knew that Glen would have enjoyed every minute of it.

'We're at the drop-off point.'

If we had to talk it would be in a low whisper from now on. As we clambered from the vehicles I motioned to Sarah for both of us to stand out of the way. We got underneath one of the small stumpy trees which made up this olive grove, the stars giving us just enough light to move in without bumbling. The thing I'd always loved most about the Middle East was the stars; it felt as if you could see the whole universe, and so clearly.

The Regs were putting their bergens on and sorting themselves out. The glow of the town could be seen coming from the dead ground about five ks beyond the target. The night air was cold after the warmth of the people carrier and I couldn't wait to get moving.

The driver came over, holding up a small magnetic box. 'The keys,' he said. 'Both vehicles, rear nearside wheel arch.'

I glanced at Sarah as we both nodded. She had a smaller bergen than mine, containing her trauma kit, with fluid, and anything else she would need. Once the patrol kit was packed, what else went in was down to personal choice.

Glen joined us with a jolly 'You OK?', as if he felt he had to bolster Sarah's morale.

She looked at him blankly and said, 'Let's get on with it, shall we?'

There was a pause as he let the tone of her reply sink in. He didn't like it. 'OK, let's go.' He pointed at her. 'You, behind me. Nick, behind her, OK?'

On the track between the olive groves I could see shadowy figures shaking out into single file. My only job was to protect her; we hadn't let Glen in on this, but if there was a drama, the two of us were going to fuck off sharpish. We'd just let them get on with it and die. As we joined the snake I wondered about the times I'd done jobs while in the Regiment, not realizing that no-one really cared.

We moved off into the shadows, weapon butt in the shoulder, index finger across the trigger guard, thumb on the safety catch. Sarah was carrying only a Beretta for self-defence. We were there to do everything else for her.

For about forty minutes we moved through wide groves. When we finally stopped I could only hear the crickets and the wind in the trees. Ahead of us now was the target, a row of six or seven low-level, brick-faced light industrial units with flat aluminium roofs and windows. The entire complex was surrounded by a three-metre-high chain link fence, with just one entrance, which was gated off for the night. The road was lit by yellow street lamps every thirty metres, and there were floods on the fronts of the buildings, facing down the walls and lighting up the shutters.

There were also lights on in some of the units, but no sign of movement. Apart from the fence there seemed to be no security, which would be about right for units that supposedly housed nothing more serious than JCB spares.

The buildings gave off enough light for us to see what we were doing, but we were still in the shadows of the grove. Glen came alongside me and said quietly, 'This is the FRV (Final Rendezvous). The target . . . if you look at the nearest building on the left . . .'

We were looking at the long sides of three rectangles. He indicated the closest one. 'You see the lights on?' I nodded. 'All right, count three windows from the left. That's where we reckon he is – or was last night.' The 'reckon' would have been a bit of a judgement call: the latest pictures we had of the Source were three years old. I didn't even know his name. Only Sarah did, and only she could positively identify him.

I could make out two small mobile satellite dishes and a wire half-wave dipole antenna on the roof, looking like the world's longest washing line. You didn't need that lot for road building.

I sat against a stubby tree while the patrol prepared itself, bringing out kit from their bergens very slowly to eliminate noise. There was no light from the town to the north, which was lost completely in the dead ground. Reg 1 and 2 checked in with Glen, then moved off. Glen pulled an antenna out of a green twelve-by-eight-inch metal box and began to press buttons. I didn't have a clue what the box was called, but I knew what it did. A little red light came up, which no doubt was a test to make sure he had comms with whatever devices were rigged up at the electricity substation which supplied the power to this area. I imagined they'd be using a number of small stand-off charges, something about the size of a Coca-Cola can, to penetrate the cast-steel casings. All they'd need to do was make a hole big enough for the coolant to drain out of and the generators would quickly burn themselves out.

Sarah wanted confirmation about the target. She pestered Glen, 'Are you *sure* that's the building? Are you *sure* he's in there?' He was already pissed off with her, and told her politely that she might be in overall command but he was the commander on the ground, so shut the fuck up and let him do his job. Good one, Glen, I thought.

We were kneeling around him at the edge of the grove as he made his final checks on the target and confirmed the orders with the rest of us. There were no changes to the plan. It was Sarah who would give the final Go or No Go now. She nodded at him.

'OK, everybody, here we go.' Glen got his box of tricks and pulled up the antenna the last few inches. 'Standby, standby . . .' I heard the click of a button being pressed. There was a delay of about two seconds, then a bright flash in the distance, beyond the glow from the industrial units. Then, after twenty seconds, there was total darkness as the lights went out in the compound.

Glen was back to enjoying life, despite Sarah's presence. He grinned. 'OK, let's go.'

We moved off at a slow jogging pace along the edge of the trees. Once level with Reg 1 and 2, we turned left over the waste ground and went straight for it. They were pulling at the straight line of the cut they'd made, making a big upside-down V for us to get through.

We took advantage of the darkness and sprinted the fifty metres to the target building. There was the odd outburst of hollering and shouting through an open window – nothing frantic; the voices just sounded pissed off that the power had failed, probably halfway though the Syrian version of *EastEnders*. Now and again I saw the glint of torchlight from inside.

We reached the edge of the target building and everybody got against the wall, Glen looking towards the nearest corner. Round that, to the left and next to the shutters, was our entry point. Sarah was between us, catching her breath and trying to keep the noise down.

The other three in the crew were on their knees, nearer the corner. If the door was locked they'd have to blow it. They started to get the prepared charges from their belt kit. I watched as they worked together, slowly unwinding the det cord, which looked like white washing line, only filled with high explosive.

They stood up with the charge. Everything was nice and slow and controlled. As they started to move, the door burst open.

Voices were shouting in Arabic from around the corner. The door charge was quickly placed on the ground. I saw hands reach into belt kits. They would have to remove the threat, but quietly.

The voices got closer and closer and I could hear the sound of flip-flops slapping against feet. Two boys rounded the corner wearing dishdashes, arm in arm, both smoking and still shouting about something, maybe what Grant Mitchell was up to in the Queen Vic.

Two of the Regs climbed aboard them, and almost at once I heard a distinctive buzz and crackle. The boys were getting Tazered good style, at the same time as being dragged out of sight towards us. Tazers are cattle prods for humans. As the two electrodes touch a body, you press a button and 100,000 volts zap through the target. They are a great weapon as you can hold the victim at the same time as you fuck them up big time, without getting zapped by the current yourself.

As the blokes got them down on the floor, I could hear them moaning and groaning under the hands that covered their mouths. They were still being dealt with as Glen put on his NVGs. We did the same.

Glen looked back at Sarah to check we were ready. Following his cue, we moved towards the corner with Sarah still between us. It was now one of those situations that couldn't be stopped. We just had to get on with it. The fuck-it factor had taken over.

We piled in through the door. A Reg secured the entry point and waited for the other two to join him, dragging the two dazed Syrians. The corridor was dark and silent. In a loud whisper Glen said, 'With me, with me, with me.' We moved like men possessed down the breeze-block passage, the world through our NVGs looking like a light-green negative film.

We turned right, and through the windows to our left I could see the outside of the building; on the other side there were ply-

25

wood internal doors leading, I guessed, to rooms or offices. The smell of cigarettes, cooking, coffee and the sweat of not too much air conditioning was almost overpowering.

We came to a T-junction. Glen stopped on the left, Sarah right up behind him. I came up level, on the right. I wasn't too sure which way we were heading. Glen would tell me. I looked over and he was moving his IR torch beam, attached to his weapon, to the right.

I cleared the corner, moved forward three or four metres and stood my ground, waiting. I knew Glen would be clearing the other way. I saw his weapon's IR splash against the walls as he turned towards me, then they both passed on my left. Sarah still had her pistol holstered and was keeping close to Glen. The floor was tiled or concrete, it was hard to tell which. All I knew was that there was an echo of footsteps and squeaking rubber as we moved.

Glen stopped and pointed at a door. He took his weapon out of the shoulder, put his back against the wall to the left and reached for the door handle. I moved to the opposite side, weapon still up in the shoulder, ready to make entry. He nodded; I took off my safety and nodded back. He turned the handle and I moved inside, pushing the door with me.

I was blinded. The NVGs were totally whited out. It was as if someone had let off a flare in front of my face.

Glen shouted, 'The fucking lights are back on!'

I fell on my knees and ripped off the NVGs, blinking hard as I tried to get back some normal vision. I made out movement in the right-hand corner and rolled to the left, trying to make myself a harder target. As my eyes adjusted I saw a middle-aged guy, his head bald apart from wiry side hair. He was curled up against the far wall, his hands protecting his face, flapping even more than I had just been – as you do when, just as the lights come on, a man with a weapon bursts in on you. Fuck it; they must have had standby power.

I became aware of bits of electronic machinery – PCs, screens and computer stuff all over the place, whirring and crunching now the power had returned.

26

I lifted my weapon into my shoulder and pointed it at him. He got the message. I called for Sarah.

She came in and confirmed, 'That's him.' She gobbed off in Arabic and he immediately did as he was told, sitting down on the sofa against the other wall, away from the desk with all the machinery on it. He didn't move; his eyes were like saucers, trying to work it all out and listen to Sarah at the same time.

From my bergen, I pulled out six magnesium incendiary devices. All I needed to do was to get them sparked up and we could be on our way.

It was then that Sarah pulled a laptop and some other gear from her bergen and started plugging it in and revving things up, still talking to the Source, referring to the Arabic script displayed on two of the screens. He replied at the speed of sound, trying his best to stay alive.

I was confused. This wasn't in the plan. I tried to keep a calm voice. 'Sarah, what are you doing? Come on, it's time to go.'

Glen stayed outside in the relit corridor, giving protection. I knew he would feel exposed soon and would want to move out. After all, we'd got who we'd come for. I said, 'Sarah, how long's this going to take?'

She was still scrolling down the screen. I was getting pissed off. This wasn't what we were supposed to be here for.

'No idea – just do your job and keep everyone back.'

I needed to underline the problem we faced. 'This is going to turn into a gang-fuck soon, Sarah. Let's just grab him and go.'

She wasn't even looking at me, just hitting one of the keyboards.

The Source sat tight, looking as confused as I felt.

Glen was starting to get agitated. He stuck his head back into the room. 'How much longer?'

She said, 'What's with you people? Wait.'

Sarah seemed gripped by the information she had before her. I walked towards her, trying to be the good guy. 'Sarah, we've got to go. If not, we're in a world of shit.' I grabbed her arm, but she pulled away and glared at me. I said, 'I don't understand the problem. We have the Source, so let's grab him and go.'

27

We were inches apart, so close I could feel her breath on my face as she spoke. 'There is more to do, Nick,' she said, slowly and quietly. 'You don't know the full brief.'

I felt ridiculous. Very near the bottom of the food chain as usual, I'd obviously been shown only one piece of a much bigger jigsaw puzzle. They'd justify it in terms of 'need to know' or 'op sec', but the real reason was that people like me and Glen simply weren't trusted.

Just as I took a step back the silence was broken by shouting, then the distinctive signature of AKs on auto, their heavy calibre 7.62 short rounds flying around outside the building.

'Shit . . . don't move!' Glen shouted into the room. We had gone noisy: not good. He left us and ran down the corridor. I closed the door.

I could hear the lighter sound of Car 15s returning fire, and lots of shouting, from our guys as well as the Syrians. It didn't matter that the Syrians could hear us shouting in English – there was now so much gunfire and confusion that it was irrelevant – much more important was to get the communications right.

I tried to sound calm. 'Sarah, time to go.'

She turned her back on me and carried on working. Our new friend on the sofa was getting more worried by the minute. I knew just how he felt. There was another exchange of fire outside.

'Fuck this, Sarah, we've got to go. Now!'

She spun round, her face tight with anger. 'Not yet.' She almost spat the words. She jabbed her finger towards the direction of the contact as more rounds were fired. 'That's what they're paid for. Let them get on with it. Your job is to stay with me, so do it.'

Glen was at the end of the corridor, screaming to me at the top of his voice. 'Get them out! Get them out now!'

I moved across the room towards the Source. He was curled into a ball, like a terrified child. I grabbed his arm and started to drag him off the sofa. I hadn't even put on the plasticuffs. 'Let's go, Sarah, we're . . . going . . . now!'

She turned, and as she did I realized that she was drawing

28

down on me, her pistol aimed at my centre mass. She stepped back so there was too much distance for me to react to it.

My new friend didn't want anything to do with this. He just stood next to me, his arm still half elevated by my hand, gently and calmly praying in a low Arabic moan as he waited to die.

Sarah had had enough. 'Sit him down.' She said something in Arabic which must have been to the effect of, 'Shut the fuck up!' because he jumped back on the sofa. She levelled her eyes on me again. 'I'm staying here, what *we* are doing here is important. Do you understand?'

It doesn't matter who it is, if somebody's pointing a gun at you, you get to understand very quickly. Whatever her agenda was, it must be important. She turned calmly, holstered her weapon and went back to work on the keys.

I had one last try. 'Can't we just take him, plus the computers, and fuck off?'

She didn't even bother looking at me. 'No. It has to be done this way.'

I couldn't do both – take her and the Source. I was still working out what to do when I heard Arabic voices inside the building. The best way to do my job and protect her was to go forward, to get out of the room and stop the threat before it came screaming in to get us.

'I'm going outside,' I said in an urgent whisper. 'Don't move until somebody comes to get you. Do you understand me?' I checked my mag was on tight as she looked up from the computer and sort of acknowledged.

I put the Car 15 into my shoulder, and holding the pistol grip to keep the weapon up, opened the door with my left hand.

The lights were still on in the corridor and the sounds of contacts were louder to my right, but my immediate concern was the noises to my left in the corridor. I decided to move down to the next junction and hold it there; that way there would be a weapon at each end with Sarah in the middle.

I closed the door behind me and started to run. After seven or eight strides I was moving past an external door when it burst inwards. The thud as it hit me full-on was as hard and sudden as if I'd walked into the path of a moving car. I was hurled against the opposite wall, stunned and winded. Worse, my weapon had been forced out of my hands. I had lost control of it.

There was yelling on both sides; me from the pain, once I got my breath back, and the Syrian from the surprise. He jumped on top of me on the floor and we grappled like a couple of schoolkids. I tried to get to the pistol on my right thigh, but he had me in a solid bear hug around my armpits. I was pinioned with my arms out like the Michelin Man.

I tried to kick and buck out of position, then to head-butt him. He was doing exactly the same. Both of us were screaming.

The bloke stank. He had a week's bristle on him and it was rough against my face and neck as he squeezed and squeezed, his eyes closed, snorting through his nose as he cried for help. He was a big old boy, packing maybe sixteen stones of solid weight.

I needed help, too, and screamed for Sarah. There was no way she couldn't have heard me, but she didn't respond. I wasn't entirely sure what this boy was trying to do, whether he wanted to kill me, or if he was just fighting to protect himself.

I yelled again. 'Sarah! Sarah!'

He responded by lifting his head slightly to scream out even louder. It gave me a momentary window. I head-butted him, trying to make contact wherever I could. He did the same. Then something happened that moved the situation on. You don't normally feel pain during a fight, but I felt a stinging in my left ear. His teeth were sinking in. I could actually hear the skin break and then the sound of him straining to bite harder. The fucker had a gristly bit of my ear lobe in his mouth and was starting to pull his head back.

I felt the capillary bleeding at once, warm and wet, splashing the side of my cheek as his heavy breathing spat it out. He was in a frenzy, growling at me through clenched teeth, snot and saliva. I was still trying to get my hands down towards my leg so I could reach my pistol, which wasn't helping keep my ear intact.

I managed to get my legs around his gut. I tried to squeeze, but could only just about get my feet together. I felt the snorting from his nose move away from my face slightly, which wasn't good news for my ear. Then his head jerked back, taking part of the lobe with him. The pain felt like a blowtorch on the side of my head, but now that he'd moved back a bit I could start to get my hands around his head. I could see the blood on his face and snot running down from his nose as he fought to breathe through his still-gritted teeth. My fingers reached his eyes and he squeezed me up even more, shaking his head and screaming as I began to get a good hold on his face and dig deeper with my thumbs. He tried to bite my fingers. I moved my right hand so I had a flat palm underneath his chin, then switched my left to just below the crown of his head and grabbed a fistful of his hair.

You can't just whip a head round to break someone's neck. The design is too good for that. What you have to do is screw it off, as if you were untwisting the cap on a jar of Marmite. You're trying to take the head off at the atlas, the small joint at the base of the skull. It's relatively easy if you're doing it against somebody who's standing, because if you get them off balance, their body is going down and you can twist and turn at the same time, so their momentum works against them. But I couldn't do that; all I could do was keep my legs around him and try to keep him in one place.

I managed to get my boots interlocked, and at last I could squeeze and push down with my legs, at the same time twisting up with my arms as hard as I could. I kept on turning as we both screamed at each other. The fucker didn't like it; he knew what was going on, but fortunately for me he was too old and too fat to do much about it.

His neck went without too much of a crack. He slumped down, and there wasn't much noise coming from him; there wasn't even a body jerk. He just went very still. My hands were covered in blood, snot and saliva. I rolled over and kicked him off.

My weapon was only about five feet away. I picked it up and checked that the magazine was on tight, and that I still had a round in the chamber. I started to move back to Sarah, then stopped. I ran back to the Syrian. I could hear firing again, and

31

people screaming and shouting, both Brits and Arabs, maybe just thirty metres away. It's funny how these details take a back seat when you're worrying about other things.

I scrabbled around and eventually found the piece of my ear still in his mouth. I couldn't be arsed trying to stop the bleeding on the side of my head because I knew it wouldn't; capillary bleeding goes on for ever. It would sort itself out. But I would want to get the severed bit sewn back on. It wouldn't be too good with a chunk missing because I'd have a VDM (visual distinguishing mark); but worse than that, I knew a couple of people with bits of their ear missing, and it looked fucking ugly. The only alternative was to have a 1980s Kevin Keegan haircut to cover it up.

I got back to the room and banged on the door. 'Sarah, it's me. I'm coming in, I'm coming in.'

Glen was still at the end of the corridor. When he heard my voice he shouted, 'Come on, for fuck's sake! Drag her fucking arse out . . . now!' He was right.

Enough was enough, we were all going to die here soon.

I pushed it open and Sarah was still standing over one of the PCs with her laptop plugged into some other shit. I looked over at the Source. He was sitting in the same position I'd left him in, as if he was watching the TV.

A small amount of blood was trickling from a hole in his shirt, but it was the one in the front of his head that gave the game away. Blood was oozing out like lava flow. The back of his head lolled against the sofa; it had ballooned out slightly, but the skin was keeping all the fragmented bone in place. It looked like a car windscreen that's been punched; the glass goes out in the shape of a fist, but it's still held together. Blood and gooey grey tissue were dribbling onto the sofa. You didn't have to be George Clooney to know this boy wouldn't be surfing the net any more.

Not even looking at me as she manipulated the keyboard, she said, 'He tried to attack me. But he is happy – God would have sent him *seqina*.' She knew I wouldn't have a clue what she was on about, and added, 'Tranquillity.'

I looked at him again. He hadn't moved from where he'd been when I'd left the room and there was no look of tranquillity on his face. He hadn't attacked her. So what; as if I gave a fuck. It was probably part of the alternative brief she'd been given. AK fire called me back to the real world.

'Come on, let's go. Now, Sarah!'

'No.' She shook her head. 'I'm going to be a few seconds more.'

The incendiary devices were still on the table. One of my jobs, unless she was going to tell me that had changed too, was to destroy any equipment on target.

She hit the final key. 'OK, we can go.' She started to pack herself up. I went to the sofa, pulled the Source away and let him roll onto the floor. Picking up one end of the sofa and dragging it across the room, I leaned it against the bench of computers. I got the waste-paper bin, scattered the contents on the bench top and added a rug from the floor and a couple of chairs. I wanted as much flammable stuff as possible near the incendiaries.

I said, 'Are you *sure* you're ready now?'

It was the first time she'd looked at me since I'd returned to the room. I saw her studying the red mess on the side of my head. I pulled the pin of the first device and positioned it on the table between two VDUs. The handle flew off, and by the time the last one was placed two were already burning fiercely. I could feel the heat, even through my jump suit.

I ditched the bergen; everything I needed now was in my belt kit. The air was filling with the noxious black fumes of burning plastic. I grabbed hold of Sarah, who had her repacked bergen slung over her shoulders, and headed for the door. I opened it a couple of inches and shouted to Glen, 'Coming through! Coming through!'

He yelled back, 'Shut the fuck up and run! Run!'

I didn't look left or right, just ran for the door by the same route we'd come in. Within less than a minute I was in the cold night air, my eyes peeled for the gap in the fence. It was pointless worrying about getting shot; I just ran in a stoop to make as small a target as possible, keeping Sarah in front of me.

I caught a glimpse of Glen behind me, plus another bloke still further back. They followed as we sprinted towards the fence, rounds thudding into the ground around us. The Syrians were firing far too many rounds in one burst and couldn't control their aim.

Reg 1 pulled open one half of the upside-down V. Sarah slid into the gap like a baseball player going for base. I prepared to do the same. I caught up with her as her slide stopped on the other side, and kicked her out of the way so I wasn't blocking the gap for the other two.

'Move! Move!' I expected them to do the same to me. Nothing happened.

Reg 1 had already seen the reason why: 'Man down! Man down!'

Looking back through the gloom, I could see a shape on the ground about twenty metres away. Whoever was with him already had his hand in his loop and was trying to drag him towards the fence. Each of us was wearing a harness, a large loop made of nylon strapping between our shoulder blades with which a downed body could be dragged or hooked up to a heli winch for a quick extraction.

'Stay here – don't move!' I could see from Sarah's expression that for once she was going to do as she was told.

I ran out to the dragger, and between us we pulled Glen towards the hole in the fence line. He was moaning and groaning like a drunk. 'Shit, I'm down, I'm down.'

Good. If he was talking, he was breathing.

I could see that the legs of his coveralls were shining with blood, but we'd have to look at that later. The first priority was to get him, and us, out of the immediate area.

I slid through the fence, turned on my knees, got hold of Glen's harness and dragged him through the gap. Sarah said and did nothing. Her bit was done; she was way out of her depth now. Reg 1 and 2 were waiting with her; the other two patrol members were giving covering fire from the olive-grove side of the fence as we moved towards them, letting off double taps at anything that moved. They needed to conserve ammo; we didn't have Hollywood mags.

34

Reg 1 was shouting commands. 'Move back to the FRV, move back.' He had a sat comm out, its miniature transmission dish pointing skyward, telling the world that we were in the shit. I didn't know who he was talking to, but it certainly made me feel better.

Every other man carried a poncho stretcher – a big sheet of green nylon with loop handles – as part of his kit. Reg 2 laid his on the ground as I removed Glen's belt kit and bergen and put it on my back. So much for travelling light. As we rolled him onto the stretcher he was still conscious but, if he hadn't already, he'd soon go into shock.

It was then that I heard an ominous slurping noise in time with his breathing. He had a sucking wound to his chest: air was being sucked inside his chest cavity instead of going through his mouth. It was going to need sorting out quickly because otherwise the fucker was history. But there wasn't enough time to do it here – that way we'd all die. We'd have to wait until we reached the FRV.

Reg 2 heard the noise, too. Grasping Glen's hand, he placed it on his chest. 'Plug it up, mate.' He wasn't that out of it, he understood what he needed to do. With a chest wound we couldn't give him morphine; he was going to have to take the pain.

Two of us got hold of him, one either side of the stretcher, and started to hobble along with him as quickly as we could, Sarah following at my heels. I didn't look at what was going on behind us, but I heard the rate of covering fire from Reg 1 and 2 step up as we moved off.

We hit the tree line, Glen's moans distorted by the jolting as we ran. We got further into the grove, and only then moved to the right, under cover. He was still conscious and breathing noisily as we laid him on his back. The light from the target area was just enough to see my hands moving as they worked on him. There was no need to worry about clearing his airway, but his hand had fallen from his chest. I put my hand over the wound to form a seal. Hopefully, with his chest now airtight, normal breathing would return. I could see the anguish in his eyes. His throat spluttered as he coughed and fought the pain. 'What's it like?

35

What's it like? Oh shit.' He screwed up his face even more as Reg 2 moved him. It was a good sign: he could still feel it, his senses hadn't given way yet.

Reg 2 finished checking him. 'No exit wound.'

First you've got to plug the leaks, then you have to put in fluid to replace what's been lost. I watched as Reg 2 grabbed the field dressings from Glen's belt kit and ripped them open. You always use the casualty's own dressings; you might need yours later. The packaging was Israeli, but they looked the same as ours, like big fat sanitary towels with a bandage attached. Their job, in any language, is to block up wounds and stop bleeding by the application of direct pressure.

A round from an AK had also ripped through the muscle mass on his thigh, like a butcher's knife slicing open a side of beef. He was losing blood fast. Reg 2 started to cavity-pack the wound.

The downside of Glen still breathing was that we couldn't shut him up. Over and over he groaned, 'What's it like? What's it like?'

I looked down at him. He was covered in sweat, and the dust had caked onto his face. 'Shut the fuck up,' I said. 'It's nothing, we'll fix it.' You should never let a casualty see you looking concerned.

Sarah was several paces behind me, watching the route we had just taken, weapon out. I half whispered, half shouted, 'Sarah! Come here!'

She moved towards me. I said, 'Put the heel of your hand over this hole when I take mine off, OK?'

He was losing consciousness. Close to his ear, I said, 'It's OK, you can speak to me now.' There was no response. 'Oi, come on, speak to me, you fucker!' I pulled on his sideburns. Nothing.

I pulled up the left sleeve of his coveralls to expose the six-inch band of tubigrip on his forearm. Underneath that was the catheter, already inserted in a vein before we left Delhi. You'd have to be mad not to; a bit of anti-coagulant in the catheter to stop the blood from clotting and it will last for a good twenty-four hours. You are a bit sore afterwards, but it will save your life. It's hard to get a vein up to insert a catheter once you've lost fluid, especially under fire and in darkness.

Reg 2 had nearly finished packing the thigh wound. It would have been no good just piling bandages on top, because the muscle underneath was still going to bleed. You have to really pack the cavity, keeping direct pressure on the wound, and that, in turn, will stop the bleeding. That done, he now needed fluid.

Glen's breathing was very rapid and shallow, which wasn't a good sign. I felt the pulse on his neck; same problem there. His heart was working overtime to circulate what fluid was left around his body.

Shots were now being fired at us from about a hundred metres away but all my attention was focused on Glen.

Reg 2 shouted at Sarah. 'Watch him and tell us if his breathing starts to slow down. Got it?' She nodded and started to take notice.

I pulled the plasma expander from his belt kit, a clear-plastic half-litre container shaped like a washing-up-liquid bottle. I ripped it out of its Israeli plastic wrapper and threw that on the ground. I bit off the little cap that kept the neck of the bottle sterile. Fuck hygiene – infections could be sorted out in hospital. Let's keep him alive so he can get to one first.

By now I also had his IV set out of its protective plastic coating, and was biting off the cap to the spearhead connector and jabbing it into the self-sealing neck of the bottle. I undid the screw clamp, took off the end cap and watched as the fluid ran through the line. I heard it splash onto Glen's face. He didn't react. Bad sign. Rolling the screw clamp on to stop the flow, I wasn't concerned about air bubbles in the line; a small amount doesn't matter – certainly not in these circumstances. Let's just get the fluid in.

There was more gunfire from the target area, too close for comfort, and for the first time since we'd been in the trees our blokes fired back. The Syrians had found us.

Reg 1 was still in command. He was down at the tree line waiting for us to sort Glen out. 'How much longer up there?'

37

Reg 2 called back. 'Two minutes, mate, two minutes. I need your fluids.' As he jumped up with his weapon to collect the kit I unscrewed the end cap of the catheter and screwed the IV set into it.

Sarah was still plugging the hole. I could hear her breathing quickly in my ear as she leant over Glen. 'Nick, listen to me. Let's leave them to it, let's go.'

She was right, of course. The two of us would stand a far better chance on our own.

I ignored her and carried on working on Glen, gently squeezing the bottle to get the fluid into him. She whispered, a bit more urgently, 'Come on, we need to go now, Nick. Remember, this is what they get paid for. And you are paid to protect me.'

Glen had to be dangerously low on fluids, but he was still conscious – just. 'Sarah, pass me your fluid, quick.'

She used her free hand to pull the bergen straps off her back to get to it. The first bottle was now empty. I turned off the IV with the screw clamp. Sarah had her fluid in her hand. I said, 'Open it.'

I heard her ripping the plastic with her teeth as I pulled off the empty bottle. She handed it over. The sound of gunfire was still very much in the background.

Reg 2 came back, packs of fluid pushed down the front of his jump suit, panting as he collapsed on the floor next to us. I jabbed the new bottle into the set and opened up the screw cap. Reg 2 was studying Glen. All of a sudden he shouted, 'Fuck, fuck, fuck!' and leaned over, grabbing Sarah's hand and lifting it.

There was a sound like a rush of air escaping from the valve of a car tyre and a fine geyser of blood sprayed in all directions. The round must have pierced his lung, and as he breathed in, the oxygen was escaping from the lung and going into the chest cavity. The pressure had built up so much in his chest that his lungs hadn't been able to expand and his heart couldn't function properly. That was why Sarah had to watch and listen, because the pressure on the heart and lungs would make him breathe much slower than he needed.

Reg 2 went ballistic, still gripping her arm. 'Fucking bitch! Fuck you. Do it right! What are you trying to do? Kill him?'

38

She said nothing as the air gush subsided. Then, very calmly, she reminded him who was boss. 'Let go of my arm at once and get on with your job.'

Reg 2 placed Sarah's hand back over the wound. Glen was just about conscious but still losing blood internally. Reg 2 got right up to his face, 'Show you can hear me, mate . . . show me . . .' There was no reply. 'We're going to move you, mate. Not long now before we're out of here. OK? OK?' All he got in reply was a low moan. At least there *was* a reply.

Reg 2 had to turn him to check the leg dressing. Blood started to run out of the hole and down Sarah's fingers. She looked at me, pissed off, as another fluid set was being connected. She wanted out of here.

The others were rolling into the FRV, out of breath and confused about what had happened. 'Is everyone here?' Reg 1 counted. He came over to us and looked at Glen. 'Is he ready to go?'

Reg 2, still looking at the casualty, said, 'I think we're just about to find out.' Using one of the large safety pins that came with the field dressings, he pinned Glen's tongue to his bottom lip. Glen was out of it; he couldn't feel a thing. The danger was that, in a state of unconsciousness, his tongue would roll back and block his airway.

I turned to Sarah as they sorted their shit out for the next phase and whispered in her ear, 'Our best chance now is with these boys. If you don't want to come, that's fine, but you leave the bergen. I'll take it back.'

The look on her face said she knew she had no choice. She wasn't going to leave; she couldn't do it without me.

Reg 2 placed one of the ripped plastic coverings over the wound to seal it better and instructed Sarah, 'Get your hand back on that.' He and another Reg picked up the casualty. Reg 2 kept the bottle high for the fluid to run freely by holding the hanging loop in his mouth.

It wasn't a tactical move to the wagons, it was a case of getting out of there as fast as we could, bearing in mind the weight of the casualty and his comfort. I didn't know what was going on

39

behind me, back at the target area, and I didn't really care.

We reached the vehicles about thirty minutes later. I grabbed Sarah and took her to one side. There was no point getting involved in what these blokes were doing; we were just passengers. That wasn't good enough for Sarah. 'Come on,' she hissed, 'why aren't we moving yet?'

I pointed at the rear Previa. They had got the back door open and were pulling the seats down to create a flat space for Glen. Looking beyond them I noticed that the town was still dark. I was right, the industrial units must have had emergency power.

The driver of our vehicle retrieved the key, opened the door and motioned us inside. Another of the team got in the front. He leaned back towards us. 'As soon as they're ready we're going to move to the ERV (Emergency Rendezvous).'

We were sitting in darkness, the driver with his NVGs on. There was tension in the air; we needed to get going. If not, it wouldn't just be Glen who'd be in the shit. I didn't talk to Sarah; I didn't even look at her.

At last, the other vehicle started to move off slowly and ours manoeuvred in front of it and took the lead. It wasn't long before we hit the metalled road. Behind us headlights came on, and Sarah took this as her cue to get out her laptop. A few seconds later she was going shit or bust on the keyboard. The screen glowed in the darkness, lighting up her sweaty, dirty face. My eyes moved to the maps, diagrams and Arabic script in front of her, none of which meant anything to me, and then down at her well-manicured fingers which were tapping away furiously on the keys and smearing them with Glen's blood.

We drove like men possessed for twenty minutes. Then, after an NVG drive into the desert with IR filters on the wagons' lights for another ten, we stopped.

Apart from the engine gently ticking over and the noise of Sarah's fingers hitting the keys and her mumbling the Arab script she was reading, there was silence. A beeping noise came from the laptop. She muttered, 'Fuck it!' Her battery was running out.

There were shouts from the other Previa. Somebody was

working hard on Glen, yelling at him, trying to get a response. Silence was obviously out of the question now. It's hard to be quiet when you're fighting to keep a man alive.

The driver looked at his watch after about five minutes. He opened the door and shouted, 'Lights!' then started to flash the wagon's IR light between dipped and full beam as he hit the Firefly and stuck it out of the window. Even as this was being said, I started to hear a throbbing noise in the distance, and less than a minute later the sky was filled with the steady, ponderous beat of an incoming Chinook. The noise became deafening and stones clattered against the windscreen and bodywork as the Previa rocked under the downwash from the rotor blades. The pilot wouldn't be able to see the vehicles or the ground now due to all the sand and crap his rotors were throwing up.

A few seconds later a figure loomed out of the dust storm, bent double, his flying suit whipping around him. He flashed a red light at us and the driver shouted, 'That's it, let's go.'

Our vehicle edged forwards. We drove for several yards into the maelstrom of wind and dust before things started to calm down. Red and white Cyalume sticks glowed around the open ramp and the interior was bathed in red light. Three loadies wearing shoulder holsters, body armour and helmets with the visors down were beckoning to us urgently with a Cyalume stick in each hand. As if we needed any encouragement.

Our Previa bumped up the ramp as if we were driving onto a cross-Channel ferry, and one of the loadies signalled us to a stop. The other vehicle lurched in behind us, and as soon as it had cleared the ramp I could feel the aircraft start to lift off its hydraulic suspension. Moments later, we were in a hover.

We swayed to the left and right as the pilot sorted his shit out and the loadies lashed down the tyres with chains. Hertz were going to be one very pissed-off rental company.

We were no more than sixty feet off the ground when I felt the nose of the Chinook dip as we started to move off and turn to the right.

Chaos erupted inside the aircraft. The Regs spilled from their vehicles, shouting at the loadies, 'White light! Give us white

41

light!' Somebody hit the switch, and all of a sudden it was like standing on a floodlit football pitch.

The inside of the other wagon looked like a scene out of *ER*. Glen was still on his back, but they'd ripped open the front of his coveralls to expose the chest wound. Blood was everywhere, even over the windows.

Reg 2 ran over to a loadie who was still at the heli ramp checking it had closed up correctly. He shouted as loudly as he could against the side of the guy's helmet and pointed to the rear wagon. 'Trauma pack! Get the trauma pack!'

The loadie took one look at the bloodied windows, disconnected the intercom lead from his helmet and sprinted towards the front of the heli.

Everybody had a job to do; mine was simply to get out of the way. I left Sarah sitting in the back of our Previa sorting out her laptop, and moved to the front of the Chinook. I knew where the flasks and food would be stowed and, if nothing else, I could be the tea lady.

As I moved to the front of the aircraft I met the loadie on his way back with the trauma pack, a black nylon bag the size of a small suitcase. I stepped to one side and watched him open the bag as he ran, bouncing off the front wagon and airframe as he momentarily lost his balance.

At that moment Sarah jumped out between us with the laptop and power lead in her hands. She was shouting at him, 'Power! I need power!'

He went to push her aside, yelling, 'Get out of the fucking way!'

'No!' She shook her head angrily and put her hand on him. 'Power!'

He shouted something back at her; I didn't know what because he was now facing away from me, pointing towards the front of the aircraft.

She moved quickly past me towards the cockpit, so bound up with her own obsession that she didn't even see me. I continued on, heading for the bulkhead behind the cockpit. I picked up one of the aluminium flasks, which was held in place by elastic cargo netting, and started to untwist the cup. Coffee not tea, and it had never smelled so good.

As I turned and started to walk down towards the rear Previa, flask in hand, I could hear them, even above the noise of the heli, shouting with frustration. Two drips were being held up and a circle of sweaty, dusty and bloodstained faces was working on him. As I got closer I could see they were rigging him up in shock trousers. They're like thick ski salopettes, which come up past your hips and are pumped up to apply pressure to the lower limbs, stemming blood loss by restricting the supply and so keeping more blood to rev up the major organs. It was a delicate procedure, because too much pressure could kill him.

Reg 2 looked as if he was on the case big time. He was holding Glen's jaw open, breathing into his mouth with the safety pin still in place. I was close enough to see his chest rise. Someone had his hand over the chest wound, ready to depressurize. Once Reg 2 had finished inflating his lungs a few times he shouted, 'Go!' Another was astride him, both arms outstretched and open hands on top of each other on his chest. 'One, two, three . . .'

There was obviously no pulse and Glen wasn't breathing. He was technically dead. They were filling him up with oxygen by breathing into his mouth, then pumping his heart for him, whilst simultaneously trying to make sure that no more of his fluid escaped from any of the holes he had in him. Glen's chest was just a mess of blood-matted hair.

The team were going to be too busy to drink coffee, so with nothing useful to do I pulled up my left sleeve and peeled back the tubigrip. Ripping off the surgical tape holding the catheter in place, I carefully pulled it out, pressing down on the puncture wound with a finger until it clotted.

I looked around for Sarah. She was in a world of her own, sitting near where the coffee flasks were stowed. She'd found the power point and an adaptor that fed a two-pin plug, and her fingers were tapping frantically at the keyboard once more.

I looked back at Glen. There was still lots of shouting and hollering going on in there; I just hoped that whatever was on that computer was worth it.

I looked out of one of the small round windows and saw lights on the coastline. We had a bowser inside the Chinook, feeding extra fuel. It looked like this was a direct flight and that we were on for tea and toast in Cyprus later that morning. I took a sip of coffee.

As we crossed the coast and headed out to sea, I stared out of the window, my mind starting to focus on the deep sound of the two big rotors throbbing above us. I was cut out of the daze by a despairing shout: 'Fuck it! Fuck it!'

I looked up in time to see the bloke who'd been astride Glen's chest climbing down slowly onto the deck, his body language telling me everything I needed to know. He swung his boot and kicked the vehicle hard, denting the door.

I turned my head and stared back out of the window. We were flying low and fast across the water. There wasn't a light to be seen. My ear was hurting. I reached into my pocket and checked around for the lobe. I sat there toying with it, thinking how strange it was, just a small lump of gristle. Hopefully they'd stitch it on all right – but what did it matter how bad I looked? I was alive.

I stood up and went over to Sarah. It was my job to look after her, and that included keeping her informed of what was going on. She was still immersed in her laptop.

I said, 'Sarah, he's dead.'

She carried on tapping keys. She didn't even look up to see me offering her a flasktop of coffee.

I kicked her feet. 'Sarah . . . Glen is dead.' She finally turned her eyes and said, 'Oh, OK,' then looked straight back down and carried on with her work.

I looked at her hands. Glen's blood had now dried hard on them and she didn't give a shit. If it hadn't been for her fucking about and not telling us that the job wasn't as straightforward as we were first told, maybe he'd still be here, a big fucking grin on his face. Maybe Reg 2 was right, maybe she had been trying to kill Glen at the FRV. She knew that I would have binned the patrol and gone with her if he wasn't still in with a chance.

The team were sitting against the wagon, opening flasks

44

and lighting up, leaving Glen exactly as he was. We'd all been doing what we got paid to do. Shit happens. This wasn't going to change their lives, and I certainly wasn't going to let it change mine.

As Sarah carried on hitting her computer keys I drank coffee and watched the line of the Cyprus coast appear, trying to work out what the fuck I was doing here.

APRIL 1998

1

FRIDAY 24 APRIL 1998

'Three gallons a day, that's your lot,' the bosun barked. 'But two gallons have to go to the cook, so there's one gallon – I'll tell ye again, just one gallon – left over for drinking, washing and anything else ye need it for. Anyone caught taking more will be flogged. So will gamblers, cheats and malingerers. We don't like malingerers in Her Majesty's Navy!'

We were lined up on either side of the deck, listening to the bosun gobbing off about our water ration. I was trying not to catch Josh's eye; I knew I'd burst into a fit of laughter which Kelly wouldn't find amusing.

There were about twenty of us 'new crew', mostly kids, all dressed in the standard-issue sixteenth-century sailors' kit: a hessian jerkin and shirt, with trousers that stopped about a foot short of the trainers we'd been instructed to bring with us. We were aboard the *Golden Hind*, a full-sized reconstruction of the ship in which Sir Francis Drake circumnavigated the globe between 1577 and 1580. This version, too, had sailed round the world, and film companies had used it as a location so often it had had more makeovers than Joan Collins. And now it was in permanent dock serving, as Kelly called it in her very American way, as an 'edutainment' attraction. She was standing to my right, very excited about her birthday treat, even if it was a few days late. She was now nine, going on twenty-four.

49

'See, I told you this would be good!' I beamed.

She didn't reply, but kept her eyes fixed on the bosun. He was dressed the same as us, but was allowed to wear a hat – on account of all the extra responsibility, I supposed.

'Ye slimey lot have been hand-picked for a voyage with Sir Francis Drake, aboard this, the finest ship in the fleet, the *Golden Hind*!' His eyes fixed on those of each child as he passed them on the other line. He reminded me of my very first drill sergeant when I was a boy soldier.

I looked over at Josh and his gang, who were on the receiving end of his tirade. Joshua G. D'Souza was thirty-eightish, five feet six inches, and, thanks to being into weights, about fourteen stones of muscle. Even his head looked like a bicep; he was 99 per cent bald, and a razor blade and moisturiser had taken care of the other 1 per cent. His round, gold-rimmed glasses made him look somehow more menacing than intellectual.

Josh was half-black, half-Puerto Rican, though he'd been born in Dakota. I couldn't really work that one out, but nor could I be bothered to ask. Joining up as a teenager, he'd done a few years in the 82nd Airborne and then Special Forces. In his late twenties he'd joined the US Treasury Department as a member of their Secret Service, in time working on the vice-presidential protection team in Washington. He lived near Kelly's dad's place, and he and Kev had met, not through work, but because their kids had gone to the same school.

Josh had his three standing next to him, working hard at understanding the bosun's accent. They were on their last leg of a whistlestop tour of Europe during their Easter vacation. Kelly and I had collected them off the Paris Eurostar just the day before; they were going to spend a few days seeing the sights with us before heading back to DC, and Kelly was really hyper. I was pleased about that; it was the first time she'd seen them since 'what happened' – as we called it – over a year ago. All things considered, she was pretty well at the moment and getting on with her life.

The bosun had turned back and was moving up our line. 'Ye will be learning gun drills, ye will be learning how to set sail and repel boarders. But best of all, ye'll be hunting for treasure and singing sailors' shanties!' The crew was encouraged to respond with their best sailor-type cries.

All of a sudden, competition for the loudest noise came from the siren of a tourist boat passing on the river, and the bark of its tannoy, as the first sailing of the day 'did' London Bridge.

I glanced down at Kelly. She was quivering with excitement. I was enjoying myself, too, but I felt just a bit weird standing there in fancy dress in full public view, aboard a ship docked on the south side of London Bridge. At this time of the morning, there were still office workers walking along the narrow cobblestoned road that paralleled the Thames, dodging the delivery vans and taxis on their way to work. The trains that had got them this far were slowly trundling along the elevated tracks about 200 metres away, making their way towards the river.

The pub next to the ship, the Olde Thameside Inn, was one of those places that supposedly dates from Shakespeare's day but which, in fact, was built maybe ten years earlier on one of the converted wharves that line the river. The office crowd, plastic cups and cigarettes in hand, were making the most of the morning sun on the terrace overlooking the water, having picked up their late breakfast from the coffee shop.

I was hauled back to the sixteenth century. The bosun had stopped and was glaring theatrically at Kelly. 'Are you a malingerer?'

'No sir, no sir!' She pushed herself into my side a bit more for protection. She was still a bit anxious about strangers, especially adult men.

The bosun grinned. 'Well, seeing as you're a special crew, and I know you're going to work hard, I'm going to let you have your rations. You'll be getting some special sailors' nuggets and Coke.' He spun round, his hands in the air. 'What do you say?'

The kids went bonkers: 'Aye aye, sir!'

'That's not good enough!' he bellowed. 'What do you say?'

'AYE AYE, SIR!'

The kids were shepherded by the bosun and the rest of the permanent crew towards the tables of food. 'Small sailors first,' he ordered. 'The tall sailors who brought you here can wait their turn.'

Kelly ran over to Josh's three – two girls, Dakota and Kimberly, aged eleven and nine, and a boy, Tyce, who was eight. Their skin was lighter than Josh's – their mother was white – but they looked just like their dad, except they still had all their hair. Which was a good thing, I thought.

Josh and I turned and looked out over the deck towards the Thames. Josh waved back at some tourists who were waving from the boat, either at us or at the coffee morning still going strong to our left.

'How is she coping?' he asked.

'Getting better, mate, but the shrink says it'll take time. It's affected her schooling big time, she's way behind. The last lot of grades were shit. She's an intelligent girl, but she's like a big bucket with holes, all the information's going in, but it just drips out again.'

'You think about what she's been through, man, for sure it's going to take some time.'

We turned to see all four of the kids throwing chicken nuggets down their necks. It was a strange choice for breakfast, but then again, I liked choc ice and chips first thing in the morning when I was a kid. The elder daughter wasn't getting on with Tyce today and Josh had to do a dad thing. 'Hey, Kimberly, chill! Let Tyce have his Coke – *now*!'

Kimberly didn't look too happy but obeyed. Josh turned back towards the river, took off his gold-rimmed glasses and gave them a wipe. 'She looks happy enough, that's a good sign.'

'It's the best she's been for ages. She's slightly nervous around adults, but with her friends she's OK. It means so much for her to see your lot. Besides, it gives her a rest from me.' I couldn't bring myself to say that I found it wonderful to see him as well. I hoped he knew anyway.

We both looked out over the river with not a lot to say. He broke the silence. 'How's the job? Are you on permanent cadre yet?'

I shook my head. 'I don't think it will ever happen. They know

52

I was involved in a lot more of the Washington stuff than I let on.'
It pissed me off, because I needed a regular income these days. I
had the money I'd rescued from last year's gang-fuck, but that
wouldn't last for ever. I grinned. 'Maybe I could turn to crime.
Couldn't be worse than the shit I do now.'

He frowned, not sure if I was being serious or not, and tilted his
head in the direction of the huddle of small sailors, as if to remind
me of my responsibilities. He put his specs back on and focused
on a black guy in an old, shiny blue tracksuit who had set up
shop at the corner of the pub, selling the *Big Issue* and chatting up
the women walking past.

'It's OK for you,' I said. 'We don't have a training wing where
I can go and put my feet up and still get paid.' I thought Josh was
going to give me a lecture, so I put my hands up. 'OK, I surrender.
I *will* sort my shit out – one day.'

In a way, I had sorted myself – a bit. With the money I'd
diverted from the Washington job, £300,000 once the dollars were
converted, I'd bought myself a house up on the Norfolk coast in
the middle of nowhere. The village had a Co-op on the corner and
that was about it; a traffic jam was when the three fishing boats
came into the harbour and their vans arrived at the same time to
take the catch away. Otherwise, the busiest it got was when the
postman rang his bell as he was going round the corner. I didn't
know anyone; they didn't know me. If anything, they all had me
down as an international drug dealer or some weirdo. I kept
myself to myself, and that suited everybody just fine.

I'd bought a motorbike, too. At last I had the Ducati I'd always
promised myself, and I even had a garage to put it in. But what
was left – about £150,000 – wasn't enough to retire on, so I still
had to work – and I only knew one trade. Maybe that was why
Josh and I got on; he was much the same as me, running his life
like a conjuror, trying to keep all the plates spinning on top of
their poles. His plates weren't spinning so well at the moment.
Now that Geri had gone, one income wasn't enough, and he'd
had to put the house up for sale.

Josh had had a fucker of a year. First his wife had got into yoga
and all that mind-body-spirit stuff, then she'd ended up going to

Canada to hug trees – or, more precisely, to hug the yoga teacher. Josh and the kids were shattered. Something had to give. He could no longer travel away from home with the vice-presidential crew, so he became one of the training team out in Laurel, Maryland. It was a very grand-sounding outfit – Special Operations Training Section – but a shit job for a man who was used to being in the thick of things. Then, two months after his wife left him, his friends Kev, Marsha and their other child, Aida, were hosed down, and he found he was an executor of the will – along with some dickhead Brit he'd never heard of called Nick Stone.

Between us we looked after Kelly's trust fund, and we'd been having some problems selling the family home. When it came down to it, who was going to buy a house where a whole family had been butchered? The property company was trying to pull a sleazy deal so it could get the land back. The insurance companies had been trying to give Kelly a lump sum instead of making regular payments, because it was cheaper for them. The only people getting any money were the lawyers. There was something about it all that reminded me of my divorce.

I turned to him. 'It is good to see you, mate.'

He looked back and smiled. 'Same here, *mate*.' His piss-taking accent sounded more Australian than English. Maybe they got *Neighbours* in his part of Virginia, too.

There was really nothing more to be said. I liked Josh and we had a fuck of a lot in common, but it wasn't as if we were going to be sharing toothbrushes or anything like that. I'd decided after Euan turned me over to bin any idea of friendship with anyone else ever again, and to restrict myself to acquaintances – but this did feel different.

'Talking of shit,' I said, 'how's the quilt shaping up? The kids sounded really ecstatic about it last night.'

His eyes looked up at the sky. 'Fuck, man, it's been a nightmare. Two months of hoo-ha and the kids getting so high they might as well be on drugs.'

I had to laugh. I'd been following the build-up to this from Josh over the phone, but no-one was going to stop him honking about it a bit more now. 'I've been to meetings, meetings about meetings, sewing classes, discussion groups, you name it; that's been my life for the last two fucking months.'

There was going to be a summit between the Israelis and Palestinians in Washington DC. Clinton was out to look the big-time statesman, brokering the peace deal, and somebody had come up with the bright idea of making the world's biggest peace quilt to commemorate the occasion. Kids from all over had been sewing like crazy in preparation for the world's biggest photo opportunity on the White House lawn.

Josh said, 'I mean, do you have any idea how many stitches it takes to sew on just one fucking little shape?'

'Don't worry about it, mate,' I said. 'They'll turn it into a TV commercial for Coke and then you'll all be rich.'

The bosun wanted us. 'Oi, you two! Come down and get your rations or ye'll swing from the yardarm!'

'Aye aye, sir!'

'I can't hear you. What did you say?'

Josh got into 82nd Airborne mode, snapped to attention and screamed, 'SIR! – AYE AYE – SIR!'

The old boy flogging the *Big Issue* started to cheer and clap, though I wasn't too sure whether the bosun liked the competition. Josh collected his food and sat down amongst the kids, trying to pinch some of their breakfast.

I got my ration of authentic Elizabethan nuggets, doughnuts and pirate cola. A train from London Bridge station rattled along the elevated railway line behind us, the bells of Southwark Cathedral just fifty metres away fired off a salvo, telling us it was 10.30 a.m., and here I was wondering for the millionth time how I'd landed myself with all this. Josh told me he'd always loved the idea of being with the kids, but had never realized the stress of looking after them all the time until his wife left. Me, I loved it when I was with Kelly, but hated the idea of it. The responsibility filled me with dread. When it came to the world of emotions I was a beginner.

My birthday girl was holding court, telling Josh's kids about her boarding school. 'I got a twenty pence fine because I didn't wear my slippers to the shower room last week.' She loved the idea of being the same as the other girls; the fact that she had been fined meant she was one of the crowd.

'Yes, and who has to pay the fine?' I said.

She laughed. 'My manager.'

Her school had been fantastic about everything, even though they knew only the bare bones of what had happened. I agreed with Josh that it was the best thing to do, taking her right away from the US and an environment that would bring back memories and screw her up even more. She never brought up the subject of what had happened the day her parents and sister died, but she had no problem talking about them if things came up in daily life to remind us of them. Only once had I made a direct reference, and she'd just said, 'Nick, that was a long time ago.'

She began telling everyone about the week's plans. 'Nick couldn't see me on my birthday and had to leave me with Granny and Grandad the day before. But this week we're going to see the Bloody Tower.'

'What?' Josh's mouth dropped open. He might be ex-Airborne at work, but within earshot of his kids not even the mildest cuss would pass his lips.

'She means the Tower of London,' I said. 'There's a place called the Bloody Tower; it's where the Crown Jewels are kept, I think. Something like that.' History had never been my strong point.

Kelly's face lit up at the thought of seeing all those jewels. As a child, I'd never known that sort of joy. My mother and stepfather never took me anywhere; all they ever gave me was promises. When I was about eight, HMS *Belfast* docked by Tower Bridge and became a museum. All the kids on the estate went, but not me – all I got for weeks was IOUs. At last I was told I was going with my Auntie Pauline. I spent hours trailing round the local shops behind her, asking when we were going. 'In a minute, son, not long now.' The bitch was lying, just like my parents. The whole thing had been a ploy to get me off their hands while they went out on the piss. After that I didn't even bother to ask. Fuck 'em. I had another eight years before I could leave home; I'd treat it like a waiting room.

'. . . then we're going to have a sleepover at the place where all

56

the mummies are. There's a museum where you can spend the . . .'

She was interrupted by the bosun, who'd maybe guessed that the tall sailors needed a rest.

'It's time for some seafaring tales while ye have your feed. So listen in, all ye crew, small and tall!'

It was while we were sitting there listening to the sea tales, and I was digging a chicken nugget into my red sauce, that I felt my pager go off. I liked the fact that people needed me to do things they couldn't do themselves, but I always kept it on vibrate because I hated the noise it made; it always spelled trouble, like an alarm clock that wakes you on a morning you're dreading.

I took it out of its little carrying case, which was attached to the drawcord of my trousers, and checked the screen. It was displaying only a phone number. I was aware that Josh was looking at me. He knew exactly what it was. The other kids were too busy listening to stories of doom and gloom on the high seas to notice, but Kelly never missed a trick. She shot me a concerned glance, which I ignored.

Pager networks cover a larger area than mobile phones, which was why the Intelligence Service used them. I preferred them anyway, because it gave me time to adjust mentally before someone bollocked me – or even worse, gave me the job from hell. I'd only had the pager for about six months. I wasn't too sure if it was a promotion to be given one, or if it meant I was considered a sad fuck and always available, locked away like a guard dog until needed, then once done, given a bone and sent back into the kennel.

Josh raised an eyebrow. 'Dramas?'

I shrugged. 'Dunno, I'm gonna have to phone. Can you hold the fort?'

He nodded. 'See you in a few.'

The stories were still going on and the rest of the crew were producing tubs of ice cream for the spellbound kids. I slipped away and went down the stairs to one of the lower decks, where we were going to be sleeping that night. Mattresses were spread out on the floor, and we'd had to bring our own fluffy sleeping bags, just like sixteenth-century sailors did, ho ho. I rummaged in my holdall for some small change, and went upstairs and tried to sneak off the boat without Kelly seeing me.

I should have known better. She must have been watching me like a hawk; as I looked round and saw her, I put my hand up and mouthed, 'Be back in a minute,' pointing at the pub. She looked puzzled, and more than a bit anxious. Josh was still with them, nodding and grimacing and generally joining in with the tales of seafaring derring-do. The cathedral bell rang out to tell me it was now eleven o'clock.

I found a payphone in the pub hallway. The Olde Thameside Inn had its first customers of the day: traders from the fruit market drinking pints, rubbing shoulders with the City dealers and their bottled beer. As I stood with my finger in my ear trying to listen for the dialling code, I found myself looking at racks of tourist flyers, rows and rows of the things telling me how great the Tower of London was, all of them seeming to point the finger at the scurvy mutineer who might be jumping ship.

I pushed a couple of coins into the slot and dialled the number, putting my finger back into my other ear to cut out Oasis on the juke box. After just one ring a very crisp, efficient female voice said, 'Hello?'

'It's Nick, returning the page.'

'Where are you?'

She knew exactly where I was. Every call to the Firm is logged on a digital display. They put as much effort into spying on each other as they do against the enemy. It was pointless tapping in 141 before the number, and saying, 'I'm in Glasgow and can't get back,' because whatever I did the display would still tell her I was at a payphone in Southwark.

I said, 'London.'

'Please wait.'

She pressed the cut-out button. Two minutes later she came back. 'You need to be at Gatwick at three thirty this afternoon.'

My heart sank, but I already knew I was going to be there. 'How long for?' Not that it mattered much, I was already a couple of jumps ahead, thinking about how I was going to make excuses to a recently turned nine-year-old.

She said, 'I don't have that information.'

Once she'd finished with the details of the RV, I put the phone down, expecting a refund of my unused coin, but I got nothing. The phone box in the pub was one of those private ones where you can charge whatever you want. For a pound I got all of sixty seconds.

I walked back, making my way around the crowd outside which had moved with the sun towards the ship. I was racking my brains thinking of what I was going to say. Not to Josh – that wouldn't be a problem – but to Kelly.

I saw Josh looking for me. It was only about twenty or thirty metres to the gangplank, and I was looking up at him and slowly shaking my head, getting some of the message across in advance. He knew exactly what was happening; he'd been there himself.

I went up the gangplank, pretty certain I would be in the shit, and no doubt starting to look suitably guilty. This was the first occasion Kelly and I had had any decent time together since she'd been in the UK; it was like a newly-wed leaving his honeymoon to go back to the office.

As I got on deck she and a few other kids were helping to clear up the plates under the bosun's instructions. For a horrible second or two I had a flashback of her in her house just before her family were killed, laying the table for her mother in the kitchen. It made me feel even more guilty, but I told myself we'd both get over it. She would be upset but I could make it up to her when I came back. Besides, she'd seen Josh and the kids, and we'd had a whale of a time. She'd understand. Plus, she could see her grandparents now.

Josh knew what was on the cards. He bent down to his kids. 'Yo!' He clapped his hands together as they waited for the instruction. 'OK, kids, let's get all these plates back to the bosun,' and he dragged them away.

I said, 'Kelly?'

'Mmm?' She didn't look up, just carried on being too busy picking up plates. She wasn't going to make it easy for me to give her the news.

'That was my boss on the phone. He wants me to go away.'

59

She still didn't look me in the eye as she put the plates in a bin. She said, 'Why?'

'They've got a job for me. I told them that I was going to be with you for the week and I didn't want to go in, but they said I must. There's nothing I can do.'

I was kind of hoping she'd buy the line that they were to blame, not me. She stopped what she was doing and spun round. Her face told me everything I didn't need to know. 'Nick, you promised.'

'I know, I can't help it. I've just been bleeped—'

'No,' she stopped me. 'It's beeped!' She was always giving me a bollocking for getting it wrong.

Her face had gone bright red. Tears were starting to well up in her eyes.

'Listen, Kelly, we can always do this again some other time. Just think, Josh and his children have to leave for home in a few days and won't have a chance to see all these places, but we can come back.'

'But you said . . . you promised me, Nick . . . you said you wanted to have a holiday with me . . .' The words tumbled out, punctuated by angry gasps for air. 'You said you'd make up for not seeing me on my birthday. You promised me then, Nick . . . you promised.'

She didn't just have her hand on my heartstrings, she'd braided them into ropes for extra purchase and was pulling on them big time. I said, 'I know I did, but that was last time. This time it will be different, I really mean it.'

Her bottom lip was starting to go and her eyes were leaking down her face. 'But, Nick, you *promised* . . .'

I stroked her hair. 'I'm sorry, I can't help it. I've got to go to work. Oh, come on, Kelly, cheer up.'

What the fuck was I saying? I always hated this. I didn't know what to do or say, and to make things worse I reckoned I was starting to sound like my Auntie Pauline.

The cry had become heart-rending sobs. 'But I don't want you to go . . . I want to stay here and be a sailor . . . I want you to stay here . . . I don't want to sleep on this boat without you.'

'Ah,' I said, and the way I said it was sufficiently ominous to make her look up. 'You won't be sleeping on the ship. I'm going to take you to see Granny and Grandad. Listen, I promise, I really do promise, I'll make this up to you.'

She stared at me long and hard, then slowly shook her head from side to side, deeply wounded. She'd been sold down the river, and she knew it. I wondered if she'd ever trust me again.

There was nothing I could say, because actually she was right. Just to make sure I avoided the issue, I walked across to the bosun. 'We've got to go,' I said. 'Family problem.' He nodded; who gives a fuck, he just gets paid to wear the hat and growl.

Josh came back. His kids were halfway through a lesson on how to hoist the sails. I said, 'We've got to go, mate.'

I tried to pat Kelly's head, but she flinched away from my hand. I said, 'Do you want to go downstairs and change? You can say goodbye in a minute. Go on, off you go.'

As she disappeared I looked at Josh and shrugged. 'What can I say, I've got to go to work.' And then, before he had the chance to come up with all sorts of different ways that he could help, I said, 'I'm going to take her down to her grandmother's now, then I'm off. I'm really sorry about this, mate.'

'Hey, chill, it doesn't matter. These things happen. It was just really good to see you.'

He was right. It had been really good to see him, too. 'Same here. Have a good flight back. I'll give you a call as soon as I've finished this job, and we'll come to you next time.'

'Like I told you, the beds are always made up. The coffee, white and flat, is always hot.'

It took me a moment to understand the white and flat bit. 'Is that some kind of Airborne saying?'

'Kinda.'

I said goodbye to his kids and they got back to pulling ropes and getting bollocked by the bosun. Then I went down below and changed.

2

We stopped at a pedestrian crossing to let a blue-haired New Age guy saunter across. I laughed. 'Kelly, look at that bloke there! Isn't he weird!' He had big lumps of metal sticking out of his nose, lips, eyebrows, all sorts. I said, 'I bet he wouldn't dare walk past a magnet factory.'

I laughed at my own joke. She didn't, possibly because it was so bad. 'You shouldn't make personal remarks like that,' she said. 'Anyway, I bet *he's* been to the Bloody Tower.' Her school work might be suffering a bit but she was still as sharp as her old man.

I looked across at her in the passenger seat and felt yet another pang of guilt. She was reading about how wonderful London was from a flyer we had in our hire car; she was sulking away, probably wondering what could be so important in my life that instead of taking her to see the Crown Jewels, I was dumping her back with her dreary old grandparents who she already saw enough of during the weekends out from her boarding school.

We drove through Docklands in the East End of London, past the outrageously tall office block on Canary Wharf; then, as we followed signs for the Blackwall Tunnel, the Millennium Dome, still under construction, came into view across the Thames. Trying anything to lighten the mood, I said, 'Hey, look, the world's biggest Burger King hat!'

At last I got a reaction; a slight movement of the lips, accompanied by a determined refusal to laugh.

Still heading towards the tunnel that took us under the Thames and south, we came to a petrol station just past the Burger King dome. I needed to call her grandparents.

It seemed that fuel was a sideline for this garage; it sold everything from disposable barbecues to lottery tickets and firewood. I undid my seat belt and tried to sound happy with life. 'Do you want anything from the shop?'

She shook her head as I got out to use the payphone on the wall. I'd get her something anyway. A nice bundle of kindling, maybe.

After pulling various bits of paper from my jacket pocket I found Carmen and Jimmy's phone number on a yellow Post-It note, its sticky bit covered with blue fluff from my jacket. Kelly was still sitting in the car, belted up and staring daggers at me, both for what I had done and what I was about to do.

I knew that they'd be in at this time of day. They always had lunch at home; in nearly fifty years of marriage they'd never eaten out. Carmen didn't like other people preparing her husband's food, and Jimmy had learned better than to argue. I also knew that Carmen would answer the phone; it seemed to be a house rule.

'Hello, Carmen, it's Nick. How are you both?'

'Oh, we're fine,' she said, a little crisply. 'Quite tired, of course,' she added, to introduce a tone of martyrdom at the first available opportunity.

I should have ignored it and got straight down to business. 'Tired?' I asked, and as I said it I suddenly remembered something.

'Oh yes, we stayed up until well after *News At Ten*. You said Kelly would be calling us.'

They hadn't heard from her since I'd taken her away for the trip, and I'd promised she would call. Mind you, Kelly hadn't exactly gone out of her way to remind me.

'I'm sorry, Carmen, she was so sleepy last night I didn't want to wake her.'

She didn't go for that one and I didn't blame her. She was right; at ten o'clock last night we were both filling our faces with Double Whoppers and chips.

'Oh well, I suppose we can talk to her now. Has she had her lunch?' What the question actually meant was: Have you remembered to feed our granddaughter? My thoughts went out to Jimmy, married to her for half a century, and her son, Kev. No wonder he'd headed west just as soon as he could.

I tried to laugh it off; for Kelly's sake I didn't want to rise to this emotional blackmail.

'Carmen, look, something has come up. I have to go away tonight. Would you be able to have her and take her back to school on Monday? I was going to take her out for the five days to "do" London, but she might as well go back now.'

There was excitement in the air, but she still had to carve off her pound of flesh. 'Of course. When will you be coming?'

'That's the problem, I haven't enough time to get her to you. Could you meet us at Gatwick?'

I knew they could. In fact, chances were that Jimmy was already being dispatched with an impatient motion of her hand to get his eleven-year-old mint-condition Rover out of the garage. The new door that had just been built gave direct access from the bungalow; he was very proud of that. I could picture him in there, wiping any stray finger marks off the paint work.

'Oh . . . can't you come here? It would mean we wouldn't get back until late.'

They only lived an hour from the airport, but anything to fuck me about.

'I can't, I'm afraid. I'm a bit strapped for time.'

'But where would we meet you?' There was an edge of panic in her voice at the thought of having to do something so challenging, mixed with annoyance that today's minute-by-minute routine was being disrupted. It must have been a riot growing up as Mr and Mrs Brown's little boy.

I'd sensed from the beginning that they – or rather, she – didn't really like me. Maybe she blamed me for their son's death; I certainly knew she resented the fact that I was the person he'd

64

appointed as their granddaughter's guardian, even though she knew very well that they were too old to look after her themselves. But fuck it, they'd be dead soon. I would just feel sorry for Kelly when that day came; she needed other people to support her, even if they were as suffocating as the Browns.

When I got back to the car Kelly was pretending to be engrossed in another flyer, and without looking up she greeted me with a downright martyr's sigh. I'd have to sort her out soon, or she was going to turn out like her poisoned granny.

I kept it upbeat. 'They're really excited about you coming to stay today instead of next weekend, they can't wait to see you and hear all about your time on the ship with everyone.'

'OK. That means that I go back to school when everybody else does?'

'Yes, but you'll have a great time with Granny and Grandpa first.'

She didn't share my optimism, but she was switched on enough to know that, even though they might be boring, they loved her dearly. It was the only reason I put up with them.

We got back onto the main drag and headed for the tunnel, me thinking about the RV details I'd been given. From Kelly there was nothing but brooding, oppressive silence and I didn't really know how to break it.

Eventually I said, 'I'll phone you at school one lunchtime next week, OK?'

She perked up. 'You will? You'll phone me?'

'Sure I will. I don't know when it will be, but I will.'

She looked at me and raised an accusing eyebrow. 'Is that going to be another one of your promises?'

I smiled and nodded my head. I knew I was digging myself a very deep hole here, because every time I promised I seemed to fuck up; I didn't have a clue what I'd be doing, and I knew it was a short-term gain. I hated this part of my responsibilities, I hated letting her down the way I'd been let down.

I said, 'Not just a promise – a double promise. We'll talk about all the things we'll do on our next holiday. I'll make it up to you, you'll see.'

She was studying my face, sizing me up. Having gained an inch, she was going to go for the full mile. 'Do I have to go to Granny and Grandad's?'

I could guess how she felt. She'd told me that when she was with them, she spent most of her time pulling her jumper back out of her jeans after Carmen had pulled them up to her armpits 'to keep out the cold'. I wouldn't want to be going there either, but I said, 'It'll be fine, don't worry about it. You were going to stay with them next weekend after school anyway. Another weekend won't hurt. I'll have a little chat and see if they'll take you to the aquarium to see those sharks we were talking about.'

She gave me a look to let me know the aquarium trip wouldn't happen. I knew she was right and ploughed on. 'One thing's for sure, I don't want them to take you to the Bloody Tower; that's our special thing, OK?'

There was a slow acknowledgement, even though she probably knew there was more chance of her grandmother meta-morphosing into Zoë Ball overnight. I indicated to get off the M23 on the last stretch towards the airport.

Signs welcomed us to the North Terminal and I headed up to the short-term parking. I kept up my goodness-me-I'm-so-excited voice. 'Right, let's go and see if Granny and Grandad are here yet, shall we? Tell you what, if they aren't, we'll go and have some-thing to eat. Hungry yet?' That should keep Granny happy.

She didn't say it, but the look she gave me as she got out of the car said, Cut the crap, dickhead, I've had it up to here. She'd been hung out with the washing; she knew it, and she wanted me to know that she knew it. I got hold of her hand and bag, because there was traffic all over the place, and followed the signs to the North Terminal.

I'd arranged to meet them in the Costa Coffee shop. It would be easy enough to find; even they could do it.

I looked at my G-Shock, the one I'd bought to replace the one I'd lost. It was a Baby-G this time – the new one – and when you pressed the backlight button, a little surfer came up on one of the displays. I quite enjoyed that, even though it was the same little

66

man doing the same little surfing thing every single time. Sad but true.

It was just past one o'clock. They weren't there yet. Trying to ease my guilt I took Kelly on a sightseeing tour of the shops and she landed up with bars of chocolate, an airline teddy bear and an All Saints CD. It was the easy way out; I knew it wouldn't achieve anything, but it made me feel a bit better.

We went back to the Costa Coffee shop and sat on bar stools with a view of the terminal entrance. She had an orange, I had a flat white, if that was what they called it, and we both had a sandwich as we sat watching a packed airport get fed, catch planes and generally spend more money in one hour than they would in an entire day on holiday.

Kelly said, 'Nick, do you know how long it takes before an elephant is born?'

'Nope.' I wasn't really listening; I was too busy bending over my coffee and looking out for Wallace and Gromit, resisting looking at my watch.

'Nearly two years.'

'Oh, that's interesting,' I said.

'OK, do you know how many people were in the world in 1960?'

'Three years.'

She'd sussed me out. 'Nick . . . Three billion. But very soon the world will have a population of six billion.'

I turned to look at her. 'You're very clever for a—'

Then I saw what she was doing: reading facts off the back of sugar packets. 'That's cheating!'

At last I got a smile from her. It turned into an actress's smile when she said through gritted teeth, 'Oh look, Granny and Grandad.'

'Well, off you go then and say hello!'

Muttering under her breath, she got off her stool and ran over to them. Their faces showed a mixture of relief at finding us and self-congratulation at being brave enough to be out and about in such a big, busy place. Kelly gave them both a hug; she did love them, it was just that they weren't the sort of people you'd want

67

to spend all day with, let alone a bonus weekend. Their trouble was, they didn't actually do anything. They didn't take her to the park or on outings; they just kind of sat there expecting her to draw pictures and drink cups of tea.

Jimmy was wearing cream flannels and a beige anorak; Carmen wore clothes from the sort of catalogue that had Judith Chalmers on the cover. Jimmy's face seemed to have no features whatsoever; he looked as if he'd been designed in a wind tunnel. Kev must have got his dark skin and eyes from his mother, who still looked attractive, even if she did believe people really thought her jet-black hair was natural.

The pair of them were busy fussing all over her, asking her what she'd done as they walked towards me. I got in there first, flicking my eyes between them as I spoke. 'Jim, Carmen, how are things?' And before they could debrief me on the road conditions and the exact route they'd taken I got straight down to it. 'Look, I'm sorry about this, but I've got to go. You sure you're OK for the rest of the weekend?'

They were both very happy. It was like Christmas again, except that that time it had been Heathrow and Kelly had had to be picked up four days early. They never understood why someone so erratic had been chosen as her guardian; they didn't even know me and I was clearly not suited to the task. I bet they had me down as one of Kev's wife's friends. They never did like Marsha. When they weren't blaming me for their son's murder, they were probably blaming her, not that she was around to answer back.

Carmen busied herself doing up the top button of Kelly's shirt and tucking the whole thing back into her jeans. You can't take any chances, the draughts you get in airports.

I made sure they saw me take a quick look at my watch. I had loads of time, but it didn't mean I wanted to stay. 'I've really got to go now. Kelly, give us a hug and a kiss.'

She wrapped her arms around me and I bent at the waist so we could kiss. Carmen hated that, because Kelly didn't show them the same sort of sustained affection. She did with them only what she knew was expected, and I had to admit that made me feel good.

68

I looked her in the eye and mimed a mock phone call with my hand. 'I promise.'

She raised an eyebrow and gave me a withering look. 'Is that a Nick promise?' she said quietly, so that only I could hear it. I suddenly saw about twenty years into the future; she was going to grow up into the sort of woman who could light a fire just by looking at it.

'No,' I said, equally quietly, 'it's an NPP.'

'What's that?'

'Normal person's promise.'

She liked that one and nodded.

I knew I'd dropped myself in the shit even more, just as my parents had done with me. By now it was almost unbearable. Carmen and Jimmy were uncomfortable with our private intimacy, and I really didn't know how to behave in these situations. I was feeling more guilty than ever. I just wanted to leave.

The look on Kelly's face made me remember my thirteenth birthday. My parents didn't. They made up for it by running to the corner shop and buying a board game in the shape of a robot for seventy-five pence. The reason I knew that was because it wasn't even wrapped up, just in a bag with the price tag still on. I knew how it felt to be let down by the ones who are supposed to love you most.

I whispered in her ear, 'I've got to go.'

As I stood up, Carmen's nod told me I should have left ten minutes ago. She said, 'We'll be hearing from you, then?' in that special way of hers that suggested she wouldn't exactly be holding her breath.

'Of course we will, Granny,' Kelly said. 'When Nick makes a promise he always keeps it.' She might be lying through her teeth, but she knew when to back me up.

I grinned. 'Yeah, something like that. Bye now.'

Jimmy smiled weakly. I couldn't tell if he was happy or just had wind. I couldn't remember the last time I'd heard him speak.

Carmen decided it was time for Kelly to cut from me. 'Oh, that's nice, you've got a record, have you?' she said. 'Who's it by?'

'All Saints.'

'Oh, they're good, aren't they? My favourite is the ginger one with the Union Jack dress.'

'That's the Spice Girls.'

'Oh, is it?' Carmen glared at me as if it was my fault, then rounded on Jimmy. 'Grandad doesn't like any of them; he doesn't go for all that piercing.'

Kelly looked at me and rolled her eyes. As the look changed to one of desperation, I turned on my heel and walked away.

3

I made as if to go back to the carpark, but instead jumped onto the transit train that would take me to the South Terminal. I kept thinking about the fuck-up and how Kelly must be feeling, but I would have to cut from that soon. I decided to use the two-minute journey to sort out my guilt, then bung the work cassette into the back of my head before I got off the train.

The shuttle was full of all the usual airport suspects: young couples in matching football shirts, him with a team holdall, her with copies of *Hello!* magazine and wordsearch puzzle books; and businessmen in suits, carrying briefcases and laptops and looking in dire need of *The Little Book of Calm*.

I walked into the South Terminal, following the signs to the short-term carpark, and took the lift to the top floor. I was in work mode now; everything else had been put to one side in another compartment.

The exposed roof level was about three-quarters full. The deafening sound of aircraft taking off blanketed all the other noises of cars and clattering luggage trolleys. I half closed my eyes to protect them from the glare of sunlight as I started walking down the aisles.

In a row of wagons, down the middle, I spotted what I'd been told to look for: a Toyota Previa people carrier, dark blue with tinted windows. Maybe the Firm had found a use for the ones brought back from Syria after all; it wasn't as if Hertz would have been too happy to have them back. I went to the rear of the row of vehicles and started to follow the line of cars towards it.

Since the change of government in 1997, every department seemed to be using people carriers. I didn't know if it was policy or just that Tony Blair used one, but they were a great improvement – much more room for a briefing, instead of sitting hunched up in the back of a saloon with your knees around your head. Besides, they were easy to find in a hurry.

As I got closer I spotted a driver in the front seat, filling up the right-hand side of the cab area, reading the *Evening Standard* and looking uncomfortable in his collar and tie. None of the windows were open. The size of his head and his flat-top haircut made it look as if it should have been sticking out of the turret of a Panzer.

I approached casually from the rear, checking the number plate. I couldn't exactly remember the full registration but I knew that it would be a P. The thing I was looking for was the VDM, and sure enough, above the Toyota sign, on the bottom left side of the tail, was the small chrome outline of a fish, the trademark of heavy-duty Christians. This was the one; I went up to the sliding door on the side and waited, listening to the engine purr.

The door opened out a few inches, then slid back to reveal the two rows of passenger seats. I looked inside.

I hadn't seen Colonel Lynn for nearly a year, but he hadn't changed much. He hadn't lost any more hair, which I was sure he was happy about. His clothes were the same as always, mustard-coloured corduroy trousers, a sports jacket with well-worn leather elbows, and what looked like the same Viyella shirt he'd been wearing the last time we'd met, just a bit more frayed around the collar.

I climbed in and slid the door closed behind me. I could feel the air-conditioning working overtime as I took my seat next to him and we shook hands. Lynn had that fresh-from-the-shower officer's smell about him; maybe he'd taken in a quick game of squash at the Guards' barracks in Chelsea before coming to the meeting. Between his feet was a dark-blue nylon daysack, which I recognized. It was my quick-move kit.

There was somebody else in there, in the rear row of seats, who I also recognized. I turned and nodded politely at her. She returned the gesture, refolding her copy of the *Daily Telegraph*. It was only the second time that I'd met Elizabeth Bamber in person. Last time hadn't gone too well; she was on the selection board which refused me permanent cadre. It seemed that our cultural differences didn't endear us to each other during the interview.

Permanent cadre are Ks – deniable operators on a salaried retainer – not freelancers like me, called on to carry out shit jobs that no-one else wants. The pay I got was £210 a day for ops, £160 for training days. I wasn't too sure what the retainer was, but I knew that, like all other payments, it would be handed over in a brown envelope with no tax or national insurance to pay. It was a bit like casual labour, which made me feel used and fucked over, but I liked the money – what there was of it. In any case, it was the only line of work I'd ever known, and I was more afraid of what I would become without it.

I didn't know exactly what Elizabeth did, or for whom; all I knew was that she was one of those women who, if they weren't working for the Intelligence Service, would probably own a stable full of racehorses. She probably did anyway. She had that sort of broken-veined, no-nonsense, out-in-the-fresh-air look about her. She was medium height and in her late forties – or at least looked it, especially with her shoulder-length hair, which was 60 per cent grey, with a centre parting and a little fringe, though I doubted she gave much of a fuck about it. In fact, having hair was probably a bit of an inconvenience for someone like her, because it took valuable time to comb the stuff.

She was wearing a very smart, sensible, grey two-piece that looked as if it had cost a fortune; it would have been economical in the long run, however, because she probably wore it every third day, alternating it with the two other equally expensive out-fits she bought every year in the Harvey Nichols sale. Under her jacket was a blouse with a long scarf attached, which was tied into a bow. The smart but practical look was complemented by an almost total lack of make-up – it probably took too long in the morning to put it on, and she couldn't be bothered with that: she had a country to protect.

I made a half-turn back towards Lynn so that I only had to move my head to see each of them. There was silence for about half a minute, broken by the rustling of a newspaper in the front. I glanced to my left and saw the driver's huge neck sitting on a very wide back and slightly hanging over his collar. I could see part of his face in the rear-view mirror; his pale skin and near-Slavic looks gave the game away: he was a Serb, no doubt promised passports for his entire family if he spied for us during the Bosnian war. This guy would now be more loyal to the UK than most Brits, myself included.

Still we just sat there. Elizabeth was looking at me; I was looking at her. Come on, I thought, let's get on with it. It always felt as if they were toying with me.

It was Lynn who kicked off. 'We haven't seen you for a long time, Nick. How's life?'

As if he cared. 'No complaints. How long am I going to be away?'

'It will depend on how quickly you can get the task done. Listen to what Elizabeth has to say.'

Elizabeth was primed, ready to go; she didn't even have notes. She levelled her gaze on me, and said, 'Sarah Greenwood.' It was delivered more as a question than a statement, and her eyes narrowed slightly, as if she was expecting an answer.

My reaction when I heard the name surprised me. I felt as if I'd just been told I had a fatal disease. My hard drive was spinning. Was she dead? Had she fucked up? Had she got me in trouble? Had she been lifted? I wasn't going to show these people anything more than I had to; I tried to remain casual and unconcerned, but all I really wanted to do was ask, 'Is she OK?'

She said, 'You know her, I believe?'

'Of course I know her – by that name anyway.' I didn't say how I knew her name, or what jobs I'd done with her. I didn't know how much Elizabeth knew, so I just played it straight, which is always the best thing to do. In my experience, the less you say, the less drama you get yourself into. It's good having two ears, but even better to have just one mouth.

'Well, it seems that she has disappeared – and of her own accord.'

I looked at her, waiting for the follow-on, but she let it hang. I didn't exactly know what she was getting at, yet she was looking at me as if I should know.

Lynn saw the problem. 'Let me explain, Nick.'

As I turned my head towards Lynn, I caught him just finishing eye contact with Elizabeth. He was playing the peacemaker here.

He said, 'Two years ago, Sarah Greenwood was posted to the Washington desk. You are aware of that?'

Of course I was. I always tried to keep tabs on where she was and how she was getting on, though I never kidded myself that the interest was mutual. I'd half hoped that she'd make an appearance during my debrief over last year's fuck-up in the States, but she didn't. I realized he was still waiting for an answer. 'No, not really.'

There was a pause as Lynn glanced again at Elizabeth. It looked as if he needed the nod to continue; he must have got it, because he said, 'Sarah has been UK liaison with the Counter-terrorism Center, a new intelligence cell set up by the CIA to provide warnings against potential terrorist attacks. It's a central clearing house, if you like, for intelligence on terrorism worldwide. Here is the problem. As Elizabeth has already said, Sarah has disappeared – we know she's still on the US mainland, but we don't know where or why she has gone. We fear that her reliability and judgement are, how shall I say it, in doubt.'

I couldn't help a smile. That was the standard fuck-off when what they were really saying was: 'We don't like you any more. You have done something wrong and you are no longer one of us.'

Now it was time for Elizabeth to join in. She said, 'Let's just say, since her posting in Washington she has been engaging in too many initiatives of her own.'

Still looking at Lynn, I smiled again. 'Oh I see – too many initiatives.' I gave her word the full five syllables.

I hated it when they beat around the bush. Why didn't they just get on with it and tell me what the fuck was happening and what they wanted me to do about it? Before I could get an answer we were interrupted by the arrival of some punters.

'Oi! You're not on holiday now; give a hand with these sodding bags!'

'All right, don't get out yer bleedin' pram!'

Everything stopped as we all looked over to the driver's side of the wagon. I couldn't see Lynn's face, but Elizabeth's registered disgust. Two couples were standing by a Ford Escort XR3i. While we'd been waffling away they'd turned up, opened the boot and were loading their luggage. One young couple, both in their mid-twenties, had come to pick up the other one. The girl back from holiday was wearing white cut-down jeans with half her arse hanging out to show us how brown she was, but the effect was spoiled a bit by all the exposed skin being goose bumped, what with this being Gatwick rather than Tenerife. Just in case we didn't get the message that she'd been away, her bottled blond hair was in beads where it had been braided by a beach hustler.

Our man in the driving seat was keeping an eye on them continuously, still with the paper up, still on the same page, the skin of his massive neck hanging over his collar even more as he looked right in his wing mirror checking everything out. These boys had to be jacks of all trades, offensive and defensive drivers, as well as body guards to protect their 'principals' and great joke-tellers to entertain them. Maybe that was why the Serb worked for Elizabeth. She wasn't the sort of person who understood jokes, and judging by the Serb's expression as he tried to follow the Estuary English outside, he wasn't up to speed on banter either. I just hoped he wasn't learning his English from these two in the wagon – people would think that Prince Charles had been hitting the gym.

The entertainment was over. We all turned back to our original positions and Elizabeth carried on, physically affected by what she had just seen. Her breed found such people a terrible stain on their ordered lives. 'We are concerned that there might be a conflict about the ethics of her employment.'

I tried not to laugh. 'Ethics? That's not Sarah. She's got ethics filed under "Things to worry about when I'm dead".' I risked a chuckle, but either Elizabeth didn't understand, or she got the joke and didn't like it. The atmosphere felt so frosty I wondered if the Serb had adjusted the air-conditioning. I was slowly welcoming myself out of this wagon.

Elizabeth continued as if I still hadn't spoken. 'We feel that this could expose current operations and put operators' lives in very real danger.'

That stopped me smiling. 'How do you know Sarah might be putting operations at risk?'

'That', she said, 'you don't need to know.' I could see she'd enjoyed saying that. 'However, let me give you an example of the problem we face. The information that Sarah Greenwood retrieved from Syria – I understand that you were part of that operation? – the material delivered to us was in fact incorrect. It would appear that she quite deliberately distorted information she knew was important to us and the Americans.'

So they had wanted what was on the computers after all. And, as usual, I had been one of their mushrooms, kept in the dark and fed on shit.

She was on a roll now. 'It was most unfortunate that the Source was killed – after all, that was your task: to bring him back. We still don't know what intelligence the Syrian operation would have revealed – because you destroyed the computers on site, I believe.'

She made it sound as if I'd done all that on some kind of whim. I let her carry on, but inwardly I was ready to punch her lights out.

'The Americans were not pleased with our efforts, and I have to say, it was hardly one of our finest hours.'

I wasn't going to let her rev me up even more. For years we'd done jobs for the US that Congress would never sanction, or which were against the 1974 executive order prohibiting US involvement in assassination. The job had been false-flagged as an Israeli operation because the US could not be seen to be screaming into Syria and kidnapping an international financier, even if he did happen to be the right-hand man of the world's most prolific terrorist. However, by making it look like a joint operation between the Israeli military and Mossad, everyone was a winner: America would get the Source, the UK would have the satisfaction of doing a difficult job well and Israel would reap all the kudos. Not that they knew about it when it was happening – they never did – but they would still take all the credit.

I thought back to Syria and Sarah's frantic work on the laptop, and the fact that she had killed the Source. Sarah had certainly sounded convincing during the debrief, and after that I didn't even think about it, it was finished. Whatever had happened since then didn't worry me either; it wasn't going to change my life. Well, maybe it was now.

Elizabeth continued, 'She could have caused a major change in foreign policy, and that, I must say, would have been most detrimental to the UK's and US's balance of payments and influence in the region . . .'

She was talking crap. I bet the reason she was pissed off was because Clinton had recently signed a 'lethal presidential order' against Bin Laden. He had authorised, in advance, an aggressive operation to arrest him if the opportunity arose, at the same time recognizing that some of those involved might be killed. In other words, Clinton had found a way round America's strict anti-assassination rules, and the Firm would be done out of some work. I could see that Sarah fucking about wouldn't help matters.

I waited for the part Elizabeth had forgotten to emphasize. There are three things they like to give you at a briefing, when they eventually get round to saying what they really mean. One, the aim of the task; two, the reason why the task has to happen; and three, the incentive for the operator. I saw her eyes move fractionally up and to the left. She was lying.

'. . . as well as putting operators at risk in the area. Which is, of course, our most important consideration.' Not a bad incentive, I thought – even if she was talking bollocks – especially if it was me operating there.

'As to her motives, well, that's not for you to worry about.'

I was starting to feel uneasy about all this. I turned to Lynn. 'If you were worried about this back then, why didn't you just give her a bung?'

From behind me Elizabeth said, 'A bung? A bung?'

Lynn looked over my head and said, in the voice of a QC patiently explaining a blow job to a High Court judge, 'Money. No, Nick, we didn't offer her a bung. You know as well as I do that the service never bribes or pays anyone off.'

I couldn't believe he'd said that and I somehow managed to keep a straight face. Amazingly, so did he. They look after their own in the Intelligence Service. Even if the IG's been given the sack for gross misconduct, whether it's for being a paedophile and getting blackmailed for it, or for just screwing up the job, he goes into a feeder system where he gets work, and that does two things – it keeps tabs on him, but it also keeps him sweet, and, more importantly, quiet. That's what a bung is all about: keeping the house in order.

I wished they would give me one. Only a few months earlier I'd been escorting an IG called Clive to a service apartment in London. These apartments are paid for, furnished and run by the Intelligence Service. Nobody lives in them; they're used for meetings, briefings and debriefings, and as safe houses.

Clive had had a bit of a drama with Gordievsky, the Russian dissident who'd years ago defected to the West with a headful of secrets. The former KGB chief was briefing the Intelligence Service at one of the training establishments near the Solent on the south coast. Clive and two others refused to go to the presentation, on the grounds that Gordievsky was a traitor, and it didn't matter which side he came from. I happened to believe they were right, but they still got cut away. After all, it was very embarrassing for HMG to have its people calling an inbound defector a scumbag. Two went quietly with a pay-off and jobs supplied by the Good Lads' Club – the City. Clive, however, refused to go. The best way, it seemed to the service, was to offer him a bigger wad than the other two. If that was refused, then he could have as much pain as money can buy.

I persuaded him into a flat in Cambridge Street, Pimlico, and listened as they offered him 200 grand to shut up and fuck off to the City. Clive picked up the money, ripped it out of its plastic bank wallets, opened the window and scattered it like confetti. As the hundreds of notes fluttered down onto the corner pub on Cambridge Street, the punters must have thought Christmas had been brought forward to June. 'You want to fuck me off?' Clive said. 'Then it's going to cost you a fucking sight more than this.'

I thought it was great and wanted to join the pub crowd fighting for fifty-pound notes. To my mind the boy had done good; nobody likes a traitor, no matter what side you think you're on. I really hoped Sarah wasn't one, because I liked her. Actually, I liked her a lot.

I asked Elizabeth, 'And you're sure that she hasn't been lifted?'

She looked at Lynn. 'Lifted?'

It was a bit like being at Wimbledon, sitting between these two. Lynn had to interrupt again because Elizabeth seemed about as switched on to real life as Mickey Mouse.

I asked, 'So what do you want me to do about it?'

Elizabeth kept it very simple. 'Find her.'

I waited for the rest of the sentence. There was nothing. It was the most succinct aim I'd ever been given.

'Do you know where she could be? I need a start point.'

She thought for a while. 'You will start in Washington. Her apartment, I think, would be best, don't you?'

Yes, I didn't disagree with that. But I had another question: 'Why don't you get the Americans to help you? They'd have the resources to track her down much faster.'

She sighed. 'As I thought I was making clear to you, this matter needs to be handled with the least possible amount of fuss, and speedily.' She looked at Lynn. He cleared his throat and turned to face me. 'We don't really want to involve any American departments yet. Not even our embassy staff are aware of the situation. As you might imagine, it's somewhat embarrassing to have one of our own IGs missing in the host country. Especially with Netanyahu and Arafat in the US for the Wye summit.' He paused. 'If you fail to find her they will have to know, and they will have to take action. This is a very grave situation, Nick. It could cause us a lot of embarrassment.'

I had been given the shortest aim ever, and now I'd also been told the clearest reason why. Lynn showed the worry on his face. 'We need to find her quickly. No-one must know. I emphasize, no-one.'

I hated it when these people used the word 'we'. They're in the shit, and all of a sudden it's 'we'. If the job went wrong it would have no father but me.

I calmed down. 'That's why you want a K – it's a deniable op?'
He nodded.

Why me? I said, 'Isn't this a job for the security cell? They're used to investigations. This isn't my sort of work.'

'This isn't something that needs to go any further within the service.' There was irritation in Elizabeth's voice. 'I particularly wanted you for the job, Mr Stone, as I understand you know Sarah better than most.'

I looked at her, still trying not to show any emotion. She'd raised a knowing eyebrow as she said it. Shit. I tried to look puzzled. 'I know her, if that's what you mean, and I've worked with her, but that's about it.'

She tilted her head slightly to one side. She knew I was lying. 'Really? I was informed that the relationship between you was somewhat cosier. In fact I was told that the reason for your divorce after leaving the military was due entirely to your relationship with Sarah Greenwood. Am I mistaken?'

She wasn't, and I now understood even more. They had chosen me because they thought I knew her well enough to have a chance of finding her. They were fire-fighting, and they were using me as Red Adair. Fuck 'em, let them sort their own shit out. I might be pissed off, but I wasn't stupid. It was excuse time. 'It's not going to work,' I said. 'The US is a big place, and what am I going to do on my own? I haven't seen her for ages and we weren't that close. What can I do? What's the use of even getting on a flight?'

Lynn bent down to pick up my quick-move kit. 'You will be going on the flight. You will start an investigation to find her. If not, I'm afraid you will find yourself in gaol.'

I felt like saying, 'Come off it, that's the sort of line I use myself when I'm threatening people. You can do better than that.' But I had learned the hard way to keep my mouth shut, and it was just as well I did. Lynn had my daysack on his knees now.

'Credit us with a little intelligence, Nick. Do you really think we don't know the full events of last year?'

My stomach lurched and I knew my cheeks were starting to burn. I tried to remain calm, waiting to hear what he had to say.

'Nick, your version of events leaves out a number of details, any of which will put you behind bars if we so choose. We haven't investigated the money you kept, or the unlawful killings you performed.'

That sounded rich coming from a man who had sent me out routinely to 'perform' unlawfully. But I knew that they could stitch me up if they wanted. It was par for the course; I'd even been part of the stitch-up sometimes. I now knew how it felt.

There was an outside chance they were bluffing. I stared at him and waited to see what else he had to say. I soon wished I hadn't, because it gave Elizabeth another opening.

'Mr Stone, let us consider your situation. What, for example, would happen to the child in your guardianship if you were imprisoned? Her life must be difficult enough as it is, I should have thought: new country, new school . . .'

How the fuck did they know all this? I thought I'd already been given my incentive, but obviously not. They didn't come any less subtle than this. I had to clench my fists to control myself. I felt like kicking the shit out of both of them. They knew it, and maybe that was why Godzilla was in the driving seat. It's always unwise to fuck with a man who has a neck bigger than your own head, especially if he probably has enough weaponry in the footwell to shoot down a jumbo jet. I took a deep breath, accepted I was in the shit and let it out again.

Elizabeth carried on as Lynn opened my daysack. 'Having found her, report back where she is and what she's doing. Then await further instructions.'

I turned back to Lynn. I knew she had finished and he would now give me the details I needed. I could hear the newspaper being unfolded. She was probably checking which of her horses were running tomorrow. I tried to keep my breathing under control. I felt angry and helpless, my two least favourite emotions.

Lynn was unloading the bag and handing me the items. My cover documentation, driver's licence, passport and even an advert for books from a local paper, showed that, as from now, I lived in Derbyshire. There were three credit cards. These would have been serviced every month, and used so that I ended up with a normal bill like everyone else. The family who covered for me made sure of that; years ago we used to keep all this stuff with us all the time, but there were too many fuck-ups, with people getting corrupt and using the credit cards to pay for new cars and silk underwear for their mistresses. An audit a few years earlier had unearthed two K operators who had never even existed, and somebody somewhere was drawing off the money.

Lynn said, 'There's the photography kit to Mac anything down to us.'

I had a quick look inside. From the way that Lynn said it, I knew he'd just got the briefing on this kit, and it sounded all exciting and sexy. I nodded. 'Great, thanks.'

'Here are your flight details and here are your tickets.' As he got them out of the bag he checked the details and said, 'Oh, so you're Nick Snell now?'

'Yep, that's me.' It had been for quite a while now, ever since I became operational again after . . . well, after what I'd thought I'd got away with.

Then he produced two flash cards from envelopes and handed them to me. 'Your codes. Do you want to check them?'

'Of course.' He passed the bag to me. I took out the Psion 3C personal organizer and turned it on. I'd been trying to get the new 5 Series out of the service, but unless the funds were for building squash courts, it was like trying to get blood from a stone. All the Ks would have to put up with the 3Cs they'd bought two years ago – and the thing I had was one of the early ones, which didn't even have the backlit display. Their attitude to kit was the same as that of a thrifty mother who buys you a school uniform several sizes too big, only in reverse.

I put the cards into both of the ports. It would be no good getting on the ground and finding that these things didn't work. I opened up each one in turn and checked the screen. One just had a series of five number sequences; I closed that down and took it out. The other had rows of words with groups of numbers next to each word. All was in order.

'The contact number is . . .' Lynn started to reel off a London number. The Psion held the names and addresses of everyone from the bank manager to the local pizza shop, as you would have as part of your cover. I hit the data icon, and tapped the telephone number straight in, adding, as I always did, the address 'Kay's sweet shop'. I could sense Elizabeth's eyes burning into the back of my head and I turned round. She was looking disapprovingly at me over the top of her paper, clearly put out that I was entering her contact number in the 3C. But there was no way I'd remember it that quickly; I'd need to go away and look at it, and once I had it in my head I'd wipe it off. I'd never been clever enough to remember strings of telephone numbers or map co-ordinates as they were given to me.

Lynn carried on with the details. 'Once in DC, make contact with Michael Warner.' He gave me a contact number, which I also tapped in. 'He's a good man, used to work in communications, but had a car accident and needed to have steel plates in his head.'

I closed down the Psion. 'What's he do now?'

Elizabeth had finished with the racing section and turned to the share prices. The driver still hadn't turned a page. Either he was learning the recipe of the day by heart or he'd gone into a trance.

Lynn said, 'He's Sarah's PA. He'll let you into her apartment.'

I nodded. 'What's the cover story?'

Lynn looked impatiently at his watch; maybe he had another squash game to get to. 'He knows nothing, apart from the fact that London needs to check out her security while she's away on business. It's time for her PV review.'

Personal vetting is carried out every few years to make sure you aren't becoming a target for blackmail, or sleeping with the

Chinese defence attaché – unless you've been asked to by Her Majesty's Government – or that you, your mother, or your great aunt haven't chucked in your lot with the Monster Raving Loony Party. Not that that would have meant that much in the past. Once you were 'in' as an IG things seemed to flow along without much in the way of monitoring, unless you were at the lower end of the food chain – my end – when it was a completely different story.

'He is a bit strange at times; you may have to be patient.' Lynn started to smile. 'He had to leave the comms cell because his steel plate picked up certain frequencies and he used to get terrible head pain. He's good at his job, though.' The smile faded as he added pointedly, 'And more important, he's loyal.'

I shrugged. 'Fine.' Chances were that Metal Mickey was loyal because he couldn't get a job anywhere else, apart from as a relay station for Cellnet.

I was packing everything back into the bag. I couldn't wait to get into the fresh air; I was fed up with being scrutinized and fucked over by these people. But Lynn hadn't finished. He had one more item, which he shoved right under my nose. It was a sheet of white A4 paper, requiring a signature for the codes. I used Lynn's pen to scribble mine and handed it back. No matter what happens, you've still got to sign for every single thing. Everyone needs to cover their arse.

I pushed open the door and slid it back, picking up the day-sack. When my feet were on the concrete I turned and said, 'What if I can't find her?'

Elizabeth lowered the paper and gave me the sort of look she'd given our friends in the Ford Escort.

Lynn glanced at Elizabeth, then back at me. 'Get yourself a good barrister.'

I picked up the daysack, turned away and started to walk towards the lift. I heard the door slide closed, and moments later the Previa moved off.

4

I walked towards the lift trying not to get myself into a rage. I didn't know what had brought it back on – the fact that the Firm knew about both Sarah and Kelly, or the fact that I'd been stupid enough to think they didn't. I tried to calm down by telling myself that, in their shoes, I would have done exactly the same, would have used it as a lever to make me do the job. It was a fair one, but that didn't make me any happier about being on the receiving end.

I got to the lift and jabbed the button. I looked at the red digital display above the door. Nothing was moving. An elderly couple arrived, having an argument about the way their bags were stacked on the trolley. We all waited.

The lift stopped at every floor but ours. I stabbed at the button six times in rapid succession and the elderly couple shut up and moved to the other side of their trolley to keep out of my way.

Maybe it was Sarah I was pissed off with, or maybe I was just pissed off with myself for letting her under my guard. Elizabeth was spot on, she had been responsible for my divorce.

The wait for the lift was starting to turn into a joke. More people had arrived with trolleys and were milling about. I took the stairs. Two levels down, I followed the signs to departures across the skywalk, fighting my way against a stream of pedestrian traffic with suntans. Several charter flights must have come in at once.

I couldn't get the briefing out of my mind. How was it that they knew everything about last year's fuck-up? I'd kept my mouth shut all along and just let them have the barest of facts.

There was no way I was going to let them take the money off me. Did they even know about it? I had a brainwave and started to feel better. They couldn't know everything. If so, they would know that I had enough evidence to put a few of the fuckers behind bars for ever, and if they knew that, they wouldn't risk threatening me. Then I felt pissed off again: they could do what they wanted, because they knew about Kelly. I'd seen grown men's emotions getting fucked over and used against them when it came to their kids, but I'd never thought it would happen to me. I cut all the conjecture from my mind and started working.

Departures was the normal mayhem – people trying to steer trolleys that had other ideas and parents chasing runaway two-year-olds. A gaggle of pubescent schoolkids with tin grins were on a trip somewhere, and an American kids' orchestra were sitting on their trombone and bassoon cases, bored with waiting to check in.

I went to the cashpoint, then to the *bureau de change*. Next priority was to find myself some plausible hand luggage. I bought myself a leather holdall, threw in my quick-move daysack and headed for the pharmacy for washing and shaving stuff. After that I hit a clothes shop for a pair of jeans, a couple of shirts and spare underwear.

I checked in at the American Airlines business-class desk and fast-tracked airside into the lounge, where I got straight on my mobile to contact my 'family'. They were good people, James and Rosemary. They had loved me like a son since I boarded with them years ago, or that was the cover story, anyway. James always seemed like a father should be; he was certainly the sort of man who would have taken his eight-year-old around HMS *Belfast*. Both civil servants who had taken early retirement, they had never had any children because of their careers, and were still doing their bit for Queen and country. I even had a bedroom – they called it 'Nick's room' – in the loft. If all your document-ation shows that's where you live, you must have a room, surely?

These were the people who would both confirm my cover story and also be part of it. I visited them whenever I could, especially before an op, with the result that my cover got stronger as time passed. They knew nothing about the ops and didn't want to; we would just talk about what was going on at the social club, and what to do with greenfly on the roses. James wasn't the best gardener in the world, but this sort of detail gives substance to a cover. While I was in the area I would use my credit cards at one or two local shops, collect any mail and leave. It was a pain to do, but details count.

'Hello, James, it's Nick here. Quick change of plan. I'm going for a holiday in America.' I might have changed names, but not James and Rosemary. They just got used to the change of details; after all, I was their third 'son' since retirement.

'Any idea how long for?'

'A couple of weeks probably.'

'All right, have a good holiday then, Nick. Be careful; it's a violent country.'

'I'll do my best. See you when I get back. Say hello to Rosemary for me.'

'Of course, see you soon. Oh, Nick . . .'

'Yes?'

'Local council elections. It was a Lib Dem who got in.'

'OK, Lib Dem. Male or female?'

'Male, Felix something. His ticket was to stop the planning per-mission for the superstore.'

'Oh, OK. Will he block it?'

'Don't be stupid. And talking of blockages, the problem with the septic tank got sorted out yesterday.'

'OK, cheers. I tell you what, I'm glad your shit is sorted out there, because I'm up to my neck in it here.' We were both still laughing as I pressed 'end' and watched the businessmen frantically bent over their laptops.

There was nothing else to do now but wait for my flight, my

head slowly filling up with Sarah. I didn't want to do this job. She'd fucked me up, but I still missed her. I could see that if what I was being told was right, she definitely needed to be stopped; it was just that I didn't want to be the one to do it.

5

I settled into my business-class seat, listening first to the screams and banter of the zit-faced, hormonal boys and girls from the band twenty rows behind me, then to a very smooth, west coast American voice saying how wonderful it was for the flight crew and cabin staff to be able to serve us today.

They filled us with drink and a meal of chicken covered in stuff, and it was only then that I closed my eyes and started to think seriously about how I was going to find Sarah.

Even in the UK, a quarter of a million people go missing each year, over 16,000 of them permanently – not, for the most part, because they've been abducted, but out of deliberate choice. If you go about it the right way it's a very simple thing to do. Sarah knew how to do that; it was part of her job. Finding a missing person in the UK was bad enough, but the sheer size of the USA, and the fact that I couldn't turn to anyone for help, meant it was going to be like looking for a needle in a haystack, in a field full of haystacks, in a country full of fields.

Whatever was going on in her head, like most people in this business, Sarah would have her security blanket tucked away. Part of that would be another identity. I had two back-up IDs, in case one was discovered. Everybody finds their own way to build one up and, more especially, hide it from the Firm. If you ever had to do a runner from them, you'd need that head start, and if

Sarah had it in mind to disappear it would have been well planned. She wasn't the sort of person to do anything at half-cock.

Then again, nor was I. I thought about my new mate, Nicholas Davidson, who I'd bumped into in Australia the year before. He was a bit younger than me, and had the same Christian name, which is always a good start, as it helps when reacting to a new ID. But more importantly, both Nick and Davidson are very common names.

I found him in a gay bar in Sydney. It's usually the best place for what I had in mind, whatever country you're in. Nicholas, I soon learned, had been living and working in Australia for six years; he had a good job behind the bar and a partner with whom he shared a house; most important of all, he had no intention of going back to the UK. Pointing out of the window, he said, 'Look at the weather. Look at the people. Look at the lifestyle. What do I want to go back for?' I got to know him over two or three weeks; I'd pop in there a couple of times a week, when I knew it was his shift, and we'd have a chat. I met other gay men there, but they didn't have what Nicholas had. He was the one for me.

When I got back to the UK, I opened up an accommodation address in his name. Then I went to the town hall and got Nicholas registered on the electoral roll for the area of the address and applied for a duplicate of his driver's licence. It arrived from the DVLC three weeks later.

During that time I also went to the Registry of Births and Deaths at St Catherine's House in London and obtained a copy of his birth certificate. He hadn't liked to talk to me about his past, and I could never get anything more out of him than his birthday and where he was born, and trying to dig any deeper would have aroused suspicion. Besides, his partner, Brian, was getting pissed off with me sniffing around. It took a couple of hours of scouring the registers between 1960 and 1961 before I found him.

I went to the police and reported that my passport had been stolen. They gave me a crime number, which I put on my application form for a replacement. Added to a copy of the birth certificate, it worked: Nick Davidson the Second was soon the proud owner of a brand-new ten-year passport.

I needed to go further. To have an authentic ID you have to have credit cards. Over the next few months I signed up with several book and record clubs; I even bought a hideous-looking Worcester porcelain figurine out of a Sunday supplement, paying with a postal order. In return, I got bills and receipts, all issued to the accommodation address.

Next I wrote to two or three of the high-street banks and asked them a string of questions that made it sound as if I was a big-time investor. I received very grovelling letters in reply, on the bank's letterhead, and written to my address. Then all I did was walk into a building society, play very stupid and say I would like to open a bank account, please. As long as you have documentation with your address on, they don't seem to care. I put a few quid in the new account and let it tick over. After a few weeks I got some standing orders up and running with the book clubs, and at last I was ready to apply for a credit card. As long as you're on the electoral register, have a bank account and no bad credit history, the card is yours. And once you have one card, all the other banks and finance houses will fall over themselves to make sure you take theirs as well. Fortunately, it appeared that Nick One had left no unpaid bills behind when he'd left. If he had it would have been back to the drawing board.

I was thinking about going one step further and getting myself a National Insurance number, but really there was no point. I had money and I had a way out, and anyway, you can just go down to the local DSS and say you're starting work the next Monday. They'll give you an emergency number on the spot, which will last you for years. If that doesn't work, you can always just make one up; the system's so inefficient it takes for ever for them to find out what's going on.

As soon as I had my passport and cards up and running, I used them for a trip to confirm they worked. After that, I carried on using them to keep the cards active and to get the passport stamped with a few entries and exits.

Just as I would do if I needed to disappear, Sarah would be

leaving behind everything she knew. She wouldn't be contacting family or friends, she would completely bin all the little day-to-day experiences that made up her life, all the little eccentricities that would give her away.

I started to think back over what she'd told me of her past because, without any outside help, that was the only place I had to go. I really knew very little, apart from the fact that she'd had a boyfriend a while ago, but binned him after finding out he was also seeing another woman. The story went that he lost a finger during the row with her; and that was the sum total in that department. Maybe metal-headed Mickey Warner could help, if I made it sound like a PV question. In fact, there would be plenty of questions for him to answer.

As for the family and her upbringing, she'd never told me much. All I knew was that, though we might have come from different ends of the social spectrum, we seemed to share the same emotional background. Neither set of parents had given a monkey's. She was fucked off to school when she was just nine, and me, well, I was just fucked off. Her family life was a desert, and it would hold no clues. The more I thought about it, the smaller the needle became and the larger the haystack.

What it boiled down to was that if she wanted to disappear she could – nobody was going to find her. I could be on her trail for months and still not be getting any warmer. I racked my brains, trying to remember something, anything, that might help, some little clue she might have revealed at some point which would give me a lead.

I pressed the 'call' button and ordered a couple of beers, partly to help me sleep, partly because, once I got to DC, there would be no more alcohol. For me, work and drink never mixed.

Maybe Josh could help. I could get hold of him when he returned from the UK, and maybe he could access some databases and run some covert checks. I wondered whether I should tell him the truth, but decided against. It could land both of us in the shit.

The thought suddenly struck me that part of me was hoping I wouldn't find her. I felt depressed, but resolved to crack on and get it over and done with. I would go straight to her flat, meet my new mate Metal Mickey, and take it from there.

The beer turned up and I decided to veg out for the rest of the flight. As I watched a film my mind drifted to Kelly. She was probably sitting at the table with her grandad, drawing pictures and drinking tea and trying to pull her jumper out from her jeans every time her grandmother tucked it back in. I made a mental note to call her.

I took another swig of beer and tried my hardest to think of something else, but I couldn't get Sarah out of my mind.

In 1987, two years before the end of the Soviet occupation of Afghanistan, the UK and US were sending teams in-country to train Afghani rebels, the mujahedin.

The Soviet Union had invaded Afghanistan eight years earlier. Peasant villagers got their first experience of modern technology when they were pounded by Moscow's jets, tanks and heli-copters. Three million were killed or maimed; six million others fled west into Iran or east into Pakistan. Those that were left standing took on the Russians, living on stale bread and tea, sleeping on rocky mountainsides.

Eventually the mujahedin put out an international plea for help. The West responded with $6-billion worth of arms. Congress, however, would not give permission for the rebels to be armed with American Stinger ground-to-air missiles to take down the Russian gunships and ground-attack aircraft, so our job was to train them in how to operate the Brit Blowpipe missiles instead. The CIA reasoned that if Congress was shown that the Afghans had a piss-poor ground-to-air missile capability – which they certainly did with Blowpipe: you needed to be a brain surgeon or have two right hands to use the thing – then they would eventually be allowed to have Stingers instead. They were right. We stayed and generally trained them how to fuck the Russians over.

Not that I knew it at the time – I was more concerned about not losing a leg on the hundreds of thousands of anti-personnel mines the Russians had dropped – but in Saudi Arabia, a few years before, a young civil-engineering graduate called Osama

Bin Laden had also responded to the rebels' plea for help, packing himself and several of his family's bulldozers off to central Asia. An Islamic radical from an influential and enormously wealthy family, whose construction company had been involved in rebuilding the holy mosques in Mecca and Medina, Bin Laden was inspired by what he saw as the plight of Muslims in a medieval society besieged by a twentieth-century superpower.

At first his work was political. He was one of the Saudi benefactors who spent millions supporting the Afghan guerrillas. He recruited thousands of Arab fighters in the Gulf, paid for their passage to Afghanistan and set up the main guerrilla camp to train them. Then he must have gone a bit loopy. With all that money he decided to take part in the fighting himself. I never saw him, but every other word from the mujahedin would be on the subject of how great he was. They loved him, and so did the West at that time. He sounded like a good lad, taking care of widows and orphans by creating charities to support them and their families, all that sort of stuff.

Our team had just finished a six-month tour in the mountains north of Kabul and was cleaning up back in the UK before a two-week holiday when we got called to London for orders. It looked as if we were going back to visit our new best mates a bit quicker than we thought. Aboard the helicopter, the rumour going round was that we were needed to protect a civil servant during meets with the mujahedin. We groaned at the thought of having to nanny a sixty-year-old Foreign Office pen-pusher while he did an on-site audit of arms expenditure. Colin had been picked to be with the principal at all times when on the ground, while the rest of us would provide protection from a distance. 'Fuck that,' said Colin. 'It'll be like getting stuck in an episode of *Yes, Minister*.' He promptly wriggled out of it and handed the job over to me.

Colin, Finbar, Simon and I were part of the team. We were sitting in a briefing room in a 1960s office block on the Borough High Street, just south of London Bridge, drinking tea from a machine and gobbing off as we waited for others to arrive. A woman we didn't recognize entered the room, and all four of us, as well as a few of the advisers and briefing personnel, did a double take. She was stunning, her body hardly disguised by a short black skirt and jacket. She nodded to people she knew and sat down, seemingly oblivious to the many pairs of male eyes burning into her back.

Colin would fuck the crack of dawn if he had the chance. He couldn't keep his eyes off her. She took off her jacket, and the sleeveless top beneath showed off her shoulders. They had definition: she trained. I could sense Colin getting even more excited.

He leaned over and whispered to Finbar, 'I need a lawyer.'

'Why's that, wee mon?' Finbar always called him that, which was strange, as the Irishman was about a foot smaller than Colin.

'I'm getting a divorce.'

We were all intrigued to know what she was bringing to the party; it came as a bit of a shock when she was introduced as the civil servant we were going to protect. I had to smile. I knew what was coming next and, right on cue, Colin leaned towards me. 'Nick . . .'

I ignored him, making him suffer a bit more. 'Nick . . .'

I turned and gave him a big smile.

'I'll take my job back now, mate.'

I slowly shook my head.

Listening intently to the briefing officer, she crossed her legs, and the rustle of the material was just about the most wonderful sound I'd ever heard. I was sure we were all paying more attention to that than to the briefing. She was now comfortable in her seat and her skirt had ridden up enough to show the darker tops of her tights. It was impossible to tell if she was doing it on purpose. She didn't turn her head or glance around to check for effect.

When she stood up to speak, her voice was low and very confident. If the Intelligence Service didn't work out for her, she could always find a job on an 0898 number.

Sarah explained that what she wanted to do was lay her hands on – and get back to the West – an airworthy, Russian-built Hind ground-attack helicopter, the true capabilities of which, she said, were still not understood. Better still, she added, she'd like a pair. She was the one who was going to strike the deal with the Afghans, and it was a simple case of, 'we'll scratch your back by carrying on showing you how to fuck the Russians, you scratch ours with a helicopter or two.'

From day one of the two months that we were moving in and out of Pakistan to the rebels' mountain hides, she was a consummate professional to work with. She made life so much easier for us – sometimes on jobs like this we could spend just as much time massaging the fear factor out of the poor fucker who had to make the meet as we would preparing for it ourselves. But she was different. Maybe she wasn't scared because she had just as much of a fiery temper as the truculent rebels. That often led to delays in negotiations – more so than the fact that she was a woman. But it was obvious to me that she had the knowledge, language and background to hold her own with these people, for whom we all had the greatest respect; after all, they were fighting a superpower, and winning.

I saw that Sarah had a love and understanding of this part of the world that she couldn't have hidden, even if she'd tried. On top of that, she was switched on and didn't flap when the meets got heated. She knew I was there, and that the other three were around somewhere, watching. If the shit had hit the fan, the Afghans wouldn't have known what had hit them – unless the shit was Russian, in which case our orders were to bail out and leave the rebels to it.

We were on a shopping trip, but with a difference. Everyone had a weapon and everyone was at war – not only with the Russians, but also with each other as they fought to gain control of the country. Sarah played one group off against another to get what she wanted. It only went wrong once, when two young men discovered what was going on and confronted her. I had to do a little confrontation of my own at that point, and make sure the bodies were never found.

Another time she lost her cool when the rebels told her they wanted to sell the Hind to her, not simply hand it over. They had screamed and shouted at each other and the meet had ended with her storming off onto the mountainside. We drove to the border in silence, while she sat and brooded about what had happened. At length she said, 'Not a good one for me, Nick. What do you think I should write in my report?'

I thought for a moment. 'PMT?'

She laughed. 'Never mind, we'll just have to come back and try again soon, but not for the next five days.' It was the first time I'd seen her really laugh. As we tried to make it back to Pakistan before one of the helicopters she was so keen to get hold of found us, she was giggling like a schoolkid.

It turned into a ritual. After it happened for the third time I would just nod and say, 'Fuck 'em if they can't take a joke.' She'd laugh, and we would then just spin the shit until we got to the safety of Pakistan.

Later she had a report that PIRA (the Provisional IRA) were passing technical information to the mujahedin on how to make home-made explosives and timer units. London reckoned the Afghans would be paying PIRA back with buckets of their US- and UK-sourced weapons.

She looked concerned. 'What are we going to do about it, Nick? London wants me to find out who their contact is.'

I cracked up. 'You already know them.'

She looked puzzled. 'I do?'

'Colin, Finbar, Simon and me.'

She was now totally confused.

'Think about it. Who has been fighting a terrorist war for years? *We* showed the Afghans what PIRA use, *we* showed them how to make the timer units. PIRA's stuff is easy to make, reliable and it works. It's the best improvized kit in the world. We even use it ourselves, so why not show our new best mates? That's our job right: to help fuck up the bad boys.'

The next evening in Pakistan was spent constructing a sit rep that took the piss out of the int collator who'd thought up this little PIRA gem, and she found it as funny as I did, which was all rather nice, because I was finding that I liked the way her nose twitched when something amused her and her face creased into a big, radiant smile.

It was strange that we got on so well, because in many ways we were chalk and cheese. I had joined the Army because I was too thick to do anything else. I'd seen the adverts that said I could be a helicopter pilot serving Queen and country, and an uncle of mine, who was an ex-serviceman, told me that girls loved a uniform. As far as I was concerned, all you had to do to get permanently tanned and laid was saunter down to the recruiting office. To a sixteen-year-old kid who thought that the world beyond my south London housing estate was just hearsay, it was no wonder the posters sucked me in. I couldn't wait to go to Cyprus – wherever that was – and fly my helicopter over beaches packed with girls who were just gagging for me to land and let them play with my joystick.

Strangely, however, that wasn't quite the way things turned out. I took the entry tests, but the army seemed to take the view that somebody who could only just about do up his own boot laces without getting confused was not about to take sole charge of a multimillion-pound Chinook. So, the infantry it was, then.

Sarah, on the other hand, was smart. Private Benjamin she wasn't. Not that I knew much about her; ironically, she was just as good as I was at not giving anything away. No, I realized later, she was better. And to be honest that pissed me off. I wanted to know all about her strengths and weaknesses, her hopes and fears, her likes and dislikes, because armed with that information I could properly plan and carry out an attack on her expensive designer underwear. Since part of our cover while in Pakistan was that we were a couple and had to share the same hotel room – much to Colin's fury – I thought I might be in with a chance. At least, that was at the back of my mind at the start. I soon surprised myself by finding that, more than to get into her pants, I wanted to get inside her head. I realized I actually liked her. I liked her a lot, and I'd never felt that way about anyone before.

As time went by, however, I was making no progress. I could never get any sort of handle on who this woman really was. It was like playing a computer game and never getting past level one. It wasn't that she was aloof; she was a great mixer. She'd go out with the team, and even accepted dinner with me a couple of times. She had a way of making me feel like a puppy jumping around at her feet waiting for a doggie drop. I knew, though, that I had the dreamer's disease, and that nothing would happen between us. What the fuck would she want from someone like me, apart from my ability to rip people apart for her if they got too scary?

On that point I'd obviously acquitted myself all right, because Sarah was the one who suggested that I apply for a job with the service once I left the Regiment. Even now, after five years, I still didn't know if I should kiss her for that, or give her the good news with a two-pound ball hammer.

I drank more beer and tried to watch the TV screen in front of me, but really I couldn't be arsed. I thought back again to the Afghanistan job. The United States and its allies gave tens of thousands of assault rifles and rocket-propelled grenades, millions of rounds of ammunition and hundreds of Stinger missiles to the mujahedin. By the time the war ended in 1989 the muj's stock of Stingers was far from exhausted, and the CIA soon had a multimillion-dollar reward operation going, in an attempt to get them back before they were sold to any terrorist group who fancied a couple to play with. As far as I knew, the offer still stood.

I turned onto my side, trying to get comfortable, and thought that maybe I should be going back to try and get some of that reward for myself. It was about time I made some money. I didn't know where they were, but I knew an Afghan who'd got Sarah's Hinds for her, and he just might.

It's strange how things change. During that time Bin Laden was most certainly in the West's Good Lads' club. Now he'd had the idea of blowing up things on the American mainland, he was public enemy number one. I wondered what sort of reward the US had on his head.

The flight ended in Dulles airport, just outside of Washington, and I joined the long snake of people lining up for Immigration. It took about twenty minutes to shuffle to the desks, gradually zigzagging my way backwards and forwards between the ropes.

It reminded me of queuing for a ride at Disneyland. The immigration personnel looked like policemen and behaved like bouncers, pushing and herding us into position.

My immigration official glared as if he was trying to spook me, maybe because he was bored. I just smiled like a dickhead tourist while he stamped the visa waiver and wearily invited me to enjoy my stay in the United States of America.

The automatic doors parted and I walked into the frenzy of the arrivals lounge. Drivers were holding up felt-tipped cards, families were clutching flowers and teddy bears, and they were all looking hopefully at each face that came through the sliding doors. All I wanted was a big dose of caffeine.

I wandered over to Starbucks and got myself about a pint and a half of cappuccino. Tucking myself away in the corner, I got out the 3C and the mobile and switched them both on.

I found the number I wanted and waited an age for the mobile to get a signal. The new Bosch mobiles worked on both world-wide and US frequencies; there wasn't 100 per cent coverage here yet, but it was getting better. They had completely changed the way we worked. Phones had been around for ages which could do the same job, but they weren't available commercially. On covert ops you can only use what you can buy at the Carphone Warehouse; if not, you'd stand out like dogs' bollocks. I hit the keys.

'Hellooo, Michael speaking.' The voice was camp and highly pitched, more like a game-show host than the personal assistant of a member of the 'other Foreign Office'.

'My name's Nick Snell,' I said.

'Oh yes, I've been waiting to hear from you,' he said, and it was a mixture of warmth, excitement and pleasure, as if I was a long-lost friend. 'How are you?'

I was a bit taken aback. We didn't know each other, and going by the sound of his voice I wouldn't even buy a second-hand washing machine from him, yet he was talking to me as if I was his best mate from way back. 'I'm fine,' I said, feeling a smile spread across my face. 'How are you?'

He came back with, 'I'm just Jim Dandy!' Then he tried to switch

101

to serious mode. 'Now then, where do you want to meet me?'

All of a sudden I wondered if I was on a radio stitch-up show and started to laugh. I said, 'I'll leave that to you. After all, it's your town, isn't it?'

'Oh and what a town!' He clearly couldn't wait to share it with me. There was a little pause, then he said, 'I tell you what, I'll meet you at the Bread and Chocolate Bakery. It's a coffee shop on the corner of M and 23rd. They do fantastic mocha, and it's not far from the apartment. Now, do you know where M and 23rd is?'

I knew the area and I could read a map. I'd find it. 'I've got to pick a car up first – I'll be there in about two hours' time. Will that fit in with you?'

For reasons best known to himself, he came back with a mock-Texan drawl. 'Why sure, Nick.' He laughed. 'I'll be the beach ball with the blue shirt and the red tie; you won't be able to miss me.'

I said, 'I'm wearing jeans, a blue checked shirt and a blue bomber jacket.'

'See you there. By the way, parking is an absolute bitch this time of day, so good luck to you. See you there, M and 23rd. Byeeee!'

I hit the 'end' button and shook my head. What the fuck was that all about?

6

I was only two blocks away when I got held up in slow-moving traffic. With its tall buildings and narrow roads, the area around M and 23rd reminded me of the more upscale areas of New York. Even the weather was the same as on my visits to the Big Apple: cloudy, but warm. Trust Sarah to live around here, I thought, but in fact it made sense. It wasn't far from Massachusetts Avenue, which more or less bisects the city from north-west to south-east, and all the embassies, missions and consulates are in the area, mainly in the north-west section.

As I filtered forward I saw the problem. The junction ahead was sealed off by DC police bikers, and we were being rerouted to the right. As I made the turn, a fleet of black Lincolns with darkened windows screamed through the crossroads. At the rear of the convoy was a bunch of four-wheel-drive Chevy escorts and two ambulances, just in case the principal cut his finger. It looked as if either Netanyahu or Arafat was already in town.

The grid system in DC works with the lettered streets running east–west and the numbers north–south. I found the junction I wanted easily enough, but there was no way I could stop. The one-way circuit on M street had a mind of its own, and Metal Mickey was right, parking was a gang-fuck. The street was lined with cars that had a firm grip on their meters and weren't letting go for anyone; another three laps of the block and I finally found a Nissan pulling away from a space on M, just past the junction I wanted.

I locked up, fed the meter and walked. Bread and Chocolate turned out to be a small coffee shop on the street level of an office and apartment building, just fifteen metres further down on the left side of 23rd. There was another coffee shop opposite, attached to a grocery store, but this was the better of the two. The interior looked so clean I felt I should have scrubbed up before going in. Long glass display cases were filled with Danishes and a million different muffins and sandwiches, and on the wall behind them was a coffee selection menu which went on for ever. Everything looked so perfect I wondered if people were allowed to buy anything and mess up the displays.

The tables were white marble, small and round, just big enough to seat three. I sat facing the glass shopfront and ordered a mocha – a small one after the mother lode at the airport. The place was about a quarter full, mostly with smartly dressed office workers talking shop. I nursed my caffeine for the ten minutes that remained before our RV.

Right on time, in he walked, and a beach ball he certainly was. He had skin that was so clear it was virtually see-through, and black hair that was slightly thinning on top, which he'd gelled and combed back to make it look thicker. On his cheerful, chubby face he had fashionably round, black-rimmed glasses, behind which a pair of clear blue eyes were looking twice their natural size because of the thickness of the lenses. He was wearing a shiny, grey single-breasted suit, bright blue shirt and red tie, all set off nicely by a little bum-fluff goatee beard. He must have been about three stones overweight, but was tall with it, over six feet. His jacket had all three buttons done up and was straining to contain the load. He spotted me just as easily and came over, hand outstretched.

'Well, hellooo. You must be Nick.'

I shook his hand, noticing his soft skin and immaculate, almost feminine, fingernails. We sat down and the waiter came over immediately – maybe Metal Mickey was a regular. Pointing at my coffee, he looked up and smiled. 'I'll have one of those, please.'

The aroma of the mocha was no match for his aftershave.

The moment the waiter was out of earshot, he leaned forward, unnaturally close to me. 'Well then, all I've been told is to help you while Sarah's away.' I was about to reply, but he was off again. 'I must say, I'm quite excited about it. I've never been involved with someone else's PV review before. Just my own, of course. Anyway, so here I am, all yours!' He finished in a grand gesture, with his hands in the air in mock surrender.

Grabbing my chance, I said, 'Thanks, that certainly makes things a lot easier. Tell me, when was the last time you saw her? I'm not too sure how long she's been away.'

'Oh, about three weeks ago. But what's new? She's here, there and everywhere, isn't she?'

The coffee came and Metal Mickey's head turned as he said thanks to the waiter. The light caught it just right and I could see the scarring where the plate had been inserted – an area about three inches by two of slightly raised skin. I just hoped that no-one on a nearby table answered their cellular phone, because he'd probably leap up and start doing the conga.

He picked up his coffee cup, got his podgy lips over the rim, and sucked away at the froth. He put it down again with a big, 'Ah!' and smiled, then was straight back into it. 'Yes, three weeks ago was the last time. I don't worry much about her comings and goings. I just make sure things are running smoothly here.' He hesitated, like a child who wants something from a parent and is trying to pluck up courage. I was almost expecting him to start playing with his fingers and shuffling his feet. 'I've been thinking, is her review because she's due to return to the UK? If so, it's just that I wondered . . . would I have to go back too? I mean, not that I wouldn't want that, but it's just . . .'

I caught his drift and cut in. 'I don't think she, or you, will be going home soon, Michael. Unless you want to.' I decided not to hit him with any questions at the moment. He was too nervous, and would naturally be loyal to Sarah. Besides, I might as well get to grips with the apartment, then hit him with everything in one go.

There was visible relief in his face. I went on, in a more upbeat tone, 'You have the keys for her apartment?'

'Sure do! Shall we go up there now?'

I nodded, and sucked down the rest of my coffee while he pulled some notes from a slim, tidy wallet to pay for the coffees. At the paydesk he carefully folded the receipt and tucked it away. 'Expenses,' he sighed.

He carried on as we walked out onto 23rd. 'I don't know when she's coming back. Do you?' He held open the glass door for me.

I thought, Who's supposed to be asking the questions here? 'No, I'm afraid I don't. I'm just here to do the review.' I thought I'd leave it at that. I didn't know if he'd seen how a PV review was really carried out – which wasn't like this – but he nodded as if he knew it was all part of the procedure.

'Did you manage to park near?'

'Just round the corner, on M.'

'Well done, good boy!'

I started to go to the right, towards the car, thinking we were about to go for a drive.

'No, no silly,' he said, pointing the opposite way. 'She lives at the end of the block, on N.'

It was strange; the one thing I didn't get from Lynn was Sarah's address. Mind you, I didn't ask. It must have been shock at the thought of seeing her again.

As we walked the short distance along the narrow, tree-lined street to the next junction, I saw what he was pointing at. The apartment block was right on the corner of 23rd and N. Its jutting balconies and combination of red brick and white stone made it look like a game of Jenga played with Liquorice Allsorts. I couldn't make up my mind whether that was how it had been designed, or if the builders had been pissed when they put it all together.

We carried on towards the junction and I decided to chance a question. I knew I'd resolved not to press him just yet, but this was one that I was very curious to have an answer to. 'Tell me about boyfriends,' I said.

He looked at me with a mixture of surprise and disapproval, and sounded quite defensive. 'I don't think that has anything to do with this PV.' He paused, then said, 'But yes, as a matter of fact, I do . . .'

'No, no, not you,' I laughed. 'Sarah. Do you know of any men that she's been seeing?'

'Ohhh, Sarah. None at all. Well, not after what happened last time.' His tone just begged the question.

'Why, what happened?'

'Well, poor Sarah was in love with a guy from the real Foreign Office. He was back in London, but he came here from time to time. They would disappear for a week or two, to the middle of nowhere. Not my sort of stamping ground, let me tell you.'

I looked at him expecting to share a smile, but he was thinking of the next bit and had begun to look sad. 'Something very unfortunate happened, and I'm afraid it was me who was the bringer of bad news . . .'

He was waiting for the panto reply, and I obliged: 'What bad news?'

'Well, I get a call from Sarah, telling me that Jonathan' – he took a breath, getting really sparked up about him – 'is arriving at the airport and she wants me to pick him up and take him straight to the restaurant she's booked for a surprise dinner. They planned to leave for the lakes the next day.'

I nodded to show that I was hanging on every word.

'I get to the airport to pick him up. He's never seen me before, of course, but I've seen photographs of him. Anyway, so there I am, waiting. Out he comes, arm-in-arm with another woman. All over her like a wet dress, I ask you! I put my name card down sharpish, I can tell you, and followed to see what happened next. I even got in the taxi line with them and listened. She was called Anna . . . Ella . . . Antonella – that was it. Anyway, a stupid name if you ask me, but spot on for a Sloaney slapper, which was what she looked. Too many pearls round her neck; didn't suit her . . .' He left a gap. Maybe he wanted me to feel part of the show.

I said, 'What happened next?'

'Well, what was I to do? I call Sarah at the restaurant an hour later to say that I couldn't find him. She says, "Not a problem, he's called me on my cellphone." You can imagine, Nick, I struggled all night about what to do. Do I tell her or do I not? Well, it's none of my business, is it? Anyway, the next day the decision was made for me.' The smile on his face told me that it had been a good one. He was trying to suppress a giggle.

'Go on.'

'Well, poor old Anna whatsherface had been mugged downtown. In such a mess she was, lost her money, cards, the poor girl was in hospital for days, you know. Well, who does she ask the police to contact but dear Jonathan, care of the embassy? The call comes through, I get to hear about it, and guess what – it only turns out he's her fiancé! So, I had the contact number and she was in hospital. Poor girl. I suppose I feel sorry for her now.'

I laughed, but wondered who in their right mind would two-time with another woman when they already had Sarah. 'What happened?'

He held his hand up, with his index finger folded down. 'The bitch lost his finger; she slammed the car door on his hands! That will teach him to mess with Sarah. If you knew her like I do, Nick, you'd know that she's a wonderful woman. Far too good for a man like that.' Someone must have powered up a mobile near us – Metalhead was off on a tangent. 'And she wears such wonderful clothes, you wouldn't believe!'

As we got to the junction I saw that the entrance was on the N Street side. A Latino in a blue polo shirt and green work trousers was hosing down the street directly outside the main doors, while the greenery along the front of the building was getting a drenching from the irrigation system.

The main doors were made of copper-coloured alloy and glass. To the left, a brass plate welcomed us to the building; to the right, a touch-screen TV entry system made sure the welcome wasn't abused. Metal Mickey took out a long plastic key, which looked as if it should be used to wind up a kid's toy. He slipped it into the keyhole and the doors parted.

We walked into a world of black marble floors, dark-blue walls and ceilings you could freefall from. The elevators were ahead of us, about twenty metres further down the atrium. To the right of them was a semi-circular desk – very Terence Conran, with a shiny wooden top and black marble wall beneath. Behind it sat an equally smart and efficient-looking porter, who would have looked at home on the door of a five-star hotel. It appeared that Metal Mickey knew him quite well. He greeted him with a cheery, 'Why, hello, Wayne, how are you today?'

Wayne was fortyish, and obviously having a really good day. 'I'm very good,' he smiled. 'How are you doing?'

It was obvious that he didn't really know Metal Mickey's name or he would have said it, but he recognized the face.

'I'm just Jim Dandy,' Mickey grinned. Then he looked over at me and said, 'This is Nick, a friend of Sarah's. He's going to be using the apartment for a few days while Sarah's away, so I'll show him what's what.'

I smiled at him and shook his hand, just to prove to him that I wasn't a threat. Wayne smiled back. 'Anything you need, Nick, just dial H–E–L–P on the in-house phone and it'll be done.'

'Thanks a lot. I'll need Sarah's parking space, if she has one.'

'You just tell me when you want to collect the pass key.' He beamed.

There was one more thing I needed. I leaned towards Wayne, as if letting him into a secret. 'If Sarah comes in, please don't tell her I'm here. I want to surprise her.'

Wayne gave me a knowing, between-men sort of nod. 'No problem. Tell you what, I'll call you on the in-house if I see her.'

Metal Mickey and I took the elevator to the sixth floor. The door opened onto a corridor that was every bit as plush as the entrance hall downstairs, with the same coloured walls and subtle, wall-mounted lighting. You could see the vacuum marks on the thick blue carpet.

Metal Mickey was quiet for a change as we walked along the corridor, his hands in his pockets as he sorted out some keys. He stopped outside the door to apartment 612. 'Here we are.' He undid the large, five-lever deadlock first, then the equivalent of a Yale lock, and pushed the door open for me.

I stepped in before him and blocked the doorway, which opened straight into the living room. He got the message, dangling the keys between his thumb and forefinger in front of me. 'Do you want me to stay and make you some coffee, or do you need anything else?'

I said, 'There will be a few things I need to talk to you about – work stuff, you know. Later on. But apart from that, mate, no. But thanks a lot for everything. I just need a little time on my own, to sort myself out; it's my first one, I need to do a good job.'

He nodded as if he knew what I was talking about, which was just as well because I didn't; it had just come into my head. It was nothing personal, I just didn't want him around.

He gave me his card. 'My home and pager.'

I took it from him. 'Thanks, I'll try not to call you out of hours. I can't imagine there'll be any need. It can all wait until Monday.'

It always pays to be nice to people, because you never know when you might need to use them. And besides, Metal Mickey was harmless. As he started to walk back towards the elevator, I poked my head round the doorframe and called out, 'Thanks a lot, Michael.' He just waved his right hand in the air and said, 'Byee, and remember, anything else you need, just call.'

I closed the door and remained standing on the threshold while I keyed Metal Mickey's numbers into my 3C – cards always get lost. Once done, I looked around at nothing in particular, just tuning in to the place rather than charging in and not noticing anything. I knew there wouldn't be any letters under the door, because they all went via the central mailbox. I also knew that there'd be nothing tangible, like a notebook with a detailed plan of what she was up to, but if you don't take your time you can go straight for the sixpence and miss the five-pound note.

I went to lock myself in so no-one could enter; it was a natural reaction to being in someone else's house when I shouldn't, but on this occasion there was no need. I wanted her to come in; it would certainly make my job a lot easier, and if Wayne kept his eyes open I'd get a warning.

A strange thought struck me. I'd seen Sarah so many times in short-term accommodation, when we'd stayed in hotels or flats, but this was the first time I'd seen where and how she lived for real. I felt like a voyeur, as if I was watching her undress through her bedroom keyhole.

Basically it was just a large one-bedroomed apartment, furnished, I could see at once, by the 'accommodation pack' – the standard furniture provided on the diplomatic circuit. Very plush, very expensive, very sophisticated, but not much of it, which the FCO (Foreign and Commonwealth Office) probably called minimalist because that way it sounded fashionable. The rest of it you bought yourself with an allowance. She obviously hadn't got round to that yet.

In the main room there was a slightly lighter blue carpet than in the hallway outside, and a matching blue sofa and chairs. In the far left-hand corner was a long sideboard with three drawers, facing a large window which looked out on to the rear of the building and one of the creeks that ran into the Potomac. Next to the window was a bookcase, its four shelves filled with hardbacks. I went over and scanned the spines. Quite a few titles seemed to be concerned with the Middle East and terrorism, and there was a complete set of the 1997 *Economist* world reports. One shelf started with biographies – Mandela, Thatcher (of course, she would have that), JFK, Churchill – and ended with a couple of Gore Vidal's books, plus a few heavy-going ones on American history and a collection of Oscar Wilde's plays. The bottom shelf held what looked like large-format, coffee-table-type books. They were lying flat because of their size and I had to twist my head to see the titles. I recognized *The Times World Atlas* because it was the free offer of that which had enticed me into one of the book clubs I'd used when becoming Nick Davidson, and then there were several pictorial ones on different countries in the Middle East, and one about the US.

The sideboard and bookcase were both made from a light wood veneer, and the walls were emulsioned off-white. There had been no effort whatsoever to personalize this flat. It was as anonymous as my house in Norfolk, though at least she had a sofa and a bookcase.

There were a few society, news and what's-on-in-Washington magazines beside the sofa on the floor, piled on top of each other. A phone was lying on top of the mags, its digital display telling me there were no messages. The walls were bare apart from some bland views of DC which were probably taken when JFK was boss. There were two lamps: a normal table lamp on the floor just in front of the sofa, its wire snaking away across the carpet, and a standard lamp over by the bookcase, both with matching white shades. That was her all over; she might be highly professional in her job, but when it came to her personal admin she was a bag of shit. But what did I expect from someone who wouldn't even know her way around Tesco?

There wasn't a television set, which didn't surprise me. She'd never watched it. If you asked her about *Seinfeld* and *Frasier*, she'd probably say it was a New York law firm. My eyes moved back to the bookcase. On the bottom shelf sat a large glass vase, but there were no flowers in it, instead it was filled with coins and pens and all the rest of the shit that people pull out of their pockets at the end of the day. Near it was her social calendar: thick, gilded invitations for drinks at eight at British Embassy or American Congress functions. I counted seven for the last month. It must be a terrible life, having to scoff all those free vol-au-vents and knock back glasses of champagne.

On the sideboard was a bog-standard, all-in-one, solid-state CD player, probably quite inexpensive, but serving its purpose. About a dozen CDs were stacked on top of each other, and as I walked over I could see that three of them were still in their cellophane. She hadn't had enough time to play them yet – maybe next week. There was also a boxed set of five classical operas. I turned the cases to read the spines. *Cosi Fan Tutte* was there, of course – one of the few things I did know about her was that it was her favourite.

I looked at the rest of the music: a couple of 1970s Genesis albums, remastered on CD, and what looked like a bootleg cover of a group called Sperm Bank. I'd have to have a listen to that one, it was so out of place. She and I had never really talked that much about music, but I knew she loved opera – whilst I'd hear things on the radio and think, That's good, I'll buy that, but then lose the tape before I'd even played it.

The standby light was still on. I pressed 'open', put in the Sperm Bank CD and hit 'play'. It was some kind of weird Tahitian rap/jazz/funk, whatever they call it – very noisy but very rhythmic. I turned the volume up a bit so I could hear it big time, and felt very fashionable. Fuck it, the chances of her coming back here were ziff.

I'd had my first cursory look in the living room, now I'd try the kitchen. It was about fifteen feet square, with units completely filling up both sides of the wall, so that it ended up being more like a passageway. The hob, oven and sink were all built-in.

I had a mooch in the cupboards above the work surfaces, trying to get some idea of how this woman lived. It was nothing to do with the job now. I was just curious to see this other side of her. There was hardly any food, and probably never had been. There were cans of convenience items, like rice and packet noodles, which could just be opened and boiled, and a couple of packs of gourmet coffee, but no spices or herbs or anything else you'd need if you cooked at home. On the few occasions when she wasn't at embassy dos, or being dined in restaurants, she probably got by with the microwave.

I opened another cupboard and found six of everything – the accommodation pack again – plain white crockery, six cups, six glasses. Over 60 per cent of the cupboard space was empty. In the fridge was half a carton of milk, which wasn't looking too healthy – it smelled and looked as if it held the cure for HIV. Next to that were some bagels, still in their plastic bag, and half a jar of peanut butter, and that was it. Not exactly Delia Smith, our Sarah. At least I had some cheese and yoghurt in mine.

The bathroom was between the kitchen and the bedroom. There was no bath, just a shower, sink and toilet. The room had been left as if she'd got up normally, done her stuff and dashed off to work. A dry but used towel lay on the floor next to a laundry bin which was half full of jeans, underwear and tights. No sign of a washing machine, but I wasn't really expecting one. Sarah's clothes would go to a dry-cleaners, or to a laundry for a fluff and fold.

The bedroom was about fifteen by twenty feet, with a walk-in wardrobe, but no other furniture apart from a double bed and a single bedside lamp sitting on the floor. The duvet was thrown to one side where she'd just woken up and thrown it off. All the bedding was plain white, the same as the walls. There were pillows for two people, but only one of them looked slept on. Again, there were no pictures on the walls, and the venetian blinds on both windows were closed. Either she'd just got up and gone to work, or this was simply how it always was.

The walk-in closet had mirrored sliding doors. I pulled them open, expecting the scent of a woman's wardrobe, that slight waft of stale perfume lingering on jackets which have been worn once and are back on their hangers before they find their way to the cleaners. In fact, there was almost no smell at all, which wasn't surprising. The rows and rows of expensive-looking clothes were all in dry-cleaner's plastic wrapping, and even her blouses and T-shirts were on hangers. Out of curiosity I checked a few labels, and found Armani, Joseph and Donna Karan. She was obviously still slumming it. On a shelf above the dresses was the just as expensive luggage to match. Nothing seemed to be missing or out of place.

In front of me was a small stand-alone chest, just a white Formica thing with about five or six drawers. One of the drawers was open; I looked inside and found knickers and bras, again all very expensive.

All her footwear was arranged on the floor on the right-hand side of the wardrobe, and looking very orderly: formal, summer, winter and a pair of trainers. To the left of the wardrobe, and also on the floor, was a shoe box. I bent down and lifted the lid. A Picasso dove greeted me, on top of more old Christmas and birthday cards. Flicking through them, I found a picture of her arm-in-arm with a tall, good-looking man. They were in woodland, looking extremely happy, both dressed the part in waterproofs and boots. Maybe this was Jonathan, and presumably in happier times. Sarah looked a little older than when I'd seen her on the Syria job; the bob had had three years to grow out and her hair was about shoulder length, still very straight and with a fringe which was just above those big eyes. She hadn't put on weight, and still looked fantastic as she smiled that almost innocent, childlike grin towards me. I realized I was looking at the man beside her and wishing it was me as I dropped the photo back in the box and lay down on the bed. There was no smell of her, just that of dry-cleaned cotton.

114

*

We had been in and out of Afghanistan those first two months, with no result. The rebels had managed to get a major offensive off the ground in between their internal feuds and were kicking the arse out of the Russians. No-one would be talking to us for a while, so we got out of the way, taking time off and generally having fun. We could only hope that one of the rebel groups with an entrepreneurial flair would attack a heliport and see us all right with a couple of Hinds.

Both of us could have gone back to the UK with the other three and done our own thing, but she wanted to go trekking in Nepal and I knew the country well. It seemed a simple swap: she showed me the historical and religious sites, and I showed her the bars and dives where, as a young infantry soldier on an exchange with the Gurkhas, I'd been separated from my money. It was an education for both of us.

It was during the first week off, staying in Katmandu before moving to Pukara for our week's trek, that things changed. By now she would take the piss out of my accent: I called Hackney 'ackney, and she called it Hackerney. We'd just finished a run one day, and were both getting our key cards from our socks, when she leaned into my ear and said, in her bad cockney accent, 'Awright darlin', you wanna fuck or what?'

Three weeks later, and back with the rest of the team in Pakistan, the cover story of being a couple was now played out for real. I even had fantasies of maybe seeing her later on once the job had ended. I'd been married for four years and things hadn't been going well. Now they were in shit state. With Sarah I enjoyed the intimate talks and learning about things I'd never bothered to find out about, or even knew existed. Up until then, I'd thought *Cosi Fan Tutte* was an Italian ice cream. This was it. Love. I didn't understand what was happening to me. For the first time in my life I had deep, loving feelings for someone. Even better, I got the impression she felt the same. I couldn't bring myself to ask her, though; the fear of rejection was just too great.

When the Afghanistan job finished, we were on the flight home from Delhi and well into our descent to Heathrow before I plucked up enough courage to ask her the big question. I still didn't know that much about her, but it didn't matter, I didn't think she knew that much about me either. I just really needed to be with her. I felt like a child being dropped off by a parent and not knowing if they will ever come back. Courage or desperation, I wasn't sure which, but I kept my eyes on the in-flight magazine and said, very throwaway, 'We're still going to see each other, aren't we?'

The dread of rejection lifted as she said, 'Of course.' Then she added, 'We've got to debrief.'

I thought she'd misunderstood me. 'No, no . . . I hoped, later on, we might be able to see each other . . . you know, out of work.'

Sarah looked at me, and I saw her jaw drop a fraction in disbelief. She said, 'I don't think so, do you?'

She must have seen the confusion on my face. 'Come on, Nick, it's not as if we're in love with each other or anything like that. We spent a lot of time together and it was great.'

I couldn't bear to look at her, so I just kept my eyes fixed on the page. Fuck, I'd never felt so crushed. It was like going to the doctor for a routine check-up and being told I was going to have a slow, painful death.

'Look, Nick' – there wasn't a hint of regret in her voice – 'we had a job to do and it was a success. That means it was a success for both of us. You got what you wanted out of it, and so did I.' She paused. 'Look, the more intimate we were, the more you would protect me, right? Am I right?'

I nodded. She was right. I would probably have died for her.

Before she could say another word I did what had always worked in the past, ever since childhood: I just cut away. I looked at her as if I'd just been asking her out for a drink, and said, 'Oh, OK, just thought I'd ask.' I'd never been fucked off with such casual finesse. I kicked myself for even having considered that she would want to be with me. Just who the fuck did I think I was? I was definitely suffering from the dreamer's disease.

It was only a month after we'd landed at Heathrow that I left my wife. We were just existing together, and it didn't seem right to be sleeping with her and thinking of Sarah.

When the Syria job came along I didn't know she was going to be on it. We met for orders in London, this time in better offices – Vauxhall Cross, the new home of SIS overlooking the Thames. She acted as if nothing had ever happened between us. Maybe it hadn't for her, but it had for me. I made a plan. Never again would she, or any other woman, fuck me over.

I sat up on the bed and put the lid on the shoebox. That could wait. I needed to tune in to this place and try to get a feel of it.

I went back into the kitchen, filled the coffee percolator with water and ground beans and got it going. Then I went back into the living room. Sperm Bank – or the Sperm, as I now liked to call them – were still rattling along big time.

I slumped sideways in one of the chairs, with my back against one arm, my legs over the other. I'd found nothing at all on the first sweep. I would have to give each room a thorough going over, digging everything out. Somewhere, somehow, there could be a slight clue, a tiny hint. Maybe. The only thing I knew for sure was that if I rushed it I wouldn't find anything.

As I looked around me my thoughts drifted. Sarah wasn't that different from me really. Everything in my life was disposable, from a toothbrush to a car. I didn't have a single possession that was more than two years old. I bought clothes for a job and threw them away once they were dirty, leaving hundreds of pounds' worth of whatever behind me because I didn't need it any more. At least she had a photo; I didn't have any mementos of family, schooldays or the Army, not even of Kelly and me. It was something I was always going to get around to, but hadn't.

I went back to the kitchen, realizing I was thinking more about myself than her. And I wasn't looking for me. I was starting to feel quite depressed. This was going to be a long, long job, but I had to do it by the book if it was going to work.

I poured myself a cup of coffee and went to the fridge, then remembered that the milk was only good for medical research. I couldn't find powdered creamer, so I'd have to have it black. I took the pot with me, and was walking back into the living room just as the Sperm decided to sign off. I threw myself back in one of the chairs and put my feet up again on the coffee table, sipping the hot coffee and thinking, I've got to make a start; it'll be like most things, once you get stuck in, everything's fine.

I finished the first coffee, poured another, got up and wandered over to the sideboard. I plonked the cup next to the CDs, then started to take off my Timberlands. I'd worn boots like this for years; they always seemed the thing to wear with jeans, and I always wore jeans. It felt like I hadn't taken them off for days, and it was time to let my feet and socks add to the apartment's atmosphere.

To work, then. Starting from the top, I opened the first drawer and took out a sheaf of dry-cleaning receipts, theatre stubs and folded-up back copies of *Time*. I studied each item in turn, opening each page of every magazine to check nothing had been ripped out, scored or ringed. Had I found anything missing, I'd have had to go to a reference library and get hold of the issue to find out what was so interesting that it had been removed. But there was nothing like that.

The second drawer was much the same, just as full of shit. The other drawers were completely empty, apart from one solitary safety pin, still stuck into yet another dry-cleaning ticket.

I was becoming bored, pissed off and very hungry. It was nearing time for my first Mickey D's of the trip. I'd just heard on the radio that McDonald's mission statement for the USA was something like, that no American was ever more than six minutes away from a Big Mac. In the UK that would make most heroin addicts jump for joy: scales were old hat for measuring out deals; McDonald's 100-milligram spoons were absolutely perfect.

Before I went to fill my face, however, I decided to give the bookshelves the once over. I took out each book in turn, doing exactly the same as with the magazines. I got quite excited at one stage because a book on political terrorism had passages which had been underlined in pencil and notes in the margin, until I looked inside the cover and discovered it was a textbook from her university days.

It took about an hour, but I eventually got to the bottom shelf. Turning the pages of a photo-history of North Carolina, I admired the tree-covered mountains, lakes and wildlife, with bullshit blurb in the accompanying captions, 'deer drink contentedly from the pool, next to families enjoying the wonders of the great outdoors.' I could almost hear Kelly groaning a 'Yeah, right!'

I took a look at her other books, about Algeria, Syria and the Lebanon, but they contained nothing but photograph upon photograph of mosques, cypress trees, sand and camels.

I threw them on the floor to check through later and started flicking through the atlas. Then I had second thoughts, deciding to go back to the chair with the atlas and the other three books and do the lot now. As I started a careful, page-by-page check, I found my attention drifting to the traffic in the street below, which I could just about hear through the double-glazing. But it wasn't just my hearing that was wandering. For some reason my mind kept going back to the book about North Carolina.

It usually pays to listen to that inner voice. I stopped looking at the books and just stared at the wall, trying to work out what it was that I was trying to say to myself. When I thought I understood it, I got up and went into her bedroom.

I picked up the shoebox and tipped the contents out onto the bed. When I'd found what I was looking for it was back to the living room.

Turning the pages of the North Carolina book, I tried to match the photograph with the terrain – the type of trees, the background hills, the lakeside. Nothing. The spark was soon put out. It might not necessarily have meant anything, but it might have been a start. My head was starting to hurt. It was time for that burger. I'd be back in an hour to start again. I went to my boots and pushed my feet in, tucking the laces inside, too idle to do them up.

Two minutes later I was standing waiting for the elevator, staring at my boots, when it hit me.

I ran back to the apartment door, opened up and headed for her dressing room.

Sarah must have been the Imelda Marcos of the Washington section. She must have had about thirty pairs of shoes in all, but there were no hiking boots. All the times I'd been with her, she had always worn them when out on the ground. Like me, when it came to footwear, she was a creature of habit.

I was starting to get sparked up again. I turned and checked the rails. Where was the Gore-Tex jacket? Where was the fleece liner? She had always worn that sort of clothing, and she had it on in the photograph. It wasn't so much what I saw as what I didn't. Her outdoor clothing; it wasn't here.

I couldn't go to McDonald's. I had to keep thinking about this. I went into the kitchen and threw some noodles into a pan, filled it up with water and got it boiling on the stove.

I realized that was what had been bugging me. I'd known it all along but hadn't switched on, and the ironic thing was that it was Sarah who'd taught me.

She was in the middle of one of her very heated, noisy meetings. We'd been stuck in a cave for hours, the smoke from a large fire stinging my eyes and casting dark shadows in the background, just where I wanted to see the most. Two mujahedin were sitting cross-legged on the floor, wrapped in blankets and cradling their AKs. I'd never seen them at other meetings before, and they seemed out of place amongst the other three members of their group who were by the fire.

Sarah was also sitting on the floor, draped in blankets beside the fire with the other three muj. They were all drinking coffee as Sarah got more sparked up with them. The two men in the shadows started muttering between themselves and looking agitated, and eventually they pushed off their blankets and grasped their weapons. In a situation like that there are only seconds in which to make a decision to go for it or not. I did; I put my AK into the aim as I stood over Sarah.

The result was a Mexican stand-off, like something out of a spaghetti western. For two or three seconds all that could be heard was the crackling of the fire. Sarah cut the silence. 'Nick, sit down. You're embarrassing me.'

I was very confused as she talked to all the mujahedin. She sounded like a parent apologizing for her toddler's behaviour in the playground. Everyone looked at me and started to laugh, as if I was some sort of schoolboy who'd got it all wrong. All

120

weapons were dropped and the talking continued. Even the two boys sitting at the back looked on me as some sort of mascot. I was expecting them to come over and ruffle my hair at any moment.

It was only when we were on our way back to Pakistan that she explained. 'There was no danger, Nick. The old guy – the one we saw last month?' She smiled as she thought about the event. 'He is the only one with the power to have me killed, and he wasn't there. Those guys at the back were just showing face. Nothing was going to happen.' She sounded like teacher as she added, 'It's not only what you see, Nick. Sometimes what isn't there is just as important as what is.'

She might have been right that time, but in a similar situation I would still have done the same. Shame for her that she hadn't remembered her own lesson.

I sat down to work out what I wanted to say to Mickey, and the way to say it. I'd already forgotten where I'd put his card, so I got out the 3C, tapped in his name and rang his number.

'Hellooo.' He was eating by the sound of it.

'Hello, mate, it's Nick.'

'Oh, so soon.' He sounded quite surprised. I could hear soft rock in the background and an American voice, just as camp as his, enquiring who was on the phone. His voice became distant. 'Gary, go and do something useful in the kitchen. It's the office.'

Gary, it seemed, took the hint. 'Sorry about that, he is sooo nosey.' I could hear drink being poured and a sip being taken.

'Michael, remember what you were saying about Sarah and Jonathan going to the middle of nowhere?'

'Uh-huh.'

'Can you remember exactly where it was? I need it for the report.'

He took a quick swallow. 'Yes. Falls Lake.' He broke into a terrible Southern accent. 'North Carolina, y'all.'

'Do you have an address, or the contact number? You did say that you had a number, remember? You used it to call her.'

121

He laughed. 'Sarah took it off file when old Jonny boy got his come-uppance.'

I had reached another dead end.

Then he added, 'But I think I can remember most of the number; it was almost the same as my mother's old one. Tell you what, give me five and I'll ring you back, OK?'

'Give it three rings, put down, then ring again. I wouldn't want to pick it up and find I'm talking to her mother or anything like that. OK?'

'Ooh, just like James Bond.' He giggled. 'No problem, Nick. Talk soon, byeee.'

I flicked though the book again. Falls Lake did exist, but it covered a vast area. What a dickhead! Why hadn't I asked him for more detail when he told me the story? Just as well I wasn't in the security cell.

Something was smelling bad. I jumped up and ran into the kitchen. The water had boiled away and I pulled a pan of very hot and smelly black noodles from the stove.

I couldn't be arsed to clean it up, just put the pot to one side and turned the cooker off. The phone rang. I walked back into the room, counting. It stopped after three. Good news, I hoped. I let the new call ring twice before picking it up.

'Hellooo, Michael here.' I could hear Gary singing to himself in the background.

'Hello, mate, any luck?'

'The last four digits are *exactly* the same as my mother's old number in Mill Hill. Isn't that freaky?'

I really didn't have an answer for that. I contained my eagerness. 'Oh, and what was it?'

'Double four six eight.'

'Thanks, mate. You sure that's all you know?'

''Fraid so, Nick. I was just given the contact number. Sorry.'

'No problem. I'll let you get on with your evening.'

'OK. I'm here if you need me. Byeee.'

I looked at my watch. It was about half-past nine – according to my body clock, 2.30 a.m. – and I was starting to feel knackered. In the absence of any noodles, it was soon going to be time to RV with Ronald McDonald, but first I had a phone call to make.

I rang a London number. A very clear female voice answered immediately. 'PIN number, please?' The tone was so precise she sounded like the speaking clock.

'Two four four two, Charlie-Charlie.'

'Please wait.' The line went dead; five seconds later the voice was back.

'Charlie-Charlie. Details, please.'

I gave her the same details as Metal Mickey had given me and asked for the address. I could hear the clinking of keys as she entered the details. She checked with me: 'To confirm. North Carolina, address that ends with call number 4468, perhaps in the vicinity of Falls Lake. It should take approximately thirty minutes. Reference fifty-six, fifty-six. Goodbye.'

Charlie-Charlie stands for 'casual contact'. The people in London can work from even the smallest amount of information, and you can inquire via the phone for speed, or ask for a written report, which would give more detail but take longer.

A phone number or car licence plate can lead to you finding out almost everything there is on record about the contact, from the name of his doctor to the last time and place he used his credit card, and what it was he bought. A Charlie-Charlie was about the only perk of the job; I'd used it a few times when trying to find out about women I wanted to take out. No-one ever asks what you want the information for, and it makes life easier if you know in advance what sort of social life they have, whether they're married, divorced with kids, or have a monthly champagne bill the size of an average mortgage.

All I needed this time was an address. These sorts of requests were routine, and wouldn't mean I had gone against Lynn's need-to-know policy.

I walked downstairs. I couldn't see Wayne anywhere. I got to the car, took the parking ticket off the windscreen and threw it in the back. I was committed west, towards Georgetown on the one-way system. That was fine, and in fact McDonald's were right. Within five minutes I passed the big yellow arches; the only problem was that I couldn't park up anywhere. I decided to cruise on M until I found an easier place to stop.

Dead on thirty minutes later I called London. The speaking clock was back. 'Reference please.'

'Reference thirty-two, fourteen.'

There was a gap as the line went dead. She was checking the reference number I'd just given her. All I had to do was subtract my PIN from her reference number. It's a quick and easy confirmation system for low-level inquiries.

She came back on line. 'I have three addresses. One . . .'

The first two locations were nowhere near Falls Lake. One was in Charlotte, another in Columbia. The next one sounded warmer. 'The Lodge, Little Lick Creek, Falls Lake. This is now a disconnected line. Do you want the zip codes and user names on any of these?'

'No, no that's fine. Thank you, that's all.' I hung up. I didn't care who the disconnected line used to belong to. It wouldn't help me one bit.

As I drove, I couldn't get Falls Lake out of my head. I passed a Barnes & Noble bookshop, its neon window sign telling me it was open and selling coffee until 11 p.m. I drove on.

A 7-Eleven came to my rescue with a sandwich and coffee. I turned the car round and passed the Barnes & Noble again while filling my face. I couldn't resist it; I parked up, ditched the coffee and finished off the chicken sandwich as I fed another meter.

I went straight to the reference section and pulled out a small-scale atlas of North Carolina. I found Falls Lake and Little Lick Creek. It sounded like a commune for oral-sex fans.

North Carolina was only a short flight away. I could get down there maybe tonight, and if it turned out to be a fuck-up I'd be back by tomorrow night. I got out my phone and started to make some enquiries.

I drove back to the apartment with a ticket for the 0700 from Dulles. I would still check out her bedroom and kitchen, though, just in case.

7

I took the slip road off Airport Boulevard, following the signs for Interstate 40. According to the map, if I kept on this highway heading east I would hit the Cliff Benson Beltline, which would take me north through Raleigh and on to the lake.

The weather was a lot warmer here than in DC and the clouds were dark and brooding, almost tropical. It had been raining quite heavily by the look of the large puddles that lined the road, and the sandy soil was dark with moisture.

The whole area was going through a massive rebuild. The airport itself had been having a makeover, and a new highway, not yet on the map, was under construction. On each side of me as I drove east, yellow bulldozers were going apeshit, flattening everything in sight to make way for the steel skeletons of yet more buildings. From reading the local information magazine on the flight, I knew that the area was fast becoming 'science city USA', with the largest concentration of biochemical, computer and technical research establishments, and Ph.D.s per capita, in the entire USA. It's amazing the stuff you'll read when you're bored shitless on a plane.

Rows of pristine, glistening, black or silver glass-fronted buildings sat in acres of manicured gardens with lakes and fountains – not at all what I had in mind for the American South after all the redneck jokes I'd heard over the years.

It took about fifteen minutes to get onto the beltline. I drove clockwise heading north around the city, keeping my eyes peeled for signs for exit ten towards Falls Lake. The new money that this transformation had sucked in was impossible to miss, with grand houses and new business fighting hand-to-hand with the old, and demonstrably winning. Smart new office blocks looked down on decrepit trailer parks strewn with abandoned cars and kids, both black and white, whose arses hung out of their dirty jeans, their parents fucked without the skills needed to take advantage of the new opportunity.

I got to exit ten in another ten minutes or so and headed north on Forest Road. From the map, I knew that the Falls Lake area covered about 200 square miles. It was a very long and winding waterway, with hundreds of inlets, like the coastline of Norway, just the kind of place you could disappear into.

After seven miles the road became a single carriageway. Tall firs interspersed with smaller seasonal trees looming on either side. Four more miles and I reached the Falls of Neuse and entered forest proper. The Falls was a small collection of neat little homes made of natural wood or painted white on the eastern side of the lake area. Even here, the new was winning out over the old and rubbing its nose in it. Tracts of land were being carved out of the woods to make way for 'communities' of enormous mansions to house the middle classes who were streaming in for the new Gold Rush of high-tech jobs. At the entry point into each community was a twee, shiny sign announcing 'Carriageways' or 'Fairways', and at each junction a barrage of estate agents' signs directed buyers to even more land which was up for grabs.

I headed west on Raven Ridge, driving deeper into the forest. The new was gradually less and less evident, until it was the old that prevailed once more: dilapidated shacks with car wrecks for garden furniture, and rundown stores built of bare breeze-block, with peeling signs advertising bait and beer. I passed trailer homes that looked as if they'd just been dumped twenty or thirty metres off the road, with no paved access, just trampled ground, and no fences to mark their territory, just corrugated iron leaning around the bottom of the trailers to make them look as if they belonged. Outside, washing hung on lines getting even wetter. Inside, probably, were the stars of the *Ricki Lake* or *Jerry Springer* shows. Fuck knows what the future held for them, but one thing was for sure: new carriageways would be scything through here within a year or two.

The only buildings that weren't falling down or apart were the churches, of which there seemed to be one every mile along the roadside, standing very clean, bright and white. Each projected a different recruiting message on the sort of signboard that cinemas use to advertise their movies. 'You can't even write Christmas without Christ' one said, which was true but strange to see in April. Maybe they liked to think ahead.

I drove for another twenty minutes past trailers and churches, and now and then the occasional neatly tended graveyard right on the side of the road. I came across a small green sign to Little Lick Creek. It wasn't the creek itself I was after, but the point at which it entered the lake, and where one of the spurs had the same name. Going by the waterproof hunting map I'd bought, there were two buildings in that area which weren't accounted for by a symbol on the map legend, so they were probably private houses.

I turned off the tarmac and headed down a gravel road that was just wide enough for two cars to pass. There was a steep gradient each side, and the forest seemed to be closing in, the trees here even higher and more densely packed.

A sign chiselled into a slab of grey-painted wood warned, 'Firearms Strictly Prohibited'. Fifty metres further on, another said, 'No Alcoholic Beverages'. Soon more friendly signs welcomed me to Falls Lake, and directed me to the carparks and recreational areas and hoped I enjoyed myself – but only if I kept my speed to 25 mph.

Up ahead, a motorhome as big as a juggernaut was bearing down on me. I noticed a small track that obviously took wheeled traffic, because there were tyre grooves worn down on each side of a wet grassy central strip, but I didn't have time to get in there. I slowed and pulled over to the side of the road, my car leaning drunkenly to the right. The Winnebago was a massive vehicle, with enough canoes and mountain bikes strapped onto its exterior to equip the US Olympic team, and the family hatchback towed along behind. A wall of spray splashed onto my windscreen as it passed. I didn't even get a wave of acknowledgement.

I drove for another kilometre or so through the forest before I came to a large carpark. Crunching and squelching across a mixture of gravel and mud, I pulled up next to a big map in a wooden frame. Pictures around the edge displayed various indigenous birds, turtles, trees and plants, as well as the tariff for the camp site and the inevitable: 'Enjoy your stay – take only pictures, leave only footprints'. It was possible that I would be taking pictures, but I hoped I would leave no footprints whatsoever.

Driving on for another hundred metres or so, I caught my first glimpse of Little Lick Creek. It wasn't quite the picture postcard scene I'd been expecting. Tall ranks of firs seemed to have marched right to the lake's edge. The water was smooth and as dark as the clouds it mirrored, like the smoked glass of a Raleigh office block. Maybe when the sun was out the area was idyllic, but just now, especially with the trees so claustrophobically close to the water, the atmosphere was more like the brooding menace of a penitentiary.

Over on the other side, 500 metres away and on higher, more undulating ground, sat two houses. They were the ones I wanted to have a look at.

A dozen or so vehicles were already in the carpark, mostly clustered around a wooden boat shed on the lake's edge which had been designed to look like a fort. Canoes and rowing boats were lined up near it in the water, plus the statutory Coke machine and another selling chocolate bars. I'd watched a documentary once which claimed that the Coca-Cola company was so powerful in the US that it had even got a president into power in the 1960s. I wondered how their mission statement compared with Ronald McDonald's. It certainly seems that no matter where you are in the world you will always be able to get a Coke; I'd even been offered one by a six-year-old on a mountainside in Nepal. Out trekking with Sarah in the middle of nowhere, a kid no older than eight came along the track with a tin bucket filled with water and about six battered cans of Coke inside, trying to sell them to the walkers as they made their way up the mountain. Sarah gave him some money but refused the Coke. She had this hang-up about cultures being contaminated by the West and spent the next hour bumping her gums about it. Me? I was thirsty and just wished he'd had Diet instead of Regular.

As I drove past the fort I could see that it was manned by two young lads lounging in the shadows, who didn't look as if they were coming out unless they had to.

At the far end of the carpark was a picnic area with built-in grills and a wooden canopy covering the seating. A family barbecue was underway; a bit early in the season, but they were having fun anyway. Granny and Grandad, sons, daughters and grandchildren all filling their faces.

Beyond it I could see the tops of brightly coloured, family-sized tents. It looked as if each pitch was surrounded by its own individual little coppice. I turned the car through a 180, so I was facing back the way I'd come, and drove towards the toilet block. I nosey-parked between two other cars, front against the toilet block wall, back to the lake.

Picking up the binos and bird book I'd bought at the tourist shop along with my maps, I got out of the car and locked up. Straight away I was hit by the humidity; having air-conditioning in a car almost makes you forget the reason you turned it on in the first place.

Everyone seemed to be having a giggle in the barbecue area. A boom-box was playing some Latino rap, and even Granny was dancing rapper style with the kids. In the car to my right were a couple of senior citizens who'd no doubt driven for hours to get here, parked up at the lake and stayed in the car to eat sandwiches with the air-conditioning going full blast and their hats still on.

I wandered down towards the boat shed, keeping an eye on the spur at the other side of the creek. The larger house of the two was on the left, with a gap of maybe 100 to 120 metres between them. There was no movement around either.

129

I went to the Coke machine and threw in a handful of coins. I didn't really want a drink, certainly not at a dollar a go, but it gave me a chance to look around.

The two teenage lads were probably doing a school vacation job. I didn't know whether they were stoned or just bored shit-less. Both were barefoot but wearing the company uniform: blue shorts and red polo shirt. I nodded at them through the small swing doors; they'd obviously been told to be pleasant and said they hoped I had a nice day. I wasn't sure that I would.

I sat down on the wooden jetty and immediately felt the damp-ness soak into my jeans. To my right were a father and son, with dad trying to get his boy sparked up about fishing: 'We'll only catch something if you sit very still and watch the float.' The kid, in his Disney poncho, was as uninterested as the two in the boat shed – as you would be if you'd much rather be eating ice cream and playing computer games.

I was very overtly carrying the binoculars and bird book; today I was the dickhead tourist with his feet dangling over the side of the jetty, taking in the magnificent view over the water.

Half a dozen boats were moored at various points around the lake. Through the binoculars I could see that each one held two or three very fat, middle-aged men who were dressed for trap-ping bears in the Yukon, their hunting waistcoats festooned with fishing flies, their pockets bulging with all sorts of kit, and fear-some knives hanging in sheaths from their belts.

I panned with the binos along the opposite side of the spur, starting from the far right-hand side. I made out a track cutting though the trees just short of the lake on the higher ground, the one I'd stopped by to let the motorhome past. It looked as if it should lead to the houses. I followed it along and, sure enough, it passed the smaller of the two. I couldn't see anything about the building that gave me any information; it was just a square, two-storey, flat-roofed structure, built into the hill and with stilts holding the forward two thirds. There was a boat and a 4x4 vehicle underneath the stilted area, but no movement. Then two kids came running round from the front of the house followed by a man. They were laughing and throwing a

130

football at each other. Happy families; I'd give that one a miss.

I put the binos down for a while, and had a look at the book. This part is all about third-party awareness, because you never know who is looking at you; they might not be saying, 'Is he doing a recce of those houses over there?' but if all I did was bino at the house and didn't move or do other things, it would look pretty strange. The trick is to give the impression that whatever reason you have for being there is so straightforward no-one gives you a second glance. I just hoped a fellow anorak didn't come up to me and start on some serious bird talk.

I put the book down, much more intimately acquainted with the lesser-spotted something or other, and started to look at the other target. By now enough humidity had condensed on my head for droplets to run down my face, and I was starting to feel sticky and damp all over.

The second house was very much like the first, but about a third bigger and with an extra floor. It, too, was wooden and had a flat, felted roof, but its stilted area had been enclosed with plywood sheeting. Two large doors opened onto a concrete slipway which led down to the water's edge. A boat, a four-seater fibreglass job, ideal for fishing, was parked on the land, still on its trailer, nose facing down towards the water, the outboard engine towards the house.

All the curtains seemed to be closed. I couldn't see any rubbish bags outside, or towels or anything else which might indicate that the house was occupied. However, the garage doors were only three-quarters closed and the rear of a black 4x4 was protruding, which made me think that maybe there was another one inside.

I heard a groan from the two boys in red polo shirts. A man was coming towards the fort with three kids, all highly excited about hiring a canoe and already fighting about who was going to have the paddle.

I put the binos down and had a swig of Coke, which was now warm and horrible, like the weather. I binned it and got another one, then I took a walk back to the car.

The rave at the picnic area was still going strong; the kids were dancing, and the adults, beer cans in hand around the barbecue, despite the signs forbidding alcohol, were putting the world to rights. Even from this distance I could hear the loud sizzle as steaks the size of dustbin lids were dropped onto the smoking griddles.

The old couple were still in their car, her struggling to drink a can of Dr Pepper through her false teeth, him reading the inside pages of a newspaper. Nice day out.

I could read the headline, even through the windscreen. It looked as though I'd been right: the black convoy that had held me up in DC must have been carrying either Netanyahu or Arafat, because both boys were being welcomed to America.

I got back to the car and slowly rolled out along the gravel road to the main drag, turning left, back towards the Falls of Neuse and the beltline. I didn't follow the signs back to Raleigh, though. This time, I wanted the road to Fayetteville.

8

Fayette Nam, as some people in the States call it, due to its high casualty rate, is the home of the 82nd Airborne and US Special Forces. They were stationed at Fort Bragg, the only place I knew in North Carolina. About an hour south of Raleigh – or so they told me at the gas station – I'd first gone there in the mid-1980s for a joint exercise training with Delta Force, the Regiment's American counterpart.

'Deltex' was designed to further an atmosphere of co-operation between the two units, but all it did for me was induce huge amounts of envy. I could still remember being bowled over by the sheer size of the place; you could have fitted the entire town of Hereford twice over into what they called a 'fort'. The quantity and quality of equipment on show was beyond belief. Delta had indoor 7.62 and 5.56 shooting ranges; at Stirling Lines we only had the 9mm equivalent. We also had only one gym, while they had dozens of them, including jacuzzis, saunas and a massive climbing wall for their Mountain Troop. No wonder we renamed the place Fort Brass. They had more helicopters in one unit than we had in the whole of the British army; come to that, there were more personnel in just that one base than in all of the British armed services put together.

Fayetteville is effectively a garrison city, with every business geared up for the military. The troops are the ones with the money and the desire to burn it. Like them, in all the times I'd been there I'd never felt the need to venture out of the city limits.

The 401 was a wide single carriageway. I drove through a few small towns which would have made great locations for 1950s films or, better still, could have done with a couple of thousand-pounders to put them out of their misery, before the area started to open up into cornfields and grassland. Houses and small industrial units dotted the route, alongside open barns filled with tractors and other agricultural gear, and every few miles, in case people needed reminding that they were in the boonies, I came across a road kill, a mess of blood and fur as flat as a pancake in the middle of the blacktop.

I knew I was getting near when I hit the Cape Fear river. The water was about 300 metres across at this point, getting wider as it got closer to the sea, and sure enough I passed the 'City of Fayetteville' sign before long and kept my eyes peeled for anything directing me to Fort Bragg.

Bragg Boulevard was a wide dual carriageway with a grass central reservation, but as I passed rows of car showrooms with new 4x4s and sports cars under miles of red, white and blue bunting, it changed back to two lanes. The buildings on either side were mainly one-storey breeze-block warehouses behind a shop front. Korean pawn shops and tailors jostled with Vietnamese restaurants and takeaways, representing a weird chronicle of all the conflicts the USA had ever been involved in. They just needed an Iraqi kebab stall to complete the set.

I was beginning to see the kind of outlet I'd come here to find. Neon signs and posters announced boot-shining specialists, tattoo artists and gun shops – 'Test fire before you buy – we have our own range'. On every sidewalk, young men and women strode around in smartly pressed BDUs (combat uniform) and very short haircuts – the men usually had a 'whitewall' with a little lump on top. It felt very strange to see uniformed soldiers on the streets without a weapon and not on patrol; the terrorist situation in Europe meant that off-duty soldiers were forbidden to walk around in uniform; they'd just be ready-made targets.

I drove on base and got my bearings. American military

installations aren't like European ones, which resemble World War Two prisoner-of-war camps, again because of the terrorist threat. This place was open and sprawling, with vehicle pools and groups of men and women on route marches, singing cadence, their unit flag carried proudly at the head of the column.

I couldn't remember the name of the road I wanted, but I followed my nose, driving along roads with buildings on each side which looked more like smart apartments than barrack rooms. I found it – Yadkin, a long road that came out of the base and moved into the city area. There had been quite a bit of building since my last visit in the late Eighties. Roads coming off the main drag had names like Desert Storm Boulevard, or Just Cause Road. I wondered if the Firm would ever get round to naming thoroughfares after its operations – if so, they'd have to be called things like Blackmail Lane, or Stitch Them Up Big Time Street.

I carried on along Yadkin until it took me off base, past Kim's No. 1 Sewing, Susie J's (I wasn't too sure what service she was offering) and whole blocks of military supply shops. There was one I remembered, called US Cavalry. It had been a complete department store for the start-your-own-war nut, glass counters displaying sharp, pointy things, racks of BDUs, military T-shirts and combat helmets, rows and rows of boots, and shelves of posters and books with such politically correct titles as *Ragnar's Big Book of Home-made Weapons* and *The Advanced Anarchist Arsenal: Recipes for Improvised Incendiaries and Explosives* – always good for that last-minute Christmas present.

I drove past shop fronts displaying murals of airborne assaults. One had a giant poster of John Wayne in uniform in the window. After another mile I saw the store I wanted and drove into the carpark. Jim's was the same size as a small superstore; the front had a wooded ranch look about it, but the rest was whitewashed breeze-block. The front windows looked almost cottagey from a distance, with lots of little square panes, but as you got nearer you could see the panes were just white-painted bars behind the thick plate glass. And the anti-ram barriers one third of the way up the windows weren't there to tie your horse up to either. Through the foyer I could see keyboards, VCRs and rows of TV

135

screens all showing *Jerry Springer*. It was to the left of all that, however, a place where there were no windows at all, that they kept what I'd come here for.

I walked onto a small verandah where a large red sign warned me, 'Before entry weapons will be unloaded, actions opened and thank you for not smoking'.

The inside of Jim's Gunnery was L-shaped. To my right was a pawn shop; the rest disappeared around the corner to my left, past a counter selling magazines and sweets. Opposite was a small shop within a shop, selling jewellery. The place smelled more like a department store than a pawn shop. It was very clean, with a polished, tiled floor.

I turned left towards a series of glass display cases, all containing pistols – hundreds of them – and behind them, in wall racks, rifles, with something to suit every taste, from bolt action to assault. After I picked up a wire basket, I was greeted by a very well-fed white guy in his mid-thirties, wearing a green polo shirt with Jim's logo on it, a Glock .45 in a pancake holster on his belt and a big smile. 'Hi, how are you today?'

In my bad American I replied, 'I'm good, how are you?'

I wasn't worried; the transient military population made it a lot easier to get away with a dodgy accent. Besides, they'd only think I was Australian – Americans always do.

'I'm good, sir. Is there anything I can do for you today?'

'Just having a look round, thanks.'

He beamed. 'If you need anything, just holler.'

Heading towards the weapons counter, I passed shelves stacked supermarket fashion with boxes of ammunition and everything for the hunting man, even down to Barbour jackets and shooting sticks, which surprisingly didn't look out of place.

Anti-mugging sprays hung from racks. I couldn't decide whether to have the CS gas or the pepper spray, so in the end I put both in my basket.

The footwear section sold camouflaged Gore-Tex boots and an assortment of wellingtons and leather footgear. What I wanted, and eventually found, was a normal pair of high-leg assault boots, a mixture of cross-trainer and boot. The Gore-Tex and go-faster boots were all well and good, but I could never really be bothered with trying to keep my feet dry. Once they were wet, which they would be tonight, that was it, I just got on with it. I didn't bother to try the boots on; it wasn't as if I was going to be tabbing for six days across the Appalachians. I got them in a size ten; I was size nine, but remembered from a very painful few days in a pair of new US trainers that their sizes are one up from those in the UK.

I went over and had a look in the weapon cabinets. There were hundreds of revolvers and semi-automatics to choose from. I could see what I wanted and waited my turn to be served.

Next to me, a woman in her early thirties had a two-year-old in a carry-rig on her back. She was being helped by one of the assistants to choose a new nylon holster for her Smith & Wesson .45 CQB, and they were also chattily discussing the pros and cons of various models. The one she was carrying was the stainless-steel version. As she was saying to the assistant, the matt-black, alloy version was lighter, but the steel one was more noticeable and therefore a better deterrent. It was a fantastic weapon, and would always have been my weapon of choice were it not for the fact that I preferred 9mm because the magazines carried more rounds. Mind you, if she needed more than the seven in the mag plus one in the chamber, she was in the shit anyway. The conversation moved back to the new holster as opposed to keeping it in her handbag.

A bit further along, a young black guy in a blue tracksuit was being briefed on the merits of a .38 revolver over a semi-automatic. 'With this baby y'all don't even have to aim,' the sales pitch went. 'Especially at the range y'all be using it at. Just point it like your finger at the centre mass and it will take them down.' The customer liked that; he was going to take it.

The woman had gone and the assistant came over to me. 'Hi, how can I help you today?'

It was bad accent time again. 'Can I have a look at your Tazers on the bottom shelf there.'

'Sure, no problem.' The assistant was black, in his mid-twenties, and dressed in the house green shirt. He was also

137

'carrying'. It was a Sig 9mm, held in the same sort of nylon pancake holster the woman had been interested in. He bent down and pulled out the tray of Tazers.

They were selling all different types, from little handheld ones, to the sort that fire out prongs on a wire which you can use to attack someone from a five-metre range, right up to big ones which resembled police truncheons. I was tempted by a handheld one called 'Zap-Ziller – the monster of stun guns!' mainly because of the slogan. There was even a picture of a dinosaur on the box that told me it packed 100,000 volts of stopping power.

I read the packaging to make sure it suited my needs: 'A short blast of a quarter-second duration will startle an attacker, cause minor muscle contractions and have a repelling effect. A moderate length blast of one to four seconds can cause an attacker to fall to the ground and result in some mental confusion. It may make an assailant unwilling to continue an attack, but he will be able to get up almost immediately.

'A full charge of five seconds can immobilize an attacker, cause disorientation, loss of balance, falling to the ground and leave them weak and dazed for some minutes afterward. Note: Any blast lasting over one second is likely to cause your assailant to fall. If you do not help them down, gravity may injure them.' I hoped so. They'd certainly done the business in Syria.

In the clothing area I picked out a set of 'woodland camo' Gore-Tex, choosing one two sizes too big so it was nice and baggy. Gore-Tex had changed a lot since it was first invented by God in answer to every infantryman's prayers. In the early days it had made a rustling noise as you moved, which wasn't good if you were moving on target, and as a result we'd had to wear it under our combat clothing. But nowadays it was much more like textile than plastic.

I cruised round the aisles and filled my trolley with a few other bits and pieces I thought I'd be needing. I didn't think I'd need a weapon, but seeing them all made me feel strange about being on a job without one. It would take too long to apply for a gun legally. The US laws aren't as crazy as people in Europe imagine, and I didn't want to take the risk of stealing or buying one illegally. Normally, if I knew I was going to need one, I would plan to obtain it in-country, because that meant I wouldn't have to worry when travelling on commercial flights. If that wasn't possible, I'd put one in the diplomatic bag, along with any other special kit I needed, and then pick it up at the embassy. This wasn't happening on this job, however; the timings hadn't allowed it. Besides, I was carrying out a PV review; what would I need a weapon for?

The hunting-bow section at the rear of the store caught my eye. Three customers in their early fifties, baseball caps on their heads and beer bellies hanging over their belts, were trying to outdo each other with their war stories. I overheard, 'When I was in Da Nang there was a whole week I thought the good Lord was going to take me away . . .'

I saw some crossbows that took my fancy. They were small, but I knew they were powerful. Since the UK government had banned handguns, the pistol clubs had had to find another sport, and many now used their ranges to fire crossbow bolts instead of pistol rounds. The club where I'd been shown how to use one was in Vauxhall, just across from the Firm's HQ.

I picked up one model and examined the optic sight and the attachment to keep spare bolts. The price tag said $340, which was all right, but the other side was disappointing: a label told me it needed a North Carolina weapons licence.

The only option left to me was an ordinary bow, and I wasn't short on choice. There were racks of them to choose from, with names like Beast 4x4, Black Max and Conquest Pro. Made of carbon fibre, aluminium or composite resin, with cams that worked like gears at the end of the bow to give the bow cable more power, these modern versions of the longbow would have had Robin Hood creaming his Lincoln green.

I found one I liked the look of, the Spyder Synergy 4, proudly boasting thirty-two inches of throbbing manhood end to end, cammed and cabled up, ready to go – as long as I had some arrows. I wanted the smallest ones I could find, just like the bow. Looking along the racks I worked out it was the two-footers I was after, and picked up a box of six. But that wasn't the end of it. I then had to choose the arrowhead. I went for the Rocky Mountain Assassin; it looked like Thunderbird Three with its tail fins, which were in fact razors. It also seemed to be the only one that came with ready-assembled fins.

I was quite enjoying myself at the bow mix 'n' match counter, and the next item I needed was a quiver. These, too, were cammed up and fixed onto the bow, so that everything was secure and close to hand.

I carried on and got the rest of the stuff on my mental shopping list, and with enough kit to bow-hunt until Christmas I went to the checkout. The woman with the baby was examining a necklace in the jewellery department. She obviously hadn't liked the holster, because the stainless steel .45 CQB still gleamed from her open bag on the counter.

Behind the checkout a woman in her early twenties sat bored out of her skull, apparently not that interested in the latest style of handgun or waterproofs. Her hair was gelled to her forehead, and she didn't even look at me as she said, 'Card or cash?' I couldn't keep my eyes off her fingernails. They were two inches long and nearly curling, like Fu Manchu's, and were painted with an intricate, black and white chequer-board pattern. I couldn't wait to describe them to Kelly.

I replied, 'Cash,' did the transaction, lifted my bags, put my twenty cents change into the 'Candy for Kids' box and left. While I was loading the boot of my car, the woman with the baby came out and got into a people carrier. I couldn't help but smile as I saw the stickers plastered across the back:

'This vehicle insured by Smith and Wesson.'

'A proud parent of a terrific kid, sponsored by Burger King.'

And, best of all: 'The driver carries only $50 . . . OF AMMO!'

In amongst all of these was a large silver Born-Again Christian fish sign with the word Jesus in the middle. It was just like old times, part of the crazy kaleidoscope of contradictions that made me love America so much. It was a good job I hadn't made a mistake the last time I was looking for a wagon with a fish sign on it, and climbed into this woman's vehicle. No doubt the vehicle's insurers would have given me a greeting to remember.

There were still a few other odds and ends I needed, so I drove away from Yadkin and towards the city centre – or what I thought was the centre. After ten minutes I had to stop, open the boot and get the maps out, hoping that on one of them there might be a town plan. I worked out where I was and where I was going to: a shopping mall, the nearest one I could see. It was about a mile away.

It turned out not to be the single, contained area I'd been expecting. The main mall building looked more like the Pentagon, but clad in something like York stone, and the remaining outside shopping areas and carparks must have straddled an area of more than eight square kilometres, with traffic jams to match. The big blue sign for WalMart was exactly what I wanted, and the store was part of the outer shopping area. I waited at the lights, peeled off right, and went into the carpark. There was the usual line-up of stores – Hallmark Cards, post office, shoe superstores, a Lone Star steak house, then my mate, WalMart.

As I got a trolley I was greeted by an elderly male welcomer with his happy face on. 'Hi, how are you today?'

I smiled back at him. He had a WalMart baseball cap on which was a size too big for his head, and a T-shirt over his long-sleeved shirt which told me how happy WalMart were to see me. There was an ATM machine just past the turnstile. I took the opportunity to get some more cash out on my card and off I went. The place was full of Airborne soldiers, screaming kids and stressed-out mothers.

I selected food that was both ready, and quiet, to eat. No crisps or cans of fizzy drink; instead, I picked up four big tins of Spam, four large bottles of still mineral water and a bumper pack of Mars bars. Then a couple of laps around the gardening section, and I was done.

There was a little self-service café which I'd missed as I entered, maybe in the excitement of my welcome to WalMart. After paying, I left my trolley with my new friend – it was also his job to keep an eye on them when people went to the café. I picked up a tray and got myself two large slices of pizza and a Coke.

As I ate I ran through my mental checklist, because I didn't have that much time left to mince around. Deciding I had everything I'd need, I finished the pizza and Coke and headed for the exit. I felt a stirring in my bowels; I couldn't find the toilet, but no matter, I'd go to a coffee shop. However, the pangs made me think about something I'd forgotten: I went back to the pharmacy section and picked up a couple of party-size packs of Imodium.

Thinking about it, the pizza hadn't been too bad, so I went back in and bought two full-sized Four Seasons.

As always, I'd chosen the trolley with one dodgy wheel, so as soon as I was outside on the concrete I was all over the place, pushing it at a crazy angle in order to go forwards. When it came to supermarket trolleys, my lucky number was zero.

I threw everything into the boot; I'd sort it all out later. As I got behind the wheel, I got the phone out, turned it on and checked the battery level. It was fine. All the same, I fished out the spare battery, swapped it for the one I'd just checked and then plugged it into the recharger. I was going to need both batteries full up and ready to go.

One last check of the map and I nosed out into the solid traffic.

9

I drove out of town and back towards the lake. It had started to rain a little and I had to put the wipers on intermittent, turning them off again just before Raleigh when they started to rub on the dry windscreen. Soon afterwards I spotted a rest area, pulled in and got sorting.

Bending into the boot I started to pull off the sticky-back price tags from the Gore-Tex and my other purchases, stuck two on my hand, then packed all the stuff into the hunting bergen. I made a point of putting the secateurs in one of the little pouches on the outside, together with the string and gardening gloves, as I'd be needing them first. The gloves were a bit embarrassing as they were like Marigold washing-up gloves with lots of little lumps on the fingers for grip, and worst of all they were yellow. I should have opened them up and checked the colour. It was too late now to do anything about it; I needed to get back to the lake. All the other items, including the plastic petrol container, went in the main compartment of the bergen.

All I had to do now was prepare the food. I folded the big sections of pizza in on each other and wrapped them in clingfilm. I ripped the Mars bars out of their wrappers and clingfilmed them together in pairs. Then I opened the tins of Spam and also clingfilmed the contents, and the whole lot went into the bergen. Peeling the labels from my hand, I stuck one on top of the other

143

and then both over the small battery light on my phone. Then I went into the menu and turned off all the sound facilities.

It was then down to a good smearing of insect repellent. I didn't know if I'd need it or not, but better safe than scratching. I got back into the car and headed for the lake. The rain had died down, at least for the moment.

Flicking through the radio channels, I found myself listening to a woman who was talking about Southern females spending more time and money on their hair than those from any other area of the USA. 'That's why we should buy this magical mousse that—' I hit the seek button. There was someone else explaining the reason why the weather was all screwed up: El Niño. 'We're lucky here in North Carolina, unlike the main areas hit, like Alabama; they had twisters.' I hit the switch and landed on a Christian station. This one was telling me that it was God, not El Niño, who was responsible for climate changes. Apparently the good Lord was not best pleased with all our sinning and was sending us a warning. However, the first step towards salvation might be to buy one of the channel's leatherbound Holy Bibles, available for only $98.99. All major credit cards accepted.

I was back in the woods. It was just past seven o'clock and nearing last light, especially under the canopy of high trees. That was absolutely fine by me; I wanted the maximum amount of dark to get on target and sort myself out before first light, then find out whether or not she was in the house. I hoped she was, otherwise it was back to DC and a great big empty drawing board.

I hadn't had time to think about a good drop-off point for the car, but maybe the lake attracted families in the evenings, and the carpark had looked a very likely lovers' lane. Either way it meant other vehicles and my car would blend in.

I was about half a K short of the carpark when I finally had to turn my lights on. I had a quick spin round; there were a few lights in the tent area, but only one other car, which presumably belonged to the young couple I could see having a romantic interlude under the canopy. Well, they were until my headlights hit them and they had to hold their hands up to shield their eyes.

144

I parked as near as possible to the barbecue area, but not so close to the young couple that I was going to have to go 'Hi' when I got out. Not that they would have noticed me; from what I could see he seemed totally engrossed in trying to get his hand up her skirt, though unfortunately for him she appeared to be more interested in the food they were cooking.

Looking across the lake, I could see lights on in both houses. I was still gagging for a shit, so I decided to walk over to the toilets with my new boots and ring-lace them while I relieved myself. The weather was still warmish, and the crickets were really going for it, drowning the noise of my footsteps on the mud and wet gravel. The stars were trying to break though the clouds, and the surface of the lake was as flat as a mirror. I hoped it stayed that way and didn't rain.

The toilets were moulded, all-in-one, stainless steel units, with just a handle sticking out of the wall, so nothing could be vandalized. It was hot, dark and muggy in the cubicle, the only light coming from outside the main door. Swarms of buzzing things had been waiting on the ceiling for some poor unsuspecting arse to show up on the radar. As the first two or three dived in I heard a laugh from the girl by the barbecue. Maybe he'd found his target as well.

I pulled out a few sheets of toilet paper from the container and its hard texture gave me a flashback to twenty-odd years ago, and the juvenile detention centre: 'Three squares only,' the staff had barked. 'One up, one down, one shine.'

That reminded me, I needed to bung myself up; I'd better take some Imodium. With my Timberlands in my hand and my shiny new boots on my feet, I trogged back to the car. The lovers were nowhere to be seen, but their car was still there and the barbecue was glowing. He must have scored and they'd moved somewhere more secluded; it's amazing what you can get away with if you make a woman laugh.

I opened the boot and got out the bergen and bow, checking that I hadn't left anything I'd be needing for the job or which would compromise what was going on if the car got nicked. In went the Timberlands; I wasn't going to fuck them up, I'd only just broken them in. I opened a foil pack of Imodium and swallowed four capsules. The instructions said two, but that was a problem I'd had all my life: I never listened to advice.

Slinging the bergen, which now had the bow strapped onto it, over my right shoulder, I had a last study of the lake and the target houses to get my bearings, and set off. My plan was to follow the shore, cross the creek, then follow the shoreline again to the target – that way I avoided the track. There was too much risk of transport going up and down it, and I didn't know how aware anyone in the buildings would be. I might compromise myself before I'd even reached the target. Do it properly and then you don't have to worry about those sorts of things.

I passed the lovers' car. The windows were very steamed up, but I could see some strange movement going on inside.

A few paces further on, nailed to the barbecue canopy, was a large sign with 'WARNING' stamped on the top. I stopped to read it; the more information, the better. 'Caution Hikers,' it said, 'Hunting activities involving the use of firearms and other legal weapons may take place on the Wildlife Resources Commission Gamelands immediately adjacent to the park during hunting season.' It further warned, 'Please stay on the marked trail during hunting season to avoid the danger of possible serious injury or death. Wearing an item of bright-orange clothing is strongly suggested.' That was all well and good, but when was the hunting season?

I carried on and got level with the tented area, encountering a two-metre-high wooden fence which seemed to surround the site. I followed it until I got to the grandly named Recycling Center, which, in fact, was three galvanized dustbins for plastic bottles, glass and aluminium cans, and clambered over. A swathe about ten yards wide had been cut into the forest from the water's edge. Tree stumps an inch or two high jutted from the sandy ground, and I kept stubbing the toe of my boots as I took the beach route.

After five minutes or so, when my night vision kicked in, the going got easier. It takes a long time to adjust to darkness. The cones in your eyes enable you to see in the daytime, giving colour and perception, but they're no good at night. What takes over then are the rods on the edge of your irises. They are angled at forty-five degrees, because of the convex shape of the eye, so if you look straight at something at night you don't really see it, it's a haze. You have to look above it or around it so you can line up the rods, which will then give you a picture. It takes forty minutes or so for them to become fully effective, but you can start to see better after five.

Every now and then I could hear the clinking and clanking of people in tents doing their evening stuff; I couldn't really make out what they were saying, but I was sure it would be something along the lines of, 'Whose idea was it to come camping anyway?' I also heard a portable TV being tuned in, and the sound of jingles.

I was hardly behind enemy lines here, but all the time I was thinking, What if? What if I bump into someone? Answer, I'm on holiday, I'm hiking. I'd play the dickhead Brit abroad on holiday thinking he's having fun, and try to turn it to my advantage and learn as much as possible about the houses. You've always got to have a reason for being somewhere, so that if you're challenged, you won't be fumbling around trying to come up with bone excuses. It also gives you a mindset, and you can then do what- ever you're doing with more confidence.

I moved off the lake shore as it petered out, and into the wood between the water and the fence. It was hardly secondary jungle; the larger trees were five or six feet apart, with smaller saplings scattered in between. It was wet and muddy, but being flat it was easy enough to negotiate.

I was just coming level with the end of the tented area when, from very close quarters, I heard a young woman's voice. 'Jimmy! Jimmy!' Before I knew it I'd stumbled on the couple from the barbecue, and from the way their clothing was rearranged, she'd forgotten what was on the barbecue entirely. It confused me; I'd thought they were in the car.

This sort of thing can go one of two ways – either they're embarrassed, so they make their excuses and move on, or if you're unlucky, the guy decides he's got to demonstrate what a big man he is.

I checked my stride and moved to the right to go round them. I tried to make it look as if I was concentrating on my footing as I passed, but without losing him from vision. He shouted, 'Who the fuck are you, man?' and it was obvious which way this one was going to go. He stopped me in my tracks with his hand on my shoulder and held me there. I had my head down in order to look confused and unthreatening, but also to protect my face in case this kicked off.

I stuttered, 'I'm sorry to disturb you.'

He went, 'What? You some kind of sicko stalker, or what?'

'Jimmy!' The girl was trying to look as if she was brushing sand off her skirt. I couldn't see her face in the darkness, but it was obvious from her tone that she was embarrassed and wanted to get away. He had managed to pull up his Levis and fasten the top button, but there was a big gaping hole where the rest of his flies were still undone. The white of his underwear glowed in the dark and I had to try hard not to laugh.

My voice was my normal really bad American one, but at the same time trying to sound scared and submissive. I said, 'Nothing like that, I'm just going to see some of the turtles.' Hopefully that would be enough to make him satisfied that he was the tough guy around here, so I could move on. It would hardly square with having a bow, but I was hoping he couldn't see that, wedged between my back and the bergen.

'Turtles? Who are you, Mr Nature from the fucking Discovery Channel?' He liked that one; he guffawed and turned to his girl-friend for approval.

I said, 'On the other side of the lake, they're making their nests. This is the only time of year they do it.' Unlike your good selves, I added to myself. I carried on waffling about turtles coming onto the beach and digging and laying their eggs – something which, ironically, I had in fact learned from the Discovery Channel. Plus, my bird guidebook told me they were here.

Lover Boy laughed; honour had been satisfied. I wasn't a weirdo, just an anorak. Now he didn't really know what to do, so he laughed again. 'Turtles, man, turtles.' And with that he put his arm around the girl and they walked off towards the beach.

I'd got away with it, but it was annoying that it had happened, because two people might now be able to identify me. It didn't mean anything at the moment, but if there was a drama at a later date they might remember the encounter. It could have been worse: at least he wasn't a nature fan himself.

It was nine twenty-seven and it had taken two hours and getting my trousers wet up to my arse crossing the creek, but I'd eventually got to within maybe sixty metres of the target. I was right on the lake shore, which was the only way I'd been able to get a decent view of the house because the ground was so undulating. The terrain was different here; the National Parks people hadn't cleared a swathe, and the treeline extended almost to the water's edge.

Some lights were still on on the first floor, but the curtains were drawn and I couldn't see any movement. It was a question now of finding a position that would give me cover, but with a good aperture with which to view the target. That could only be achieved by carrying out a 360-degree recce of the area around the house.

I took my time, picking my feet up carefully to avoid making noise by hitting any rocks, stones or fallen branches, then slowly placing the edge of my boot down on the ground first, followed by the rest of the sole. The technique puts quite a strain on your legs, but it's the only way to have any sort of control over the noise you make.

When I reached the water's edge, I stopped after about ten metres and listened, pointing my ear towards the target and slightly opening my mouth to overcome any body-cavity noises, such as jaw movement. I couldn't hear anything apart from the lake lapping against the shore; certainly nothing from the target house. I had a look at where I wanted to go on my next bound, and started picking my way carefully over the rocks. There were still lights on in the other house as well, but I couldn't make out much detail because it was too far away. At least the rain was holding off.

I did my next move and got to within about forty metres of the house. I realized that, because the ground was up and down like a yo-yo, it was going to be very difficult to be stood off from the target and watch from any distance. Yet if I went right up on the higher ground behind, all I'd see was the roof. I couldn't site the OP (observation point) between the houses. Kids are very inquisitive and by mid-day tomorrow they'd probably be in the OP with me, sharing my Mars bars and pizza. My options were so limited that there was no point doing a 360; it wouldn't achieve anything.

I went back down to the shore, took off the bergen and left it by a big overhanging tree. That way, even if there was a major drama, I knew I'd find it again; all I'd have to do was run down to the lake, keeping to this side of the house, turn right and I couldn't miss it. What was more, the lighter and less bulky I was, the less noise I made while I found a good hide position. For all I knew at this stage, although I hadn't seen or heard anything, there could be dogs, or even worse, geese – they're food for virtually everything that moves, so they spark up at the slightest noise; the ancient Egyptians used them as an alarm system. I learned this from living in my new house in Norfolk because the guy who lived nearest me kept geese, and the fucking things never failed to wake me up in the middle of the night. I'd had two in my oven so far. Kelly thought that I bought her favourite Sunday roast from the Co-op.

I went back towards the house, taking my time, moving slowly; stopping, looking at the target, looking at the area, listening, working out my next bound and then moving off again. With any OP, the closer you are to the target, the better you'll be able to observe what's going on, but the greater the chance of com- promise. The further away you are, the less chance of compromise, but you might see fuck all. The ideal with this particular target was probably to be stood off miles away, maybe placing a remote, high-powered camera on the house and view- ing it from the other side of the lake – but I didn't have the necessary optics. You have to make do with what you've got.

The sky had cleared and a few more stars were out. I could still hear the lake lapping on the shore, but there was now also a splashing as the turtles came to the surface and dived down again.

I got to within about twenty-five metres of the house. The tree line stopped and the 'garden' began, an area of rough grass with tree stumps which hadn't been pulled out after creating the clearing for the house. From this position I could see the whole of one side of the target, plus the boat and the lake.

There were three floors, and beneath them a garage, with its doors still slightly open to fit the wagon. There was a light shining on the first floor, towards the lakeside, but only small cracks of light from behind the heavy curtains. I couldn't see any movement. A door was facing me on the ground floor which looked as if it went to the garage.

A light came on on the second floor. No visible movement.

A few seconds later a toilet flushed. At least there was movement inside, unless the flush was electronic and on some sort of security timer to operate every hour with the lights. I hardly thought so; in another place, yes, but not here.

I started to cast around to find somewhere to dig in before first light. I found one possible site – a bush set back a little from the tree line. It came up to about chest height and was four feet or so wide, with other, smaller bushes around it. It looked ideal, but first I'd have to check I could see the target while I was lying down in it. Anyone who has ever done OPs has horror stories of digging in under cover of darkness, only to find at first light that all they can see is mud. I got to the bush, taking care not to disturb any of the foliage, then lay down right in front and checked. I could see only the top floor, and that was no good to me.

I moved further up the hill. The tree line curved right, bringing me no more than twenty metres from the target, which I didn't really want. I'd be able to hear snoring at that distance, but I also stood a good chance of being heard myself. I moved back down the hill, towards the lake.

There was one other bush, about thirty metres from the house, but this one was only about waist height. Again it was about four feet wide, but the foliage didn't seem as dense as the other one. I was running out of choices. I lay down level to where the aperture would be, and found I could see the whole shebang – all three floors, the garage, the side door from the garage and the lake. I could also see the distant lights from the camp site, so I knew that in daylight I'd be able to see movement in the carpark. It looked like this was going to be the one.

I got behind the bush, out of sight from the house. So far, so good. The next thing was to check that there was a mobile-phone signal. If I saw her, London would need to know. Without the mobile phone I'd have to lie concealed all day, leave at last light, and either get to a location with a decent signal or find a public call box, which would not only mean a possible compromise, but also loss of eyes on target.

I switched on the Bosch, put my hand over the backlit display and waited. I gave it a minute, keeping my eyes on the house. The toilet light had gone out now, but the first-floor one was still on. I made a tunnel over the display with my hand, pressed one of the buttons and the backlight came on again. The display showed that I had three signal bars out of a maximum four, and that was good enough for me. I turned it off again.

I sat there for another five minutes, tuning in. Somebody crossed behind the gap in the curtain. I couldn't tell if they were male or female.

The temperature had dropped a few degrees and it was starting to feel a little bit nippy now that I'd stopped moving. Not freezing, but it felt cold where sweat had trickled down my spine and where the hair on my head was wet around the edges. My jeans were still damp and felt uncomfortable, but they would dry. I stood up slowly, feeling wet clothing make contact with skin. I turned and started to move in a line directly away from the house, and as soon as I found myself in a decent dip of dead ground, I changed direction and headed straight down to the lake.

I retrieved the bergen and bow, checked that everything was done up, and carefully ran my hand around on the ground to make sure I hadn't left anything. Then I retraced my route to the OP. By now it was just before midnight, which left me plenty of time. First light wasn't until about five o'clock in the morning.

I dropped the bergen directly behind the bush. Nothing and

no-one goes forward of an OP from this point on, because that's what the enemy can see.

I opened the side pocket and pulled out the secateurs and string, hunkered down at the rear of the bush and started to cut. I felt like James pruning his roses. What I was trying to do was make a hole in the bush, as small as possible, but through which I could crawl. It's pointless just pushing a bush apart and charging inside; you'll distort the shape, make noise getting in and, once inside, make yet more noise and movement, because the bush is pressing on you. If you're going to do it, do it properly. As the first branches were cut, I tied them together with one end of the string, like a bunch of flowers. I ran out a spare couple of metres of string, cut it and put the bundle to one side.

There was no need for my nice yellow Marigolds after all, because it wasn't a prickly bush. But I was still glad I'd brought them. I'd never believed in being macho about building hides with my bare hands. Why scratch or cut yourself when even a minor injury can slow you down? If you've got a pair of gloves and you need them, use them. The object is to get into the bush, not to show how hard you are.

I was still mincing away, making progress into the bush, cutting slowly and deliberately so as to reduce noise and not fuck up. I didn't need to create too big a space; all I wanted was to be able to crawl inside, get up to the front of the bush, make an aperture and observe the target. I was edging my way in, pruning it piece by piece. Anything that could just be moved out of the way and not cut, I would leave, sometimes using string to hold it back; it all added to the density of foliage around me.

It took the best part of an hour to tunnel my way in, and I had about six inches of movement area around me and about a foot of bush in front. Now it was a matter of rigging up the rest of the OP.

I wriggled back out, unloaded some stuff from the bergen and pushed them into the hide. First out was the digital camera, with its small tripod and cable release. I crawled inside and rigged it up.

Next was the hunter's individual camouflage net that I'd got at Wars R Us. I got on my back, put the camouflage over the front of my chest, and then started to shuffle into the hide. Once in, I pushed the net gently against the bush so it snagged, tying it with string where necessary. By the time I'd finished I had created a snug little tunnel. The aim of the cam net was to give the bush more density; without it, if direct sunlight came into the bush the gap would be glaringly evident. If I hadn't found a cam net, a dark green blanket would have done just as well.

The most annoying thing about building an OP at night is that you can't check it, so it's all down to practice and experience. After my check at first light, I wouldn't be able to move from the hide, and if it hadn't been done right, there wouldn't be a second chance. I'd been doing this shit since 1976 when I first joined the infantry, so I'd got it down to a fine art by now. All you've got to do is have patience and know the techniques – and have the aptitude to lie there for days, sometimes weeks, on end, just waiting for five seconds of exposure of a target. Some people defined this aptitude as self-discipline; me, I saw it as being just too idle to do anything else.

10

Very slowly and deliberately, trying not to take laboured breaths and make noise, I started to lift the rest of the stuff I'd be needing out of the bergen. I would normally keep everything there, but being so close to the target, I wanted to cut down movement. I placed the pizzas and the rest of the food into the side of the bush and covered them with the sandy soil to try and hide the smell from animals and insects, and to prevent the clingfilm from reflecting shine – not that there was likely to be too much of that tomorrow if this weather continued. The phone, the 3C, the passport and any other essentials would go in my pockets if I had to run; it was just like being a soldier again and keeping belt kit on. Finally, I pushed the bergen inside the OP.

I carefully put on the Gore-Tex, then got on my knees and felt around on the ground with my hands, both to check there was nothing left lying exposed, and to smooth out any sign I had made. The final check was that my pockets were done up and the kit was secure inside them. Only then did I crawl into the hide, and start pulling in behind me the bouquet of branches that made up the bung. I was now sealed in.

For two or three minutes I lay still, listening and tuning in to my new surroundings. There was no noise from either of the houses, and the light was off in the target house; all I could hear was the lapping of water. The turtles seemed to have gone to bed.

I waited for another couple of minutes, and then it was time to sort myself out, to make sure everything was in place, and make minor adjustments. Moving more stones and damp sand from under me, I built it up around my sides, slowly digging a shallow grave to conceal myself even more. Once past the first couple of wet inches, the ground was quite easy to move.

I got my wrist in front of my face and had a look at Baby-G. It was just after 2 a.m., which meant I had about three hours until first light. Whenever there's a lull in the battle, you should eat or sleep, because you never know when you'll next have a chance for either. I decided to get my head down; the light would wake me up, and so would any movement. After all, I could hear them flush the toilet from here; if I was any closer I'd be able to wipe their arses for them.

I lay on my front and closed my eyes, but it wasn't working. The only stone I hadn't moved seemed to be against my hip. I shifted it, only for another one to rise to the surface and replace it. I got reasonably snug inside the Gore-Tex, which was acting as a kind of sleeping bag, but the ground at this time of the morning feels like ice and you find yourself thinking, What the fuck am I doing here? And even if the weather isn't bad you still get cold. Total inactivity means your body isn't generating warmth, and you become a lizard who needs sunlight. You brood about the fact that, as well as the cold, it's bound to rain soon, otherwise it wouldn't be an OP. Sometimes the wait pays off and you forget about all the discomfort, but I had lain in hides for days on end, wet and freezing, only to find fuck-all.

I started to laugh to myself, thinking about an operator called Lucas. We were tasked to OP a meeting point on the Polish border with Germany. It was a farm complex, where weapons-grade plutonium was being traded for heroin by Russians. The plan was to fuck up the meet and get hold of the plutonium. Lucas was a keen diver, and the scheme he came up with was to get into dry bag (military slang for a waterproof diving suit) and bury himself in the mountain of horse manure by the house. He lived there for four days. The meet never took place and it took a week to get the smell off him – mainly because, instead of telling him to lift off straight away, we left him simmering in the heap for a bonus forty-eight hours.

When I woke up it must have been just before 5 a.m., as I could just see first light coming up. As soon as I could see outside properly, it was time for me to move out and check. Not that anyone finding anything was going to say, 'Oh look, there's an OP,' but if it's an attractive item, someone could come over to pick it up, then they're right on top of you and the chance of compromise is big time. I slowly pushed the bung out with my feet and, lifting myself on my elbows and toes, eased out backwards.

I could see a couple of footprints left from my clean-up in the dark, so I pushed myself out a little bit more and used the bung to brush them away. Whilst I was doing that I looked at the bush itself. It was looking all right; I was quite proud of my handiwork.

I started to inch myself very slowly in again, feet first this time, carefully pulling the bung into the entry point. I then rolled some of the cam net around the base of the bung and tucked it in as if I was tucking a child in for the night. Then I got into the centre of the little grave I'd dug, curled up and turned myself around, being careful not to create movement in the bush. I didn't know what the targets were doing; they could be up there, standing at the window, taking in the view of dawn over the lake, only to see a bush mysteriously shaking . . .

The next priority was to check the camera, since the only reason I was in this hole at all was to see if Sarah was here, and then confirm it to London photographically. Lynn and Elizabeth took nothing at face value, and they certainly weren't going to trust me.

It was now just light enough to see through the view finder. I made a small hole in the cam net facing the target. It didn't have to be the same size as the lens; as long as light was getting into the centre of the lens it could be as small as a pencil prick. I positioned the lens at the hole – this was now the aperture – and focused it exactly on the area around the garage and the side door. It looked the natural way in and out. If there was

157

movement, I wouldn't have to fuck about positioning the camera, all I'd have to do was press the cable release. Not only would it cut down on movement, which would mean less noise, but I could look at whoever was moving and ID them, instead of trying to focus a lens.

Once done, I put sand and stones around the tripod to keep it stable. A final check that the cam net wasn't obstructing the lens, then I made sure that the cable release was on correctly.

It was time to have something to eat and drink before the fun started. I opened one of the mineral-water bottles and took a few gulps even though I wasn't really thirsty. I wasn't particularly hungry, either, but I munched my way through a slab of luncheon meat, all the time keeping my eyes on the target.

Once I'd finished with the clingfilm from the Spam, I wrapped it in a ball and covered it with soil. The last thing I wanted was a swarm of insects hovering over my OP like a big pointing hand. After eating and drinking, there were other bodily functions that might need attending to, but hopefully the Imodium was going to do its stuff.

I was lying on my stomach with the camera just above my head and to the left, staring at the target with the cable release in one hand. My hands were crossed in front of me and my chin was on my forearms, and that was it: there was nothing else to do except look and listen. I'd always found it mind-numbingly boring, but I knew that sod's law dictated that any exposure of Sarah would last for no more than five seconds, and it would be a pisser to miss it. I had to be switched on and fight the boredom. I looked at my watch. It was just after five thirty.

I started to think about her again. If she was here, what was she up to? I didn't really understand what was going on, but then again, at a time like this I didn't want to know. Just as I had that thought, another took over and said I was lying. I was dying to know.

I could see the house quite clearly now. It was white weather-boarded and could have done with a lick of paint. Each of the three floors had two or three windows on this side; no shutters, just two window frames which opened from the middle.

I also saw security lights with motion detectors which I had to assume would be covering all approaches. If they were powered and had covered my location, last night would have been a very bright one indeed. Building my OP would have been piss easy.

On the first floor some French windows led out onto a small verandah overhanging the garage and facing the lake. Below it, the garage doors were still ajar, with another light and motion detector covering the entrance.

The boat, a dirty-cream four-seater with the driver's seat in the middle, looked as if it hadn't been moved since I'd bino'd it yesterday. The engine was still facing the doors and the nose of the trailer was still down on the floor at the water's edge.

The garage walls were made from white trellis work fixed against the stilts, with hardboard backing. Facing me and set into the wall was the side door which seemed to go into the garage. A rotary washing line stood to its left, but there was no washing on it, which wasn't particularly strange, given the weather. There was no condensation on the windows from people asleep inside.

There weren't even any visible rubbish bins I could take a look at later tonight to see if she was here. A person's eyes may be the windows to their soul, but their dustbins are the windows to a fuck of a lot else. It never ceased to amaze me that even the most switched-on people seem to think that once stuff they have discarded is out of their house, it's safe. Reporters find vast amounts of information by sifting through people's bins. In some South-East Asian countries, all the rubbish from hotels with international guests is routinely picked through by the intelligence services. Sarah wouldn't be that careless, but I knew, for example, that she didn't eat any processed food unless she had to: if there were organic food wrappers in the refuse, it might be a significant indicator.

The birds were well into their morning chorus. There was a slight wind, causing a bit of rustling in the trees, but that was only welcome if you were hiding in an OP because it hid noise. The main problem was that, where there was wind, rain would surely follow. In the meantime, as long as the rain kept off it would be almost idyllic.

An hour or so later I heard the first man-made noise of the day, the gentle chug of a small outboard. The big-game fishermen were on the lake, chasing the early fish. I couldn't see anything, but I could just hear it behind me somewhere near the entrance to the creek.

In the background the *putt-putt* got louder then stopped, and I heard the splash of an anchor. The fishermen were close by. I could even hear mumbles now and again on the breeze.

A curtain twitched on the first floor. I guessed they were checking out the fishermen, but if you were up and about and you could hear it, why not just throw them back and have a proper look? This was significant; maybe no trip back to DC after all. My finger tensed on the cable release in case a door opened.

There were shouts from across the lake. Maybe someone had had a bite. But still no-one moved the curtains to see what it was all about.

At about eight o'clock the front door opened and two men came out.

I had just four or five seconds in which to act. I couldn't wait for perfect poses because they mustn't be allowed time to get acclimatized to the outside environment. In the first few seconds after leaving the house they'd still be tuned in to whatever was going on indoors, maybe the sound of a washing machine or the television, mixed with their own walking and talking. Once they'd been outside for anything more than four or five seconds they would be listening to the noise of the trees rustling and the movement of water on the lake. Before that happened, I had to act, then keep very still again, so the only things that were moving would be my eyes. I squeezed the cable release, taking about five or six pictures. Thanks to the digital camera, I didn't have to worry about the noise of the rewind and shutter.

That done, I had time to study the two men with my own eyes. It was obvious they hadn't been awake that long. One of them had a pair of leather boots on, laces undone and a rumpled blue sweatshirt which hung out over creased, faded blue denim jeans. It looked as if they were the clothes he'd been sleeping in. His jet-black hair was sticking up, and he had a few days' growth on his face. He was in his thirties and didn't look too much of a threat: he was only about five feet five inches, and very slim. As Josh would have said, he was too slight to fight, too thin to win. The most striking thing about him was that his features were distinctly Middle Eastern.

The other guy had the same skin tone, but was just over six feet and broader in the shoulders. He was wearing trainers, a *Men In Black* T-shirt under a dark-green fleece jacket and a pair of black tracksuit bottoms. He, too, seemed the worse for wear, with a cigarette in his mouth which flopped down the left-hand side of his face. He had a string of prayer beads, which looked very much like a Catholic rosary, looped over the middle and index fingers of his right hand. He was flicking them so that they closed around his fingers, then flicking them again to unwind them.

They stood by the door looking out at the lake, and there was mumbling between them as the taller one put his right hand down the front of his tracksuit and started to scratch. The inflection and cadence of the mumbling sounded Arabic to me. They sauntered outside, closing the door and walking past the washing line towards me.

I froze, allowing myself just short, shallow breaths. Their footsteps sounded like Godzilla's.

They gazed out at the lake as they walked, probably watching the fishermen. They weren't aware, but I had to accept that I could be in the shit. I was sure the fuckers would see me; I looked to my right, where the bow was lying no more than four inches away from my hand. No movement; calm down and wait.

My body was tensed, ready to react. But how would I get myself out of this? Fight – that was the only answer. I could hardly just smile and claim to be lost. If I was quick enough, and didn't get entangled in the cam net, I could threaten them with the bow. No, that wouldn't work. I would just make a run for it and hope they weren't carrying. I mentally checked that all the important stuff was in my pockets.

They stopped. They exchanged a few more words, then Men In Black took a last drag on his cigarette, dropped it on the ground near his feet and stubbed it out with the toe of his trainer. He obviously hadn't read the signs asking him to leave only footprints.

They turned right about ten metres short of my position, moving uphill towards the track. They were taking the easy route as the ground right next to the house was steeper. Too Thin To Win led the way.

They walked up onto the track, and I realized that they were checking the ground. They were looking to see if there was any sign left by anyone during the night. They moved off the track and downhill, but stopped short of the house and didn't move any closer to it. I wondered why, and then I realized: there must be proximity alarms. As well as the motion detectors, which would trigger the lights, there must be sensors that informed them of movement outside. Judging by the route the two of them took, I worked out that the proximity alarms were probably covering an area about twelve to fifteen metres out from the house.

MIB lit up again as they went back onto the track, then disappeared behind the house, still playing with his beads. I used the time to check the cam, the bung behind me and that my pockets were done up.

After four minutes I watched them emerge from the opposite side of the house, the lake side, and walk towards the boat on the trailer. They clambered aboard and started up the engine, revving it until I could see the blue two-stroke smoke pumping out of the exhaust. Then, just as suddenly, they killed it, and jumped out with lots of talking as they disappeared through the gap between the garage doors. I heard the wagon start up. It wasn't going anywhere because the boat was in the way. It meant these boys were good: they were checking everything, including their getaways, in the event of a drama.

The vehicle engine cut and there was silence. They didn't re-emerge.

I now knew there were at least two in the house, and I also knew that there must be access to the house from the garage.

That was it for another couple of hours. I just lay there,

watching, resting one eye at a time. Now and again I could hear a *putt-putt* on the lake, and a couple of times the sound of a toilet flushing. Occasionally there was the far-off screaming of kids, possibly in a boat or playing in the water, but otherwise nothing unusual.

At ten fifteen I watched as Mom, Dad and kids from the other house started to push another boat towards the lake; that was probably them out of it for the day. Well, until it rained anyway.

After that, nothing at all happened. It was pizza and Mars bar time.

At about eleven thirty I started to get movement from the garage doors. Still nibbling at the last bit of my third Mars bar, I moved my thumb over the cable release.

MIB came out. I watched him and slowly swirled the camera to the right, wishing I had a wider lens. He walked to the front of the trailer and stopped near the hook-up point. He seemed to be waiting; sure enough the wagon sparked up.

Sarah walked out. Gotcha! She was wearing blue jeans and a blue sweatshirt with the Quiksilver logo on the back. I knew her gait, I even recognized her walking boots. She stopped to look at the sky. Yes, it was going to rain. I hit the cable release and hoped I'd got her. If so, the job was just about over. It felt so strange, seeing her after so long, and in this way. She still looked just like the picture in her apartment, but without the smile. It gave me a strange sense of power over her by being hidden, watching.

As the boat was in the way, the garage doors couldn't open fully. She and MIB twisted the boat so that it was parallel to the water, then they opened the garage doors fully and out came a black Ford Explorer. One up. It was Too Thin To Win, and going by what I could see of his top half, he'd smartened himself up – probably had a shit, shower and shave.

The engine revved as he came screaming towards me, then uphill towards the track. I craned my head in an attempt to catch the registration. I couldn't get any detail, but it definitely had a North Carolina plate with the 'First In Flight' slogan and a picture of the Wright Brothers' aircraft on a white background.

163

My eyes jumped back to Sarah. She was helping to turn the boat round so that it faced the water again, ready to go. This was an escape route, for sure. Once they had done that, they went inside and the garage doors were closed fully behind them.

Very weird shit. It seemed that London were right to worry about her after all.

11

I slowly got out the 3C and slid open one of the ports, inserted a flash card from my jeans pocket and turned it on.

A flash card stores information in much the same way as a floppy disk does for a PC. What came up on the screen from this one was a selection of about 200 words or phrases, each with a five-figure sequence of numbers beside it. The letters of the alphabet were also encoded, so that uncommon words could be spelled out. To compose my message, all I had to do was scroll through to the word or phrase I wanted and write down the corresponding five-figure group on my notepad with a pencil. I preferred pencils to pens because you can write with them in the rain. I always used one that was sharpened at both ends, so that if one lead broke I could still use the other.

The first parts of the message I was going to send were standard and didn't need the codes. My PIN was 2442, but since the numbers had to be in groups of five for the code to work, I made it 02442. I followed this with the time/date groups: 02604 (26th April). I had a look at Baby-G and wrote down 01156 (1156 hrs; times are always local). It was then just a matter of scrolling through the codes to make up the message.

The first I looked for was 'tgt loc. 6 fig grid'. I gave the map sheet details, plus the six-figure grid reference of the target. Just to make it clear, I told them that it was the easternmost building of the two.

My message continued: 'ECHO ONE (Sarah) LOCATED WITH TWO BRAVOS (males) MIDDLE EASTERN. ARE AWARE. NO WEAPONS. MAC DOWN. WAITING FURTHER INSTRUCTIONS.'

I ended the message with my PIN again – 02442 – and that was it. It worked out that I had twenty-one groups of numbers.

I put the second flash card into Port B, took out A and put it back in my jeans pocket. I could run the Psion with both cards in, but I didn't like doing it; if there was a drama and I was caught, it meant the whole system would be accessible all at once. At least with them separated I had the chance to hide or destroy a key part of it.

The second card held a series of numbers, also in groups of five, called the 'one-time pad'. Devised by the German diplomatic service during the 1920s, the OTP is a simple encoding method consisting of a random key used only once. There are a few variations on the OTP theme. The Brits first started using it in 1943. Still widely used by the intelligence services of all countries, it is the only code system that is unbreakable, both in theory and in practice.

I started by writing down in my notebook the first group from the OTP under the first group of the message, my PIN. I carried on until all twenty-one groups had another set of numbers from the one-time pad under them. What I had to do then was subtract 14735, the first group of the OTP, from 02442, my identification code, and came up with 98717 – not because my maths was shit, but because in spyland sums, you don't carry the ten over, you lose it. Bloody typical.

At the London end, they knew the message would start with my PIN, and groups are always used in the order they are laid out in. It would be easy for them to add the groups on their corresponding OTP from the groups that I'd transmitted, and they'd come up with the original set of numbers again, because they would also do spyland sums. Referring these back to the code book, they'd produce my intended word or phrase. Once used, those groups would never be issued again.

I did my spy-type sums one more time to confirm my arithmetic, and was ready to send. I turned on the phone, tapped in the PIN code and waited for a signal. I tapped out 'Kay's' on the Psion to retrieve Elizabeth's number; I hadn't got round to learning it after all. After two rings a recorded message from a synthesized but happy-sounding female voice said, 'Please leave your message after the tone.' Two seconds later, there was a beep.

I tapped out the message of twenty-one groups on the number pad, then pressed Hash and listened for the auto-acknowledgement. 'Thank you for your' – there was a pause, then a different electronic voice – 'twenty-one group' – then the original voice 'message.' It cut off and so did I.

I put the flash cards back in their separate jeans pockets. I wrapped the piece of paper up in a sheet of clingfilm and tucked it under a branch in the mud. I didn't want to get rid of it yet, because I didn't know if I was going to need it. If London came back and told me they couldn't work out my message, it might be because I'd fucked up the encoding or spy sums. The system can be time-consuming, but used properly it works.

The next part of the job was to 'Mac down' the pictures. I plugged the lead into the phone, clipped it into the receiver end of the camera and clicked on its internal modem. I dialled the same London number and got the same recorded message. I pressed Send on the camera; the telephone was taking the information from the digital camera and bouncing it off a satellite up there somewhere. Pictures would come up on an Apple Mac screen at the other end and hard copies would be made. Within minutes Elizabeth and Lynn would have my nice holiday snaps of Sarah and her two playmates on their desks.

After transmission, I switched off the phone to save the battery. It was pointless leaving it on; they weren't going to get back to me straight away. If they did, the phone's message service would intercept the call anyway, so no problems. I was in no rush; even if they said, 'End-ex,' I couldn't come out of here until nightfall.

Events had moved on since my briefing. I tried to imagine what would be going on in London. Elizabeth would probably be at home, as it was the weekend. A car would be sent to her country seat to bring her to the operations room in Northolt, North London. The opening scene of James Bond's *Tomorrow*

Never Dies, with large screens and computer projections on VDUs, wasn't that far from the truth. The people receiving my int wouldn't have a clue what it was about, or who it was from. Elizabeth would lock herself away with Lynn somewhere and look at it, probably complaining that it had taken me so long, and then drink some more tea. From what I could remember, it seemed very fashionable to drink a herbal blend at the moment. But not her, she'd be throwing Earl Grey down her neck. Meanwhile, I waited out in this hole.

Elizabeth, not Lynn, would make the decision on what I was to do next. I wished again that I knew who she was; I hated it when people had so much power over me, and I didn't know who had given it to them or why.

I had my fingers crossed that they wouldn't want a technical device put in to find out who these people were and what they were up to, because that would entail me doing a CTR (close target reconnaissance) to help whoever was being sent to do the job. That would mean getting into the house and working out the best way to bring the technical device in, as well as describing the make-up of the general area, the size of the house, how many storeys, the kind of doors, the kind of locks. A locks recce is a task in itself; it means going right up to the door or window to study them in detail. Sometimes you put a little bit of talcum powder on the lock, then press Plasticine into the key-way, pull it out and put it in a secure container so you can take imprints later. Then, of course, you have to remember to remove all the dust from the lock.

A CTR has to answer every conceivable question that might be asked by a third party who's been tasked with making entry. Are the windows locked? What is the area of clear glass? Of frosted glass? What are the main access routes to and from the target? Is the target overlooked by any buildings? Are there any garages or outbuildings or carparking spaces? How many doors are secured, how many are loose? Do they make a noise when they open? They would need to know to take in some oil, to stop any creaking.

Are there any good approach routes? Any major obstacles? Is

there lighting? What are the weather conditions like? What are the routes to the target? What's the general condition of those routes? What would you need to get to the target? What type of ground – ploughed, pasture, boggy? What sort of natural obstacles are there? What is the time and distance from the DOP (drop off point)? Where is the DOP? Are there any animals about? Dogs, horses, geese? And that was assuming I could get onto the target at all, past the proximity lights.

The list of questions can seem endless, especially when you're two hours into a CTR, first light is approaching and you only seem to be a third of the way down the list. Where are the best places to put OPs in? In this particular case, that was easy: I was in it. Where would be the best place to put long-range technical devices in for a video soak? That would be somewhere over the other side of the lake. Could we have a helicopter trigger? Could we have a helicopter that just flies around maybe three or four Ks out?

Once I'd gathered all that information on the exterior, I would have to CTR inside the house. For that I'd need to take in an infra-red camera, or buy commercially available infra-red filters to fit my camera, so that I could take pictures without disturbing the people in residence. They'd want to know the full estate agent's monty. What are the dimensions and layouts of every room? Where is the electrical supply? If you're putting listening or picture devices in, batteries only last so long, so you might have to tap into the mains. Where is the best place to put a listening device? And that might entail looking at the direction of the floor-boards, because if you're trying to hide an antenna, you'd put it in the gaps between them; but that also means taking a compass bearing of the floorboards, so the scaleys (communications personnel) can work out their antenna theory.

Stuff like this takes days and days to organize, and it would be my job to stay and wait with eyes on target while everything was prepared. If my stores ran out I would have to be resupplied via a dead letterbox and outside help – and even that would be a pain in the arse to sort out.

As far as I was concerned, my job was now finished. I'd found

Sarah and confirmed it with photography. I didn't want to be a part of anything that happened next.

I cut away from it by thinking about a job I'd done in the jungle once. We'd got to our report line, it was pouring down with rain and we were gagging for a hot brew, which we couldn't sort out because we were on hard routine. We transmitted our sit rep, something to the effect of, 'We are at the river head, what now?'

We were told, 'Wait out.'

About four hours later they came back to us and said, 'OP any track.'

What the fuck did they mean, OP any track? What good would that do us? We asked, 'What track?'

They came back, 'OP any track that runs west to east.'

They had to be mad. We sent back: 'We can't find one running west to east. However, we've found one running east to west and we're going to OP that one.'

All we got back was, 'East-west is good, out.' Either they were taking the piss, or the world's most useless officer was manning the desk that night. We never found out which. You never do.

Nothing was happening. Even the fishermen had gone back to their tents for lunch.

I'd just decided it was pizza time, and was about to reach for one of my wraps when I heard movement on the ground, and soon afterwards, rapid, heavy breathing.

The distinctive, metallic tinkle of a name tag on a collar became louder as the dog got nearer. I hadn't seen anything around the target that identified it as having a dog, so it probably wasn't from the house. But the name tag meant the animal was domestic, and that meant there would probably be people with it.

I began to hear aggressive sniffing; seconds later, a wet, dirty nose was nudging the hide. Maybe he was a fan of WalMart's Four Seasons.

I moved my hand slowly to my pocket, easing out the Tazer and the pepper spray. I didn't know if the pepper would work on dogs; they can be immune to some of this shit. One thing I knew for sure: he wouldn't enjoy the Tazer. But then again, the yelping would alert everybody – and what if the shock killed him stone dead? I would have to drag him in with me and have a smelly, wet and very dead dog as my new best mate.

The sniffing seemed just inches from my ear. This dog was excited; it knew it could be din-dins time.

A young woman called, 'Bob! Where are you? Here, Bob!' I recognized the voice.

Bob carried on sniffing around the OP. Straight away I thought, I'm a British journalist working for a tabloid newspaper. I'm doing a story on the famous people hiding in the house, and I want to get pictures of their illicit affair. I'll jump straight in with questions before they can ask any. Do you know anything about them? Do you live round here? You could make a lot of money if you tell us what you know about them . . .

The brain has two orbs. One side processes numbers and analyses information, the other is the creative bit, where we visualize things – and if you visualize situations, you can usually work out in advance how to deal with them. The more you visualize, the better you will deal with them. It might sound like something from a tree huggers' workshop, but it does the business.

My eyes were glued to the target, but my ears were with the dog. It's nearly always this sort of third-party shit that compromises you, and dogs can be the worst of all. They can detect your every breath and movement from as much as a mile away under favourable conditions – which it seemed I had given him. Dogs have very poor eyesight, only half as good as man's, but their hearing is twice as good. The wind was blowing from the lake towards the dog. He might have heard me, but I was sure it was an odour that was attracting him. It's not just food smells that provide a target; so does body odour, or clothing, especially if it's wet. Soap, deodorant, leather, tobacco, polish, petrol and many others are all a giveaway – you name it. Who knows what it was in this case.

The more Bob sniffed, the more I came to the conclusion that he was after the pizza. No matter how much I'd wrapped it up, his nose wasn't fooled. Cannabis smugglers wrap eucalyptus leaves around their stuff to put off sniffer dogs, but it doesn't work: the

171

mutts can smell both at the same time and know they're going to get a nice chocolate drop as a reward.

I heard a man's voice no more than twenty metres behind me, but I hoped he was in one of the dips. 'Bob! Where are you? Come . . .'

I recognized his voice as well. I'd tripped over these guys last night, and now they were going to return the favour.

The girl said, 'Where is he, Jimmy?'

Jimmy was angry. 'I told you we should keep the dog on a fucking leash, man, or back in the car.'

She sounded as if she'd started to cry a little. 'My parents will kill me.'

He started to creep. 'It's OK, Bob will be OK. I'm sorry.'

I hoped they were more interested in making up than they were in following Bob into my bush. But I was ready, I'd just stick with my tabloid story; they'd be able to see the camera. Besides, if I was a reporter I wouldn't have told him last night. I'd just have to keep the bow hidden.

They obviously had no idea that I was there yet, but Bob did, the nosey little fucker. The girl was still fretting. 'I gotta go back. My parents will freak if I'm late with the car *and* I've lost Bob.'

He wasn't impressed. 'OK, OK, I told you I'd get you home on time.' He sounded pissed off; he could see all hope of a midday knee-trembler in the woods evaporating.

I heard giggling; he was giving it one last try. 'Jimbo, not here! I gotta get home. Bob, come on, boy, let's go!'

Bob was having none of it. He was sniffing big time at the OP. Next thing I knew, the dog's face was straight in front of me, demanding his share of the pizza. I gently scooped up a handful of earth and flicked it at his eyes. Bob now thought the pizza man was putting up a fight. He backed off, but not as much as I'd hoped, and started barking. I had fucked up but I'd had no choice. As soon as he barked, they knew where he was.

The girl must have come over the brow. Her voice was much clearer. 'Bob! Oh, look, Jimmy, he's found something. What have you found, Bob?'

I got myself ready.

'What have you found, boy?'

The moment she saw me, I would launch into my reporter's spiel.

'What's going on, Bob?'

Bob's arse was in the air, his shoulders more or less on the ground with his front legs splayed, and he was jumping back and then coming forward and barking. I kept my eyes on target and now my ears on her as she started to walk directly towards the hide.

I heard the guy shout from somewhere behind me, very pissed off: 'Come on, let's go. Bob . . . come!'

I saw the first-floor curtains twitch.

Bob was still leaping around with excitement, and on top of that I heard a vehicle. The tyres rumbled along on the dirt track.

As Bob's nose once again came up to the cam net I decided to give him the good news with the pepper spray. He jumped back, whelped and ran to Mommy.

I heard the girl: 'Bob, see, serves you right! Stop messing around!' She probably thought he'd got his nose bitten by something.

I listened as they shuffled through the sand. Jimmy was still behind somewhere, complaining. Next time they slipped into the woods he'd lock Bob in the car again to steam up the windows, like last night.

I got my head back on the ground, watching and listening, just waiting for shit to happen.

The Explorer had come back. Two up. I looked up just before it turned left off the track and downhill towards the garage.

It came down the hill and headed away from me, towards the garage. Too Thin To Win was still in the driver's seat. I couldn't make out his new playmate in the passenger seat.

The wagon stopped just short of the garage and the side door of the house opened. Sarah again. She was looking at the woods behind me, keeping a wary eye out for Bob and his friends. I watched her and tried to keep contact with her eyes. I would know if she suspected anything. I watched her scan the tree line, uphill and then back down again, towards me. As her eyes approached my OP I moved mine out of contact. I couldn't look at her. A sixth sense can sometimes let you know when you're

173

being looked at, and I didn't want to take the chance.

I knew I was doing the wrong thing. Even if her plan was not to react to anything she saw, but to go back into the house, then return with an automatic weapon to hose down the area, I knew her well enough to see it in her eyes. I could feel sweat running around the back of my legs and neck. I waited three or four seconds more, then moved my eyes up again.

She was finishing off her scan, past me and down to the lake. Once there, she quickly turned her head to the wagon and walked up to the passenger door.

A white guy clambered out. By his style of dress I would say he was American. He was wearing a black nylon bomber jacket, tight blue jeans and white trainers. He was above-average height and build, about mid-thirties with black, fairly long, curly hair, and a moustache like the sheriff's in the Bugs Bunny cartoons. He looked good enough to be the hunky lumberjack in any soap.

The meeting with Sarah was intimate: they hugged, kissed each other on the mouth, then held the embrace. They spoke in low voices as Sarah ran her hand across his back. There was something odd going on, though. They looked pleased to see each other, but the talking wasn't loud and they weren't going overboard.

I got two pictures of them during the thirty or so seconds that they were together.

Too Thin To Win had the tailgate down on the Explorer. He was looking quite smart in jeans and a dark check jacket. He pulled out a brown suit carrier with an airline tag on the handle.

Sarah had disappeared inside the garage with the white guy, followed by Too Thin To Win, who closed the door behind them. It was time to send another sit rep.

12

I had just started to prepare my message when Too Thin To Win emerged from the side door with MIB. He, too, had had a shit, shower and shave, and was dressed a lot smarter in brown trousers and jacket. They both got into the Explorer, Too Thin To Win in the driver's seat. The wagon backed round to point uphill. They weren't talking to each other, smiling, or looking at all happy. Something was happening.

The 4x4 bumped along the track and disappeared from sight. I looked back at the house. All the windows and doors were closed, and so were the curtains. That was strange; if someone was arriving at such a nice spot, surely you would show him the view? Maybe she had better things to do with him. Maybe he was just another sucker that she was using. But for what exactly?

It was nearly two hours before the Explorer returned. There were bodies in the back, but I couldn't work out how many as it turned downhill, my eyes flicking between the wagon and the side door of the house, waiting for it to open. When it did, it was the American who appeared. Sarah was nowhere to be seen. He was looking aware, checking the lake and, as MIB had done, playing with worry beads. I watched him, listening to the slow rumble of tyres past my OP. His denim shirt tails were hanging out of his jeans and showing below his bomber jacket. I was right, he and Sarah did have better things to do than look at the scenery.

The wagon stopped and I counted an additional two heads in the rear seats. All four got out and I pressed the cable release.

The two newcomers were both dark-skinned. They hugged and kissed the American on both cheeks. It looked as if they knew him pretty well. All the same, there were no loud shouts of welcome or smiles, and everyone spoke in a murmur I couldn't understand. The meeting also seemed to have an air of relief about it.

Too Thin To Win and MIB had opened the tailgate and were pulling out two square aluminium boxes which were plastered with what looked like old and torn 'Fragile' stickers and airline security tape. They started to move the boxes inside the garage via the side door. The luggage area of the 4x4 was still full of sports bags, another suit carrier and a black plastic cylinder which stretched from the back seat to the gear selector at the front. It was about two metres long and covered at each end. Either it was the world's biggest poster tube or they had some serious fishing rods with them – I didn't think. One of the new guys motioned to the other one and the American to give him a hand.

I snapped some more. This guy looked much older than the others. He was short and bald, with a very neat, black moustache, and he was a bit overweight, mostly around the stomach. He looked like he should be in a film as the gangster boss, the Bossman. The other newcomer was more nondescript, of medium build and height, and looked about twenty years old. He could have done with a few plates of what the bald guy had been eating.

After a couple of trips, with the boys lifting what seemed to be heavy kit, the 4x4 was empty and everything was stowed inside the garage. The side door closed and the area once more looked as if nothing had happened all day. What was going on here?

Ever since we'd first met, it had seemed to me that Sarah was sympathetic to the Arabs. She'd been involved with them in one way or another for most of her life. Come to think of it, we'd even had a row once about Yasser Arafat. I said that I thought he'd done a good job; she thought he was selling out to the West. 'It's all about homeland, both spiritual and cultural, Nick,' she'd say every time the subject arose, and nobody who'd been within sight of a Palestinian refugee camp could argue, but I wondered whether there was more to it than that.

A faint drizzle was starting. It hadn't penetrated my hide yet but could clearly be seen falling on the open ground in front of me. I could hear outboard motors in the distance as the intrepid fishermen set out in pursuit of a six-ounce carp. Lunchtime must be over.

There's more to surveillance than just the mechanics. A report that says, 'Four men get out of vehicle, two men pick up bags and go inside,' is all very well, but it's the interpretation of those events that matters. Were they looking aware? Did they seem to know each other well? Were they, perhaps, master and servant? These people were meeting up, in hiding, and with kit. I had seen this before with ASUs (active service units). The boxes looked as if they'd seen a lot of air time during their life, but not on this trip. There were no airline tags on the handles or on the bags. Maybe they'd driven to an RV point and then transferred the kit. If so, why? Whatever was happening here, it wasn't about the turtles.

Things were starting to spark up and Lynn and Elizabeth needed to know that there were now four Arabs, one American and Sarah. Maybe London could make sense of what was happening; after all, they would know far more than they had told me. With any luck, Elizabeth would now be at Northolt, poring over my previous message and images, with her tea so strong you could stand the spoon in it.

It was 15:48, time to switch on the phone. It had been a couple of hours since my last transmission, and they should be calling me back with an acknowledgement and maybe even a reply.

I took it out of my pocket and switched it on, placing it in the shell scrape so I could see when I had a signal while I got out the codes from my jeans, and encoded my sit rep. As I retrieved the 3C, I started to feel like I needed a shit. So much for the Imodium: it should have bunged me up, but maybe the combination of pizza, Mars bars and Spam weren't the most binding of materials. I knew from bitter experience that fighting the urge never works;

177

if you've got the time, however inconvenient that might be, you never wait until the last minute: if you do, sure as anything, a drama will occur at the target the moment you get your trousers down.

I got the roll of clingfilm from the bergen and pulled off the best part of a metre. Leaning over to my left, still trying to keep my eyes on the target, I undid the buttons of both sets of trousers with my right hand, and pulled them down, along with my pants. I then got the clingfilm in my left hand and tucked it under, ready to receive. I started to want to piss; I wasn't going to rummage for the petrol can at this stage of the proceedings, so I just had to restrain myself while I got the main event out of the way. I wrapped the first handful in the clingfilm and put it to one side, pulled off another length, put it underneath, and carried on. Having to do this in the field is never an easy procedure, especially when you're lying on your side and in fits and starts, because it's got to be controlled. It's unpleasant, but there's no way round it.

The drizzle was now trying hard to become something more grown-up. I could hear the first raindrops hitting the leaves above me. I was about halfway through the second lot of clingfilm when the LED on the phone told me I had a message waiting.

At the same moment, I heard a voice – male and American. I switched off the phone and thrust it and the 3C in my pockets. I looked out of the hide at the movement of the trees, trying to gauge the direction of the wind. It was still coming in from the lake. The American was on his own, coming out of the garage doors and heading towards the boat.

Trying desperately to control my sphincter and bladder, I watched as he moved the boat out of the way of the garage doors. I guessed he was going to park up the Explorer. He climbed into the driver's seat and revved the engine. All the curtains in the house were still closed and there was no other sign of movement.

There are quite a few times on tasks when you really have no alternative but to shit yourself, especially on urban OPs where you're in a loft space and there are people downstairs. You try not to do it, because you might have to go out into the street straight afterwards and operate like a civilian, but sometimes, if there's no room to move, it's just got to be done. The only precautions you can take are to not eat before the op, drink as little as you can, and pop some Imodium – then hope for the best. It's a bit like the KitKat commercial, with the photographer outside the panda house at the zoo: you could have been lying in an OP for four weeks, but the moment you get the clingfilm out, the panda emerges and does a quick impersonation of Fred Astaire.

I'd guessed correctly. By now the 4x4 was in the garage, the boat was back in position and he'd gone back into the house. I finished off the job with the clingfilm and petrol container and pulled up my trouser bottoms. I was feeling quite sorry for myself; the only consolation I could think of was that clingfilm probably did the job better than the shiny stuff in the carpark toilets would have done.

I tore off another big length of it, wrapped up all my offerings and popped them straight into the bergen. It would help to hide the smell, which in turn meant it wouldn't attract flies and animals. I then tucked the fuel canister back into the bergen as well, doing my bit for eco-tourism.

I'd learned my lesson. I dug around in the daysack for the Imodium and took another six capsules, probably enough to constipate an elephant. I lay down again with my hands resting under my chin, looking at the target, but after a couple of sniffs I decided to rub them with soil and keep them away from my face for a while.

On target, nothing else had changed. The curtains were still closed. In the hide, it was now wet and miserable. The rain was starting to fall more heavily; the noise of it hitting the trees increased and it was dripping from the foliage, through the cam net, and running down my face and neck. I brushed away a small twig which had stuck to my cheek. Sod's law of OPs was at it again; I knew it would only be a matter of time before it percolated down onto me in a steady stream.

I got out the phone again. Sheltering it under my chest, I

179

switched on the power, tapped in my PIN and dialled Kay's sweetshop then *2442. They would be transmitting one-time pad number groups to me, exactly as I'd done to them, except that the groups would have been recorded on a continuous tape, which would keep running until I acknowledged that I had received it.

I cradled the phone to my ear and listened as I switched the Psion to word-processing mode. As the woman's voice recited groups of five-digit numbers, I tapped them into the keyboard. It was easier than writing them down.

'Group six: 14732. Group seven: 97641. Group . . .'

I knew it had got to the end of the message when she said, 'Last group: 69821. End of message. Press the star key if you require the message repeated.' I did. I then had to wait a few moments for the message to repeat itself so I could receive the first five groups. Up it came again: 'You have a' – pause, different voice – 'sixteen' – back to normal voice – 'group message. Group one: 61476. Group two . . .'

When the taped message had come full circle, I switched off the phone, put it away and transferred the groups onto paper. I'd never been up to doing the maths on the Psion, and by the time I'd got the hang of it I would have been up for retirement.

The rain was coming down in earnest. Keeping my eyes on the house, I pulled the hood up around my neck to cut out what was pouring through the cam net. I couldn't cover my head, however, because that would degrade my hearing.

Armed with the number groups, I was now going to do the reverse of what I'd done earlier: look for the recognition group on the one-time pad, then subtract each group from the ones that I had on my OTP.

Once I'd done that, I put the flash card back in my jeans pocket and got out the one that held the codes. They came up on the screen and I worked out the message. The first lot of groups were the introduction – date, time groups, all that sort of stuff. Then I got to the meat of the message:

61476 EXTRACT
97641 TARGET

02345 BY ANY MEANS
98562 CUT OFF TIME
47624 DTG (date time group, times local)
82624 27 APRIL
47382 0500HRS (times local)
42399 FOR
42682 T104
15662 ACKNOWLEDGE
88765 02442

'Extract target' was easy enough to understand: they wanted me to remove Sarah from the house by 5 a.m. tomorrow morning. Fair enough.

It was the next bit I couldn't believe: 'T104.'

'T' plus a numeral is a code within a code, for brevity. There are quite a few T commands, and they have to be learned parrot fashion, as nothing about them is ever written down by anyone, anywhere. They don't officially exist, and the reason is simple. T is a command to kill.

They wanted me to kill Sarah.

Not only that, but 104 meant without trace: the body must never be discovered.

Elizabeth must have been more pissed off at being summoned to Northolt on a Sunday than I'd thought. Either that, or they'd told me even less about the operation than I suspected they had.

The wind gusted and the heavens opened, as if to confirm my feeling about the T104.

13

I redialled.

The recorded voice said, 'You have no new messages.' There was a pause, then she started to give out the introduction for the groups already sent. I checked them against the ones I'd written down, and went through all the codes again.

As I protected the 3C from the rain I knew there was no mistake. I took a deep breath and let it go slowly, wiping away some water which had splashed down my cheek.

I'd been a young infantryman when I'd killed my first man, an IRA terrorist. I'd felt good about it. I thought that was how you were supposed to feel. After all, it was what the Army did for a living. Later, I got more satisfaction from stopping death than causing it. However, if the task was to kill, it didn't particularly worry me. I didn't celebrate the fact, but neither did I complain. I understood that they had sons and daughters, mothers and fathers, but they were players like everybody else, including me. And at its most basic level, if somebody had to die, I'd rather it was them than me. My only concern was to try to make it as quick as possible – not so much for their benefit, but to make it safer for me.

This T104 was different. This was the second time I'd had to kill someone I'd been close to. Considering there was only Josh left who resembled anything like a friend, I couldn't help wondering what the fuck was going on in my life. Euan had been my best mate for as long as I could remember, but he'd used me – worse than that, he'd used Kelly. Now the only woman I'd ever felt really involved with had got herself into a world of shit that I had to wipe clean. I was starting to feel sorry for myself, and realized it. I had to cut out of this; I needed to get real.

I deleted from the flash card the groups that had been used for the two messages, and ate the small piece of paper I had used. No-one would ever be using that combination again – that was why it was called a one-time pad – and no evidence of any T104 would ever be seen, since all details are destroyed once used. I put the two flash cards back into separate pockets in my jeans and turned off the 3C, getting it out of the rain.

Everything that Elizabeth and Lynn had said was making sense to me here on the ground. They knew the big picture, I was sure of it; maybe the imagery I'd Mac'd down to them had confirmed their fears. Was there a connection with what she'd got up to in Syria? I didn't even bother to think that much about it. I didn't really give a fuck. Even if, say, this group was planning to hit Netanyahu, Arafat, Clinton or even the whole job lot – so what? I remembered the footage after Rabin had been assassinated, and sure, I saw his niece, or whoever it was, speaking at his funeral. I understood that it must be sad, but I wasn't personally affected. To me, it was just one more dead person amongst the thousands on both sides in Israel who'd been bombed and shot over the years. I didn't get worked up about political murders, even when they were closer to home, which usually meant Northern Ireland. Fuck 'em, we all have to die some time. Live by the sword, and all that. They were all as bad as each other.

For all I knew, there could be massive ramifications to what-ever Sarah was involved in. This crew could be plotting the murder of thousands of people. Maybe the USA's fear of chemical or biological weapons being used in their backyard was becom-ing a reality here and now, in a holiday home in North Carolina. It would be quite easy to contaminate, say, the entire water supply of DC. Even if it was partial contamination, the right sort of disease would quickly spread itself around. Making one person history can often mean saving many others; it was simplistic, but I always saw such Ts in terms of putting a round into Hitler's skull in 1939.

I knew I was trying to keep emotions out by looking at it logically.

Maybe the Americans had now been told what was going on, and would be hitting the target as soon as they got sorted? In which case, it stood to reason that Elizabeth wouldn't want Sarah to be found on target. So extract her, drop her, make sure she's never found. Who knows?

I forced myself to cut away from conjecture; it had no bearing on the order I'd received, and I'd probably come to the wrong conclusion anyway. Either way, I just didn't want the job.

I was watching the house through the misty rain in a sort of daydream. I gripped myself again. Fuck it! If I carried on thinking like this, I'd end up howling at the moon and dancing round the maypole – or whatever tree-huggers do. Maybe I'd been reading too many books about kids and their emotions; maybe all the touchy-feely crap was getting to me. I decided to bin it; get the tree-hugging cassette out of my head and put the work one back in. Sarah might have lots of plans, but as far as I was concerned long life wasn't going to be one of them.

The rain was bucketing down. I pulled on the hood string, trying to stop the water running down my neck. I was getting very cold. I forced myself to focus on a mission analysis, and to look at the factors that could affect it; only then could I carry out the task and have a chance of getting away with it. If I wanted to kill the president of the United States, nobody could stop me, but getting away with it would be the hard bit.

The first thing I had to do was understand my mission. What was required of me? It broke down into just two parts: first, I had to get her out of the target area by 0500 hours tomorrow morning; the second part, the T104, wasn't important at the moment. Besides, I already knew how I was going to do it.

I broke down the first part of the job into five phases: one, approach the house; two, make entry; three, locate Sarah; four, lift and exfil from the house; five, exfil the area.

Next I had to look at what might stop me carrying out those five phases. The first obstacle was obviously the men with her. There were far too many of them for comfort, and for all I knew there could be even more inside who hadn't poked their heads out yet. What were their intentions? Fuck knows. It was a safe bet, though, that they weren't there for the canoeing. It looked as if the place was an RV point. At some stage, therefore, they were going to leave, and maybe that was the reason she had to be lifted before five o'clock in the morning, because they wouldn't all be staying together in one place for long.

The next question: What were their tactics, training, leadership and morale? I could only guess. Certainly their leadership would be good; either Sarah would be in charge herself, or if she wasn't, then whoever was would have to cut the mustard, or she wouldn't be working with them. As for their morale, that looked just fine. They seemed confident about what they were doing, whatever that was. Ninety per cent of people's confidence can come from total stupidity and no understanding of what's going on, and only 10 per cent because they are well trained and well prepared. Sarah would only be in a group where confidence was backed up with ability.

What were their capabilities? And did they have weapons? I had no idea. All I knew about was Sarah as a person and an operator, so I knew that she was professional, ruthless, focused and capable of killing. If I got into the house and she saw me first, she'd kill me if she had to. She would fight rather than be taken. Strangely enough, that meant that I wasn't so worried about her, because she was quantifiable; but the other guys – I didn't know if they would fight, and what with. I had to assume the worst; it always pays to assume that the other players are better than you are, and plan accordingly.

I didn't have a lot of information to go on, but what was new about that? It wouldn't be the first time that I'd had to go into a situation blind. It just pissed me off that I'd positively ID'd her. Maybe it would have been better if I hadn't. Maybe. I found myself half hoping that everyone in the house would clear off in the next few hours. Then there would be nothing I could do but start on the trail again.

I began to run through everything I'd seen so far, trying to think of something I'd forgotten. The subconscious is wonderful, because it never forgets what it has seen or heard. Every sight, sound and fragment of perception is tucked away in there somewhere – all you've got to do is drag it out. Maybe, for example, I'd seen a weapon without actually realizing it? Nothing came to me.

Now I had to look at the ground where I was going to carry out the mission. First of all the general terrain, and that was of no concern because I was sitting on it. I could almost spit at the target; it wasn't as if I was heading into an area I'd never seen before.

The one factor that did worry me was the 'vital ground', which in this case was the fifteen metres this side of the house that I reckoned to be within range of the proximity sensors and lights. How was I going to approach the target, let alone penetrate it?

I scanned all the doors and windows for any information that would help me make entry. I had seen through the binoculars that the lock on the garage side door was just an ordinary pin tumbler inside a large knob handle, much like those on motel doors – very common, and not difficult to defeat. The far bigger problem would be whether I could get near the lock in the first place without the detectors going apeshit.

I had a clear picture of what my mission was. I knew all that I could about the enemy at this stage, and I knew all that I could know about the target – or as much as I could for the time being. Now what I needed to work out was 'time and space' – how much time I had to do what I had to do. As I lay looking at the target, pushing my hair from my forehead as it was starting to act as a channel for the rain, I thought about the five phases and tried to work out plans for each one.

I looked at the approach. I visualized all the different routes, as if I was sitting in comfort, looking at a monitor connected to a live-feed camera with someone who was moving along each possible approach in turn.

I next considered different ways of making entry. I visualized working on the locks, and what to do if I couldn't get in that way.

Not that it would necessarily work, but at least I'd have an alternative. Deniable operations are not a science. People might have an image gleaned from spy movies of precision and perfection, and assume it all runs like clockwork. In reality it doesn't, for the simple reason that we're all human beings, and human beings are liable to fuck up – I knew I did about 40 per cent of the time. James Bond? More like James Bone. Add to that the fact that the people we are working against are also fallible, and it isn't a formula for guaranteed success. The only true measure of human intelligence is the speed and versatility with which people can adapt to new situations. Certainly once you are on the ground, you have to be as flexible as a rubber band, and what helps you be flexible is planning and preparation. With luck, when the inevitable fuck-up did occur, I wouldn't be a rabbit frozen in the headlights. As Napoleon, or somebody like that, said, 'If your opponent has only two possible options, you can be sure that he will take the third.'

Eventually I came up with a workable plan – well, I thought I had. I'd soon find out. I checked my watch – just gone 5.32 p.m. That gave me just over eleven hours to get into the house and get her away. But that was merely the physical timing; the factors that mattered even more were light and dark. I couldn't move in daylight; all my movements had to be under cover of darkness.

London wanted her lifted by 5 a.m. I knew that first light was at about five thirty, but it would take a little longer to arrive in the forest. I needed to get hold of her and be away from here by 3 a.m.; that would give me about two hours of darkness to get clear of the area. Last light was at just after seven o'clock, but I wouldn't get full cover of darkness until about an hour later. On the face of it, that effectively gave me seven hours of working time. But I couldn't go in there while they were still awake, so what would I do if they were still up and about at two o'clock in the morning?

By now, I'd dehumanized the people I was up against. To me they were targets, the same as the house. From now on I wouldn't refer to them, or even think of them, as people. I couldn't, otherwise I wouldn't be able to do the job. Ironically, Sarah had once asked me about that. I told her I didn't like to analyze myself too much because I wasn't sure I'd like what I found. I knew I'd done some really terrible things, but I didn't think I was too bad a person. The question that always bugged me more was, Why was I doing this shit in the first place? My whole life had been spent sitting in wet holes. Even when I was in the Army I would ask myself the same thing: Why? I couldn't answer fully then, and I couldn't now. Queen and country? Nah. I didn't know anyone who'd even considered that. Pride? I was proud, not necessarily of what I did, but certainly of the way I did it. Being a soldier, and later a K, was the only thing I was good at. Even as a kid I was just odd socks and scabs, my mother was always telling me I'd never amount to anything. Maybe she was right, but I liked to think that, in my own little world, I was among the best. It made me feel good about myself, and I got paid for it. The only downside was that I'd have a little bit of explaining to do when I was standing at the Pearly Gates. But who doesn't?

The wind had died down, and the rain wasn't falling quite so hard. Lights came on in the house, which was natural enough; it was nearly seven o'clock, it would be dark inside. The lights were showing on the first floor, the same as last night. I strained to listen, but couldn't hear anything, not even a radio or TV. What I wouldn't have given to know what was going on in there. I hoped they were packing their bags and fucking off.

You can always improve on a plan, so I kept on visualizing. What if I got to the door just as they were coming out with their bags? What would I do? Where would I go? Would I just barge in there and kill her, or would I try and get her out? Arnie and Bruce go in and take on a dozen bad guys at a time, but it doesn't work like that for the rest of us: against a dozen people, you die. A job like this was going to call for speed, aggression and surprise. I'd have to get in there, and get out quickly, but all with minimum risk to me. It wasn't going to be a good day out at all.

Eyes and ears glued to the house, I went through the whole lot again. And again, wondering if there was anything I'd missed. For sure there would be, but that was what I got paid for: to improvise.

Nothing else mattered now but the task. To achieve the aim is to have a chance of staying alive. This was not the time to think about skipping through meadows or getting in touch with my feminine side. Sarah was now a target. To think any other way could put me in danger, and that wasn't the way I wanted it. Kelly and I still had a Bloody Tower to visit.

14

The lights on the first floor went off. It was just before eleven thirty, and another forty gallons of rain had fallen on the OP since I'd last looked at Baby-G thirty minutes before. I packed the camera.

I pushed the bung with my foot and eased myself out of the hide backwards on my arms and knees, dragging the bergen and bow with me. The rain hadn't stopped, but at least the wind that brought it had died. I stayed on my knees and retrieved the two flash cards from my jeans, and with the plier part of my Leatherman I cracked and bent them into unusable shapes. I put them in two separate pockets of the bergen, along with the 3C.

I slowly got to my feet and stretched, stiff as an old man, a wet old man at that, and then listened carefully. Nothing from the house, just the noise of the rain hitting Gore-Tex and leaf. Unfortunately, the next part of the plan entailed me taking my jacket off.

Shivering as the cold air got at my skin, I spread the jacket on the ground, then pulled off my Gore-Tex trousers and put them to one side. Finally, everything else I was wearing came off, apart from my skiddies, and was quickly placed on top of the jacket.

There was one last thing I remembered to do before carrying on. I retrieved my shirt and, with the knife of the Leatherman, cut off both sleeves at the shoulder. I tucked them into a pocket of my jeans, then started to wrap up the bundle of clothes in the jacket, shivering big time after being cocooned in so many layers.

Next I cut four or five lengths of string and used a couple of them to secure the bottoms of the trouser legs by twisting. I shoved the jacket and bundle of clothes down one of the trouser legs, then tied up the waist. Finally I twisted and folded over the trousers and tied the complete bundle. Once done, it went into my bergen.

I wasn't concerned about any of the kit that I'd left in the OP as none of it was traceable to me, apart from my clingfilmed shit. If the extraction of Sarah did turn into a gang-fuck and the hide was discovered by the police or whoever, then by the time anyone got a DNA analysis done I should be well out of the country. Besides, unless I got caught and the UK denied me, the Firm would ensure that any DNA records or follow-up became history.

My passport, phone and credit cards had been in my jacket, clingfilmed, since the beginning. I made the decision to take them with me instead of going into the house sterile. If I got caught now, chances were I'd be dead anyway. And besides, Sarah knew who I was. It wouldn't exactly take a Mastermind contestant to work out what I was there for.

The bow was wedged into the frame of the bergen with the six arrows inserted in the quiver. I took the fifth length of string and tied one end to the bergen, attaching myself to the other by looping it round my wrist a couple of times. At the first hint of trouble, I could let go and part company with it.

Once done, I checked that the bergen straps were done up as tightly as possible, then looked at the house yet again. Still no lights.

I replaced the bung and smoothed away any sign. Maybe archaeologists in the next millennium would unearth my little time capsule and scratch their heads at the cache of Four Seasons pizza, a gas can full of piss and a couple of handfuls of shit in clingfilm.

I moved down to the water's edge, watched, listened, then slowly waded in. The bottom sloped gently to start with, but by the time I'd done four or five paces I was in up to my knees, and

191

freezing. It was just a matter of fighting it and persuading myself that I'd be warm again soon.

I lowered the bergen into the water in front of me, and it floated with the bow just above the water. Even when fully laden, there's always enough air trapped in a bergen to make it buoyant. It had been years since I'd done anything like this. In the jungle, it always used to rain heavily. It would often take us an entire day to cross a main river, and the Regiment had lost more people doing this sort of thing during training than by any other drill.

I kept wading further in, until the water came up to my waist, then my neck. The rain was jumping off the lake's surface and hitting my face; being so close, the splashes sounded louder than they really were. The shock of the cold took my breath away, but I knew I'd get used to it in a minute or two.

I took one of the mangled flash cards from a bergen pocket, dropped it in the lake and checked it sank. Then, pushing the bergen in front of me and keeping parallel to the shore line, I walked towards the house, taking my time so I didn't create a visible bow wave or make any noise. At night, and at that distance, even if they were looking at the lake, the bergen would pass as a floating log. In any event, it was the only way I could get on target without triggering the alarms.

After a dozen or so steps I stopped, checked the house again, and dumped the remaining flash card as the rain pelted the taut nylon of the bergen.

I kept moving slowly towards the target, at the same time wanting to get there as quickly as possible. My balls were so cold I thought they might make a dash for my armpits. Underfoot it was rocky and a couple of times I hit an obstruction and got entangled in weed.

It was time to discard the 3C. I wouldn't be needing it any more, because if everything worked to plan, the next time I contacted Elizabeth I'd be back in the UK – and if it didn't and I was in the shit, Sarah would know how to extract information from it and the flash cards.

I got level with the house and turned to face it. The curtains were closed and there were still no lights on. Placing my wrist behind the bergen to shield it from the target, I pressed the back-lit display on Baby-G. It was just after midnight. I started to shiver even more now that I'd stopped. I needed to get out of the water and back into some clothes.

I moved forward in a direct line towards the slipway, pushing the bergen in front of me. The boat was now dead ahead, and all I could see of it was the bow tilted down towards me.

I inched my way, eyes glued on the target; the only sound was the rain as it hit my bergen and the water. As I got closer and the floor started to rise, I forced my body lower by bending my knees and hunching down. A few metres from the end of the slipway I had to get right down on my stomach to keep as much of me in the water as possible to make a smaller profile. I had to use my hands and knees to work myself forward.

A metre from the edge the bergen hit bottom. I stopped, looked and listened. The echoey sound of the rain hitting the fibreglass of the boat took over from the splash of it hitting the water.

Now came the wriggly bit. I had to cross open ground to get to the boat and shelter under the hull. Ideally I would have taken maybe as long as an hour to cover the five metres, but I didn't have that time to spare.

I unravelled the string attached to my wrist and, lifting myself up on my elbows and toes, I kitten-crawled forward, four inches at a time, trying to hold and control my breath and stop my teeth from chattering. I could feel stones and water moss pushing against my legs and stomach, moving with me as my trunk touched the bottom. The fact that it was cold no longer mattered; I knew I was doing it correctly from the pain in my elbows as they took my weight on the gravel. I was more interested in trying to make sure my trunk didn't scrape along the ground and make a noise. I was now at the slipway.

Lifting the bergen a fraction, I edged it forward another few inches, lowered it onto the concrete and eased myself up behind it. Then I stopped, listened and repeated the move. Inch by inch I neared the boat, in a direct line with the point where the tow bar touched the concrete slip. As long as I moved slowly enough and kept flat, the motion detector shouldn't pick me up, and once I was in the lee of the boat I'd be completely safe. Fifteen minutes later, I was there, where I wanted to be, under the boat. The rain hammered the fibreglass. It was like being in a greenhouse in a thunderstorm.

The garage doors were still only semi-closed. I could see the back of the Explorer and the pitch-dark beyond.

I was staring into the darkness and contemplating my next move when a light came on to my right, spilling through the gap in the doors. It came from the rear of the garage. My heart skipped a beat, then started to pump at warp speed. If I'd been discovered, there wasn't much I could do.

I gripped myself: Stop, calm down, watch.

Almost immediately another light came on, this time on the other side of the garage. Through the gap, I could see what was happening. Someone had opened the lid of a chest freezer; the glow from the interior light showed the face of a man, as if he was shining a torch under his chin, like we used to at Hallowe'en. I wasn't sure which of the targets it belonged to, just that it wasn't Sarah. He rooted around for a moment, then pulled out three or four small boxes of food, stood up and seemed about to close the lid again, but instead, he looked back inside and picked out some more stuff. With his arms full, he walked away. I could make out the lower part of his body, he was wearing trainers and check, knee-length shorts.

I tried to count how many cartons he had. There seemed to be five. Did that mean that five people were still awake and about to have a meal, or was it just a big snack for one very hungry man?

I heard a door close, and the light went out.

I waited a few minutes for everything, including me, to calm down, then crawled the length of the boat until I reached the stern. I looked up. As I'd hoped, I was well hidden from the sensor and directly under the first-floor landing. The sensor might not even be linked to an alarm, it might just have been a helpful detector to switch on lights as people neared the garage. Whatever, I was this side of it and that was what mattered.

The garage doors were less than a foot away from me. I moved to the right of them, still under the landing and out of the way of the sensor and the rain. The priority was to get some clothes on and get warm, but if you're moving, you're making noise. The more slowly and deliberately I did it, the less noise I was going to generate. At least the downpour gave me some cover.

Gently unclipping the bergen, I lifted the flap, got hold of the toggle which held the drawstrings together, pressed the button in and opened it up, all the time looking and listening, and checking to see if anything was happening in the house next door.

I lifted the Gore-Tex bundle from inside the bergen. It was soaking wet on the outside, but my knots had worked. Wet clothes would make noise and leave sign, so I took off my underpants and slowly put on my dry stuff. It had been worth getting so cold just to feel the sensation of dry socks.

I checked that the Tazer was still in the right-hand pocket of the jacket, and that everything else was where it should be. Then I dug out the gardening gloves and put them on. I might get lifted when I tried to get out of the country, and I didn't want the police to be able to make a connection with something as stupid and basic as fingerprints at a crime scene. I couldn't guard against every shred of forensic evidence, but I could do my best to minimize the damage. Last of all, I ruffled my hair with my fingers, trying to get off as much water as possible so that a stray drop didn't blur my vision at a vital moment. I was ready to go.

I picked up the bergen and weapon, and edged my way round to the doors. I had a quick look at the gap in case they'd rigged a trip.

It was totally dark inside.

15

The space between the rear of the Explorer and the garage door was going to be a bit of a tight squeeze. I pushed the bergen and bow through and placed them on the floor to the right, then got myself side on, breathed out and squirmed through.

The sound of the rain was immediately muffled, as if a switch had been thrown. I became aware of a different ambient noise, coming from above me. I stopped by the 4x4, opened my mouth, looked up and listened; there was a vague mumbling, which at first I took to be talking, then I heard a shout, gunfire and a burst of music. They were watching TV.

I stayed where I was, just past the tailgate of the Explorer, and continued to tune in. The mumbling went on, then there was a metallic rattling within the garage as the freezer motor kicked in, followed by a low buzz. A floorboard creaked above me, over to the right. Maybe someone getting up from their chair. The noise didn't move anywhere; he must have sat down again.

Baby-G told me it was one thirty-one. This wasn't good; I had just one and a half hours left in which to do what I needed to. I got the mini-Maglite out of my jacket, held it in my left hand and twisted the head to turn it on. The beam shone through my fingers. I could now see that the Explorer was the only vehicle in the garage; it was only jutting out because there wasn't enough room to drive it all the way in.

I stepped over the bergen and checked along the wagon. All its windows were closed and there wasn't a key in the ignition. I slowly tried the driver's door; it was locked. No chance of using the vehicle for a quick exit. In a drama, the boat would have to get me to my car.

As well as a washing machine and the freezer, the garage was packed with gardening tools, canoes standing on end, bikes on racks, and rusty old bits and pieces that had accumulated over the years, and it had a smell to match. At least it was dry and quite warm.

Moving further along the side of the 4x4, I shone the torch over its bonnet. In the far-left corner I saw the side door I'd been watching from the OP. At right angles to it was another door; the staircase behind it was boxed in, and the shape of it went up to the next floor. There were more piles of clutter underneath.

I could still hear the vague mumble of the TV above me and the creaking of floorboards as people upstairs shifted in their chairs. That was fine by me; the only thing I didn't want to hear was excited shouts or rapid movement to signal they knew I was there.

I picked up the bergen with both hands to control the noise, and with the torch in my mouth I made my way over to the staircase doors. The beam shone on plastic bags under the staircase, containing the world's largest collection of empty Kraft ready-made dinner containers. They weren't putting the rubbish out; they were hiding it. They were taking no chances. Nor was I; I took the bow from the bergen and laid it down so that as I picked it up with my left hand the cable would be facing me, and the arrows were ready to access.

There wasn't any light shining through the gaps round the staircase door. I put my ear to the wood and listened. The voices on the TV were louder, but still indistinct. There was more shooting and police sirens, and a fairly constant murmuring, which I could distinguish from the TV; it seemed as if the household was having a long night of telly, munchies and chat.

An inspection of the lock told me it was an ordinary lever type. I gently pushed on the area of the door by the lock, then pulled it

197

forwards, to see if there was any give. There was about half an inch. Then, with my hands down at the bottom of the door and still on the same side as the lock, I pushed hard and slow to see if it had been bolted. It gave way an inch, then moved back into position. I did the same to the top of the door. That also gave way, this time just over half an inch, and I gently eased it back into position. It seemed that there were no bolts on the other side, just the one lever lock to deal with.

Holding my breath, I slowly twisted the handle to check the door was locked. You could spend hours picking the lock only to find the thing was already open; best to take your time and check the obvious. I'd always found that holding my breath gave me more control over slow movements, and it made it easier to hear if there was any reaction to what I was doing. As I'd assumed, the door was locked.

The next move was to check all the likely places where a spare key might be hidden. Why spend time attacking a lock if a key is hidden only feet away? Some people leave theirs dangling on a string on the other side of the letterbox, or on the inside of a cat flap. Others leave it under a dustbin or just behind a little pile of rocks by the door. If a key is going to be left, it will nearly always be somewhere on the normal approach to the door. I checked the shelving above the washing machine, under the old rusting paint tins by the door, and along the top of the door frame and all the obvious places. Nothing. I would have to work on the lock.

I got down on my knees, listening all the time to the TV show, and looked through the keyhole. I could still see nothing but darkness. I shone the torch through and had another look. There was a glint of metal. I smiled; piece of piss. They'd left the key in the lock.

The glow from Baby-G in this darkness was outrageous, but it told me it was now nearly 2 a.m. I'd give it just another thirty minutes, and maybe by then these fuckers would be in bed. Meanwhile, if they came downstairs for more munchies, I'd need to know, so I sat on the floor with my ear to the door listening to the rain and the TV. The police cars were still screaming and the shooting had become more intense. A floorboard creaked above

198

me, then another. I looked up and followed the sound, trying to picture where he was. The movement continued across the floor to more or less directly over my head.

Picking up the bow, I turned and looked through the keyhole to see if he was going to turn the light on and come downstairs. The key obscured most of my vision, but I'd be able to see light, as the teeth were still up in the wards of the lock. There was a faint glimmer, but it was ambient light from quite a distance away, maybe way up at the top of the stairs. No-one was coming down. The light disappeared. There were more creaks above me, then the muffled talking started again. The adverts must be coming on.

There was nothing to do but wait while the minutes ticked away. All I knew was that I had to get in there and do it at two thirty, no matter what. How, I didn't know; I'd just play it by ear. I sat down again and got back to listening to the TV and the rain.

I was quite thirsty after the exertions of the night. The chest freezer started to rattle again; I tiptoed over and lifted the lid very slowly. The light came on. I had a quick look at all the goodies. There were boxes of Kraft dinners, macaroni and microwave chips. It was obvious that nobody had been giving a lot of thought to the culinary side of this trip, which I bet Sarah didn't like, and none of it was any good to me. Then I found something I could munch: a Magnum bar. I closed the freezer, took off the wrapper and put it in my pocket, sat back down by the door, put my ear against it and started eating as I joined in the film.

It was now two twenty. This was cutting it really close to the bone.

I finished the ice cream, and the stick joined the wrapper in my pocket. I looked at my watch yet again. Two twenty-five. I couldn't afford to wait any longer.

With the Maglite in my mouth, I opened the screwdriver part of the Leatherman and worked it into the keyhole. When it had a firm purchase I started to turn the key along its natural line to unlock the door, at the same time pulling the door towards me to release the pressure on the bolt as it lay in the door frame. The key turned until it hit the lock; it would need a lot more pressure now to open it, but that would make noise. I waited. Whoever was pissing off the cops would be doing it again, really soon. Thirty seconds later, it happened: shouting, gunfire and sirens. I gave the key the final necessary twists and switched off the torch.

With the door ajar a couple of inches I could hear the TV much more clearly. Going by the intensity of the shooting, screaming and shouting, the whole State police force was out trying to get the bad guys.

There was no distinct light shining down from above, just a faint glow. I picked up the bow and prepared an arrow. Keeping it in place with my left hand, I got my right hand on the door handle, ready to go. I was going to have a rolling start line: remain covert for as long as possible, and only go noisy if they did. It wasn't much of a plan, but it was enough. If you worry too much about these things, you never get down to starting the job; just get on with it and half the battle is won. Then hope that experience, knowledge and training will get you through the rest.

I checked that nothing was about to fall out of my pockets, then gently pulled the door towards me, ready to stop at the slightest creak, holding my breath so I could hear it happen. There wasn't a sound from the people upstairs. It must be a good show.

I was facing a flight of worn, bare wooden stairs which climbed directly to the first floor. There was a wall on either side; on the left it was the external wall of the house, and on the right it was plasterboard, which sealed the stairs from the garage, then became a bannister on the right-hand side where the first floor began. Anyone standing up there could easily look down and see me.

Beyond the top of the staircase, and facing me, was another wall, and just off to the right-hand side was a door that was closed. Apart from that, all I could see were flickering images, composed of different tones of light from the TV screen as they flashed on the wall and the closed door facing me. I was happy about that; if the TV was facing the top of the stairs, it meant that the fuckers would have their backs to me as I went up.

The smell had changed. The mustiness of the garage had given way to a more domestic odour: spray polish and cigarettes, the smell of good housekeeping, heavily overlain with nicotine. They must be having a Camel-fest up there; I'd have to be quick about this or I'd be going down with lung cancer.

Drawing the cable half back, focusing my eyes and the weapon on the top of the stairs, I placed my left foot very carefully on the bottom step, then my right. I stopped and listened.

I lifted my left foot again and put it down on the second step, easing my weight down gently, hoping there wasn't going to be a creak. I had both eyes open, cable half drawn and ready to fire. My ears had cut away from the sound of the rain; they were totally focused, on the alert for signs of movement upstairs. I pulled the bow cable back a little bit more and took another step.

16

The music and the police chase suddenly stopped. So did I, foot raised, bow at the ready. I must have looked like the statue of Eros. A very macho American voice boomed out, 'Back soon, with HBO's movies for guys who like guy movies.' There was a long burst of machine-gun fire, no doubt as bullet holes sprayed over the titles. Then it went into a commercial for a fitness plan that could change all our lives in just fourteen days.

I couldn't tell how many people were in the room, but the one thing I knew for sure was that Sarah was unlikely to be one of them. She wasn't a guy who liked guy movies.

There was some mumbling coming from the room. I couldn't understand what was being said, but something was agreed on. Floorboards creaked again. I hoped he wasn't coming back down to the freezer; if he was after the last Magnum he wasn't going to be a happy teddy.

The shadow of a moving body hit the wall at the top of the stairs, blocking the dancing reflections from the TV screen. It got bigger and higher. I slowly brought the bow up the last two inches, into the aim. The cams at each end of the bow started to strain as I tensed the cable almost to full draw, stopping about three inches from my face. I wasn't too sure if I needed as much power for the arrow to do its job at this range. But fuck it, I wasn't taking any chances. I could smell the rubber gardening gloves as I waited, motionless.

The shadow became the body's back and I saw it was MIB. He now had the TV flickering on his shirt. He didn't turn and come down towards me. Instead he went straight ahead and through the door to the right of the top of the stairs. Fluorescent lights came on to reveal kitchen cabinets and brightly coloured mugs hanging from hooks.

There was the sound of crockery and cutlery being moved about. The others were talking amongst themselves, maybe about the film, and there was a little laugh as someone made a funny. Still no sound of Sarah, though, which tended to confirm what I'd thought.

A bit more clanging came from the kitchen. I kept the bow in the full draw position. The strain on my arms was starting to take its toll; sweat was pouring down the sides of my face and I knew it wouldn't be long before it got into my eyes.

I heard the *ffsshhht!* of a ring-pull being opened in the TV room, then another. Maybe this meant there were three of them in all. With any luck the cans they were opening held beer: if they'd been soaking up alcohol while watching the film that should slow down their reaction times rather nicely.

Mr Macho Voiceover was with us again: 'We're back with movies for guys who like guy movies.' He was greeted by a *ffsshht!* from the kitchen. MIB emerged, can in hand, muttering away. The others immediately gave him a hard time and he stepped back a few paces and switched off the light, left the door open and went back to join them.

I let the cable relax, brought my arms down and wiped away the sweat.

There was more gunfire. It sounded as if the final big shootout was underway. People were screaming at each other as only actors in cop thrillers do. I'd probably seen it, and was trying to work out what movie it was, so I could guess when the noisy bits were and when they'd finish – anything to help get Sarah out of there without us all getting involved in our own 'movie for guys who like guy movies'. But no luck.

Someone in TV land was being really brave and shouting for covering fire as he took on the bad guys single-handed. Dickhead.

203

I really couldn't delay any longer. I still didn't know where Sarah was in the house, and this stairway was my only entry point. I checked that the spare arrows were still fixed in the quiver, and that everything on me was secure. I didn't want the Maglite clattering to the floor the moment I moved.

Keeping the bow in my left hand, arrow still in place, I took a deep breath and lifted my right foot. To reduce creaks, I used the very edge of the stair, then stopped to listen. The shooting had finished and there were murmurs from the audience again. I carried on.

When my eyes got level with the top stair I lay down with my head against the end of the bannister. The cloud of tobacco smoke was thick enough to make me choke. I checked the bow to make sure it was out of my way, then eased myself up on my toes and the heels of my hands, tilted forward and looked around.

I could see at once that the TV was in the far-right corner of the room, facing me. On the screen, someone was getting a doctor to patch his gunshot wound.

Three men were watching; two on a sofa with their backs to me, one of them swigging back on his can; the other guy, MIB, was in an armchair, and at an angle, so that he half faced the kitchen wall. He still had the beads in his right hand, and was feeding each one individually through his fingers as he watched. The room was like a Turkish bath, except with smoke instead of steam. There was also a strong smell of pizza and beer. On the floor beside the sofa on the right-hand side was a twenty-four-pack of Bud, ripped open.

I checked for access to the next floor. This wasn't going to be easy: the stairs were at the far side of the room, opposite me. I'd have to cross over twenty feet of open floor space.

As I moved my head back into cover, I heard the cardboard of the twenty-four-pack being ripped further open, then the hiss of a ring-pull. They were going to be here a while.

Should I wait it out? No, they could be up all night. Besides, if they moved they would see me. I lay there and thought for a while, and felt the blood pumping in my neck.

If I burst into the room and tried to hold them in position, it wouldn't take them long to work out that I could maybe take on one of them, but the other two would be climbing all over me before I could reload, restring, or whatever it's called.

There was only one thing I could do, and that was to try to cross the room without being seen. If I got pinged, I'd just have to 'deal with the situation as it develops on the ground' – the last thing the Firm always said when giving orders; it meant they could transfer any blame onto you if it went wrong, or take the credit for a success.

I pushed myself away from the stairs with the heel of my hand and slowly stood up. I checked the arrow position for about the hundredth time and moved onto the final step. I edged out, and was in the room.

With my back pressed against the wall, I started to move towards the next flight of stairs, moving one leg in front of the other very, very slowly, my eyes riveted on the three watching the TV, my left hand on the bow, my right on the arrow, holding the cable one quarter drawn.

I got to the kitchen door and could hear the microwave working overtime. I moved on. They had eyes only for Robert De Niro. I silently thanked him for such a spellbinding performance.

The light of the TV was projected onto the faces watching it. MIB was totally absorbed, as were the other two on the sofa, Too Thin To Win and the younger of the two who'd arrived today. I was maybe twenty feet away from them. MIB was squinting as he inhaled on a cigarette held between the index and middle fingers of his right hand, the glow illuminating his face even more as he played with his beads in the other.

As he blew out the smoke, the screen went blank for a second, then a bright graphic appeared, accompanied by machine-gun fire. 'Back soon with movies for guys who . . .'

I had fucked up big time. I hadn't taken into account the commercial break. A pain hit me in the throat and shot down into the pit of my stomach.

Too Thin To Win gobbed something off to the others and moved his head a bit to the right – just a bit too much.

He must have seen me, but these things take a while to sink in when you're not expecting them, and especially when you've been concentrating so intently on something else. But he had detected movement in his peripheral vision and I knew what was coming. It would take him maybe two seconds, no more, to register that something was wrong. Straight away, the body reacts to that: fight or flight. Blood surges into your hands to fight and into your legs to flee, and you can feel it. I had just two seconds up on him. It was all going to be over soon, one way or another.

To me it was all happening in slow motion. As I brought up the bow, Too Thin To Win jerked his head further to the right, did a double take and stared straight at me. By the time his eyes were widening with shock the bow was in the aim and at full draw.

He shouted something, but I didn't know what. Everything closes down in a situation like that. All I could hear was the voice in my own head, and as my knees started to bend automatically to make me a smaller target it was screaming, Fuck! Fuck! Fuck!

Too Thin To Win became a non-target as he threw himself to the left and jumped down below the settee. It was MIB that presented himself as the nearest threat, and at the same time the easiest target. He was up on his feet and had already turned and was facing me, trying to absorb and interpret this new stream of information. I kept my eyes fixed on his and brought the bow round. As soon as I had what I hoped was the correct sight picture, I released the cable and hoped these things were as good as the salesman had said. I was aiming at the centre of the body mass, the centre of what I could see in front of the blinding glare of the TV screen. He took the hit with a dull thwack and went down.

I didn't know where the arrow had got him because I was too busy loading the next one and wishing I'd practised archery as much as I'd practised firing pistols over the years. I stretched out my left arm and, at the same time, pulled back the cable with my right, quickly trying to feed the head of the arrow into place above my left hand. Then it was straight back up into the aim, the arrow being held in position on the cable by my fingers. I still couldn't see Too Thin To Win; I was aiming at the young one, who had now decided to run round the settee and try to get to me before I could release. In fact, he was so near that I didn't so much have time to aim as just vaguely point it at him.

There was a whoosh and a twang as the cable released, then a thud as the arrow punched into him. He didn't make a sound. I didn't care whether or not he was dead; there was still one more to deal with.

As I moved towards the settee I could see that Too Thin To Win had remained on the other side of it; I didn't know what he was doing, and I didn't care. I just had to get to him. There was no time to reload. I pulled an arrow out of the quiver and launched myself at him.

He was leaning over one of the aluminium boxes I'd seen them unload from the wagon. I swapped the arrow from my left hand to right, gripping it firmly, like a fighting knife, making use of that extra blood now pumping through my hands.

As I fell on top of him, my weight pushed him down onto the box. We both grunted with the impact. While trying to cover his mouth with the crook of my left arm, I jammed the arrow into his neck with my right. Only one of these actions worked. I had managed to cover his mouth, but as I thrust with the arrow I felt it hit bone. Arrowheads are designed to zap into the target at warp speed, and I'd done no more than rip his skin. He was screaming big time beneath my arm. I increased the pressure to try and get better coverage over his mouth.

I raised the arrow in the air again and rammed it down hard. It hit against the bone again, but this time slid off and lodged deeper into his neck. I felt him stiffen, his muscle tensing up to resist the penetration. The gardening glove gave a good grip as I pushed harder, twisting the arrow shaft to maximize the damage. I was hoping to cut into his carotid artery or spinal cord, or even find a gap to penetrate his cranium, but instead I ended up severing his windpipe. Now I just had to hold him as he asphyxiated. I put all my weight on him to press him against the edge of the box, trying to stop his body-jerking from getting out of hand and becoming noisy. Once I knew I was in control, I looked quickly around me to make sure that no-one else had arrived on the scene as I waited for him to die.

Finally, he was going down. His hands started to scrabble behind him, towards my face. I bobbed and weaved to avoid them, and his movements gradually subsided to no more than a spasmodic twitching in his legs. The last reserve of strength he'd found as he saw his life slowly get darker was now exhausted. By the flicker of the TV I could see dark blood oozing out of the wound; it followed along the shaft of the arrow to my glove and dripped onto the floor. When I moved my arm away from his mouth he made no sound.

Still on top of him, I turned round, and could see that MIB had taken a poor shot but I'd been lucky: I'd been aiming at the centre of body mass, but the arrow had entered his head above the left eye and there was about four inches of arrow protruding out the back. His beads lay at his feet.

I didn't have a clue about the young one. He was slumped with his chest on the floor. Blood was coming out of him from some-where and being soaked up by the rug.

I started to shake. I'd never been so scared in my life, nor so relieved that something was over. Lesson learned: always get a pistol, whatever it takes.

Young One was still alive; blood was gurgling in his throat as he tried to breathe. I lifted myself off Too Thin To Win, guiding his body as it slumped from the box onto the floorboards. I went over to Young One and checked him. His glazed eyes turned to follow mine as I moved my body around him, feeling him for any hint of metal. He wasn't carrying. His eyes were reflecting the TV screen as they pleaded with me for help.

As I looked away, my eyes caught the aluminium box. When I saw what was inside, I felt much better about what I'd just done. Too Thin To Win must have been flapping big time trying to get to the contents; if he had managed it, I might not be here now.

The TV baddie was dying from a gunshot wound given to him by the cop. It must have been near to the end of the film. I went over to the box. Stowed inside were three collapsible-stock Heckler & Koch 53s, virtually the same weapon as the MP5 used by the Regiment, but firing a larger 5.56mm round. With their thirty-round mags, Too Thin To Win could have taken my head off and still had change.

I picked up one of the weapons and two of the mags. I could now see that on the bottom of the box there were also three silenced pistols, again with mags.

I took one round out of the 53 mag and pushed down on the remainder to check the spring worked. Young One was still moaning as the film credits rolled. He was watching me. I thought for a while. Why take the 53? If I had to use it, I would alert the people in the house next door and maybe even the whole camp site. I picked up one of the pistols. I didn't have a clue what it was, only that, going by the markings, it was made in China. I looked in the mag. The rounds were 9mm. I loaded and made ready with one mag, and took a few rounds out of another and looked inside. These mags held nine rounds a piece. I didn't know why I checked. I never counted them as I fired, I was always too busy flapping.

I replaced the rounds and put the five spare mags in my jeans. This Chinese thing looked quite good. If total silence was required, there was a catch that would keep the working parts in place when you fired. You then had to manually unload and then reload. If not, and you could get away with a suppressed weapon on semi-automatic, all you had to do was take the catch off and the working parts would move and feed another round to fire. The baffling would still do its job in stopping the weapon report; you'd just hear the working parts moving. With my thumb I pulled down on the catch, safety on, then jammed it into my jeans.

I got hold of Young One's arms and pulled him up against the settee, and as I did so I could see where he'd been hit. The arrow had entered his stomach, and as he'd fallen it must have been pushed right up into his ribcage. I got him so that he was sitting on the floor with his head lolling over to the left-hand side, resting on the seat. His eyes were still begging me as I placed a cushion under his head, stepped back, and gave him a round in the head.

There was just a noise like someone tapping the edge of a

wooden table with their finger. The cushion and settee helped to suppress the round completely as it came out of the back of his head. He just lay there, eyes still open, blood shining in the TV light.

I'd never worked out how I felt about things like this. He would have killed me if he'd had the chance, and I'd just put him out of his misery. I took the catch off, unloaded and fed another round into the chamber, letting the catch down to lock the working parts in place.

I stood, watched and listened. There were a couple of plates on the floor covered with dried sauce and stubbed-out cigarettes, two or three full ashtrays, countless crushed cans of Bud and now these three bodies.

HBO told me they were now going to show *Road House* with Patrick Swayze. I wiped the blood from my gloves onto the settee and changed magazines, gently pushing a new, full one into position, listening for the click that told me it was engaged.

As I moved away from the TV set, a loud *ping!* sent my heart leaping into my throat. I spun my head and weapon round, expecting to have to react. The rest of my body followed about half a second later, both eyes open and the weapon up in the aim. I found myself pointing at the microwave oven in the next room.

I needed a minute to calm down and sort my shit out and decided to put the weapon into semi-auto mode. Time to move on. I was still left with two that I knew of, the American and the Bossman, plus Sarah – and there were still another two floors to clear.

I didn't need the bow any more so I left it on the floor. The TV was still bumping its gums: 'Guys who like guy movies . . .'

I started to move slowly but purposefully, trying to keep the noise down, both eyes open, weapon up. I had the light from the TV screen shining behind me, projecting my shadow on the wall. I got to the stairs and checked upwards. It was dark up there. Eyes and weapon glued to the top of the stairs, I started to move.

I knew this feeling all too well. My heart was pumping so hard I could feel it banging against my chest wall, and I had a horrible, dry, rasping feeling in my throat. My head was so far back that sweat was running into my eyes and down the folds of skin at the back of my neck. I flicked my head to the side, attempting to get rid of it.

It started to get darker and quieter as the glow and noise of the TV faded, and soon all I could hear was the sound of my own breath. I did my best to suppress it because I imagined three people upstairs listening and following my progress.

Moving upstairs like this is physically demanding. Every movement has to be so slow and deliberate that all your muscles are tensed; your body needs oxygen, and your lungs, in turn, need to work harder, but you don't want them to because that makes noise, and on top of all that, at any moment, somebody could be trying to kill you.

I reached the landing of the second floor. I immediately noticed a nice polished smell up here, a different world to the one I'd just left behind me.

There was a wall to my left, with a door that faced the corridor which ran to my right. It must be the bathroom where I'd heard a toilet being flushed last night.

As I looked to the right, I could see that the corridor ran the length of the house. Right down the middle was a single strip rug, which would help muffle noise. In the light thrown from a door that was slightly ajar at the far end I could see a table about ten feet away, on the left. The open door showed a sink shining in the light. It didn't sound as if anyone was in there, and I didn't hear water running or a cistern filling up. Maybe they were just scared of the dark and wanted a light on for when they came out for a piss. I looked at the crack under each of the other doors to see if there were any signs of life or light from within the rooms. Nothing.

Across from me were the stairs to the top floor. I stayed where I was and listened. I could just about hear the low drone of the TV downstairs, but the sound of my heartbeat seemed louder. I could feel my carotid pulses banging in my ears. I couldn't just wait here all night until she needed the toilet.

With my knees bent, shoulders hunched over, arms out, staring down the thick baffled barrel of the weapon, I started to move along the centre of the corridor, using the rug. I reached the first door on the right and edged over, putting my ear to it, but kept the pistol where it was.

I could still hear the TV and the rain. My antennae were out, trying to take in every possible sound, but it was very distant, very indistinct. From inside the room came the noise of snoring. Sarah never snored, but there was always a chance she could be sleeping with someone who did.

I carried on along the corridor to the next room. I listened outside it. Nothing. As if I was going to hear her singing along to a CD.

I went on, passing a fire exit on my left, which I hadn't noticed earlier. It had bolts top and bottom, which I gently eased back, and a pin-tumbler lock in the middle, which I also undid.

I moved on to the next two doors past the table, hearing nothing. I stood by the lit-up bathroom. This could go on for ever. Fuck it, there was no time to do anything but take my chances with whoever was back down the corridor. I just knew I had to do something, and quickly.

Holding the pistol in my right hand, I checked with my left that everything was in place. The Tazer was in my right-hand bomber jacket pocket, with the handle outwards, ready to grab.

I got out the torch, placed the lens against the wall, and twisted it on to check it still worked. The light hit the wall but wasn't going anywhere else. I turned it off and kept it in my left hand, with my thumb and forefinger at the ready.

I put my right thumb on the weapon's safety catch and pressed down, checking it was off and ready to go. Then I pushed the mag in the pistol grip to make sure it was engaged.

With my left hand I lifted the latch. I wasn't going to try to do it gently; once you've decided you're going in, you might as well get it over with. I pushed the door open a few inches, and at the same time brought my left hand up and switched the torch on, using my body to open the door fully.

As I came into the room I moved to the right to avoid silhouetting my body in the doorway. I three-quarters closed the door with my shoulder, and the torchlight hit a pile of men's

212

clothes on the floor. I also saw a watch and a glass of water on a bedside table. There was a shape in the bed. I knew straight away by its size that it wasn't Sarah. The body stirred, maybe as a reaction to the change in air pressure as the door opened, or the fact that light was shining in his face.

As he turned I saw that he was bald and dark-skinned and had a moustache. It was Bossman. His eyes opened fully as he settled. He wouldn't be able to see me, just the torchlight.

I moved quickly, getting my left knee on one side of him and my right on the other so I was astride him, pushing him down onto the bed. He was pinioned by the sheet across his chest and gave a quick grunt of protest.

I dropped the torch onto the bed. I didn't want him to see my face and, in any case, I didn't need light for what I was about to do.

With the pistol jammed against his clenched teeth he gave a long drawn-out groan as he tried to resist. I got hold of the back of his head with my left hand and forced the weapon down harder. The metal of the silencer scraped against his teeth and he eventually opened up. I pushed the muzzle in until it was nearly at the back of his throat and the suppressor was filling his mouth good style.

He struggled on for a while, not trying to escape, just wanting to work out what was going on and to breathe. He was flapping and snorting like a horse. I moved with his chest as it went up and down. At length he lay back. No-one will fuck around once they realize they have a pistol in their mouth.

I leaned towards his left ear. In my bad, fluctuating American accent I whispered, 'If you speak English, nod slowly.'

He did. I could feel the pistol moving up and down.

I heard him slurping and retching as his Adam's apple worked overtime. With his jaw wide open he'd lost the ability to swallow.

'You have two choices,' I said. 'Die if you don't help me, live if you do. Do you understand?'

It's always better to take your time at moments like this. If you've got somebody who's flapping and you say, 'OK, where's

213

Sarah?' he can't talk because he's got this thing stuck in his mouth, so he gets all confused about what you expect of him. It's better to do it as a process of elimination, and then you know you have the right information. That is, if he knows it in the first place.

There was still a bit of hesitation here. He was still flapping too much and not thinking enough. I said, 'Do you understand?' and underlined the point with a jab of the pistol. He finally got the message and I felt the pistol move up and down.

His body smelled of shampoo and soap. Shame he hadn't cleaned his teeth. His breath smelled like road kill.

Now that he understood the facts of life, I whispered, 'You've got one woman in the house. Yes?'

I felt his immediate sense of relief. His body relaxed; it wasn't him I wanted. He nodded.

'One woman?'

He nodded again.

'Is she on this floor?'

The pistol shook from side to side.

'Is she on the floor above this one?'

Up and down.

'Do you know which room she's in?'

I could hear his breathing and slurping, but there was just a touch too much hesitation: he was thinking about what to say. He shook his head slowly.

I gave a weary sigh and said, 'Then you're no good to me, and I'm going to kill you. I think you're lying.'

No response.

I said, 'Last chance. Do you know what room she's in?'

I started to rise. He got the idea. He nodded. I came back down to his ear.

'Good. Now think about this. Is she on the left-hand side of the corridor as you go along it from the stairs?' I was assuming it was the same sort of configuration upstairs as down. I didn't know yet, but it was a good enough place to start.

He thought about it and nodded.

'Good. Is it the first door on the left?'

214

He shook his head. Saliva was oozing out of his mouth and running down his chin. I could feel his chest rising and falling more and more quickly; he was fighting to get oxygen in and there were too many obstructions.

'Is she in the second door on the left?'

He nodded.

'Good. If you're lying, I'll be back and I'll kill you.'

He nodded that he understood, semi-choking on the suppressor because I pushed it a little more to the back of his throat, just to the point where he was starting to gag. At the same time, I reached down with my left hand, closed it around the Tazer, slid off the safety catch and gave him the good news right on the pectoral muscle. I counted the crackle for about five seconds. If I remembered correctly, that should result in the person being 'dazed for some minutes afterwards'. He jerked about, and then got very dazed indeed.

I climbed off him, picked up the torch and put it in my mouth, then turned round and started to look for his socks amongst the clothes that were on the floor. I found one and shoved the toe end of it into his mouth, pulling down on his jaw to force him to take it all. Noise comes from the throat and below, not the mouth; for an effective gag, you have to ram obstructions down there as far as they can go, so that when the person tries to scream the sound can't amplify in the mouth. A strip of gaffer tape over the face isn't enough to achieve the desired effect. A sock stuffed in the mouth also calms people down, because they become more worried about choking than about raising the alarm.

I could hear moans and groans from the back of his throat as he began to come round. I couldn't have him alerting the others, so I gave him another three-second burst. That settled him down again, and gave me time to finish filling his mouth. Once that was done, I got his shirt from the floor and wrapped the sleeve around his face to form a seal over the sock. I kept his nose free because he had to be able to breathe, but wrapped the sleeve as tightly as I could around his lips.

I pulled a leather belt from his trousers which was about an inch and half wide, with a brass buckle, and grabbed the tie-backs from the curtains, lengths of rope with shiny tassels. I tied his knees together with the first tie-back; if you can move your knees, you can crawl and manoeuvre, if not, you haven't got much scope for movement.

Next I tied his ankles together. He was semi-conscious, breathing and moaning in the back of his throat. I turned him over on the bed and got his hands behind him, tying them tightly together with the belt, making sure that I'd left the buckle and some of the other end free. It was going to hurt him, and he was going to have hands like balloons by the morning, but he'd live.

By now my breathing was almost as laboured as his. This was physical stuff, spinning him round, trying to do it quickly, but also trying to keep everything quiet to cut down on noise. I got hold of his shoulders and pulled him down gently, so that his head and his shoulders were on the floor, then I grabbed his legs and dropped them down, too.

There was still a little bit of moaning, especially when I got hold of his ankles and brought them up towards his tied hands. I put the ends of the belt around the tie-back that secured his wrists, did up the buckle, and that was him trussed up like an oven-ready chicken.

He was coming round again. I held the Tazer on his thigh and gave him the good news for another five seconds. He tried to scream, but the sock did its stuff. As I lifted the Tazer away from him I still had the button depressed; the bolt of electricity crackled brightly as it arced between the two terminals. The glow that it cast added to the torchlight, and I could see the suit carrier, now open, hanging on the wardrobe. Inside was a grey business suit, white shirt and patterned tie, already knotted and hanging round the hanger.

I got to the door, checked the corridor and turned left towards the stairs. This flight was different, the stairs turning back on themselves to reach the top floor. As I climbed and turned left, up the next flight, the distant TV mush disappeared, its place gradually taken by the constant bass-drum rhythm of rain bouncing off the roof. It was almost soothing.

I got to the top and lay down on the stairs. I looked left along the corridor, but this time there was no light to help me and I couldn't see any coming from under the doors.

I twisted the Maglite and headed directly to the second door on the left. There was no rug up here. I moved slowly. Between the first and second door, against the wall, there was a semicircular table with a lamp on it.

I got to the door. It was exactly the same as the one downstairs, with the latch on the right. I crossed over and got against the right-hand wall. I just had to get in there, be hard and aggressive, grab her and get out before my new mate downstairs started trying to become Houdini.

I listened for a few seconds, just in case she was in there expecting me and loading up her 53. Then, with the Maglite in my mouth, I put my hand on the latch and pressed.

There was a small bundle in the bed, and I knew at once that it was Sarah. I could smell the familiar fragrance of her deodorant. It was the only one that didn't leave white powder marks on her clothes.

I started moving towards her. Her jeans were on the floor, crumpled, as if they'd just been pulled down and stepped out of. There was a bedside cabinet with some water and headache pills by the lamp.

I was going to have to grip her so hard that she thought there were twenty people piling in on her. I had to confuse her, scare her, faze her, because I knew that, if I didn't, she was more than capable of killing me.

17

I moved towards her, Tazer in my left hand, pistol in my right, torch in my mouth, adjusting my head to keep the beam pointing into her face. The sound of the rain hitting the window was louder than my footsteps.

She started to turn, and her eyes reacted to the light as I moved the final pace, dropped the pistol on the bed, then smacked my open hand over her mouth. She gave a muffled scream and fought against me and her mouthful of bloodstained glove. The torch got knocked sideways, scraping against my teeth, as she thrashed about. I heard the pistol fall off the bed and onto the floor. I hit the Tazer's 'on' button and her eyes widened as she saw the current crackling between the metal prongs, inches from her nose. Then she hit her own 'on' button and began struggling so violently I thought she was having a fit.

She got the good news in her armpit. The 100,000 volts shot through her body and fucked her up big time. With her body jolting up and down, I was finding it hard to keep my hand on her mouth to dampen the scream. The bed springs sounded as if she was having sex. Five seconds later she was a rag doll, just a little groan as she fell back onto the bed. It wouldn't last for long.

I needed the pistol. I got the torch out of my mouth and retrieved it from under the bed, shoving it into the waistband of my jeans. Next, as weak coughing told me she was starting to regain her senses, I got out the two sleeves I'd cut from my shirt. She coughed again and I looked at her. The bedclothes had been kicked off during the struggle, and she lay spread out on the mattress like a starfish, in just a white T-shirt and white knickers. Outside, the wind had come back. I could hear it thrashing the rain against the windows even more now.

With the torch back in my mouth I was soon dribbling and breathing like the Bossman downstairs. I prised open her jaw and started ramming the first sleeve into her mouth. She was just conscious enough to realize what was happening, and tried her best to resist. I had to give her another two or three seconds with the Tazer, getting my hands out of her mouth just in time as it snapped shut in the first of another series of convulsions.

When she relaxed, I stuffed in the material until it must have gone halfway down her throat. I then got the second sleeve, placed it over her mouth like a conventional gag and tied the ends tightly at the back of her neck with a double knot. There was going to be no noise from her now.

I pulled the belt from her jeans and used it to tie her hands together, front loading her. She was now ready to go and so was I – nearly. All that was left was to gather up as much of her ID as I could find. A T104 meant leaving no trace, which wasn't going to be easy. I didn't know where all her stuff was. I hoped it wouldn't be too much of a drama if anything was left behind; with any luck she'd be using cover docs that she'd got by chatting up some gay woman in an Australian bar.

I found her bag on the floor near the bottom of the bed. It was a small black nylon affair with a shoulder strap; inside was a nylon sports-type purse, passport and a few loose dollar bills. I quickly scanned the rest of the room with my torch. A green sports bag lay open on the floor, and clothes were strewn all around it. A glint of metal caught my eye. I shone the torch beyond the bag and saw the barrel of an HK53. Its black Parkerization had been worn off over the years. I also saw four mags, taped together to form two sets of ammo.

She started moaning and retching, trying to expel the material from her mouth. She still didn't know who was doing this to her;

it was too dark, and even if she could see straight at the moment, all she was getting was a powerful torch beam in her eyes as I moved towards her, putting her bag strap over my head.

It was time to grip her and get the fuck out of there before the authorities screamed in – or whatever was going to happen after 5 a.m. I got back to her, switched off the torch and put it in my jeans. With my left hand I got hold of her at the point where the back of her head met the neck, and banged the web of my right hand hard up under her nose. I felt her jolt as it slammed into her face. Bending my legs, I pushed up with both hands, making sure that all the pressure of the lift was against her nostrils. Her hands raised, then fell again. She couldn't resist, she had to go with it, her moans of pain getting louder.

I got her sitting bolt upright, and put the crook of my left arm around the front of her neck, jamming her tight against me. Her face was still tilted upwards. With the pistol in my right hand, I moved my right forearm behind her neck to complete the head lock, and stood up. She was fighting for oxygen. No way was she not coming with me.

I started to move and she didn't like it at all. Her back arched more as her legs hit the floor and she tried to take more weight off her neck. She was recovering quicker now that she was in pain, but I had total control. If she fought back too strongly I'd just give her another bulletin with the Tazer, but that would be a last resort. I wanted to move quickly, not be dragging a dead weight.

I made my way across the room and, checking the pistol's safety with my right thumb, opened the door. The corridor was still dark and silent. I reinforced my hold on her by jerking my knees and gripping her neck more tightly. She seemed to be concentrating on holding onto my left arm so that she could relieve some of the pressure on her neck, probably too worried about being asphyxiated to resist.

I stepped out into the corridor, her head still jammed against my chest, the rest of her body following behind me. She gave no resistance at all, and once we got past the table I understood why. She started to buck and spark up, her legs kicking out as she held onto my arm for even more support. She kicked the table side-ways, knocking the lamp onto the floor. Its stained-glass lampshade shattered across the floorboards.

It had gone noisy; no need to tiptoe around any more. I started to motor towards the stairs, dragging her with me. At first she continued to buck and kick, her feet banging on the wooden flooring, then she must have realized that if she didn't help her-self by trying to keep her back arched and her legs on the floor, she could break her own neck.

We got to the staircase, and I was just about to turn right and go down when I heard the sound of a latch lifting to my left.

I swung round as the door opened and light burst from the room. Sarah swung with me, a muffled scream coming from her throat as the movement wrenched her neck.

It was the American. His reactions were quick. I fired into the door as he shoved it closed. I gripped her and started moving aggressively down the stairs.

The American was thumping on the floor, screaming, 'Wake up! Attack, attack! Wake up!'

Sarah's heels and calves were taking a good hammering; she was squealing like a stuck pig inside the gag, and trying to tense up her muscles to help with the pain. We were sounding like a herd stampeding, with my heavy footsteps and her feet bouncing off the wood.

I didn't look behind me, I just ran for it. I wasn't going to head for the fire exit on the next floor as I'd thought I might. There were too many rooms on either side of that corridor, and I had no idea if there was anyone else in the building that I hadn't accounted for. The way my luck was going, there was bound to be. My new plan was to get down to the garage, a route I knew, then just make a run for it.

I turned right to go down the next flight of stairs. As I took the first few steps I could see that the second floor corridor below me was now lit up like a football stadium.

Above me the American screamed, 'Sarah! One of them has Sarah! They have Sarah!'

From below me a voice shouted above the babble of the TV, 'Where? Where are they? Help me here.'

I froze no more than six feet from the bottom of the stairs. It wouldn't be long before these two got their act together and I'd be dead. I just wanted five seconds in which to calm down and think.

A shadow approached from the left on the corridor below. It turned into Bossman, now in jeans and carrying an HK53. Fuck, how did he get free so quickly? I kept looking down on him, weapon in the aim, gripping Sarah even tighter to stop her disrupting my sight picture.

He turned and looked up. I blatted three quiet rounds until he went down, not dead, just screaming and writhing on the ground. The 53 clattered down the stairs to the floor below.

Above me the American half groaned, half yelled, 'What's happening? Talk to me. Someone talk to me here.'

I went down more stairs, stopped short of the corridor and, still holding Sarah with my left arm, put my pistol round to the left and loosed off the rest of the rounds blindly. Being suppressed, it wouldn't have quite the same effect as rounds going off with a loud report, but people would hear them splintering the wood-work and get the general idea. I willed Bossman to carry on screaming and scare the shit out of anyone listening. Maybe it worked, because there was still no firing back at me. Either that, or there were no more people.

I ran out of rounds and started to change mags. Pressing the mag release catch I jerked my hand downwards to help the mag fall out. It hit the stair and bounced down, onto Bossman's back. I looked at him, face down on the floor, his blood spilling across the polished wood. Then, turning to look up the stairs, waiting for the American, I placed a new mag into the weapon right next to Sarah's face. As I turned back to check chamber, we had eye contact for the first time. The shock of recognition was plain to see; her eyes were wide with amazement and disbelief. I looked away, more concerned about the job in hand.

I moved straight across the gap without looking, just making sure I didn't trip over Bossman, whose screams were fading. I rammed down the last flight of stairs, feeling and hearing Sarah bumping down behind me, sometimes lifting up her feet to take the strain, sometimes stumbling.

I carried on straight across the room towards the garage stairs, passing Too Thin To Win and his friends. Shouts and screams came from the TV as we passed the kitchen door.

Just as I neared the bottom of the flight and was about to enter the garage, I heard shouting upstairs, and then four or five rounds went off.

I wondered what the American was firing at, then I realized: he'd probably run downstairs, seen figures by the TV in semi-darkness and fired off at them straight away without looking. The flickering light from the screen, and the scariness of the situation, had probably got him jumping. It certainly had me.

I closed the door behind me to add a bit more to the confusion. He wouldn't dare barge straight through; he couldn't guarantee what was on the other side. We moved alongside the Explorer, and I could hear the American's voice above me. I couldn't make sense of what he was saying, but he didn't sound too happy about the way his day was shaping up.

The rain stung as it lashed my face. It was then that I remembered the bergen, but it was too late now. Fuck it. I turned left, towards the other house, and had taken no more than three steps when the proximity lights came on. With my head down I started pumping, but was restricted by the weight I was dragging.

I'd covered maybe ten or fifteen metres when the first burst from a 53 was fired from one of the upper floors. Its short barrel and the power of the round makes the muzzle emit a fearsome flash; it's the only weapon I'd ever seen that looks like the ones you see in films. It was great for close-up work as it scared the shit out of people. I kept on running; I'd be out of the light in a few more strides.

As soon as we hit darkness I glanced back. All the lights in the house were blazing. Smoke was drifting from the windows on the second floor. It looked almost like that house in *The Amityville*

Horror, shrouded in rain and mist, except that it wasn't mist, it was cordite from the rounds.

A couple of lights were on upstairs in the place next door. My new plan was to get in there, point a big fat gun at them, take their pickup and fuck off. The next thing I knew, however, the external light on the family's 4x4, mounted on the driver's side wing, burst into life, and a million-candle-power beam sliced through the darkness towards us. A man's voice shouted a warning: 'Don't come near – stay away! I'm armed – I've called the police!'

For good measure he whanged down a couple of rounds at us from a rifle. He probably had 'My land, my country, my gun' on his bumpers, and a few other stickers that he'd bought at Jim's, but he was protecting his family, and that was a fair one.

I felt a thump as one of the rounds rammed into the ground far too close to me. Either he was good, and he meant to aim a warning shot, or he was trying to hit us and this time we'd been lucky. I didn't want to find out which. I jinked left and ran between the two houses, uphill, towards the dirt track. Change of plan again: we were going to make it on foot back to my car, as I'd been aiming to do all along, but without all this drama.

Another rifle shot rang out, but this time I didn't hear the answering thud. There was the burst of a 53; fuck knows where that went.

I got to the track, crossed it and stopped to try and assess the situation. We were in darkness and on higher ground. I heard shots and saw a couple of foot-long muzzle flashes coming from the direction of the target house, and more from the area around the pickup. Shotgun Ned must be zapping and shouting at anything that moved. His spotlight swept left and right, looking for targets.

It wasn't the only light I could see. Red and blue flashing lights were glistening in the rain on the other side of the lake and I suddenly realized that I stood more chance of being struck by lightning than I did of getting back to my car. Acting as the situation demanded, I changed plan again. We were going to get out of here on foot. I stood still, knees bent, waiting to regain my breath. It was colder than before, and the wind and rain were loud against the leaves.

I started moving through the forest again. Sarah's bare flesh was getting zapped left and right by branches, and I could hear her suffering. I put my head down and pumped uphill, leaving everybody down there to get on with it. It seemed that my lucky number for house clearing was the same as for shopping trolleys: zero.

18

I gripped Sarah and plunged on, slipping and skidding on the wet mush, stumbling over rocks and fallen branches, flailing to regain my footing. She was screaming as best she could beneath the gag, partly because of the tree branches that whipped at her bare body and the ground cutting her legs, partly just trying to keep her airway clear. At least I knew she was breathing.

I tripped again and went down. The pain as my knees hit rock made them feel as if they were on fire. She moaned loudly under the gag as she took the brunt of my fall, and she had to arch her back to relieve the strain on her neck. I stayed on my knees, screwing my face up as I took the pain, waiting for it to die down. There was nothing I could do but accept it. I just hoped I hadn't smashed a kneecap. My chest was heaving up and down as I tried to catch my breath. Sarah gave up the struggle to keep her body off the ground. She collapsed in the mud beside and slightly below me, her head, still in the neck hold, resting in my lap and moving up and down in unison with my breathing.

There was plenty of commotion going on behind, the odd rifle round and automatic burst, followed by shouts. Looking down and behind me through the trees and rain, I could make out the lights of both houses some 150 metres away. I wasn't in dead ground yet, and it was going to be light soon. I needed to get distance.

Shotgun Ned was having a ballistic fit, screaming and hollering, like something out of one of the movies for guys who like guy movies. I couldn't tell whether he was enjoying it or hating it, but he was vocal, that was for sure. I got myself to my feet, pulling Sarah upright with me, and started moving again.

I could hear rotor blades in the sky behind. Moments later a blindingly bright Night Sun searchlight penetrated the darkness and began to sweep the area towards the houses as the helicopter hovered over the lake. It wasn't venturing too near the scene just yet, probably for fear of someone taking a pot-shot.

More gunshots echoed in the background. Almost immediately I heard returned bursts of fire and saw the brilliant, almost white, muzzle flash of a 53. I turned back and started to move off.

My throat was parched; God knew what Sarah's was like. She must be in shit state. I kept checking behind me as I moved and could see the lights in the houses slowly fading into the dark and rain. We would be in dead ground soon. As I moved, the Night Sun briefly lit up the area around me as it realigned itself while the heli orbited the lake, making hundreds of shadows in the trees as the rotor blades groaned, trying to keep it in a stable position in the wind. The campers were no doubt outside their tents, trying to watch the re-enactment of the Waco siege from the safety of the other side of the lake, pleased that their washed-out holiday had turned out quite exciting after all.

Below me I could only see the flat roofs of the two houses. More blue flashing lights cut through the trees, but this time on my side of the lake, coming from the left along the track. Yet more police vehicles were also arriving in the carpark across the lake. They'd all got here too fast. My guess must have been correct. My report must have confirmed Elizabeth and Lynn's speculation about what was going on, and they wanted Sarah out before the seventh cavalry moved in. It seemed that I'd fucked that up a bit; it wouldn't be long before the area was choked with police and FBI trying to stop the Third World War.

Shotgun Ned would be a national hero after this. He'd probably be given his own fucking talk show. The police, however, had mortgages and kids to think about; while it was dark they would do no more than contain the area. By first light, however, they'd have all their shit together, maybe even have the Army or National Guard on standby.

I crested a rise, and as I moved downhill it blocked out all the noise behind me. My first priority was to put as much distance as possible between us and the target before first light.

As I moved, I could feel Sarah shivering and shaking beside me, screaming inside her gag. If I was feeling bad, she must be in shit state.

I crossed another small ridge, started to move downhill, and lost my footing in the mud. As I slithered and tumbled Sarah fought to break free and save herself. I had a split second in which to decide whether to hold onto her or let go.

The decision was made for me. We took another half tumble and slide and came to an abrupt stop against a tree trunk. I'd landed on my back, with Sarah on top of me, her wet hair in my face, breathing hard through her nose like a Grand National winner. My pistol, which had been pushed into the front of my jeans, had gone.

I let go of Sarah; she wasn't going anywhere, the weapon was the priority. I never wanted to be without one again. Maglite in hand, the bulb covered by my fingers to minimize the spill of light, I crawled around on my hands and knees sifting through the leaves and mud like a kid searching for a lost toy.

My knee caught a metal edge as I moved. I checked the safety, wiped off the worst of the mud and shoved it back into my jeans. Scrambling back towards Sarah, I noticed she was breathing much more loudly. That wasn't right. Then I heard a loud, hoarse whisper, 'What the fuck do you think you're doing? Get this belt off me – now!'

She had somehow untied the gag, and was coughing and trying to relieve the soreness in her mouth. 'Come on!' She lifted her hands. 'Get this fucking thing off!'

She couldn't see it, but I was trying to hide a laugh. People with accents like hers shouldn't swear, it just doesn't work. Besides, she was practically naked, streaked with mud, yet trying to order me around.

'Do it, Nick. Hurry, we must keep moving!'

There were no more weapon reports from behind us, and a loud-hailer was now being used, probably to give instructions to anyone left in the house. The rain prevented me from hearing what was being said. The heli was out there somewhere, the throbbing of its rotors carried in on gusts of wind.

What did she mean, *we* need to keep moving? I looked at her, and couldn't help it – I started to laugh, and that pissed her off even more.

'Don't be ridiculous, hurry up and untie me!' She held her arms out. 'Get me out of here before this becomes even more of a fucking fiasco!'

The rattle of the helicopter getting closer made us both shut up. It was hard to tell which direction it was coming from. I was peering up, but could see jack shit.

'Come on, get this belt off me and give me your coat!' She started to use her teeth to pull the knot apart. It wasn't working. The leather was too tight and wet, and she was shivering too much to get a good grip.

The helicopter roared overhead. I caught a glimpse of its navigation lights through the trees. At least it wasn't hovering, or moving in a search pattern – not yet, anyway. I guessed it would be soon. I could see the glimmer of first light beyond the canopy.

She wanted my attention again. 'Nick, get this off me and give me your coat. Please.' Her arms were still thrust towards me. I grabbed hold of the belt and started to drag her along in the mud.

First light had started to penetrate to the forest floor, relieving the gloom just enough to show my footprints. The rain was starting to ease off; the noise of it hitting the leaves was dying down, along with the wind in the trees. I was starting to feel depressed; I was soaking wet, cold and confused. What was worse, we were leaving an unmissable trail in the mud.

She could obviously see that I was in no mood for discussion as we moved and she shut up. We came over another rise. Down below us, about one or two hundred metres away at the bottom of a steep gradient, was a river. Maybe thirty metres wide, it was in full flood, a maelstrom of fast-flowing water and foam.

As we scrambled downhill, all I could hear was the rush of water in front of us. Sarah called out, 'Slower, slower,' trying to get her footing. I wasn't listening. We had to find a way across. With luck it would be the psychological boundary of the search; hopefully they would start from the house and fan out as far as the bank, assuming that no-one would be mad enough to try and cross.

At that moment I had to be the only person in the world with a good thing to say about El Niño. In theory, it should have been nice and sunny at this time of the year in the Carolinas. Conditions like this would slow the searchers down, and if the weather closed in any further the heli might not be able to fly.

Closer to the water the tree canopy started to thin. Out in the open it was virtually daylight, and looking up I could see a really thick, grey, miserable sky. It had stopped raining, but in dense woodland you'd never know that; all the moisture is held on the leaves and it still works its way down to the floor. What the fuck, I was soaked to the skin anyway.

Sarah's hair was wet and flat against her head. Dried blood ringed her nostrils; I must have slammed my hand into her face quite hard on the bed. She was bleeding from several cuts on her legs, with goose bumps the size of peanuts, and in any other circumstances she'd have needed hospital attention. She was covered in mud, sand, bits of leaves and twigs, and shivering uncontrollably in her drenched and now transparent knickers and T-shirt.

I let go of the belt and studied the river, trying to look for a safe place to cross. It was pointless. If I'd doubted the strength of the current I only had to look at the chunks of uprooted tree that were surging downstream and crashing over the rocks. Wherever I chose, it was going to be a major drama. So what was new?

Sarah was switched on; she knew what I was thinking. She sat in a foetal position against a rock on the bank with her arms wrapped around her legs, trying to cover her body for warmth. She looked at the river, then at me. 'No, Nick. Are you mad? I'm not going, not here. Why don't we—'

I cut her off mid-sentence, grabbing hold of the belt and

dragging her a short distance back into the canopy for cover. I
didn't talk to her; there was too much stuff churning round in my
head. Instead I started to pull out my shirt from my trousers, then
the bottoms of my jeans where they'd been tucked into my boots.
I undid the cuffs on my jacket sleeves until everything was nice
and loose and water could flow more freely around me. If your
shirt is tucked in when you swim, the weight of trapped water
that collects can slow you down, then it might drown you. The
gloves came off; it was pointless wearing them at the moment,
and besides, they looked ridiculous. Sarah was all right, she had
fuck all on anyway. I stuffed all my docs, plus hers, into one of the
gloves, then pushed that inside the other one and put it back
in my jacket. I wondered about the bag; fuck it, I'd have to
take it with me. I didn't want to leave any more sign than was
necessary.

The wind had started to gust strongly and the trees at the top
of the canopy on the opposite side of the river were bending and
swaying. I looked at Sarah hunching down behind a tree for
shelter. Only feet away the water crashed angrily against the
rocks.

I looked along the opposite bank, following the river's current,
trying to work out where we might land up. I could see downstream for about 250 metres, then the river bent round to the right
and disappeared from view. The opposite bank was about two or
three feet above water level, with plenty of grab provided by
foliage and tree roots exposed by the current as it carved into the
soil. I had to assume the worst, that there was a massive waterfall
just after the bend, and that meant that we had just 250 metres in
which to make our way across and get out.

The ambient temperature wasn't freezing but it was bitterly
cold. On land, we wouldn't die of exposure if we kept moving,
but the river would be another matter. Sarah saw me looking at
the water and back at her. She dropped her head and buried it in
her arms. The gesture was one of resignation, and recognition of
the fact that, if she was telling the truth about wanting to get
away, I was her only means of escape.

The heli was somewhere behind us, doing its stuff between the

231

river and the houses; I couldn't tell exactly where it was, but it had to be near or I wouldn't be able to hear the rotor blades groaning as it tried to keep a low hover.

I went over to her, grabbed hold of the belt and pulled her to her feet. She looked into my eyes. 'Nick, why not take this thing off? Please. I'm not going anywhere, am I?'

I ignored her. Gripping the belt with my left hand, I moved down to the water's edge, keeping my eyes lifted to the sky. I tried to convince myself that the only thing that mattered right now was the helicopter.

A spit of rocks extending about five metres out looked as if it would give us some sort of platform to begin our crossing; water sluiced over the top and there was no way of telling how deep it was on either side. I hoped Sarah could swim, but if she couldn't, tough, she should have said. I looked at her eyes and suddenly saw fear there, then I looked at the river again. It was a fair one. There was no way I couldn't remove the belt. I needed to keep her alive. Her death had to be at a time and place of my choosing.

As I undid the knot she said very quietly, 'Thank you.'

I caught her eye, trying to read the message there, then nodded and moved on, throwing the belt into the bag. She stepped gingerly over the small stones at the water's edge. 'Come on!' I snapped.

She kept her head down, watching her footing. 'I'm trying, it's hurting my feet.' As we started to wade in she gasped, 'Oh fuck, it's so cold!'

She was right; the water temperature had to be near zero. I told myself just to get in there, get it done, and worry about warming up again on the other side.

I fought the current until I was up to my waist, with Sarah behind me grasping the strap of her bag which was still over my shoulder. Then, with my next step, I was into fast-flowing water, the current tearing at my leg, threatening to throw me off balance. I grabbed her hand, whether to support myself or to help her, I didn't know, but no sooner had I lifted my other leg than the weight of water whipped it away from under me and I was being swept downstream. I still clung to Sarah, both of us kicking and thrashing to keep afloat and make some progress towards the opposite bank, but the current was starting to drag me under. If you're trapped against a rock by water that's just half a metre high and moving at 12 mph, you'd need to be able to bench press 550 pounds to lift yourself away. We were no contest for the tons of water surging downstream.

My head was forced under and I swallowed a mouthful of freezing river. I kicked back to the surface, forcing myself to breathe in through my nose, only to choke as I inhaled yet more water. I let go of her. We each had to fight our own battle now. She looked at me, her eyes the size of saucers as she realized what I'd done. That wasn't my problem; it would only become one if I couldn't find her body before they did. She still had to disappear without trace.

I saw her through wet, blurred vision, trying to keep her head up, kicking and swimming and wading like a seal. Then she was sucked under by the current and I couldn't tell how far across I was. The water kept taking me under, and I was more concerned about sucking in air than getting to the other side. I couldn't see Sarah at all now, but there was nothing I could do about that. I was in enough shit of my own.

As I came up again and snatched a lungful of air, I heard a scream. 'Oh God! Oh God!' I looked around for her, but saw nothing above the torrent.

I was dragged back down and inhaled more river water. Scrabbling my way to the surface, I saw that this time I was almost at the far side. The current wasn't dying down, though, because the river curved around to the right and I was on the outside of the bend, where the force of the water was at its fiercest. An eddy caught me and the momentum threw me against the bank. I threw out my hands, trying to grasp an exposed tree root or an overhanging branch, anything I could.

I shouted for Sarah, but all I got in reply was another mouthful of river. I coughed, trying to force my eyes open again, but they stung too much. Thrashing around blindly, my left hand connected with something solid. I made a grab, but whatever it was gave way. The next thing I knew, my right arm had hooked into a large tree root. The current swung me round and pressed me against the bank, and my feet connected with solid ground. I clung to the roots and took deep breaths to slow myself down. Downstream, nothing was moving in the water but branches and lumps of wood.

I struggled against the weight of water until I could reach with my free hand and grab another root higher up the bank. I finally hauled myself up until only my feet were left in the water, being forced sideways by the current. One more grab and pull and I was lying on the bank, fighting for breath. I'd never felt such relief. I lay there for more than a minute, coughing up water and slowly feeling some strength return to my limbs.

As my head cleared, I realized my problems weren't over. I'd now have to find Sarah, and she could be anywhere downstream. Clearing the banks would expose me to view from the ground, and the river was a natural route for any follow-up to be taking. As if that wasn't bad enough, the heli, if it came back, would ping me at once.

There was nothing I could do about any of that; I just had to get on with it and retrieve what I could from this gang-fuck. Turning my head, I could make out the river behind me, blurred by the water in my eyes. There was still no sign of Sarah.

My soaking clothes weighed me down as I started to stumble along the bank, leaning over the edge from time to time to double check that she wasn't concealed behind rocks or in some kink in the ground below me. If I couldn't find her and she was discovered downstream, or even on the coast, I'd just have to accept that it was a big-time fuck-up. However, not yet.

As I moved, I kept my eyes skinned for somewhere to hide her body if she was dead. Hiding her wouldn't be the ideal solution, but there was fuck-all else I could do. It would slow me down, carrying her out of the area, and I could always come back in a month or two and finish the job. It needed to be a spot that I could ID at a later date, and perhaps after a change of season, and one that wasn't near a hikers' route or a water course.

As the current reached the bend and changed direction, its noise became almost deafening. I followed round, the dead ground gradually coming into view. I couldn't believe it. Just 300 metres further downstream, resting on timber supports driven into the riverbed, was a small footbridge. The story of my life. If I'd been looking for one, it wouldn't have existed.

I stopped, looked and listened. The bridge would be on their maps, and anyone sent to follow us would use it to cross.

As I got to within maybe 150 metres of the structure, I could see that it was made of three thick wooden supports rising up from the river on each side. The walkway, made of what were probably old railway sleepers, was maybe two metres above that.

In any search pattern the police would use this bridge as a key point, somewhere that it would be natural to go to. Maybe they had already identified it and had a team hidden, waiting for us to cross.

Should I move into the canopy a bit and then come back to the river further down once I'd boxed round it? No good: I needed to search the whole bank. The way things were going she was probably just a metre from the bridge, dead. I watched for a while longer. The wind bent the treetops and the water crashed along at warp speed.

At first I thought it was the white water pushing itself against the middle support, with the occasional plume of foam being thrown into the air. It wasn't. It was Sarah, clinging to the post and reaching up, trying to make the two metres to safety. Time and again her hand moved up the support, only to be ripped away again as the current got hold of her. For a split second I hoped she'd be washed away; then I could concentrate on saving my own arse and getting away, taking any flak when I got back to the UK. Then reality kicked in. There was still a chance I could pull her out and do my job properly.

I moved back into the canopy and made my approach towards the bridge, lying down about twenty metres short for one last look. She wasn't making a sound. Either she was switched on enough to know not to scream, or she was just too scared. I didn't care which, as long as she stayed quiet.

There didn't seem to be any other activity, but then again, if the police were switched on I'd be very lucky to ping them. It was decision time: I could either get her out and complete the task, or let her get carried away and drown. Then it hit me that there was a third option. She could be swept away and survive.

I looked around for a branch that was long enough to do the job. It didn't have to be strong, just long. Jumping up, I grasped one with both hands and pulled down with all my weight. Water sluiced onto me from the leaves. The branch snapped. I twisted and pulled, and it finally parted from the tree. I didn't bother stripping it of its smaller branches, just headed down towards the bank.

I stopped to pull off first my boots, then my jeans. For a moment I fantasized that maybe I could be doing the world a great service here. Maybe London knew that she was going to be the next Hitler. Then my jacket came off and the wind bit into me. What the fuck was I doing, freezing cold in the back of beyond, with the police after me, taking my kit off to save a woman's life just so I could kill her somewhere else? I gave myself another reality check. 'Shut the fuck up, Stone. It's point-less honking, you know it has to be done.'

I secured my weapon and the contents of my jeans in the bag and put it back over my shoulder. With my boots back on, but my jeans and jacket in my hands, I left the canopy and ran out towards the bridge. I must have looked like someone doing a runner after being caught in bed with another man's wife.

As I hit the railway sleepers that made up the walkway, I could see her still playing the limpet, the current pushing her head against the support as she fought to keep it out of the river.

She saw me. 'Nick, Nick. I'm here . . . here!'

As if I didn't know. I leaned over the handrail. 'Shut up!' I had to holler above the noise of the water as I started to pass down the end of one jeans leg, knotted to help her grip. The other was tied to one of the sleeves of my jacket. I could never remember the name of the knot. If I'd wanted to know it I would have joined the Navy. The other sleeve also had a knot at the end, to help me.

'Take the jeans end only,' I shouted. 'Now listen to me, OK?'

She looked up, shaking the water from her face. Her eyes kept flicking towards the knotted jeans leg that was her lifeline. They were wide with fear.

I kept hold of the knotted sleeve as I dangled the material so that it would be easy for her to get hold of, yet still keep in contact with the support. Her teeth made contact with the material first and she bit down, turning her head to bring it closer to her hands. Once there I could see by the determination in her expression that she wasn't going to let go.

'Sarah, look at me.' I wanted her to understand exactly what was expected of her. When people flap they nod and agree to everything without really understanding what's being said. 'I'm going to drop the rest of this lot into the water, and retrieve it on the other side of the bridge. When I shout, I want you to let go of the support and just hold on to the jeans. Got it?'

'Yes, yes. Hurry.'

'Here goes.' I checked again to see if anyone was watching, then I threw the rest of the makeshift rope under the bridge.

I switched to the other side, lying on my stomach on the sleepers and leaning down. My jacket was snaking from side to side in the current. Looking back upstream under the bridge, I could see her coughing and spitting out water, only to take another mouthful.

Moving the branch down into the water, I made contact on the third attempt and pulled up the free end of the rope. Wrapping the knotted end round my wrist, I braced myself against the wood supporting the handrail, ready to take the strain. I could no longer see her.

'Now, Sarah. Now!'

She must have let go and the current swept her under the span. There was an almighty jolt, then what felt like the world's biggest dog pulling on its lead. I held on to the jacket sleeve like a man possessed.

'Kick, Sarah. Kick.'

She didn't need telling twice. The combination of her efforts and the pendulum effect of the current swept her in towards the bank like a hooked fish.

I got to my feet and managed to reel in two more twists of the jacket, taking a few steps towards the end of the bridge. By the time I reached the bank I had hands full of jeans. I dropped

237

to the ground above her and we linked arms. She didn't need to be told what to do next. I heaved and rolled and she used my body as a climbing frame. A moment later and she was lying beside me on solid ground.

I thanked whichever guardian angel was looking over me that day.

She was coughing and fighting for breath. She wasn't going to be in any condition to help herself for a little while, and we had to get away from here. I hauled myself to my feet, bent down and scooped her up in a fireman's lift over my shoulder. I picked up the knotted jeans and jacket as I moved off, staggering more than running into the trees. I needed us to be out of sight of the helicopter, and to find some shelter.

Ahead of me was a steep rise. I put her down while I got some breath back. I was shivering violently, and Sarah moaned as she, too, fought the cold and shock. I wanted to get beyond the rise into another lot of dead ground, so we couldn't be seen from the other side of the river.

Her head lolled over my shoulder, her face close to mine. I was looking straight ahead and focusing on the trees, but I still heard the words. 'Thank you, Nick.' I tilted my head towards her and did my best to shrug. It felt strange to be thanked like this, and for the second time.

Safely inside the tree line, I stopped and helped her to the ground. I turned away and leaned against a tree, my lungs greedily sucking in air. 'Can you manage on your own?' I asked.

To my surprise, the reply came from very close. I felt her hand on my shoulder as she said, 'I can do it. Let's go.'

I moved off with her following, over the rise and onto dead ground. We couldn't be seen from the opposite bank any more, but we still needed cover from the air and the biting wind. It wasn't as strong as last night, but wind-chill could really slow us down after what we'd just been through.

Normally, when looking for shelter from the elements, the last place you want to be is in a valley bottom or a deep hollow, because hot air rises, but we needed the cover. We also needed to try and find a place where we could preserve what little body warmth we had left, and away from the noise of the river so I could listen out for pursuers.

As I bustled her through the canopy, needles pushed themselves sharply into my face, and bucketfuls of water spilled off the disturbed branches.

The best hide I could find was a massive fir about 100 metres from the river, whose branches hung down to the ground. Sarah was clearly in pain as she crawled towards the base of the trunk. The branches started about a metre up the trunk and met the ground about a metre away from us. There was no noise here, except for the wind against the outer branches. It was just as wet inside as out, but it felt wonderful just to be under cover. It's a psychological thing; get up against, or under, something and you begin to imagine you're a bit warmer.

We huddled against the trunk, both of us shivering and shuddering. Adrenalin had kicked in when we were on the move, but its effects were subsiding. I just wanted to lie there, but I knew that if I made an effort it would pay off. I pulled the strap of Sarah's bag over my head and dropped it on the ground. Then I took out the knots with cold, numb and very fumbling hands and teeth. With my foot on the collar of the jacket, I got hold of the rest of it and started to twist out the worst of the water.

Sarah looked at me like an abused puppy, huddled up and shivering. I untwisted the jacket and threw it at her. I wanted her to stay alive for two reasons now: I still didn't want to have to carry a dead weight out of the area, and I wanted her to answer some questions.

She put the jacket around her shoulders and hungrily wrapped herself up in it. Then she wriggled backwards until she was resting against the tree, cuddling herself, trying to tuck the jacket around her legs.

I took off my shirt and T-shirt, and wrung them out, too. I was shivering so badly that it felt as if my muscles were in spasm, but it had to be done. I had to get the water out and some air into the fibres so that my body heat – what was left of it – could sustain itself. Not that cotton has that many air pockets. 'Cotton kills,' the saying goes in outdoors circles, and for good reason, but what I

239

was doing was better than nothing. It made me think of Shirts KF, the thick woolly shirts we had to wear in the infantry. I'd never found out what the letters KF stood for; all I knew was that the material used to itch and scratch, and in summer make you feel as if you were wearing a greatcoat, but in the field during winter they were great – wet or dry, the fibres retained heat.

I put the shirt and T-shirt back on, then knelt to take off my boots, fumbling to undo the laces with numb, trembling fingers. Finally I wrung out my jeans, taking care to keep the pistol away from Sarah's grasp.

When I was dressed again I tucked everything in, trying to minimize the number of ways in which the wind could get to me. I pushed the pistol into the back of my jeans by the base of my spine, where she wouldn't be able to get at it.

I sat back against the trunk, with Sarah on my left. She was still in the same position as before, sitting in a curled-up ball and using the jacket as best she could to keep herself warm, her hands keeping the collar pulled up around her face.

It's always best to share body warmth, and two people of opposite sexes huddled together generate five per cent more warmth than two of the same sex. I nudged her with my elbow, held out my arms and motioned with my head for her to move over. She shuffled across, sniffing, her hair soaking wet and plastered over her face.

High above, a strong gust of wind made the tree sway. I straightened my legs and she arranged herself in my lap with her left side against me, then I lifted my legs to press her closer to my chest, which insulated her from the ground, and got more of her skin in contact with mine. Her wet hair was over my shoulder as her body pushed into mine. I put my arms around her. Neither of us could control our shivering. She snuggled into me, her head against my chest, and I could feel the benefit almost immediately. There was a silence during which we both willed ourselves to get warm. I looked down on her wet, muddy hair, flecked with pine needles and bits of bark.

It almost took me by surprise when she spoke. 'I suppose they told you I'm a runner?' Her body was shaking. She didn't move

240

her head for me to see, but I could tell by her tone that her period of compliance was coming to an end.

'Something like that.' I bent my head to listen for any follow-up, and raised my knees more to pull her nearer for warmth.

'And I suppose you believed them? Christ, I've been putting this operation together for over four years, Nick. Now it's destroyed by some dunderhead who's sent to fuck me over.'

The dunderhead bit pissed me off. 'Four years to do what? What operation? What the fuck are you talking about, Sarah?'

Her speech was slow, the tone that of a schoolmistress trying to show patience as she explains simple things to tiny minds. It was only partly working; her shivering was making her speech disjointed. 'Four years to infiltrate deep enough to discover their network in the US and Europe – that's what I am talking about.'

'Infiltrate who? What? Why didn't London know?'

'London . . .' She paused. 'The reason London doesn't know is because I don't know who I can tell. I don't know the whole network yet, but the more I learn, the more I know I can't trust anyone.'

There was another pause. She intended it to give me time to think, but I left it for her to fill. After pulling the collar up further around her face to fight the cold, she took the hint. 'I suppose they sent you to kill me?' Her voice was slightly muffled by the jacket.

'No, just to get you back to the UK for questioning. It seems you are becoming an embarrassment.'

She scoffed at my answer. I could feel her shoulders shaking as she covered her mouth to hide the noise of her coughing laugh.

'Ah, London . . .' The laughter stopped and the coughing took over. She looked up at me. 'Listen, Nick, London have got it wrong. This isn't about embarrassment, for Christ's sake. It's about assassination.' I must have had that vacant expression on my face again, because she reverted to her kindergarten-teacher voice. 'The team in the house; they were planning a hit on Netanyahu.'

To be honest, I didn't really give a shit about Netanyahu, so I couldn't help a grin. 'The hit has failed. They're all dead, apart from one.'

241

Her head started shaking like a mechanical toy. She was deadly serious, or as serious as you can be when all your extremities are purple, including your nose. 'No, you're wrong. There are still two more members of the cell. They were going to RV with us at the house today. You don't understand, Nick; it's not a job to them, it's a quest. They will carry on.' There was real frustration in her voice. 'Believe me, if Netanyahu dies, you *will* give a shit. It will change the way you live, Nick. That is, if you do.'

I hated all this beating around the bush; it was like being in the middle of a conversation with Lynn and Elizabeth again. 'What the fuck are you on about, Sarah?'

She thought for a while as she buried her head back into the jacket collar. The sound of the rotor blades kicked in to join the wind above us, then died as quickly as it came.

'No, not yet. I'm going to keep that as my insurance; I need to make sure you get me out of here. You see, Nick, I don't believe you're here to take me back to London. It must be more important than that, or they wouldn't have sent you.'

She was right, of course, I would do exactly the same if I was in her position.

'Look, Nick. Keep me alive and get me out of here, and I'll tell you everything. Don't let them use you; give me time to prove it.'

I hated not having control. I wanted to know more, but at the same I wasn't so desperate that I would lie awake at night with worry. I didn't reply; I had to think. And I was going to take her out of there anyway, whether she liked it or not.

She adjusted her body on my legs, and looked up again and stared into my eyes. 'Nick, please believe me. I've got involved in something where nobody can be trusted – and I mean nobody.'

She kept her eyes locked on mine. She had just opened her mouth to speak again when we both heard the sound of somebody crashing through the trees.

Whoever it was wasn't having much luck with their footing. They hit the ground with a loud curse. 'Shittt!' It was a man's voice.

I didn't need to say anything to Sarah. She jumped away from me and my hand reached for the pistol.

The man must have got up, only to fall down again immediately with a grunt as he scrambled to recover. 'Oh fuck, fuck . . .'

On my hands and knees, I moved slowly to the edge of our hide and pushed my face against the branches. It was the American. He was stumbling around in the mud, his clothes soaking, his moustache looking like a drowned rat. He was heading in our general direction, looking as bedraggled as we were. But he wasn't just running, he was looking for ground sign. He was tracking us.

I crawled back to Sarah and whispered in her ear, 'It's your American. Go bring him in.'

She shook her head. 'It won't work.'

'Make him.'

'He won't fall for it.'

'You're the one that needs his clothes, not me.'

She thought about it, then nodded slowly and took a deep breath. I watched as she turned away from me and crawled out of the hide.

I heard her call, 'Lance! Over here! Lance!'

I moved to the opposite side of the tree, pushing back under the branches, just in case Sarah decided to become Lance's best friend again. I lay down and brought my pistol up into the aim, the barrel just clearing the branches.

I could hear her talking to him as they got nearer. It was Arabic, but spoken rapidly. She was still gobbing off to him at warp speed as she shuffled backwards into the hide. I started to feel vulnerable now. Why was she talking to him like this? I'd already heard him speak English. It could only mean trouble. But fuck it, whatever she was planning was about to happen.

243

19

The first things to appear were his hands, the backs of which were covered in hair and looked way too big for his wrists. Then his head and shoulders, face down to avoid the low branches as he pushed his way in. He was nodding and agreeing with whatever it was that Sarah was saying as she followed him in.

He didn't look up until he was right inside the shelter. When he did, he saw me crawling out of the branches opposite him. His eyes widened as he saw the weapon, and he shot a glance back at Sarah, looking for some kind of clarification or reassurance. He looked back at the weapon, then at her again, trying to work it out. After a couple of seconds he gave a deep sigh and lowered his head, rocking it slowly from side to side.

Sarah was level with him now, and jerked her head to indicate for him to crawl forwards a bit more; he did as he was told. She ran her hands underneath his jacket. I watched her like a hawk, ready to react if she tried to grab his weapon and draw down on me.

She looked at me and shook her head.

I motioned him to move to the left of the hide and he shuffled over on his hands and knees. I stopped him before he was too close to me, in case he fancied his chances.

The black bomber jacket he was wearing had a Harley-Davidson motif on the left-hand side and looked warm. I motioned with the pistol.

'Clothes.'

Still on his knees, bent over with his back parallel to the ground, he started to remove the jacket. His gaze switched between me and Sarah; he didn't say a word, still trying to work it all out. Sarah was sitting against the tree with her hands in her jacket pockets and her knees against her chest.

I grabbed the American's jacket and started to put it on, making sure I put Sarah's bag back over my shoulders. 'Now the rest of your stuff,' I said. 'One hand.'

He put his left hand on the ground and fiddled with his belt buckle with the other. Sarah was impatient and very cold, and she snapped at him in Arabic. She must have been feeling grim, covered from head to toe with mud, leaves and pine needles, and her legs were wet, dirty and bleeding.

Lance was wearing Nike trainers, and Sarah decided to help him by pulling them off from behind. His Levis were next, and when he'd finished she stretched out on the ground, arched her back and raised her backside to get the big jeans on. She was doing up the belt and he was pulling off his T-shirt when I heard the helicopter again. The two of us looked up, which was pretty fruitless considering the tree's canopy meant we couldn't see anything. Lance's T-shirt was over his head but not his shoulders. I put my left hand on the back of his neck and rammed his face into the mud, the barrel of my pistol pressing into his neck.

The throbbing of the rotors was virtually overhead. The heli was hovering. It stayed there for several seconds, the trees flexing under the downwash. Shape, shine, shadow, silhouette, spacing and movement: those are the telltales that can betray your location. But we were in good cover; Sarah knew that, too, and continued slowly pulling on the warm clothes.

The heli moved away about fifty metres, hovered again, then moved on. The sound of its rotor blades disappeared completely. I took the muzzle away from the American's neck and told him to carry on. He finished taking off his T-shirt. Sarah took off the jacket, put on the T-shirt, and replaced the jacket. All that was left were his socks and boxers. It was Lance's turn to shiver, the thick hair on his back plastered flat by the rain.

I could see in his eyes that he was starting to flap. He must have thought he was going to be killed, and started mumbling some sort of prayer to himself. But it wasn't a plea, the tone was more of acceptance.

I said, 'It's OK, Lance, you don't need Allah yet, you're not going to die. Just shut the fuck up.'

Sarah was sorted, kneeling with her hands in her jacket pockets, wearing size eleven trainers and jeans with the gusset hanging halfway down to her knees, with turn-ups so big they looked like some sort of fashion statement.

The boy was still mumbling away to himself on his knees, bent forward with his forearms resting on the ground, his hands clasped together in prayer. He was trying his best to be the grey man.

Sarah looked at me. 'What about him?'

I said, 'Let's get moving while the heli's gone. I'll tie him to the tree with my belt. He'll be fucked off, but he'll live.'

She shook her head.

I said, 'No, just leave him. Come on, let's go. We need to make distance.'

She gave a sigh as I took the belt from the bag and kicked Lance over to the tree and began to secure him to it. An hour or two and he would free himself; if not, he deserved to die anyway. He was still muttering to himself, and as I tightened the knot he blurted out some insult to Sarah in Arabic. He was probably telling her what a bitch she was for fucking him over like this, after all they had been through together and all that shit. She ignored it. I felt like telling him I knew how he felt.

I had a quick look around to check we hadn't left anything, and started to crawl out of the shelter. Sarah followed, or at least I thought she did. The Arabic mumblings got fainter.

I was still on my hands and knees, my head just emerging from the branches, when the loud report of a weapon came from behind me. Instinct flattened me to the ground. In almost the same instant I realized it wasn't me who'd been shot and slithered out of the way.

My first thought was that he'd somehow got Sarah. I jumped

246

to my feet and ran round the tree to approach him from the other side. I started to crawl in, weapon at the ready. Pushing through the branches on my stomach, I saw him. He was still being held up by his secured hands, but his body was sagging and his legs were splayed, like the crumpled victim of a firing squad. There was no way Lance would be feeling the cold any more. Sarah had head-jobbed him with a semi-automatic. She was on her knees, putting the weapon into her jacket pocket.

What the fuck was it with this woman? Every time she was left alone with a man she landed up killing him. 'Give me the gun, Sarah . . . Give it.'

She looked up into the sky, as if I was being boring, pulled it from her pocket and threw it over to me. I crawled back out. It was pointless keeping a low voice now; half the State would know where we were. I snapped, 'What the fuck are you doing?'

'He wouldn't stop, believe me. He would try and join up with the other two or carry on himself. I know these people. I know Lance very well. Look, the other two – they know where, how and when to do the hit. What you did this morning won't stop them.' Her face had taken on a manic look. 'For fuck's sake, Nick, I'm beginning to wish I'd just killed you and opted to carry on with him.'

There was no time for debate. We'd been compromised. We had to be like animals now and run as fast as we could; it didn't matter where, we just had to get out of that immediate danger area. Only when we were a safe distance away could I stop and assess.

Assuming the shot had been heard, there would be chaos at the police control centre as it was reported over the radio net. They would just have been starting to work through all their post-incident procedures when, literally, *bang!*, another problem. Initially they'd be confused, but they'd soon figure out where it had come from, and direct the helicopter and follow-up our way.

We legged it. We could move much faster now than before, even with Sarah wearing her size-eleven Nikes. I was severely pissed off with her for what she'd done, but tried to control it.

Once you allow yourself to get angry, you stop concentrating on the aim, which in this case was to make distance. Whether or not she was lying wasn't an issue at the moment, I didn't care. The only thing that mattered right now was escape.

The helicopter swooped over the canopy. We stopped in our tracks and took cover beneath the trees. But the aircraft wasn't hovering this time, it was moving fast and low. It crossed directly overhead, blasting torrents of rain water from the trees onto our heads, then roared away at speed.

I decided to keep going in the same direction, a straight line away from the house. I wanted to find a road or some habitation. A house should mean a vehicle.

It was fully light now. Our faster pace had got some body warmth going, and if anything I was starting to overheat. Just like me, Sarah was puffing and panting as we scrabbled up the rises and stumbled headlong downhill. There was no need to explain to her what I was doing. She was actually a help, because it was so much easier to have two sets of eyes and ears.

After thirty minutes of hard running we finally hit a road. It was a single carriageway, potholed and no more than three or four metres wide. I paralleled it to the right, running through the trees about ten metres to its side. We hadn't gone far when I heard a vehicle. We stopped, got down, and I rested on my elbows and knees to keep myself out of the mud and preserve body warmth. It was approaching fast from behind us, engine roaring and tyres splashing on wet tarmac.

A blue and white appeared and sped past, its roof-mounted red and blue light bar flashing brighter than was normal in daylight because of the cloud cover. The police would have things squared away by now; they were probably placing a cordon round the whole area. They'd then either wait for us to emerge, or come in and flush us out.

The moment the cruiser disappeared from view we got up and started moving. The wind had strengthened and I could see waves of heavier rain coming in ahead. After twenty minutes of running through deeply rutted, puddled ground we came to a large open area, a perfect square of about five acres cut out of the forest, with a white cattle fence around the perimeter. Sitting in the middle, and approached by a driveway from the road, was a two-storey ranch house built of wooden slats, with a pitched roof, tiled with grey slates. A square extension had been added onto the far end, and I could see an open garage at ground level. Inside were a pickup truck, two other cars and a small powerboat on a trailer. The building and two of the three vehicles looked as if they'd seen better days.

There was no approach to the garage that avoided open ground. I guessed there would be windows on every side of the house, to take advantage of the views. Six or seven horses were loose in the field, but there was no evidence of dogs and the house itself seemed quiet enough. Maybe everybody was still tucked up in bed.

'You stay here,' I whispered to Sarah. 'I'm going to go and get a wagon. When you see me drive out, move up to the road.'

'Why aren't I coming over with you?' She sounded suspicious, as if she thought I'd get in a vehicle and just leave her stranded. If only she knew.

She was in no position to question my decisions, but I answered. 'Number one, it's quieter if I go on my own – I know what I'm doing, you don't. Number two, I don't want you killing anybody else. And number three, you have no choice. I have your documents in here.' I half turned to show her the bag on my back. 'You want me to help you, you wait here.'

The plot of land was as flat and green as a pool table, not a single fold in the ground. Checking the road for vehicles and the sky for helis, I set off across grass which was about three inches high and full of moisture, running but trying to keep as low as possible. I didn't know why, because it didn't make me any less visible, but it just seemed the natural thing to do. I was leaving a clear track in my wake through the wet grass, but I couldn't do anything about that.

I kept looking at the windows for movement. As I got closer I could see that the upstairs curtains were drawn. I wondered if Mr and Mrs Redneck were sitting in bed watching the news about last night's events down the road. For sure, there'd be more news crews at the lake by now than there were police.

Reaching the house, I bent down below a side window with open curtains. In this weather there would have been a light on if people were up and about, and there wasn't, but even so I didn't chance looking inside. I held it there for a few seconds and listened. Nothing. Now that I was close up to them I could see that the slats weren't wood at all, but aluminium painted to look that way, and the roof was just felt, masquerading as tiles.

I moved around to the opposite side of the house, towards the garage extension, making sure that I kept low to avoid the windows.

I shook my head to get the rain out of my face. There were no wet tyre marks on the garage floor or rain on the wagons. There had been no movement since at least last night.

The first thing to do was check whether any of the vehicles were alarmed. I couldn't see any warning signs, flashing LEDs, or other telltales. An alarm would probably have cost more than the two cars anyway. I tried all the doors on the vehicles, starting with the pickup truck, then the two others – a small, rusting red Dodge, a bit like a bottom-of-the-range Rover, and an elderly, olive-green estate car, with fake wood panelling along the sides that made it look like a stagecoach. Everything was locked. The rain was drumming on the garage roof as I went back to the muddy white Nissan pickup. It had a double cab, with a flat bed on the back, protected by a shaped, heavy plastic liner. I had a quick mooch in the boxes next to it against the wall, then moved aside the plastic bottles of two-stroke mix for the boat engine, looking for something to jemmy it open with.

I found a toolbox and was bending over it, moving the tools really slowly and carefully so I didn't make any noise, when there was a shout that made me jump.

'Don't move! Freeze, yo' son of a bitch!'

Whoever it was, he must have spent his life stalking animals in the woods, because I hadn't heard a sound. I didn't move a muscle. 'Keep still or I'll shoot yer so'ry ass,' he said in a really cool, calm, deep Southern drawl. He was directly behind me.

Fucking right I stood still. I also made sure he had a good view of my hands. I had a pistol tucked down the front of my jeans, and another in my jacket, but they were staying where they were. I didn't know what he was pointing at me, or even whether he had anything at all, but I wasn't going to take the chance. I stayed bent over the toolbox and kept my mouth shut; I didn't want to say anything that might antagonize him, especially in my bad American accent.

I could hear his feet scraping on the concrete floor of the garage. I listened intently; I wanted to estimate how far away he was.

'Surn of a bitch, stay whar y'are.' He sounded an oldish man, maybe in his early sixties.

He was shuffling towards me. I moved my eyes so that I could catch his reflection in the door window of the pickup. As he moved closer I could clearly see an outstretched hand holding a snub-nosed revolver.

'D'ya know whose truck this here's is, feller?'

I shook my head very slowly.

'Muh surn's. Muh surn's a State Trooper. He's out thar lookin' fer yer ass right now. But yer in muh house. You belong t'me. Surns o' bitches, shit, dammit . . .'

Either I was right – they had been watching breakfast TV – or Mr and Mrs Redneck's little boy had been on the telephone to fill him in on events.

He carried on. 'The troopers is comin' now t'drag yer ass in, feller. Shit, thet's muh surn's truck, he worked dadburned hard fer thet . . . mutherfucker, shit . . .'

I kept watching the reflection in the window. He took another couple of steps towards me, but he shouldn't have done; you never get too close to someone when you're holding a pistol – what's the point, it's designed to kill at a distance.

Another step and I could see the detail of the weapon. It was a .38, the same type as the young black guy had been buying at Jim's. As the salesman had told him, 'Just point it like your finger at the centre mass and it will take them down.' The hammer was back, which wasn't good for me. Revolvers work on a double

251

action: to fire, you have to make a very positive squeeze on the trigger, which works both actions, pulling the hammer all the way back, and letting it then go forward. That serves as the safety device on a revolver, instead of having a safety catch, which you get on most semi-automatics. But he'd cocked it; the hammer was pulled back, the first action had already been taken up – all he had to do now was gently squeeze that trigger with less than seven pounds of pressure and the thing would go off. A year-old baby can exert seven pounds of pressure with his index finger, and this was a big old boy who was pissed off and sparked up.

I remained passive. He had me; what could I say?

The reflection moved and he was almost on top of me, and then I felt cold metal in the back of my neck. He jabbed the pistol, moving it up and down, and, knowing that he had his finger on the trigger, I started to flap. I closed my eyes ready to die.

'Fuckin' surns o' fuckin' bitches,' he ranted. 'Why dirn't you fucks git a job like ev'ry other mutherfucker? . . . Shit . . . not jest come an' take . . . yer not gonna take here . . .'

I opened my eyes and looked in the window. He had his arm fully extended and the muzzle was still in contact with my neck. Either he was going to kill me by accident if that second pressure was pulled, or I was going to get fucked over well and truly once the son and his trooper mates arrived on the scene.

If I was quick enough on the initial move, I'd be safe for a second; it was what I did afterwards that would decide whether or not I lived. I was going to get caught or I was going to die, so anything I did before that was a bonus.

I didn't want him to see me taking the three deep breaths to fill my lungs with oxygen, so I just let him get on with jabbing the muzzle into my neck while I closed my eyes and got ready. He cackled at his own humour as he said, 'Muh surn's gonna kick yer sorry ass, you fuck.' He was getting more angry as he gained confidence. 'Why is you here doin' yer killin'? Git home an' do yer killin' thar . . . shit . . .' He was thinking of something to add. He found it: 'surns of bitches.'

I took the final breath and opened my eyes. Fuck it, just go for it.

ARRGGGHHHHHH!

Stepping forward with my right foot, and at the same time swivelling left on the other, I raised my left arm, bellowing like a lunatic. I was hoping for two things: that it would confuse him, and that it would also spark me up. It didn't matter to me which part of my left arm hit his weapon arm, as long as it did. My arm connected and I could no longer feel cold metal against my head.

My left forearm now had to keep contact with his weapon arm as I carried on swivelling round so that I was facing him. He was bigger than I'd expected. His unshaven face looked like crinkled leather and it was topped with a riot of uncombed grey hair. I grasped the material of whatever he was wearing on his weapon arm, trying to keep the .38 facing anywhere but at me.

A round went off, and the report echoed around the garage. He probably didn't even realize he had pulled the trigger.

I kept turning, and he started to scream back at me and holler for 'Ruby'. His face was no more than six inches from mine, and I could smell his bad breath and see his toothless mouth, wide open.

For the full two seconds my move had taken, my eyes had never left the pistol. In theory, the rules of squash apply: never take your eye off the ball. But I'd always found it hard; sometimes I reckoned it was just as effective to look at the other player, because just before he hits the ball his eyes will tell you if he's bluffing a hard one and is in fact going to hit it gently. It wasn't something I'd been taught, it was just something I found myself doing instinctively in that situation; maybe that was why I was such a crap squash player.

As I turned further, so did he. The look on the old boy's face was not a happy one. A couple of seconds ago things had been going really well for him, and yet now he thought he was about to meet his maker. His head and body were turning away from me, presenting his back, and with my right hand I was able to slam his head against the wagon. There was a thud on the window as he made contact, with me still gripping what I could now see was the blue overall sleeve on his left arm. I pushed him hard against the pickup with the weight of my whole body, knocking

253

the air out of him. I pushed with my right knee against the back of one of his kneecaps and he buckled. I held his head to control his fall.

I didn't say a word. I didn't have to. He was on his knees, spreadeagled against the wagon, his face pressed against the door. I gripped his weapon arm and shook it. The .38 clattered to the floor.

But that wasn't the end of it. This boy wasn't giving up. Spit and blood flew out of his mouth as he raged, 'You surn of a fuckin' bitch, thet's all yer want t'do, come here an' take . . . shit.'

I was worried about his wife; was Ruby on the phone to the police, or getting out the shotgun? I stepped back and drew my own pistol, kicking his left arm to get him right down on the floor. Then I delivered a couple of persuaders for him to get under the pickup. Now what? I ran.

I sprinted out of the garage, turned left past the front of the house and legged it across the grass, following the track I'd made on the way in. The rain was pelting down.

I heard a woman shout behind me, but I didn't look back. There were no shots.

I vaulted the fence and made my way through the woods to Sarah. She was on her haunches, against a tree. I collapsed next to her, panting on my hands and knees. I looked up and we exchanged a glance. What could I say? I'd fucked up. You can be so close to civilization, yet when you're wet, cold, hungry and don't exactly know where you are, it can seem so far.

There was a gap that she filled. 'What now?'

'Let me think . . .' I looked back at the house. There was no movement. Ruby was probably in the garage, dragging her husband out from under the pickup before heading back to the phone.

My mind was racing through all the options, but the decision was made for me. A cruiser ripped along the road from the opposite side of the house, a blue and white blur in the driving rain. No sirens, no lights, just a foot flat down on the gas pedal. If it was Mr and Mrs Redneck's little boy responding to the call, he wasn't going to be happy with the way I'd abused his father's Southern hospitality.

I got up and started to move. They would be following up big time, tracking the sign I'd left in the grass. I ran back the way we had come, then hung a right towards the road. At that moment I heard the helicopter rattling through the sky. We got into tree-hugging again. The moment it had flown past, and not even bothering to look behind me to check for Sarah, I started motoring through the forest. She would just have to keep up.

Reaching the edge of the wood near the road, I dropped onto my hands and knees, watched and listened. The only sounds I could hear were my own laboured breathing and the rain hammering on the tarmac and leaves. Sarah flopped down beside me.

I crawled to the very edge of the tree line and looked out. The wet, potholed, single-carriageway road was deserted.

20

We both lay there in the mud, lifting our heads and checking for movement like a pair of meerkats. I couldn't see anything, just solid walls of rain.

Finally I nodded to her. She acknowledged. I got up and sprinted across the road, but instead of going into the tree line, I cut left and started following the edge of the tarmac.

She shouted, 'Nick, what are you doing? Come on, let's get under cover!'

I turned and waved her towards me.

She hesitated a moment, then understood and ran to join me. I kept to the roadside for another thirty metres, checking backwards, forwards and upwards for movement. I chanced about ten metres more and knew I was tearing the arse out of it. I ducked to the right and moved into the tree line. Even if they followed up with dogs, it would take them a while to re-establish our trail, for the surface scent would be washed off the tarmac by the heavy rain, slowing the dogs down severely. It would then be up to the trackers to cast for sign in both directions and along both sides of the road, because for all they knew I might have doubled back. Only when, or if, they refound our trail could they get the dogs back on the scent.

For the next half-hour I picked my way through dense forest. The ground was undulating and littered with knolls; it was hard going, but excellent cover, the sort of terrain that a light aircraft might crash into and never be found. I was heading in this direction for no other reason than that I wanted to; sometimes there is no absolutely correct answer.

Every ten minutes or so the heli clattered across the sky, casting around for movement or visible sign. This time it got a bit too near. We stopped and hid, using the chance to catch our breath. Both of us were still soaked to the skin with rain and sweat. As the heli came in low over us, the trees swayed with the down-wash and another sixty gallons of rain cascaded through the canopy. My throat was dry and rasping as my chest heaved, the only positive thing being that all this effort was keeping my body core nicely heated.

Still the helicopter didn't move out of the area. He was there, somewhere; low and slow. I looked back the way we'd come and saw the ground sign we'd left. It would be easy enough even for the untrained eye to follow, but for anybody who knew what they were doing, possibly with dogs, it was a floodlit motorway.

Deep down, I knew it wouldn't take them long to find where we'd crossed the road. From there it would be simple; we were travelling through wet forest, over stinking ground, in rain and fog – perfect terrain and conditions for keeping a scent glued in position. What was more, they would be following on fresh legs and able to call up reinforcements at will, and after a while they'd be able to predict our direction of travel so that others could intercept us. Then again, maybe they didn't have dogs or trackers on the case yet; it wasn't as if such things were on twenty-four-hour standby. Visual tracking is not the most popular skill for a person to take up, and exponents are in short supply; maybe it would take them hours to mobilize somebody, and maybe they lived on the other side of the state. Maybe . . . maybe. Whatever, every man, but hopefully not his dog, would be out looking.

I had to admit to myself that I had no idea where we were going, and we were gradually exhausting ourselves. A decision had to be made: Did we hide up and wait until dark to move out of the area, preferably by vehicle? Or did we take our chances now?

The heli's blades chopped the air above us. It didn't seem to be going anywhere. This was strange; it wouldn't be able to see a thing under the canopy, and in a backwoods area like this it was unlikely to be fitted with thermal-imaging equipment. It was a full ten minutes before I heard a change in engine pitch, and the aircraft rattled off into the distance. I moved from under the tree and continued running. Our pace was slowing perceptibly. I was fucked. My footprints were getting closer and closer together as my strides shortened: to a visual tracker or trained dog it would be the encouraging sign of a slower-moving quarry. I glanced behind me. Sarah looked like death on legs.

I tried to think of positives. If you run at 10 mph for one hour in an unknown direction, you could be anywhere in a circle of just over 300 square miles. An hour later that will have become an area of 1,256 square miles. In *The Lone Ranger*, Tonto used to stop and say, 'Five wagons, two hours ago. That way, kemo sabe.' Luckily, real life isn't that easy – and Tonto lives in Arizona.

I decided to lie up and wait until last light. With no compass or stars to guide us, I could be going round in circles for weeks. During darkness, the plan would be to move to a known quantity – the road – and parallel it until I could get my hands on a vehicle.

I carried on for another ten minutes or so, with Sarah now up with me. About sixty or seventy metres away to my half right, there was something which looked as if it could work: a fallen tree on higher ground, its branches still intact but decaying. It had fallen down a sharp bank. It would give us ideal cover from view from the air as well as the ground and, just as important, it would give us cover from the elements. If the police didn't get hold of us, I didn't want the weather to finish us off. It wouldn't be long before exhaustion and cold would take their toll.

'What are we doing now?' Sarah asked. 'Why have you stopped?'

I didn't bother replying; I was looking back at the route we'd taken. Then I turned round again and looked forward at the tree, off to my half right. The ground ahead was the same as behind, rises, with lots of dead ground beyond.

I turned half left and started kicking my feet, leaving obvious sign. I wanted them to see my direction change away from the fallen tree. Sarah followed on behind, puffing and panting, struggling to keep the size-eleven trainers on her size-five feet.

Over a rise, and in the dead ground beyond, was a stream a couple of metres wide. I headed down and waded straight into the freezing water. I checked behind me and couldn't see the tree.

Sarah stood her ground on the bank. 'What are you doing?'

'Get in.'

The water came over my knees. I turned left and moved down-stream, stopping every dozen or so paces and looking back to make sure I couldn't see the tree. I had trudged about fifty metres, with Sarah splashing along behind me, before I decided this was far enough. I didn't know why, it just felt right. I got out on the far side of the stream and stood still. I could hear Sarah's trainers squelching as she came up beside me, visibly thankful for the rest.

I gave myself a minute to collect my thoughts, looking at her, soaked and bedraggled, fir needles splattered on her face, twigs in her hair. Not exactly how she'd choose to appear at one of her embassy parties, but she was doing well; she'd obviously kept herself in shape.

'Ready?'

She nodded and took a deep breath to prepare.

We moved up and down for another 300 metres or so, in a direct line away from the stream. Sarah was starting to feel the strain, and I could only move at her speed. I decided that this was far enough; it was time for one last bit of deception. I stopped and moved over to an outcrop of rock. Sarah came up level with me, and we both had our hands on our knees, panting for breath as if we'd just finished a 200-metre sprint.

'Sarah, take off your knickers.'

She looked at me blankly. She'd heard me say that before, but not in a situation like this. 'What?'

'Your knickers, I need them.' I'd already taken off my jacket and was pulling off my shirt. I was after the T-shirt underneath. Her expression told me that she wasn't sure about this. 'Sarah, trust me. They must have dogs.' She didn't bother to ask, just

259

moaned to herself about getting undressed. In any other situation it would have been quite nice to watch her drop her jeans and peel off her underwear, but that was the story of my life: wrong time, wrong place.

I got my shirt back on and shivered as it touched my skin. Sarah was busy doing up her jeans. I picked up her knickers and placed them with my T-shirt between the rocks and a bush. If we were being tracked visually or by dogs they would get to this point. The mutt doesn't know what's really happening and what exactly he's looking for; to him it's just a game. A dog can confuse an item of clothing with the quarry and assume victory with its find. Then the handler has to get the dog sparked up again before it will continue.

Dogs pick up scent in two different ways: from the air, and from contact with the ground, trees, plants and buildings. Airborne scents don't last long; they are quite quickly blown away by the wind. Ground scent, however, can be obvious to a dog for anything up to forty-eight hours, and can be generated not only by leaving your smell on things you touch, but by your movement itself. If you're walking on grass, or pushing through vegetation, you'll crush leaves and stems with every step.

Even on bare ground your footprints will release air and tiny quantities of moisture which have been trapped in the earth, and they smell quite different from the air above ground. From your 'scent footprints', a dog can even tell which direction you are moving in, because as you push off each step with your toes, the front of the scent print is more obvious than the heel, and it doesn't take long for a well-trained dog to work out what that means.

Just as each person's footprints look slightly different to the human eye, so does the mixture of scents in a smell footprint to a dog. If he's really switched on, he might even be able to track one individual where there are a number of people travelling together.

A dog could out-hear, out-smell and out-run me. But I could out-think him. 'The strongest odour is from the sweat glands,' I said to Sarah. 'But at the moment I think your underwear will smell more than your T-shirt.' I grinned. 'Nothing personal.'

She thought about it and nodded; she had to agree on that one.

'OK, follow me. Step by step. Don't touch anything, not even to lean on.' I started to pick my way over the outcrop, sticking to the highest rocks to keep out of any areas where scent could be trapped. Hopefully, they would be washed clean by the rain.

We moved into dead ground, carefully picking our way to prevent leaving sign. I started to move back down to the river. I got seventy-five metres short of the water and moved left until I saw the fallen tree.

From nowhere, the heli reappeared.

We hurtled under the trees, hugging them as if they were long-lost relations. I heard the groan of the rotors again, moving deliberately over the top of the canopy. It got so close I could feel the downwash. I suddenly made sense of what it was doing – it was following the line of the stream, maybe patrolling any exposed waterways because that was all they could see down here. It moved off and so did we.

The fallen tree looked quite promising. There were enough branches to hide under, and we could even get under the trunk where it lay clear of the ground. It was going to be a squeeze, but we'd be needing to huddle together anyway to share body heat.

Sarah was down on her knees trying to catch her breath. She searched my face as I motioned her in. 'Why aren't we running?'

'I'll explain later, just get under cover.'

She squeezed in and I followed. The underside of the trunk was just as wet and cold as the open air, but we were hidden and had a chance to rest. I wasn't too sure any more if this was a good decision, but it was too late to worry now.

I made sure I could see the first turning point before the stream by scraping away the mud between the trunk and the ground. I'd used the same tactic time and again in the jungle, where it was standard procedure to 'loop the track' and put in an instant ambush on your own trail. If we were being followed, they would pass no more than sixty or seventy metres away and move half left, away from us and into the dead ground. There they'd find the stream, and start trying to cast over the other side to pick up our scent or ground sign again. That would give us vital time in which to act; if I saw dogs while lying up, I'd just have to make a run for it.

The heli passed overhead yet again, this time at speed, but we were well concealed. It could stay there all day if it wanted to, it wouldn't make any difference. Sarah was looking at me, waiting for an explanation.

'We wait until last light and go back towards the road.' I pointed uphill. 'That way.'

She wasn't enjoying this outing, but she cuddled into me. I was wedged against the trunk, looking out; she was behind me, her body spooned against mine with her arms around my chest. I could feel her warmth. I tried hard not to think about how much I liked her depending on me. Continuing to look out, I tilted my head towards her. 'Concealment is our best weapon. It's going to be cold, and you'll think you're about to die, but you won't – as long as we keep close and keep each other warm. Do you understand that?'

I felt her nodding, then she squeezed herself a little more tightly against me. Even in these circumstances, I had to admit it felt good.

There were three situations I'd hated all of my life: being wet, cold or hungry. Four, if you included having to shit in the field. All our lives, even as children, those are the three things that most of us try to avoid, but here I was, doing it again, and I couldn't help feeling that, at thirty-eight, I should be seriously concentrating on getting a life. The one I had seemed to be going nowhere fast.

As the minutes ticked by my body started to cool, even with Sarah snuggling in behind me, and the ground itself seemed to become colder and soggier. I could feel her body warmth at the points where she was making contact with me, but the rest of me was freezing. Every time she fidgeted to get comfortable, I could feel the cold attack the newly exposed area.

She fidgeted again and muttered, 'Sorry, cramp,' as she tried to stretch out her leg and tip up her feet in an effort to counter it.

I kept stag, listening to the stream, the wind in the treetops, the

262

rain dropping onto the leaves and debris on the forest floor. There was a murky, calf-high mist permeating the woods which reminded me of stage smoke. That could work either for us or against us: it would give us some visual cover if we were forced to move, but it was also good for the dogs.

As time passed without any hint of a follow-up, I started to feel better about our situation. I looked at my watch: seven forty-six. Only another twelve hours or so until last light. Doesn't time fly when you're enjoying yourself? At least the Baby-G surfer was keeping cheerful.

Sarah had settled down and wanted to talk. 'Nick?'

'Not now.' I needed time to think. I wanted to take a long hard look at what she'd told me, and to think about all that had happened. Was she bluffing about the Netanyahu plot? How did they plan to kill him? How had she been planning to stop them?

My head was full of questions, but no answers. Now wasn't the time to ask. Tactically, noise had to be kept to a minimum, and besides, I needed to keep my head clear for the task in hand. I had to get out of here alive, preferably with Sarah still alive, too, for there was still another job to do.

21

An hour later Sarah and I were chilled to the bone and shivering violently. I tried to combat the cold by tensing up all my muscles and then releasing them; that worked for a while, but I was soon shaking again. I didn't have a clue how Sarah was coping, and I didn't care now; my head was in hyper mode trying to work out my options. Was she telling the truth? Should I call London if I got out of this? Should I get help from within the US? From Josh, maybe? No, he wouldn't be back from the UK yet.

I heard a noise and hoped that I hadn't.

Peering through the mud hole, I opened my jaw to improve my hearing. My heart sank. I turned my head to look at Sarah, who was just about to tell me that she'd heard the dogs, too. The sounds were coming from the direction of our approach. I couldn't see them yet, but they would be on us. It was only a matter of time.

My eyes and puckered lips told her to stay quiet, then I moved my head back to the hole in the mud.

Sarah put her mouth against my ear. 'Come on, let's go.' I whispered for her to shut the fuck up; they were coming over the brow of the rise. There was a gang of them. The first thing I noticed was the two big snarling dogs on long leads, steam rising off their wet coats, their handler fighting to keep control. The good thing was that they were German Shepherds; they weren't tracker dogs, but 'hard' dogs – there to bridge the gap between us and the pursuers if we were spotted. The other good thing was that they didn't look quite so big with their coats wet against their skin.

The pursuit consisted of a six-man police team. One of them had a springer spaniel on a lead, its nose to the ground, loving the whole business. Apart from the tracker-dog handler, none of them was dressed for the hunt; they were wearing just their normal brown waterproof jackets, and two of them were even in shoes, with mud splattered up their pressed brown and yellow-striped trousers.

They passed us in a haze of dog noise and steam as our tracks took them half left, away from us and towards the stream. The moment they were in dead ground I turned to Sarah. 'Now we go.'

I squeezed under the trunk and immediately broke into a run in a line directly away from the river. Maybe my hide-until-dark plan hadn't been such a good idea after all. The only option now was to outrun the team. It was unlikely the dogs would tire, but they could only go as fast as their handlers, so I would just have to get them exhausted. The police had looked wet and hassled, and were breathing hard. Even in our shit state we should be fitter than they were.

I pushed on, looking for a point where we could hide a change in direction. It might not stop them, but it would slow them down. After close to thirty minutes of hard running through thick woodland I had to stop and wait for Sarah to catch up; she was panting deeply, clouds of her breath fusing with the steam coming off her head. When we moved off again I checked my watch. It was ten thirty-nine.

We went for it for another solid hour. Sarah was lagging further and further behind, but I pushed the pace. I knew she would keep going. When we used to train together in Pakistan she would never give up, even on a silly fun run. And then it was only her pride at stake, now it was a bit more than that.

We were in low ground and I could see sky about 200 metres in front of us, through the tree trunks. I heard the sound of a car, and then splashing on tarmac.

I crawled up to the tree line. It wasn't a major road, just a single carriageway in each direction, and not particularly well kept, probably because it wasn't used that much – the sort of back-woods road that looked as if the tarmac had just been poured from the back of a slowly moving truck and left to get on with it. It might even be the same road as the last one, there was no way of telling. The rain wasn't firing down like a power shower any more, just a constant drizzle.

I still didn't have a clue where we were, but that didn't matter. You're never lost, you're only in a different place from the one you wanted, and at a different time. Sarah had crawled up next to me and was lying on her back. Her hair had clumped together, so I could see the white skin of her skull. We looked as if we both had our personal steam machines strapped to us.

I decided to turn right – it could have been left or right, it didn't really matter – and just follow the road; at some stage we'd find a vehicle, or at least discover where we were, then work out what we were going to do. 'Ready?'

She looked up and gave a nod and a sniff, and we crawled backwards, deeper into the tree line. I got to my feet and she accepted my outstretched hand. I hauled her upright and we started running again, paralleling the road. After only a minute or two I heard a car; I got down and watched as it splashed through the potholes, lights on dipped, side windows misted up and the wipers on overtime. As soon as it had disappeared from view we were up and running.

The next vehicle was a truck loaded with logs; its wheels sank into an enormous pothole and threw up a wall of water which fell just short of us. There seemed to be a vehicle of some description every five minutes or so. Most were going in our direction, which was a good sign. I didn't know why, but it felt that way.

After another two kilometres or so I began to see lights forward of us and on the opposite side of the road. As we got closer, I could see that it was a gas station-cum-small general store with a tall neon sign saying, 'Drive Thru – Open' in orange letters. It was a one-storey, flat-roofed, concrete building with three pumps on the forecourt, protected by a high tin canopy on a pair of steel pillars. The place had probably been state of the art when it was built in the Sixties or early Seventies, but now the white paint was grey and peeling, and the whole fabric of the building was falling apart. I knew how it felt.

There were windows on the three sides of the shop that I could see; above the ones at the front were large, red, raised letters telling me the place was called Happy Beverage & Grocery. Faded posters advertised coffee and corn dogs, Marlboro and Miller Lite. They were all the same, these sorts of places, family-run as opposed to franchised mini-markets, and I knew exactly what this one would smell like inside – a mixture of stale card-board and cona coffee, fighting with the aroma of the corn dogs as they rotated in their glass oven. All rounded off, of course, with a good layer of cigarette smoke. The main sound effect would be the hum of fridges working overtime.

Even the pumps outside were early Seventies. This place was in decline; maybe years ago, when the road was first built, it was a major hot spot, but once the freeways had been laid to move the growing population of North Carolina, the traffic went else-where. Happy Beverage & Grocery looked like it was already history.

I stopped just short of the Drive Thru sign on the other side of the road and got down. Sarah joined me, and I told her to wait where she was. I crawled forward. I'd been right; now that I could see through the windows my eyes hit on packets of every-thing from Oreos to Cheerios, and a line of glass-doored fridges which were less than a quarter full of milk cartons and Coke cans. A large glass pot of coffee was stewing away on a hob, alongside a whole range of polystyrene cups, from two pints down to half a pint, depending on how awake you wanted to be. If you wanted cream, it would be powdered, without a doubt.

On her own, as far as I could see, and sitting down behind the counter, was a large woman in her mid-thirties. I could only see her top half; she had peroxide-blond 'big hair', which was prob-ably kept that way with a can of lacquer a day; she must have been one of those Southern women the radio programme had been talking about. The T-shirt was probably her daughter's,

267

going by its tightness. I couldn't see her bottom half, but no doubt she'd be wearing leggings that were about four sizes too small. She was eating a corn dog and reading a magazine, and somehow managing to smoke at the same time.

I crawled back to Sarah.

'Can we take a vehicle?' she said.

'Not yet. It doesn't look as if she has one.'

Beyond the shop was another tarmac road that met this one at a T-junction. The only thing that interested me was that, where you have junctions, you nearly always have signposts.

We headed for the junction. The neon light was reflecting off the rainswept road and the hard standing of the pump area. I had to remind myself that it was still daytime. The sign said, 'Drive Thru', and I'd do just that, given half a chance.

I started to envy the woman with big hair. She was sitting in there with a TV or radio on, and the heaters would be blasting away to keep the condensation off the windows; in fact, she was probably keeping so hot that she might need to knock back a Coke after the corn dog. I wondered how she'd keep the cigarette in her mouth.

We passed the shop and carried on to the junction. I motioned for Sarah to wait, but she'd got her breath back, and with it some of her old habits. She'd never liked being ordered around and not being part of the show. She came with me.

I moved forward the last ten metres and spotted a signpost, green tin on a tin stake. To my left, the way we had come, wasn't signed; to my right was a place called Creedmore, which was no good to me – I didn't know it from a hole in the ground. But I knew where Durham was. It was just west of the airport; lots of people and traffic, somewhere we could get lost. The sign said that the road facing me was going that way.

It passed the gas station at the junction on the left, went uphill for about half a mile, with muddy drainage ditches on each side, then disappeared to the right behind a line of tall firs. That was where I wanted to go once I'd lifted a vehicle, but before I did anything I had to make sure the woman couldn't call for help. My eyes followed the phone lines from the building across the junction. They paralleled the road running from my left to right.

I moved in the Creedmore direction, about twenty metres beyond the junction, and crawled back up to the road, looked and listened. Absolute silence. I got to my feet, nodded at Sarah and we sprinted across. Once back in the trees, I followed the phone lines until I found a pole about five metres short of the junction.

I started taking my belt off, and asked Sarah for hers. This time she didn't question me. She followed the line of my gaze as I studied the top of the pole. 'Are you going up there?'

'I want to cut the line to the gas station.'

'Are we going to rob it?'

Sometimes she only had a nodding relationship with reality. I stopped pulling my belt off and looked at her. 'Are you serious?' I wondered about what had happened to all those expensive years of university training. She had enough brain power to move a glass without even touching it, but sometimes she didn't seem to have even an Eleven Plus in common sense.

'We're just going to get a car and get the fuck out of here,' I said. 'We have guests arriving, remember?' I mimed a dog biting with my hand.

I took her belt and buckled the two together to make one big loop. Hers was the American's heavy biker's belt, with a Harley-Davidson logo that said, 'Live to ride, ride to live'. I dropped the loop at the bottom of the pole, hooked my feet inside either end, gripped the pole with my hands, and started to climb. I'd learned how to do this from a documentary on the South Pacific, when I'd seen blokes use similar devices to climb coconut trees. You slid your feet up as high as you could, keeping the strap taut, then pressed down until it gripped. It was then a matter of reaching up and gripping the pole with both hands, lifting your feet again, and so on. That was the theory; the pole was so wet and slippery, however, that it took me several attempts to master it. At the end of the day, though, I was rather impressed with myself; if ever I was marooned in Polynesia, I wouldn't go hungry.

I heard the hiss of tyres and the drone of an engine getting closer. My heart missed a couple of beats while I wondered how I'd explain myself, then both sounds changed direction and died

269

as the car turned and headed towards Durham. It happened twice more. Each time, I stopped and waited until the vehicle had gone. At least the treetops gave me some cover.

I had just another couple of feet to go when I heard a fourth vehicle approaching, but this time from the direction of Durham. It was going slowly and coming close.

I looked down for Sarah, but she was already moving away from the pole and into cover.

The car drew up at what I guessed was the junction and stopped. I heard a door open and the sound of radio traffic. It had to be a police cruiser.

I couldn't reach down for my weapon, because it was taking all my strength and grip just to stop myself sliding back down the pole. I wondered about climbing up the last couple of feet so I could rest on a cross spar, but the way my luck was going I'd probably fuck it up and come hurtling down like Fireman Sam and land on their heads.

I heard a burst of laughter and looked down again. Sarah was nowhere to be seen, but a smoky-bear hat was, covered in clear plastic, shaped so it kept the felt dry. It moved into the woods, above a dark-brown raincoat that stuck out at the sides. State troopers have zips up the sides of their coats to enable them to draw their pistols easily, but this guy wasn't doing that, he was undoing his front zip. I saw his knees jerk as he released himself, then the sound of piss hitting the tree just a few feet below me. Steam rose in front of the hat. I didn't want to make the slightest sound. I didn't even want to swallow. My fingers were starting to lose their grip on the rain-slicked pole.

I searched frantically for the trooper's mate. I couldn't see him; he must have stayed in the car, as you do when it's raining. I could see raindrops ricocheting off the garage roof, glistening in the light from the Drive Thru sign. The stream of urine against the tree subsided as he finished off, then he let go a resounding fart.

I started sliding. I pressed down hard on the belt with my feet, and gripped the pole like a drowning man. The sounds below had stopped, and I watched him jigging up and down to shake off the drops. He packed himself away, checked his coat, and strode off.

I heard the troopers joking to each other. The car door slammed, and then they drove off. I let out all the air I'd been holding in my lungs, inching myself further up the pole to increase my range of vision. The cruiser was finally driving into the gas station. Why the fuck didn't he go in there in the first place? Maybe he was trying to chat up the woman and the last thing he wanted was for her to hear him farting away and stinking the place out.

I reached the top and hooked my left arm around the cross spar. I took a few deep breaths to calm myself down, then looked for Sarah. She was emerging from the bush she'd been hiding in, and I wondered if she knew how lucky she'd been: it looked a very inviting bush, and she might easily have got drenched by old fartypants.

I followed the telephone line to make sure it was the one to the gas station, reached down and retrieved the Leatherman from my pocket. Where these lines come in to a pole, they get hooked up to take the tension from the line, and then there's a nice little loose bit which carries on through. I leaned out, squeezing hard with the rubber soles of my feet, got the pliers part of the Leatherman over the line, and snipped. Then it was just a case of sliding down the pole nice and slowly so I didn't land up with half a ton of splinters in my arms and legs.

Sarah was straight in at me: 'Give me a gun, Nick. What if he'd seen you?'

It made sense but I felt uneasy. Giving Sarah a weapon seemed to be a lot like giving Popeye spinach. On the other hand, if he'd spotted me she could have done something about it. I still wasn't sure whether she would fuck me over, but decided she still needed me too much. I'd let her have it for now.

I got Lance's semi-automatic, 9mm Eastern-bloc thing out of my jacket and handed it over. She said a sincere 'Thanks' as she pushed back the topslide half an inch and checked to see if there was a round in the chamber.

The cruiser was driving out of the gas station and coming back in our direction. We both got down, and she used the time to put her belt back on. The blue and white passed us heading towards Creedmore; maybe they were helping to man a roadblock or something further up the road.

I wanted her to stay where she was while I went back to the gas station to hijack a vehicle. She insisted on coming with me. 'Listen,' I said, 'a man and a woman turning up at a gas station, stealing a vehicle – don't you think there's a bit of a chance they'd make a connection with the lake?'

'Nick, I'm coming with you. I'm not going to take the chance of us getting split up and this all going wrong. We're going to stay together.'

She was right; without realizing it, she had reminded me what I was here to do. If there was a drama with the police or whoever, and it was obvious I was about to lose control, I would have to kill her before they could get her. Not the ideal option, but at least she'd be dead. Looking at her with my not-happy-about-it face on, I gave in to her demand. 'Fuck it, come on then.'

We finished doing up our belts, moved back up the road for more distance and crossed. We turned right and paralleled to a point where I could get a clear view of the pumps and the shop again.

One car, a white Nissan saloon, was already on the forecourt, but it was four up, with two couples in their mid-twenties. The driver had just started the engine and out he rolled. I heard a distinctive *ding-ding* as the tyres ran over a rubber tube sensor. He got to the road, stopped, turned his wipers and dipped lights on, laughing with the rest of them – probably about the woman with the corn dog – turned left and off they went. We lay there, waiting in the rain.

During the next ten minutes, two news vans with satellite dishes scuttled past along the road, headlights blazing, windscreen wipers working furiously, on their way to get the story.

Another car rolled onto the forecourt. It was a Toyota, full of a family. I was half up, ready to go for it, like a big cat watching the herd. The car was ideal, a normal family saloon. Dad got out and, avoiding the rain, ran straight into the shop. I saw him give Big

Hair a few bills, then he came out again and filled up. I decided against. I was looking at the family – two kids in the back, window half steamed up, the kids beating each other up, the mother turning round and shouting at them. There were just too many people in the car. It would be a nightmare to drag two screaming kids from the car.

Ding-ding. They took the Durham road.

Sarah looked over at me. 'I thought we were in a hurry?'

Big Hair was walking across to the machine to get herself another bucket of coffee. She went and sat back by the till, next to the window, looking out, wistfully stirring her bucket with a spoon. I was right, it was packet creamer. Perhaps she dreamed that one day Clint Eastwood would drive onto her forecourt, come in to pay for gas, and bang, *The Bridges of Happy Beverage County*. Until then, nice work if you can get it.

A sign to the left of the shop entrance announced, '24 Hour Video Surveillance', together with the fact that they only carried fifty dollars in the register and the rest was slipped into a night safe that the attendant didn't have access to. I turned to Sarah. 'When we go to lift the wagon, I want you to get your T-shirt and pull it over your head, so you can only just see out of it.'

Ding-ding. Another vehicle drove in towards the pumps from our left. This time it was a really old van, late Seventies, early Eighties, the sort of thing Mr T and the A Team used to run around in, but a very tired grey. The windows were half steamed up, so I couldn't see how many were inside, but as soon as the driver opened the door I knew this was the one. He was in his early forties, and the important thing was that he got out and didn't take the ignition key with him, but just waved at the woman. He must be a local, because he was trusted enough to fill up and pay afterwards.

We got back into our big-cat positions, and I studied our prey. He was wearing a pair of green overalls that had seen better days, with oil stains and rips in the knees. His baseball cap should have been white but needed burning more than bleaching now. He was skinny and of average height, with about three days' stubble and four years' worth of wet or very greasy hair over his shoulders.

273

The tank was full, the filler cap went back on. I whispered, 'You ready?'

She nodded. He turned and, with his hands working their way into his overalls for money, jogged towards the shop. I jumped to my feet and started to run. With my left hand I pulled my T-shirt up over my face, and so did she. We must have looked like a couple of sperm. I kept my eyes moving between the van and the shop. I didn't really bother about what Sarah was doing; the plan was for her to go to the near side of the van, to the passenger door; I was to go round the rear, because I wanted to hide myself as much as possible, then get in the driver's seat and go for it.

The glass panels had been smashed out of the back doors and were covered with cardboard, and the whole thing was a rust bucket. I turned the corner of the van and moved along the side towards the driver's door. I had to skip over the loop of the pump lines and slipped on the diesel-stained floor. I recovered without falling and got to the door. Still holding the T-shirt over my head with my left hand, I got hold of the door handle in my right. It was a rickety, rusty old thing, hardly any chrome left on it; I pulled and it all but came away in my hand, hanging on by one edge.

The window on the other side was misted up and I couldn't see what Sarah was doing. All I knew was that she wasn't getting in. She must have the same problem; her handle must be busted.

The driver's window was down about three-quarters of the way. That must be how he got in – just reach in and open up from the inside. I jumped up slightly, got my right hand in . . . and then chaos. The furious barking from the back of the wagon made me jump back as if I'd been given the full twenty seconds with a Tazer.

I glanced towards the shop. The guy was staring out, mouth wide open. Someone trying to nick his van must have been the last thing he expected. The black thing in the back of the van was leaping up and down, going ballistic. I had to put my hand inside again; it had to be done, I was committed now. I reached in, yelling for Sarah to do something.

I was jumping up and down, trying to find and grab the inside handle, the dog was reacting as if it had had to wait three days for lunch, and to the left of me the distraught owner was coming out of the shop shouting, 'My dawg! My dawg!'

'Sarah, fucking do something!'

She did. I heard a loud, quick double tap from Lance's 9mm.

It couldn't get worse than this. I jumped away from the window, leaving the dog in the van going apeshit, and ran round to the front of the vehicle. 'Sarah, fucking stop shooting! Stop!' Then I realized she wasn't firing at the driver, she was drawing down on the two German Shepherds that had come out of the treeline and were now about five metres away from giving us the good news. It had just got worse.

She took one down; it fell over itself and kicked around on the ground, yelping. The other one kept coming. Sarah turned to fire but it was too close to me now. My right hand flew down to draw my weapon at the same time as my left went to pull up my bomber jacket so that I could get to the pistol. It was too late for both of us.

It's pointless trying to evade an attacking dog so close; without a weapon, you can't do anything about immobilizing the fucker until it's committed itself to an attack. You've got to let the thing sink its teeth into you, and take it from there.

I had to get him onto me. I turned half left, let go of the bottom of my jacket and presented my forearm, still trying to get to my pistol with my right.

He didn't want to miss this. He leapt up, his jaws opening with a deep growl, his lips pulled back to bare his teeth so he got a good bite first time. I saw his eyes roll back as he launched himself at me.

I stood my ground and braced myself for the hit. I felt his saliva fly onto my face as he opened up and his head flicked back.

There were probably other things going on, but they were lost on me now. I couldn't hear anything but the snarling of my attacker. I felt the weight of the dog hit me, and then him closing his jaws on my arm. His teeth sank straight through the jacket into the skin of my forearm and I started to shout. 'Sarah! Sarah!' I wanted her to come and shoot this fucking thing. 'Sarah!'

275

I staggered backwards with his weight, and he came with me. I got my hand around the pistol grip; not completely, but enough to pull it out of my jeans. The dog was jumping up on me, trying to get me to the ground, his hind legs scrambling against my legs and waist. His legs hit my hand and the weapon fell. 'Sarah!'

There was fearsome pain as his teeth tore into my skin. It was like having multiple injections with pen-sized syringes. I had to let it happen. I had to make sure the dog had confidence in himself, that he sensed an easy victory. If I went with the flow, he'd keep his teeth in one place, thinking he had me, he wouldn't thrash around all over the place. Forget the old wives' tales about grabbing a foreleg in each hand and splitting them apart: it only works with chihuahuas – and that's assuming you can catch the little shit in the first place. In real life dogs are like monkeys, they're much stronger than they look.

I continued to move back under its weight as the German Shepherd jumped up and snarled. I could smell his raw-meat-eating breath mixed with mud and the shit on his coat from the follow-up. He took a deeper grip on my arm and I screamed out for Sarah again as I felt more flesh being mangled. She was nowhere to be seen.

I heard several gunshots as I staggered back towards the driver's side of the van. I was trying to look and act submissive; I didn't want to fight this fucking thing, I just wanted Sarah to come round and hose him down. The dogs' handler and the police wouldn't be far behind. We needed to get moving.

The animal's growl changed tone as he shook his head from side to side like a mad thing, trying to get a deeper grip. His rear legs were now on the floor, with his front pads on my chest, walking back with me like a circus performer, still attempting to join his jaws together, but through my arm. Now the black thing inside the van sparked up again as I heard more gunshots, but there was no instant, miraculous release of the grip on my arm. It wasn't going to happen. I'd have to do it on my own.

The dog was feeling really confident now; he knew he'd got me. I bent down and, with my right hand, grabbed hold of his left rear leg. The limb twitched as if he was doing an Irish jig as he tried to kick away.

I started to pull the back leg up towards me. The dog was confused and pissed off, biting more and moving his head from left to right. I was grappling to keep hold of his leg. It was dancing away like Michael Flatley on speed.

I got a firmer grip on the spindly bit at the bottom of the dog's leg and, with my right arm, pulled it up as hard as I could towards my chest, at the same time starting to turn. The dog yelped with surprise, and I started to pirouette, as if I was spinning a child in a game. I did three, four, five turns, and the dog started to rise with the centrifugal force, anchored by its teeth in my arm and my hand on his leg. He had to make a decision, and he did: he let go of my arm. I didn't reciprocate by letting go of the leg; I kept hold now with both hands and swung him round and round as violently as I could. Still spinning, I managed to take two steps towards one of the concrete pillars supporting the forecourt canopy. On the third step, the dog's head connected with the pillar. There was a thud and a weak yelp and I let go. My own momentum carried me on round for another one and a half turns. My head was spinning as I tried to get my bearings.

I found the van. Sarah was sitting in the cab, firing out of the window. I screamed at her, 'The door! The door!' She leaned across and opened it up. I looked down; my pistol was by the pump line. Bending down to pick it up, and keeping bent to avoid getting hit, I half jumped, half collapsed, into the driver's seat and slammed the door closed. As I did, the black thing in the back tried to scramble over the driver's seat.

Sarah shouted, 'Let's go. Come on, let's go!'

I was still in a semi stoop over the steering wheel, trying to present a smaller target, when the police started firing back at us.

All the windows were steamed up, probably from the dog's panting, which was good for us, because at least it hid us from the video. Just as well, as the T-shirt ploy had gone to ratshit the moment the dogs arrived on the scene.

I hit the ignition and the engine turned over, but it failed to engage. It sparked up on the second go. Sarah fired a few more rounds towards the tree line. The mutt behind me wasn't biting, but it was making more noise than the weapon reports.

The shots that hit the van reminded me of being in a helicopter under fire; because it's so loud inside the aircraft, you don't know you're being attacked until you see holes suddenly appearing in the airframe, accompanied by a dull *ping* as the rounds penetrate.

The driver was screaming his head off inside the shop, jumping up and down, but no way was he coming out until the shooting stopped. The woman was on the phone, shouting into the useless receiver, and as we rolled off the forecourt the driver started running along inside the shop, keeping up with us, his arms waving in the air as he screamed at the top of his voice. It was wasted on us. He was inside the shop and his fucking dog was making enough noise to drown the roar of a helicopter.

Ping. Sarah was still screaming, 'Come on, come on, come on!' And the dog was adding his tuppence worth. He wanted out. Didn't we all.

I turned left onto the road. There was a coffee-holder on the dash, with a half-full poly cup of coffee in it, with a cigarette butt floating on the top. As the van lurched, the whole lot went over my jeans. Then, surreally, the radio suddenly came on of its own accord. Sarah fired a few more rounds into the tree line. There was a return.

I looked in the wing mirror. The police were on the road, assuming proper firing positions. I put my foot down.

I jerked my thumb at the dog and shouted at Sarah, 'Sort that fucking thing out!'

I turned left again and started to drive up the hill. I looked behind me and saw this big black mangy thing. Fuck knows what it was, just a wet, dank dog in the back, jumping up at the newspaper Sarah was trying to hit and distract it with, barking and yelping away at us both.

We started to take the right-hand bend in the road. The moment we were out of sight of the junction and shop I hit the brakes. I yelled, 'Get that fucking thing out!'

'How?'

'Just get it out!'

She opened the door and tried to grab hold of the dog, but it was already scrabbling its way out, its claws tearing against her seat. It clambered over and fucked off. It probably hadn't been trying to have a go at us at all, it had just been frantic to get back to its owner.

She closed the door and I hit the gas pedal. I'd noticed some bags and stuff in the back. 'Why don't you check that out?'

She didn't need telling again. She was straight in there.

22

'Is there a map?' My arm was killing me as I gripped the steering wheel. The wagon's heating system wasn't up to it, so I used my sleeve to wipe the condensation from the windscreen. Even the wipers only worked on half speed. At least now I could sort of see where I was going, even if I wasn't too sure where that was.

The bend eventually straightened out and trees loomed up on either side. Above them, all I could see was thick grey cloud. Great; the worse the weather, the less the chance of the heli still operating.

'Nothing, just crap.' Sarah was back in her seat. She wound down the window and started to adjust the wing mirror to keep a check behind us. I kept my foot down, but the vehicle was only making about 60 mph with the wind behind it, the threadbare tyres not exactly gripping the road big time. All the shit in the back was rattling, and bits of paper were flying around in the draught rushing through the open windows. I just hoped the brake pads were in better shape than the bits of the wagon I could see.

She tried to pull open the glove compartment on her side, which probably hadn't been done for years. It gave way, and out spilled bits of fishing wire, lighters, greasy old garage receipts, all sorts. But no map. She shouted, 'Shit, shit, shit!' I kept quiet, letting her frustration play itself out.

I drove on for about three miles, during which we didn't say a word to each other. We got to a T-junction with the same sort of road. There were no signposts. I turned right.

I was feeling exposed. I didn't know if the police back at the gas station had comms, which would depend on whether they had relay boards in the area to bounce radio signals off. I couldn't help a smile: Metal Mickey's head would have come in handy.

I shouted at her so I could be heard above the noise of the wind. 'Did you drop any of the police?'

She was wiping the wing mirror. She seemed to have calmed down a bit. 'I don't know, I don't think so. Maybe.'

I started to feel even more depressed. Whatever had happened, if we didn't get out of the area very soon and hide up, we'd be in a world of shit.

Less than two minutes later the chance came when I saw dipped headlights in front of us. 'I'm going to take it, Sarah. Make sure you don't say a word, OK?'

She nodded. 'What do I do?'

'Just point the gun at whoever's in there. *Do not* shoot anyone. Just keep your finger off the trigger . . . please.'

I slowed down to about 20 mph and swung the van left, blocking the road. The car kept coming towards us. I couldn't see how many were in it, but it was a blue four-door saloon.

Sarah was waiting for instructions. 'Come out this side and follow me. We have broken down, OK?'

I jumped out, trying to watch the car as well as listen for a heli. The car slowed. It was a Mazda, one up, and going by the big hair blocking half the windscreen she was the twin sister of the woman at the gas station. She wasn't too happy about what was going on. I had to be quick, in case she reached for a weapon; for all I knew, she might be one of Jim's best customers.

The car stopped. I ran over to the driver's side with a very thankful face on. She hit her window button and let it down only a couple of inches, but at least she wasn't going for her handbag or the glove compartment.

I got to the window and drew down on her, screaming, 'Look down! Look down!' My accent was getting worse.

She was maybe in her thirties. Her hair must have taken all day to tease into that beehive. Her make-up was about two millimetres thick and looked like wet cement now she'd started to cry.

I yelled, 'Out, out!'

The door was locked. I kicked it and made out like a madman, which wasn't far from the truth. She finally relented; Sarah heard the clunk of the central locking and started moving towards the car as the woman got out. I motioned with my hand for her to take the driver's seat; she passed the woman, who was standing on the road sobbing her heart out. 'I have babies. Please don't kill me, please. Take the car, take the car. Take my money. Please don't kill me.'

I wanted to tell her, Shut up. You're not going to die. I'm playing the madman because I want to scare you; that way you don't go for a weapon, and we all stay alive.

Sarah was in, door closed; I ran round to the other side and joined her. Before I'd even shut the door she was slamming the car into a three-point turn. I looked under my legs to see what I was sitting on. It was Big Hair's bag. No point in fucking her up completely; I got the barrel of the pistol hooked in the bag and threw it out to her, just as Sarah finished a really bad turn with lots of braking and tyres screaming in the wet.

'Get your foot down.'

She didn't need any prompting for that.

The car interior smelled of fresh perfume and coffee. A large polystyrene cup with a lid was resting in the console holder; I lifted it out and gave it a shake. It was half full and the contents were still warm. I took a couple of sips and handed it over. The air-conditioning was on; I turned a couple of dials and it soon changed to hot, hot, hot.

'Where to, Nick? Where am I going?'

I wasn't sure. 'Just keep going until we see a sign.'

Ten minutes later we hit a main drag and were welcomed to Route 98 – Raleigh was to the left, Durham to the right.

'Go left, left!' It was still a single carriageway, but wider than before and with houses dotted along the way.

Before long we were joining other vehicles on their daily

migration towards the city, and in no time we were in main-stream traffic and had some cover.

I said, 'Have you got any rounds left?'

She gave me her weapon. I checked and refilled her mag from the spares in my pockets, and passed it back. She placed it under her right thigh with a 'Thanks'.

I started to recognize our surroundings. Traffic was starting to slow up; every time we hit a major intersection there was another bunch of lights letting people out from all the suburbs around the city. We couldn't see any of the houses, though, because of the trees and low-level industrial units that hemmed us in on either side.

We had stopped at a set of lights alongside some other people drinking their breakfast. Some of them had big paper cups from drive-ins, some had mugs that looked like Apollo space capsules, really wide at the bottom so they didn't fall over in the car, then narrow at the top with a nozzle to drink through. All of a sudden I saw people in different cars around us smiling or laughing out loud to themselves. Sarah saw what was happening and she wanted to listen in. She hit the radio buttons on preset and cruised through the stations. Three goes and she got it. A man and a woman were talking about people's choices of bumper stickers. The woman said, 'One is OK, but hey, more than that reads a ten on my geek meter.'

The guy replied, 'Have you seen the one that says, "A mind is like a parachute. It only works when it's opened . . ." Come on, man, that's like, off the scale!' There was some canned laughter, then he quickly returned to the airwaves.

'Hey, morning! It's Q98 comin' attchaaa . . .' The ads started to roll.

Everyone was laughing with us in the traffic. Then it got worse as they saw the same thing we did. The van four or five vehicles ahead had that very sticker in its rear window. I couldn't stop laughing as we started to move on green. I looked over at Sarah, who was joining in the fun; it wasn't that the joke was that funny. I think we were just so relieved to be back in civilization.

We hit the beltline, saw signs for the airport and swung right at the intersection onto the highway. About halfway round we were on an elevated section, and down below us were low-level square buildings, mostly motels and burger joints, islands in a sea of neon. The rain had slackened to a drizzle.

I directed Sarah off the ramp and we cruised around, looking for a motel that would work for us. She drove past a Days Inn, standing in its own lot. It was a T-shaped building, with the reception at the top and three storeys of brown doors making up the stem. It had seen better days, but was just what was needed. I let Sarah carry on past it so I could check out the area. That way I knew which way to run if we got bumped once we were inside.

'Turn left here.'

She drove into the parking lot of an adjacent single-storey sportswear outlet. There were about 200 cars in the 400-capacity carpark; she found a space in the middle and parked. We wiped the car interior of our prints, got out and did the same to the outside – not that it mattered that much, as they would have our prints from the van; it would just slow them up a bit.

Walking back towards the motel, we made an effort to clean ourselves up, brushing the mud and pine needles off our clothes. It didn't seem to make much difference. We got a few strange looks in the carpark, but nothing too serious; Americans know better than to stare at dishevelled strangers. The motorway roared above us with the morning's traffic, and a truck's brakes hissed loudly as it stopped to make a delivery.

As I peeled the gloves and clingfilm from the docs, I gave Sarah our story. 'OK, we're Brits – boyfriend-girlfriend, travelling up from the Cape Fear coast, had a puncture. We've been out in the rain trying to fix it, and all we want to do now is sort our shit out.'

She thought for a few seconds. 'Got it.'

I cleaned up the jacket sleeve the dog had ripped as best I could, wiping the dried blood on my hand against my jeans. A last quick spit and rub on the more stubborn stains did the trick.

We'd put our hands through our hair in a last minute effort to sort ourselves out as we went through the door. We still looked rough, but so did the motel. The carpet in reception needed replacing and a new coat of paint wouldn't have gone amiss. To my left, a TV blared by the coffee and vending machines as the glass doors closed behind us.

The receptionist went through the automatic company welcome: 'Hi, how are you today?' still looking down at something more important. She was about seventeen or eighteen, and wore a maroon polyester waistcoat and skirt, with a white blouse. Her name tag said she was Donna. She was a black girl with relaxed hair put into a side parting, a big, round pair of glasses and, now that she was actually pointing it at us, a great big brilliant smile. It might not be sincere, but at least she was the first person we'd been close to for a while who wasn't shooting at us.

Her smile evaporated as she took in our appearance. 'What's happened to you folks?'

I did my best stupid English tourist impression. 'We had a puncture this morning and the car went off the road in all this rain. Look at us. It's been a nightmare; we just want to clean up and sleep.' I stopped my waffle and looked sorry for myself while showing her the state of my jeans.

She agreed, we were in shit state. 'Wow!' She looked down at the computer and hit the keys. 'Let me see . . .' She didn't sound too hopeful. 'It's early and I don't know if any rooms will be ready yet.' She smiled as she read the screen, and I knew we were in luck. 'Hey, you know what? I have a double room – but it's smoking.' The way she said it, I knew that when the time came for her to have a child, she'd sue someone lighting up even two states away. She looked up, waiting for us to share her distaste.

I said, 'That will be fine, thank you.' She looked at us as if we were somewhere below subhuman. 'We don't smoke, but at the moment anything will do.' I smiled. We became normal again and were given a big smile back.

She continued to hit the keys. 'Sure. I have a special at the moment: thirty-nine dollars ninety-nine, plus tax.' Her expression now said that I should be jumping up and down with joy. I took the hint.

'That's great!' I pulled out my wallet and gave her my credit card. She could have been asking for $139.99 plus tax, I wouldn't have given a shit.

'Thank you' – she studied the card – 'Mr Snell.'

She swiped the plastic and the machine clicked and hummed as I filled in the registration form. I put down any shit I could think of for the vehicle registration. They never look at it anyway, and if she did, I'd just say, sorry, Hugh Grant type character Brit abroad.

'OK, you're room two sixteen. Where are you parked?'

I pointed out and to the left. She started to direct with her hands. 'OK, go round back to the left, up the first flight of stairs, and it's there on the right-hand side.'

'Thanks a lot.'

'You're welcome. Y'all have a good one.'

We walked out of reception and I placed my arm around Sarah, talking shit about what a night it had been. We turned left to go to our non-car and worked our way round the motel to our room. There was a chance that anyone putting two and two together after watching the news might call the police, especially if the gas station was already news. But this girl looked as if she didn't even know what day it was. There had to be a point where I had to accept I'd done all I could for now. It was time to clean up, get our act together and then move on.

It was a typical, low-rent motel room that could have been any-where in the world, with a queen-sized bed, faded flower-pattern cover and white melamine-veneered chipboard furniture. The curtains were closed and the air-conditioner was off to save electricity.

I took the Do Not Disturb sign from the inside handle and put it on the outside as I fiddled around trying to find the lights. Sarah passed me as I closed the door and pulled the latch across. I went over to the air-conditioner and, leaving the curtains closed, switched it to full-blast heat.

Sarah was sitting on the bed, pulling her trainers off. I walked back to the other side and checked the window, a sealed, double-glazed unit which overlooked the landing. The only way out was by the door. I visualized my escape route. There were two staircases; I could either get down to the ground or onto the roof. Once on the ground I would head back to the carpark and hijack a vehicle. If push came to shove, I'd kill her here beforehand. I picked up the remote from the bedside cabinet – it was attached to a curly bit of wire so I couldn't nick it – and started flicking through the channels trying to find some news. The faded silver plastic TV must have been about ten years old – so were most of the programmes.

Sarah went towards the air-conditioner, pulling off her jacket and muttering, 'I need a shower.' She started to take off the rest of her clothes, placing them item by item on the heater, then weighting them with ashtrays and a telephone directory to keep them in place. The air was blowing them about as if they were on a clothes line in a gale.

I watched her undress as I lay on the bed. I couldn't stop thinking about what she'd said the guys in the house were planning, and about how lucky we'd been to get away. I just hoped she hadn't killed any police; even if she was telling the truth about the assassination plot, we'd be in deep shit over that.

I'd made a conscious decision to let her keep the weapon; if any police had been killed, she had the weapon that linked her to that, and to the Lance killing. London would have to do a mega-deal with the Americans.

I watched her naked body walk across in front of me, heading for the bathroom. She'd always been at ease with nudity, almost nonchalant, in the way models are. Her body was beautiful and still well trained. I watched her thigh muscles flex as she moved; her skin was usually so healthy it glowed, but with those cuts and bruises she wouldn't be showing her legs off in short skirts for a while.

As the shower started splashing I lay back against the headboard, flicking through the channels with the sound on mute. I couldn't see anything of use yet, like the news, but if I'd wanted to buy a diamond necklace and earrings or an ab-cruncher, it was my lucky day. My chin was resting on my chest, my back propped up by the pillow. I could smell myself: wet, mushy and, like her, in need of a shower. Looking in the mirror to the left of the TV, I saw a scarecrow who needed a shave.

I finally hit a news channel that was showing pictures of forests, then the lake. I didn't bother turning it up. This must be it; we were famous. There was film of different emergency vehicles toing and froing, police and ambulance crews running around with waterproofs over their uniforms. Then a policeman gave an interview with the same sort of thing going on in the background. I really didn't want to know what he was saying. If there were dead police, a picture of them would soon be on screen. It wouldn't change what I had to do, even though it might make it harder.

The news was replaced by a commercial. I was in a semi-daze, trying not to nod off. My eyes were stinging as much as my forearm now; at least that had started to scab up a bit. I'd sort it out later. If I'd got tetanus I'd be finding out very soon. I smiled at myself in the mirror as I thought, I could always sue the police department. This was America, after all.

I watched a child's toy commercial, where two small girls were playing with dolls. Shit! I leaned over to the bedside cabinet that held the phone and a Days Inn notepad and pen combo, and wrote a big 'K' on my left wrist. Next to the pen was a small book of matches; I put it in my jeans pockets, along with the mags.

My body was aching all over. I forced myself up, and pulled the phone book off Sarah's jeans. They fell to the floor and I couldn't be bothered to pick them up.

I trawled through the Yellow Pages, looking for car hire, called a freefone number, and was told that, for a charge of $43 a day, plus tax and insurance, they'd be with me inside an hour and a half.

Sarah came out of the shower just as I was putting down the receiver. She had a large towel wrapped around her, and a smaller, still-folded one in her hands. As she walked across to check her clothes I could smell the soap and shampoo.

'Who was that?' she demanded as she threw the towel by the TV and bent down to pick up the jeans and put them back on the heater.

'I've hired a car.'

'Excellent. How long before we move?'

I didn't know why she was so pleased. We weren't going anywhere she wanted. 'We?' I said. 'What the fuck's with this *we* business?' I always seemed to regress to South London gobby twang when pissed off. 'All the bollocks you're on about is your problem, not mine. The only *we* about this, Sarah, is that *we've* got the North Carolina police, FBI and whoever else wants overtime looking for us, and if you have killed a policeman and they catch up with us, we're in a very big world of shit. Take my word for it, we won't survive any containment; they'll hose us down on sight.

'*We* are going to do nothing. What *I* am going to do is, first, get us out of this shit; then I am going to get us both back to the UK. End of story. I don't care what is happening elsewhere, or what you want to do about it. I have enough shit here to deal with. Fuck Netanyahu.'

She sat on the end of the bed and looked at me. I knew she was going to give me a sales pitch, but tough, I wasn't going to let her get to me.

'Nick, I'm going to tell you anyway. It's important. I need your help.'

I cut in. 'Sarah, I'm not interested in your stories. Not now, OK?'

She wasn't going to give up. 'Look, I am the UK liaison in a contact group set up by the CIA. It's called the Counter-terrorism Center, and we're based at Langley. Our general remit is to disrupt terrorist—'

'Sarah, I told you, shut the fuck—'

Her voice got a bit louder. '—to disrupt terrorist operations; my particular cell is co-ordinating a US effort with European and African nations to roll up Osama Bin Laden's networks.'

'Bin Laden? What the fuck . . .'

She looked at me, waiting for me to continue. I didn't, but she knew I was now starting to take an interest. She drew a breath and continued. 'Yes, Bin Laden. We had a common cause while he was fighting in Afghanistan, that's true. But the problems began after the 'eighty-nine Russian withdrawal and his return to Saudi. As far as he was concerned, Nick, Afghanistan wasn't destroyed by the Russians, but by Afghans who had turned their backs on their religion and their country for money and power. Once he returned home, he saw the same corruption in all the Arab nations that had adopted Western values – above all, in Saudi, the land of the two most holy places, Mecca and Medina.'

I looked at her blankly, wondering if she would be saying all this if she knew her life depended on it.

'The whole situation was made worse by the Gulf War. To him, the presence of hundreds of thousands of American and other foreign troops on Saudi soil was a desecration of Islam, the return of barbarian Crusaders to defile Islam's holy places. He vowed to wage war against their presence in Saudi, and against the Saudi leaders who had brought them into the country. As far as he was concerned it had become an American colony. He wanted to strike back at the West – in fact, at anyone who was non-Muslim and in Saudi.

'The thought that former mujahedin would one day come to the United States and conduct operations didn't enter anyone's head at the time.' She allowed herself a small smile. 'The CIA has a word for it: blowback – a poisonous fallout, carried on political winds, drifting back home from a distant battlefield.' The corners of her mouth went serious again as she added, 'Bin Laden has become, over the last several years, the international terrorist posing the most serious threat to Western interests. He has an incredibly effective infrastructure and, of course, he has lots of money to fund it all himself. The ASU at the lake was funded by him. That's why I was there.'

I shrugged. 'Listen, if there's shit on, call Washington, London, whatever. Let them sort it out. There's the phone, call them.'

She looked across at the bedside cabinet, but made no movement towards it. Her eyes stayed fixed on mine. I wasn't too sure if she was actually listening, or just waiting for me to say more.

I got up and went over to the vanity unit outside the bathroom. It had a sink, mirror, shaving plug, soap and hand towels; it was time to clean up my arm. If she was telling the truth, all she had to do was pick up the phone.

I took off my jacket, pulled up the shirtsleeve, and surveyed the damage: two rows of nice clean puncture wounds that any German Shepherd would be proud of. If I collected any more scarring I'd start to look like the Cabbage Patch doll Kelly said I was. I turned on the taps and Sarah remained silent for a few seconds as I rinsed the dried blood and mud off my arm. The puncture wounds were deep, but less jagged than I'd expected.

'Nick, don't you imagine that I've already thought of that?'

I glanced in the mirror and saw her sitting on the bed.

'Making contact with anyone is not an option, because it's not a solution.'

I washed the wound slowly with soap and waited for that first horrible stinging to die down, trying to work out if what she'd said was any more than her usual cocktail-party performance. The room heater was working overtime and making my eyes sting.

'Nick, how do you think the ASU were going to get close to their target here in the US? Just walk up and give him a little tap on the shoulder?'

I shrugged. It didn't matter if I knew or not, she was going to tell me. It came at me in a flood. 'Nick, Bin Laden has a highly placed source. We think it's possibly as high as the National Security Council. Think about what that means: the group that blew up the World Trade Center . . . and Khobar Towers in Saudi, remember? Nineteen American servicemen dead. They also did the 'ninety-five bomb in Saudi. Another five Americans killed.

'Those are the people who have someone within the administration. That's why I can't just pick up the phone and get inside help: the source would find out, then close down for a few years and never be found. He is the key to stopping Bin Laden.'

I could see the passion in her eyes as she continued. 'Nick, the source has access to Intelink. Not only does that mean he would know before virtually anyone else of any contact I made, but just think about what information is being passed on to Bin Laden

291

and anyone else he then decides to sell or give it to. Don't you think I would love to call this in?'

Well, if all this was true, that was the phone call question taken care of. Intelink is a top-secret network, through which all the US and some Allied intelligence agencies share information, very much like their own private Internet. Within it, all agencies also have their own intranets, separated by firewalls from the main system. There are about a hundred sites that need top-secret security clearance to get access to. Whoever the source was, if he or she had access to it, then they must be big time.

I washed, thought and said nothing. If she was telling the truth and Netanyahu was killed and the source did exist, it would be a drama, but it wouldn't make much of a dent in my life. Come to think of it, would it affect anyone else's very much?

I could still see her reflection in the mirror. 'Hey, kill one Israeli prime minister,' I said, 'another pops up. So what?'

It seemed that something I'd said had amused her, because her nose twitched and a big smile lit up her face. 'They're not going to kill just Netanyahu, Nick. The main target is Arafat. Bin Laden hates him – hates him even more than Netanyahu, for reining in Hamas and other Islamic fundamentalists and supporting the peace process.'

I looked down at my arm, trying to hide my smile. 'He's not too keen on making friends, old Bin boy, is he?'

My joke wasn't appreciated; she just carried on as if she was Elizabeth giving me a brief. 'For Bin Laden, the important thing about this attack is what it will say to the world. When CNN asked him about his plans, he said, "You'll see them and hear them in the media, God willing." Since then, the Islamic Jihad group have sent the United States a warning: that they would soon deliver a message to Americans "which we hope they read with care, because we will write it, with God's help, in a language they will understand".

'His message is that nowhere is safe for United States citizens and their friends. It's the logical extension of the bombing of American interests overseas. The one place that should be safe – here in the US – isn't. Think about it, Nick. Two world leaders

292

killed while guests of the most powerful nation in the world. A perfect demonstration that Allah's avenger can strike wherever and whenever he wants. Just think what a boost that would be for the fundamentalists. As you would say, there'd be shit on. And the source is there, Nick, every step of the way.'

She stood up and started to walk towards me. I concentrated on dealing with my arm. I said, 'And what about the guy we were sent in to lift in Syria? Where does that fit in?' I hoped I wasn't sounding too interested. 'And you changed the data. London told me everything.'

She was now standing next to me. 'Ah, London again. I killed him because I had to, Nick. He knew the real data. If he'd come back to the UK the corrupt stuff I gave them wouldn't have stood up.'

'Why change it in the first place?'

She sighed. 'To try to confirm if the source really existed, and where in the NSC food chain he was. Those were early days, Nick, nothing was confirmed. At that point he was just a myth.'

She clearly felt more had to be said. 'Look, I needed to do it so that when the source – if he existed – got a look at the data, he would have to inform Bin Laden that everything was OK, nothing had been compromised. That way, not only did it confirm he existed, but meant that perhaps he could be tracked down. Whoever sent you here will not know everything, Nick.'

There was a lull. I knew she was waiting for me to ask another question. I patted my arm with a hand towel, turned and leaned back against the sink. I looked at her, two feet away. 'We should have been told there was a change of plan once on the ground. You fucked a job up that killed Glen.'

She looked at me, confused.

'Reg Three, remember?'

There was no reaction in her face. 'Yes, of course. I'm sorry about that.' I knew she really didn't give a shit about Glen. Come to think of it, nor did I any more. It was a long time ago. Even in the Regiment he would have been long forgotten, apart from by his family and a few close friends on Remembrance Day. His wife would probably have married another member of the Regiment and would be getting on with her life.

I got back into the present. 'So why are you in the shit about all this, if it was part of the job?'

She looked at me with her small-child-in-trouble face. 'That's the problem.' She hesitated. 'They didn't know. I thought that if no-one was aware there would be no leaks.' She was starting to look depressed, as you would if you'd severely fucked up. 'In fact, it was a cock-up from start to finish. The FBI confirmed shortly afterwards that the source did exist. They call him Yousef, but they didn't know at what level of the NSC he was. I decided not to tell them about anything I was doing. In fact, they don't even know about what I was doing at the lake.'

It was all making sense now. It was so typical of Sarah to be going it alone, hoping to collect all the Brownie points and smoothe her way up another rung of the career ladder. 'So now you want me to help you get out of your fuck-up.' I couldn't help smiling. Actually, it felt good.

'I couldn't tell anyone, Nick. If I had, the whole thing might have been compromised. I wouldn't – couldn't – risk it.' But she was risking it with me. That also felt very good, which was making things even more difficult for me.

She turned back towards the bed, sat down and hit the 'off' button on the TV remote control, knees drawn up and her arms around them, counting the number of piles there were per square inch of carpet. 'The problem is, Nick, I still don't know the identity of the source – no-one does. No matter how I did it, that has been the aim of this last four years: to find him, and to force the whole network down.'

She had finished with the carpet and turned back to me as I continued to tend my arm. 'The two others who were arriving at the lake today are the only ones here in the US who know who he is. I've only met them once. I don't know their names, contact details, nothing. But my plan was to play along with the hit, and get them lifted – I wasn't quite sure how. But once we had those two, we'd get the source as well. It won't stop at Netanyahu and Arafat, unless we can neutralize the top man.'

She brushed back her hair with her fingers as it was drying. My breathing was very slow and heavy as I tried to think of questions to help me feel right about what I was thinking.

'Nick, you are the only—'

The phone rang. Sarah jumped up and started to throw her things on, picking up her weapon and checking chamber. With her jeans halfway up her legs, she pulled the curtain slightly to see outside. She shook her head. I picked up the phone. She carried on dressing.

It was reception; we exchanged a few words and I replaced the receiver. 'It's the car. Take everything, get into the shower room and wait.' She picked up the rest of her clothes, towels and bag and took them with her. I put my jacket back on to hide the wound and the fact that my shirtsleeves were missing and changed channel, checking it wasn't on a news programme. I turned up the volume to cover Sarah.

There was a knock on the door. As I walked across the room, even I couldn't help noticing how dank the room smelled. I looked through the spyhole. It was a young black guy wearing a blue T-shirt. He had all the forms on a clipboard under his left arm, and a runner for the credit card in his hand.

I sat down with him on the bed to fill out the forms. Showing my driving licence was always a bit of fun, as most people outside the UK don't have a clue what they're looking at – a damp piece of pink paper that says nothing much at all, and doesn't even have a picture. He was turning the page over for the details he needed, trying to appear as if he knew what he was about. I couldn't bear to see him in pain. 'The number's there.' He smiled at me in relief.

As he got up, I could see him trying to work out the smell. I laughed. 'We were using a friend's car for our holiday. It broke down last night in the middle of nowhere.'

He nodded, not really caring. When he left, Sarah came out of the bathroom, taking her jeans off again to dry.

If she was telling the truth, maybe I would take her back to London. The problem was that although I hardly knew where I was with Sarah, I did with Lynn and Elizabeth. It might be G&Ts

at seven, dinner at eight for them, but if I didn't carry out my job they would fuck me over big time, maybe even organize my own personal T104. I needed more information from Sarah; the fact that she'd killed the American gave me a pretty clear idea of whose side she was on, but I needed solid evidence. I sat on the bed as she finished undressing and put her clothes back on the heater.

'When are they going to do the hit?'

She came and sat next to me. She looked up at me with excitement, then her face changed. 'You still don't believe me, do you, you bastard?' She gripped my arm with her hand. 'You must help me. I'm the only one who can identify the two who are left, and I know them, Nick. They won't rest until they've finished the job.' She stared at me. I didn't answer; I knew she was going to continue. 'What are we here for, Nick? How will you look at yourself in the mirror if you don't help me to stop it?'

Mr Spock would have been proud of her. The emotional stuff didn't work too much for me, but the story did sound logical. But she'd already fucked me over once, and looking at myself in the mirror had never been high on my list of priorities.

I got to my feet and went towards the door. 'I'm going for a cruise round to see if I can get us some clothes. What size are you?'

'Eight US, shoes six. Why don't I just come with you?'

'They're looking for a couple now. They may even have a video grab from the gas station. Sit here, I'll be back.'

Out in the corridor, I closed the door behind me but didn't walk away immediately. Ripping two matches from the book I'd picked up I wedged them between the door and the frame, one a foot above the lock, one below. I heard the locks being closed from the inside as I went downstairs.

The rain came down in a constant drizzle as I got into the car, a red Saturn, and turned over the ignition. The heater blew at its highest setting, the radio blared and the windscreen wipers thrashed from side to side. The urgent *bing bing bing* told me to put my seatbelt on. I did, inhaling the new-car smell, put it into drive and headed for the road.

In case she was watching, I drove out of her line of sight before going round the back of the motel, crossing over the main drag and parking up in the lot for Arby's, a hot sandwich shop. Looking through the power, telephone and stop-sign lines which hung above the main drag I now had a trigger on the motel door; I'd even be able to see where she walked to, as I had the stairs and ground floor in view. If she did something that showed she was lying, at least I'd know, and then I'd have control again. Plus, I could see if the police turned up. What Sarah was going to do once that happened I didn't know, and I wouldn't wait to see. If she followed her usual pattern, she would probably kill a couple of them and hopefully get killed herself. It was a risk, not keeping her with me, but worth it. Besides, there was something I had to do alone.

I kept watching the motel door as I turned on the power of the mobile, hit the PIN and eventually keyed in three digits. An operator answered. 'Yes please,' I said. 'North Carolina, Century Twenty-one Realtors, on Skibo Road, Fayetteville.'

Century 21 was a family-owned estate agency franchise, letting out apartments. I'd gone there once when I was in the Regiment, when a couple of us were staying in Fayetteville for six weeks. We spent one week in Moon Hall, a military hotel on the base, which was fine enough, but with the allowances we'd been given we decided to treat ourselves to an apartment. The only reason I could remember the name was that the 'Ski' in 'Skibo' was pronounced Sky and I always got it wrong.

I kept the engine running so the window wouldn't fog, and my eyes on the trigger. As I waited, I hit the wiper arm to clear the windscreen. The number was given to me and I dialled.

The call was quickly answered by a female voice in turbo mode. 'Century Twenty-one, Mary Kirschbaum and Jim Hoeland Property Management Inc. How may I help you?'

I switched to my bad American. 'Hi, I'm looking for an apartment to rent – three bedrooms, maybe.' The bigger it was, the more chance there was of the kitchen having the facilities I was going to need.

I heard the sound of a keyboard being tapped at warp speed, and within a nanosecond she replied, 'I only have one or two

bedrooms available. Do you require furnished or unfurnished?'
She gave me the feeling this wasn't her first day on the job.

'Two bed, furnished, would be fine.'

'OK, how long do you require the property for? I need a
day's notice for weekly rentals and a week's notice for monthly
rentals.'

She had obviously decided that for someone like me, who
didn't seem to have a clue what he wanted, it would be better to
explain right away instead of wasting her time.

'Two weeks, but could I get it today?'

There was a pause. I'd fucked up the procedure, but she recovered with style. 'Right now I have a two-bedroom apartment
available to rent for one seventy-five a week or five fifty a month,
plus electric and tax. If you decide to stay longer the monthly
rental rate would start on month two.'

Once I'd heard the first nine or ten words I didn't even listen to
the rest. 'OK, that sounds great. What's the kitchen like? Does it
have a freezer?'

I thought she was going to ask if I'd just arrived from Mars.
'Yes, they all have a full kitchen. Freezer, dishwasher, range—'

I cut in before I got the whole list. 'And I can definitely have it
today?'

There was another pause.

'Sure.' The computer keys were going into meltdown. 'You
need to come into the office today before five thirty so I can book
you in. It will be a two-hundred dollar deposit in cash, plus one
week's rental, plus tax in advance, cash or card only. Can I have
your name?'

The keyboard was given another brief respite as I slowed the
process down by talking at a normal speed. 'Snell. Nick Snell.'

By the time I'd finished, it was on the hard disk.

'OK, I'm Velvet, the rental assistant. I'll see you here before five
thirty.'

I came off the phone feeling dizzy. I had to hit the wipers again
as I kept both eyes on the motel door. I looked at the half washed-
out 'K' on my wrist, then at my watch. It wasn't too early. I dialled
call number two and got the answer, 'Hello, lower school office.'

'Hello, Mr Stone here. I'm sorry to call outside of social hours, but is it possible to talk to Kelly? I'm working and I—'

Before I'd even finished a very prim and proper voice, straight out of a 1950s black and white film, said, 'That's perfectly all right, Mr Stone. One moment.'

I was treated to an electronic version of 'Greensleeves'. I'd thought that had been banned by the music police years ago.

I knew it wasn't 'perfectly all right'. The secretary would have to drag her out of class, or whatever goes on in boarding schools at that time of the evening. *Him* calling again, the wrong line, wrong day and always with excuses – but I paid the bills, and on time. It must piss her off. I made a mental note to find out who this woman was and what she looked like next time I visited. I imagined a cross between Joyce Grenfell and Miss Jean Brodie.

She came back on the line. 'Can you ring back in a quarter of an hour?'

'Of course.'

'Not bad news, I hope. She's been so excited today, because they sang a belated "Happy Birthday" in assembly. She's feeling a very special young lady indeed.'

I turned off the power with fifteen minutes to kill, while keeping my eye on the motel and listening to the radio, feeling really pleased that I'd got it together to call. It would surprise her. I was cut out of the daydream by a news headline.

'. . . the deadly gun battle only minutes away from vacationing families. We'll bring you more from the scene after these messages . . .'

Once I'd listened to an important announcement about this week's sportswear specials at Sears, a very serious voice tried to give weight to the popcorn-style report he was presenting. They had found bodies at the house, and they were thought to be Middle Eastern. However, police were not yet releasing further details. His voice dropped an octave for extra gravitas. Unconfirmed reports suggested that the dead men could be terrorists.

At least there was no mention of any dead police, which meant no pissed-off cops hunting for the Bonnie and Clyde who'd murdered their best mates. I sat and listened to the rest of the news, very aware of the uncomfortable dampness of my jeans.

It was about seventeen minutes past twelve. I powered up the phone and called the UK again, flicking my eyes between the keypad and the motel door. I got the ringing tone and turned off the radio.

Our conversations when she was at school were normally quite strained, because she was in the office and people were listening in, and, like the grandparents, they still didn't understand how someone as erratic as me could be in charge of a child's welfare.

It rang, she answered. 'Hello?'

'Hi, how are you today!' I always tried to sound really happy to put her at ease.

'Fine. Where are you?'

I could hear phones ringing and Miss Grenfell-Brodie fussing around in the background.

'I'm in London, still working. How's school?'

'Fine.'

'And Granny and Grandad? Did you have a good time?'

'It was OK.' Her tone suddenly shifted. 'Hey, Nick, it's really cool you called!'

It was great to hear her voice as well. 'See, I promised I'd ring you, and I have, haven't I? You see, a normal person's promise. Are you impressed, or what?'

She started to spark up. 'Yes, and do you know what? The whole school sang "Happy Birthday" to me today in assembly. Well, Louise, Catherine and me. They had birthdays in the holidays, too. Are you impressed, or what?'

I imagined Miss Grenfell-Brodie giving Kelly a disapproving look.

'We don't say "or what," remember? Anyway, was it embarrassing?'

'No! My class have bought a present for me. A book of amazing facts; it's really cool.'

'Wow!' I said, trying to work up some enthusiasm. 'So what have you been doing today?'

'Hmmm, mostly the Geography project, I guess.'

'That's good. I used to love that at school.' I looked skywards in case a bolt of lightning was heading my way.

'We had wet breaks all day today,' she chatted on. 'Is it raining in London?'

'Pouring, I got soaked. It was raining cats and dogs. Especially dogs.'

We both laughed. She said, 'Have you talked with Josh yet? Are they back home?'

'No, they won't be home until tomorrow.'

'Oh, OK. We need to send a card to say thank you for them coming to see us.'

I thought I was the one who had to come up with the grown-up, parent-type stuff. 'OK. Can you be in charge of that? It would be a really nice surprise for them. Tell them a few amazing facts while you're at it.'

'I will, during Letters.'

'Great, they'll love that.' Letters was an hour set aside each Saturday after study time, when the kids who were boarders had to write to their parents. Or, if you were Kelly, guardian and grandparents.

A truck parked between me and the motel. She was still prattling on while I moved in my seat to keep the trigger, and at the same time used the opportunity to adjust my damp jeans. 'I wished we could have stayed with them, Nick. Can we go back to the ship?'

'Yeah, no problem.' I realized I was still feeling guilty. She could have asked for anything at that moment and I'd have agreed to it. The traffic was still screaming past between the target and me, throwing up clouds of water.

'Can Josh and everyone come?'

'Of course. As soon as we go on the next long holiday. Make sure you ask Josh in the card, OK?'

Even as I heard myself saying it, I knew it wasn't going to happen. The chances of Josh being able to get over to the UK with his kids again were slim because of the expense. I said, 'I've got to go now. You have a really, really happy birthday time tonight.'

'OK, are you going to ring me again soon?'

'I hope so. I won't be able to this week, but I'll definitely call after the weekend, promise. NPP. Are you seeing Granny and Grandad at all?'

'Yes. There's no Drama on Saturday, so after Study Time and Letters Granny said I can go stay with them.'

I was pleased about that, because if they weren't able to have her some weekends she didn't get to leave the school grounds.

'OK, listen, have a great day.'

'I will. I love you.'

It always felt weird when she did that. I liked it, but I could never say it unless she did first. If I did, it made me feel like I was intruding. 'I love you, too. Now there's another amazing fact! OK, back to class. I'll speak to you soon, all right?'

She laughed and the phone went dead. I guessed she knew she had to make the first move.

She was happy that I'd called – and I was happy that I'd remembered to. What was more, it was a lot easier to do now that I knew the Firm knew about her. I didn't have to get out of the car and use a public call box. I cleared both numbers from the recall menu and closed down.

The truck had moved, so I no longer had to sit like a contortionist to keep the trigger. I sat there for a minute just looking at the motel door and the traffic cruising between us, feeling very pleased with myself.

I switched back into work mode, pulled $5 out of my wallet and went and bought a Coke, trying my best to 'keep dog' on the target through the windows. Once out on the forecourt with my pint and a half of Coke and ice in my hand, I went to the bank of four phones which stood beside the Burger King next door.

I pulled out the handset to its full extent so that I could still see the motel. The roar of the traffic was almost deafening. I put my money in to call directory assistance. Pushing my finger in my ear and pulling on the handset for that last inch of line to keep the trigger, I shouted, 'Washington DC, British Embassy, Massachusetts Avenue, please.' I had to say it again because of the traffic, plus she couldn't understand my Australian accent.

302

I dialled the number and finally got through to who I wanted. 'Michael, it's Nick. I need some help, and I've decided to take you up on your offer.'

There was a slight pause as Metal Mickey mulled this one over. 'Well, that depends on what exactly the offer was.' I could imagine the smile on his face.

'It's just some questions that need answering, nothing that'll get you into trouble.' I could hear myself shouting down the phone to overcome the traffic noise.

'Good. I would just hate to be a naughty boy.'

I bet he would. 'No, mate, no trouble. Have you a pen?'

He gave a slow, 'O–K,' as he looked for it.

'I need anything that you can find on a handling name – Yousef. Anything you can get.'

He sounded surprised at my plain speech on the phone. 'Nick, aren't you the naughty one! You're supposed to be the one concerned with security.' He giggled like a schoolboy.

'I know, mate, but this is important and I haven't any time to mess about. The other thing I need to know is what exactly Sarah's been working on these last two years in the US, plus, what did she do the two years before that? I know you don't know now, but I just know you'll be able to find out.'

'Why, Nick, you old flatterer, you.' He started to laugh as he wrote a note to himself. 'Aren't you supposed to be the one in the loop?'

I let out a sigh. 'Yeah, I know, mate, but I've fucked up and got myself in a muddle. I don't really want to call London and get it sorted out. First time doing this sort of job, and all that. It would be very embarrassing.'

He let out a squeal of delight. 'Oh, tell me about it!'

I didn't have a clue what he was on about and just carried on before he had the chance to tell me. 'Finally, I need to know what Netanyahu and Arafat are getting up to this week. You know, times, places, that sort of thing.'

'O–K. You are a busy boy, aren't you?'

'Oh, and one last thing. I need to know the names and

backgrounds of the four men killed last night at a place called Little Lick Creek in North Carolina.'

There was a pause; I could almost hear the cogs churning as he linked this to Sarah and her country breaks. I was expecting a reply along the lines of, 'I don't feel comfortable with this, Nick,' but instead got a very nonchalant, 'When do you need this by?'

'Later this afternoon would be great. Do you think you can?' I had to turn back towards the booth to hear him as three trucks thundered past.

'No, but I know a man who might. I can't wait to call him.'

'Thanks for that, Michael, I really appreciate it. There is no-one else I can ask – you know how it is. But I would like this one to be just between you, me and the gatepost, OK?'

'You, me and the gatepost, mmm, sounds interesting. Byeee!'

I stepped back into the booth and hung up. I would rather have been talking with Josh, but I couldn't – until he got back from the UK, Metal Mickey would have to do.

The rain had given me a new layer of wet on the shoulders of my jacket and hair. My forearm was starting to sting again. Walking to the car, I lifted up my jacket cuff to investigate. Not good. There were scabs forming, but the bites were deep and needed cleaning and dressing by someone who really knew what they were doing. At least when it scarred I wouldn't have to explain anything. The teeth marks said all there was to say.

I did a drive-past of the motel, checking to see if there was anything abnormal, such as sixteen police cars and twice as many shotguns, ready to pounce. Nothing. I parked up and walked past the reception. Looking through the glass doors, I could see that Donna was still at reception, still reading whatever was so riveting below the desk. There was a tray of Danishes next to the coffee machine for the guests, and a bowl of big red apples. Everything looked absolutely normal.

I put my relaxed face on and headed through the door. Three children were fighting over who was going to carry what bag. I smelled the coffee and remembered I was hungry. Leaving the family to sort out its shit, I walked over to the machine, picked up coffees, four apples and the same amount of pastries, and then went back over to Donna.

'We've decided to check out early now we have a replacement car,' I said, breaking the corner off one of the Danishes and taking a bite.

'Sure, no problem, but I'm afraid I'll have to charge you full price.' She printed out the bill and I checked it to see if there were any phone calls logged. There weren't. I signed the card counterfoil.

I went to the room. The two telltales were still in place. Knocking on the door, I made sure she could see me through the spyhole as I pulled them out.

The heat was stifling, and the moisture from the drying clothes and bodies had made it as humid as a greenhouse. She'd gone back to watching TV, sitting on the edge of the bed, still with a towel around her. She took her plate and coffee without looking at me, her eyes glued to the screen. 'It's the third bulletin I've seen.'

As I joined her on the bed, I could see that it was a rerun of what I'd heard on the radio. A reporter was talking with a background of police cars and vans, and then the woods. He was wearing a brand-new blue Gore-Tex jacket, probably bought on expenses at Sears on the way to the lake; the hood was down so that you could see his very perfect, plastic hair and face, and he was talking in that earnest here-we-are-at-the-scene tone of voice. The shootings had happened hours ago, but he had to make it sound like the bad guys could reappear any minute.

I said, 'Have they mentioned any details?'

She was sounding quite excited. 'Yes. They've all said it was two men at the gas station, but there are unconfirmed reports that one of them could be a woman. The FBI are at both scenes, but there's been no official statement yet.' She took a bite of Danish and spoke through a mouthful of pastry. 'That woman in the blue Mazda must have been really scared if she couldn't see I was female.'

I had to agree. But then again, maybe they were going on the dogs finding Sarah's knickers. After another mouthful she added, 'There's been no mention of Lance.'

I wasn't bothered by that; I knew they wouldn't be giving the media everything they knew. Unless they hadn't found him yet. The main thing was that no police had been killed.

I stood up and walked over to the window. Her clothes were mostly dry now. 'It's time to move. Get your kit on, let's go.'

She pulled her jeans on, and I knew what they would feel like – stiff and horrible. She got them on, bent her knees and did little squats to make them a bit more pliable, dusted off the mud and got her top back on. As she put on her size-eleven trainers she looked up at me. 'Where are our new clothes?'

'I forgot. Let's go!'

We got into the car and I drove. She didn't seem to notice to start with, because she was busy eating her apples and drinking coffee, but when we got onto the highway it was obvious we were driving away from the airport, not towards it. She frowned. 'Where are we going?'

'Fayetteville.'

She picked up the A4 map sheet of the state that the hire company had left for us. 'But that's even further away from Washington. Why Fayetteville?'

'Because that's what I want to do: I want to be out of here and in a safe area that I know. Then I'll sort my shit out.' I kept my eyes open for signs for the 401 south.

Her face fell. 'You are going to help me, aren't you, Nick?'

I didn't answer.

23

Keeping to the speed limit so as not to attract any police attention, I drove along the same road as before towards the city. Crossing the Cape Fear bridge, I noticed a carpark on the other side, on the riverbank below the bridge, to allow fishermen and boats to get to the water. As we reached land and passed the slip road down to it, I made a mental note.

Soon afterwards we hit Fayetteville city limits, which seemed to consist entirely of fast-food joints. 'Why Fayetteville, Nick? Why are we here?' It was the sort of America she'd never seen, nor wanted to, by the look on her face.

'This is the only place I know in North Carolina. I plan to stand off here until London decides how they're going to get you, and me, back to the UK. They'll have to sort this gang-fuck out with the State Department before we go anywhere, or do anything. Until then, we need to keep out of the way of the police – in fact, everyone.'

I glanced across and thought I saw her stiffen. I knew she was rattled about all this, but she was fucked if she was going to show it.

I drove down Skibo, and Century 21 was just as I remembered it, a log-cabin-style converted home set amongst pine trees, with a small carpark in front and a large neon sign jutting out from the side of the road. But I wasn't ready to go in yet; I needed to sort my act out and look at least halfway presentable.

I drove some more and found a shopping area set around an open square. Beyond that, way over to my left, I saw the 'Pentagon', and realized that this must be part of the shopping mall I'd been to before. A large banner hung from a York stone façade the size of a row of houses. It announced that Sears department store was ready and waiting to take my money any time with its fantastic sportswear sale. I pulled in and buried the car amongst a whole lot of other vehicles.

She was staring at me. 'What now?'

'Clothes. I'll go on my own. What size are you?'

'I've already told you – I'm an eight, and my shoe is six, both US.' Then she gave me a look that said, Can't you remember? You used to know that stuff.

Looking at her as she smiled, I closed the door and walked towards Goody's Family Clothing Store.

Half an hour later I came back with two bulging nylon sports bags. We went into the Pentagon and changed in the public toilets. I washed my face and made an attempt to dress my arm injuries with some of Goody's finest dishcloths. I should have found a pharmacy, but I just couldn't be arsed; there seemed to be more important things to do. Besides, I was the original one-stop shopper. Once washed and changed I waited outside the washrooms with my bag of old clothes. Near by was a cellphone shop; I went in and bought two $20 call cards and stopped off at the ATM.

Sarah and I looked quite the devoted couple in our matching suburbanite jeans and sweatshirts, with neat nylon bomber jackets for the rain. It certainly made me feel a lot better to be out of my minging old kit, but my eyes were stinging with fatigue and I had trouble focusing on anything for too long. We got back to the car and threw the old stuff in the boot.

I was now into a new phase of the job. 'You drive,' I said, throwing the keys at her. 'I'll tell you where.'

We drove onto the Century 21 lot and parked up amongst the fir trees. The engine was still running, and I looked across the carriageway towards a gas station, not really concentrating, but getting myself ready for the next few minutes. These things have to look natural, and that can only happen if you act natural. That takes just a bit of preparation.

She was confused. 'What are we doing now?'

'Like I said, *we* are doing nothing. *I* am getting us somewhere to stay. The fewer people that see us together, the better. Wait here.'

I left the keys with her again. It was no drama, she was going nowhere; she wanted me to help her. Besides, she knew that if she drove off I'd have to call it in, and she would then be OTR (on the run) – not only from me, but also from the police, as the Firm would have no option but to stitch her up.

I left her counting trucks and went inside the office. I recognized Velvet from her voice as she took another phone enquiry at the speed of sound. Her hair was long, past her shoulders, and she had a dyed-blond perm which was long overdue for a refit. It had so much spray on it that the hairs looked like strands of nylon. The skin on her arms and hands showed that she was in her twenties, but her fingers were yellow and she already had crows' feet from screwing up her face to stop the cigarette smoke getting in her eyes. She looked pretty enough on the outside, but I wouldn't have wanted to look down a fibre-optic scope into her lungs. My eyes were stinging more than ever.

She finished her call and looked up. 'Hi. How may I help you?'

'Hi, my name's Nick Snell. I booked an apartment with you this morning.'

Before I'd finished she was already going into her files, and moments later she flourished a key. 'I'll need you to fill out this form. I forgot to ask if you have any pets. If so, they mustn't weigh more than twenty pounds each and you are only allowed two. How are you paying?'

'No I don't, and cash.'

At last, a reaction from her that wasn't fully automated; maybe she liked the way I pronounced the word 'cash'. Two minutes later I was heading back to the car.

I opened the map and looked for North Reilly Road, which

309

Velvet had told me was only a few minutes' drive away. Stewart's Creek turned out to be a private 'community' with just one road in and out; it opened up into an area of about forty acres, on which sat twenty or so blocks of green, wooden-façaded apartment blocks, three storeys high. We observed the 15 mph limit as we entered our new neighbourhood.

'It's apartment one seven one two,' I said, looking from side to side. 'I guess that's building seventeen.' Sarah nodded and we splashed our way through the puddles, looking at the numbers on the large grey mail boxes arranged outside each block. We passed the community pool and tennis courts, beside which stood a row of call booths and Coke and newspaper machines.

'Got it.' Sarah turned into number seventeen's parking lot.

We climbed the wooden stairs and entered the apartment. The first impression was, brown. There was a brown sofa and chair around a TV, and a log fire in the fake-stone fireplace, with a chain-mail curtain to protect the brown carpet. The living area was open plan, with the kitchen area facing us as we went in. At the far end of the room was a set of sliding patio doors with insect mesh on the outer side, which led to a small balcony.

The place smelled clean and looked comfortable. In the bedrooms, blankets, sheets and towels were all laid out, ready for use. In the kitchen there was a welcome pack of coffee, powdered creamer and sugar. Sarah went into the bedrooms, closing the blinds. I slipped into the kitchen area and switched on the freezer, turning the dial to 'rapid'. The sound of the motor powering up was too noisy, so I put the fridge on as well.

She came back into the living room as I was putting the kettle on. 'Now what?' she asked, closing the patio-door blinds to cut out prying eyes.

'Nothing. You stay here, I'll go and get food. I'm starving. The kettle's on, why not make a brew?'

I drove to the nearest store, which was part of a gas station, and bought the normal supplies – a couple of subs, crisps, canned drinks, washing and shaving kit. Then I used my call card to dial Metal Mickey from a phone booth on the forecourt. There was no answer from his extension at the embassy, not even voicemail, and the switchboard wouldn't take messages. Baby-G told me it was 18:36. He must have finished for the day. I tried to remember his home number; I couldn't, shit. It got binned with the 3C.

I returned to the apartment. Sarah was lying on the sofa half asleep, TV on and with no coffee made. I threw her a sub and a bag of crisps, and turned to reheat the water. The yellow freezer light told me it was still working overtime to achieve quick freeze.

Sarah eventually reached out and started to pull open her food. I poured water into the coffee mugs.

The annoying thing was that everything she'd said made sense; she'd done nothing to show she was lying. Why should she trust anyone back in London? I knew from first-hand experience that the Firm were as slippery as eels in baby oil.

I turned round to face her as I placed the coffee on the break-fast bar. She was lying back with the sub on her chest, one mouthful missing. She'd closed down. I knew how she felt. I was knackered and my head was starting to spin. I desperately needed sleep. I checked that the front door was locked and crashed out on one of the double beds, on top of the piles of sheets, towels and blankets.

It was still dark when I woke. I turned and felt another body next to me. I hadn't heard or felt her come into the room.

As my eyes adjusted to the dull light from the streetlamps through the blind, I could make out her shape. She was facing me, curled up, her hands together, supporting her head. It sounded as if she was having a bad dream. She mumbled to her-self and started to move her head against the folded blanket. She'd never appeared more vulnerable. I just lay there, looking at her.

Her skin glowed in the warmth of the room, but her brow was furrowed. For a moment, she almost seemed to be in pain. I reached out to touch her, just as she gave a small cry, tossed and turned once, then settled again. I could still smell the scent of apple shampoo in her hair.

311

I figured I'd been pretty good at keeping people at arm's length ever since I was a kid. It didn't make life completely fucking brilliant, but it kept me going and it sure as hell helped avoid disappointment. This was different, though. Very different.

She murmured again and snuggled closer to me. I didn't know how to deal with this at all. First Kelly, now Sarah. Any minute now I'd be checking out estate agents' particulars for the dream cottage with roses round the door. The full catastrophe. It scared the shit out of me.

I'd never been the world's best when it came to staying in one place, and I started to have this uncomfortable feeling that keeping on the move suited me so well because it meant I didn't have to think too much about what I was running away from, or what I was heading towards.

I could hear the TV still going in the next room. A woman was trying to sell us a great deal on a barbecue set. I rolled over, sat up and pulled at the corner of the blind. It wasn't raining, but I could see from the rivulets on the windows that we'd had another downpour during the last few hours. The backlighter of Baby-G told me it was 02:54.

I stood up slowly, trying not to disturb her, and made my way towards the kitchen. Rubbing my eyes back into life as I passed the mirror on the living-room wall, I saw the face from hell; creases and blotches from sleeping on the towels, and my hair thick with grease, sticking up as if I'd had a good burst from a Tazer. I shuffled to the kitchen, scratching every fold of skin I could reach. It was coffee time.

Sarah must have heard me banging about. Her voice behind me matched the way I felt and looked. 'I'd like one of those, please.' The TV went quiet as she hit 'off' on the remote.

She sat on the sofa, looking sheepishly at the carpet, her arms between her legs, as if she'd been unmasked as human after all. I was expecting her to say, 'Please don't tell anyone,' but she didn't. Instead she said, 'I'm sorry about that, Nick, I just felt so alone and scared. I needed to be close to you.' She looked up at me. Her eyes were full of pain, and something else I couldn't quite identify, but found myself hoping was regret. 'You did mean a lot to me, Nick. I just didn't know how to deal with it at the time. I'm sorry for how I behaved then, and I'm sorry for being so stupid now.' She paused, searching my face. 'I won't do it again, I promise.'

I turned back to the coffee and tried to sound upbeat. 'That's OK, no drama.'

What I really wanted to do was grab her, hold her tightly and pretend for a moment that I could make everything all right. But I was frozen between my memory of what she'd done to me in the past and what my orders were for the future.

I plugged in the kettle, feeling more and more confused. I had a crack at dragging myself back to the present. 'I need Michael Warner's home number.'

It didn't register with her at first. 'Who?'

'Michael Warner. I want his home number.'

I turned and glanced at her. It dawned on her that I'd been to Washington. She said, 'What did you tell them?' I didn't think I'd ever seen her look more miserable.

'That I was reviewing your PV. Anyway, I've only talked to Metal Mickey.'

I tipped last night's mugs into the sink and started again.

'Metal Mickey.' She started to laugh. 'Great name!' Then her mood changed again. 'Why do you need his number?'

I brought the coffee over to her, placing it on the low table in front of the sofa. 'I had some questions I wanted him to research. He might think it odd if I don't call to get the answers.'

She thought for a while as she took her first sip, and then recited the number. I didn't have a pen, but scratched it onto the front of the phone book with my car key and ripped the piece off. 'I'll be back in a minute.'

She put down her brew and stood up. 'It's a bit early, isn't it?' She was right, but I wanted to know.

'Fuck him. He's paid twenty-four hours a day, isn't he?'

The call boxes by the pool and courts were only about fifty metres away across the road. To the right of them were the newspaper vending machines, one with *USA Today* and the other with the *Fayetteville Observer-Times*. Under the street lighting I could just make out a picture of the forest on the front page of the *Times*. I couldn't be arsed to find out what they were saying.

It really had been raining while we were asleep, and quite heavily, judging by the size of the puddles. It was warm and damp and my sweatshirt was starting to stick to my back. I wished this weather would make up its mind. I got out my bit of phone book and the call card and dialled.

There was a sleepy 'Hello?' from Metal Mickey, very drowsy, but slow and wary.

'It's me. Nick. Sorry it's so early but I couldn't get to a phone. Have you had any luck?' I heard the rustling of bedclothes as he got comfortable with the phone in his ear.

'Oh, mmm yes, let me get my eyes on and I'm all yours.' There was a gap as he fumbled around for his glasses.

I didn't want to be on the phone to him all night. 'Our two friends we spoke about, what are they up to for the rest of this week?' I turned round to check if anyone was watching. Not that it would be unusual to be out telephoning at this hour, as these apartments didn't come with a phone. You had to connect your own.

'Well, they've finished their work and will spend Wednesday and a bit of Thursday just pressing flesh and having photo opportunities to show how nice they are and how well things have gone during their visit. Isn't that nice?'

'I'm sure it is, but where? Where is all this happening?'

'Don't really know. In and around DC, I suppose.'

'OK, mate. Now what about our American friend?'

'Ah now, I think we need to meet for that one, Nick. I don't really want to discuss him on a land line, and a lot of paperwork has come my way that I think you may want to read. I also have the information you wanted about your other friend.'

Had he found something sensitive, or was he just worried that when his PV review came up, gobbing off on the phone would reflect badly on him?

I said, 'OK, mate, I'll tell you what. Same place as before, at 12.30 p.m. today. You sponsor it.'

'Lovely, I'll see you then.' There was a pause. 'But what about

. . . the others?' He was sounding more like the village gossip with every word.

'What?'

'About your other four friends. You know, the ones who go on holidays to the lakes.'

'Oh yes, those friends. I'd forgotten, I have so many.'

'I know just what you mean, Nick. It's soooo hard to keep track.' He paused again. I was going to have to work for this.

'Who are they?'

'Can't tell you! Well, not over the phone, Nick. I think you need to read what I have for you. It all links in very nicely with Girlie. It's like a great big jigsaw puzzle. Isn't it exciting! See you tomorr—'

'Remember, you sponsor.' I had to cut in to make sure he knew.

'Byeee.' I didn't know if he'd understood what I meant, but I'd find out soon enough.

I replaced the receiver and turned to walk back to the apartment. Sarah was halfway across the carpark and storming towards me. I stayed where I was and let her come to me.

She was shaking with anger. 'Are you going to kill me?' She jabbed my chest with every word. 'Is that what the phone call's all about?'

'Don't be stupid,' I said. 'Why would I drag you all the way here—'

'I saw the freezer light, Nick. Don't lie to me.'

'What? It must have come on when I turned on the fridge.'

'Bullshit! They're on separate plugs. Do I look stupid? You're lying to me, Nick!'

I looked around to make sure no-one was watching. This wasn't exactly Times Square, and raised voices on the street in the early hours of the morning were sure to bring police or private security cars. I put my finger to my lips. She lowered her tone, but still laid into me. 'Why don't you believe me, for Christ's sake? Why don't you believe what I'm trying to tell you?' Her throat tightened and tears welled up in her eyes. It was the first time I'd ever seen her cry. 'I can't believe you were going to do that. I thought I meant something to you.'

I discovered I was feeling guilty, probably as guilty as I ever had.

'What after you froze me, Nick? Was it the wood-shredder to grind me up, like you did with those two in Afghanistan? Bag me up, then down to the river and feed the fish? They ordered a T104, didn't they? *Didn't they*?'

I shook my head slowly. 'You're wrong, Sarah, you are—'

She wasn't having any of it. 'You were going to do the same to me as you did to those two muj, weren't you? Weren't you, Nick?'

I held her by the shoulders. 'You're talking shit, the freezer must have been on already. Listen to me, I believe you, I really do, but it changes nothing. I am still going to take you back to London.' The words were said with conviction; I wasn't lying about either of those things now. It made it easier as I looked into her eyes.

'But, Nick, if you believe me, you've got to help me. You're the only one I can trust.' She shook her head and turned her back on me. 'Hah! What a fucking irony!'

'Sarah, listen, I don't care what happens in Washington. The only thing I do care about is getting out of here with *both* of us alive.'

She turned back to me, tears streaming down her face, then wrapped both arms around my waist and buried her head in my chest. She started to cry even harder; I wanted to do something, but just didn't know what. I looked up at the clouds and let her get on with it.

The crying switched back to anger and she pushed me away. 'You used to care for me, Nick. Haven't you any fucking boundaries?' She covered her face with her hands, wiping away the tears. 'I can't believe you were going to kill me, or even think of it.'

'No, Sarah, no . . . I wasn't . . .'

The crying changed to convulsive sobs. It sounded as if she was having a breakdown. 'I got it so wrong, Nick, so fucking wrong . . . I thought I had it all worked out . . . all under control . . . I even trusted you. How could I have been so stupid?'

I stroked her cheek wordlessly, then ran my fingers through her hair as she carried on.

'You were right ... you were right. I wanted to be the one, I wanted to do it all myself ... I wanted it so badly, it just got out of control. Once it started I couldn't go anywhere for help, I had to go it alone.' She squeezed me hard and carried on sobbing. 'What am I going to do, Nick? Or maybe you don't care?'

It was pointless asking me. I was still trying to get over my own guilt. Fucking hell, I'd got so far down the line that I'd switched the freezer on. How could I have done that to her? Maybe I didn't have moral boundaries like normal people. Was I always going to be the freak without emotion?

She was still in remorse overload; it was as if she was talking to herself. 'I could have done something about it in the beginning, but no, I wanted to be the one to get the credit. I'm so sorry, so sorry. Oohhh shit, what have I done, Nick?'

She squeezed her arms around me even more, desperately wanting support. I put my arms around her and she sobbed her heart out. I wanted to give her the comfort she needed, but just didn't have the tools. I'd never really needed them.

'I don't know what to do, Sarah,' I whispered.

'Just hold me, Nick, just hold me.'

I hugged her tighter. I felt strangely good about what I was doing. We stood there for minutes, rocking gently in each other's arms, her sobs slowly subsiding. I doubted there were any more tears left for her to cry.

She wiped her face on my shirt. I tried to lift her chin, but she resisted. 'I'm sorry, Nick. I'm just so sorry ...' She moved away from me and wiped her face with her palms, the sniffles starting to slow down in frequency as she regained some of her composure.

'Sarah, where are they going to make the hit?'

She looked up, breathless. 'The White House, tomorrow.'

'How? How will they do it?' I needed to know for when I called London. It would be my justification for returning with her alive. She was in the shit, I understood that, but so would I be if I

317

helped her and hadn't prepared my tuppence worth for the inquiry that was bound to follow.

She sniffed loudly. 'There's a photo call on the White House lawn with Clinton, Arafat and Netanyahu. They'll give a press conference, then there'll be a ceremony with white doves and songs for peace, kids singing, all that sort of nonsense for the cameras. I don't know any more. The two that were arriving yesterday from Washington had all the details. The team works in just the same way as we do: no details until the last minute. All we knew was that we were already accredited to enter the White House as news crew.'

'So that's why the old guy had a suit?'

She nodded. 'We were going to be part of Monica Beach. Oh shit, Nick, how did I ever think I could do this on my own?'

Monica Beach was what the media called the area of the White House that TV crews gave their reports from, because ever since the Lewinsky affair, it had been even more crowded than Santa Monica beach.

My first reaction was that it sounded more like something out of a B movie than a real plan. 'It wouldn't work; they'd never get out of there.'

The tears started again. 'Nick, these people don't care. Survival isn't an issue. Look who they have for their inspiration. Bin Laden's devoted his life to driving the Russians out of Afghanistan, and is now doing the same to drive the Americans from Saudi. He both finances and inspires them. Pakistani, Palestinian, even Americans. Dying is not an issue with these people, you know that.'

I found myself nodding. 'If you can't attack your enemy, you attack the friend of your enemy. And what better way to show the world that even the mighty USA can't protect anyone from Allah's vengeance, even in its own backyard.' As I spoke, I realized what a fucking idiot I'd been, just keeping my head down, concentrating on the job, trying not to think about where all this was heading. 'Shit, Sarah, explain to me in detail, the kids singing and white doves bit.'

I could see her scrolling through her memory for the information; she took a breath and wiped her nose as she gathered her thoughts. 'After a press conference, there's going to be a ceremony involving about two hundred kids. They'll present a peace blanket made from patches sewn in the US, Israel and Palestine to the three leaders on the White House lawn, in front of the North Portico. The kids will sing songs of peace and white doves will be released as Netanyahu, Arafat and Clinton hold the blanket for the cameras.'

Now I knew what had been troubling me. My heart started pounding and I thought I was going to vomit. I sounded surprisingly calm for someone whose mind was working at warp speed. 'My friend's kids are going to be there. . .'

There was a look of horror on her face. 'Oh shit. Nick, one of the options was a bombing. It wasn't their first choice, but now, who knows? Without the assault weapons, it will be the easiest way.' She started to cry again.

I grabbed her and forced her to look me in the face. Her eyes were puffed up, her cheeks wet and red. 'Sarah, I've got to make a call.'

She started to beg. 'Please don't, Nick. Calling won't solve it. Your friend's children might be saved, but the others will still die.'

I put my hand up to her mouth. I understood what she was saying. I couldn't call Josh anyway: he would only get back just in time for the final rehearsal. Did I give a fuck about the other kids? Yes, of course I did, just not as much as I did about Josh's.

'I have to call someone to get his number, that's all.'

I strode back to the bank of phones, got the phone card out and dialled. Miss Grenfell-Brodie answered. I said, 'Hello, it's Nick Stone again. I'm very sorry to bother you, but would it be possible to talk to Kelly? I'll phone back in fifteen minutes if that's all right.'

She was obviously getting used to this. I could almost hear her sigh. 'Yes, of course, but please try not to do this too much, Mr Stone. It disrupts her routine. Phone calls can be arranged through this office at a more convenient time for everyone concerned.'

'Thank you for telling me, I wasn't aware of that. It won't happen again, I promise. Could you ask her to bring her address book with her?'

'Yes, of course. She will be brushing her teeth. She's just had breakfast. I will fetch her.'

'Thank you.' I put the phone down. I did know about booking calls. But then again, fuck 'em. Who was paying the bills?

Sarah arched an eyebrow. 'Who is Kelly?'

'Never mind.'

We stood there waiting. I could see that she was dying to say something more, but she knew me well enough to know I wasn't in the mood to answer.

As I stood by the phones, more and more anxious about being seen, I realized that I no longer had to be. I could call Kelly from the mobile. We walked back towards the apartment in silence, Sarah still with her arm around my waist.

As I closed the door behind us, she went to wash her face. I put the kettle on. I thought about what Sarah had said. I didn't normally remember the deaths I'd seen, but I could see the body of Kelly's little sister as clearly as if she'd been slaughtered yesterday. Whatever happened, Josh's kids weren't going to go the same way. But should I tell him, and risk him doing his job and telling the Secret Service? I would in his shoes, but did it even matter? Would the ceremony go on if he did? Yes, of course it would. But what about the source? Would it affect the timing of the hit?

As the kettle did its stuff I bent down to pull the deep-freeze plug from its socket, then stopped myself. Things had changed, but pulling it would show her that she'd been right about me. I decided to leave it where it was.

I walked around the breakfast bar towards the sofa. What the fuck was I going to do about this situation? My first reaction was to tell Josh and get him not to tell a soul, but that wasn't going to work. Even if, like me, he didn't give a shit about the brass in the White House, he would about the kids. Then he'd be smack in the middle of the same predicament as me. Some of them must be his friends' kids, and then friends of his friends. Soon every fucker would know the score.

Sarah came from the bedroom, her eyes still red, even after her wash-up. She saw the steam rising from the kettle and walked past me to make the brews. I checked my watch.

A different female voice answered this time. 'Oh yes, she's on her way, she should be here any moment.'

'Thank you.' I cradled the phone in my shoulder, expecting a wait, but almost at once got, 'Hi! Why are you calling me again, what's up?'

At first I thought I should try not to sound as if I was talking to a child, then I decided not to bother. 'Nothing, just checking you've cleaned your teeth.' It got a laugh out of her. 'Have you got your address book with you?'

'Sure have.'

'All right then, I'm after Josh's number, because I'm going to the airport in a minute. Guess what? I'm going to Washington and maybe I'll get to see him.'

'Cool.'

'I know, but I need the phone number and I've left it at home.'

'Oh, OK.' I could hear the pages flicking in her Spice Girls address book. At the bottom of each page was a multiple-choice profile and a space to insert the 'cool factor' of the person the page was about. I'd felt quite proud to see that she'd circled 'funny and weird' as my description, and given me a CF of 8 out of 10. But that had all crashed before my eyes as I turned to the next page and saw her grandparents circled as 'kind and gentle' and given a CF of 10. Perhaps I'd have to start tucking her pullovers into her jeans all the time if I wanted to up my cred.

She reeled off the number and I scratched it on the piece of phone book, then tapped it into the phone as we talked.

'Nick, why are you going to America?'

'I'm going with a friend. Her name is Sarah.'

I looked over at her. She was staring quizzically, trying to work it out. I was sure she knew it was a child. Those things are hard to hide.

I said, 'My friend Sarah is going to do some work in

Washington and I'm going with her. Hey, would you like to speak to her?'

'OK.' There was a slight reluctance in her voice. Maybe she sensed that things were about to get complicated. I didn't want to tell her they already were. Sarah came to the settee with two full coffee mugs.

I passed over the phone and said, 'Sarah, this is Kelly. Kelly wants to say hello.'

She fixed her eyes on me as she spoke. 'Hello?' There was a gap, then, 'Yes, that's right. Sarah.'

I kept looking at her and hoped this was the right thing to do. It might come in handy, later. Sarah was still talking. 'Yes, I'm going to Washington. What do I do? I'm a lawyer. Yes, I'm just going over to work, just for a few days, and Nick is coming with me.' She was obviously getting the third degree. 'Oh yes, a long time, but I hadn't seen him for years. Yes, OK, I'll pass him back. Nice to talk to you, Kelly, goodbye.'

'Will you still call me next week?'

'I promise. Don't worry, this isn't instead of next week's phone call. I'll see you soon, no worries.' I was just about to carry out our normal routine at the end of a call, but checked myself. This one was different. Shit, this could be the last time I spoke to her. 'Hey, Kelly.'

'What?'

'I love you.'

She sounded slighty quizzed at me saying it first, but very happy nonetheless. 'I love you, too!'

'Bye bye.' I slowly took the phone away from my ear and switched it off, not feeling too sure how I felt about letting it all hang out.

'How old is she?'

'Nine last week.'

'You kept that quiet, didn't you?'

'She's a friend's child.'

'Of course.'

'No, she is.' I thought about telling her about Kev and Marsha, but decided against it.

She sat next to me on the sofa and cupped both hands around her coffee, still puffy-eyed.

'You OK?'

She nodded, trying to regain some sort of composure. 'Yes. Look, thanks for . . . I don't know what came over me.'

As we drank our coffee I explained my plan. We would go to DC, and I would look at what Metal Mickey thought was so worth looking at. Depending on what I found, I would then decide whether to tell Josh, or just go for it ourselves.

I was feeling uncomfortable about the Josh situation, but cut away by trying to justify it to myself by the fact that he wouldn't be back until early this afternoon, and by then I'd be with Mickey. So it wasn't as if I was abusing our friendship. I took another sip and decided that was bollocks. Deep down, I knew I was.

Everything we did now would be paid for and ordered by Sarah, in the name of Sarah Darnley. It was part of her security blanket. There must not be any movement detected on my credit card or phone. We went back down to the call box and called the ticket line. We were going to leave for Washington National on the 8.50 a.m. from Raleigh.

After showering and sorting our shit out we drove north, back towards Raleigh. There was a constant flow of early morning commuter traffic. It was cloudy, but no need for wipers yet. First light had passed us by as we headed out of the city, stopping only to buy some coffee and a plain blue baseball cap for Sarah from a gas station. I had one hand on the wheel and was sipping coffee through the gap in the top of the container when Sarah, who'd been keeping one eye on her wing mirror, turned off the radio. 'Nick, we have a problem.'

Behind us, and to our right, was a Fayetteville blue and white. I stopped at the lights as Sarah started to draw her pistol, placing it under her right thigh. On the basis of her performance so far, the mere sight of it got me flapping.

'Sarah, let me do this.'

She didn't reply. The cruiser came up level. My heart started to pound big time. Both of the patrolmen, one black, the other Hispanic, were wearing black, short-sleeved shirts and sunglasses, even at this time of the morning. Their chests looked bigger than they actually were, due to the protection they wore under their shirts. The driver was staring at us both, the Hispanic was face down, looking at a screen attached to the dash, probably carrying out a plate check on our car. I smiled like an idiot at the driver. What was I supposed to do? He wasn't giving me any instructions.

It was Sarah who switched on. She opened her window, and at the same time I could see the black trooper doing the same. His moustache met his glasses, with acne-scarred cheeks each side. I couldn't see his eyes, only what he was looking at in his mirrored lenses, but his demeanour told me that I wasn't on his Christmas card list.

Sarah came to the rescue. 'Hello, Officer, can I help you? Is there something wrong?' Her voice was outrageous; it was the fluffiest damsel-in-distress impression I'd ever heard.

The policeman would have heard it many times before, only not in Cambridge English. He drawled, 'Yes, m'am. The driver of this vehicle is violating the Federal Highway Code by consuming a beverage whilst at the controls of a moving vehicle.'

She said breathily, 'I'm so sorry, Officer, we didn't realize. We're just on vacation from England and . . .'

The black policeman got the OK from his mate. The check had come through. He nodded back at him, then turned towards us. He looked at me and jutted his jaw. 'Sir?'

The lights had changed to green, but no-one was going to hit their horn. I smiled like the dickhead tourist I was determined to be. 'Yes?'

'Sir, please don't consume beverages on the highway. It's an offence.'

'I'm sorry, Officer, it won't happen again.'

Trying hard not to let a smile reach his face he drawled, 'Y'all have a nice day,' and they drove off.

*

At the airport I abandoned the car in the long-term carpark. Formalities such as handing it back to the rental company didn't figure on my list of things to do today.

I waited outside the terminal while Sarah went in and got the tickets. I needed to call Josh's number, hoping to leave a message. Getting it clear in my head what I wanted to say, I hit the keypad.

A heavily Hispanic female voice answered, 'Heelo? Heelo?'

'Oh hi, is this Josh's number?'

'Jish?'

'Yes. Can I leave a message for him?'

'No Jish.'

'Can I leave a message?'

'Jish no here.'

'I know that. I want to leave a message.'

'I say to Jish. Goodbye.'

The phone went dead. I felt as if I'd wandered into *Fawlty Towers*. I redialled as Sarah came out of the terminal. She saw me and headed over. She passed, handed me my ticket and carried on walking. We were going to travel as two separate individuals.

'Heelo? Heelo?'

I could hear a vacuum cleaner in the background. I said, 'Please say to Jish, Nick is flying to Washington today.'

'OK. Ees Nick.'

We were getting warmer.

'What . . . time . . . is . . . he . . . home?'

'He no home.' Maybe not so warm.

'*Muy bien, muchas gracias, señorita,*' I said, using rusty stuff I'd learned while garrisoned on Gibraltar as a young squaddie. Then I added the only other Spanish phrase I knew: '*Hasta la vista, baby.*'

I checked in and made my way to the gate area. The front pages of the state newspapers glared at me as I passed the news-stand. The main picture seemed to be a fuzzy black and white still from a CCTV video of Sarah and me lifting the van. She was still looking like a sperm, T-shirt over her head; I was side-on with my head uncovered. It must have been taken at the point when

325

the dog and I were about to have a major disagreement.

I decided not to buy the paper or hang around. The news-stand was part of the shop where I'd bought the maps of the lakes; maybe it would be the same woman behind the counter, and she could put two and two together. I walked to the gate area and waited.

24

The hour-long flight was late landing. The Ronald Reagan National Airport, Washington's main domestic terminal, is a stone's throw from the capital, on the west bank of the Potomac river and south-west of DC, near the Pentagon. You can see the traffic jams around Capitol Hill as you land.

I disembarked behind Sarah, who was following the rest of the herd towards the baggage area. We'd both packed our weapons in our bags; being a domestic flight, there wasn't much of a risk. I collected my holdall from the carousel and walked off to the phones. It was 10.27 a.m.

My Mexican friend was quick to answer. 'No Jish,' she said. '*Mas tarde*. He home two o'clock.' Then she put the phone down.

Getting anywhere in DC by taxi at this time of day is a wish. If you're in a hurry, the best bet is the Metro. As I headed towards the airport station, Sarah linked up with me with her head down, baseball cap on. At the machines I checked the map and put in two one-dollar bills for my ticket. 'RV back here, by the machines, at two o'clock?'

She shook her head. 'No, not here. I'll meet you somewhere in town. There's more chance of me being seen here.' It was clear by the way she studied the instruction panel that, in all the time she'd lived in this city, she'd never used the Metro. I took the change out of the cup with my ticket and put in some more money for her as she looked at the map. 'I need to keep out of town for now,' she said. 'No need to expose myself too much. I'll go south and hold off for a while.'

'Do you know the Barnes and Noble on M, in Georgetown?'

Still studying the map, she nodded. 'Two o'clock.'

As we moved towards the barriers, I checked the signs and pointed her to her platform. 'See you at two.' The peak of her cap nodded and headed down the escalators.

The rules of the Washington Metro are simple: the answer to everything is No. No smoking, no eating, no Walkmans, litter or pets. If you're good boys and girls you can read the newspaper. The station was as stark and clean as the set of a sci-fi film, with its streamlined, dark-grey concrete and moody lighting.

The lights set into the platform flooring started to flash, warning that a train was about to arrive. Moments later, a string of sleek silver carriages whispered alongside and the doors opened silently.

I was heading north on the Blue Line. It would take me past the Pentagon, which has its own Metro station, and the Arlington National Cemetery, then eastwards under the Potomac to Foggy Bottom, the nearest stop for Georgetown and the M and 23rd Street junction. I came out of the Metro and onto the busy street feeling cleaner than when I'd gone in. Checking the map on the wall at the station entrance, I saw that I had just over a ten-minute walk to the RV. As I headed north, I noticed the improvement in the weather. Only 50 per cent cloud cover and no rain. Compared with the downpours of the last couple of days, it was heaven.

Bread and Chocolate on 23rd was teeming with office workers enjoying a lunchtime sandwich and coffee. I had just crossed M, and was on the opposite side of the road, walking towards Sarah's apartment. Metal Mickey seemed a bit of an airhead and I didn't want to get fucked over and lifted while tucking into a sticky bun and cappuccino. I didn't expect the RV to go wrong, but these things have to be done right; complacency is a tried-and-tested shortcut to a disability pension, or worse. Anyone could have been listening to his calls, or he might simply have got cold feet and decided to seek advice. They would then use him to get to me, the K who should have been in North Carolina dealing with Sarah.

I bumbled on, not looking directly through the window, but checking things out all the same. If a trigger was on the shop and a weirdo walked past staring at the place, it would be a good bet that he was the target. Things were looking fine; I couldn't see anyone sitting in cars or hanging about, but that wasn't necessarily significant. Whether or not I was getting set up by Metal Mickey, they could just as easily have put a trigger on him. And if he'd said anything to the Firm, I'd know as soon as I met him; I didn't have him down as the sort of man who could tell lies with his body language.

I walked past the 7-Eleven-type store on my right and noticed it had a small coffee and Danish area, busily taking its share of the office workers' dollars. There wasn't much going on in there, either, just people filling their faces and catching up on gossip.

I got to the junction and turned left on N. Walking about another thirty metres, I was more or less level with the entrance to Sarah's block. The water system was working overtime again on the flower garden. If I'd been triggered as I did my walk-past they would now be behind me, thinking that I was heading for the apartment.

Two attractive black women were approaching from the opposite direction, coffee and pretzels in their hands. I would have no more than three seconds in which to check. They passed, laughing and talking loudly. Now was the time. I turned to give them an admiring glance in that way that men think they do so unobtrusively. The two women gave me a You-should-be-so-lucky-white-boy look and got back to their laughing.

There were three candidates beyond them. A middle-aged couple dressed for the office turned the corner, coming from the same direction as me, but they looked more preoccupied in staring into each other's eyes for as long as possible before it was time to go home to their wife or husband. Then again, good operators would always make it look that way. The other possible was coming from straight ahead, on N Street, on the same side as Sarah's apartment. He was wearing blue jeans and a short-sleeved, dark-green shirt with the tail hanging out, the way I would if I wanted to cover my weapon and radio.

I faced back the way I was walking. You can only do so much checking. If these were operators, the couple would now be overtly cooing to each other; but instead of sweet nothings they'd be reporting on what I was getting up to, on a radio net, telling control and the other operators where I was, what I was wearing, the colour of my bag and which shoulder it was being carried on. And if they were good, they would also report that I could be aware, because of the look back.

I carried on the last twenty metres to the end of the block and turned left. I was now on 24th Street and paralleling 23rd. This was the second corner I had turned; if there was a technical device or trigger on our RV, there could be people stood off around the other side of the block, waiting for the word to move. Nothing seemed to look that way, just lots of traffic and people lining up to buy lunch at the pretzel stalls.

The couple were still with me. Maybe they wanted pretzels, or maybe they'd told Green Shirt that they could take the target round the corner, towards M Street. Stopping at the last of the three stalls, I bought a Coke and watched the area I'd just come from. The lovers were now at the middle stall, doing the same. I moved off, got to M and turned left, back towards 23rd and the RV. Three corners had now been turned in a circular route; an unnatural thing to do. I moved into an office doorway and opened my Coke. If the lovers came past, I would bin the RV, but then again, any good operator wouldn't turn the third corner. I hated clearing an area, especially if it was me going into the RV. It was so hard to be sure.

Nothing happened during the five minutes it took me to finish the can, so now seemed the ideal time to get my weapon out of the bag; apart from anything else, fishing around like a tourist looking for a map gave me an excuse to be standing there now that I'd finished drinking. I sneaked together the Chinese thing and its mag, which I'd split for the flight, and tucked it into my jeans, ensuring that the jacket covered it and the catch was off, so it could be used in the semi-auto mode. Moving off again, I eventually turned back onto 23rd and into the 7-Eleven.

I bought a Danish, a newspaper and the biggest available cup of coffee, and sat at a table that gave me a good trigger on the RV. There were twenty-five minutes to go.

I watched as people walked past from both directions, on both sides of the street. Were they doing walk-pasts to see if we were in there? This wasn't paranoia, it was attention to detail; it doesn't work like it does in the movies, with fat policemen sitting in their car right outside the target, engine running, moaning about their wives and eating doughnuts.

No-one went in and came straight out again; no-one walked around muttering into their collar. All of which meant either they weren't there, or they were very good indeed.

Cars, trucks and taxis trundled past from right to left on the one-way system. As the traffic stopped for a red at the junction with M, I pinged Metal Mickey sitting in the back of a cab, well down in his seat with his head resting on the back. I couldn't see his eyes, but I hoped that he was also taking the trouble to clear his route. Maybe he wasn't as much of a numb nut as I'd thought. The traffic moved on and he went with it.

If there was one thing I hated more than clearing an area before a meet, it was the meet itself. It's at simple events like this that people get killed, in the way that a traffic cop stopping a car for jumping a red light might land up getting shot by the driver.

I sat, watched and waited. It wouldn't look abnormal to the staff or anyone else for me to be spending that amount of time there. The place was packed and the size of the coffee signalied that I wasn't a man in a hurry. I checked around me again, just to be sure that I wasn't sitting next to a trigger. It had happened to me once, outside Derry; it was late at night, and I was waiting in a car waiting to lift a player, only to discover, as a JCB tried to crush the car and me with its bucket, that I was parked in front of his brother's house. Maybe they'd always done that with any dickhead they spotted picking his nose outside.

Mickey appeared right on time, but not from the direction I was expecting him to. He came from the right, the same direction from which he'd approached in the cab. He was dressed in the same loud suit and neon shirt as before. Perhaps he thought I'd have problems IDing him. He was carrying a laptop bag, with the strap over his right shoulder. Was what he wanted me to see on hard disk, and the dickhead had actually brought it with him? Maybe he wasn't so switched on.

I knew from our last meet that he was right-handed, and noted that his jacket was done up; chances were, he wasn't carrying. Not that it meant that much at this stage, but these things needed to be thought about in case things went tits up.

Having cleared his route, he showed no hesitation about going into the café. Good man. He did understand about sponsoring the meet. He knew I'd be watching him, and covering his arse as well as mine.

I watched for another five minutes past the RV time; if I didn't walk over to meet him he would wait another twenty-five minutes before leaving, then try again tomorrow at the same time. Nothing that I could see told me the RV was compromised. I got off my stool and binned the rest of the coffee and Danish, checking that my weapon wasn't about to clatter onto the floor. I hated not having an internal holster; I'd already lost my weapon twice because of it. I walked outside and checked once more as I crossed the road. Nothing. Fuck it, there's only so much checking you can do.

As I pulled the door towards me I saw his back in line at the counter. The place was still packed. I walked past him and did my surprised, 'Hi! What are you doing here?' He turned and smiled that happy I-haven't-seen-you-for-a-while look, and we shook hands. 'Great to see you, it's been . . . ages.' He beamed. 'Join me for a coffee and something sinful?'

I took a look around. All the seats were taken. 'Tell you what,' I said, 'the place across the street isn't so full, let's go there.' His smile got even bigger as he agreed. When we got out onto the street he slapped me on the shoulder. 'I'm sooo glad you said that. It's like that every lunchtime, you know. I don't know why I bother going there.'

To my surprise, he didn't make as if to cross the street, starting instead to walk towards N. I fell into step beside him and shot him a quizzical look. Mickey put his arm around my shoulder and said, 'We'll go to Sarah's, it's a bit more private.' He patted his computer bag. 'I've even brought some milk to go with the Earl Grey. Do you know, there's a little shop in Georgetown that gets it straight from Sir Thomas Lipton himself!' He was very pleased with himself; maybe he was hoping I'd take special note of his initiative when I filed my report. Fuck the milk; I wanted to see what was next to it.

As we walked along 23rd, I carried on playing the part of best mate in nice-to-see-you mode. I couldn't decide whether he was really good, or away with the fairies. Either way, I was glad I could run faster than him and had a weapon.

'I'll leave the clearing to you now,' he said. 'You're probably much better at it than I am.'

I laughed and nodded in response, so that anyone watching would assume he'd just made a joke.

'By the way,' he grinned, 'the man sitting on the corner? He's always around here; he works in the apartments. I know you'll be keeping an eye on him.'

I looked round and saw Green Shirt, sitting on the wall to the right of Sarah's apartment, smoking.

'Just in case you started to worry. You may have seen him on your area-clearing. I certainly did on my drive-past; in fact I always look out for him. It makes me feel better to know he's there.' He gave me a cherubic smile.

We reached the entrance and the water system was still drowning the flowers. Wayne was behind the desk, leaning back in his chair and reading a newspaper. It was like watching an action replay; they both had the same clothes on and even the dialogue was the same: 'Hello, Wayne, how are you today?'

Wayne put down his paper and grinned like an idiot. He was obviously having a really good day again. 'I'm very good. And how are you today?'

'I'm just Jim Dandy.' The corners of Mickey's mouth were almost touching his ears. As we walked towards him, Wayne turned his full attention to me. I really felt as if I was being welcomed to the asylum. 'How are you today? Do you still need that car space? If you want it, you got it!'

I said, 'I'll certainly bear it in mind. Thanks.'

He put his hand up. 'Hey, no problem.'

We reached the desk and Metal Mickey switched his camp game-show host's voice into overdrive: 'Wayne, I bet if you looked in the delivery drawer you'd find a large UPS envelope addressed to Sarah.'

Wayne had a look, rummaged around for a moment and handed it over. 'Why, thank you, Wayne, I hope you continue to have a very nice day!'

We said our goodbyes and walked to the elevator. He saw me looking at the envelope; as the elevator doors closed he raised an eyebrow. 'Why, Mr Snell, you didn't expect me to carry the material around with me, did you?'

Sarah's apartment was just as I'd left it. There was even the faint aroma of burned food hanging in the air. Metal Mickey wrinkled his nose.

'Cooking – the other night,' I explained, closing the door behind us.

'Ooh, that's what it is.' He walked towards the kitchen. 'I'd ask for the recipe, but . . .' He twitched his nose again. 'Can I get you some tea?' He threw the envelope onto the settee and unzipped his bag.

I walked over and sat down beside it, checking my watch. The envelope looked quite thick, but I had plenty of time before my RV with Sarah.

I heard the kettle being filled as I ripped open the UPS plastic outer. Inside was a brown, A3 envelope, sealed with Sellotape.

Metal Mickey came back into the room. 'They're printouts, and they are now your responsibility.' He couldn't help looking rather pleased with himself.

'How did you get all this?' I asked.

He gave an impish smile and his eyes twinkled. 'Ask no questions, you'll be told no lies; that's what my dear mother always used to say.' He came over and sat down next to me.

334

'However, I have a friend,' – his fingers mimed quote marks – 'who has access to Intelink.' He clasped his hands together between his legs and did a pretty good impression of a Cheshire cat. It was the most pleased I'd seen him, and he had every reason to be.

Intelink was switched on in 1994. The need for real-time intelligence had never been so acute, as the Gulf War demonstrated when General Schwarzkopf very loudly complained that the spooks had failed to produce satellite imagery fast enough. The network was soon being used as a central pool by all thirty-seven members of the United States Intelligence Community, from the CIA to FINCEN (Financial Crimes Enforcement Network), plus other groups connected with national security and the military. I knew that at least 50,000 people had passwords, with varying levels of access.

We both heard the kettle boil and click off. Mickey jumped up. 'Tea! Milk, sugar?'

'Strong. Shaken, not stirred.'

I heard him giggle as I pulled out the wad of A4 paper, filed in three clear-plastic sleeves. It was definitely stuff off Intelink. On the top file I could see the META tagging: <"IL.CIA" Executive Order 12958: Classified National Security Information"> META (Megadata) is a system for pulling down the documents needed from hundreds of thousands on call. The information available is nearly half a million electronic pages; just over 80 per cent of all the National Security Agency's output can be accessed in two hours.

The rest of the title went on to give its level of security. This document was tagged Intelink-P – in other words, managed purely by the CIA and top secret, available only to policy-makers.

Mickey came back with the tea. I had just finished skimming through the rest of the tags. This was looking good. There was another Intelink-P and an Intelink-TS – classified secret, about a third of the intelligence community have access at this level. I was quite looking forward to having a read. I looked at Mickey as he held a sugar lump on a spoon for me. I shook my head. 'How on earth did your friend get this stuff?'

He sat down and proceeded to put four lumps in his cup. 'Well, the objective is the eventual flow down, or up, of information as various security classifications impose themselves. Right now, standard COTS tools are used, but they're not specially augmented with multilevel security. These tools don't provide the right hooks, so for now different levels of security are provided by different physical levels of security, so there's an issue regarding upgrading and downgrading information between security levels.'

I gave up listening to him halfway though his waffle. 'What the fuck are you on about?'

His spoon fought a battle with the amount of sugar in his cup. 'If they say something is an "issue", it means they haven't got that sorted out yet. Now and again you can confuse the system. Especially when it's new and is taking a while to sort itself out.'

He went back into Cheshire-cat mode and took a sip of what must have been very sweet tea. I was waiting for his teeth to drop out as he spoke. 'The only one that can't be got into at the moment is a new, fourth level. It hasn't even got a name that I know of. Maybe it's only for the president and a few of his best buddies, who knows?'

I didn't touch my cup, just kept flicking throught the pages, looking for things I understood. I heard him slurp another mouthful of tea, and then a loud swallow. 'There will be a lot in there that is of no use to you whatsoever. He just pulled down any document containing information that might be relevant. He's such a nice boy. Drink your tea, Nick, it'll get cold.'

I nodded and didn't say a word. He got the hint; I heard the cup go down on its saucer. Mickey stood up and went back into the kitchen, then returned with his laptop bag. 'Nick, I hope you find it interesting reading. I've left the milk and tea for you.'

I looked up at him. 'Thanks, mate.'

'Of course, you'll destroy all the files before you leave?'

'No problem.'

He got to the door and turned, dangling the apartment keys between his thumb and index finger. 'By the way, send my love to Sarah. Tell her, if she needs these, I'll be leaving them with Wayne.'

I looked at him, trying to look confused. 'Er, what?'

His eyes twinkled. 'Oh, you are so transparent, Nick! PV? Pants, that's what it is, a load of frilly old pants. I'm not that mad, you know. I bet they told you I was, didn't they? Well, let's just let them think it. Pension, that's what it's all about, my absolutely gorgeous disability pension.' Still highly amused with the whole thing, he turned to leave.

I said, 'Michael, thank your friend for all his help.'

He looked back with a smile that suggested it had already been taken care of. 'Been there, done that. Now remember, say a special hello to Sarah for me. Byeee.' The door closed behind him. I got off the settee and turned the lock. If anybody decided to hit the place, it should at least give me enough time to get the papers down the toilet.

I checked out Baby-G. An hour to go before the RV with Sarah. I pulled out the papers that were tagged Intelink-P: Executive Order 12958. I turned the pages, but they meant nothing to me, just lots of directions on security of documents. Maybe Mickey's friend had a sense of humour.

Next was Executive Order 12863 on the PFIAB (President's Foreign Intelligence Advisory Board) and Executive Order 12968: Access to Classified Information. I thumbed through acres of stuff that was full of abbreviations and acronyms. I understood ziff.

Then I saw the reason I had been given it. One of the sub-paragraphs was entitled, 'Yousef'. I felt a jolt of adrenalin.

I read slowly, making sure I understood every word.

Since 1995, several senior officials in Clinton's administration had been under surveillance by the FBI. At first they suspected that one of them was spying for the Saudi government, but more recently that information was being leaked to Bin Laden. According to this report, the hunt for Yousef had narrowed to include a senior official on the National Security Council, the 1,200-strong body that advises the president on intelligence and defence-related matters. Its office is in the White House.

I picked up my lukewarm tea. It tasted shit; I'd have to make a new brew. I went to the kitchen with the files. There was plenty of jargon and junk, but it was clear that the hunt for Yousef had begun after the interception of a message between Washington and Bin Laden's farm in the Sudan that hinted about an agent who might be able to get a copy of a secret letter signed by Warren Christopher, then secretary of state, which spelled out American commitments to the Palestinians in the Middle East peace process.

The handler in the Sudan had replied, 'That is not what we use Yousef for.'

The report carried on to say that they believed there was little chance of discovering Yousef's identity after the intercept, because he would have been one of the first to learn about it on Intelink. All communication between him and his handlers would have ceased. I had a quiet laugh to myself. Maybe that was what the fourth level of Intelink was all about: trying to keep people like him out of the loop.

There were references to other documents relating to Yousef, but Mickey's friend hadn't included them. I placed the cup on the floor and picked up the other Intelink-P file. Its tag told me it was a CIA document, entitled simply, 'Counter-terrorism Center'. It wasn't the whole document, just the introduction, but even that ran to fifteen pages. I definitely needed more tea.

When the Clinton administration endorsed the idea of specialized units to infiltrate terrorist operations and disrupt them, the CIA established the Counter-terrorism Center as a central clearing house for intelligence. Its aim was to 'give the president more options for action against foreign terrorists to further pre-empt, disrupt and defeat international terrorism'. These options included covert operations designed to prevent terrorism, or to take revenge for successful attacks on Americans. New cadres of undercover CIA officers were sent overseas, and the use of CIA teams was expanded to assess and predict threats against United States military personnel deployed abroad.

Part of this strategy was a new level of co-operation between the intelligence agency and the Federal Bureau of Investigation, its traditional rival. Senior FBI agents stationed overseas held long and successful meetings with CIA station chiefs – the first at the United States Embassy in Rome, the second at the embassy in London – to work out ways to co-operate against terrorists and other international criminals.

The kettle boiled and cut out. I left it for a while; this was getting interesting. I knew that such a meeting would have been unthinkable as recently as two years ago, when the two agencies were at each other's throats over their conduct in the investigation and arrest of Aldrich Ames, a spy for Moscow inside the CIA.

I put the file down, threw a teabag into a cup and poured. The next page dealt with Sarah's group. The unit had scored several successes. British police raided the London home of an Algerian named Rachid Ramda and found links with the Armed Islamic Group, an Algerian organization suspected of seven bombings in France that killed seven and wounded 180 in 1997. The police also discovered records of money transfers, and traced them to Bin Laden's headquarters in the Sudan.

In Egypt, security officials uncovered a conspiracy by the extremist group Islamic Jihad to assassinate President Hosni Mubarak. It seemed that Sarah's group was investigating evidence that Bin Laden helped fund the plot. They also had evidence that Bin Laden was the major backer of a camp in Afghanistan called Kunar, which provided training for recruits of Islamic Jihad and the Islamic Group, both Egyptian terrorist organizations. This was in addition to the three terrorist training camps in northern Sudan, which Bin Laden helped to fund, and where extremists from Egypt, Algeria and Tunisia received instruction.

I threw the teabag into the sink, added milk and wandered back to the settee to read some more. Sarah's explanation of events was becoming more convincing as the minutes passed. I sat back down. To track Bin Laden's activities, the National Security Agency's eavesdropping satellites were used to listen in on telephone and e-mail conversations throughout the world. CIA analysts were able to determine that in January he had held a meeting with leading members of his network to prepare for a new wave of terrorism. Soon afterwards he publicly announced his intentions when he issued a fatwa calling on Muslims to kill Americans.

I had a drink and held the cup on my chest, slumped on the sofa. American officials are barred by executive order from planning an assassination. But after the fatwa was issued, Bin Laden was named in a secret presidential covert action order on terrorism, signed by Bill Clinton, which authorized intelligence agencies to plan and carry out covert operations that might lead to death. Such a measure was necessary, the report concluded, for two reasons:

'1. We believe that Bin Laden is planning new terrorist acts against American interests.

2. We believe that the question is not whether Bin Laden will strike again, but when.'

I bent my neck forward and drained the cup. I checked my watch; thirty minutes to go to the RV.

I went back into the kitchen and turned on the electric hob, then placed my cup and the two files I'd read on the worktop.

It was time for file number three. This one came from an acronym, DOSFAN, which I didn't recognize. The document discussed the investigation and arrest of several of Bin Laden's operators worldwide.

The hotplate was red. I saw a smoke alarm on the ceiling, and stood on the sink unit to pull out the batteries. Then I touched one of the papers I'd read to the plate. Once it was in flames I placed it in the sink, put a few more on top and carried on reading.

The first few pages detailed those responsible for the World Trade Center bombing: Mohammed Salameh, a Palestinian, and his room-mate in a Jersey City apartment, Ramzi Ahmed, an Iraqi who'd fought in Afghanistan and arrived at Kennedy International Airport on a flight from Pakistan in September 1992. After the bombing, he spent most of the next three years until his eventual arrest at a guest house called the House of Martyrs in Peshawar, Pakistan, which was owned by Bin Laden.

On that same flight in 1992 had been Ahmad Ajaj, a Palestinian fresh from Afghanistan, whose suitcase was full of bomb-making manuals. Ajaj was convicted in the Trade Center bombing, as was

Mahmud Abouhalima, who raised money for the rebels. Arrested in Egypt, he told his captors that the bombing was planned in Afghanistan by veterans of the jihad.

Meeting at a New York mosque, Ramzi Ahmed recruited Mohammed Salameh, Nidal Ayyad and Mahmoud Abouhalima. They helped him buy and mix explosive chemicals in cheap apartments and a rented storage space in Jersey City. Abdul Rahman Yasin, an Iraqi, was also recruited.

From time to time, I fed the fire in the sink. Halfway down the third page I found out what DOSFAN stood for: Department of State Foreign Affairs Network, <Mid East policy group>.

The report went on to detail individuals from one particular cell that was under scrutiny, and their names tallied with those Sarah had given me. I finished the last four pages and burned them, too. I felt as if I'd been speed-reading Tolstoy's *War And Peace*.

I turned the tap on and pressed the button for the waste-disposal unit. There was the wailing of metal as it took the black ash. I got a grip on myself and decided it didn't change a thing. All I cared about was Josh's kids.

Another thing Sarah had been right about: there was no-one to turn to. Josh couldn't be trusted not to approach one of his superiors. Even if his kids didn't go to the ceremony, the others would still be at risk, and he'd want to do something about it.

I watched the last bit of ash swirl down the hole, and turned off the tap and waste disposal. Only five minutes left to the RV. I was going to be late, but it wasn't as if she had anywhere else to go.

Fuck it, I'd have to get her into the White House without Josh knowing what we were up to. I didn't know quite how I was going to do it. Once again, I felt more bonehead than Bond.

I walked into the bookshop after clearing the area. The coffee shop was to the rear, and I spotted Sarah at one of the tables, nursing a tall latte. She was dressed much smarter than when I'd last seen her. The baseball cap was gone, and in its place was a grey trouser suit and designer loafers that must have sent her credit card into meltdown. Her facial appearance had been totally changed by a pair of black, rectangular, thick-rimmed glasses.

As I approached she smiled and gave me the hello-so-nice-to-see-you RV-drill look. I looked surprised and delighted – not that I had to fake it – and she stood up for the lovey-lovey kiss on the cheeks. 'How are you? It's so good to see you.' She voiced her pleasure for the benefit of the people around us.

We sat down and I put my nylon bag beside her new leather one and matching briefcase. She noticed my raised eyebrow and said, 'Well, I should be looking the part. I am a lawyer, remember?' I smiled, and she gazed at me for several seconds before taking a studied sip of her coffee. Then she gave me the smallest of smiles. 'Well?'

What could I do but nod. 'Yep, let's get on with it. But we do it the way I need it to be done, OK?'

She nodded back, her smile slowly widening into a victory grin. 'I was right, wasn't I?'

We left the bookshop and walked along the main street. I told her everything, from what Lynn and Elizabeth had said to the attack on the house. I just left the T104 out of the story, and kept the return to the UK in its place. She never asked. I also told her about Kelly, the events that made me her guardian and where Josh stood in all of this. It would undoubtedly come into any conversation once we met up.

'We met when we did, OK? The dates and everything will work. You used to work for us as a secretary.' She nodded. I said, 'We didn't see each other because it was all too complicated. Then we met up again. How long ago was the Syria job?'

'Late 'ninety-five – about three and a half years ago.'

'OK, we met again four weeks ago, in London, in a pub in Cambridge Street, and we sort of got back together, saw each other, nothing big time. And this is our first trip together. We've come here because you've never been before and I like Washington, so we thought, Fuck it, let's do it.'

She cut in, 'But I told the kid I'm a lawyer and I'm working.'

I didn't like her calling Kelly that, but she was right about the story. 'OK, you're in the States to meet a client, in New York, and I wanted to show you DC. The rest you can busk.'

'Fine. There's only one problem, Nick.'

'What's that?'

'What's your name? Who are you?'

'I'm Nick Stone.'

She laughed. 'You mean that's your real name?'

'Yeah, of course.'

And then it dawned on me, after all the years that we'd known each other, I didn't know her name, either. I'd only ever known her as Greenwood. 'I've shown you mine, you show me yours.'

She was suddenly a bit sheepish. 'Sarah Jarvis-Cockley.'

It was my turn to laugh. I'd never known anyone with such a fucked-up name. 'Jarvis-Cockley?' It was pure Monty Python.

'It's a Yorkshire name,' she said. 'My father was born in York.'

Stopping at a call booth, I tried Josh's number. It would be pointless travelling there if he hadn't got home yet. He was in, and sounded excited about seeing us both.

We got a cab, crossed back over the river and followed the Jefferson Davis Highway south-west, away from DC, towards the Pentagon. We didn't talk. There was nothing left to talk about; she'd told me what the two players looked like while we waited for a cab. It was hardly worth the wait. Neither appeared to have any special features that were likely to make them stick out. From the sound of things, we'd be looking for Bill Gates and Al Gore, only with darker skin.

We were both too tired to say any more. It was easier for us to leave each other with our own thoughts, and mine centred on how the fuck I was going to do this. She put her arm in mine and squeezed my hand. She knew what I was thinking. I had a feeling she usually did, and somehow that felt good.

We approached Arlington National Cemetery: I could see aircraft emerging above the trees on the opposite side of the road, as they took off from the National Airport by the river. At least the sun was trying to come out, even if it was in patches through the cloud.

I gazed at the row upon row of white tombstones standing in

immaculate lines on the impossibly green grass to our right. Heroism in the face of idiocy was an everyday job for me, but it was difficult not to be affected by the sheer scale of death in this place.

I knew the Pentagon was just around the corner as the highway gently turned right. The traffic wasn't that bad now; it would be much worse in a few hours, as the staff of the world's biggest office complex headed home. The carparks each side of us were the size of Disneyland's.

The Pentagon came into view. It looked just like the Fayetteville mall, except that the stone was a more depressing colour. We lost sight of it momentarily as we went under a road bridge. One of the supports still bore a crudely painted white swastika. Josh had seen it as a sign of democracy. 'The day they clean it off', he once said to me, 'is the day no-one can speak out.' I just saw it as the halfway marker between his house and DC.

'About another twenty minutes,' I said. Sarah nodded and kept on staring at the massive stone building. A Chinook helicopter was lifting from the rear of it, the tailgate just closing. I always liked it once the gate closed; it kept the cold out.

I'd been to Josh's house many times before while we sorted out Kelly's future. They lived in a suburb called New Alexandria, which was south of Alexandria proper and quite a way south-west of DC, but people who lived there called it Belle View, after the district next door. That way it didn't sound as if they wanted to live in Alexandria but had been forced to buy a little further away. The nearer your house was to DC, the bigger your bank balance had to be.

Josh's house was on the Belle View road, overlooking the golf course. As we turned onto it I gave the taxi driver directions. 'Halfway down, mate, on the right.'

Sarah moved closer to me and leaned to whisper in my ear. 'Thank you for believing me, Nick. I'm glad you're here.'

I knew how lonely she felt. I put my fingers between hers.

The golf course was to the left, and facing it were rows of three-storey, brick-built homes that in the UK would be called

344

town houses. The whole area was green and leafy, and probably a wonderful place for kids to grow up in. I half expected snowflakes to start falling and James Stewart to appear round the corner.

'Just behind that black pickup.' The Asian driver grunted and pulled in. Parked on the drive outside Josh's was a double-cabbed Dodge truck with large chrome bumpers and kids' mountain bikes stashed on a rack at the back. A big For Sale sign was hanging outside the house.

A middle-aged Mexican woman in a cream raincoat emerged from the front door, which was about ten very worn stone steps above pavement level. She looked at us and smiled, then just carried on past. I looked at Sarah. 'That must be my new friend.'

Josh appeared at the door, all smiles, his head and glasses shining as brightly as his teeth. He was wearing a grey sweatshirt tucked into belted grey cargo fatigue trousers and a pair of walking boots. As he came down towards us he was still grinning away, but concentrating more on getting a good view of Sarah through the sun bouncing off the taxi windows.

He opened the door for me, and I stepped out after paying off the driver, who took my money with another grunt. We shook hands and he reminded me that he had the strongest grip of anyone I knew. He said, 'Great to see you, man. I didn't think we'd link up again so soon.' He lowered his voice. 'How did the job go?'

'Not too bad, mate. It took a day, that was all.' It was good to see him. He released my hand and I pumped it, trying to get some blood back.

Sarah came round the front of the taxi, between the two vehicles. I held my hand out towards her. 'Josh, meet Sarah.'

'Hi, Sarah,' he shook her hand and I saw her reaction to his grip.

'Nice to meet you, Josh. Nick has told me a lot about you.' She must have been reading too many books; whoever says that in real life? Josh just gave her his biggest smile. 'I don't know what he's said, but when we get inside I'll tell you the truth.'

He ushered us up the steps and through his front door.

The first thing Sarah asked for was the bathroom. Josh pointed up the stairs, 'First on the left.' As an afterthought he called after her, 'We're going into the living room, so you make as much noise as you want.' That was something I'd forgotten to warn her about; Josh didn't change his sense of humour for anybody. I wondered if that was one of the reasons his wife had eloped with a tree-hugging yoga teacher.

The holiday cases were still in the hallway. 'Where are the kids?' I asked as we walked past them.

'Jet lag is not an option with kids. It's rehearsal time in DC, man. The big day is tomorrow.'

I wasn't going to pursue the subject. It made me feel too much of a lowlife, and besides, it was too early to hit him with the real reason I was here. 'Of course they are. I hope they have a good time.'

The house hadn't changed at all. The flowery three-piece suite and thick green shag-pile carpet were still in place. The pictures were the same, and you couldn't move for them: Josh as a soldier, Josh becoming a member of Special Forces, Josh and the kids, Josh and Geri, the kids, all that sort of stuff, plus all those horrible school photographs, rows of gappy-toothed kids in uniform, with that really stupid grin that they only do when there's a camera pointing at them.

He closed the door and said, 'So, my friend, how does it all square with Sarah? What does she know?'

I stepped closer to him. 'All she knows is that Kelly's family were killed and I'm now her guardian. She knows what Kev did, and how I knew him. You're the other executor of the will. That's how we became friends. She thinks I work for a private security firm. We haven't got down to details yet.'

He nodded. That was more or less all he knew about me anyway. 'Cool. Now a couple of details to get out of the way, mate. Do I get Maria to make up one bed or two?' It had always sounded really funny to me when Americans said 'mate', because of the accent; the word sounds like it should only come out of Antipodeans or Brits, but Josh had got into the Brit way

346

of speaking with me. Either that, or he'd been taking the piss all this time.

It was a good question, and I had to make the answer sound convincing. I smiled. 'One, of course.'

'All rightttt!' A big, conspiratorial grin lit up his face. We both sat down, him on a chair, me on the settee.

'Next important question, how is Kelly? She get to her grand-parents OK?'

'She's fine. Yes, everything went OK. I spoke to her today; she's missing you and the crew. I think you'll be getting a thank-you card from her soon.'

The small talk was already killing me. Normally I would chat happily about that sort of shit; it was what our relationship was all about. But at the moment all I could think about was the fact that I was about to fuck him over big time – even though I knew it was the right thing.

The door opened and Sarah came in. Josh stood up. 'Anyone for a brew?'

I laughed. To Americans, a brew means a beer; I'd once been with Josh and had said, 'Do you fancy a brew?' He'd looked at me as if I should be certified. One, we were driving; two, we were looking after kids, and three, it was nine o'clock in the morning. It had been a bit of a standing joke ever since.

Sarah was out of this one. She sort of smiled to look as though she got it, but she probably wasn't used to being offered a brew at embassy cocktail parties, and it certainly wasn't going to be a big thing in her social circle.

He turned to Sarah. 'Coffee good for you?'

'Thank you.'

He turned and walked towards the door, talking as he went. 'The kids will be back from singing practice soon and all hell will break loose. It'll be so cool for them to find you here.'

We listened to him pottering around in the kitchen. Sarah went and sat on one of the chairs – only a short distance from me, but significant in the circumstances. I said, 'Sarah, we're sharing a room tonight.'

347

She got it immediately, stood up and came and sat next to me. 'What now?'

It was pointless bullshitting her. 'I don't know, switch on and take my lead. It's far too early yet.'

She looked anxiously at the carpet. 'I'm worried, Nick. This has got to work.'

'Trust me. Look over there,' I nodded towards the books to the right of the fireplace. 'Second shelf down.' What had caught my eye was *Designing Camelot – the Kennedy White House Restoration.* I looked at her through her glasses. 'That's got to be a good omen.' I hoped I sounded more confident than I felt.

She saw it, and her expression gained a new determination. Josh came back with the coffee pot, mugs and biscuits as she was pulling it from the shelf. He started to pour. 'Flat white?' he asked. We nodded.

He saw Sarah flicking the pages, admiring the pictures of the White House interior.

She looked up and caught his eye. 'Now there's a classy lady.' She turned the book round so we could see the picture of Jackie O.

'Yes ma'am, she certainly turned this town upside down. That's her in the State Dining Room. She was our Princess Diana, I guess you could say. Geri loved her. I bought her that book for her birthday, just before she left.'

He started to open the packet of biscuits. 'I have to hide these from the kids, otherwise there'd be none left.

'You know what?' he said through a mouthful of biscuit, 'I didn't realize all the things you have to do when you're looking after kids single-handed. I've had to learn so much.'

Sarah looked surprised.

Josh looked over at me, quite happily, 'You didn't explain?'

'I thought I'd leave it to you,' I said, trying to turn it into a joke. 'Yeah, leave it to you, then I'd tell her the truth later on.'

He looked at Sarah. 'Geri had gotten more and more involved in local projects and classes, that sorta thing, so that she could' – he pulled a face to underline the words – 'better herself.' He passed a mug of coffee to her. 'One of them was yoga. You know,

I guess I was too busy working and stuff to see what was going on. I just didn't notice the classes were lasting longer as the months passed.'

I smiled in sympathy as he passed me my mug, and we had eye-to-eye. 'In fact, she got to like the classes so much she never really wanted to come home.' I could see him looking at Sarah for her reaction. He'd managed to make it sound like a joke, but I knew that deep down he was devastated. I felt guilty as hell as I listened to Sarah doing a number on him, but I knew it was the only way.

Nodding towards the pictures above the gas log fire, Sarah continued to reel him in. 'What about the children? They're such beautiful kids; whatever got into her to make her leave them?'

He picked up his coffee and sat back. 'The yoga teacher, that's what got into her.' He tried a laugh, but it was starting to really hurt him now.

Sarah took a second or two to get that one, but I could see from her eyes that she'd picked up on Josh's sadness.

'She calls once a week,' Josh said. 'The kids miss her real bad.'

'How long has it been?' she asked quietly.

'Must be about nine months or so.' He looked over at me. I nodded; the timing was about right. Not that he didn't know; I bet he'd counted every single day. He took a sip from his mug, deep in thought.

We all sat in silence for a while, until Sarah asked a couple of polite, ice-breaking questions about the children, and Josh told her what she already knew. She was good; they were bonding. He was almost enjoying having a woman listen to the story and appear to understand his point of view.

There came a sound of crashing and slamming, and shouting in heavily accented English. Maria was back with the kids and telling them to slow down. She put her head through the door. 'Hola!'

A second or two later, the kids came surging past her to see their dad. At that moment they spotted me. 'Nick! Nick! Is Kelly here?'

Then they stopped and got embarrassed because they saw somebody they didn't know.

'Hiya,' I beamed. 'No, Kelly's at school. Did you enjoy your time in London?'

'Yeah, it was cool. It's a shame Kelly can't be here, though.' They were all excited. They went over to their dad, kissing and cuddling him until he was buried. 'You guys, this is Sarah, Nick's friend. Say hello to Sarah.'

All together they shouted, 'Hello, Sarah.'

'Hello everybody, very nice to meet you.' She shook each of them by the hand.

Formalities over, it all changed. It was straight into, Dad, can I do this? Dad, can I do that?

'Dad, it's really cool! There are kids from everywhere, even New Mexico. Some of them are going swimming. Can we go swimming?'

Josh said, 'Yes, yes, yes – but later. Maria'll arrange it. Go and have something to eat. Go, go, go.'

The kids went out in a whirlwind and headed for the kitchen. I heard the radio go on, tuned in to a Latin music station. We heard them all squabbling, and Maria making the most noise of all, telling them to keep the noise down.

I carried on looking for a time when I could hit him with my pitch. The kids went out, came back, eventually went to bed, and Maria went home. By then we'd seen the new garden shed, we'd talked about Christmas, Easter, even about Thanksgiving and the different ways Americans and Brits stuff their turkeys. I still preferred Paxo to peanuts. Josh told Sarah about tomorrow's events and what the kids were going to be doing. He couldn't disguise his pride that his kids were part of it all. He was going to be watching it with some of the ERT (Emergency Response Team) people, whose kids were also involved.

Sarah was perfect all the time; maybe it wasn't even put on, because something told me she genuinely liked Josh. I was glad, as these were the only two adults I had any feeling for. I wanted them to like each other. It mattered to me. Fuck the job in hand; I knew it had to be done, and soon, but we seemed to be moving into something more important between us. I hoped so. Once the job was finished, I needed Josh to appreciate our reasons for keeping him in the dark.

Before we knew it we'd had pizza, nachos, a couple of bottles of wine, and it was nearly ten o'clock. We seemed set to spin shit all night, but I knew I had to wait for the right moment. I listened to the other two as they put the world to rights.

I heard Josh saying, 'Have you met Kelly yet?'

Sarah was just sitting back drinking wine next to me. 'Kelly? No, I haven't, not yet. You know Nick, he keeps his cards very close to his chest.' She gave me one of those strange looks couples give each other when they're talking about one thing, but thinking about something else. 'I have spoken to her, though.' She was keeping the lies close to the truth. It was always the best way.

Josh said, 'She's a really good kid, you'll like her a lot. Maybe if Geri was here Kelly would have come to live with us and the kids. It's been really hard for her.'

Sarah looked at me to carry on the story. I began to think she was liking this, finding out about me.

'Yeah, but me and her, it's all right,' I mumbled.

Sarah reached out and grasped my hand.

Josh broke the silence. 'Ah . . . you sure you two don't want to be alone?'

We all started laughing. I looked at Josh and remembered that I had a job to do, and now was the time to do it. 'Mate, I've just had a brilliant idea. Well, good for us, but maybe hard for you to sort out.'

He sat back and took a sip of wine. 'Yesss . . . and what could that be?' He suddenly sounded like my dad.

'Well, if there was any chance of a trip round the White House for us – you know, like the time you took me round before? – Sarah would love me for ever.' I smiled at her.

She picked up the ball, blushed and her eyes lit up. 'That would be absolutely brilliant. Can you really fix that, Josh?'

Josh wasn't looking too sure. 'Well . . .'

I decided to jump in and keep it all upbeat. Looking at Sarah, whose face now resembled that of a child at a funfair, I said, 'This boy is the greatest. He took me round the White House last year. He was running the vice-presidential protection team.'

'Oh, I'd love that. That would be fantastic!' She was making all the right noises.

I said, 'There's a bowling alley in the basement so Bill can go and have a bit of a practice, and some of the stonework still has scorch marks from when the Brits tried to burn it down in eighteen hundred and something or other.'

She turned to Josh. 'Is he bullshitting me?'

He shook his head as he took another sip of wine. 'No, the Brits came to Washington and burned the lot down. It was Eighteen fourteen.'

I said, 'Come on then, mate, what do you say? I'll even buy a crap tie to make me look like Secret Service if you want. What do you say?' I always took the piss out of the way they dressed. The White House team's uniform seemed to be either a grey suit, or a blue blazer and dark grey trousers. The only thing they were allowed to have choice over, it seemed, was their ties. I had never seen so many Daffy Ducks and Mickey Mouses in one place, apart from the window of Tie Rack. Josh had an impressive display of sheep jumping over gates and Bugs Bunny eating carrots.

It was time for him to insult me in return. 'Lard-arse, you will never look like an agent. No matter how hard you try.'

Sarah stood up. 'This is way over my head,' she grinned. 'So I'm going to pop upstairs again.' She knew it was time to leave us alone. She raised an eyebrow at Josh. 'I'll shut the door this time, so you won't be embarrassed if I make a noise.'

Josh rocked back on his chair and started laughing as the door closed behind her. He looked at me. 'She's cool, man, real cool.' I could see his smile tighten; I was sure he was thinking about Geri and how much he missed her. I felt sorry for him, but I didn't want to let him off the hook. 'What do you reckon then, mate? Any chance? It would be great for her, and on top of that I'd score an unbelievable number of Brownie points, if you know what I mean?'

He sat back in his chair, holding his arms up in mock surrender. 'Whoa, man, chill. Chill out on trying to sell it to me. I got it.'

He put his arms back down and got serious. 'I'll try, but I can't say for sure,' he said. 'I'll phone up in the morning. What's your cut-off time?'

'It's got to be three at the latest. We're on the six-something flight from Dulles to Newark.'

He held up his hands again. 'OK, OK, I'll see what I can do. Tomorrow's a big deal up there, but maybe we can go in the morning. Nothing's going to kick off until around midday, and the kids won't be doing their thing until one.'

He put his glass down, filled it up again and offered me some. I nodded and passed mine over. He hadn't noticed that I was only sipping whilst he was knocking it back.

Josh held up his glass. 'It's really good to see you, man.'

I raised mine. 'And you, lard-arse.'

Sarah walked back in, probably having listened behind the door the whole time. I gave her a big smile as she sat down. 'Josh says we might be able to get in tomorrow before we go back to New York. He's going to see what he can do.'

She gave him the sort of look that would have made a blind man's heart beat faster.

His face lit up. 'Hey, you know what? I have a neat idea. If I can't take you in myself, I could probably get you onto one of the tours. You could always come back and go round with me another time.'

Sarah carried on looking excited, but I knew that she'd be flapping inside.

Josh continued. 'I could organize tickets for you both without much trouble. You won't see the bowling alley or the pool, just the main building reception rooms, but hey' – he looked straight at Sarah – 'the important thing is you get to see the State Dining Room, and that's the only part left that Jackie O furnished. It's the room in the picture you showed me.'

Sarah reached across and touched his hand. I could see she wished she'd never mentioned the woman. 'Thank you, that would be great. I just hope that we'll be able to do it with you; it would be much more fun.'

Josh just about melted. 'Yeah, I know what you mean, it would be kinda cool to show you around. I promise I'll call in the morning; that's all I can do, man.'

'It's going to happen, believe me,' I said to Sarah. 'I told him, if it didn't, I'd tell the White House about the rubber duck.'

'The what?'

Josh looked at me with an embarrassed smile.

I said, 'There's this yellow rubber duck that gets passed around all the different sections in the Secret Service – and the Unit.'

She cut in. 'The Unit?'

She was well aware of what I was referring to, but she knew Josh would expect her not to be. 'Delta Force,' I explained. 'Sort of the American SAS. Anyway, the big thing is to have a picture taken with the duck in the most unusual places. Josh's task was to get photos taken in the White House, so he had one of it floating in the president's toilet in the private apartments, and he even managed one on the desk in the Oval Office . . .'

Josh yawned politely and started rising to his feet. 'On that happy note . . .'

As we said our goodnights, Sarah picked up the Kennedy book and put it under her arm, and we all trundled up the stairs. At the top landing, Josh went left to check on his kids; through their open doors I could see night lights glowing below a poster of a basketball hero, and a big picture of their mother. Duvets and toys were strewn everywhere.

Our bedroom was further along to the right. It was exactly what might be expected of a spare room in one of these houses: very clean and new looking, with a polished-wax pine bed with shiny nuts and bolts showing either side. I got the feeling the design choices had been Geri's, not Josh's, because it was all matching flowery curtains, pillow cases and duvet covers; if anything good was to come of Geri leaving, it was that Josh could sort out the decor in the next house. The bed was made up, with one corner of the duvet pulled back invitingly. Maria had done such a professional job that I half expected to see a note with tomorrow's temperature and a chocolate on the pillow.

I closed the door behind us, and right away Sarah was into her bag. She picked up her weapon and mag, and went into the *en suite*, leaving the door ajar. I watched as she loaded it by pulling back the topslide, placing a round in the chamber and letting the action go forward under control to cut out any noise, then just pushing the last two millimetres into place against the round. She then pushed the magazine in quietly until there was a click.

I laughed. 'You expecting a rough night?'

She turned and smiled, then checked safety. I got up and joined her in the bathroom. Sarah turned on the tap in the basin and started to clean her teeth. The danger with whispering is that you can make an even louder noise by doing it incorrectly than you would by talking. I leaned into her ear and said, 'If he does get us in, then no matter what, we don't harm him. OK? We don't harm him or anyone else; have you got that?'

She nodded as she spat out toothpaste.

I said, 'We're all on the same side here. If we get caught, or even challenged, we don't fight back. Nobody gets killed, and we don't take weapons, OK? They stay in the bags.' The security would be so tight we'd never be able to get them in. 'Anyway, we don't need them.'

She rinsed her teeth, turned and nodded her agreement, offering me the toothbrush.

'Thanks.' Our eyes met, then she smiled and went into the bedroom.

I watched her undress as I brushed my teeth. She laid her clothes neatly over the chair, and when she was completely naked she started taking off the price tags from the new lace underwear she'd bought to wear the next day. As ever, she wasn't shy about her body, but I sensed this was different from her performance in the motel. That was business, whilst this was . . . well, whatever it was, it felt good. I watched her in the glow of the bedside light.

Digging into her bag again, she took out a new shirt, unwrapped it and put it on the chair. Then she looked up at me and smiled. I finished my teeth as she came back in and we swapped rooms again.

As the bathroom door closed, I sat on the bed and started to pull my clothes off, thinking about the prospects for tomorrow. I

355

could hear Josh, opening and closing doors somewhere along the corridor, checking on the kids again, I guessed, or locking up, or whatever he did at this time of night. The toilet flushed, and after a while Sarah appeared.

She pulled back the duvet and climbed in beside me. I smelled toothpaste on her breath and soap on her skin. Her leg touched mine – I wasn't sure how accidentally. Her skin felt cool and smooth.

We both lay there, thinking our own thoughts. I wondered whether her thoughts were anything like mine. After a while she turned to me. 'What are you going to do after this, Nick? After you've left the service, I mean?'

It was something I had always tried not to give any thought to. I shrugged. 'I don't know. I never think that far ahead, never have. Tomorrow night – that's far enough. And I hope I'll be celebrating that we're all still alive.'

'I don't think I'll stay in,' she said. 'I'll probably do what everybody else does – get married, have children, all that sort of stuff. I sometimes wish I had a child.' She lifted herself up on one elbow and looked into my eyes. 'Does that sound crazy?'

I shook my head. 'Not since I've had Kelly.'

'You're very lucky.' She moved her face closer, and I could feel her breath on my neck. 'Maybe I'll write my memoirs.' She brushed my face with her hand. 'But where could I possibly start the story?' She paused, her eyes shining. 'And what would I say about you?'

'Hmm.' I smiled. 'Not easy.' Fuck, if she carried on like this I'd go to pieces and tell her I was in love with her or some shit like that. I couldn't handle it at all.

Her lips brushed against my forehead too lightly for it to be a kiss, then moved down to my cheek. I turned my head and my mouth met hers. I closed my eyes and could feel her body half on top of mine, her hair brushing my face.

Her kiss was long, gentle and caring, then suddenly more urgent. She pressed her body hard against mine.

25

I was woken by the screams of 200 kids – or at least that was what it sounded like. I kept my eyes closed and listened to the din. Maria had arrived and was trying to shush and organize them, and in doing so she was stirring things up even more.

A herd of elephants went downstairs, followed by Mexican commands to 'put on clean sock' as she went past our door. I opened my eyes and looked at Baby-G. It was six fifty-eight.

I yawned, turned and saw Sarah. She was sitting up, flicking through the Jackie O book. I muttered, 'What was that you were saying about children last night?'

Eyes firmly fixed on the page, she nodded, not listening. I hoped this wasn't going to be one of those terrible mornings-after when both of us desperately wished we were somewhere else and neither of us could bring ourselves to be the first to go for eye contact. I hoped not, because I knew it would only be that way for me if it was for her.

'Time spent on reconnaissance is seldom wasted, Nick,' she said, glancing at me and smiling. Things were looking up.

I propped myself up and checked the scabs on my arm. They were sealing up OK; the bruising was now very dark and swollen. I moved closer and looked at the book. It was mostly about the decor of each of the main rooms that Jackie O had changed in the 1960s. The useful stuff was at the back in an appendix: floor plans of both wings, west and east, plus the executive mansion in between. There was no way of telling if the layout was still the same, but that was all we had, apart from my memory of Josh's guided tour.

I looked up to read her eyes, and they told me she was already walking into the White House press room. Her work cassette was in.

I threw off the duvet and headed for the shower. I came back ten minutes later, drying my hair with a towel, to find her already dressed, apart from her jacket and shoes. 'Let's go down and find out what's happening, I'll shower later.' She waited while I threw on my clothes and followed her.

Armageddon was well underway in the dining room. Spoons crashed into cereal bowls, chairs scraped on the wooden floor, the toaster popped, Maria tutted and fussed. In amongst all this the kids were practising their songs. The problem was they were all in different time. It sounded like cats on heat. I tried to remind myself that this was a celebration of peace, rather than a declaration of war.

Josh had his back to me, doing some magic act with lunch boxes. He looked like a TV chef cooking ten things at once, wrapping sandwiches in clingfilm, washing apples, throwing in handfuls of cheese snacks. He was wearing navy-blue suit trousers and a freshly ironed white shirt; I could see his white T-shirt underneath, and the dark skin of his arms. I couldn't wait to see his tie. The thing that worried me was that he had a light-brown pancake holster just behind his right hip, and a double mag carrier on his left. I just hoped he didn't end up having to use what would be going in there on us two. I checked with Sarah. She'd clocked his gear, too.

Josh didn't even look round as I came in; he just called out, 'Morning! Coffee's in the machine over to the left.' I could see the percolator bubbling away. 'Bagels are by the toaster. Can't stop, got to get these ready before Puff Daddy and his backing crew here are picked up for their gig.'

I went over and split some of the pre-cut bagels, putting a couple in the toaster as Sarah poured some coffee. We put on a good show, as if I knew that she liked nothing better than toasted bagels for breakfast and didn't even have to ask, and she knew exactly how I liked my coffee. She asked Josh if he wanted some and he looked up from the lunch boxes for a second, nodded and smiled.

She poured. 'So what are our chances, Josh?'

He had his back to us again, jamming too much food into a Little Mermaid lunch box. 'I was going to give them a call at the top of the hour,' he said, 'just after the shift change.'

He finished loading up the Little Mermaid and glanced at his watch. 'Tell you what, let's see if I can get hold of the guy now.'

He walked over to the wall telephone and dialled, hooked the receiver with about a ten-foot lead between his shoulder and ear, then walked back to put the lunch boxes into the kids' daysacks. He had sold out: his tie was just plain old blue. He saw me looking at it in disgust, annoyed that there was nothing I could take the piss out of. He grinned back at me.

The daysacks were made of clear plastic – the only sort of bag that could be taken into some American schools now, because the kids had to show they only held books and lunch boxes and not guns. I imagined that White House security would have thought them a good idea, too.

I could hear cartoons on the TV next door. That worried me; it meant they'd finished breakfast and were killing time. In this house, there was never any TV while there were meals to be eaten or work to be done. I looked at my watch. It was seven thirty-two.

He got an answer. 'Yo, it's Josh.' There was a gap. 'Yeah, absolutely fine, I'll be there today anyway to watch my kids; we can talk then.' They spun more work shit for a while, and had an in-joke about their president.

The toaster popped up. I picked up the bagels and went to the fridge, digging out some spread. Sarah's eyes followed me as she crossed to sit at the kitchen table. She looked like a student waiting for her finals results.

I deliberately didn't look at Josh; if he turned I didn't want any eye-to-eye. Our unconscious bubbles away inside, and mostly we manage never to let people see in; the only place they can is our

359

eyes. I'd spent most of my life controlling it, but Josh knew the score. He'd been there too. I just concentrated hard on the bagel as I spread, and listened.

He finished waffling and got down to business. 'Who's the shift co-ordinator today? Ah, right. Is Davy Boy in?' He sounded pleased.

I walked across the kitchen and sat next to Sarah. She had her hands round her mug, just sipping slowly, taking fantastic interest in the coffee's molecular structure. Josh was still gobbing off on the phone with his back to us and zipping up the daysacks. Once he'd done that, he walked over to us and dumped them on the table, still waffling.

'I've got two really good friends here, over from the UK, and I want to bring them in for a visit. What do you say, bud?' He smiled at whatever was being said at the other end. 'Yeah, today . . . yeah, I know, but it's their only chance, man . . . yeah, that's OK.' He looked at his watch, placed his thumb on the cut-out, looked at us and said, 'Call back in thirty.'

Both of us managed a genuine look of happiness, but I was bluffing big time. We had a problem if the kids left before we got the OK for the visit.

I checked my watch again. It was now seven thirty-nine. Josh smiled, too, feeling good about himself as he sat down at the table with his coffee. Sarah sounded excited. 'I'll go and get ready, then. See you both soon.' She gave my shoulder a loving squeeze and disappeared.

Josh checked the kitchen. His jobs were done. We drank coffee in silence. He ate a bagel and listened to Maria still shouting at the kids in the next room. I said, 'When do the kids leave, Josh? It's a bit early for a one o'clock start isn't it?'

'About eight. A school bus will pick them up and take them downtown. Dress rehearsals, man. I'll be glad when this is all over; this quilt business seems to have taken over my life.'

I nodded. I knew exactly what he meant.

I tried to fill the silence. 'What's the dress code?' I said. 'I don't want to let you down.'

'Hey, no problem, man. I just gotta look good; it's my job.'

We continued to drink our brews and gob off. I asked if I could borrow one of his ties.

He was about to clip me over the head when a shout came from the dining room. 'Daddy! Daddy!' There was some whingeing going on and Maria was just about to go ballistic. He got up. 'Back in five.'

He went out with a smile on his face; mine dropped. I checked again. Seven forty-five. Fifteen minutes till the kids left, but closer to twenty-five before we got the go or no go for the visit. Not good; I needed the kids here just in case we had a no go, otherwise plan B wouldn't work. Time to get my finger out of my arse and get in gear. I put my coffee down and went upstairs. Sarah's shower was running and she was standing naked by the curtain, just about to step in. I said nothing, but went to my bag and pulled out the 9mm, checked chamber and put the safety on.

She came over to me, putting her mouth right against my ear as she asked what was happening.

I placed the weapon in the waistband of my jeans and pulled out my shirt to cover it. 'The kids could be leaving before Josh gets the go or no go.'

She leaned over the chair, got her clothes and started to dress, muttering, 'Shit. Shit. Shit.'

'You wait here and stand by. If I have to go for it, you'll hear. If so, get down to me and be quick about it. Remember, don't kill him, OK. Do you remember what to do?'

She nodded as she tucked her shirt into her trousers. I still wanted to run through it with her. We couldn't afford to fuck up now. 'If it's a no go, I'll hold them here, and you will have to go with Josh on your own. Can you handle that?'

She nodded again, without looking up.

'Good. Remember, he will do whatever you say if the kids are hostages. Make sure you keep reminding him about his kids.'

This time she stopped dressing and looked up at me.

'Good luck,' I said quietly.

She smiled. 'And you.'

Checking my shirt, I went downstairs, leaving Sarah as she

checked that there was a round in the chamber, ready to go.

The bags had gone from the kitchen, but kid-type noise was still coming from the TV room. Josh came back in from giving them their daysacks. 'What's the score up there, then, eh?' He jerked his head to indicate upstairs. 'Is it serious?'

'I think so, mate. I hope so.'

He had a big smile on his face. 'She's magic, man. She'd make my head spin.'

'Tell me about it.' I sat down to finish my coffee, with a sly check of Baby-G. It was seven fifty-seven. Three minutes and the kids could be leaving; still over ten before the call.

Dakota came into the kitchen, very excited about the day's programme. 'Hi, Nick. Are you and Sarah hanging out with Daddy today so you can see us sing? It's going to be so cool!'

Josh tried to calm her down. 'Wow, chill. We don't know yet, we're waiting on a call. You'd better say goodbye to Nick now, just in case.' With that he went back into the TV room to usher the others into the kitchen.

Dakota came over and gave me a hug. It must have felt as strange for her as it did for me. I was holding back; I didn't want her to feel the weapon.

'If I don't see you this afternoon, I'll call you all soon – with Kelly, OK?'

By now the others were coming through, more interested in what they were missing on the TV than in saying goodbye.

Josh was getting them organized. 'All go upstairs and say goodbye to Sarah. Holler through the door if she's in the shower.' Off they scrambled. I heard their shouts, and hers in return.

Josh was on the doorstep with Maria. It looked as if she was finished until this afternoon. Good: one less to worry about.

It was eight o'clock. Things could start getting scary soon. I made sure my work cassette was in, and stayed there. At least Josh's holster wasn't full yet; it never was with the kids around. I heard the hiss of air brakes outside.

'The bus is here, kids, let's go!' There was a thumping on the staircase and one in my heart as I walked into the hall to stop them, hand now reaching under my shirt.

362

They saw me. 'Bye, Nick, see you this afternoon!'

The phone rang and Josh came past me, back into the kitchen, sounding exasperated. 'Come on, kids, get your bags. Bus is waiting!'

Through the open kitchen door, I saw him answer the phone. I was standing in their way as they were about to turn left towards the door that led from the hallway into the TV room. I put my hand around the pistol grip. I knew it would work; people don't fuck about when it comes to their children.

Sarah was at the top of the stairs, weapon strong, five steps behind. The worse scenario I could imagine couldn't be stopped now. She was walking down the stairs, pistol behind her, in case one of the children looked back.

I slowed the herd. 'Hey, hey, don't go yet. I think your dad wants you all in the kitchen. He's finding out if Sarah and I are coming to see you all sing today.' They turned left through the door to their dad. I had eye-to-eye with Sarah. She was nearing the bottom of the stairs and was placing her weapon in her trouser band.

'Remember what I said.'

She nodded as we both went into the kitchen with the last of the kids. He got to the end of his call and the kids were all over him, wanting to know.

'Right, we're on at ten!' He beamed.

The kids cheered and we both cheered with them.

'Well done!' I had a big smile on my face. 'Thanks a lot, mate. Brilliant!'

He remembered the bus. 'What are you guys doing here? Go, go!' He shooed them out towards the front door.

I heard the hiss of the bus's air brakes and the chug of diesel as it dragged itself down the road. Josh came back into the kitchen and collapsed onto a chair with a loud sigh, pouring himself some more coffee as he looked up at Sarah. 'Come back, Geri, all is forgiven.' He looked at me. 'Great news, huh? To tell you the truth, I'm quite looking forward to it myself.'

Sarah laughed, more out of relief than anything else.

'Say, do you guys have a camera?'

363

We didn't.

'No problem, we can pick one up from a store. I'm quite look-ing forward to going downtown. I miss working the team, man.' He took another slug of coffee. 'This job is driving me crazy, know what I'm saying? I've got to get back on ops.' Tilting his head back, he killed the coffee. 'I'm going to make a call to arrange parking. It's a nightmare up there.'

Sarah stood up. 'I'll finish getting ready and pack.'

I followed her out to the stairs and passed over my weapon. 'In the bags.'

I was back at the coffee percolator as Josh finished his call. I motioned to see if he wanted more, and he nodded. The phone went back on the wall and he came to the table.

I took a seat beside him. 'We'll just have to wait now while she puts her face on.'

He smiled as he unfolded the newspaper. I started to flap as the *Washington Post* was laid out on the table top, but the chances of the story still being in there after three days were pretty slim, especially given the amount of column inches devoted to events at the White House.

'Anything interesting?'

'Hell no, just the normal shit.'

He turned the paper round to show me the front page: pictures of Netanyahu and Arafat in town yesterday. The subject was a bit too close to home for me at the moment.

He turned the paper back as I asked, 'What do think, mate? Think it will work? You know, the peace deal?'

He started to give his views on the summit. Not that I was listening, but I wanted him to talk, which was why I'd asked the question in the first place. The more he was gobbing off, the more I could just sit there and nod and agree or throw in the odd question, but at the same time get myself revved up for the job. I was in my own little world, so relieved the call had brought good news.

I heard Sarah coming down the stairs. It brought me back to the real world. He was now honking about all the roadworks and the DC traffic as Sarah came into the room with our bags and my jacket. She may not have had time for a shower but she'd made up for it with eye-liner and lip gloss.

Josh stood up, looking at his watch. 'OK, let's saddle up!'

I picked up our two bags while Josh ran upstairs. He didn't say why, but we both knew that it was to fetch his weapon.

26

A bleep came from the pickup and the lights flashed. Josh jumped into the cab, and Sarah and I went round to the passenger side. As I opened the door a toy racing car fell out. Crayons, a colouring sheet from McDonald's and other kids' crap littered the footwell. I put our bags in the back; our weapons were inside now, and would stay there. Sarah picked up the toy from the sidewalk and climbed in. I followed; there was room enough for three in the front seat.

The morning sky was still overcast, but bright when the sun came out between the clouds. I had to squint as I looked through the windscreen. A pair of mirrored sunglasses were hanging by their cord from the rear-view mirror. Josh put them on over his shiny head and fired up the ignition. The engine gave a big four-litre growl, and out we backed, the antenna automatically starting to rise.

The radio came on, and to my surprise it was a woman talking about the place of Jesus in today's world. Josh looked at me, obviously feeling that my unasked question needed an answer. 'Christian channel,' he said, not at all defensively. 'A couple of guys got me into listening. It's been a help. I've even started going to a few meetings with them.'

I said, 'That's good, Josh,' and wondered if his bible studies had got as far as Judas yet.

We headed north, back along the route by which the taxi had brought us. Josh chatted about how long it had been since he'd been to the White House, and what he missed about working there. The thing he didn't miss, he said as we gradually crawled our way to DC, was the traffic. He hated it. As if we didn't know by now.

Sarah saw a filling station coming up and reminded Josh to stop for a one-shot camera. Twenty-five minutes after leaving the house, we were back on the Jefferson Davis Highway approaching the Pentagon. Instead of passing it, however, we took a right onto a bridge that took us across the Potomac. Josh became the tourist guide. 'Left, that's the Jefferson Memorial, and further over is the Lincoln Memorial. Sarah, you've gotta get Nick to take you to the Reflecting Pool at sunset; it's real romantic, just like the movies.'

We had plenty of time to admire the view, as the traffic was backed up from halfway over the bridge. Eventually we started heading north on 14th Street, bisecting the vast stretch of grass that is the National Mall, running from the Capitol building all the way down the Lincoln Memorial by the Potomac.

Once over the Mall we made a few turns. Josh said, 'Here we are, where all the dirty deeds are done!' We drove past the target, leaving it to our left. 'We have to go round because of the one-way system. But that's cool, you get to see it from all sides.'

Once we'd done a circuit anticlockwise, we landed up on 17th Street. The front of the White House faced north, sandwiched between two gardens, Lafayette Park, which was part of the pedestrian area in the front, now that Pennsylvania Ave was closed to traffic, and, at the rear, backing onto the National Mall, the Ellipse, a large area of green that looked as if it had become a giant carpark for government permit holders.

The White House was flanked to the west by the old Executive Office and to the east by the Treasury Department. Each of the two buildings had an access road between it and the White House, but both were closed to traffic. West Executive Avenue was closed off to pedestrians as well, but East Executive

Avenue wasn't, to allow the public entry through the east wing of the White House.

We turned left and slowed down. Rows of cars were parked on the grass of the Ellipse, and in amongst them was a line of about a dozen yellow school buses.

Josh indicated again. The road had originally bent round, away from the White House, but had since been blocked off to create yet another carpark. We passed the gates to West Executive Avenue and stopped on the corner of State Place. Josh opened the window and put his hand out. 'Yo!'

He got a nod from a man dressed in a grey single-breasted suit and what looked like a reddish tie. He'd been standing by the gates and started to amble towards us.

'Davy Boy! Long time!'

'Yo, Josh, good to see you!'

Sarah and I looked at each other as they exchanged greetings. She had the same concern as I did: Was this guy going to stay with us?

'How goes it Davy, get a place for me?'

Davy continued towards the wagon. I could see his tie now – lots of small Dalmatians on a red background. 'Hey, you know what, just park in the West Exec duty pool.'

As we got out of the vehicle Josh clapped Davy enthusiastically across the shoulders. 'Come here, let me introduce you to my friends from the UK. This is Sarah.' They shook hands. 'And this is Nick.' We pressed the flesh.

'Hey. Good to see you. Welcome.' Davy was in his mid-thirties, and very open and friendly. He was also tall, fit, good-looking and had all his own teeth – white and perfect. If he hadn't been in the Secret Service, a great career would have beckoned as the Diet Coke man.

Davy had everything arranged. 'I'll take you guys to the gate house, get you an ID pass each and take you in. As you know, it's kinda busy today, but we'll do what we can for you.'

Sarah and I gushed our thanks as we started to walk off with him. Josh cut in from behind us, 'See you folks in a few.' I heard his door close and the wagon start to move.

Davy did all the small talk. 'Take long to get here?'

I looked at my watch. It was ten sixteen. 'No, not really, just over an hour.'

'That's good. Was he complaining about the traffic?'

'He did nothing but moan.'

Davy Boy liked that one. It seemed that nothing had changed with his old workmate.

Josh's black Dodge passed us on the way to the gates that would let him into West Executive Avenue. We were going there as well, but via the security gatehouse. Josh stopped at the big, black iron gates, which opened automatically for him. The gate house was to the left, with a turnstile and airport-style metal detector. From a distance it had looked as if it was made of white PVC and glass, like a conservatory. As we got nearer, I could see that it wasn't; the white paint covered steel, and the glass was so thick I could only just make out movement inside.

As the gates closed behind him, I could see Josh parking in line, nose in to the pavement, about fifty metres up on the left-hand side.

There was a big round of applause to my right, and the roar of excited children's voices, coming from a huge marquee which had been erected in the rear White House gardens. Davy grinned. 'There are about two hundred of them in there. Been practising all morning.' He screwed up his face as the applause continued. 'At least they think they're good.'

I could see more clearly into the gatehouse now that we'd gone through the fence, turned right and were standing by the metal detector. Just beyond that was the turnstile. Two bodies were inside the gatehouse. The door opened and one of them came out. An electric buzz came from the turnstile as Josh came through to join us. The guard was white and in his forties. His Secret Service uniform was a very sharply pressed white shirt, a black tie, black trousers with a yellow stripe and black patent-leather belt kit, holding a semi-automatic pistol and spare mags. He couldn't wait to have a go at Josh.

'Things must be getting desperate round here if they're bringing you back!'

369

Josh laughed; he'd obviously had this for years from this guy, because he gave him the finger as he replied. 'I've been sent to get rid of all the dead wood, so you'd better watch out, lard-arse.'

Everybody contributed to the banter as the fat one slapped his stomach. Sarah and I were the gooseberries in this, so we just kept our mouths shut and concentrated on looking awestruck at standing so close to the official residence of the most powerful man on earth.

I could see that Lard-arse and a younger black guy who was still inside the gatehouse were also responsible for manning a bank of TV monitors and radios. Davy got hold of a clipboard and went through the signing-in procedure. 'Nick, surname please?'

'Stone.' Being with Josh, there was no option but to reply truthfully. 'OK, S–t–o–n–e.' There was a few seconds' pause as he finished writing.

'And Sarah?'

'Darnley.'

He frowned, and she spelled it for him as she wiped her new glasses with a tissue from her pocket. 'OK, if you can just sign here and here for me, please.'

The first signature was for the ID card, the second for the entry log. Josh then signed himself in as well. Davy gave the clipboard back to the guard, who handed Sarah and me each an ID card. Lard-arse smiled at Sarah as he passed her card over. 'You're not going to let these two losers show you around, are you?'

'I guess I'm stuck with them for now.'

He smiled and shook his head. 'The only place these two know is the canteen. You'll just be eating doughnuts and drinking coffee all day, and look what that did for me!' He looked down at his belly.

We joined in the laughter. Mine was out of sheer relief at getting even this far. It appeared that we weren't quite in the Good Lads Club because we didn't have our cards on nylon straps – we had clips, with a black V on a white background – not for visitor, but volunteer. It must have been part of the deal, today being busy: no visitors. It seemed Davy and Josh had made a real effort for us. I hated that. It made me feel even more guilty, but I'd live. At least, I hoped I would.

Our IDs looked quite different from the ones Davy and Josh were wearing. Theirs had a blue edge surrounding their pictures, and some red markings underneath. We clipped ours onto our jackets and Davy clapped and rubbed his hands together. 'OK, people, let's do this thing.' He walked around the detector and waited with Josh as we walked through it.

As we all went through the turnstile I didn't know which feeling inside me was stronger, elation at getting past the first hurdle, or concern that I was now fenced in and the clock was ticking.

We walked north along West Exec Ave. We weren't inside the actual grounds yet, as the iron fencing that stretched away from the gate divided the White House from the road. We seemed to be aiming for an entrance about fifty metres further up, which opened onto the front White House lawn. Looking through into the gardens, I could see the rear of the main building and the marquee. A member of the Emergency Response Team was standing under a tree, talking into his radio as he watched the road, and us. He really looked the business. He was dressed from head to foot in black: black coveralls, black belt kit, body armour and boots. He had a baseball cap with ERT on the front and a pager that was hooked onto the leg strapping that went round his thigh to keep his pistol and holster in place. It looked as if his main weapon, probably an MP5, was covered by a black nylon support across his chest.

Josh took a back seat as Davy started to give us the brief while we continued towards the gate. 'Regardless of what people think, this place is basically just an office complex. Over to the left-hand side' – we looked over at the old Exec Building in perfect unison, like a group of Japanese tourists – 'that's where the VP's office is, and that's also the Indian Treaty Room. It's a fantastic sight, I'll try and get you in there later on, especially if our little tour the other side of the fence is cut short.'

We carried on up the road between the two buildings, basically just listening to Davy Boy. The more you listen, the less you have to say and the less you can fuck up – and the more time you can

371

spend looking for anyone who looks remotely like a dark-skinned Al Gore or Bill Gates.

Walking purposefully between the two buildings, via the gate, were men in conservative suits and women in identical two pieces, each with an ID card dangling on a nylon cord. Television and power cables snaked across the tarmac, and at the top of the road, where it met Pennsylvania Avenue, satellite trucks were jammed onto every available square inch of space.

As we got to within ten metres or so of the gate I saw Monica Beach in front of me, on the White House side of the fence. I looked at Sarah. She'd seen it, too. Multi-coloured umbrellas were pitched high to keep the light out of the camera lenses. Spotlights were rigged up for the reporters to look good in front of the cameras, and there were yet more power cables. They seemed to have a life of their own. The whole place looked like a Hollywood location.

Beyond Monica Beach I could see another gatehouse, which I guessed was the press entrance point from Pennsylvania Avenue. Throngs of people with videos and cameras jostled against the railings to get a good shot of the building. They seemed to be photographing everything that moved, maybe in the hope of capturing some celebrity to show the folks back home. If this all went to ratshit in a few hours' time, I guessed the police would be appealing for them to hand in their footage.

Davy continued to give us the general picture as we stood at the gate. There was a bit of a bottleneck as ERT and uniformed Secret Service security scrutinized the IDs of everybody who was waiting to go through. 'The White House can be broken down into three main parts. The east wing' – he pointed to the far side of the main house; we looked, but I was more intent on scanning the faces of the news crews that were walking from the building up to the beach – 'then, in the middle, the executive mansion. That's the part you always see in newsreels. As you can see, just outside, on the lawn, is where the ceremony will take place. The kids will be doing their thing in front of the stage.'

Arranged on the stage were a couple of rows of chairs, and two lecterns emblazoned with the presidential seal. The flags of Israel,

Palestine and the United States were being unfurled on flagpoles. The scene looked idyllic.

Sarah was watching the hordes of tourists poking their video cameras through the fence. 'Isn't it dangerous to be so exposed to the road?'

Davy shook his head. 'No, they'll close off Penn Ave soon.' He pointed to our side of the Executive Mansion. 'This here is the west wing, used mainly for administration and press briefings, as you can see.' He nodded over to the TV crews behind us.

We turned, and it gave both of us an opportunity to have a good look at the personnel. I couldn't see anyone who looked remotely like our targets. In any case, these guys were technicians sorting out camera gear, not reporters. We just had to get back to playing the tourist.

'The Oval Office is in the west wing and not in the Executive Mansion,' Davy went on. 'That's why these guys' – he pointed at the crowd by the fence – 'never get to see him. They're always looking at the wrong place and from the wrong side. The Oval Office overlooks where all the kids are at the moment.'

Still we waited, shuffling forward towards the security. Now and again Josh and Davy waved at somebody they recognized. We moved out of the way so that a group of sharply dressed men and women could come through the gate onto the road. One of the women recognized Josh. 'Well, Mr D'Souza! What brings you to town?'

Josh stepped to one side with a larger than normal smile on his face. 'I thought I'd just drop in and say heyyy.' We stood and waited for a few seconds so that he could finish his conversation. I could hear him talking about his kids being part of the ceremony. Sarah suddenly remembered something. 'Oh no, the camera. I've left it in the car.'

Josh heard and turned his head. 'Hey, no problem, I'll open the truck.'

Sarah didn't want to mess up the conversation. 'That's OK, I'll do it.' She held out her hand for the keys and Josh presented them.

I'd forgotten it, too. We were going to need it, as we were

373

tourists on a once-in-a-lifetime trip. Josh looked at me as if I was a mophead. 'We now know who's the one with the smarts!' Then he turned back to his conversation.

We waited until Sarah ran back to us with the camera in her hand, and Davy continued the tour. 'Come on, I'll show you something that you see on the news every day.' Following yet more power cables, we were walking along the pathway that led from the gate to the front of the east wing. We went down a few steps and past a door with a small white semi-circular canopy over it. More power cables spewed over the ground and a portable generator was chugging away to my left. Every time we passed groups of people, I watched Sarah for a reaction. She was the only one who could give a positive ID on these people. I could only make possibles.

'Here we are.' We'd arrived at a large glass-panelled door. I looked to the left and saw a satellite truck backed up against the side of the main stone staircase, which was the North Portico of the Executive Mansion. Under the staircase were open doors leading into the ground floor. A flight above it led to the first floor and the main entrance. Davy ushered us through and we were immediately confronted by a very familiar sight, the lectern with the presidential seal from which I'd seen so many White House statements delivered. The room looked very purposeful and businesslike, but was much smaller than I'd imagined. Facing the lectern were plastic chairs, arranged in rows with a centre aisle. It looked more like the set-up for a community meeting in the local village hall, except that there were wires everywhere on the floor, with camera crews sorting out TV equipment and mikes. I was busily scanning the room, looking at the dozen or so people who were in a frenzy preparing for the afternoon's events.

Josh looked at us both, 'You got your camera?'

I played dumb. 'What?'

'Your camera?'

There was a big laugh. He said, 'Go on, get up there!'

Sarah and I looked at each other and I thought, Fuck it, we've got to do it, it would be unusual not to. Josh took pictures of each of us at the lectern, and one of us together; we put our arms around each other for it and smiled. He threw the camera at me as we walked towards him. 'Something to show your grand-children!' On cue, Sarah and I exchanged the expected coy smile.

We came out of the press conference area and back onto the pathway. Davy was looking at the satellite truck. Josh was still saying hello to everyone he knew and explaining to them why he was here. Davy had made up his mind. 'Hey, you know what? I think we will go round the other side. It's kinda busy in there.' Shading our eyes from a sudden burst of brilliant sunshine, we started to walk up the small flight of stairs that would take us to the same level as the main entrance staircase.

Still no Al or Bill, but we were a bit early. What we were going to do when we pinged them, I hadn't actually worked out yet. It all depended on the situation. I hoped we could get Josh to take action, alert him that something was wrong, or maybe I'd say that I'd seen people I could positively ID as terrorists. Whatever, it didn't matter, as long as these people stopped them. All we had to do was find them first.

I asked, 'Davy, when do the rest of the media arrive, mate? Do they go anywhere to get instructions and stuff like that?'

He pointed back to the press room. 'The media get a briefing in there at noon. The TV presentation guys won't pitch up until then. They just have their sound and lighting people rig up first.'

I looked excited. 'Would it be possible to see the briefing? I'm a bit of a media junkie, I really like that sort of thing.'

Davy looked at me as if I was mad. How could something like that be interesting? 'Sure, no problem.'

I looked over at Sarah as we walked. She knew what I was doing. All we had to do was keep this up until midday. If the players were going to show, they'd be at the media brief.

We'd reached the bottom of the stairs of the North Portico lead-ing into the mansion. Davy pointed to the stage on the grass opposite, still receiving its finishing touches. He nodded towards Pennsylvania Avenue. 'The cameras will be on that side of the stage, with the TV reports made from the media area we passed earlier.' We both nodded and looked extremely interested, which wasn't difficult. Josh wasn't so enthralled. He asked Davy, 'Where to now?'

'You wanna see the alley?'

We continued to walk past the Executive Mansion towards the east wing. The drive we were walking on went from the white gatehouse the press used and swept in a semicircle to the far right of the lawn, where there was a similar security post. An ERT guy was walking towards it from a line of black Chevy pickups parked in line on the driveway. Their red and blue light racks, darkened windows and antennae made me remember that there were probably more guns within a 200-metre radius of where we were standing than Jim's had sold in its lifetime. We would have to be careful not to get zapped ourselves when they took on the players.

We now had an uninterrupted view down into the lower area the other side of the staircase. I couldn't help noticing the paint. It was more cream than white, and it was peeling. We moved a bit further along and went down some steps that took us below the level of the grass. At the bottom, Davy turned and walked backwards so he could face us as he explained, 'This is the part the public don't get to see.' We bent down to get past some large steel ventilation pipes. He pointed at the Executive Mansion. 'This is really the ground floor. Behind this wall are some of the state rooms, like the Diplomatic Reception Room, the China Room, that kinda thing.' He indicated the area below us. 'But this is more interesting ... the basement, that's where it's at. In fact, there are two basements. Bowling, rest areas, paint shop and repairs. There's even a bomb shelter down there.' Looking to the right, I saw windows that opened onto rooms under the White House driveway and lawn.

We came to a white, glass-panelled double door. Actually, it was more grey than white, now. You could tell this was the admin area. Davy kept the door open for me and Sarah. Josh followed.

We were now under the main staircase. Across the way the satellite crew were working under the eagle eye of an ERT escort. Davy gave him a wave. 'Hi, Jeff, good to see you, man.'

Davy steered us towards the door that was nearest the other

entrance, into which all the cables seemed to lead. Once through it, I was hit straight away by the smell: the heavy odour of school dinners and cleaning products that I'd known as a child and which, as I got older, I came to associate with army cookhouses or stairways of low-rent accommodation. We were in a hall about four metres wide, with polished floor tiles. The walls were stone, with a plaster skim and many years' worth of cream gloss paint. Grooves and concave shapes had been gouged into the plaster by carelessly pushed food trolleys, an empty one of which was parked up in the corridor.

Following the cables, we passed a lift and staircase on our left, then went through another door. It was like walking into a different world. We emerged into the opulent splendour of marble walls and glass chandeliers, hanging from high cross-vaulted ceilings. The smell had disappeared. Blocking the view to our left were two tall brown screens, positioned like a roadblock. Davy and Josh muttered greetings to the ERT and two Secret Service agents who were in the area. One of them had a blue tie with golfers in various poses, the other had a yellow one covered in little biplanes.

Davy said, 'This is the ground floor hallway. We can't see down it today as the president will be here later on. He won't want to see all this stuff trailing around.' He was pointing to the cabling.

Sarah wanted to know more. 'Why, what's happening in here? I thought everything was going on outside?'

Two television technicians walked past from left to right, escorted by their ERT minder. Josh was still talking quietly to the two Secret Service guys.

Davy whispered, 'At about eleven, Arafat, Netanyahu and the president will be in the Diplomatic Reception Room for coffee.' He nodded his head towards the TV crew, who were now walking back towards us. 'These guys are rigging up a remote for CNN that's going to put out live coverage. The leaders stay there for twenty to thirty minutes, then move out for an early lunch.'

Sarah was trying to work out where the Diplomatic Reception Room was, pointing past the screens. 'That's the oval-shaped room down there on the right, isn't it?'

Davy nodded. 'Yeah, after lunch they then move to the Blue Room. That's the same shape and directly above on the first floor. Then, at one o'clock, they walk out onto the lawn and get blasted by the heavenly choir.' He screwed up his face again at the thought of 200 kids out of tune.

Josh came over and joined us. 'Hey, guys, I think we'd better move on.' We got the hint. The Secret Service guys didn't want us around so near coffee time.

We started down the corridor to the right, following the cables. Davy sparked up, pointing at a large white double door at the end of the corridor. 'That leads to the west wing, where the briefing area is.' The cable went through a door on the left of the corridor. We turned right and entered one of the admin areas. The smell came back to me. To the left was another lift. 'That's the service elevator for the State Dining Room.' Davy was clearly enjoying his role as tour guide. 'It's directly above us on the first floor.' To the right of the lift was a spiral staircase.

We stopped by the elevator. Davy had a huge grin on his face. 'I gotta show you folks the burn marks you Brits made last time you made an unannounced visit!'

A trolley headed towards us, pushed by an efficient-looking, mid-fifties black guy in black trousers, waistcoat, tie and a very crisply laundered white shirt. It was laden with coffee pots, cups and saucers, biscuits and all sorts. The guy said, 'Excuse me, gentlemen,' then saw Sarah and added, 'and lady,' in a very courteous manner as he cruised past, the cups rattling on the metal trolley. Basically, of course, he was just telling us to get the fuck out of the way. He was a man with a mission.

We climbed down the spiral staircase as Davy continued his running commentary. 'We have two other elevators, one hundred and thirty-two rooms and thirty-three bathrooms.'

Josh chipped in. 'And seven staircases.'

I tried to raise a smile of acknowledgement. At any other time this would be interesting, but not now.

At the bottom we stopped by a pair of fire doors with thick wooden panels inset with two rectangular strips of wired, fire-resistant glass, and covered with dirty handmarks where they got continuously pushed. Above them sat a large slab of stone supporting the archway. Black scorch marks were clearly visible.

'We've kept them there just as a little reminder of the sort of thing that happens when you guys come to town. Not that you stayed that long; we'd had more than enough of you by then.'

There was more laughter. I saw Sarah check her watch.

Davy said, 'You know, people think that it was called the White House after you Brits burned it down. Not so, it only got its name in 1901, under . . .' He turned to Josh for the answer.

'Roosevelt.' Josh looked at us sheepishly. 'Hey, if you work here you have to know these things.'

There wasn't much we could say, and there was only so much burned stone we could look at. After a minute or so, Davy said, 'OK, let's go bowl a few.'

27

As we pushed our way through the fire doors, I could see maybe twenty-five or thirty metres of white painted corridor in front of me, each side of which were white wooden doors slightly inset into the walls. The whole area had a functional feel. It was lit by strip lighting, with secondary lighting boxes positioned at key points in case of power failure or fire. The same cookhouse-and-polish smell hung in the air. There was no activity down here at all. Our footsteps squeaked on the tiles and echoed along the corridor.

We came to a pile of cardboard boxes and bulging bin liners stacked against the wall. 'It's just like any other house,' Davy said. 'All the junk goes into the basement.'

We passed several of the white doors and came to a grey metal one with a slowly flashing red bulb above it. Davy pointed up. 'Let's see who's in.' He swiped his ID card through a security lock and said, 'Welcome to Crisis Four.'

He opened the door and gestured us in. I followed Sarah into a darkened room which contained a bank of at least twenty CCTV screens, set into the wall in banks of three. Each carried a different picture, with a time code bar at the bottom ticking away the milliseconds. The coloured views were of large, richly decorated rooms, and hundreds of metres of corridors and colonnades. On a desktop that ran the whole length of the console, illuminated by small downlighters, were banks of telephones, microphones and clipboards.

I went in and moved to one side so that Josh could follow. The temperature was cooler in here; I could hear the air-conditioning humming gently above me. Lined up in front of the bank of screens were four office chairs on castors. The sole occupant of the room was sitting on one of them, dressed in ERT black, his baseball cap illuminated by the screens as he mumbled into one of the phones.

I looked at Sarah. Her eyes were glued to the screens; I could see the light from them reflecting off her face.

The phone went down and Josh called out, 'Yo, Top Cat! How goes it?'

TC spun round in his chair and raised both arms. 'Heyyya, fella! I'm good. It's been a while.' He was white and looked in his mid-thirties, with a very smart, well-trimmed moustache.

They shook hands and Josh introduced us. 'This is Nick, and this is Sarah, they're from the UK. Friends of mine. This is TC.' We both walked over to him, and he stood up to shake hands. His chin already had shadow and he looked as if he needed five or six shaves a day; either that, or he'd been on duty all night. He was maybe about five foot six, with short dark-brown hair under his black cap.

TC's firm grip contrasted with his very soft Southern accent, but both oozed confidence. 'What have you seen so far?'

'Josh has been showing us what happened the last time the Brits were down here.'

Sarah had a question to ask Davy. 'Do you think it would be possible to see the State Dining Room? It's just that I'm a big fan of Jackie O and . . .'

Davy looked at TC, who shrugged apologetically. 'I'm sorry to have to tell you folks that no-one can go upstairs today.'

Josh felt that he had to explain. 'Access depends on what is going on. Just about any other day would have been fine. Hey, thousands of people visit most days; it's one of Washington's biggest attractions.'

Sarah and I both started waffling variations on the theme of,

'It's no problem, it's great just being here. We're really enjoying it.'

Davy sounded like he had a good idea. 'I tell you what, from here you can see it all anyway.' He pointed at the screens, and then proceeded to give us a quick rundown. 'As I said, this room is Crisis Four. It's one of the control centres from where any incident in the White House or grounds can be monitored and controlled. Which control centre is used depends on where the incident occurs.'

Sarah and I were all eyes and ears as we looked at the screens, especially the one that showed the press briefing room. Not much had changed in there. I kept my eye on it, though.

TC took over the brief as he went back to his chair. 'Crisis Four could be used, say, if anything happened upstairs – the president and first lady would be moved down here to the secure area. It also doubles as the bomb shelter. There's a kinda neat room beyond this for the VIPs.' He pointed at a screen. 'There's the State Dining Room. That's kinda neat, too.'

It didn't look as if lunch was going to be served there today. The long dark wood table just had silver candelabras placed along its centre. Apart from that it was bare. Sarah studied the picture for a while, as if taking in all the detail of the decor. My eyes were focused on the shot of the briefing room.

'Is that the Diplomatic Reception Room?' Sarah put her finger on a screen to my left, pointing to a doorway. Looking over, I could see the brown screens blocking off the ground floor corridor, and the ERT escort standing over the CNN guys, who were still fiddling about with cables.

TC confirmed it. 'That's right. Any minute now you'll see the big three appear and walk in there. At the moment they're across the hall, in the library.'

As I watched the picture he was indicating, flicking back to check the briefing room every few seconds, our friendly waiter came out of the reception room and walked back towards the brown screens. This time his trolley was empty. I heard comms mush coming from TC's earpiece. 'The coffee's there, all we need now are the drinkers.' The ERT guy began to move the CNN people out of the corridor, back towards their wagon. I flicked my eyes over at one of the screens again. Shit! Bill Gates was in the briefing room. At least, the hair and glasses matched what I thought he looked like. He had walked in and was just looking around. I needed Sarah to confirm, but she was the other side of Davy as we all stood around TC in his chair. I kept looking at her, trying to catch her eye. I couldn't say anything yet; I could be wrong. Why wasn't she also checking that screen? They were focused on the other one with the four Secret Service men at the far end of the corridor.

More mush was coming from TC's earpiece. 'Here they come . . .'

A few seconds later the three world leaders walked out into the corridor and turned towards the camera. They were moving quite slowly so that Arafat could keep up. I checked Bill Gates. He was now sitting down and writing. I looked back at the other screen, then at Sarah. Come on, look at me, check the screen, do something! She was oblivious to anything but the three leaders as a group of advisers followed them, clutching folders and nodding with each other as they walked.

'Hey, let's give you folks a listen.' TC leaned over the desktop and hit a button on the console. A speaker in front of us burst into life. A very quick, but calm New York voice was giving commands over the net. People were acknowledging him in just the same tones. It sounded like mission control at Houston. Small red buttons were now lit on three of the microphones on the desk. I checked Bill Gates. He hadn't moved.

They walked along the corridor for a short way, Clinton between the two others as they moved in line abreast. A few paces more and they turned left into the Reception Room.

I looked across at Sarah. She was checking the large green digital display clock on the wall. It was 10:57; they were right on time. 'Hey, Sarah, isn't that Gatesy? You know, that reporter friend of yours?' I couldn't think of anything else to say. I pointed and everyone turned to look.

Sarah took a step forward and looked at the figure sitting down, reading his notes. Standing back, she looked at me. 'No, it's not. His hair is much darker. But they do look similar.'

TC stood up 'That's it, folks, I've gotta go.' He hit the console button. The sound and red microphone lights died.

We all shook hands again. 'I hope you people have a good trip. Ask these two nicely, see if they'll take you over to the Treaty Room.'

Davy said, 'It's on the itinerary, after the alley.'

TC nodded as he headed for the door. 'See you guys. Hey Davy, don't forget, four thirty this afternoon, we've got that meeting.' They ran through a few details of their work admin while Sarah and I, the gooseberries, just stood by, keeping an eye on the briefing-room screen.

We followed TC out of Crisis Four. When we were all out in the corridor he made sure the door was secure, then turned right and walked off towards the fire doors with a cheery wave of the hand.

A couple of Hispanic women came squeaking along in white overalls and white patent-leather shoes, looking like a cross between cleaners and nurses, and talking at 100 mph in their own language. They stopped as they passed us, nodded and smiled, then returned to their warp-speed conversation. We turned left and moved further down the corridor.

Josh had an idea. 'Hey, you know what? I'll go over and see if I can get us into the Treaty Room, and maybe even the VP's office.'

'That would be great,' I said. 'Would we still be able to watch the press brief?'

Sarah joined in. 'Yes, I'd love to see that as well. I have—' Josh smiled as he put his hands up defensively, like a parent fending off an overenthusiastic child. 'Hey, no problem. In a few.' He turned and walked towards the fire doors. Sarah and I exchanged a relieved glance as Davy led the way. We stopped two doors down.

Davy grinned. 'This is the best room in the house.' He opened the door. Inside was an open space, maybe fifteen feet by fifteen, with stackable plastic chairs arranged around the walls, the same as in the briefing room. Beyond that, in shadow, was a single-lane bowling alley.

The floor was highly polished lino. The walls were painted white, and covered with a couple of posters of bowling teams, and pushed against it was a large wooden box, also painted white, with compartments which looked as if they were holding about eight or nine pairs of bowling shoes.

There was whirring and clicking as all the bits and pieces of alley machinery came to life and the strip lighting along the alley flickered on.

Davy smiled back at us as he walked towards the shoes. 'I've got a great story for you guys.'

By now the bowling balls were rolling up onto the stand and the pins were being positioned by the machine at the bottom of the lane.

Davy had his back to us, his shoulders rolling as he anticipated his own story. His head moved to look at us both again and he pointed at the top pair of shoes. 'You see these?' We both nodded. He looked back to pull them out. I took the opportunity for a quick look at Baby-G. Fifty-five minutes to go until the press brief.

Davy turned round to walk back to us. 'These are Bill's personal bowling shoes,' he said. 'Look at the size of the things.'

They must have been something like size sixteen, at least. 'He's a big man all right.' Hefting them in his hand, he chuckled. 'You know the old saying, big feet, big . . .' He suddenly checked himself in case Sarah didn't approve. She was smiling.

The shoes were white with red stripes. As Davy reached us, he turned them round and showed us something. 'See this?' All smiles, he pointed to the back of the shoes. I saw that each had a little mark in black felt tip. 'One day Bill came down with some of his bowling buddies. He went to get his shoes, and a couple of the advisors saw this written on the back.' He pointed again. On one was the letter "L", and on the other an "R".

'There they were, supposed to be discussing world affairs, and his aides were suddenly more worried about how he'd react to people writing on his shoes . . .

'Well, Bill picked them up, and for a moment there was silence . . .' I could tell old Davy Boy had told this story many,

many times, because the pauses were in just the right places. '...
yep, there he was, the President of the United States, the most
powerful man in the world, and someone had gotten a pen and
done that to him!

'Nobody was too sure how he was going to take it. Anyways,
he looked down at the shoes, and then Bill started to laugh. "I'll
tell you what, boys, this is just what I need . . . they are so darned
confusing, not being proper shoes and all." '

Davy started to laugh. I wasn't sure if the story was funny
or not, and nor was Sarah. I just took Davy's lead and joined
in. I could hear Sarah, standing slightly behind me, doing the
same.

The laughter died down and Davy carried on, pleased with our
reaction. 'And that's why it's still there. Apparently Bill says it
cuts his prep time by a half, so there's more time to play.'

He was going to put the shoes back. He turned away and took
two steps, and there was a thud.

Bill's shoes fell out of Davy's hands. There was no blood until
he hit the floor, face forwards, and then it started to spurt from his
head, dark and thick. I swung round.

Sarah was in a perfect firing position, standing at forty-five
degrees to Davy, with her right pistol hand out straight, pushing
the suppressed weapon at the target, her left hand cupped
around both the pistol grip and the other hand, pulling back. She
looked so relaxed she could have been on the range.

'What the fuck are you doing?' I shouted. What a bone
question; I could see precisely what she was doing.

I didn't know why, but I was half whispering, half shouting as
she lowered the pistol. 'For fuck's sake, we agreed, no killing.
What are you doing bringing that thing in? We don't need it.'

She just stood there, in a different world, calmly putting the
pistol back into her waistband.

This was out of control. No matter what happened now, we
were in a world of shit and I had no idea by whose rules we were
playing.

I started to move towards the door.

She looked at me quizzically. 'Where are you going?'

'I'm locking the door – what do you think I'm doing, letting everyone in? We're in deep shit, Sarah. Do you have any idea what you've done? This won't stop anything; it makes it worse.'

I reached the door and turned the lock inside the tumbler. It was pointless going over to Davy. There wasn't a sound from him, and dark, deoxygenated blood seeped from his mouth.

I stayed where I was, shaking my head in disbelief. 'It was under control, Sarah, for fuck's sake. Midday – the press brief, remember? What the fuck are you doing?'

She started towards the door. I moved across her, putting my arms up to stop her. 'Whoa, this is way out of control. It's time to stop this, now, and get help. Just get thinking of a fucking good story.'

I pointed at Davy as I turned towards the door once more. Why had she done it? It took two seconds before it became obvious to me why. She'd stitched me up. 'You fucking bitch!' I started to turn back towards her.

At the same instant I felt pain explode in my stomach. The wind was knocked out of my lungs as I fell to my knees. I felt a fierce burning sensation on the left side of my gut.

The left side of my forehead hit the floor, then my nose. There were sparks flashing in my head. I tasted blood in my throat. I'd never taken a round before.

I couldn't see Sarah. I was too busy curling into a foetal position as I tried to control the pain.

I started a low moaning noise that I couldn't stop. I slowly, slowly rolled my head to find her. She was crouched over Davy. His ID was now around her neck; at a casual glance she would look part of the environment. Her loafers tiptoed around him, avoiding the blood, then took the pistol from his belt and the two mags from their carrier.

I didn't want her to know that I was still alive. I lay as motionless as I could, eyes closed, trying to stifle my own moaning. It wasn't working.

I sensed her standing over me. I opened my eyes. She was just too far away for me to reach her, even if I'd been able to.

She looked at her watch and then at me. The weapon came up

and stopped in line with her eyes. For the first time in my life I thought of someone I would miss, and I decided that my last thought would be about Kelly. I looked at Sarah and waited. There was a delay, but no emotion, no explanation. Then she said, 'You have a child now. I hope you live long enough to see her.' She lowered the weapon, checking her watch again as she walked away.

The tumbler was turned and the door opened. I tried to shout, but it didn't happen. The only sound that came out was a weak rasp. 'Fuck you!' Blood sprayed out of my mouth. She glanced down at me, no reaction in her eyes.

There was a pause as she checked outside, then the door closed quietly.

She was gone.

The pain was intensifying. I looked around frantically for a panic button or a phone, but I couldn't see too well, things were getting hazy. Two others left to kill him? My arse; it had been her all along. How the fuck did I not see it?

Being curled up in a ball on the floor wasn't going to do me or the VIPs any good. I needed to do something, even if it didn't work. As I died, I would at least know that I'd tried to right my fuck-up.

My vision was starting to blur. I was taking short, sharp breaths, and my stomach muscles were tensing of their own accord. I moved my hand over a hole in my belly the size of a five-pence piece and plugged it with my thumb. At least I didn't have to worry about an exit wound; I knew it was subsonic ammunition for the silenced Chinese thing. The round would still be kicking around inside me somewhere.

I dragged myself towards the door, through a pool of Davy's blood, which had started to ooze across the lino, and I was just about to pull myself up to open it when it swung inwards and connected with my skull. Curled up again in pain as more sparks flashed up in my head, I was just about switched on enough to know that I was stopping the door from opening fully.

Encountering resistance, whoever it was got their body weight behind the door and pushed hard. I was shunted along the floor until they could get in.

It was Sarah again. She didn't talk, just closed the door behind her. Then, grabbing hold of my feet and avoiding the blood, she started to drag me face down across the room, grunting with the effort.

I felt as if I had a magnesium incendiary burning in my stomach. I tried to keep tensed up, and all I could see was a dark trail of blood where my body had just been.

After four or five paces she dropped my feet on the floor. I moaned as I curled up, trying to reduce the pain as she aimed her pistol at the door.

It opened. Josh had good news. 'Hey, guys, it looks like we're going to—'

I tried to shout a warning, but nothing came. The expression on his face was of utter shock and disbelief, his eyes looking even wider behind his lenses. Sarah was in front of him in a perfect firing position, calmly pointing at his centre mass. People take a while for this kind of information to sink in, especially if they're not expecting it, but Josh was catching on fast.

Sarah maintained her very cool, controlled voice. 'Close the door, Josh.'

His eyes flicked between the two of us, took in Davy's prostrate body, then mine, and finally settled on the pistol, no doubt trying to work out how the fuck she'd brought it in.

'Close the door, Josh.'

If Josh was scared, he wasn't showing it. He was taking in all the information; without saying a word, he did as he was told and then stood stock still, showing Sarah his hands.

She said, 'You will now turn around and put your hands on your head.'

He knew the routine. If you've got your back to the person who's pointing the pistol at you, you can't assess what's going on.

'Move out of the blood, then down onto your knees.'

Once you're on your knees, you're very vulnerable.

She had more instructions. 'With your left hand, using your thumb and forefinger, take your weapon out. Do it now.'

I was helpless, just a curled-up bundle of shit. I heard voices in

389

the corridor. I recognized the loud Hispanic accents of the two white-shoed women, walking from the direction of the fire doors. Sarah quickly checked her watch again.

Should I call out? I didn't have the strength. They wouldn't hear me. I looked over at Josh, who I could see side-on. He was considering the same option.

He wasn't flapping as he obeyed her, his finger and thumb on the pistol grip. 'I'm taking it out now, Sarah.'

'Good, Josh. Now put it on the floor behind you.'

Keeping his right hand on his head, he flicked the weapon behind him onto the lino. I could see the sweat coming down from his bald head onto his face and the wet patches in the armpits of his jacket as he raised his arm again. Fear is a good thing, there's nothing wrong with that, it's a natural reaction; you've just got to be able to control it. He'd been here before and knew what to do.

For a moment I had the strange feeling that I was in an audience, looking at actors on a stage. I knew exactly what would be going through Josh's mind. He'd be wondering how he was going to get out of this, and just waiting for the chance to do something about it – anything.

Blood is the same as milk. Drop a carton on the floor and it looks as if three have been emptied. Davy's blood had spread outwards and was mixing with mine around my face. I didn't have the energy or inclination to move, I just spat from time to time to try and keep it from going in my mouth.

Sarah threw Josh's weapon the length of the bowling alley and the clatter echoed around the walls. She checked her watch once more.

'OK, Josh, this is what you will do. Are you listening?'

He nodded.

'You will take me to the Diplomatic Reception Room. You will be my escort. Do you understand?'

He was very calm as he answered, 'I can't do that.'

Americans have this wonderful total conviction about themselves and their country. Even when they're up to their necks in ten types of shit they have this unshakeable belief that everything will be all right, that America is behind them and the Seventh Cavalry will come over the hill at any moment. After being captured during the Gulf War, as opposed to asking for things, American prisoners would demand them – they just knew they were on the winning side. In the Regiment, you always knew that if you were in the shit you would never be left behind, and that was sometimes the only thing that helped you through, but the Americans believe that at a national level. I wished I had their confidence.

Sarah couldn't quite believe what she'd heard. 'What?'

Josh said simply, 'I will not do that.'

There was a pause, and I watched Sarah's face for a reaction. It wasn't long coming. 'Josh, you've got some thinking to do, and not a long time to do it in. Think about your children. This is no time to mess about with your family, Josh. Take me to that room or you will die. I've got nothing to lose, I'm going to be dead soon anyway.' She had certainly listened to my brief on how to get Josh to do want she wanted. She checked her watch. If she needed to get to the Diplomatic Reception Room before the end of the coffee break, there wasn't much time left.

'They're great kids, Josh, and they need you. You're all they have left. Besides,' she smiled her curious little smile, 'you could even try to stop me. You can't do that if you're dead. I'm either going with you, or on my own, with you dead – in ten, Josh.'

I saw his chest rise and fall as his body took in more oxygen to suppress the shock it was experiencing. I could only guess what he was thinking: Do I die now? Or do I accept what she's saying, and try to prevent it on the way? At least then I'm going to be alive for a little longer.

I had blood in my throat and my voice was hoarse as I said, 'Take her, Josh. Just do it.'

He looked at me and our eyes locked. I could see for sure what he was thinking now: *You fucking asshole*. No matter if I had known what she was going to do or not, to him I was now the world's biggest bastard. Fair one.

I looked up at Sarah as she gave the final warning. 'It's

make-your-mind-up time.' She didn't have long until the coffee break ended.

He looked at the wall, thought for a few seconds more, and quietly said, 'OK.'

'If you try to fuck with me, Josh, know this: I will kill you before anyone has time to react. I don't want your president. I just want the other two. But if you fuck with me . . . do you understand me?'

He closed his eyes and nodded. When he opened them again he fixed them on mine. I hoped my eyes were saying: I didn't know this was going to happen, mate, and I'm sorry, so sorry.

But his expression told me it was a bit late for that.

Now that she was going to have an escort, Sarah took off Davy's ID card and put her own one back on. That was detail, and detail counts.

She said, 'Let's go.'

She stepped back from the door as Josh walked towards it. 'My weapon might be hidden, Josh, but at the slightest sign that you're fucking with me I'll ensure that I get you first.'

He nodded, looked back at me and walked out.

She followed without giving me a second glance.

28

Everything was out of focus; my head was spinning. I was losing too much blood. Between us, Davy and I had the lino pretty much covered. But now wasn't the time to worry about that; I had to accept that I'd been shot, and get on with it.

I struggled onto my hands and knees, sucked in a couple of deep breaths and started to crawl over towards the abandoned ID card. Every movement was agony. With each bend of a knee or stretch of an arm I felt as if a red-hot saw was working on my stomach. It took me what felt like for ever to cover the ten or so feet. My head was swimming as I tried to pull the nylon loop over my head without disturbing the injury in my guts. When I'd finally finished, I couldn't even remember why I'd done it.

I began crawling to the door, coughing, spitting lumps of blood, moaning to myself like a drunk in the gutter, my clothes, face and hair soaked with my blood and Davy's.

On my knees, I fumbled with the handle like a panicking child. It was a normal knob, with the tumbler lock in the middle, but I couldn't make my hands work. My fingers weren't listening to my brain, or maybe it was just that they were too slippery with warm red fluid.

I knew what I was trying to do, but I couldn't accomplish it. Maybe it's true that your life can flash before you as you die. I was suddenly looking down a long tunnel, to when I was about six years old and fell through a glass roof into a garage. I'd been with a gang of older boys, running across the roof as an initiation test. I hit the ground, cut and bruised, and had to fight with the door bolt to escape. I was so scared that I couldn't make any sense out of how to pull the fucking thing across, and once I'd gone through all that, there was no way I was going to show them how much it hurt. They let me join their gang.

My hands started to shake as they slithered around the door handle. I was losing it. I knew I was going to die soon. I didn't care; I just didn't want it to happen until I'd at least tried to stop Sarah.

I forced myself to calm down, take deep breaths and tell myself what I needed to do, just as I'd done back in that garage. It worked.

'Help . . . help me . . .' I tried to shout, but could only manage a weak splutter. Not surprisingly, nothing happened.

I couldn't just lie there in the doorway and wait. Pressing myself against the frame I scrabbled and pushed myself upright and, head reeling, I half turned, half fell into the corridor. I bent over, leaning against the wall for support, my left hand clutching my stomach. Blood smeared along the white plaster as I stumbled towards Crisis Four.

She didn't have far to go. If Josh fucked up and got zapped, she'd just have to follow those TV cables and she'd be there.

My only hope was to find TC. Anyone would be a start. I focused hard. There was no red light on outside Crisis Four. Shit. I started to look for a fire alarm, though at that moment I didn't think I'd recognize one if it hit me in the face.

I felt my reserves of strength ebbing by the second as I swiped the ID card through the machine and tumbled through the door.

There was a picture on every screen, but they were moving in a slow spin, like a kaleidoscope. I started crawling again.

I didn't know how I got to TC's chair, let alone off the floor and into it. All I knew was that, as I tried with every ounce of whatever strength I had left to focus on the screens, I could see her.

Sarah and Josh had just come out of the kitchen area. The ERT guy hadn't moved from the area of the brown screens and just turned towards them as they appeared.

Spitting out the blood and mucus that was gathering in my throat, I hit the microphone switch. 'Mayday, mayday. Black man, white woman on the first floor. Mayday, mayday . . .' I didn't know if it would mean anything to them, but I hoped they'd get the idea.

There was no reaction from the ERT guy. Then all three slipped out of focus and became a blur. I screwed my eyes shut and opened them again, spitting out another mouthful of crap onto the desk.

Refocusing, I could see the ERT guy motioning to them to either move out towards the staircase or go back into the kitchen. I lifted my head to look at the picture above, which was showing what was happening on the other side of the brown screens. There were a few people in plain clothes at the far end, but no reaction from them either.

Fuck it! I tried again. 'All stations, all stations . . .' then stopped, my head resting next to the base of the microphone. The red light wasn't on.

I started leaving bloodstains over as many buttons as I could reach, wishing I'd taken notice of which ones TC had hit when he turned off the speaker.

I got a light. 'Mayday, mayday . . . first floor, first floor. Mayday, mayd—'

The ERT guy was switched on and responded immediately, moving towards them.

Sarah was quicker. She must have seen his face react to the message from his earpiece. She drew her weapon, instinctively aiming from the stomach as soon as it was free of her waistband. Josh dived on her, but too late. She fired.

The ERT guy dropped like a bag of shit. Then, within a second of the struggle, so did Josh. Fuck, what had I done?

Sarah turned and ran as the corridor filled with blurred figures in plain clothes and black uniforms.

The cameras were now cutting from location to location as the main control room tried to get a fix on her as she disappeared off the screen. I knew where she was going.

I swivelled round on the chair, and with my left hand on my gut, forced myself to my feet. The door shimmered in front of my eyes as if I was looking through a heat haze. I staggered into the corridor. I didn't look round, just turned right and faced the fire doors.

There couldn't have been much of the stuff left to be pumped around, but adrenalin was getting me up and moving.

She'd be here soon. The Secret Service would bring the principals down to the shelter until everything was clear, and she'd aim to cut them off.

I crashed through the two doors and looked up just as Sarah was taking her last steps down the spiral stairs. She was going shit or bust, head down, pistol in hand.

I couldn't think of anything else to do but throw myself at her in some sort of rugby tackle. Perhaps it would have helped if I'd ever played a game of rugby.

I collapsed against her, throwing my arms around her waist and linking them together behind her back as her momentum propelled me backwards into the swing doors.

She was still moving, taking me with her, cracking me on the head with her pistol. By now I really couldn't feel that much. My arms slipped down to her legs and she started to fall with me.

The fire doors flew open again as we burst through. We both hit the ground and the doors swung back, trapping my lower legs.

She was stretched out, her back on the floor, and I was wrapped in a mess around her feet. I could make out the pistol was still in her hand.

My guts wrenched and screamed as I kicked my legs free from the doors and scrambled up her body, slapping my hand down heavily on her forearm to hold the weapon down. She kicked and bucked to try and get me off her. She was like an insect on its back, frantic to get upright.

I became aware of screaming, shouting and heavy footsteps echoing round the area, but it was as if a mute button had been hit, and everything was happening a long way away.

I didn't care where the noise was coming from. All that mattered was her left hand, which was going for Davy's pistol now that she couldn't use hers. I could feel it in her waistband as I moved further up her body. Her resistance got stronger; it was as if she was having some sort of fit, her head and body thrashing from side to side.

I put all my weight on her. It wasn't that difficult, I was fucked. Her hand struggled to work its way between us towards the weapon. Our heads were so close together that I could feel her breath on my face. I had to head-butt her, there was no other way. She reacted noisily. The three times I made contact, I heard the back of her head bounce off the floor. It was messy, but it slowed her up.

My head now hurt almost as much as my stomach. I was in shit state. Keeping my forehead pushed against hers, blood dripping from my mouth and nose, I prised the gun out of her grip as she tried to clear her nose and mouth.

I rammed the barrel into her windpipe and looked at her, my forehead still putting pressure on hers. She didn't return my stare as I tried to focus, just closed her eyes and tensed her body as she waited for death. Our bodies rose and fell with her laboured breathing as the doors were kicked open and I began to make sense of the shouting from behind me. The mute button had been deactivated. 'Release the weapon! Release the weapon now! Do it!'

I thought about it for the two seconds I would have before they pulled or shot me off her.

Her body relaxed and she opened her eyes and looked at me. It was almost an order. 'Do it . . . please.'

Fuck it. I tilted the gun upwards and it slid two inches until it jammed under her chin. Pointing it towards her skull, I let my head move aside. Her eyes followed mine as I flicked off the safety and pulled the trigger.

Blood and splintered bone splashed onto the side of my face.

I'd finished the job I'd been ordered to do; that was what I made myself think. A moment later I felt the pain shoot up my arm as someone kicked the pistol out of my hand.

I was manhandled onto my back. I looked up and there was ERT black everywhere, then Josh loomed over me, blocking out everything else, blood dripping onto me from the mess on his face. They tried to pull him off me as he started to give me a good kicking. It wasn't working.

I turned on my side and curled up to protect myself, and through the haze I could hear orders being shouted and the general confusion around me.

I was losing it. Josh was still screaming above me, and managed a few more kicks. It didn't matter, I could no longer feel them. What I really wanted to happen, did. I became unconscious.

JUNE 1998

June 1998

I came out of the flat on Cambridge Street, checked I'd put the key on the ring of my Leatherman and closed the door behind me. It was a strange feeling, being a virtual prisoner here in Pimlico. I'd brought plenty of worried-looking people here in the past, but never imagined that some day I'd be one of the victims myself.

The debrief was taking for ever. The Firm were trying to strike a deal with the Americans. Both sides wanted this to go away, and they weren't the only ones. It had been four weeks since I'd come out of hospital, and I'd been confined to the area ever since, under what amounted to house arrest. I was getting paid, and at operational rate, but it still wasn't a good day out.

None of my injuries hurt much any more, but I still needed bucketloads of antibiotics. The entry wound had sealed up quite well. All that was left was a dent in my stomach, coloured the same vivid pink as the puncture wounds in my arm.

Walking down the last couple of stone steps to the pavement, I looked to my left at the crowd enjoying an end-of-the-week drink at the picnic tables outside the pub. Friday evening's rush hour had turned the whole street into a carpark. The traffic fumes were cooking up nicely in the early evening sun. The heat was unusual for this time of year. It felt more like Los Angeles than London.

I crossed between the stationary vehicles, heading for the all-in-one shop on the corner. The Asian father and son combo were used to me now; dad started folding a copy of the *Evening Standard* as soon as he saw me come in. I felt like a local. Weaving back over the road, I headed for the pub. There were just as many people inside, and above the din Robbie Williams was giving it full volume on the sound system. The smell of smoke, stale beer and body odour reminded me not to come here again. It did that every night.

I worked my way towards the rear, where I knew it wouldn't be so packed, and, besides, that was where the food was. I'd started to recognize some of the regulars – sad fucks like me, with nowhere else to go, or office workers big-timing it, or old men smoking their roll-ups and spending an hour nursing a warm pint.

I asked for my usual bottle of Pils and, helping myself to a handful of peanuts from one of the bowls, headed for a booth. The one with the most room was occupied by an old man who looked as if he'd just come from a British Legion outing, all tie and association badges. He couldn't have been there long; his bottle of light ale hadn't yet been poured into his half of bitter.

'Anyone sitting here, mate?'

He looked up and shook his head. I eased myself into the seat slowly, taking care that my jeans didn't ride up and expose the tag around my right ankle. Taking a swig of Pils, I opened the newspaper.

It was all the usual doom and gloom. Ethiopian and Eritrean forces had stopped bombing the shit out of each other with their MIG 23s to give foreign nationals time to be airlifted from the war zone. That was the sort of work I liked, just plain and simple war. You knew where you stood with that shit.

I scanned the rest of the news sections, but there was still nothing about what had happened in Washington. Still no mention of the injuries to the ERT guy and Josh, and I knew now that there never would be. Lynn had given me the American party line during one of our little evening rides around town. The press release was short: a stressed-out member of the domestic staff had become temporarily deranged in the White House basement. It was a minor incident, dealt with in minutes. The three world leaders hadn't been made aware until well after the event. The most the story ever got was a column inch in the following day's *Washington Post*.

I was glad the ERT guy hadn't died. He'd just been wounded in the thigh – something to tell the grandchildren about. Josh had got it big time in the face. Lynn said the round had split the flesh on the right side and made his mouth look as if it ended by his ear. I'd been told the surgery was a success, but I doubted he'd ever be modelling for Calvin Klein.

My one hope was that his Christian thing would work in my favour. Sitting in the flat a few days earlier, waiting for the debriefing team to arrive, I'd been listening to Thought for the Day on the radio. 'If you can't forgive the sin,' the voice had said, 'at least try to forgive the sinner.' Sounded good to me. I just hoped Josh could get Radio Four in his truck.

I hadn't spoken to him yet; I'd wait a while, give him time to calm down, and me time to work out what the fuck I was going to say.

I hadn't seen Kelly since the Americans released me into the Firm's custody. We'd spoken on the phone, and she thought I was still away working. She said that Josh had called. He'd told her nothing about what had happened, just that Sarah and I had visited.

I still had no regrets about killing Sarah. The only thing that pissed me off was that every time in my life I'd let someone get close to me, they fucked me over. Everybody, that is, apart from Kelly. It seemed to be my job to do that to her.

I'd blown it again by making promises I couldn't keep. She still wanted to go to the Bloody Tower, and she wanted to go with me. Three times now I'd arranged it, only to cancel at the last minute because the debrief dragged on. At least she was going to her grandparents this weekend. Carmen and Jimmy would spoil her rotten.

I took another long swig of Pils – fuck the antibiotics, I usually forgot to take them anyway – and checked Baby-G. They started serving in twenty minutes.

The debrief was going OK, I thought, but you never knew with these people. I wasn't getting as hard a time of it as I might, mainly because Lynn and Elizabeth were potentially in just as much shit as I was and were taking measures to cover their arses. Even so, every event of those five days was being dissected in great detail. Not documented, of course. How could it be; it hadn't happened.

Not that any of it meant much. I was lying to the team, using a script supplied by the good colonel. I'd RV with him each evening, and the Serb would give us a few laps of London. As Lynn had said, 'You need guiding, Nick, on some of the more, shall we say, delicate areas of the operation.' And, of course, to avoid the slight problem of the T104, since not even the investigation crew would be aware that such things existed. The only ones in the know were lowlife like me, Elizabeth and Lynn. To the investigators, I didn't even have a name; I was just referred to as the 'paid asset'. That suited me just fine.

Lynn had already told me that I'd been sent on the job because, if anyone could find her, I could. But I knew there was more to it than that. It had become blindingly obvious that those two fuckers had known all along what she was up to, and thought I'd be so pissed off with her I'd feed her through the grinder without a second thought.

They'd even known where she was hiding, but wanted me to go through the process of finding her. They reckoned that if I thought I'd tracked her down through my own efforts, and if what I saw on the ground confirmed their story, that would put me even more in the mood.

There were still loose ends, of course. I still couldn't work out if Metal Mickey was part of Lynn's game or not. After all, Lynn did say he was loyal. But to whom? Fuck it, who cared? It just annoyed me that these people could never just tell it straight. Why bother to tell me all that bullshit? I would still have done the job if I'd known the truth. The fucking games they played pissed me off, and worse, they put me in danger.

Naturally, nothing in the big picture had been changed by Sarah's death. Bin Laden was still out there doing his stuff. Yousef had closed down, but he'd probably resurface in a year or two. And I still wasn't going to be getting permanent cadre: they said I'd be a disruptive influence on the team. I'd tried to get a bung instead, claiming that what happened in the White House might have been my fuck-up, but I did stop the president from being shot. Well . . . you have to elaborate a bit. It didn't work. Even the deafest old duffer in the pub must have heard their laughter. All I got was the promise that if a single word came from my lips that was 'off-message', I was history.

My major concern now was, what did I get up to after this? I needed to get some real money together so I didn't have to carry on getting fucked over by these people. Maybe I'd take a look at the American rewards programme. Bounty hunting terrorists, white supremacists and South American drug dealers wouldn't be so bad. Maybe I could try and recover those Stingers from the muj. Who knows?

The bottle was empty. People were three deep at the bar and it took ages to get myself another. As I rejoined my mate in the booth, I was again careful not to expose the light-grey band of plastic around my ankle, housing its two inch by two inch box of electronics. I checked my watch again; just over ten minutes till the peanuts disappeared and the menus were put on the bar. Not that I needed one. I knew it off by heart.

I thought about Sarah again. I'd learned more about her in my stints with Lynn than I had in all the time I'd known her. I'd always felt that she was holding something back from me, and in my stupid way I'd decided it was because she was scared of intimacy.

Sitting back on the cigarette-burned red velour, I started to pick at the label on the Pils bottle. The old man bent his neck as he tried to read the headlines on my paper. I passed it across the table.

The night before last had been another hot and humid one. Lynn had picked me up as usual for our daily debrief on the debrief, but this time in his new Voyager. It looked like the Firm's budget had got a bit of a boost this new fiscal year. The air-conditioner was going full blast. The Serb, as ever, kept his eyes fixed on the road.

'How was all this allowed to happen?' I said. 'How come you didn't suspect her earlier?'

Lynn kept his gaze on the real world beyond the darkened window. 'Elizabeth voiced concerns.' He shrugged. 'We took a few people aside for a word, but there was nothing we could put our finger on. The false-flag operation in Syria seemed like a good moment to put her to the test.'

Lynn obviously held a lot more pieces of the puzzle in his hand than he was letting me see, but he did tell me this much. The Syrian operation had only been taken on by the Brits as a means of checking whether Sarah was Bin Laden's best mate. It was Elizabeth's idea. Sarah changed the data, killed the Source and covered her tracks. She was good at doing that. I thought back to her giving the American a round in the head after taking his clothes in the forest. But she wasn't good enough in Syria. Without knowing it, Sarah confirmed that she didn't exactly go to sleep every night humming 'Rule Britannia'. It was then just a question of letting her lead the way to Bin Laden. The only problem for Elizabeth was that she had omitted to fill in the Americans when Sarah was posted to Washington.

Lynn had turned and looked at me as if to underline his next disclosure. 'Things got slightly out of hand when Sarah took an active part in the ASU,' he said. 'Once that had happened, how could we tell our friends across the sea? That was where you came in.'

I let that one sink in – in amongst all the other crap I was trying to make sense of.

The investigating team had been clutching at straws to explain Sarah's behaviour, and I wasn't doing much better. I asked him, 'Do you know what turned her?' He seemed to know everything else.

'We'll never completely know, will we? People are still trying to fathom out T. E. Lawrence ... and who really knows what made Philby and the rest do what they did?' There was a pause. 'A team went to Sarah's mother, to pass on the tragic news. She was saddened, of course, but very proud of her daughter's most untimely death in the service of her country.'

'I thought her parents were dead.'

'No, just her father. He died when she was seventeen. A team have been weaseling with the mother for a few weeks now. You know, trying for any links or information that may be useful.'

Sarah's father, George, they had learned, was a big-time oil executive who was a stern disciplinarian and a major-league hypocrite. He'd spent his whole working life in the Middle East without ever getting to like the Arabs – unless, that is, they were either royal or wealthy – preferably both – and took to all things Western in much the same way that flies take to shit. The right sort of Arab certainly didn't include his lower-class domestic staff and their nine-year-old son.

The friendship between Sarah and Abed had been perfectly innocent, the mother had said. The fact was, her daughter was just desperately lonely. But as far as George was concerned, inside every Arab was a rapist just waiting to get out.

The two kids were inseparable. Sarah was an only child, pushed from pillar to post all her life, with a remote, domineering father, a placid, ineffectual mother, and no opportunity to make lasting relationships. You wouldn't need to be an agony aunt to understand her joy in finding a friend at last.

George, however, was not amused. One day, Abed's mum and dad didn't turn up for work. Nor did the boy come round in the afternoon, as he usually did. The whole family seemed to have vanished. Then, just a few days later, Sarah's father pulled the plug on her education in Saudi and packed her off to a UK boarding school.

It was only after her father had died that Sarah learned what had really happened. She was helping her mother go through her father's things when she came across a gold Rolex Navigator.

Sarah said, 'I never knew Daddy had one of these.'

Her mother looked at the watch and burst into tears.

The Rolex had been given to him by a grateful business

409

acquaintance. It was George's prize possession. He had accused Abed of stealing it, and thrown the whole family out onto the streets. With a reputation as thieves hanging over them, their chances of ever working again would have been ziff. They would have seen out their days as 'dust people', the lowest of the low, outcasts from Saudi society and living on the edge of starvation. Sarah waited until her mother had finished, then left the house without another word. She never saw her again.

'Of course, I don't go along with all this nonsense about blaming everything in your life on the traumas of childhood,' Lynn said. 'My parents dragged me around South-East Asia until I was seven, then I went to Eton. Never did me any harm.'

The menus were being plonked unceremoniously on the bar counter by the girl who'd served me before. The thought of dishing out another hundred stuff and chips obviously didn't fill her with too much excitement.

I decided on the pie and another beer. The same as last night and the night before. A quick look at Baby-G told me it was seven forty-eight, just over half an hour until my RV.

Traffic was still clogging the street by the time I left, but at least it was moving. I turned left, checked my watch yet again and headed towards Victoria station. Thirteen minutes till the pick up. I turned two corners and stopped, waiting to see if anyone was following. They weren't.

Crossing the road, I cut through a housing estate that was packed with K reg Vauxhall Astras and Sierras, sat on a wall by the rubbish chute and waited. Half a dozen kids were skateboarding up and down the only bit of clear tarmac they could find – the slip road in front of me that led onto the main drag towards the station. I listened to their banter, thinking about when I was where they were.

I thought of Kelly – the girl who'd had her whole family killed, and now had a stand-in father who constantly let her down. And worse than that, much worse, I was probably the closest thing she had to a best friend. Sarah's words came back to me. 'You have a child now. I hope you live long enough to see her.'

410

I cut away from all that and got back to real life by reminding myself of the two big lessons I'd learned in Washington. The first was never again to be so soft with someone who showed emotion towards me. I had to stop kidding myself that I knew, or even understood, that sort of stuff. The second was easier: always carry a pistol. I never wanted to play Robin Hood again.

It was last light as I sat, watched and listened. Sarah's words still bugged me. 'You have a child now . . .'

The Voyager would be arriving any minute. I looked at Baby-G and thought about George's Rolex. And then I knew what I had to do. I wasn't exactly a top-of-the-range example for Kelly, but the very least I could do was be dependable. Maybe, just maybe, the one thing that Sarah had given me by sparing my life was the chance to do the right thing.

Moving swiftly away from the RV point, I jumped a fence that secured a communal garden.

Crouching in the shadows, I pulled the Leatherman from my pocket, opened the knife blade, and cut away at the plastic encircling my ankle. The pliers made short work of the half-inch steel band that ran beneath.

I knew that the instant the circuit was broken the alarm would be raised. Even as the tag was being binned in the bushes, the standby team would be running for their cars, getting briefed via their body comms (personal radios).

Jumping back over the fence, I headed towards Victoria at a controlled, fast pace. Fuck 'em. What were they going to do? Well, quite a bit, but I'd worry about that when it happened. It wasn't as if I was doing an out and out runner. I'd be back in the flat on Sunday, talking to the morons about Afghanistan. The only difference would be that I'd have acquired two new friends with necks as big as the Serb's, assigned to guard me 24/7, just in case I was overcome again by the desire to take a weekend off.

There were sirens behind me now on the other side of the estate. They must be flapping big time to call in the police.

411

As I neared the station I just hoped the investigating team had kids of their own, and would understand when I explained to them on Sunday that all I wanted to do was take my child to the Bloody Tower for a day out.

After all, I'd made her a promise. A normal person's promise.

The Colossal Cookie Cookbook

Over 425 quick and easy recipes, plus expert tips

on mixing, baking, and storing

EDITED BY
Deborah Gray

CONTRIBUTING AUTHORS:
Catherine Atkinson; Kathryn Hawkins; Dawn Stock; Janet Mannings; Katy Holder;
Fiona Hunter; Emma Patmore; Alison Austin

Colour
Library
Direct

A QUINTET BOOK

CLD 21512
This book was first published in 1999 for
Colour Library Direct Ltd
Godalming Business Centre
Woolsack Way
Godalming
Surrey GU7 1XW

ISBN 1 86155 203 3

This book was designed and produced by
Quintet Publishing Limited
6 Blundell Street
London N7 9BH

Creative Director: Richard Dewing
Art Director: Paula Marchant
Designers: Siân Keogh and
Sandra Marques at Axis Design
Managing Editor: Diana Steedman
Senior Project Editor: Toria Leitch
Editor: Jane Donovan
Photographer: Ferguson Hill
Food Stylist: Labeena Ishaque

Material in this book also previously appeared in
Breakfast Bakes; The Complete Biscuit and Cookie
Book; New Jewish Cooking, Elizabeth Wolf Cohen; The
Complete Book of Gingerbread, Valerie Barrett; High
Fibre Cooking, Rosemary Moon; Kids' Kitchen Sugar
and Spice, Nicola Fowler

Typeset in Great Britain by
Central Southern Typesetters, Eastbourne
Manufactured in Hong Kong
Printed in China

Contents

The Colossal
Cookie Cookbook

Introduction

Seeping out from the corners of every shopping centre, every pavement café and every bakery comes wafting the irresistible scent of baking butter, sugar, chocolate and vanilla. Cookies, ever-popular in America, can now be found everywhere. With the purchase of this book, the aromas from your kitchen can pervade your neighbourhood. The fruits of your labours can fill jars on the worktop, be displayed at bring-and-buy sales, be donated to parties, wing their way to distant relatives in the post, all to the delight of cookie fiends everywhere. For who can resist a cookie? Cookies seem to appeal to the child in us. They appear sweeter and more intensely flavoured than most cakes, they are crunchy and soft, nutty and chocolatey, and are easy to handle – the perfect comfort food.

Take comfort in the knowledge that this book is the only cookie book that you will ever need to own. It contains a unique collection of favourites from all over the world. The word "cookie" comes from the Dutch "koekje" meaning little cake, and this book includes recipes from Holland as well as France, Italy, Scandinavia, Eastern Europe and Australia. Every culture, it seems, has its cookies characterized by the availability of local ingredients and the temperament of its inhabitants. So rustic oaty cookies come from northern Europe, almond-studded biscotti from Italy, spicy Lebkuchen from Eastern Europe and delicate madeleines from the elegance of Marcel Proust's Paris. Then, of course, there are the American cookies themselves. Many of these are jumbo cookies stuffed with goodies or smaller, simpler cookies baked straight from the refrigerator. Here you will find recipes for family favourites and elegant classics alongside new ideas for the new millennium.

A comprehensive introduction provides all the background information in the art of cookie baking to turn you into a master of the art. Take time out to read this section before you begin, then return to your kitchen and enjoy yourself. If you have kids at hand rope them in too, they will enjoy the process of baking cookies and it's a good way to have fun with them on wet afternoons. Get them involved in the decorating, especially at holiday times, and your cookies will take on a certain home-made charm. No kids? Then why not bake with a friend? That way you'll have twice the choice without extra effort and have lots of laughs in the process. After all, you can be really serious about cookies, but who can deny that part of their charm lies in their frivolity.

The only problem with this book is the amazing choice it offers, and the wonderful photographs make all the cookies look so tempting. Maybe go for the Toll House Cookie, or the original recipe for the ever-popular Chocolate Chip Cookie or perhaps the White Chocolate and Apricot – eat one with a glass of cold milk to make the perfect snack while browsing through the other recipes to select your next cookie.

Be assured that whichever recipe you choose, the instructions are clearly written and easy to follow and the ingredients are listed in order of use. With this fabulous cookbook to guide you, you can't go wrong.

THE INS AND OUTS OF COOKIE MASTERY

By simply following the recipe instructions on the following pages you will be able to bake a huge variety of sensational cookies, but it does help to know a little about the equipment and techniques you will be using. You might want your cookies just that little bit larger, chewier or crisper than the recipe suggests and by understanding the principles of cookie production you will be able to fine tune your baking to suit your taste.

TOOLS OF THE TRADE

These are listed roughly in the order of use.

● Scales, a set of measuring spoons, and a measuring jug are all essential. Cooking is chemistry, and in order to get the optimum results careful attention should be paid to measuring the ingredients accurately. With spoon measurements, you should level the ingredient with the straight edge of a knife.

● A set of mixing bowls, preferably microwave-safe for melting butter and chocolate in the microwave as well as on top of a double boiler.

● A food mixer and/or food processor. A food mixer is great for combining butter and sugar and beating in eggs. It is still best to fold in dry ingredients by hand as it is easy to over-mix in a machine and risk making the dough tough. A food processor will blend the butter and sugar easily but will not produce quite as light, fluffy a mixture as a food mixer. However, it is probably preferable to doing it by hand with a wooden spoon, which can be quite hard on the arms. The food processor is brilliant for chopping and grinding nuts, chopping fruit and for making shortbread and pastry dough.

● A sifter or sieve.

● A wire whisk, or two – one large and one small.

● A grater for grating the rind from citrus fruits and for grating fresh ginger and nutmeg.

● Spoons. A wooden one, plus several teaspoons and tablespoons for mixing and measuring.

● Knives. A sharp pointed knife and a straight knife for levelling are both useful.

• A pastry brush.

• Two or three baking sheets. There are a lot out there to choose from. Heavy-gauge aluminium sheets are excellent as they conduct heat evenly and swiftly. Non-stick sheets are good too, but avoid those that are very dark in colour as they absorb too much heat which means that cookies may burn more easily. If yours are dark, compensate by cooking your cookies on a sheet of foil. Insulated baking sheets are not as good as they are cracked up to be – they consist of two layers of aluminium separated by a locked-in air space. Crisp cookies do not crisp well on them, and soft cookies spread out too much on them. If you are using insulated sheets, allow a minute or two extra cooking time and mound cookies generously before cooking.

To maintain optimal air circulation in the oven, baking sheets should be ten centimetres/four inches shorter and narrower than the oven. Heat circulation being what it is, if there are too few cookies placed on a large baking sheet they tend to burn. To avoid this use a small baking sheet or try turning a 20 x 20-cm/8 x 8-in baking tin over and baking on the back. Avoid using tins with edges such as Swiss roll pans, since they prevent good air circulation around the cookies as they bake.

For baking bar cookies a non-stick 32.5 x 23-cm/ 13 x 9-in and 20 x 20-cm/8 x 8-in tins are required. Some recipes also call for a Swiss roll tin. If you have to use an ovenproof glass baking dish for bar cookies, then be aware that glass retains more heat while cooking than metal. Avoid overcooking and scorched edges by reducing the oven temperature very slightly.

• A metal spatula for removing cookies from the baking sheet. Use thin, heatproof plastic if your non-stick surface will be damaged by metal.

• A timer.

• At least two wire cooling racks.

COOKIE TYPES

The ingredients for most cookies are pretty much the same – sugar, butter and a little egg, bound with flour and flavoured with vanilla, spices, chocolate, fruit or nuts. However, the proportions and treatment of these basic ingredients differ, resulting in a range of cookies with various textures and flavours.

Drop Cookies

These are probably the simplest and most versatile type of cookie. They are called drop cookies as the dough is soft enough to drop off the spoon and onto the baking sheet. Use the size of spoon recommended in the recipe and encourage the mixture to drop off the spoon by pushing with a second teaspoon. The basic batter usually consists of butter (or margarine or white vegetable fat) and sugar beaten together until light and fluffy. Eggs are then beaten in, followed by flour com-

bined with leavening ingredients and flavourings, either subtle or robust. In addition, textual ingredients are added, the most common of these being oats, coconut, nuts or chocolate chips.

Space the cookies according to the instructions which will take account of the cooking spread, and bake in a moderate oven. For soft or cakey cookies the mixture should be left well mounded on the cookie sheet. For a cookie with a deliciously soft, chewy centre and a crisp edge, remove the cookies from the oven as soon as the edges turn golden and while the middles are still soft and paler in colour. The more even the colour and the firmer the cookie to touch, the crisper the cookies will be. If you want to make crisper cookies, spread the mixture out a little using the back of the spoon before baking. Some very crisp drop cookies such as Florentines require that the butter and sugar are first melted together to begin the caramelization prior to baking, others replace some or all of the sugar with syrup. Such cookies generally contain very little flour which helps them to spread out on the baking sheet. Make sure you space these cookies far apart on the baking sheet.

Refrigerator Cookies

The advantage of refrigerator cookies is that the ingredients used to make up the dough can be made in advance and kept in the refrigerator for up to two weeks before being cooked. This encourages cooking on demand so that wonderful fresh cookies can be cooked as and when required without the need to prepare fresh dough each time you want to bake a batch. These are the perfect cookies for those who only have time to prepare food and bake at the weekend, or for anyone who doesn't have the self control necessary to leave half a batch of cookies in the storage tins!

Rolled Cookies

Rolled cookies are the delight of Christmas cooks. These tempting cookies can be rolled out and cut into shapes using cookie cutters, or simply cut into discs using the top of a drinking glass. Rolled cookie dough is similar to that made for refrigerator cookies and often requires refrigerating before rolling and pressing. After chilling, roll the dough on a lightly floured board to a thickness of 3 to 5 mm/⅛ to ¼ in. Some cooks prefer to roll the dough between two sheets of thicker quality clingfilm so that the dough can be returned to the refrigerator before cutting. Dip the cookie cutter into flour before pressing through the dough, then press down firmly to ensure that the dough is cut right through. Gently pull away any scraps, which can be combined and re-rolled. These cookies are cooked in a moderate to moderately hot oven until very slightly golden around the edges and firm to the touch. They tend to be very fragile and need to be removed from the baking sheets after they have cooled for one or two minutes. Use a thin metal spatula or fish slice to transfer the hot cookies to cooling racks. Rolled cookies freeze well for up to 1 month so they can be made before Christmas and decorated when required.

Pressed Cookies

A plate of delicate pressed cookies always looks fancy but they are simple to make using a commercial cookie press. They are the perfect cookie for those who would love to make festive cookies, but lack the skill or time to do the fancy decorations.

The dough for pressed cookies needs to be soft enough to be squeezed through a cookie press but firm enough to hold its shape. Extra care must be taken to ensure that the butter and sugar are beaten until really light and fluffy and the flour should be gently folded in

The dough for refrigerator cookies is quite stiff, so it is easiest prepared in the food mixer or food processor. The dough is then moulded into a log or into a thin, oblong brick and wrapped in clingfilm. Due to its high fat content, the dough must then be chilled for at least 3 hours to firm up so that the cookies hold their shape and become crisp when cooked. Slice the cookies according to the instructions given in the recipe using a thin, sharp blade. Space 2.5 cm/1 in or so apart on the baking sheet in a moderate oven. If you decide to increase the thickness of the cookies, decrease the temperature of the oven slightly to ensure that the cookies are crisp throughout. The best way to check that these cookies are ready is to sacrifice one and break it in half. Check to see that there is no dark, doughy strip in the centre of the cookie and that the texture is even throughout.

producing a denser and moister bar. For this reason the bars with a crumb or shortbread base often require that the oven temperature be reduced after an initial part-cooking of the base. Always cook bar cookies in the tin size recommended. Using a smaller tin will produce thicker cookies which will need a longer cooking time and would alter the proportions of crust to cake.

As a general rule these cookies are ready when a cocktail stick inserted into the centre of the tin comes out clean. However, some bar cookies, such as brownies, are best slightly softer and fudgier than most others. Remove from the oven as soon as the centre is set and the brownies are just beginning to pull away from the edges of the tin. Most soft, chewy brownies can be cut with a sharp, serrated knife when cooled. Crisp bar cookies, however, must be cut after five to ten minutes before they become firm and difficult to cut without breaking up. Do not cut bar cookies too big. Eight-centimetre/three-inch squares are ample, after all they are supposed to be cookies. Generally bar cookies keep well if left in the baking tin covered with an airtight lid or a piece of foil.

by hand. If the mixture is too stiff to press, then add a few drops of milk; if it is too soft, then place in the refrigerator until firm enough to hold its shape. For spritz-type cookies, the dough is generally pressed out onto ungreased, cold baking sheets and dredged with coloured sugar or decorated with nuts prior to cooking. To prevent the cookies from spreading and loosing their shape, the baking sheets are placed in the refrigerator to allow the cookies to firm up before baking in a moderate oven. Remove from the oven and transfer to the cooling racks as for rolled cookies.

Bar Cookies

These cookies fall halfway between a cake and a cookie. They can be thick and chewy, thin and crispy, or light and cakey. Some combine two textures having a crispy outer shell (usually shortbread or crumb based) and a rich, soft centre. Most of these cookies are baked in a moderate to moderately low oven; the cooler oven slows the process of aeration called for in lighter cakes

To Market

It goes without saying that good-quality ingredients make the best cookies but most of the ingredients required for the cookies in this book can be bought in the average grocery and are not expensive. The most important thing is to make sure that the ingredients are fresh – nuts left over from last Christmas and rock-hard apricots should be replaced, as should spices kept in a warm kitchen in full sunlight.

Flour

Most recipes call for plain flour which you can buy bleached and unbleached (the latter is probably preferable;) sifted or unsifted. It is just as well to sift even pre-sifted flour as it tends to settle when left standing on the shelf for any length of time. Always sift flour when told to do so by the recipe. Note that even the same brand of flour can vary from season to season, so the amount of liquid used in some recipes to bind the ingredients can alter slightly. Do not use self-raising flour unless it is specifically mentioned in the recipe, as this already contains leavening agents and could create dramatic eruptions in the oven if used in conjunction with other leavening agents. Substitute 120 g/4 oz of plain flour plus 1½ tablespoons baking powder and a pinch of salt for 120 g/4 oz self-raising flour.

Butter

This one is a soul-searcher. Butter has an incomparable flavour in baked goods but we all know that butter is high in saturated fat and cholesterol, both of which should be avoided. The problem is that the only substitute is regular, non-diet margarine and this is not much healthier. The process which turns liquid polyunsaturated oils into the solid fats found in margarine causes the fats to saturate, making them no better than those found naturally in butter. The softer margarines and spreads are healthier but have a greatly increased liquid content than should be used in baking. In some recipes with plenty of other flavours, hard margarine may be substituted for butter although the resulting cookie will be a little softer due to the higher water content of even hard margarine. However, where the butter is absolutely essential for a recipe, such as in shortbread, there is really no substitute. Maybe the solution is to make smaller buttery cookies and eat fewer of them.

Unsalted butter is best for baking as it allows the cook to fine tune the salt content of the cookies themselves. Always use unsalted butter when recommended in the recipe. If you only have salted butter to hand, then cut the amount of salt in the recipe by at least half. Salt was originally added to butter as a preservative, so surplus unsalted butter is best kept in the freezer in order to retain its freshness. Use butter at room temperature when making cookies that need initial beating of butter and sugar, particulary if you are beating by hand as this will cut out some of the hard work. If you need to do this quickly, place the butter on a dish and put it in the microwave on Medium and heat for 10 to 15 seconds (the exact timings vary with machines.) In other recipes where the butter is cut into the flour, very cold butter is essential as the small particles of butter in the mixture melt while cooking creating tiny air pockets resulting in the characteristic light, crunchy texture.

A few recipes call for lard, which comes from pork, or for white vegetable fat, both of which create short, flaky pastries and cookies. Use as directed on the packet. If you wish to substitute white vegetable fat for butter, then reduce the amount used by 20%.

Sugar

Sugars add flavour and texture as well as sweetness to the cookies. Use the type of sugar indicated in the recipe. Brown sugar is white sugar with syrup added to it, molasses in the case of brown sugar and generally a lighter syrup in conjunction with a little molasses in light brown sugar. Consequently, brown sugar tends to make moister cookies than white sugar. The darker the sugar the moister and more intense the flavour. Store brown sugar in airtight containers to prevent it drying out. To soften brown sugar that has gone hard, put the sugar with a slice of apple in a plastic container for a few days; alternatively, heat gently in the microwave, checking frequently until softened but not melted.

Many recipes call for granulated sugar or for the finer caster sugar. The sugar crystals in caster sugar are very small and will melt quicker than those in granulated sugar, so do not substitute.

Vanilla sugar may be asked for especially as a decoration. To make vanilla sugar simply place a vanilla pod or two in a sealed container and add about 350 g/12 oz sugar. Leave for a week to allow the flavour to infuse; add additional sugar as required and replace the vanilla pods about once every six months.

Eggs

The eggs used in this book are large unless otherwise specified. It is important to use the correct size of egg or the mixture will be too dry or too wet. Eggs are easier to separate when they are cold but are best used in baking when at room temperature. Very cold eggs tend to curdle the mixture. If you forget to bring eggs up to room temperature, place in a bowl of warm water for a few minutes. Egg whites should always be used at room temperature to ensure that they whisk to their maximum volume. Always whisk egg whites in a clean bowl that is completely dry and free of grease. If there is even a speck of egg yolk remaining with the white it will not whisk satisfactorily. Start again with a new egg.

Chocolate

The brand of chocolate you select is a matter of taste (and budget); some swear by readily available brands, others purchase special chocolate by mail order. What is not interchangeable is the type of chocolate you choose. If the recipe calls for plain chocolate that is what you should use. Be particularly careful when buying white chocolate chips that you are indeed buying chocolate and not vanilla-flavoured chips. Different chocolates contain different quantities of cocoa butter and sugar so altering the chocolate alters the chemistry of the cookie. Always melt chocolate very slowly over a double boiler or on a Medium heat in the microwave (initially for 1 minute then in 20-second bursts); either way, remove the chocolate from the heat when it is about half melted and stir well until the remainder dissolves.

Cocoa powder must be the pure thing, not cocoa or chocolate drink mixes. Dutch cocoa is probably the best type to use as it has been processed with a small amount of alkali making it less bitter to taste and darker than its untreated counterpart.

Nuts

It is important that nuts be as fresh as possible since they do go rancid over time. Buy whole nuts which keep their flavour longer, and chop in the food proces-

sor or by hand as required. Store in airtight containers, in the refrigerator if you have space. If nuts soften, place in a 300°F/150°C/Gas mark 2 oven for a few minutes to re-crisp. Some recipes call for nuts to be toasted to give a richer flavour. This is best done in an ungreased frying pan on the stovetop where they can be stirred and watched continuously. Otherwise, place on a baking sheet in a 350°F/175°C/Gas mark 4 oven and cook for about 15 minutes, stirring occasionally and watching carefully, especially towards the end of cooking as nuts burn quickly and seemingly without warning. Coconut and oats can be treated in the same way.

Dried Fruit

As with nuts, the fresher the better. As a preference, buy dried fruit loose from a reputable health shop with a good selection and a regular turnover, as this is likely to be fresher than the packaged fruit (and nuts) (this is also true for nuts and special grains as well.) You are also much more likely to find fruits that have not been treated with sulphur in the health shop. Try to avoid fruit drying out by storing it in the appropriate containers and always sealing the packet when you put it away. To re-hydrate fruit, seep hot water on to it for 10 to 15 minutes.

Crystallized Fruit

This is best bought in specialist shops, so you can be sure of buying good-quality, fresh ingredients.

Oats and Muesli

Do not confuse quick oats with rolled oats. Quick oats are rolled oats chopped finer and they absorb more liquid during cooking. Use the type specified in the recipe. Usually the recipes call for plain muesli without fruit unless otherwise stated.

Flavourings

Spices loose the intensity of their flavour quite quickly so need replacing frequently. To prolong their life keep in a cool, dark place and certainly out of direct sunlight. Use pure vanilla essence not artificial flavouring as this does not come close to the real thing. Similarly, freshly squeezed lemon and orange juice and freshly grated rind are an absolute must. Bottled juice is a poor flavour substitute.

PREPARING YOUR TIN

There are several schools of thought with regard to tin preparation. Some prefer to very lightly brush their baking sheets with a little oil using a pastry brush or mister spray, and find that sufficient to stop their cookies from sticking. Others grease with white vegetable fat using kitchen paper. However, avoid butter as it burns at a relatively low temperature and salted butter tends to make cookies stick to the sheet. Or you can line the sheets with foil, which needs oiling, or with

non-stick baking parchment paper which does not. Using liners allows you to prepare all the cookies at once then simply slide onto the baking sheets as soon as they become available. Never slide a sheet of prepared cookies onto a warm baking sheet. The sheet must be absolutely cold before it is reused or the fat in the cookies will melt and the cookies spread before they reach the hot air of the oven.

INTO THE OVEN

Cookies must be put into a pre-heated oven. Most ovens take 10 minutes to heat up to temperature so switch your oven on when you begin preparation. Every oven is different, so the times given in this book may be a little different from those in your oven. Trust your eyes and your commonsense. If you persistently find the timings at variance, test the temperature of your oven using a cooking thermometer then calibrate with the thermostat reading; alternatively call for an engineer to check your oven. For optimum heat circulation, cook one cookie sheet at a time in the centre of the oven. If you cook two sheets simultaneously, then reverse the sheets halfway through the cooking time, working quickly to prevent the oven temperature falling too dramatically. When cooking two sheets at once, the cookies will need a little extra cooking time.

For evenly cooked cookies, space as directed in the recipe for consistent air circulation.

Ingredient	Altitude		
	3,000ft	**5,000ft**	**7,000ft**
Reduce baking powder For each teaspoon reduce by	⅛ teaspoon	⅛ to ¼ teaspoon	¼ teaspoon
Reduce sugar For each 125 g/4 oz reduce by	0–1 tablespoon	0 to 2 tablespoons	1 to 4 tablespoons
Increase liquid For each cup 225 ml/8 fl oz	1 to 2 tablespoons	2 to 4 tablespoons	3 to 4 tablespoons
Increase temperature by	0–10°F/0–5°C/Gas ½	10–25°F/5–15°C/Gas 1	25–35°F/15–20°C/Gas 1½

Are They Ready Yet?

Check the cookies a couple of minutes before the suggested cooking time is up to make sure that the cookies are not already cooked. Observe the colour and touch the cookies gently to see if they spring back or feel soggy. Different types of cookies have different tell-tale signs that indicate they are ready and these will be given in the recipe. Also, follow the cooling instructions closely as some need to stay on the baking sheet to continue cooking for a few minutes while others need to get onto a wire rack fairly quickly to prevent sticking. Cut bar cookies according to the directions using a serrated knife and a gentle sawing motion. This method is less likely to rip the dough than cutting directly through the cake with a sharp knife.

High-Altitude Cooking

Many sea-level cookie recipes work well without adjustments. However, above 9,800 metres/3,000 feet the atmospheric becomes pressure lower, liquid boils quicker and evaporation is therefore greater, which concentrates the flavour more, particularly sugars; in practical terms this means that chocolate chip and other drop cookies are slightly flatter and sweeter than at sea level. To compensate, adjust the recipes if necessary using the chart above as a guide. Reducing the quantity of fat and/or increasing the quantity of flour may help too. For soured cream-based doughs do not reduce the leavening beyond ½ teaspoon per 125 ml/4 fl oz soured cream. Avoid using self-raising flour as this already contains leavening agents (120 g /4 oz of self raising flour contains 1½ tablespoons of baking powder and a pinch of salt). Getting the recipe just right may require some element of trial and error – begin with small incremental changes until the cookies are baked to perfection.

Keeping Cookies Fresh

With a few exceptions, cookies are best eaten on the day that they are cooked.

WHAT WENT WRONG

The following are the most common causes for disappointment.

PROBLEM	REASON	REMEDY
Cookies stick to baking sheet **Cookies too cool**	Baking sheet not greased or unevenly greased Greasing with salted butter	Cookies should be removed from baking sheet 1 to 2 minutes after cooking. Return to the oven for a couple of minutes and remove from sheet immediately. Follow instructions below for over-greased sheets. Salted butter can make cookies stick to baking sheets.
Cookies break or crumble when removed from baking sheet	Delicate butter-rich cookies can be very fragile	Leave on baking sheet for 2 minutes before removing to cooling rack. Lift carefully with thin metal spatula.
Cookies too Dry **Cookies are Over-baked**	Oven too hot	Check oven thermostat. Check cookies a few minutes before suggested cooking time is up. Trust your judgement when testing. Place half an apple in the storage tin with the cookies to moisten.
Cookies too moist	Cookies are underdone	Check oven thermostat. Do not remove from oven unless the cookies test ready even if the cooking time is up. Return to the oven for a few minutes.

18

PROBLEM	REASON	REMEDY
Dough too soft **Won't roll or hold its shape** **Dough too wet** **Dough too warm**	Maybe too much liquid or fat or insufficient flour	Measure the ingredients carefully. Add extra flour. Place in the refrigerator for 30 minutes.
Dough won't hold together and is crumbly **Dough too dry**	Too much flour, or insufficient fat or liquid	Check that the correct size of eggs has been used. Measure ingredients carefully. Add a little soft butter or a little milk.
Cookies spread across baking sheet and touch each other	Cookies placed too close together Baking sheet over-greased Cookies placed on warm baking sheet	Follow recipe instructions for spacing. Use a pastry brush dipped in vegetable oil and wipe the sheet thinly and evenly with oil. Allow baking sheets to cool between batches.
Cookies are not evenly cooked	Cookies of uneven sizes on one sheet Oven cooks unevenly	Always cook cookies of a similar size on one sheet. Turn cookie sheets round during cooking and reverse sheets if cooking two at a time.
Cookies burnt on bottom but not top	Poor baking sheets Over-greasing Greasing with butter Cooking too low in oven	Avoid very thin or very dark baking sheets or line such sheets with foil. This causes cookies to spread too much. Butter burns at a lower temperature – use oil or white vegetable fat. Cookies are best cooked on the middle shelf. If cooking two sheets, reverse half way through cooking time.

Cookie dough, for all but cakey cookies that contain leavening ingredients (baking powder, bicarbonate of soda, self-raising flour or cream of tartar,) will keep in the refrigerator at least overnight, some types for as much as two or three days.

Cool cookies completely before wrapping and storing to prevent them from going soft.

Dough can be safely frozen for up to four months. The flavours do become less intense after the first month after which the dough may also pick up that characteristic freezer taste. Be sure to wrap the dough well, then place in an airtight plastic container. When freezing iced cookies, place a sheet of greaseproof paper between the layers.

Store cookies in airtight containers to prevent soft cookies becoming hard and crisp cookies becoming soft. If possible store in the refrigerator to retain the freshly baked flavour. For crisp cookies do not shut the container completely – a slight air flow helps them stay crisp in all but the most humid climates. For this reason, crisp cookies are the best type to keep in ceramic containers. A little crumpled, clean tissue paper placed at the bottom of the jar to absorb moisture also helps keep them crisp. If you must keep soft cookies in jars, place them first in self-sealing plastic bags. Never mix crisp and soft cookies when storing.

To re-crisp cookies, place in a 300°F/150°C/ Gas mark 2 oven for a few minutes, remove and cool. To revitalize soft cookies that have hardened, place a piece of apple or a slice of bread in the container. Replace every day or two. This trick can be used to prolong storage, particularly in very dry climates.

Cookies keep best in the refrigerator in plastic containers. Defrost cookies in their wrappings for between 15 to 30 minutes. To accelerate the defrosting process, defrost in the microwave on Medium for about 40 to 60 seconds.

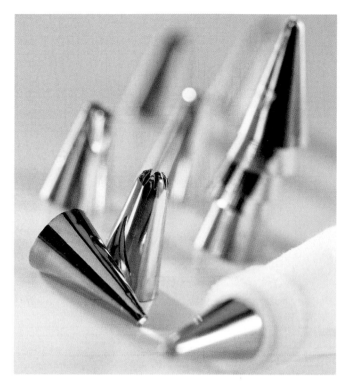

DECORATIONS GALORE

This is the point where the great cookie cook and the artist shoot off in different directions. For some, decoration means a dollop of icing or a sprinkling of sugar; others take pride in their decorating skills and pipe fancy lines and designs of great beauty.

A BASIC DECORATOR'S ICING

    225 g/8 oz icing sugar
    ½ tsp vanilla essence
    2 Tbsp milk

Beat together the ingredients until of spreading consistency and colour.

This quantity is sufficient to decorate 3 to 5 dozen cookies. Thin this mixture down a little and it becomes a useful cookie paint.

Another option is to use an egg wash. Mix together 1 egg yolk and ½ tsp water. Divide the resulting mixture if desired and tint with food colouring. This mixture can then be painted onto cookies prior to cooking. For a

blue tint use egg white in place of yolk. Tinted evaporated milk can also be used as a subtle glaze in place of egg wash.

The recipes in this book give you the information needed to decorate the cookies, but when out shopping look for unusual decorations, such as coloured sugars, sprinkles, shaped chocolate pieces and crystallized flowers that might come in handy. Small seasonal templates can be used as a stencil and dusted with icing sugar coloured with decorator's colouring dust for effective, simple decorations.

COOKIES BY POST

Cookies make the perfect gift, whatever the occasion. Wrapped in gift boxes or bags, or in seasonal storage tins they are always greeted with delight. For cookies by post, line a sturdy box or tin with foil or cellophane and place some crumpled tissue paper or cellophane on the base. Select cookies that will withstand the journey such as drop or bar cookies, or those containing fruit. Thin, delicate crisp cookies decorated with the finest piping make the worse travellers – if you must send these, place a few cookies on a piece of card, then wrap securely with clingfilm. Place plenty of crumpled tissue in between the cardboard layers in the box and around the edges. Pack other more robust cookies in layers separating each with a layer of paper or cellophane. Then pack crumpled paper in the top of the box and in any gaps around the edges. Place the box in a plastic bag and seal well (in case the package encounters inclement weather) then pack in a larger, sturdy box surrounded by a layer of packaging foam pieces or crumpled paper. Make sure that the box of cookies does not move around at all. Send for next-day delivery if possible, although most cookies can cope with a few days in the post.

All-day Cookies

Who says you can't eat cookies at any time of the day? In this chapter there are cookies for breakfast, brunch, morning coffee, lunch boxes, afternoon tea, after dinner, and night-time nibbles. Many of the cookies are quick to make, so there is no excuse – get baking and enjoy them fresh from the oven.

Breakfast

Try not to miss this most important meal of the day and there is no excuse now with this selection of tempting, nutritious cookies.

Brunch

Substantial cookies for a late brunch at weekends.

Morning Coffee

Delight your friends with the smell of freshly baked cookies when they come for coffee. These cookies make a perfect snack.

Lunch Box

The cookies in this section are hearty enough for brunches or lunches, or whenever you need an energy-giving snack. They are portable too and ideal for when you have a busy schedule but still need a quick bite to eat.

Afternoon Tea

The cookies featured in this part of the book are generally smaller and more delicate than the cookies for brunch or lunch. These cookies have also been chosen as their flavours complement the different tasting teas such as Earl Grey.

After-dinner Delicacies

These cookies are small, delicate, and bite sized; ideal to serve up after a meal of several courses with coffee when entertaining. They may be small, but they are very tempting so make a good selection for your guests to choose from.

Night-time Nibbles

Muesli Bars

Preparation time: 15 minutes ● Cooking time: 25 minutes ● Makes: 12 bars

Ideal for those who need to eat breakfast on the move, grab a bar and a piece of fruit and this will set you up for the day.

INGREDIENTS

125 ml/4 fl oz clear/runny honey

120 g/4 oz margarine

50 g/2 oz dark brown sugar

50 g/2 oz light brown sugar

225 g/8 oz rolled oats

3 Tbsp flaked almonds

3 Tbsp chopped walnuts

40 g/1½ oz raisins

40 g/1½ oz chopped dried dates

40 g/1½ oz chopped dried apricots

Pre-heat oven to 350°F/175°C/Gas mark 4. Grease a shallow 28 x 18-cm/11 x 7-in baking tin or line with a sheet of non-stick baking parchment.

● Gently melt the honey, margarine and sugars in a saucepan until well combined, taking care not to boil the mixture. Stir in the oats, nuts and dried fruits, mixing well.

● Press the mixture into the baking tin and bake in the centre of the oven for about 25 minutes, until golden. Leave to cool in the tin for 5 minutes. Cut into bars.

● Leave to cool completely before removing muesli bars from the tin. Store in an airtight container.

Maple Syrup Cookies

Preparation time: 15 minutes ● Cooking time: 12 to 15 minutes ● Makes: About 12 to 14

These simple cookies are delicately flavoured with maple syrup.

INGREDIENTS

120 g/4 oz lightly salted butter

120 g/4 oz light brown sugar

1 egg, beaten

175 g/6 oz plain flour

2 Tbsp maple syrup

Pre-heat oven to 350°F/175°C/Gas mark 4. Grease two large baking sheets or line with non-stick baking parchment.

● Beat the butter and sugar together in a mixing bowl. Beat in the egg, then add the flour and maple syrup.

● Place 12 to 14 equal-sized spoonfuls of the mixture onto the baking sheets, allowing 8 cm/3 in for spreading. Flatten the mounds of mixture a little with the back of the spoon. Bake in the oven for about 12 to 15 minutes, until pale golden. Remove from the oven and allow to cool for one minute to allow the cookies to firm, before removing with a thin metal spatula to a wire rack to cool completely. Store in an airtight container.

Banana Cookies

Preparation time: 15 minutes ●
Cooking time: 10 to 12 minutes ● *Makes: 12*

Great served with a quickly whizzed smoothie or shake.

INGREDIENTS

120 g/4 oz lightly salted butter

120 g/4 oz light brown sugar

1 egg, beaten

175 g/6 oz plain flour

150 g/5 oz dried banana chips, chopped

Pre-heat oven to 350°F/175°C/Gas mark 4. Grease two large baking sheets or line with non-stick baking parchment.

● Beat the butter and sugar together in a mixing bowl until pale and fluffy. Beat in the egg and flour. Stir in three-quarters of the chopped banana chips and place twelve equal-sized spoonfuls of the mixture onto the baking sheets, allowing 8 cm/3 in for spreading. Flatten the mounds of cookie mixture a little using the back of the spoon.

● Sprinkle the remaining banana chips equally over the twelve cookies and press in very lightly. Bake for about 10 to 12 minutes, until pale golden. Remove from the oven and allow to cool for one minute to allow the cookies to firm, before removing with a thin metal spatula to a wire rack to cool completely. Store in an airtight container.

Pine Nut Oaties

Preparation time: 10 minutes ●
Cooking time :10 to 12 minutes ● *Makes: 12*

A high fibre start to the day.

INGREDIENTS

5 Tbsp dark brown sugar

200 g/7 oz rolled oats

40 g/1 oz oatmeal

200 g/7 oz pine kernels

125 ml/4 fl oz peanut oil

1 egg, beaten

Pre-heat oven to 375°F/190°C/Gas mark 5. Grease two large baking sheets or line with non-stick baking parchment.

● Place the sugar, oats, oatmeal and pine kernels in a mixing bowl and mix together. Add the peanut oil and egg and mix all the ingredients together thoroughly to form a crumble mixture.

● Place small tablespoonfuls of the mixture 10 cm/4 in apart on the baking sheets and flatten with a fork to make 8 cm/3 in circles. If necessary, bring the crumble mixture together and place any loose pine kernels back on top of the cookies. Bake in the oven for 10 to 12 minutes or until golden-brown. Leave for 1 minute to firm before removing with a thin metal spatula to cool on a wire rack. Store in an airtight container.

Apricot Slices

Preparation time: 45 minutes ● Cooking time: 25 to 30 minutes ● Makes: About 12

The fresh tang of apricots combined with the comforting oats makes this a great breakfast cookie.

INGREDIENTS

40 g/1½ oz dried apricots

2 Tbsp granulated sugar

150 ml/5 fl oz unsweetened clear apple juice

120 g/4 oz plain flour

1 tsp bicarbonate of soda

200 g/7 oz rolled oats

50 g/2 oz light brown sugar

120 g/4 oz lightly salted butter

Pre-heat oven to 375°F/190°C/Gas mark 5. Grease a shallow 28 x 18-cm/11 x 7-in baking tin or line with non-stick baking parchment.

● Chop the apricots into quarters and place in a saucepan with the granulated sugar and apple juice. Bring to the boil, cover and simmer for 15 minutes or until the apricots have softened and absorbed nearly all of the apple juice. Leave to cool completely, then place in a blender and process until smooth.

● Mix together the flour, bicarbonate of soda, oats and brown sugar in a mixing bowl. Blend in the butter using fingertips, until the mixture resembles breadcrumbs.

● Press half of the crumbly oat mixture over the base of the baking tin. Spread the apricot purée evenly over the oat mixture, using a thin metal spatula wetted with a little cold water to help ease of spreading. Cover with the remaining oat mixture, pressing the mixture down lightly. Bake in the oven for 25 to 30 minutes, until pale golden. Leave to cool in the tin before cutting into 12 equal-sized bars. Store in an airtight container.

Pumpkin Seed and Bran Cookies

Preparation time: 10 minutes ● Cooking time: 10 to 12 minutes ● Makes: 12

Packed with goodness, try these deliciously crunchy cookies any time of day.

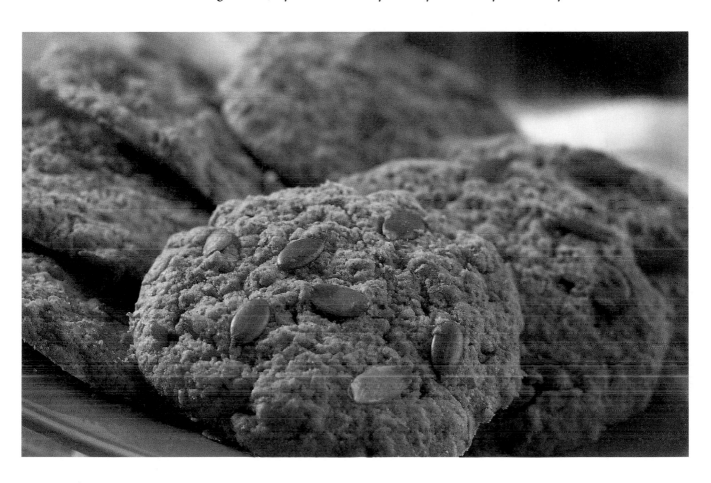

INGREDIENTS

120 g/4 oz lightly salted butter
120 g/4 oz light brown sugar
120 g/4 oz dark brown sugar
1 egg, beaten
150 g/5 oz plain flour
75 g/3 oz bran
40 g/1½ oz pumpkin seeds

Pre-heat oven to 350°F/175°C/Gas mark 4. Grease two large baking sheets or line with non-stick baking parchment.

● Beat the butter and sugars together in a mixing bowl until the mixture turns pale and fluffy. Beat in the egg, flour and bran. Stir in three-quarters of the pumpkin seeds.

● Place 12 equal-sized spoonfuls of the mixture onto the baking sheets, allowing 8 cm/3 in for spreading. Flatten the mounds a little with the back of the spoon and sprinkle the remaining pumpkin seeds evenly over the cookies. Bake for about 10 to 12 minutes, until golden and just firm. Remove from the oven and allow to cool for one minute, then remove with a thin metal spatula to a wire rack to cool completely. Store in an airtight container.

Lime Cookies

Preparation time: 15 minutes ● *Cooking time: 12 to 14 minutes* ● *Makes: 12*

Lime adds a tang to wake up your tastebuds.

INGREDIENTS

120 g/4 oz lightly salted butter

120 g/4 oz granulated sugar

1 egg, beaten

175 g/6 oz plain flour

Finely grated rind of 1 lime

2 Tbsp fresh lime juice

FILLING

75 g/3 oz unsalted butter, softened

175 g/6 oz icing sugar, sifted

1 Tbsp grated rind of 1 lime

2 tsp fresh lime juice

Pre-heat oven to 350°F/175°C/Gas mark 4. Grease two large baking sheets or line with non-stick baking parchment.

● Beat the butter and sugar together in a mixing bowl until pale and fluffy. Beat in the egg, flour, lime rind and lime juice.

● Place 12 equal-sized spoonfuls of the mixture onto the baking sheets, allowing 8 cm/3 in all round for spreading. Flatten the mounds of mixture a little using the back of the spoon. Bake the cookies in the oven for about 12 to 14 minutes, until pale golden. Remove from the oven and allow to cool for one minute to allow the cookies to firm, before removing with a thin metal spatula to a wire rack to cool completely.

● To make the filling, in a small bowl beat together the butter and icing sugar until soft and stir in the lime rind and juice for a soft icing. Sandwich the cookies together with the filling.

● Store in an airtight container.

Honey and Oat Cookies

Preparation time: 15 minutes ● Cooking time: 10 to 12 minutes ● Makes: 14

Sweet and delicious honey and oats make these a good breakfast choice.

INGREDIENTS

120 g/4 oz lightly salted butter

120 g/4 oz light brown sugar

2 Tbsp clear/runny honey

1 egg yolk

175 g/6 oz self-raising flour

Pinch mixed spice

75 g/3 oz rolled oats

Pre-heat the oven to 350°F/175°C/Gas mark 4. Meanwhile, grease two large baking sheets.

● Beat together the butter and sugar in a mixing bowl until pale and fluffy. Beat in the honey and egg yolk, then stir in the flour, mixed spice and oats until well combined.

● Divide the mixture into 14 equal-sized pieces and roll into balls using your fingertips. Place the cookies onto the baking sheets 8 cm/3 in apart, to allow for spreading. Bake for 10 to 12 minutes until golden and just firm. Leave to cool for one minute to allow the cookies to firm, before removing them with a thin metal spatula to a wire rack to cool. Store in an airtight container.

Sesame Seed Sensations

Preparation time: 10 minutes ● *Cooking time: 12 to 15 minutes* ● *Makes: About 12*

Sesame seeds have a strong flavour which bursts through the oat base in this cookie.

INGREDIENTS

5 Tbsp light brown sugar
200 g/7 oz rolled oats
40 g/1½ oz oatmeal
40 g/1½ oz sesame seeds
125 ml/4 fl oz peanut oil
1 egg, beaten

Pre-heat oven to 375°F/190°C/Gas mark 5. Grease two large baking sheets or line with non-stick baking parchment.

● Place the sugar, oats, oatmeal and sesame seeds in a mixing bowl and mix. Add the peanut oil and beaten egg and mix all the ingredients thoroughly to form a crumble mixture.

● Place small tablespoons of the mixture 8 to 10 cm/ 3 to 4 in apart on greased baking sheets and flatten with a fork to make 8-cm/3-in circles. Bake in the oven for 12 to 15 minutes or until golden-brown. Leave on the baking sheets for 1 minute to firm before carefully removing with a thin metal spatula to cool the cookies on a wire rack. Store in an airtight container.

Orange Shortbread

Preparation time: 10 minutes ● Cooking time: 1 hour ● Makes: About 16

Home-made shortbread is crisp and light and this version is delicately flavoured with orange rind.

INGREDIENTS

120 g/4 oz lightly salted butter

120 g/4 oz plain flour

50 g/2 oz icing sugar

50 g/2 oz cornflour

Grated rind of 1 orange

Preheat oven to 325°F/160°C/Gas mark 3. Grease a shallow baking tin measuring 18 x 18-cm/7 x 7-in or line with non-stick baking parchment.

● With fingertips gently work the butter, flour, icing sugar, cornflour and orange rind together in a mixing bowl. Bring the mixture together to make a soft dough.

● Press the mixture evenly into the pan and smooth the surface. Lightly prick the surface evenly all over with a fork. Bake for 40 minutes then reduce the temperature to 275°F/140°C/Gas mark 1 and bake for a further 15 to 20 minutes, or until lightly browned. Leave to cool completely in the tin and cut into 16 equal-sized bars with a sharp knife. These cookies are best eaten on the day they are made.

Currant and Almond Cookies

Preparation time: 15 minutes + chilling ● Cooking time: 8 to 10 minutes ● Makes: 16

The combination of currents and nuts in these cookies makes them both crunchy and chewy – delicious.

INGREDIENTS

225 g/8 oz lightly salted butter

120 g/4 oz light brown sugar

175 g/6 oz self-raising flour

50 g/2 oz flaked almonds

75 g/3 oz currants

Preheat oven to 400°F/200°C/Gas mark 6. Grease two large baking sheets with non-stick baking parchment.

● Beat together the butter and sugar in a mixing bowl until pale and fluffy. Beat in the flour and almonds then stir in the currants. If the dough is too soft to handle, cover and chill in the refrigerator for 30 minutes.

● Form the cookie dough into a roll about 5 cm/2½ in in diameter. Cut into 1-cm/½-in slices and place well apart on the baking sheets to allow for spreading.

● Bake the cookies in batches in the oven for 8 to 10 minutes, until light brown. Leave to cool for five minutes on the sheets before removing with a thin metal spatula to a wire rack to cool completely.

Cornflake and Sultana Cookies

Preparation time: 25 minutes ● Cooking time: 10 to 15 minutes ● Makes: 18

Soft chewy cookies that are very easy to make.

INGREDIENTS

120 g/4 oz soft margarine

120 g/4 oz light brown sugar

1 egg, beaten

150 g/5 oz self-raising flour

60 g/1½ oz cornflakes

75 g/3 oz sultanas

Preheat oven to 350°F/185°C/Gas mark 4. Grease several baking sheets or line with non-stick baking parchment.

● Beat together the margarine and sugar in a mixing bowl until pale and fluffy. Beat in the egg. Stir in the flour with the cornflakes and golden raisins and mix everything together until well combined.

● Place mounds of the mixture onto the baking sheets, leaving big spaces in between to allow for spreading.

● Bake the cookies in the oven for 12 to 15 minutes, until golden brown. Lift onto wire racks to cool completely. Store in an airtight container.

Double Banana Cookies

Preparation time: 25 minutes ● Cooking time: 12 to 15 minutes ● Makes: 16

These wholesome cookies contain oats, banana chips and fresh chunks of banana.

INGREDIENTS

120 g/4 oz soft margarine

120 g/4 oz light brown sugar

1 egg, beaten

175 g/6 oz self-raising flour

25 g/1 oz porridge oats

25 g/1 oz chopped candied pineapple

25 g/1 oz crumbled banana chips

1 banana, chopped

Preheat oven to 350°F/175°C/Gas mark 4. Grease several baking sheets or line with non-stick baking parchment.

● In a mixing bowl beat together the margarine and sugar until pale and fluffy. Beat in the egg. Stir in the flour with the oats, candied pineapple, banana chips and fresh banana and mix everything together until well combined.

● Place mounds of the mixture onto the baking sheets, leaving big spaces in between to allow for spreading.

● Bake the cookies in the oven for 12 to 15 minutes, until golden brown. Lift onto wire racks to cool completely. Store in an airtight container.

Cream Cheese Puff Swirls

Preparation time: 10 minutes ● Cooking time: 12 to15 minutes ● Makes: About 18

These cookies are so simple to make and look exquisite.

INGREDIENTS

225 g/8 oz ready-rolled puff pastry, thawed, if frozen

120 g/4 oz chopped dried apricots

120 g/4 oz cream cheese

Pre-heat oven to 425°F/220°C/Gas mark 7. Grease two large baking sheets or line with non-stick baking parchment.

● Place the puff pastry on a lightly floured surface and roll to make a rectangle measuring 28 x 23 cm/11 x 9 in.

● In a bowl mix the apricots and cream cheese together thoroughly. Spread the mixture evenly all over the surface of the pastry. Holding one of the short sides, roll the pastry up to make a roll. Cut across the pastry roll with a sharp knife to make 2.5-cm/1-in thick slices.

● Place the pastry swirls onto the prepared baking sheets allowing 2.5 cm/1 in in between them for spreading. Bake for 12 to 15 minutes, or until the pastry is golden-brown and crisp. Best if eaten warm when freshly made, but can be cooled and kept in the refrigerator for 24 hours.

36

Nut Chewies

Preparation time: 25 minutes + cooling ● Cooking time: 12 to 15 minutes ● Makes: About 36

This cookie is almost all nuts and fruit. They are soft and chewy and don't last long – especially at a picnic.

INGREDIENTS

120 g/4 oz unblanched whole almonds

50 g/2 oz pecan or walnut halves

50 g/2 oz blanched hazelnuts

120 g/4 oz plain flour

1 tsp bicarbonate of soda

¼ tsp salt

120 g/4 oz unsalted butter

120 g/4 oz granulated sugar

3 Tbsp dark brown sugar

1 egg

1 tsp vanilla essence

75 g/3 oz raisins

75 g/3 oz sultanas

Preheat oven to 375°F/190°C/Gas mark 5. Place nuts on a large baking sheet and toast until golden and fragrant, 5 to 7 minutes, stirring occasionally. Pour onto a plate and cool completely, then roughly chop. Grease two large baking sheets or line with non-stick baking parchment.

● Into a small bowl, sift together the flour, bicarbonate of soda and salt. In a large bowl, beat the butter until soft, beat in the sugar until the mixture becomes light and fluffy. Beat in the egg and vanilla until combined. Stir in the flour mixture followed by the raisins, sultanas and nuts until evenly distributed.

● Drop heaped tablespoons of the mixture, at least 5 cm/2 in apart onto baking sheets. Bake in the oven until set and golden, 12 to 15 minutes, rotating the baking sheets during cooking. Cool the cookies slightly, then transfer to wire racks to cool completely. Store in an airtight container.

Maple Syrup Tartlets

Preparation time: 30 minutes + chilling ● Cooking time: 15 to 20 minutes ● Makes: About 17

These little tartlets are delicious served warm with more maple syrup poured over the top.

INGREDIENTS

FOR THE PASTRY BASE

120 g/4 oz margarine

1 Tbsp milk

175 g/6 oz plain flour

FILLING

150 ml/5 fl oz maple syrup

TOPPING

50 g/2 oz margarine

50 g/2 oz light brown sugar

6 Tbsp self-raising flour

½ tsp baking powder

¼ tsp vanilla essence

1 egg, beaten

1 Tbsp milk

Pre-heat oven to 375°F/190°C/Gas mark 5. Grease two shallow bun tins or eight 9-cm/3½-in individual tartlet tins.

● To make the pastry base, place the margarine, milk and flour together in a bowl and mix together to make a dough. If the pastry is too soft to handle, cover and refrigerate for at least 30 minutes to become firm.

● On a lightly floured surface, roll out the pastry thinly and cut into 8-cm/3-in circles using a fluted pastry cutter. Re-roll and cut the pastry to make as many

pastry circles as possible. Line the tartlet tins with the pastry circles. Place one teaspoonful of maple syrup in each small pastry shell.

● To make the topping, beat together the margarine and sugar until pale and fluffy. Add the flour, baking powder, vanilla essence, egg and milk, mix thoroughly. Divide the mixture evenly over the maple syrup-covered tartlet bases. Bake in the oven for 15 to 20 minutes, until golden. Eat warm, served with more maple syrup or cool and store in an airtight container.

Spiced Orange Cookies

Preparation time: 40 minutes ● *Cooking time: 25 minutes* ● *Makes: About 96*

A very tangy cookie that never loses its appeal. These are great for brunch or for social parties at school, church or tennis club, for example.

INGREDIENTS

350 g/12 oz plain flour	Grated rind of 1 orange
½ tsp mixed spice	50 ml/2 fl oz freshly squeezed orange juice
¼ tsp salt	½ tsp almond essence
350 g/12 oz unsalted butter	4 Tbsp orange marmalade
200 g/7 oz caster sugar	Flaked almonds, to decorate

Pre-heat oven to 375°F/190°C/Gas mark 5. In a medium bowl, sift together flour, spice and salt. In a large bowl beat butter until creamy. Add the sugar and continue beating until light and fluffy. Beat in egg, orange rind and orange juice until well blended. Stir in flour until well combined.

● Divide the dough into quarters. Working with one-quarter at a time, fill a cookie press fitted with a ribbon or bar plate. Press 30-cm/12-in strips overlapping lengthwise, onto one side of an ungreased baking sheet, making a base about 8 cm/3 in wide. Pat down strips to flatten. Refill the press with dough, if necessary, and press a border along each side of strips, leaving a shallow trough in the centre. Press out a little dough and use to make 2 ends (this will prevent the marmalade from oozing out onto the baking sheet.)

● Bake strips for 15 minutes. Remove baking sheets from oven, and using the back of a spoon, press down a centre trench in each strip. Fill with marmalade to just below the edges.

● Return the baking sheet to the oven and bake until the edges are golden and the marmalade bubbling, 10 to 12 minutes. Remove baking sheets to wire rack and cool until set, about 3 minutes. Using another baking sheet or long metal spatula, slide each long strip onto a wire rack to cool for about 5 minutes. Slip each strip onto a work surface and while still warm, trim the edges and cut into 2.5-cm/1-in cookies.

Jam Thumbprints

Preparation time: 20 minutes + chilling ● *Cooking time: 15 to 17 minutes* ● *Makes: 14*

A cookie classic. Using a selection of jams or preserves makes a plate of these look really pretty.

INGREDIENTS

150 g/5 oz lightly salted butter
5 Tbsp light brown sugar
1 egg yolk
225 g/8 oz plain flour
14 tsp seedless fruit jam

Grease two large baking sheets or line with non-stick baking parchment.

● Beat together the butter and sugar until light and fluffy. Beat in the egg yolk and stir in the flour. Cover and refrigerate for about an hour, or until firm enough to handle. Pre-heat oven to 350°F/175°C/Gas mark 4, then divide the mixture into 14 equal-sized pieces and roll into balls using your hands. Place at least 2.5 cm/ 1 in apart on the baking sheets. Press your thumb into the centre of each cookie ball to make a hollow indentation.

● Bake in the oven for about 10 to 12 minutes until pale brown and just firm. If the centres of the cookies have risen slightly, gently pat back down with the back of a teaspoon. Fill each hollow with a teaspoon of jam or preserves and bake for a further 5 minutes. Remove the cookies to a wire rack to cool using a thin metal spatula. Store in an airtight container.

Crunchy Cheese Bites

Preparation time: 10 minutes ● *Cooking time: 20 minutes* ● *Makes: 10*

A great favourite with children and adults alike.

INGREDIENTS

50 g/2 oz margarine
50 g/2 oz plain flour
½ tsp paprika
120 g/4 oz freshly grated Parmesan cheese
75 g/3 oz Rice Crispies
1 egg, beaten

Pre-heat oven to 350°F/175°C/Gas mark 4. Grease a large baking sheet or line with non-stick baking parchment.

● Beat together the margarine, flour, paprika and Parmesan to make a crumbly mixture.

● Stir in the cereal and egg, until combined, taking care not to crush the cereal. Shape into 10 equal-sized balls and place on the baking sheet. Bake for 20 minutes, until lightly browned. Eat warm, or cool on a wire rack. These are best eaten on the day they are made.

Ginger Bites

Preparation time: 10 minutes ● *Cooking time: 15 minutes* ● *Makes: About 12*

Ginger cookies go well with cappuccino.

INGREDIENTS

4 Tbsp light brown sugar

50 g/2 oz lightly salted butter

2½ Tbsp treacle

175 g/6 oz self-raising flour

1 tsp ground ginger

½ tsp baking powder

Pre-heat oven to 350°F/175°C/Gas mark 4. Grease two large baking sheets or line with non-stick baking parchment.

● Beat together the sugar, butter and treacle until it becomes lighter in colour and fluffy. Mix in the flour, ginger and baking powder until well combined. Roll the mixture into walnut-sized balls using your hands and place 5 to 8 cm/2 to 3 in apart on the baking sheets to allow for spreading. Flatten the cookies slightly using your fingers or the back of a fork. Bake in the oven for about 15 minutes, until flattened and slightly firm to the touch. Leave to cool on the baking sheets then remove and store in an airtight container.

Popcorn Cheese Balls

Preparation time: 10 minutes ● Cooking time: 20 minutes ● Makes: 8

The popcorn adds an airy crunch to these cookies.

INGREDIENTS

50 g/2 oz margarine
6 Tbsp plain flour
50 g/2 oz grated Cheddar cheese
25 g/4 oz grated Parmesan cheese
2 eggs, beaten
175 g/6 oz ready-made plain or salted popcorn

Pre-heat oven to 350°F/175°C/Gas mark 4. Grease a large baking sheet or line with non-stick baking parchment.

● Beat together the margarine, flour and cheeses in a large mixing bowl to make a crumbly mixture. Stir in the egg. Add the popcorn and mix thoroughly, so that the cheese mixture coats the popcorn. The mixture will combine sufficiently so that it will form balls.

● Make 8 equal-sized ball-shaped cookies with the mixture and place on the baking sheet. Bake for about 20 minutes, until lightly browned. Serve immediately, while warm.

Butter, Currant & Coconut Cookies

Preparation time: 15 minutes + chilling ● Cooking time: 8 to 10 minutes ● Makes: 16

These cookies are crisp on the day they are made, but if stored in an airtight container they soften and become quite chewy – both are delicious.

INGREDIENTS

225 g/8 oz lightly salted butter
175 g/6 oz light brown sugar
175 g/6 oz self-raising flour
75 g/3 oz sweetened flaked coconut
125 g/4 oz currants

Pre-heat oven to 400°F/200°C/Gas mark 6. Grease two large baking sheets or line with non-stick baking parchment.

● Beat together the butter and sugar in a mixing bowl until pale and fluffy. Beat in the flour and coconut. Stir in the currants. If the dough is too soft to handle, cover and chill in the refrigerator for about 1 hour to firm.

● Form the cookie dough into a roll about 6 cm/2½ in in diameter. Cut into 1-cm/½-in slices and place well apart to allow for spreading as the cookies double in size. Reshape into neat rounds, if necessary.

● Bake the cookies in batches in the oven for about 8 to 10 minutes, until light brown. Allow to cool for 5 minutes to firm on the baking sheet, before removing with a thin metal spatula to a wire rack to cool.

Pear Cookies

Preparation time: 15 minutes ● Cooking time:
12 to 14 minutes ● Makes: About 12 to 14

You will want to add dried pears to many more recipes after enjoying these cookies. Other dried fruit such as apricots, can also be substituted.

INGREDIENTS

120 g/4 oz lightly salted butter
120 g/4 oz light brown sugar
1 egg, beaten
175 g/6 oz plain flour
150 g/5 oz chopped ready-to-eat dried pears

Pre-heat oven to 350°F/175°C/Gas mark 4. Grease two large baking sheets or line with non-stick baking parchment.

● Beat the butter and sugar together in a mixing bowl until pale and fluffy. Beat in the egg and flour. Stir in the chopped pears.

● Place 12 to 14 equal-sized spoonfuls of the cookie mixture onto the baking sheets, allowing 5 to 8 cm/2 to 3 in for spreading. Flatten the mounds of mixture a little using the back of the spoon. Bake the cookies in the oven for about 12 to 14 minutes, until pale golden. Remove from the oven and leave to firm on the baking sheets for one minute, before removing with a thin metal spatula to a wire rack to cool completely. Store in an airtight container.

Chocolate Swirls

Chocolate Swirls

Preparation time: 5 minutes ● Cooking time: 10 to 12 minutes ● Makes: About 18 to 20

Using ready made puff pastry makes these cookies very quick and easy to make.

INGREDIENTS

225 g/8 oz ready-made rolled puff pastry, thawed if frozen

3–4 Tbsp chocolate spread

Pre-heat oven to 425°F/220°C/Gas mark 7. Grease two large baking sheets or line with non-stick baking parchment.

● Place the puff pastry on a lightly floured surface and if necessary roll to make a rectangle measuring 28 x 23 cm/11 x 9 in. Spread the chocolate spread evenly all over the surface of the pastry. Holding one of the short sides, roll the pastry up to make a long roll. Cut across the pastry roll with a sharp knife to make 5-mm/¼-in thick slices.

● Transfer the pastry swirls onto the baking sheets allowing a little space for spreading. If necessary, reshape into neat circles and pat down slightly. Bake for 8 minutes in the centre of the oven until golden-brown, then carefully turn the pastries over and bake for a further 2 to 4 minutes until golden. Using a thin metal spatula, remove the chocolate swirls to a wire rack to cool completely.

Cheese and Peanut Shortbread Bars

Preparation time: 15 minutes ● Cooking time: 50 minutes ● Makes: 10 bars

These filling bars are tasty served with more sliced cheese or spread with peanut butter.

INGREDIENTS

225 g/8 oz lightly salted butter

225 g/8 oz plain flour

120 g/4 oz grated mature Cheddar cheese

50 g/2 oz freshly grated Parmesan cheese

225 g/8 oz salted peanuts, toasted

Pre-heat oven to 350°F/175°C/Gas mark 4. Grease a shallow 28 x 18-cm/11 x 7-in baking tin.

● Beat together the butter and flour in a mixing bowl until well combined. Add the cheeses and three-quarters of the peanuts and using your hand, lightly bring the mixture together to form a soft dough.

● Press the mixture into the prepared tin with a lightly floured hand and smooth the surface. Evenly sprinkle over the remaining peanuts and lightly press into the top of the shortbread mixture. Bake for about 50 minutes, until a pale, golden-brown and firm to touch.

● Leave to cool completely in the tin before cutting into 10 even-sized bars. Store in an airtight container. Best eaten on the day made but can be kept in the refrigerator for 2 to 3 days.

Ginger and Coffee Creams

Preparation time: 30 minutes ● Cooking time: 15 to 20 minutes ● Makes: About 25

Crisp ginger nut cookies sandwiched together with a coffee cream; perfect with a large mug of steaming coffee.

INGREDIENTS

175 g/6 oz plain flour

2 tsp baking powder

1 tsp bicarbonate of soda

2 tsp ground ginger

1 tsp mixed spice

1 Tbsp caster sugar

120 g/4 oz lightly salted butter or margarine

125 ml/4 fl oz golden syrup

ICING

120 g/4 oz unsalted butter, softened

3 Tbsp caster sugar

1 tsp coffee essence

7 Tbsp icing sugar

Pre-heat oven to 375°F/190°C/Gas mark 5. Grease or line two baking sheets with non-stick baking parchment.

● Sift together the flour, baking powder, bicarbonate of soda, ginger and mixed spice. Stir in the sugar and make a well in the centre. Melt the butter, then stir in the golden syrup and pour the mixture into the well. Mix to a soft but not sticky dough.

● Take half teaspoons of the mixture and roll into balls. Place on the baking sheets leaving space between the cookies as they will spread while cooking. Flatten them slightly. Bake for 15 to 20 minutes until set. Leave to cool for a few minutes, then transfer onto wire racks to cool completely.

● To prepare the icing, beat the butter and caster sugar together with the coffee essence until well blended. Gradually beat in the icing sugar and mix to a stiff paste. Sandwich the cookies together with the icing. Best eaten on the day they are filled, but may be stored in an airtight container for 2 to 3 days although the filling will make the cookies soften.

Apricot and Cheese Cookies

Preparation time: 15 minutes ● Cooking time: 15 to 18 minutes ● Makes: About 14

Tangy sweet apricots complement these cheese cookies.

INGREDIENTS

150 g/5 oz no-soak, dried apricots, finely chopped
75 g/3 oz lightly salted butter
225 g/8 oz plain flour
6 Tbsp grated Cheddar cheese
1 egg, beaten
3–4 Tbsp milk

Pre-heat oven to 375°F/190°C/Gas mark 5. Grease two large baking sheets or line with non-stick baking parchment.

● Cut the dried apricots into small pieces. In a mixing bowl, blend the butter into the flour to resemble breadcrumbs. Stir in two-thirds of the grated cheese, three-quarters of the chopped dried apricots and the egg. Add enough milk to form a dough.

● On a lightly floured surface, roll the cookie dough out to 5 mm/¼ in thick and cut the dough into 5 x 8-cm/ 2 x 3-in rectangular cookies. Re-roll and repeat. Place the cookies on the baking sheets, brush with any remaining milk and sprinkle over the reserved grated cheese and apricots. Bake for about 15 to 18 minutes, until golden-brown. Remove from the baking sheet with a thin metal spatula and cool on a wire rack. Store in an airtight container in the refrigerator for up to 2 days.

Apple and Cinnamon Cookies

Preparation time: 15 minutes + chilling ● Cooking time: 25 minutes ● Makes: 12

These cookies are best eaten the same day, but can be stored in an airtight container for 2 days.

INGREDIENTS

225 g/8 oz lightly salted butter
120 g/4 oz icing sugar
4 drops vanilla essence
1 tsp ground cinnamon
225 g/8 oz plain flour
150 g/5 oz cornflour
3 Tbsp apple sauce
1 eating apple, peeled, cored and diced

Pre-heat oven to 350°F/175°C/Gas mark 4. Grease two large baking sheets or line with non-stick baking parchment.

● Beat the butter, icing sugar, vanilla essence and cinnamon until well combined. Stir in the flour, cornflour, apple sauce and diced apple until it forms a well mixed but crumbly dough. If the mixture is soft and sticky, refrigerate for at least 30 minutes to firm.

● Divide the mixture into 12 equal-sized pieces and using your hands shape into balls. Place the cookie balls onto the baking sheets, 8 cm/3 in apart and flatten slightly with a fork. Bake in the oven for about 25 minutes, until golden. Leave to cool on the baking sheet for 5 minutes to firm before removing with a thin metal spatula to a wire rack to cool completely.

Chocolate and Cream Cheese Marble Fudge Bars

Preparation time: 20 minutes ● Cooking time: 40 to 45 minutes ● Makes: 12

These are very rich and sticky fudge bars which can be wrapped in greaseproof paper and make wonderful lunch box fillers.

INGREDIENTS

FOR THE CHOCOLATE BASE

175 g/6 oz lightly salted butter

75 g/3 oz plain chocolate

175 g/6 oz light brown sugar

175 g/6 oz dark brown sugar

2 eggs, beaten

120 g/4 oz plain flour

6 drops vanilla essence

TOPPING

175 g/6 oz cream cheese

75 g/3 oz light brown sugar

1 egg, beaten

4 drops vanilla essence

Pre-heat oven to 350°F/175°C/Gas mark 4. Grease a shallow 18 x 28-cm/7 x 11-in baking tin, line with non-stick baking parchment and then grease again.

● To make the chocolate base, melt the butter and chocolate in a small saucepan over a gentle heat, taking care not to boil the mixture.

● In a mixing bowl, whisk together the light and dark brown sugars with the eggs until well combined, then whisk in the melted butter and chocolate mixture. Stir in the flour and vanilla essence. Pour the mixture into the prepared tin.

● Make the topping. Beat together the cream cheese, sugar, egg and vanilla essence until the mixture thickens to a spooning consistency. Randomly place spoonfuls of the mixture over the chocolate mixture in the baking tin and, using the tip of a sharp knife, make swirling patterns drawing the knife through the two mixtures to combine lightly. Bake in the oven for about 40 to 45 minutes, or until the mixture is firm to touch and the tip of a sharp knife comes out clean when inserted into the centre of the cookie mixture. Cool in the tin and cut into 12 equal-sized bars. Store in an airtight container in the refrigerator for up to 2 days.

Spiced Molasses Drops

Preparation time: 15 minutes ● Cooking time: 14 to 20 minutes ● Makes: About 40

These cookies are bite-size, and packed with a rich spicy flavour

INGREDIENTS

120 g/4 oz plain flour

1 tsp ground cinnamon

1/2 tsp ground ginger

1/2 tsp ground nutmeg

1/4 tsp ground cloves

1/2 tsp bicarbonate of soda

1/2 tsp salt

50 g/2 oz butter or margarine, softened

120 g/4 oz shortening

4 Tbsp molasses

120 g/4 oz dark brown sugar

1 egg

GLAZE

175 g/6 oz icing sugar

3 tsp water

1/2 tsp vanilla essence

Preheat oven to 375°F/190°C/Gas mark 5. Grease two large baking sheets or line with non-stick baking parchment.

● In a medium bowl, sift together flour, cinnamon, ginger, nutmeg, cloves, bicarbonate of soda and salt. In a large bowl beat the butter or margarine, shortening, molasses, brown sugar and egg until well blended. Stir in flour-spice mixture until combined.

● Drop teaspoons of mixture 2.5 cm/1 in apart onto 2 large ungreased baking sheets. Bake until crisp and golden, 7 to 10 minutes. Cool slightly on wire racks, then remove cookies onto wire racks to cool completely. Repeat with remaining mixture.

● For the glaze, mix the icing sugar, water and vanilla until smooth. Arrange cookies on a rack over a baking sheet (to catch drips) and drizzle with glaze. Allow glaze to dry completely. Store in an airtight container.

Milk Cookies

Preparation time: 15 minutes ●
Cooking time: 15 to 20 minutes ● *Makes: About 14*

Serve milk cookies spread with savoury toppings such as cream cheeses and pâtés.

INGREDIENTS

25 g/1 oz margarine
150 ml/5 fl oz milk
225 g/8 oz flour
1 tsp baking powder
Pinch of salt

Preheat oven to 350°F/175°C/Gas mark 4. Grease two large baking sheets or line with non-stick baking parchment.

● Place the margarine and milk in a small saucepan and heat gently to melt the margarine, taking care not to boil the milk. Leave to become tepid. Place the flour, baking powder and salt in a mixing bowl and add sufficient of the cooled milk and melted margarine mixture to form a dough. Knead the mixture until smooth.

● On a lightly floured surface, roll out the dough to 2-mm/⅛-in thick. Using a plain 8-cm/3-in round cutter, cut out the cookies and place on the baking sheet. Re-roll and cut out the dough to make as many cookies as possible.

● Lightly prick the surface of each cookie with the prongs of a fork several times. Bake in the oven for 15 to 20 minutes, until lightly golden all over. Remove the cookies with a thin metal spatula to a wire rack to cool completely. Store in an airtight container.

Peanut and Lemon Crunch Bars

Preparation time: 10 minutes + chilling
● *Makes: About 6 bars*

Peanut butter is a certain favourite and makes these cookies a nutritious treat.

INGREDIENTS

50 g/2 oz lightly salted butter
50 g/2 oz light brown sugar
3 Tbsp honey
3 Tbsp crunchy peanut butter
Grated rind of 1 lemon
50 g/2 oz crisp rice breakfast cereal
50 g/2 oz cornflake breakfast cereal

Grease a 20-cm/8-in square, shallow baking tin or line with non-stick baking parchment.

● Place the butter, sugar, honey and peanut butter into a large saucepan and heat gently to melt the butter and dissolve the sugar. Do not boil the mixture. When the ingredients are melted and well combined, remove from the heat.

● Stir the lemon rind, crisp rice and cornflake breakfast cereals into the melted mixture carefully so as not to crush the cereals. Mix well. Spoon the mixture into the pan and level the surface. Leave to set for at least 30 minutes in a cool place, then cut into 6 equal-sized bars. Store in an airtight container.

Cranberry Crunchies

Preparation time: 15 minutes ● *Cooking time: 10 to 12 minutes* ● *Makes: 14*

Dried cranberries are full of flavour and would go well with a cup of lemon herb tea.

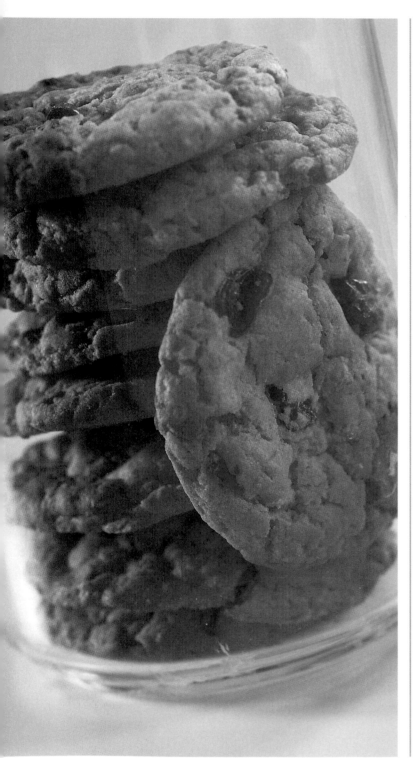

INGREDIENTS

120 g/4 oz lightly salted butter

120 g/4 oz light brown sugar

2 Tbsp honey

1 egg yolk

175 g/6 oz self-raising flour

50 g/2 oz rolled oats

75 g/3 oz dried cranberries

Pre-heat oven to 350°F/175°C/Gas mark 4. Grease two large baking sheets or line with non-stick baking parchment.

● Beat together the butter and sugar in a mixing bowl until pale and fluffy. Beat in the honey, egg yolk, flour and oats until well combined. Stir in the cranberries.

● Divide the mixture into 14 equal-sized pieces and roll into balls using the fingertips. Place the cookies 5 to 8 cm/2 to 3 in apart to allow for spreading onto the prepared baking sheets. Bake in the oven for about 10 to 12 minutes until golden and just firm. Leave to cool for one minute to allow the cookies to firm, before removing them with a thin metal spatula to a wire rack to cool. Store in an airtight container.

Maple Walnut Drops

Preparation time: 30 minutes + chilling ● Cooking time: 13 to 15 minutes ● Makes: About 48

These cookies are bursting with flavour and make a great cookie to come back to after an afternoon out.

INGREDIENTS

120 g/4 oz raisins
300 g/10 oz plain flour
1 tsp salt
½ tsp baking powder
¼ tsp bicarbonate of soda
1 tsp ground cinnamon
½ tsp ground nutmeg
175 g/6 oz unsalted butter
120 g/4 oz dark brown sugar
2 eggs
½ Tbsp maple syrup
5 Tbsp cold, strong black coffee
150 g/5 oz coarsely chopped walnuts

In a small bowl, cover the raisins with hot water, stand for 15 minutes to plump. Drain the raisins and pat dry; set aside. Into a medium bowl sift together the flour, salt, baking powder, bicarbonate of soda, cinnamon and nutmeg.

● In a large bowl, beat the butter until soft, then beat in the sugar until light and fluffy. Beat in the eggs one at a time, beating well after each addition, then beat in the maple syrup.

● In three batches add the flour mixture and the black coffee ending with the flour. If the mixture seems to stiff, add a little extra coffee or water, but the mixture should be thick enough to drop. Stir in the walnuts and raisins and refrigerate until chilled, at least 30 minutes.

● Pre-heat oven to 350°F/175°C/Gas mark 4. Grease or line two baking sheets with non-stick baking parchment.

● Drop dough by heaped teaspoon on the baking sheets 5 cm/2 in apart (keeping the remaining dough refrigerated). Bake until golden and firm to the touch, 13 to 15 minutes. Rotate baking sheets halfway through cooking. Remove the baking sheets to wire racks to allow to cool slightly, then, using a metal spatula, remove the cookies onto wire racks to cool completely. Store in an airtight container.

Blueberry Streusel Bakes

Preparation time: 20 minutes ● *Cooking time: 55 to 60 minutes* ● *Makes: 12 bars*

This recipe uses blueberry jam, but plum, apricot, or even pineapple jam would be equally delicious.

INGREDIENTS

BASE

120 g/4 oz lightly salted butter

120 g/4 oz light brown sugar

120 g/4 oz plain flour

FILLING

7 Tbsp blueberry jam

TOPPING

150 g/5 oz plain flour

½ tsp baking powder

5 Tbsp light brown sugar

120 g/4 oz lightly salted butter

40 g/1½ oz chopped almonds

Grated rind of 1 lemon

Pre-heat oven to 350°F/175°C/Gas mark 4. Grease an 18 x 28-cm/7 x 11-in baking tin.

● To make the base, beat together the butter and sugar in a mixing bowl until pale and fluffy. Stir in the flour to form a soft dough. Press the mixture down evenly over the base of the baking tin using the back of a spoon or lightly floured hand. Lightly prick the dough with a fork several times. Bake the dough in the oven for 15 minutes, until just firm. Remove from the oven and spread the blueberry jam over the dough base.

● To make the topping, place the flour, baking powder and sugar in a mixing bowl and blend in the butter, until the mixture resembles even-sized crumbs. Stir in the almonds and grated lemon rind. Sprinkle the topping over the jam. Bake in the oven for about 40 to 45 minutes until golden. Cool before cutting into bars. Store in an airtight container.

Coconut Cookies

Preparation time: 15 minutes ● *Cooking time:*
10 to 12 minutes ● *Makes: About 24*

An old-fashioned tea-time favourite.

INGREDIENTS

120 g/4 oz light brown sugar

225 g/8 oz lightly salted butter

350 g/12 oz plain flour

50 g/2 oz sweetened flaked coconut

Pre-heat oven to 375°F/190°C/Gas mark 5. Grease two large baking sheets or line with non-stick baking parchment.

● Place the sugar, butter and flour in a mixing bowl and with fingertips, blend the mixture together until it resembles breadcrumbs. Add the coconut and work the mixture together to form a dough. Do not be tempted to add any liquid as the crumb mixture, once kneaded, will come together to make a smooth dough.

● On a lightly floured surface, halve the mixture and make two long rolls about 3 to 4 cm/1¾ to 1⅓ in in diameter. Cut into 1-cm/½-in slices. Place the cookies on the baking sheets, 2.5 cm/1 in apart to allow for spreading during baking. Bake in the oven for 10 to 12 minutes, until a pale light brown. Allow to cool for 1 minute before removing to a wire rack to cool completely. Store in an airtight container.

Cinnamon Palmiers

Preparation time: 10 minutes ● *Cooking time:*
10 to 12 minutes ● *Makes: 18 to 20*

A variation on the French classic.

INGREDIENTS

225 g/8 oz ready-rolled puff pastry, thawed, if frozen

3 Tbsp dark brown sugar

1 tsp ground cinnamon

Pre-heat oven to 425°F/220°C/Gas mark 7. Grease two large baking sheets or line with non-stick baking parchment.

● Place the pastry on a lightly floured surface and if necessary roll out to a 28 x 23-cm/11 x 9-in rectangle.

● In a small bowl mix together the sugar and cinnamon. Sprinkle two-thirds of the cinnamon mixture evenly over the surface of the pastry. Fold each of the shortest pastry sides into the centre, press down and sprinkle over the remaining cinnamon mixture. Fold each pastry side in half again so they meet in the centre. Brush the pastry with cold water and fold over to make a long roll. Cut across the roll to make 5-mm/¼-in slices and place on the baking sheets 2.5 cm/1 in apart to allow for spreading.

● Bake in the oven for 8 minutes until golden, then carefully using a thin metal spatula, turn the palmiers over and cook for a further 3 to 5 minutes to brown and crisp the other side. Remove from the baking sheet with a thin metal spatula and cool on a wire rack. Best eaten when made, but can be kept in an airtight container for a few days, although they will lose their crispness.

Mini Florentines

Preparation time: 25 minutes ● *Cooking time: 10 minutes* ● *Makes: About 16*

Don't reserve these fantastic cookies for the festive season.

INGREDIENTS

50 g/2 oz lightly salted butter

2 Tbsp light brown sugar

2 tsp treacle

50 g/2 oz finely chopped glacé cherries

2 Tbsp finely chopped walnuts

2 Tbsp raisins

2 Tbsp candied citrus peel

25 g/1 oz plain flour

2 oz plain chocolate

Pre-heat oven to 325°F/160°C/Gas mark 3. Grease and line a large baking sheet with non-stick baking parchment. In a small saucepan, melt the butter, sugar and treacle over a low heat, taking care not to boil the mixture. When the ingredients are melted and well combined, stir in the cherries, walnuts, raisins, candied mixed peel and flour. Mix thoroughly.

● Place small heaped teaspoonfuls of the mixture onto the baking sheet at least 2.5 cm/1 in apart to allow for spreading. Bake in the oven for about 10 minutes, until the mixture has spread slightly and is bubbling. Remove the cookies from the oven and allow to cool slightly to firm, before lifting off with a thin metal spatula and placing on a wire rack to cool completely.

● Break the chocolate into small pieces and place in a small bowl over a pan of hot water. Melt the chocolate very slowly, taking care not to boil or get water in the chocolate. When the chocolate has melted, stir and remove from the heat. Using a pastry brush, cover the base of each Florentine with a little of the melted chocolate and leave chocolate side up on the wire rack until set. If desired, when the chocolate is very nearly set, make a wavy line pattern with the back of a fork on each chocolate Florentine. When the chocolate has set, store the Florentines in an airtight container.

No-bake Chocolate Delights

Preparation time: 15 minutes + setting ● Makes: About 18 to 20

A cross between a cookie and a truffle – and so easy to make.

INGREDIENTS

150 g/5 oz sponge cake crumbs
75 g/3 oz glacé cherries, quartered
50 g/2 oz raisins
50 g/2 oz plain chocolate
50 g/2 oz lightly salted butter
2 Tbsp milk

Place the cake crumbs, quartered glacé cherries and raisins into a mixing bowl. Break the chocolate into small pieces and place in a small heatproof bowl with the butter and milk over a saucepan of hot, but not boiling, water. Carefully melt all of the ingredients and stir into the sponge and fruit mixture. Mix together thoroughly to combine all of the ingredients and then leave to cool for a short while until the mixture is cool enough to handle.

● Using a teaspoon, place heaped spoonfuls of mixture on greaseproof paper in a single layer on a baking sheet. Chill the chocolate cookies in the refrigerator for at least 1 hour, to firm. Remove from the greaseproof paper and store in an airtight container.

Minute Meringues

Preparation time: 10 minutes ● Cooking time:
45 minutes ● Makes: 26

Tiny bubbles of airy sugar – irresistible!

INGREDIENTS

1 egg white
50 g/2 oz light brown sugar
1 tsp cornflour

Pre-heat oven to 275°F/140°C/Gas mark 1. Line two baking sheets with edible rice paper or non-stick baking parchment.

● Place the egg white in a grease-free mixing bowl and whisk until soft peaks form. Whisk in half of the sugar and all of the cornflour, until well combined. Add the remaining sugar and whisk until shiny and fairly stiff.

● Spoon the meringue mixture carefully into a piping bag fitted with a small star nozzle and then pipe small wavy lines about 5 cm/2 in long and small rosettes directly onto the lined baking sheets, leaving 2.5 cm/1 in between them to allow for a little spreading during the cooking process. Bake in the oven for about 45 minutes, until pale brown and crisp. Remove from the oven and cool completely, before removing from the baking parchment. If using rice paper, remove as much as possible, but any left on the base of the meringues is edible. Store in an airtight container.

Maple Pecan Wafers

Preparation time: 25 minutes ● Cooking time:
48 minutes ● Makes: About 24

These elegant wafers are ideal served with ice cream. Be sure to use real maple syrup, not the artificial flavouring – it makes a big difference.

INGREDIENTS

175 g/6 oz pecan halves
50 g/2 oz unsalted butter
225 g/8 oz dark brown sugar
75 g/3 oz plain flour
1 tsp maple syrup
¼ tsp salt
1 egg, lightly beaten

Pre-heat oven to 375°F/190°C/Gas mark 5. Line a large baking sheet with foil. Set aside 24 perfect pecan halves, then chop the remaining nuts.

● In a medium saucepan over a low heat, melt the butter. Remove from the heat and stir in the sugar, flour, maple syrup, salt and egg until well blended. Drop tablespoonfuls, at least 8 cm/3 in apart on the baking sheet, place a reserved pecan halve into the centre of each.

● Bake the wafers for 12 minutes, remove the baking sheet to a wire rack to cool slightly, then transfer the cookies onto a wire rack to cool completely. Cook the baking sheet and re-line, then repeat with another batch of cookies. When the wafers are cool, peel off foil and store in an airtight container with greaseproof paper between the layers.

Cardamom Cookies

Preparation time: 10 minutes ● Cooking time: 15 minutes ● Makes: 14

Fresh cardamom seeds have a distinctive but subtle flavour characteristic of the Eastern Mediterranean.

INGREDIENTS

120 g/4 oz lightly salted butter

50 g/2 oz icing sugar

125 g/4 oz plain flour

3 drops almond essence

6 cardamom pods, split and seeds lightly crushed

25 g/1 oz chopped walnuts

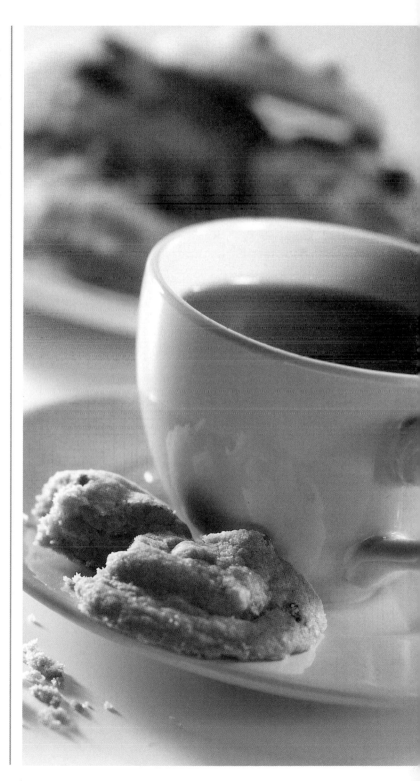

Pre-heat oven to 350°F/175°C/Gas mark 4. Grease two large baking sheets or line with non-stick baking parchment.

● Place the butter, icing sugar and flour in a large mixing bowl and beat together thoroughly. Stir in the almond essence, crushed cardamom seeds and chopped walnuts until well combined and the dough has a firm texture.

● Using your hands, shape the dough into 14 equal-sized balls and place 5 cm/2 in apart on the baking sheets. Bake in the oven for about 15 minutes, or until lightly browned. Remove with a thin metal spatula to a wire rack to cool completely. Store in an airtight container.

Chocolate Prezels

Preparation time: 40 minutes + chilling ●
Cooking time: 10 to 15 minutes ● *Makes: 30*

These delicious prezels are surprisingly easy to form.

INGREDIENTS

175 g/6 oz plain flour
¼ tsp salt
3 Tbsp unsweetened cocoa powder
120 g/4 oz unsalted butter
125 g/4 oz caster sugar
1 egg, beaten
1 tsp vanilla essence

GLAZE

1 egg white, lightly beaten
Sugar crystals, for sprinkling

Sift together the flour, salt, and cocoa powder. In a separate bowl, beat the butter until creamy, add the sugar and beat until light and fluffy. Beat in the egg and vanilla essence until blended. Gradually add the flour mixture until combined. Turn onto a piece of clingfilm and seal. Refrigerate until firm.

● Pre-heat oven to 375°F/190°C/Gas mark 5. Grease two baking sheets or line with non-stick baking parchment.

● With lightly floured hands, roll dough into about 30 4-cm/1½-in balls. Roll into a "rope" about 23 cm/9 in long. Bring each end of the "rope" together to meet in the centre. Twist the ends together, and press to the middle of the "rope" to form the prezel shape. Transfer to the baking sheets.

● Brush each prezel with egg white to glaze, then sprinkle with sugar crystals. Bake until firm, 10 to 12 minutes. Cool and tranfer to wire racks to cool completely. Store in an airtight container.

Nut Rocks

Preparation time: 20 minutes + chilling ●
Cooking time: 15 minutes ● *Makes: 12*

Crunchy cookies with a hint of oranges and almonds.

INGREDIENTS

120 g/4 oz lightly salted butter
50 g/2 oz light brown sugar
Grated rind of 1 orange
1 egg, separated
120 g/4 oz plain flour
50 g/2 oz ground almonds

Beat the butter and sugar together in a mixing bowl until pale and fluffy. Beat in the orange rind, egg yolk, and flour. Refrigerate for at least 30 minutes.

● Pre-heat oven to 350°F/175°C/Gas mark 4. Grease two large baking sheets or line with non-stick baking parchment. Using your hands, divide the cookie dough into 12 equal-sized balls and roll each in the lightly beaten egg white then in the ground almonds to coat evenly. Place the almond-covered balls on the baking sheets at least 2.5 cm/1 in apart. Bake for about 15 minutes, until just firm and light brown. Remove the cookies immediately from the baking sheet with a thin metal spatula, to prevent them from sticking, and cool on a wire rack. Store in an airtight container.

Tropical Fruit Cookies

Preparation time: 15 minutes ● *Cooking time: 12 to 15 minutes* ● *Makes: 12*

Almost every fruit under the sun is now available dried – try a new flavour or use your favourites, the choice is yours.

INGREDIENTS

120 g/4 oz lightly salted butter

120 g/4 oz granulated sugar

1 egg, beaten

75 g/3 oz plain flour

75 g/3 oz chopped ready-to-eat dried exotic fruit (papaya, mango, pineapple or melon)

Pre-heat oven to 350°F/175°C/Gas mark 4. Grease two large baking sheets or line with non-stick baking parchment.

● Beat the butter and sugar together in a mixing bowl until pale and fluffy. Beat in the egg and flour. Stir in the chopped exotic fruit mix.

● Place 12 equal-sized spoonfuls of the mixture onto the baking sheets, allowing 5 to 8 cm/2 to 3 in in between them for spreading. Flatten the mounds of mixture a little with the back of the spoon. Bake in the oven for about 12 to 15 minutes, until pale golden. Remove from the oven and leave to firm for one minute. Transfer to a wire rack and cool completely. Store the cookies in an airtight container.

Honey and Date Comforts

Preparation time: 10 minutes ● Cooking time: 12 to 15 minutes ● Makes: About 12 to 14

Comfort food at bedtime.

INGREDIENTS

125 g/4 oz lightly salted butter

250 g/8 oz light brown sugar

1 egg, beaten

175 g/6 oz plain flour

2 Tbsp honey

75 g/3 oz chopped dried dates

Pre-heat oven to 350°F/175°C/Gas mark 4. Grease two large baking sheets or line with non-stick baking parchment.

● Beat the butter and sugar together in a mixing bowl until pale and fluffy. Beat in the egg, flour and honey. Stir in the chopped dates.

● Place 12 to 14 equal-sized spoonfuls of the mixture onto the baking sheets, allowing 5 to 8 cm/2 to 3 in in between for spreading. Flatten the mounds of mixture a little with the back of the spoon. Bake in the oven for about 12 to 15 minutes, until pale golden. Remove from the oven and leave to firm for one minute on the baking sheets before removing with a spatula to a wire rack to cool completely. Store in an airtight container.

Around the World

The cookie is not a new phenomenon and most countries have little treasures that are loved by their people. Looking at the following selection, it is clear to see national influences such as almonds from Italy, spices from the Middle East, thick cream from Britain, and pecans and maple syrup from North America. There are stunning similarities too, in the use of butter, sugar, and spices which are used universally to create a treat that's always a pleasure to eat.

These cookies make excellent desserts. Espresso Biscotti would make a delightful finale to an Italian meal, serve the Spanish Churros after paella, and the Coconut Fortune Cookies after a stir-fry.

North America

The American nation has taken the idea of the cookie and run with it. Cookies are everywhere, and they are bigger, more action-packed and more adventurous than their traditional ancestors.

Britain

Known as biscuits rather than cookies in Britain, these are usually served with morning coffee or afternoon tea.

Western Europe

Steeped in history and culture, Western Europe has a long culinary tradition as clearly exemplified in its magnificent cookies as in any of its fancy sauces.

Further Afield

Eastern Europe, Scandinavia, Australia, New Zealand, India and China all have their own traditional cookie recipes. Typical ingredients include nuts, sour cream, fresh fruit juice and all kinds of spices.

Pennsylvanian Shoofly Slices

Preparation time: 40 minutes ● *Cooking time: 35 minutes* ● *Makes: 14 slices*

This cookie owes its origin to the shoofly pies popular in America's Southern States.

INGREDIENTS

175 g/6 oz plain flour
pinch of salt
2 Tbsp icing sugar
120 g/4 oz lightly salted butter

FILLING

3 Tbsp golden syrup
3 Tbsp treacle
150 ml/5 fl oz boiling water
1 tsp bicarbonate of soda
275 g/10 oz plain flour
1 tsp ground ginger
1 tsp ground cinnamon
120 g/4 oz lightly salted butter
175 g/6 oz light brown sugar

Pre-heat oven to 350°F/175°C/Gas mark 4. Lightly grease a 28 x 18-cm/11 x 7-in tin. Sift the flour, salt and icing sugar into a mixing bowl. Blend in the butter until the mixture resembles fine breadcrumbs. Add enough cold water to make a firm dough. Roll out on a lightly floured surface and use to line the base and sides of the tin. Chill the dough in the refrigerator while making the filling.

● Put the golden syrup and treacle in a heatproof jug and pour over the boiling water. Stir until well-mixed, then add the bicarbonate of soda and mix again. Leave to stand for 5 minutes.

● Sift the flour, ginger and cinnamon into a bowl. Blend in the butter until the mixture resembles breadcrumbs. Stir in the light brown sugar. Spoon half the crumb mixture evenly over the base of the tin. Slowly pour over the syrup and treacle mixture, then spoon over the remaining crumb mixture.

● Bake immediately for 35 minutes, or until lightly set. The mixture will rise a little as it cooks, but will sink again as it cools. Leave to cool in the tin. Divide the baked mixture into 14 slices.

New Orleans Oat Cookies

Preparation time: 20 minutes ● Cooking time: 10 minutes ● Makes: 20

The food of New Orleans has been influenced by African, Spanish and French cuisines as seen in these delicious cookies.

INGREDIENTS

120 g/4 oz lightly salted butter

120 g/4 oz light brown sugar

1 egg, beaten

175 g/6 oz self-raising flour

5 Tbsp fine oatmeal

175 g/6 oz rolled oats

3 Tbsp pumpkin seeds

Pumpkin seeds, to decorate

Pre-heat oven to 375°F190°C/Gas mark 5. Lightly grease two baking sheets.

● Beat the butter and sugar until light and fluffy. Add the beaten egg, a little at a time, beating between each addition. Sift the flour over the butter mixture and work into the butter mixture with the oatmeal, oats and pumpkin seeds.

● Roll out on a lightly floured surface to about 5 mm/ ¼ in thick. Stamp out rounds with a 6-cm/2½-in plain cutter. Place on the baking sheets, spacing slightly apart. Press a few pumpkin seeds on the top of each to decorate. Bake for 10 minutes, until golden brown. Leave on the baking sheets for 5 minutes, then remove and cool on a wire rack. Store in an airtight container.

Peanut Butter and Jelly Cookies

Preparation time: 25 minutes + chilling ● *Cooking time: 15 minutes* ● *Makes: 24*

The classic American combination of peanut butter and jelly (jam) not only appears as a sandwich filling, but in these giant crunchy cookies as well.

INGREDIENTS

75 g/3 oz unsalted peanuts

120 g/4 oz unsalted butter

120 g/4 oz caster sugar

5 Tbsp light brown sugar

1 Tbsp seedless raspberry jam

120 g/4 oz smooth or crunchy peanut butter

1 tsp vanilla essence

1 egg, beaten

175 g/6 oz plain flour

2 tsp baking powder

Pre-heat oven to 350°F/175°C/Gas mark 4. Lightly grease 2 baking sheets or line with non-stick baking parchment. Spread the peanuts on a baking sheet and roast in the oven for 5 minutes, until beginning to turn brown. Allow to cool, then roughly chop.

● Beat the butter and sugars until light and fluffy. Add the jam, peanut butter and vanilla essence, then beat until thoroughly mixed. Gradually add the egg, a little at a time, beating well after each addition. Sift the flour and baking powder into the bowl. Stir into the mixture with the chopped nuts to make a soft dough. Wrap the dough in clingfilm and chill in the refrigerator for 1 hour.

● Divide the dough into 24 pieces. Roll each piece into a ball the size of a walnut. Put the cookies onto the prepared baking sheets, spacing them well apart. Flatten slightly with a fork. Bake for 15 minutes or until golden brown. Leave on the baking sheets for 3 to 4 minutes, then remove with a thin metal spatula and cool on a wire rack.

VARIATION

Hazelnut Cookies

● Add 120 g/4 oz hazelnut butter and 75 g/3 oz chopped roasted hazelnuts instead of the peanut butter and unsalted peanuts.

Rocky Road

Preparation time: 25 minutes ● *Cooking time: 10 minutes* ● *Makes: 18*

Both children and adults love this sumptuously wicked treat.

INGREDIENTS

75 g/3 oz plain flour	
2 Tbsp unsweetened cocoa powder	
25 g/1 oz icing sugar	
50 g/2 oz lightly salted butter	
1 egg yolk	
1 Tbsp milk	

TOPPING

400 g/14 oz plain chocolate
120 g/4 oz unsalted butter
25 g/1 oz glacé cherries
50 g/2 oz mini marshmallows
5 Tbsp unsalted peanuts

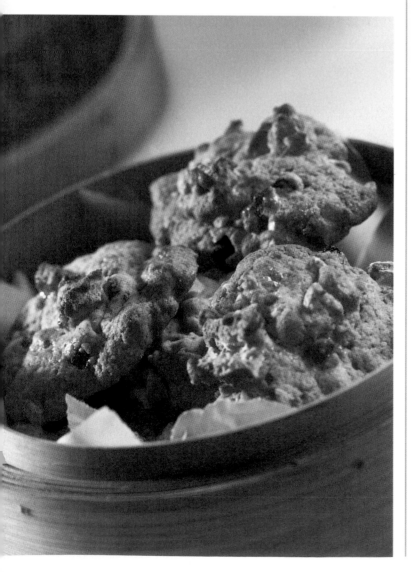

Pre-heat oven to 350°F/175°C/Gas mark 4. Grease and line the base of an 18 x 28-cm/7 x 11-in tin with non-stick baking parchment.

● Sift the flour, cocoa powder and icing sugar into a bowl. Cut the butter into small pieces and blend in until the mixture resembles breadcrumbs. Add the egg yolk and milk to the dry ingredients and mix to a firm dough. Knead on a lightly floured surface until smooth, then press into the base of the tin. Prick all over with a fork, then bake for 10 minutes. Leave to cool while making the topping.

● Break the chocolate into pieces and put in a bowl with the butter over a saucepan of near-boiling water. Heat gently until melted, stirring occasionally. Remove from the heat and allow to cool for 3 minutes. While the chocolate is melting, snip the cherries into quarters with oiled scissors. Stir into the chocolate with the mini marshmallows and peanuts.

● Quickly pour the topping over the base, gently shaking the tin to spread the mixture. Leave to set at room temperature. Cut into small squares and store in the refrigerator until ready to serve.

Raisin Rockies

Preparation time: 20 minutes ● *Cooking time: 15 minutes* ● *Makes: 16*

The raisins in these tasty cookies are soaked in orange juice to make them plump and juicy.

INGREDIENTS

50 g/2 oz raisins
2 Tbsp orange juice
120 g/4 oz lightly salted butter
50 g/2 oz caster sugar
50 g/2 oz light brown sugar
Grated rind of ½ orange
1 egg, beaten
175 g/6 oz plain flour
½ tsp bicarbonate of soda

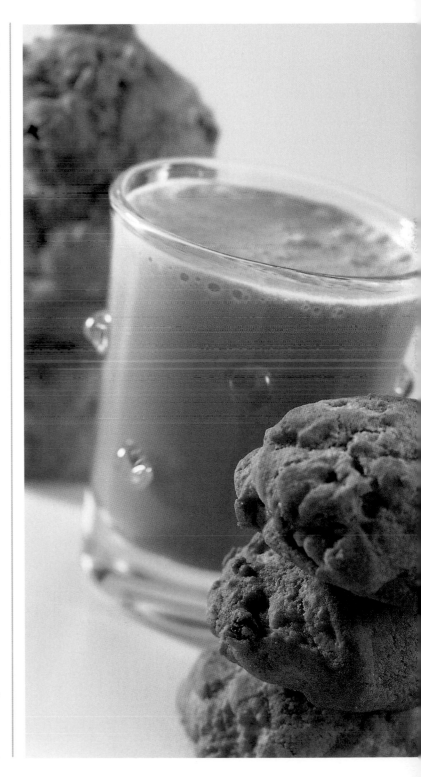

Put the raisins in a small bowl. Sprinkle over the orange juice, stir, cover with clingfilm and leave to soak for at least 2 hours, or overnight in the refrigerator.
● Pre-heat oven to 350°F/175°C/Gas mark 4. Lightly grease two baking sheets. Beat the butter, sugars and orange rind together until light and fluffy. Gradually add the egg, beating well between each addition. Sift the flour and bicarbonate together and work into the butter mixture with the soaked raisins to make a soft, dropping mixture.
● Drop heaped teaspoonfuls onto the prepared baking sheets, spacing well apart. Bake for 15 minutes until lightly browned. Leave on the baking sheets for 5 minutes, then remove and cool on a wire rack. Store in an airtight container.

VARIATION

Apricot and Almond Rockies

● Substitute 50 g/2 oz chopped dried apricots for the raisins and mix in 25 g/1 oz chopped blanched almonds.

Refrigerator Cookies

Preparation time: 20 minutes ● Cooking time: 10 to 12 minutes ● Makes: 40

**This cookie dough will keep for up to a week in the refrigerator.
It freezes well too so you can make it ahead and bake as necessary.**

INGREDIENTS

225 g/8 oz plain flour
1 tsp baking powder
120 g/4 oz lightly salted butter
50 g/2 oz caster sugar
1 egg
½ tsp vanilla essence

Sift the flour and baking powder into a mixing bowl. Cut the butter into small pieces and blend in until the mixture resembles breadcrumbs. Stir in the sugar. Beat the egg with the vanilla essence, add to the dry ingredients and mix to a firm dough. Shape into a roll about 5 cm/2 in in diameter and wrap in clingfilm or foil. Chill in the refrigerator for at least 2 hours, or until needed.

● When ready to bake the cookies, pre-heat oven to 375°F/190°C/Gas mark 5. Lightly grease three baking sheets or line with non-stick baking parchment.

● Unwrap the dough and cut into 5-mm/¼-in slices. Arrange on the baking sheets, spacing slightly apart. Bake for 10 to 12 minutes or until golden-brown. Leave on the baking sheets for 5 minutes, then transfer to a wire rack to cool.

VARIATIONS

Fruit and Nut

● Stir 50 g/2 oz chopped raisins and 50 g/2 oz chopped walnuts into the dry ingredients. Replace the vanilla essence with almond essence.

Cherry and Almond

● Stir 25 g/1 oz chopped glacé cherries and 50 g/2 oz chopped blanched almonds into the dry ingredients. Replace the vanilla essence with almond essence.

Double Chocolate Chip

● Replace 50 g/2 oz flour with 50 g/2 oz unsweetened cocoa powder and stir 50 g/2 oz plain or white chocolate chips into the dry ingredients.

Pecan Tassies

Preparation time: 30 minutes ● Cooking time: 20 minutes ● Makes: 24

These American tassies from the Southern Pecan-growing regions taste as delicious as they sound. Considered a "cookie" it is really a mini tartlet. Tender cream cheese pastry filled with a caramelized pecan centre.

INGREDIENTS

CREAM CHEESE PASTRY	PECAN FILLING
120 g/4 oz plain flour	1 egg
1 Tbsp sugar	5 Tbsp dark brown sugar
¼ tsp salt	1 tsp vanilla essence
¼ tsp ground nutmeg	25 g/1 oz unsalted butter, melted
120 g/4 oz unsalted butter, softened	50 g/2 oz chopped toasted pecan nuts
50 g/2 oz full-fat soft cheese, softened	24 pecan halves, for decoration

First, lightly and evenly butter two 12-bun or one 24-bun bun tins.

● Into a medium bowl, sift the flour, add the sugar, salt and nutmeg. Add the butter and cream cheese and, using your fingertips or a food processor, blend together until a soft dough forms. Cover the bowl and refrigerate until just firm enough to roll out, about 10 minutes.

● On a lightly floured surface, roll the pastry to 8 mm/ ⅓ in thick. Using a 6-cm/2½-in cutter cut out 24 circles. Carefully line the bun tins with the pastry circles, gently pressing pastry onto the bottom and sides. Refrigerate for 20 to 30 minutes. (If using a12-bun tin, refrigerate remaining dough and cut out once the first batch is cooked.)

● In a medium bowl, beat the eggs until foamy. Gradually beat in the brown sugar, vanilla essence, and melted butter. Sprinkle an equal amount of chopped pecans into each cup. Carefully distribute the filling in the bun tin, and top with a pecan half.

● Bake the tassies until the tops are puffed and the filling set with golden pastry edges, about 20 minutes. Remove to a wire rack to cool, 20 to 30 minutes. Using the top of a sharp knife, gently loosen the edge of the pastry from each bun tin and unmould each tassie. Either serve warm or cool completely, then store in an airtight container.

TIP

Filling can be made with toasted chopped walnuts, hazelnuts, macadamias or even pine nuts, but pecan nuts are traditional.

Grantham Gingerbread

Preparation time: 15 minutes ● Cooking time: 35 minutes ● Makes: 25

**These crisp pale spiced cookies are also known as White Buttons in the Norfolk fenlands
where they are rolled in sugar after cooking.**

INGREDIENTS

120 g/4 oz lightly salted butter

400 g/14 oz caster sugar

1 egg, beaten

250 g/9 oz self-raising flour

1 tsp ground ginger

¼ tsp ground cinnamon

Pre-heat oven to 300°F/150°C/Gas mark 2. Lightly grease two baking sheets or line with non-stick baking parchment.

● Beat the butter and sugar together until pale and fluffy. Gradually add the egg, beating well after each addition. Sift the flour and spices into the mixture and work in to make a firm dough.

● Roll into small walnut-sized balls and place on the prepared baking sheets, spacing slightly apart. Bake for 35 minutes, or until well-risen, crisp and golden. Leave on the baking sheets for 2 to 3 minutes, then remove and cool on a wire rack.

VARIATION

● For spicier cookies, sprinkle with 2 tablespoons caster sugar and ¼ teaspoon of ground ginger and cinnamon.

Wholemeal Digestives

Preparation time: 20 minutes ● *Cooking time: 20 minutes* ● *Makes: 20*

**These are sometimes spread with butter and served with cheese.
The amount of sugar may be varied, depending how sweet you like them.**

INGREDIENTS

225 g/8 oz plain wholemeal flour

50 g/2 oz fine oatmeal

½ tsp salt

50 g/2 oz lightly salted butter

50 g/2 oz white vegetable fat

4 Tbsp soft light brown sugar

½ beaten egg

2 Tbsp milk

2 Tbsp fine oatmeal, for sprinkling

Pre-heat oven to 350°F/175°C/Gas mark 4. Lightly grease two baking sheets or line the base with sheets of non-stick baking parchment.

● Put the flour, oatmeal and salt in a bowl and stir together. Blend in the butter and white vegetable fat until the mixture resembles fine breadcrumbs. Stir in the sugar. Add the beaten egg and mix to a firm dough. Lightly knead for a few seconds until smooth.

● Roll out the dough on a floured surface to a thickness of 3 mm/⅛ in. Cut into rounds using a 6-cm/2½-in plain cutter and lift onto the prepared baking sheets.

● Brush the rounds very lightly with milk and sprinkle with the oatmeal. Prick all over with a fork and bake for 20 minutes, until slightly darkened. Leave on the baking sheets for 2 minutes, then remove and cool on a wire rack.

Scottish Shortbread

Preparation time: 15 minutes+ chilling time ●
Cooking time: 30 to 40 minutes ●
Makes: One 18-cm/7-in shortbread round

Generations of Scots have baked this simple delicious recipe. As with all "traditional" recipes there are many variations, but it is always made with butter.

INGREDIENTS

120 g/4 oz lightly salted butter

2 Tbsp caster sugar

150 g/5 oz plain flour

3 Tbsp semolina or ground rice

1 Tbsp caster sugar, for dusting

Lightly grease a baking sheet or line with non-stick baking parchment.

● Put the butter in a mixing bowl and beat until soft and creamy. Stir in the sugar. Sift in the flour and mix in with the semolina or ground rice. Lightly knead on a floured surface for a few seconds until smooth.

● Roll out the dough to a 15-cm/6-in circle, then press into an 18-cm/7-in shortbread mould. Unmould onto the prepared baking sheet. If you haven't got a shortbread mould, press the mixture into an 18-cm/7-in loose-bottomed pie tin. Prick all over and mark into 8 wedges. Chill in the refrigerator for 1 hour.

● Pre-heat oven to 325°F/160°C/Gas mark 3.

● Bake for 35 to 40 minutes, or until pale golden-brown. Remove from the oven and dust with caster sugar. Leave on the baking sheet or remove from the tin, leaving the shortbread on the base for 15 minutes, then cool on a wire rack. Store in an airtight container.

Cornish Fairings

Preparation time: 15 minutes ●
Cooking time: 12 to 15 minutes ● Makes: 16

Cornish Fairings were sold in the market town of Launceston at the annual fair where maids were hired.

INGREDIENTS

175 g/6 oz self-raising flour

1½ tsp ground ginger

Pinch of freshly grated nutmeg

75 g/3 oz lightly salted butter

5 Tbsp light brown sugar

3 Tbsp golden syrup

3 Tbsp treacle

1½ tsp bicarbonate of soda

Pre-heat oven to 350°F/175°C/Gas mark 4. Lightly grease two baking sheets or line with non-stick baking parchment.

● Sift the flour, ginger and nutmeg into a large mixing bowl. Blend in the butter until the mixture resembles find breadcrumbs. Stir in the sugar.

● Gently warm the golden syrup and treacle in a small pan. Stir in the bicarbonate, then immediately add to the dry and mix together to a soft dough.

● Roll the dough into walnut-sized balls and place on the prepared baking sheets. Flatten with a thin metal spatula to about 1 cm/½ in thick. Bake for 12 to 15 minutes until slightly darkened and cracked in appearance. Leave on the baking sheets for 10 minutes, or until firm, then cool on wire racks.

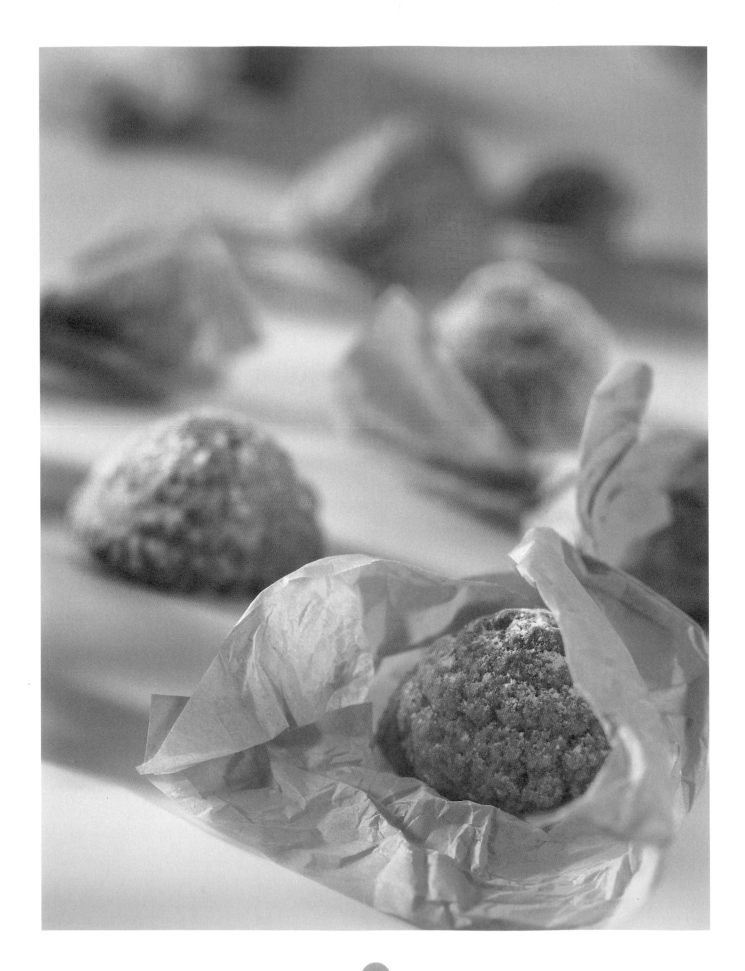

Amaretti

Preparation time: 15 minutes ●
Cooking time: 12 minutes ● Makes: 30

Wrap these almond cookies in pairs with pretty pastel tissue paper for an authentic Italian presentation.

INGREDIENTS

1 egg white
2 tsp amaretto liqueur
¼ tsp almond essence
175 g/6 oz ground almonds
120 g/4 oz icing sugar
2 Tbsp icing sugar, for dusting

Pre-heat oven to 350°F/175°C/Gas mark 4. Line two baking sheets with non-stick baking parchment.
● Lightly whisk the egg white with a fork until slightly frothy. Add the amaretto liqueur and almond essence and whisk again.
● Put the ground almonds in a bowl and sift in the icing sugar. Make a well in the centre, add the egg white mixture and stir to a stiff dough. Divide the dough into 30 pieces, then roll each into a ball. Place on the prepared baking sheets, spacing slightly apart.
● Bake for 12 minutes, or until the cookies are golden-brown. Dust with icing sugar. Leave on the baking sheets for 2 minutes, then transfer to a wire rack to cool. When completely cold wrap in pairs in coloured tissue paper.

TIP

Amaretto is a sweet almond liqueur. An orange or coffee liqueur may be used instead.

Fior di Mandorle

Preparation time: 20 minutes + chilling ●
Cooking time: 15 minutes ● Makes: 20

These sweet almond cookies, flavoured with cinnamon, are Arabic in origin, but are made throughout Sicily.

INGREDIENTS

150 g/5 oz lightly salted butter, softened
120 g/4 oz caster sugar
1 Tbsp honey
120 g/4 oz plain flour
½ tsp ground cinnamon
¾ cup ground almonds
Caster sugar and cinnamon, for dusting

Pre-heat oven to 350°F/175°C/Gas mark 4. Lightly grease two baking sheets or line with non-stick baking parchment.
● Beat the butter, sugar and honey together until light and fluffy. Sift the flour and cinnamon into the bowl and work into the butter mixture with the ground almonds. Lightly knead on a floured surface until smooth. Wrap in clingfilm and chill in the refrigerator for 30 minutes.
● Roll out the dough on a floured surface to a thickness of 5 mm/¼ in and cut into 8-cm/3-in squares. Carefully transfer to the prepared baking sheets, spacing slightly apart. Chill for a further 30 minutes.
● Bake for 15 minutes, or until light golden-brown. As soon as the cookies come out of the oven, dust with a little caster sugar and ground cinnamon. Leave on the baking sheets for 5 minutes, then remove with a thin metal spatula and cool on a wire rack. Store in an airtight container.

Espresso Biscotti

Preparation time: 20 minutes ● *Cooking time: 30 minutes* ● *Makes: 00*

They're wonderful served with steaming black coffee or cappuccino, although traditionally they are dipped into chilled sweet wine.

INGREDIENTS

75 g/3 oz unblanched almonds
250 g/9 oz plain flour
1½ tsp baking powder
Pinch of salt
75 g/3 oz unsalted butter
120 g/4 oz caster sugar
2 eggs, beaten
2 Tbsp strong espresso coffee, cooled

Pre-heat oven to 350°F/175°C/Gas mark 4. Grease a baking sheet or line with non-stick baking parchment.

● Place the almonds on a baking sheet and toast in the oven for 5 minutes. Allow to cool, then grind in a nut grinder or food processor until fine.

● Sift the flour, baking powder and salt into a mixing bowl. Cut the butter into small pieces and blend into the flour until the mixture resembles breadcrumbs. Stir in the sugar and ground almonds. Make a well in the centre. Mix the egg and coffee together and add to the dry ingredients. Mix to a firm dough.

● Lightly knead on a floured surface for a few seconds until smooth, then shape into 2 rolls about 6 cm/2½ in in diameter. Transfer to the prepared baking sheet and bake for 20 minutes until lightly browned. Leave to cool for 5 minutes, then cut with a serrated knife into 5-mm/½-in slices. Arrange on the baking sheet, cut-side down and bake for a further 10 minutes, until golden brown and dry to the touch. Store the biscotti in an airtight container for at least 24 hours before serving.

Panforte di Siena

Preparation time: 35 minutes ● *Cooking time: 40 minutes* ● *Makes: 12 slices*

A speciality of Siena in Italy, thin slices of this rich fruit and nut cookie are traditionally served at Christmas.

INGREDIENTS

50 g/2 oz candied citrus peel
50 g/2 oz crystallized pineapple
25 g/1 oz glacé cherries
50 g/2 oz papaya or mango
75 g/3 oz whole unblanched almonds
50 g/2 oz walnut pieces
5 Tbsp plain flour
1 tsp ground cinnamon
¼ tsp ground coriander
¼ tsp ground cloves
¼ tsp ground nutmeg
225 g/8 oz granulated sugar
3 Tbsp cold water
Edible rice paper
2 Tbsp icing sugar, to dust

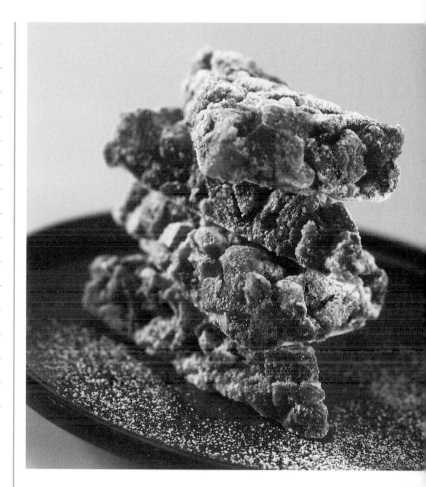

Pre-heat oven to 325°F/160°C/Gas mark 3. Cut the rice paper to fit the base of a 20-cm/8-in loose-bottomed tin. Lightly grease the tin, then line with the rice paper.

● Chop the fruit and nuts and put in a mixing bowl with the flour and spices. Put the sugar in a small heavy-bottomed saucepan with the water and heat very gently until the sugar dissolves. Turn up the heat and boil the syrup for 3 to 4 minutes, or until it reaches 220°F/104°C on a sugar thermometer. Pour the syrup over the dry ingredients and mix well.

● Spoon the mixture into the prepared tin and level the top. Bake for 40 minutes. Remove from the oven; it will still be soft, but will firm up as it cools. Leave in the tin for 5 minutes, then loosen the edges with a thin metal spatula and remove from the tin. Allow to cool on the base. When completely cold, remove the base and dust with icing sugar. Cut into very thin slices to serve. Store in an airtight container.

TIP

If you haven't got a sugar thermometer, boil the syrup to short-thread stage; remove a little syrup in a teaspoon, cool for a minute then press between finger and thumb and pull; it should form a short thread.

Pine Nut Macaroons

Preparation time: 25 minutes + cooling ● *Cooking time: 12 to 15 minutes* ● *Makes: About 24*

In Italy, pine nut macaroons are often sandwiched together with a little apricot jam – delicious.

INGREDIENTS

3 Tbsp currants

3 Tbsp Marsala, or orange juice

75 g/3 oz flaked almonds, lightly toasted

50 g/2 oz pine nuts, lightly toasted

225 g/8 oz caster sugar

1 Tbsp plain flour

1 egg white

¼ tsp almond essence

120 g/4 oz pine nuts

Pre-heat oven to 350°F/175°C/Gas mark 4. Grease or line two baking sheets with non-stick baking parchment.

● In a small bowl combine the currants and Marsala or orange juice and microwave on High for 30 to 60 seconds. Allow to sit until the moisture is absorbed, 3 to 5 minutes. Cool completely.

● In a food processor fitted with a metal blade, process the almonds, pine nuts, sugar and flour until finely ground. Add egg white and almond essence, and process until the mixture forms a dough. Stir in the plumped currants by hand.

● Place the untoasted pine nuts on a plate. Wet your hands, and using a teaspoon of the dough, shape into 2-cm/¾-in balls. Roll balls in pine nuts, pressing lightly to cover completely. Place balls 4 cm/1½-in apart on the baking sheets, flatten slightly to a disc shape.

● Bake until pine nuts are golden, 12 to 15 minutes, rotating the baking sheets halfway through cooking time. Allow to cool slightly, then transfer to wire racks. Store in an airtight container.

Vanilla Crescents

Preparation time: 25 minutes + chilling ● *Cooking time: 15 minutes* ● *Makes: 25*

Forming a horseshoe or crescent shape these "Kipferln" symbolize good luck.

INGREDIENTS

25 g/1 oz unblanched almonds
120 g/4 oz plain flour
120 g/4 oz unsalted butter, chilled
2 Tbsp caster sugar
1 egg yolk
1 tsp vanilla essence
120 g/4 oz icing sugar

Lightly grease a baking sheet or line with non-stick baking parchment. Chop the almonds very finely. Sift the flour into a bowl. Cut the butter into pieces and blend it into the flour until the mixture resembles fine breadcrumbs.
● Stir in the chopped almonds and sugar. Mix the egg yolk and vanilla essence together, add to the dry ingredients and mix to a soft dough. Lightly knead on a floured surface until smooth. Wrap in clingfilm and chill in the refrigerator for 20 minutes.

● Pre-heat oven to 350°F/175°C/Gas mark 4. Roll teaspoonfuls of the cookie dough into small crescents and place on the prepared baking sheets. Bake for 15 minutes until pale golden. As soon as you remove the cookies from the oven, thickly dredge with icing sugar. Leave on the baking sheet for 5 minutes, then remove and cool on a wire rack. Store in an airtight container.

VARIATION

● Coat the cookies with vanilla sugar. Store a vanilla pod in a sealed jar of caster sugar for at least a week. Leave the pod and top up with sugar as it is used.

Ischl Cookies

Preparation time: 30 minutes + chilling ● *Cooking time: 15 minutes* ● *Makes: 12*

These jam-filled cookies are named after the famous resort in the Austrian Alps.

INGREDIENTS

120 g/4 oz lightly salted butter

50 g/2 oz caster sugar

1 egg, beaten

1 Tbsp ground almonds

200 g/7 oz plain flour

2 Tbsp cornflour

¼ tsp ground cinnamon

3 Tbsp raspberry jam

3 Tbsp apricot jam

3 Tbsp lemon curd

1 Tbsp icing sugar

Lightly grease two baking sheets or line with non-stick baking parchment.

● Beat the butter and sugar until creamy. Gradually add the egg, beating well after each addition, then beat in the ground almonds. Sift over the flour, cornflour and cinnamon and stir in to make a soft dough. Wrap in clingfilm and chill in the refrigerator for 30 minutes.

● Pre-heat oven to 350°F/175°C/Gas mark 4. Roll out on a lightly floured surface to 3 mm/⅛ in thick. Cut the dough into 8-cm/3-in rounds with a plain cutter. Cut a leaf or flower design from the middle of half the squares with a 2.5-cm/1-in cutter. Transfer to the baking sheets. Bake for 15 minutes, until golden. Leave on the baking sheets for 5 minutes, then transfer to a wire rack to cool.

● Warm and sieve the jam. Spread a third of the uncut cookies with each of the jams and the third with lemon curd. Place the cookies with cut-out middles on top, so that the jam or curd shows through. Lightly dust with sifted icing sugar before serving. The cookies should be eaten on the same day they are filled.

Spanish Churros

Preparation time: 15 minutes ● *Cooking time: 10 minutes* ● *Makes: 25*

These are freshly made and sold as a snack on street stalls throughout Spain to be eaten while you stroll along.

INGREDIENTS

75 g/3 oz slightly salted butter

225 ml/8 fl oz water

120 g/4 oz plain flour

3 Tbsp caster sugar

3 eggs

Oil for deep-frying

Put the butter and water in a saucepan and heat gently until melted. Meanwhile, sift the flour and ½ teaspoon of the sugar onto a piece of greaseproof paper.

● Bring the butter and water to a fast boil, then add the sifted flour and sugar all at once. Remove the pan from the heat and beat vigorously. Leave to cool for 5 minutes.

● Lightly beat the eggs and gradually add to the mixture, beating until very smooth and glossy. Spoon the mixture into a piping bag fitted with a 1-cm/½-in star nozzle.

● Half-fill a pan with oil and heat to 375°F/190°C. Pipe five 10-cm/4-in lengths of the mixture at a time into the hot oil. Fry for about 2 minutes, or until golden and crisp. Remove from the oil with slotted spoon and drain on kitchen paper. Repeat until all the mixture is used up. Serve warm or cold, dredged with remaining sugar.

TIP

If preferred, dust the churros with icing sugar mixed with a little ground cinnamon instead of the caster sugar.

Parisian Palmiers

Preparation time: 20 minutes ● *Cooking time: 10 minutes* ● *Makes: 20*

These light-as-air French puff pastry cookies have a sugary glaze which caramelizes as they cook.

INGREDIENTS

120 g/4 oz caster sugar

225 g/8 oz puff pastry, thawed if frozen

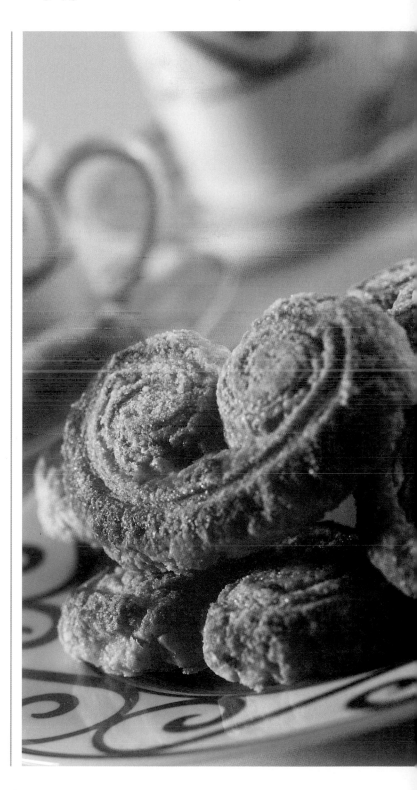

Pre-heat oven to 450°F/230°C/Gas mark 8. Lightly grease two baking sheets or line with non-stick baking parchment.

● Sprinkle half the sugar evenly over the work surface or on a pastry board, then roll out the pastry into a rectangle of about 25 x 30 cm/10 x 12 in. Trim the edges to neaten, then sprinkle with the remaining sugar.

● Roll the two longer sides to the centre to make a double roll. Cut into 5-mm/½-in slices and transfer to the prepared baking sheets, spacing slightly apart. Bake for 10 minutes, or until well-risen, golden-brown and crisp. Remove from the baking sheets and cool on a wire rack.

VARIATIONS

Cinnamon Palmiers

● Mix the sugar with 1 teaspoon ground cinnamon before sprinkling.

Jam Palmiers

● Sandwich together in pairs with 150 ml/5 fl oz double cream, lightly whipped and 3 tablespoons warmed and sieved apricot jam.

Cheese Palmiers

● Fine grate 50 g/2 oz Gruyère cheese and 50 g/2 oz Parmesan cheese. Mix with 1 teaspoon paprika and use instead of the sugar. Sandwich together in pairs with 25 g/ 1 oz unsalted butter flavoured with 2 teaspoons tomato purée.

Cigarettes Russes

Preparation time: 20 minutes ●
Cooking time: 4 to 5 minutes per sheet ● *Makes: 25*

These crisp cigar-shaped cookies make a delicious accompaniment to ice creams and mousses.

INGREDIENTS

50 g/2 oz unsalted butter
2 egg whites
120 g/4 oz caster sugar
50 g/2 oz plain flour
½ tsp vanilla essence

Pre-heat oven to 375°F/190°C/Gas mark 4. Line a baking sheet with non-stick baking parchment. Melt the butter over a low heat, then leave to cool.

● Whisk the egg whites until stiff peaks form. Gradually add the sugar a tablespoon at a time, whisking between each addition. Sift half the flour over the whisked mixture and trickle the melted butter around the edge. Carefully fold in. Sift the remaining flour over the mixture and fold in with the vanilla essence.

● Drop teaspoonfuls of the mixture onto the prepared baking sheets, spacing well apart. Spread the mixture thinly and evenly to form a circle 10 cm/4 in in diameter. Bake for 5 to 6 minutes, or until golden-brown around the edges. It is best to bake only 3 Cigarettes at a time as they need to be rolled quickly while warm, before the mixture hardens.

● Using a metal spatula, carefully remove the cookies, one at a time from the baking sheet while still hot. Roll immediately around the oiled handle of a wooden spoon. Remove and leave on a wire rack to cool. Repeat with the remaining cookie mixture until used up.

Fours Poches

Preparation time: 30 minutes ● *Cooking time: 15 minutes* ● *Makes: 30*

These tiny almond treats are perfect for serving with after-dinner coffee and can be made several days ahead. In France the word "poche" refers to a piping bag, hence the name of these cookies.

INGREDIENTS

2 egg whites
120 g/4 oz caster sugar
150 g/5 oz ground almonds
¼ tsp almond essence
Edible rice paper
Whole hazelnuts, walnut pieces and quartered glacé cherries, to decorate

Pre-heat oven to 350°F/175°C/Gas mark 4. Line two baking sheets with rice paper.

● Whisk the egg whites until stiff, then fold in the caster sugar, ground almonds and almond essence.

● Spoon the mixture into a piping bag fitted with a 1-cm/½-in star nozzle and pipe small rosettes onto the rice paper. Decorate each with a hazelnut, walnut or glacé cherry. Bake for 15 minutes, until light golden-brown. Leave on the baking sheets for 2 to 3 minutes, then cool on a wire rack. Remove surplus rice paper when cold. Store in an airtight container.

Sablés Nantais

Preparation time: 25 minutes + chilling ● *Cooking time: 15 minutes* ● *Makes: 25*

These cookies come from the French region of Nantes. "Sable" is the French word for sand, and reflects their golden crumbly texture.

INGREDIENTS

120 g/4 oz unsalted butter
120 g/4 oz icing sugar
1 tsp vanilla essence
1 egg, separated
1 egg yolk
175 g/6 oz plain flour
¼ tsp baking powder

Put the butter in a mixing bowl and beat until soft. Sift over the icing sugar and beat the mixture until light and fluffy. Beat in the egg yolks, one at a time, then beat in the vanilla essence. Sift the flour and baking powder over the butter mixture and mix to a soft dough. Lightly knead on a floured surface for a few seconds until smooth. Wrap in clingfilm and chill in the refrigerator for 1 hour.

● Pre-heat oven to 375°F/190°C/Gas mark 5. Lightly grease two baking sheets or line with non-stick baking parchment.

● Roll out the cookie dough on a floured surface to 5 mm/¼ in thickness and stamp out rounds using a fluted 5-cm/2-in cutter. Transfer to the prepared baking sheets.

● Lightly beat the egg white. Mark criss-cross patterns on top of the cookies with the back of a knife or with a fork. Brush with the egg white, then bake for 15 minutes, until golden-brown. Leave on the baking sheets for 3 minutes, then transfer to a wire rack to cool.

Rascals

Preparation time: 30 minutes + chilling ● Cooking time: 20 minutes ● Makes: 20

Known as "Spitzbuben", these Viennese vanilla and lemon cookies are sandwiched together with plum jam.

INGREDIENTS

225 g/8 oz lightly salted butter
120 g/4 oz vanilla sugar
Grated rind of 1 lemon
300 g/10 oz plain flour
1 egg, separated
1 egg yolk
3 Tbsp caster sugar, for sprinkling
120 g/4 oz plum jam
2 tsp lemon juice

Lightly grease two baking sheets or line with non-stick baking parchment.

● Beat the butter, vanilla sugar and lemon rind together until mixed. Sift in the flour and stir into the mixture with the egg yolks to make soft dough. Wrap in clingfilm and chill for 30 minutes.

● Pre-heat oven to 325°F/160°C/Gas mark 3. Roll out the dough on a lightly floured surface to a 5 mm/¼ in. Use a 6-cm/2½-in round or star cutter to cut out about 40 cookies. Transfer to the prepared baking sheets, spacing slightly apart. Lightly whisk the egg white and brush over the tops of half the cookies, then sprinkle generously with caster sugar.

● Bake for 20 minutes, until lightly browned. Leave on the baking sheets for 2 to 3 minutes, then transfer to a wire rack to cool.

● Gently heat the plum jam in a pan, then sieve. Use to sandwich the cookies together in pairs with a plain cookie on the bottom and a sugar-dusted one on top.

Eponges

Preparation time: 25 minutes ● Cooking time: 9 to 10 minutes ● Makes: 20

"Eponge" is the French word for sponge and is thought to be the name given to these cookies because they look like sea sponges.

INGREDIENTS

2 egg whites

2 Tbsp caster sugar

50 g/2 oz icing sugar

50 g/2 oz ground almonds

75 g/3 oz blanched almonds, finely chopped

75 g/3 oz seedless raspberry jam

1 Tbsp icing sugar, for dusting

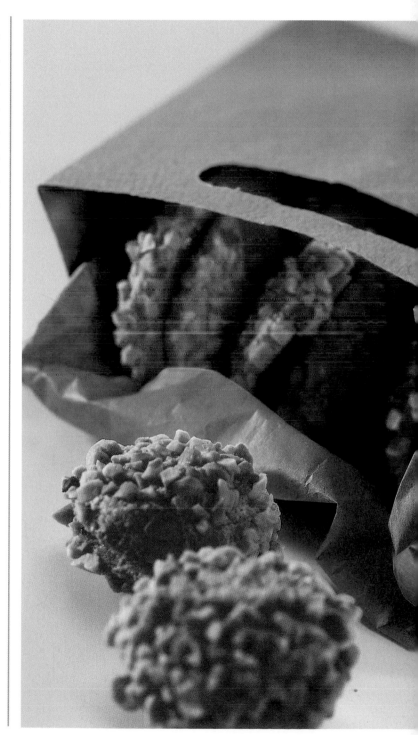

Pre-heat oven to 375°F/190°C/Gas mark 5. Line two baking sheets with non-stick baking parchment.

● Whisk the egg whites until soft peaks form, then gradually add the caster sugar, whisking after each addition until the mixture is stiff and glossy.

● Sift the icing sugar and ground almonds together and fold in. Spoon the mixture into a piping bag fitted with a 1-cm/½-in plain nozzle and pipe small rounds onto the baking sheets, spacing them slightly apart.

● Sprinkle with the chopped almonds and bake for 9 to 10 minutes, until golden. The "éponges" will rise slightly during cooking, and shrink again as they cool. Remove from the baking sheets and cool on a wire rack. When cool, sandwich together in pairs with the jam. Dust with icing sugar before serving. Eponges are best eaten on the day they are made.

Chrabeli Bread

Preparation time: 20 minutes + standing ● Cooking time: 10 minutes ● Makes: 25

**These crisp and light Mediterranean cookies are usually served with black coffee or eaten as a simple snack.
Before baking they're left on the baking sheet to dry overnight.**

INGREDIENTS

3 egg whites
50 g/2 oz icing sugar
150 g/5 oz plain flour
4 Tbsp cornflour

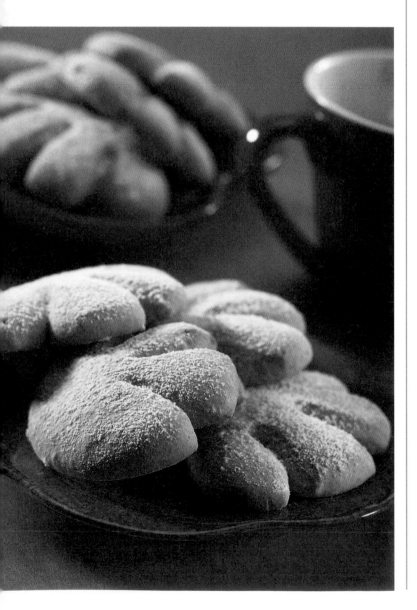

Put the egg whites in a large mixing bowl. Sift the icing sugar over the egg whites, then whisk until the mixture will hold stiff peaks.

● Sift over the flour and gently fold in until combined, taking care not to over-mix. Cover the bowl with a damp cloth and leave for 1 hour.

● Line two baking sheets with non-stick baking parchment, then lightly dust with the cornflour. Knead the dough on a lightly floured surface for a minute or so until smooth.

● Take walnut-sized pieces of the mixture and shape into ovals. Using scissors, snip three cuts down one side, then place on the prepared sheets, bending the cookies slightly to open up the cuts. Keep dipping your hands in flour when shaping the cookies, to prevent them sticking. Leave uncovered overnight to allow the cookies to dry out.

● The following day, pre-heat oven to 400°F/200°C/Gas mark 6. Bake the cookies for 10 minutes, until very pale brown. Remove from the baking sheets and cool on a wire rack.

Zitron

Preparation time: 30 minutes ● Cooking time: 10 minutes ● Makes: 20

These tangy Swiss cookies have a double helping of lemon, in both the filling and icing.

INGREDIENTS

120 g/4 oz plain flour
25 g/1 oz self-raising flour
75 g/3 oz ground almonds
120 g/4 oz lightly salted butter
2 Tbsp icing sugar
1 egg yolk

FILLING

120 g/4 oz unsalted butter
175 g/6 oz icing sugar
Grated rind 1 lemon

ICING

175 g/6 oz icing sugar
About 4 tsp lemon juice
Yellow food colouring

Pre-heat oven to 350°F/175°C/Gas mark 4. Lightly grease two baking sheets or line with non-stick baking parchment.

● Sift the flours into a bowl. Stir in the ground almonds, then blend in the butter until the mixture resembles fine breadcrumbs. Sift the icing sugar and stir in. Add the egg yolk and mix to a dough.

● Lightly knead the dough for a few seconds, then roll out on a floured surface to 3 mm/⅛ in. Cut into rounds using an 8-cm/3-in plain cutter and transfer to the baking sheets. Bake for 10 minutes, until lightly browned. Leave on the baking sheets for 2 minutes,then transfer to a wire rack to cool.

● For the filling, beat the butter, sifted icing sugar and lemon rind until the mixture is light and fluffy. Use to sandwich the cookies together in pairs.

● For the icing, sift the icing sugar into a bowl and stir in enough lemon juice to make a thick icing. Add a drop of yellow food colouring to make a pale yellow. Use to ice the tops of the cookies. Leave to set before serving.

Dutch Butter Cookies

Preparation time: 25 minutes + chilling ● *Cooking time: 15 to 20 minutes* ● *Makes: 30*

These lemon-scented cookies are known as "Botermopen" and should always be made with unsalted butter for the best flavour.

INGREDIENTS

175 g/6 oz unsalted butter
Grated rind of ½ lemon
50 g/2 oz caster sugar
50 g/2 oz light brown sugar
½ tsp almond or vanilla essence
225 g/8 oz plain flour
120 g/4 oz demerera sugar

Beat the butter until creamy, then add the lemon rind, sugars and almond or vanilla essence and beat until light and fluffy. Sift over the flour and stir into the mixture to make a firm dough. Lightly knead on a floured surface for a few seconds until smooth. Divide the dough in half, wrap each piece in clingfilm and chill in the refrigerator for 30 minutes.

● Shape each piece into a roll about 15 cm/6 in long. Sprinkle the demerera sugar over a piece of greaseproof paper and roll the cookies to coat with sugar. Wrap the rolls in clingfilm or foil and chill in the refrigerator for at least 2 hours or overnight.

● Pre-heat oven to 325°F/160°C/Gas mark 3. Cut each roll into 15 slices and space slightly apart on the baking sheets. Bake for 15 to 20 minutes or until light golden and firm. Leave on the baking sheets for 3 minutes, then transfer onto a wire rack to cool.

Polish Macaroons

Preparation time: 25 minutes ● Cooking time: 15 to 20 minutes ● Makes: 16

**These "Makaroniki" are sprinkled with poppy seeds before baking.
Halved blanched almonds may also be used to decorate these cookies.**

INGREDIENTS

75 g/3 oz blanched almonds

225 g/8 oz caster sugar

2 Tbsp cornflour

2 egg whites

¼ tsp almond essence, optional

1 Tbsp poppy seeds

Edible rice paper

Pre-heat oven to 375°F/190°C/Gas mark 5. Line two baking sheets with rice paper.

● Spread the blanched almonds on a tray and toast for 5 minutes, or until just beginning to brown. Allow to cool, then grind them finely in a nut grinder or food processor.

● Mix together the ground almonds, sugar and cornflour. Lightly whisk the egg whites and add to the dry ingredients, with the almond essence if using, to make a thick paste.

● Spoon the mixture into a piping bag fitted with a plain 1-cm/½-in nozzle. Pipe 16 rounds of the mixture on the prepared baking sheets, spacing well apart. Sprinkle each with a few poppy seeds. Bake for 15 to 20 minutes, or until lightly browned. Leave on the baking sheets for 5 minutes, then remove and cool on a wire rack. Tear away any excess rice paper when cold.

Lepeshki

Preparation time: 20 minutes ●
Cooking time: 10 minutes ● *Makes: 20*

These creamy Russian cookies are made with soured cream rather than butter and sprinkled with flaked almonds before baking.

INGREDIENTS

225 g/8 oz self-raising flour

Pinch of salt

120 g/4 oz caster sugar

1 Tbsp ground almonds

1 egg, separated

150 ml/5 fl oz soured cream

½ tsp vanilla essence

50 g/2 oz flaked almonds

Pre-heat oven to 400°F/200°C/Gas mark 6. Lightly grease two baking sheets or line with non-stick baking parchment.

● Sift the flour and salt into a mixing bowl. Stir in the caster sugar and ground almonds. Reserve 1 tablespoon egg white. Mix the rest with the egg yolk, soured cream and vanilla essence. Add to the dry ingredients and mix to a firm dough. Lightly knead on a floured surface until smooth.

● Roll out to 8 mm/⅓ in and stamp into rounds using an 8-cm/3-in cutter. Place on the prepared baking sheets, spacing slightly apart. Brush the tops with the reserved egg white and sprinkle with flaked almonds. Bake for 10 minutes until lightly browned. Leave the cookies on the baking sheets for 5 minutes, then transfer to a wire rack to cool.

Finnish Fingers

Preparation time: 25 minutes ●
Cooking time: 12 minutes ● *Makes: 12*

These golden log-shaped cookies have a crumbly airy texture and a topping of chopped almonds.

INGREDIENTS

175 g/6 oz unsalted butter

50 g/2 oz icing sugar

1 tsp vanilla essence

175 g/6 oz plain flour

5 Tbsp cornflour

50 g/2 oz blanched almonds or pistachios, chopped

FILLING

50 g/2 oz unsalted butter

75 g/3 oz icing sugar

Pre-heat oven to 350°F/175°C/Gas mark 4. Lightly grease a baking sheet or line with non-stick baking parchment.

● Put the butter in a mixing bowl and beat until creamy.

● Sift over the icing sugar, add the vanilla essence and beat until light and fluffy. Sift the flour and cornflour over the butter mixture and fold in.

● Spoon the mixture into a piping bag fitted with a 2-cm/¾-in plain nozzle and pipe 6-cm/2½-in lengths onto the prepared baking sheets, spacing well apart. Sprinkle with the chopped nuts. Bake for 12 minutes, until pale golden-brown. Leave on the baking sheets for 3 to 4 minutes, then remove and cool on a wire rack.

● For the filling, beat the butter until softened. Sift over the icing sugar and beat until light and fluffy. Use to sandwich the cookies together in pairs.

Danish Piped Cookies

Preparation time: 30 minutes ●
Cooking time: 12 minutes ● *Makes: 30*

These classic buttery cookies from Denmark melt in the mouth and are perfect with morning coffee.

INGREDIENTS

225 g/8 oz unsalted butter
120 g/4 oz caster sugar
1 egg yolk
175 g/6 oz plain flour
50 g/2 oz self-raising flour
75 g/3 oz ground almonds

GLAZE

2 Tbsp caster sugar
2 Tbsp milk

Pre-heat oven to 375°F/190°C/Gas mark 5. Lightly grease two baking sheets or line with non-stick baking parchment.

● Beat the butter in a bowl until creamy. Add the caster sugar and mix until blended, then beat in the egg yolk. Sift the plain and self-raising flours over the butter mixture and stir in with the ground almonds.

● Spoon into a piping bag fitted with a 1-cm/½-in star nozzle and pipe scrolls, fingers or whirls as liked onto the prepared baking sheets. Bake for 10 to 12 minutes until pale golden.

● Meanwhile, prepare the glaze. Mix the caster sugar and milk together in a small saucepan and heat gently to dissolve. As soon as you remove the cookies from the oven, brush with the milk glaze. Leave on the baking sheets for 5 minutes, then transfer to a wire rack to cool.

Scandinavian Slices

Preparation time: 25 minutes + chilling ●
Cooking time: 10 minutes ● *Makes: 20*

This dark, spicy cookie mixture is chilled overnight to let the flavours develop.

INGREDIENTS

120 g/4 oz lightly salted butter
120 g/4 oz caster sugar
2½ Tbsp golden syrup
2 tsp honey
50 g/2 oz flaked almonds
2 tsp ground cinnamon
1 tsp ground ginger
½ tsp ground cardamom
½ tsp bicarbonate of soda
1 tsp water
200 g/7 oz plain flour

Put the butter, sugar, syrup and honey in a small pan and heat gently until the butter has melted. Stir in almonds and spices and bring to the boil. Remove from the heat. Mix the bicarbonate and water together and stir into the mixture.

● Sift the flour into a bowl and make a well in the middle. Pour in the melted mixture and mix. Cool, then turn out and knead on a floured surface until smooth. Shape into a block 5 cm/2 in in diameter. Wrap in clingfilm and chill in the refrigerator overnight.

● Pre-heat oven to 350°F/175°C/Gas mark 4. Lightly grease two baking sheets.

● Cut the block into 3-mm/⅛-in slices and place on the baking sheets, slightly spaced. Bake for 10 minutes, until slightly darkened and crisp. Cool on the baking sheets.

Present Cookies

Preparation time: 35 minutes ● Cooking time: 15 minutes ● Makes: 11

If you can't find number cutters, trace some numbers, cut them out, and use them as a template.

INGREDIENTS

150 g/5 oz plain flour, sifted

50 g/2 oz ground almonds

120 g/4 oz lightly salted butter, cut into small pieces

1 egg yolk

120 g/4 oz chopped crystallized pineapple

DECORATION

200 g/7 oz ready-to-roll fondant icing

Food colouring

1 Tbsp apricot jam, warmed

Pre-heat oven to 350°F/175°C/Gas mark 4. Grease several baking sheets or line with non-stick baking parchment.

● Place the flour and ground almonds in a mixing bowl and blend in the butter using your fingers until the mixture resembles fine breadcrumbs. Stir in the egg yolk and chopped candied pineapple and using your hands bring all the ingredients together to form a soft dough.

● On a lightly floured surface, roll out the dough to about 5 mm/¼ in thick and stamp out squares using an 8-cm/3-in cutter. Lift on to the baking sheets and re-roll the trimmings as necessary. Prick the squares with a fork. Bake the cookies for 15 minutes or until lightly golden at the edges. Transfer to a wire rack to cool.

● To decorate the cookies, place the icing in a bowl and add a few drops of colouring, knead the icing until soft and smooth. On a surface lightly sprinkled with icing sugar, roll out the icing and stamp out the numbers "2" and "1" to make ten "21s."

● Brush the apricot jam over the surface of each cookie and lay the numbers "21" on each cookie. Cut the trimmings from the icing into thin strips and place over the squares and numbers, to represent lengths of ribbon around a present. Store these cookies in an airtight container.

Birthday Cake Cookies

Preparation time: 25 minutes ● Cooking time: 15 minutes ● Makes: 18

These cookies are made from all the ingredients you expect to find in a fruit cake, making them a clever birthday gift.

INGREDIENTS

120 g/4 oz lightly salted butter, softened

120 g/4 oz packed light brown sugar

1 egg, beaten

1 Tbsp brandy or dark rum

150 g/5 oz plain flour, sifted

¼ tsp baking powder

50 g/2 oz chopped blanched almonds

25 g/1 oz chopped glacé cherries

50 g/2 oz candied citrus peel

50 g/2 oz sultanas

1 Tbsp chopped angelica, optional

Icing sugar, for dusting

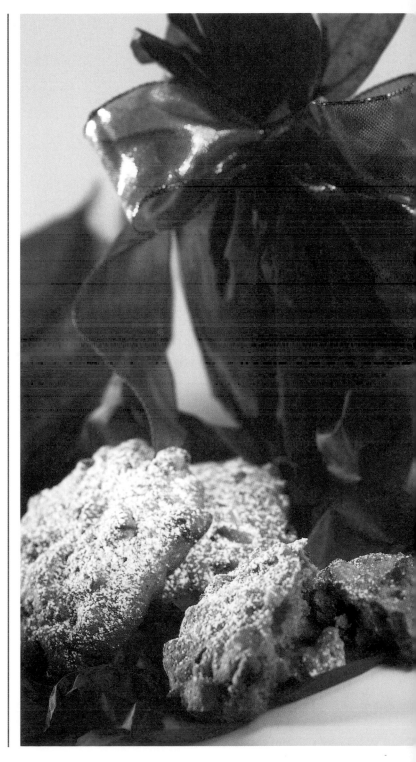

Pre-heat oven to 350°F/175°C/Gas mark 4. Grease several baking sheets or line with non-stick baking parchment.

● In a mixing bowl beat together the butter and sugar until light and fluffy. Beat in the egg and brandy. Stir in the flour, baking powder and all the remaining ingredients and mix everything together, until evenly combined.

● Place mounds of the mixture onto the baking sheets and bake for 15 minutes or until golden-brown. Lift onto wire racks to cool. Dust the cookies lightly with icing sugar and store them in an airtight container until needed.

TIP

The angelica gives good colour to these cookies, but is not essential to the flavour.

109

Coconut Meringues

Preparation time: 30 minutes ● *Cooking time: 1 hour and 30 minutes* ● *Makes: 20*

These elegant meringues, dipped in chocolate, would be perfect for a little girl's birthday.

INGREDIENTS

4 egg whites

Pinch of salt

225 g/8 oz caster sugar

75 g/3 oz sweetened flaked coconut

4 oz plain chocolate

Pre-heat oven to 250°F/120°C/Gas mark ½. Line several baking sheets with non-stick baking parchment.

● In a large mixing bowl whisk the egg whites and salt using a hand-held electric mixer until they form stiff peaks. Whisk in the sugar a little at a time until the mixture is glossy but still very stiff. Fold in the coconut.

● Using a piping bag fitted with a medium star nozzle, pipe the meringue mixture into loops to make long shapes on the baking sheets. Bake the meringues for 1 hour and 30 minutes or until they can lift off the paper easily. Store in an airtight container until needed.

● To decorate, melt the chocolate in the microwave or in a bowl over simmering water; cool. Dip one end of each meringue in melted chocolate and leave to set on greaseproof paper.

TIP

Sandwich the meringues together in pairs with 300 ml/10 fl oz whipped cream for a real treat!

110

Cassis Pink Cookies

Preparation time: 40 minutes ● Cooking time: 10 to 15 minutes ● Makes: 15

These very elegant cookies are only for the grown ups! They are flavoured with crème de cassis liqueur for a distinct taste.

INGREDIENTS

225 g/8 oz plain flour, sifted

75 g/3 oz icing sugar

150 g/5 oz butter, cut into small pieces

25 g/1 oz finely chopped blanched almonds

2 Tbsp crème de cassis or kirsch liqueur

DECORATION

50 g/2 oz unsalted butter, softened

120 g/4 oz icing sugar, sifted

1 Tbsp crème de cassis or kirsch liqueur

225 g/8 oz marzipan

Pink food colouring

1 Tbsp raspberry jam, warmed

Pre-heat oven to 350°F/175°C/Gas mark 4. Grease several baking sheets or line with non-stick baking parchment.

● Place the flour and icing sugar in a mixing bowl and blend in the butter using your fingers until the mixture resembles fine breadcrumbs. Stir in the chopped almonds and crème de cassis and mix all the ingredients together to a firm dough.

● On a lightly floured surface, roll out the dough to about 5 mm/¼ in thick. Stamp out 30 circles using a 6-cm/2½-in fluted cutter. Re-roll the trimmings as necessary and lift onto the prepared baking sheets.

● Bake the cookies for 10 to 15 minutes or until just beginning to turn golden at the edges. Transfer to a wire rack to cool.

● To decorate the cookies, first make the buttercream icing by beating together the butter and icing sugar in a bowl to give a fluffy consistency. Gradually beat in the crème de cassis. Set aside. Add a few drops of pink colouring to the marzipan in a small bowl and knead until soft and smooth. On a clean surface lightly sprinkled with icing sugar, roll out the marzipan quite thinly and stamp out 15 circles using a 6-cm/2½-in fluted cutter.

● Brush 15 of the cookies with the warmed raspberry jam and place a circle of marzipan on top, this will become the top of the cookies. Using the buttercream as the filling, sandwich the cookies together using the marzipan cookie for the top and the plain cookies for the base.

Candied Cherry Slices

Preparation time: 30 minutes + chilling ●
Cooking time: 15 to 20 minutes ● *Makes: 18 slices*

Make these chunky slices of cookie with lots of sticky glacé cherries and ground almonds for a birthday surprise.

INGREDIENTS

120 g/4 oz butter, softened

120g /4 oz caster sugar

1 egg yolk

150 g/5 oz plain flour, sifted

50 g/2 oz ground almonds

50 g/2 oz chopped blanched almonds

120 g/4 oz glacé cherries, quartered

In a mixing bowl, beat together the butter and sugar until light and fluffy. Beat in the egg yolk.

● Add the flour, ground almonds, blanched almonds and glacé cherries and using your hands bring the mixture together to form a firm dough. Shape into a 15 x 5-cm/6 x 2-in bar shape. Wrap and chill for 30 minutes. Meanwhile, line several baking sheets with nonstick baking parchment.

● Pre-heat oven to 350°F/175°C/Gas mark 4. Slice the bar into 18 equal slices and lift onto the baking sheets. Bake the cookies for 15 to 20 minutes or until evenly golden. Transfer to a wire rack to cool.

TIP

Melt 150 g/5 oz of chocolate into a small bowl, dip in one end of the cookie and place on a sheet of waxed paper and leave to set.

Vanilla Cream Cheese Cut-outs

Preparation time: 20 minutes + chilling ●
Cooking time: 10 to 12 minutes ● *Makes: 36*

These tender cookies are prefect with just a simple sugar and nut topping.

INGREDIENTS

120 g/4 oz butter, softened

75 g/3 oz cream cheese

120 g/4 oz plain flour

175 g/6 oz icing sugar

1 tsp vanilla essence

TOPPING

1 Tbsp sugar

1 tsp ground cinnamon

2 Tbsp finely chopped almonds

1 egg

Beat together the butter and sugar in a bowl until creamy. Add the flour, sugar and vanilla essence and mix to form a soft dough. Wrap the dough in clingfilm and refrigerate until firm, about 1 hour.

● Line 2 baking sheets with non-stick baking parchment. On a lightly floured surface roll half the dough to 2-mm/⅛-in thick (keep remaining dough refrigerated). Using a floured 5-cm/2-in cutter, cut out as many rounds as possible. Arrange 2.5 cm/1 in apart on the baking sheets. Repeat with remaining dough and trimmings. Chill.

● Preheat oven to 350°F/175°C/Gas mark 4. For the topping stir together the sugar, cinnamon and almonds. In a separate bowl, lightly beat the egg with 1 tablespoon cold water. Brush the tops of the cookies with the egg and sprinkle with a little of the sugar-nut mixture. Bake for 12 to 15 minutes until golden. Transfer to a wire rack to cool.

Coffee and Walnut Numbers

Preparation time: 35 minutes ● Cooking time: 15 minutes ● Makes: 14

This coffee flavoured cookie is made even more delicious by being dipped in plain and white chocolate.

INGREDIENTS

1 Tbsp instant coffee

1 Tbsp boiling water

175 g/6 oz self-raising flour

120 g/4 oz butter, cut into small pieces

175 g/6 oz caster sugar

120/4 oz finely chopped walnuts

1 egg yolk

DECORATION

50 g/2 oz white chocolate, broken into pieces

50 g/2 oz plain chocolate, broken into pieces

Preheat the oven to 350°F/175°C/Gas mark 4. Grease several baking sheets or line with non-stick baking parchment.

● Dissolve the instant coffee with the boiling water and allow to cool.

● Place the flour in a mixing bowl and blend in the butter using your fingertips until the mixture resembles fine breadcrumbs. Stir in the sugar, walnuts, egg yolk and cooled coffee and mix together well to form a firm dough.

● On a lightly floured work surface, roll out the dough to about 1-cm/½-in thick and stamp out the numbers "1" and "8" using cutters. Re-roll the trimmings to make 14 pairs of numbers and transfer to the baking sheets. Prick each cookie with a fork.

● Bake the cookies for 15 minutes, or until lightly golden-brown and transfer to a wire rack to cool.

● To decorate the cookies, melt the chocolate by placing each one in a separate bowl. Place each of these bowls over a saucepan of simmering water, stir fequently until the chocolate has melted. Dip the number "8" in the white chocolate and the number "1" in the plain chocolate and place on a piece of baking paper to set. Store these cookies in an airtight container.

Star Cookies

Preparation time: 45 minutes ● Cooking time: 10 to 15 minutes ● Makes: 16

Say "congratulations" with a crisp vanilla cookie base shaped into a star-shape and then decorated with ready-rolled white fondant icing.

INGREDIENTS

120 g/4 oz lightly salted butter, softened

120 g/4 oz caster sugar

1 egg, beaten

1 tsp vanilla essence

225 g/8 oz plain flour, sifted

DECORATION

400 g/14 oz ready-to-roll fondant icing

2 Tbsp apricot jam

Pre-heat oven to 350°F/175°C/Gas mark 4. Grease several baking sheets or line with non-stick baking parchment.

● In a mixing bowl beat together the butter and sugar until pale and fluffy. Beat in the egg and vanilla essence. Add the flour and bring the mixture together to form a soft dough.

● On a lightly floured work surface, roll out the dough to 5 mm/¼ in thick, stamp out 16 stars using a 10-cm/4-in star shaped cutter. Re-roll trimmings and place the cookies on a baking sheet. Bake the cookies for 10 to 15 minutes or until golden-brown. Transfer to a wire rack and leave to cool.

● Knead the icing until soft and smooth. Brush each cookie with warmed apricot jam. Roll out the icing on a work surface lightly sprinkled with icing sugar. Stamp out 16 stars using the same size cookie cutter and press a white star onto each cookie, re-rolling if necessary.

Pink and White Meringues

Preparation time: 30 minutes ● Cooking time: 1 hour and 30 minutes ● Makes: 20

These pastel meringues, which are as light as air and melt in the mouth, are ideal for a christening celebration.

INGREDIENTS

4 egg whites
Pinch of salt
225 g/8 oz caster sugar
Red food colouring
300 ml/10 fl oz double cream, whipped lightly

Pre-heat oven to 250°F/120°C/Gas mark ½. Line several baking sheets with non-stick baking paper.
● In a large clean bowl, using a balloon whisk or hand-held electric mixer, whisk together the egg whites and salt until they form stiff peaks. Whisk in the sugar a little at a time, the meringue should start to look glossy. Continue whisking in the sugar until all the sugar has been incorporated and the meringue is thick, shiny and stands in stiff peaks. Transfer half the meringue to another bowl, add a few drops of food colouring to create a pastel pink colour.
● Fill a piping bag with the white meringue mixture, using a 5-mm/¾-in star nozzle and pipe about 20 small whirls on to the baking sheets. Repeat with the pink meringue mixture.
● Bake the meringues for 1 hour and 30 minutes until they are dry and crisp and the swirls can be easily lifted off the paper. Leave to cool completely.
● Just before serving, sandwich the meringues together in pairs with the whipped cream. Store unfilled meringues in an airtight container. Once filled, meringues should be eaten within a few hours.

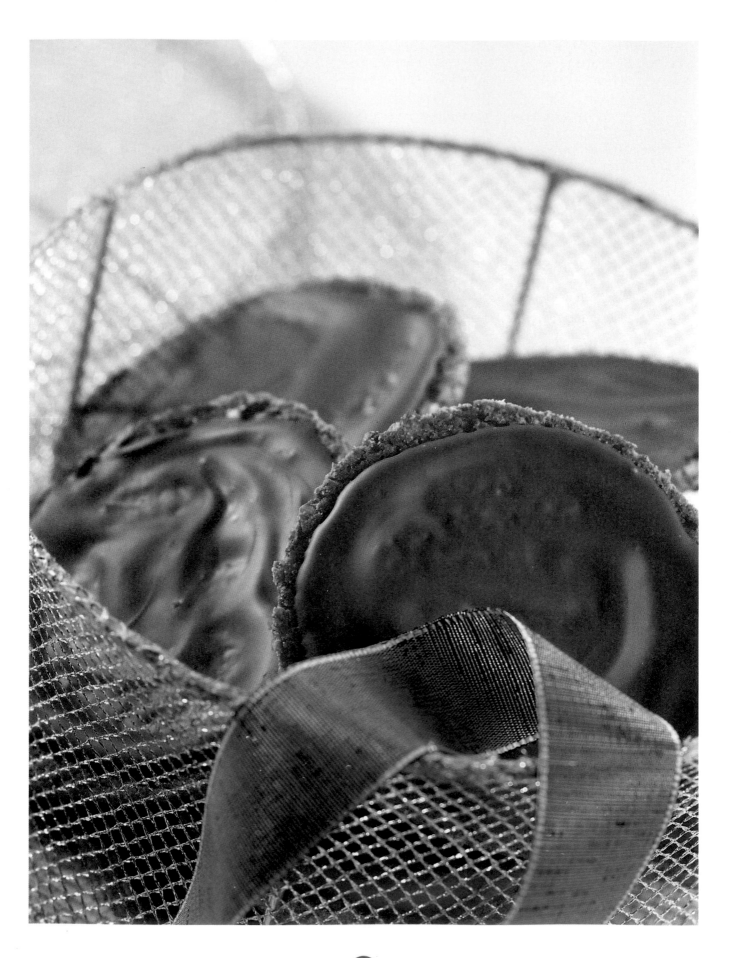

Chocolate Oaties

Preparation time: 20 minutes ● Cooking time: 20 minutes ● Makes: 16

These chunky oaty cookies with their chocolate topping will be a great edible birthday gift.

INGREDIENTS

50 g/2 oz plain flour, sifted

200 g/7 oz rolled oats

1 tsp sesame seeds

1 tsp baking powder

120 g/4 oz lightly salted butter, cut into small pieces

120 g/4 oz caster sugar

1 egg, beaten

175 g/6 oz milk or white chocolate, melted

Pre-heat oven to 350°F/175°C/Gas mark 4. Grease several baking sheets or line with non-stick baking parchment.

● Place the flour, oats, sesame seeds and baking powder in a mixing bowl. Blend in the butter, caster sugar and beaten egg to make a firm dough. Alternatively, place all these ingredients in a food processor and pulse until the mixture comes away from the sides of the bowl.

● On a lightly floured surface, roll out the dough to 5 mm/¼ in thick. Using an 8-cm/3-in cutter, stamp out 16 rounds. Lift onto the baking sheets. Bake for 20 minutes until golden-brown. Transfer the cookies to a wire rack to cool.

● Spread the top of each cookie with melted chocolate and allow to set.

Marmalade Moons

Preparation time: 25 minutes + chilling ● Cooking time: 10 to 12 minutes ● Makes: 20

Reward your child after their first day at school with these delicious moon-shaped cookies.

INGREDIENTS

175 g/6 oz plain flour, sifted

50 g/2 oz ground almonds

120 g/4 oz light brown sugar

75 g/3 oz butter, cut into small pieces

1 egg yolk

3 Tbsp orange marmalade

Icing sugar, for dusting

Place the flour, ground almonds and sugar in a mixing bowl and using your fingers blend in the butter until the mixture resembles fine breadcrumbs. Add the egg yolk and marmalade and bring the mixture together to form a soft ball. Wrap and chill for 30 minutes.

● Pre-heat oven to 350°F/175°C/Gas mark 4. Grease several baking sheets or line with non-stick baking parchment.

● On a lightly floured work surface roll out the dough to about 5 mm/¼ in thick. Using a 10-cm/4½-in round cutter, stamp out rounds, then cut away a quarter of each round making a crescent shape. Re-roll the trimmings as necessary and lift onto the baking sheets. Prick the cookies well with a fork.

● Bake the cookies for 10 to 12 minutes or until lightly golden. Transfer to a wire rack to cool. Just before serving, dust the tops with icing sugar. Store in an airtight container.

Maple Syrup Tuiles

Preparation time: 25 minutes ● *Cooking time: 8 to 10 minutes* ● *Makes: 21*

Store these very delicate Mother's Day cookies in an airtight container.

INGREDIENTS

50 g/2 oz lightly salted butter
120 g/4 oz caster sugar
2 Tbsp chopped almonds
3 Tbsp maple syrup
50 g/2 oz plain flour, sifted

Pre-heat oven to 350°F/175°C/Gas mark 4. Line 2 to 3 baking sheets with non-stick baking parchment.

● In a saucepan, gently heat the butter, caster sugar, almonds and maple syrup until the butter has melted. Remove from the heat. Add the flour and mix together until thoroughly blended.

● Spoon four teaspoonfuls of the mixture well apart on the baking sheets, bake for 8 to 10 minutes until bubbly and the cookies have spread to a lacy texture. Remove from the oven, leave to cool for one minute, then lift off with a thin, metal spatula and curl around a rolling pin to mould into tuile shapes.

● Shape the remaining cookies in the same way leave to go cold and crisp. Handle the tuiles very carefully once baked.

TIP

If the tuiles have hardened before you have shaped them, pop them back in the oven for a few seconds to soften them.

Shortcake with a Hint of Rose

Preparation time: 25 minutes ● Cooking time: 25 to 30 minutes ● Makes: 10

These thick rounds of delicate shortbread have been flavoured with rose flower-water.

INGREDIENTS

175 g/6 oz plain flour, sifted
75 g/3 oz butter, cut into small pieces
5 Tbsp caster sugar
1 egg yolk
2 Tbsp rose flower-water
Demerara sugar, for sprinkling, optional

Pre-heat oven to 300°F/150°C/Gas mark 2. Grease several baking sheets or line with non-stick baking parchment.

● Place the flour in a mixing bowl and blend in the butter using your fingertips until the mixture resembles fine breadcrumbs. Stir in the sugar, egg yolk and rose flower-water, then bring everything together with your hands to form a soft dough. On a lightly floured surface roll out the dough to about 5 mm/¼ in and using an 8-cm/3-in cutter, stamp out rounds and lift onto the baking sheets and prick with a fork. Repeat as necessary.

● Sprinkle with demerara sugar and bake the cookies for 25 to 30 minutes or until lightly golden. Transfer to a wire rack to cool.

Poppy Seed Cookies

Preparation time: 25 minutes + chilling ● Cooking time: 10 to 12 minutes ● Makes: 36

These crisp sweet cookies with a hint of orange are ideal for serving with desserts.

INGREDIENTS

75 g/3 oz plain flour, sifted
120 g/4 oz icing sugar
120 g/4 oz butter, softened
1 egg, beaten
1 Tbsp poppy seeds
Grated rind of half an orange
1 Tbsp honey

Place the flour and icing sugar into a mixing bowl and blend in the butter using your fingers until the mixture resembles fine breadcrumbs.

● Add the egg, poppy seeds, orange rind and honey and combine all the ingredients into a firm dough. On a lightly floured work surface, roll out the dough to a 23-cm/9-in log, wrap and chill for 30 minutes or up to 2 hours until firm.

● Pre-heat oven to 350°F/175°C/Gas mark 4. Grease several baking sheets or line with non-stick baking parchment.

● Slice the log into about 36 even slices and place them slightly apart on the baking sheets. Bake the cookies for 10 to 12 minutes or until lightly golden. Transfer to a wire rack to cool. These cookies can be frozen for up to a month.

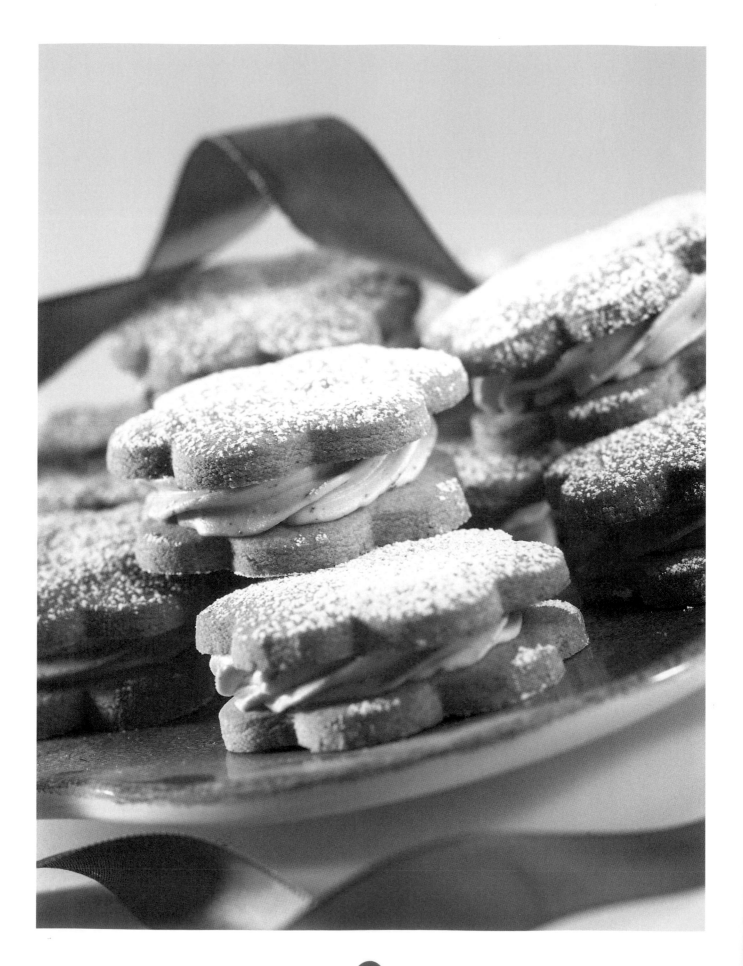

Orange Flower Cookies

Preparation time: 35 minutes + chilling ● Cooking time: 15 minutes ● Makes: 13

These pretty cookies, sandwiched together with an orange buttercream are perfect for a Mother's Day tea.

INGREDIENTS

175 g/6 oz lightly salted butter, softened

75 g/3 oz icing sugar, sifted

Grated rind of 1 orange

900 g/7 oz plain flour, sifted

50 g/2 oz custard mix or cornflour

½ tsp vanilla essence

FILLING

75 g/3 oz unsalted butter, softened

175 g/6 oz icing sugar, sifted

1 tsp grated orange rind

2 tsp fresh orange juice

Icing sugar, for dusting

In a mixing bowl beat together the butter and icing sugar until light and fluffy. Stir in the orange rind, flour and custard mix or cornflour and vanilla essence and combine all the ingredients well. Using your hands bring the mixture together to form a soft ball. Wrap and chill for 30 minutes.

● Pre-heat oven to 350°F/175°C/Gas mark 4. Grease several baking sheets or line with non-stick baking parchment.

● On a lightly floured work surface, roll out the dough to about 5 mm/¼ in thick. Using a 5-cm/2-in flower-shaped cutter, stamp out 26 flower shapes or rounds and transfer to the baking sheets. Bake the cookies for 15 minutes, or until lightly golden-brown and transfer to a wire rack to cool.

● To decorate the cookies, in a small bowl beat together the butter and icing sugar until soft and stir in the orange rind and juice for a soft buttercream icing. Sandwich the cookies together with some buttercream and dust with icing sugar before serving. Store these cookies in an airtight container for up to 1 week.

Chocolate Macaroons

Preparation time: 25 minutes ● Cooking time: 25 minutes ● Makes: 20

Show how much you care, by presenting these classic cookies to your Father on Father's Day.

INGREDIENTS

75 g/3 oz plain chocolate

2 egg whites

Pinch of salt

75 g/3 oz caster sugar

120 g/4 oz ground almonds

5 glacé cherries, halved

1 Tbsp almond pieces

Pre-heat oven to 300°F/150°/Gas mark 2. Line several baking sheets with non-stick baking parchment. Melt the chocolate in the microwave or in a bowl over simmering water. Allow to cool.

● In a large bowl, whisk the egg whites with the salt until they form stiff peaks. Gradually whisk in the sugar a little at a time. Fold in the ground almonds and cooled melted chocolate and mix well together.

● Place tablespoonfuls, spaced well apart, on the baking sheets and spread into circles about 5 cm/2 in across and decorate half the cookies with cherries and the remainder with almonds. Bake the cookies for 25 minutes or until firm, transfer to a wire rack and leave to cool. Store in an airtight container and eat within one week.

Coconut Curls

Preparation time: 25 minutes ● Cooking time: 6 to 8 minutes ● Makes: 18

These stunning cookies are ideal to serve with coffee or as an accompaniment to a cream-based dessert.

INGREDIENTS

175 g/6 oz butter

5 Tbsp caster sugar

3 Tbsp golden syrup

75 g/3 oz plain flour, sifted

2 Tbsp sweetened flaked coconut

Pre-heat oven to 375°F/190°C/Gas mark 5. Line 2 to 3 baking sheets with non-stick baking parchment.

● In a saucepan gently heat the butter, sugar and golden syrup until the butter has melted. Remove from the heat. Add the flour and coconut and mix together until well blended.

● Spoon 3 tablespoons of the mixture, well apart, on the baking sheets and spread out to a 5-cm/2-in circle, bake for 6 to 8 minutes until bubbly and the cookies have spread to a lacy texture.

● Remove from the oven, leave to cool for one minute, then lift off with a thin, metal spatula and curl around a rolling pin to mould into a curl. Shape the remaining cookies in the same way. Leave to go cold and crisp.

TIP

Handle these cookies very carefully once baked.

Classic Butter Sablés

Preparation time: 25 minutes + chilling ● *Cooking time: 15 minutes* ● *Makes: 20*

These buttery cookies will be so popular, you will be baking a double batch for the next time.

INGREDIENTS

225 g/8 oz plain flour, sifted

Pinch of salt

75 g/3 oz icing sugar

150 g/5 oz lightly salted butter, cut into small pieces

2 egg yolks

2 tsp vanilla essence

1 egg, beaten, for glazing

In a mixing bowl place the flour, salt and icing sugar. Blend in the butter, until the mixture resembles fine breadcrumbs, add the egg yolks with the vanilla essence and combine all the ingredients together to form a soft dough. Alternatively, place all the ingredients in a food processor and pulse until the mixture comes away from the sides of the bowl in a soft dough.

● Pre-heat oven to 350°F/175°C/Gas mark 4. Grease or line 2 baking sheets with non-stick baking parchment.

● On a lightly floured work surface, roll out the dough to about 5 mm/¼ in thick. Cut out rounds using a 5-mm/2-in cutter and lift onto the baking sheets. Brush the cookies very carefully with the beaten egg and chill for 30 minutes.

● Brush again with beaten egg, then mark with the back of a fork, across the cookie to make a pattern. Bake the cookies for 15 minutes or until evenly golden. Transfer to a wire rack to cool.

● To assemble the sablés, stack them together in neat bundles and tie with ribbon. Add labels marked with the names of friends or family members to the cookies. Store in an airtight container for up to a week.

Valentine Cookies

Preparation time: 30 minutes + chilling ● *Cooking time: 15 minutes* ● *Makes: 22*

This two-toned dough creates a stunning effect, guaranteed to impress your Valentine!

INGREDIENTS

175 g/6 oz butter, softened

50 g/2 oz icing sugar, sifted

250 g/9 oz plain flour, sifted

Pink food colouring

Granulated sugar, for sprinkling

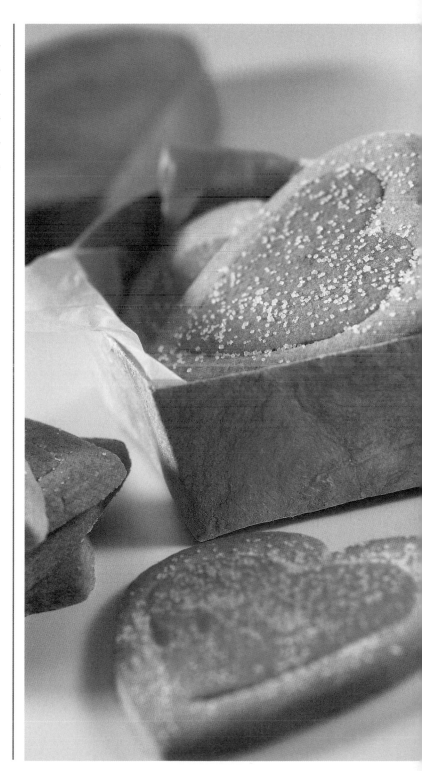

In a mixing bowl beat together the butter and icing sugar until light and fluffy. Fold in the flour and bring all the ingredients together using your hands to form a soft dough. Take half the dough and add a few drops of colouring to turn the dough pink. Wrap the two doughs separately and chill for 30 minutes.

● Pre-heat oven to 350°F/175°C/Gas mark 4. Grease several baking sheets or line with non-stick baking parchment.

● On a lightly floured work surface, roll out each dough to about 5 mm/¼ in thick. Using a 5-cm/2-in and 2.5-cm/1-in heart-shaped cutter, stamp out hearts from the dough and lift onto the baking sheets. Re-position the centres to alternate the colours. Sprinkle with the granulated sugar. Bake the cookies for 15 minutes or until lightly golden. Allow to cool on the baking sheets, before transferring to a wire rack to cool completely. Store these cookies in an airtight container.

Valentine Passion Fruit Swirls

Preparation time: 30 minutes ● *Cooking time: 15 minutes* ● *Makes: 26*

These delicately flavoured cookies are crisp to the touch but have a melt-in-the-mouth buttery taste.

INGREDIENTS

4 passion fruit

175 g/6 oz butter, softened

120 g/4 oz icing sugar

150 g/5 oz flour, sifted

Icing sugar, for dusting

Scoop out the flesh and seeds from the passion fruit and push through a fine sieve. Using a teaspoon, push the seeds against the side of the sieve to extract as much juice as possible. (You should be able to extract about 4 tablespoons of passion fruit juice, discard the black seeds.)

● Pre-heat oven to 350°F/175°C/Gas mark 4. Grease several baking sheets or line with non-stick baking parchment.

● In a mixing bowl beat together the butter and icing sugar until very soft (this will take about 5 minutes.) Then beat in the passion fruit juice and the flour to give a soft consistency. Using a piping bag fitted with a medium star nozzle, pipe small "s" shapes on the baking sheets, spacing them well apart. Bake the cookies for 15 minutes. Allow to cool slightly on the sheets then transfer to a wire rack to cool completely. Dust with icing sugar before serving. Store in an airtight container.

Chocolate Initials

Preparation time: 20 minutes + chilling ● *Cooking time: 20 minutes* ● *Makes: 18*

These incredibly crisp chocolate cookies are the perfect choice for decorating with initials.

INGREDIENTS

1 egg, separated

120 g/4 oz caster sugar

120 g/4 oz plain chocolate, finely grated

175 g/6 oz plain flour, sifted

2 Tbsp orange juice

DECORATION

50 g/2 oz plain chocolate, melted

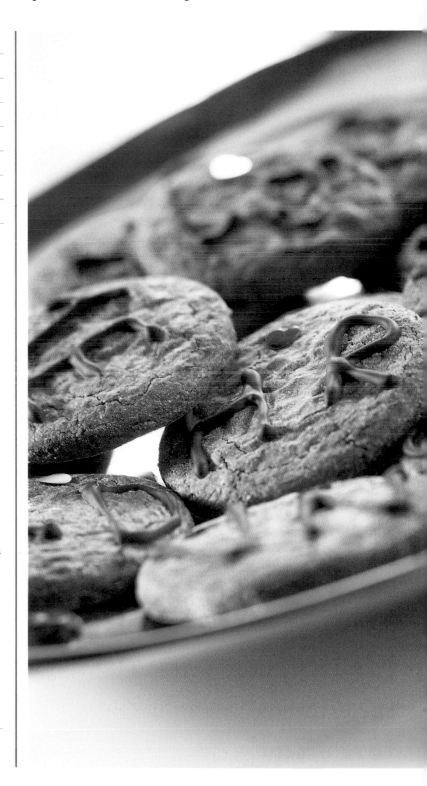

In a mixing bowl whisk the egg white until soft, but not dry and fold in the caster sugar. Stir in the chocolate, flour, egg yolk and orange juice and bring the mixture together with your hands to make a soft dough. Wrap and chill for 30 minutes.

● Pre-heat oven to 350°F/175°C/Gas mark 4. Grease several baking sheets or line with non-stick baking parchment.

● On a lightly floured work surface, roll out the dough to about 5 mm/¼ in thick. Using a 5-cm/2-in round cutter, stamp out the cookies, re-rolling the dough as necessary and transfer onto the baking sheets. Bake the cookies for 15 to 20 minutes, or until crisp. Transfer to a wire rack and leave to cool.

● Decorate the cookies by piping initials with melted chocolate using a paper pastry bag. Leave to set then store in an airtight container.

TIP

Use a selection of cutters in heart, stars, diamonds and flower shapes.

Lover's Scroll

Preparation time: 25 minutes + chilling ● *Cooking time: 15 minutes* ● *Makes: 24*

These sticky buttery cookies are delicious fresh from the oven.

INGREDIENTS

175 g/6 oz plain flour, sifted
120 g/4 oz butter, cut into small pieces
50 g/2 oz caster sugar
Grated rind of ½ lemon
2 Tbsp milk

FILLING

50 g/2 oz butter, softened
175 g/6 oz packed light brown sugar
Grated rind of ½ lemon
1 egg, beaten, for glazing
120 g/4 oz mixed dried fruit
75 g/3 oz chopped glacé cherries

Place the flour in a mixing bowl and blend in the butter using your fingers until the mixture resembles fine breadcrumbs. Stir in the sugar, lemon rind and milk and using your hands bring all the ingredients together to form a dough. Wrap and chill for 30 minutes.

● Meanwhile beat the butter and sugar together in a mixing bowl until light and fluffy, then stir in the lemon rind.

● On a lightly floured surface roll out the dough to a 15 x 28-cm/6 x 11-in rectangle. Brush with beaten egg and spread over the butter and sugar mixture, keeping within 1 cm/½ in of the edges. Sprinkle over the mixed dried fruit and glacé cherries and lightly press down.

● Roll up the pastry from one long side to the centre, then roll up the other side so the two rolls meet, brushing a little beaten egg along the point where the rolls meet. Wrap and chill for a further 1 hour.

● Pre-heat the oven to 350°F/175°C/Gas mark 4. Grease and line several baking sheets with non-stick baking paper.

● Using a sharp knife, slice the roll into about 24 even pieces and lift onto the baking sheets. Bake the cookies for 15 minutes or until lightly golden. Allow to cool on the sheets for a minute before transferring to a wire rack to cool completely.

Pine Nut Horseshoes

Preparation time: 30 minutes ● Cooking time: 15 minutes ● Makes: 10

Coated with sweet and crunchy pine nuts, these cookies say "Good Luck" in an edible way.

INGREDIENTS

75 g/3 oz white chocolate, broken into pieces

225 g/8 oz plain flour, sifted

120 g/4 oz lightly salted butter, cut into small pieces

50 g/2 oz caster sugar

75 g/3 oz chopped dried apricots

1 egg, beaten, for glazing

75 g/3 oz pine nuts

Icing sugar, for dusting

Pre-heat oven to 350°F/175°C/Gas mark 4. Grease several baking sheets or line with non-stick baking parchment.

● First melt the chocolate by placing the pieces of chocolate in a small bowl and put this in double boiler over simmering water, stir frequently until the chocolate has melted. Allow to cool.

● Place the flour in a mixing bowl and blend in the butter using your fingers until the mixture resembles fine breadcrumbs. Stir in the sugar, apricots and cooled chocolate and bring all the ingredients together to a firm dough. On a lightly floured surface divide the dough into 10 equal-sized balls.

● Roll out each ball into about 23-cm/9-in thick sausage shape and curve it in the middle to resemble a horseshoe shape. Lay a single layer of the pine kernels on a large plate.

● Brush each cookie with beaten egg, lift onto the plate and flatten slightly to coat each horseshoe with the pine kernels. Lift onto the prepared baking sheets and bake the cookies for 15 minutes or until lightly golden. Transfer to a wire rack to cool. Just before serving dust with icing sugar.

Wedding Bells

Preparation time: 45 minutes ● *Cooking time: 15 minutes* ● *Makes: 30*

These cookies contain marzipan in the dough which gives them an almond flavour that goes well with the lemon.

INGREDIENTS

120 g/4 oz white marzipan, cut into small pieces

120 g/4 oz lightly salted butter, softened

50 g/2 oz caster sugar

1 egg yolk

Grated rind of 1 lemon

150 g/5 oz plain flour, sifted

DECORATION

2 Tbsp apricot jam

Yellow food colouring

400 g/14 oz ready-to-roll fondant icing

Gold ribbon

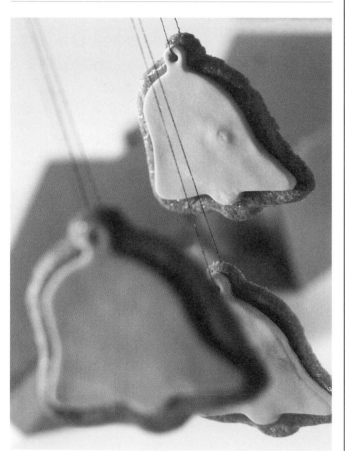

Pre-heat oven to 350°F/175°C/Gas mark 4. Grease several baking sheets or line with non-stick baking parchment.

● In a mixing bowl beat together the marzipan, butter and sugar until light and fluffy. Beat in the egg yolk and lemon rind. Add the flour and bring the mixture together with your hand to form a soft dough. On a lightly floured surface, roll out the dough to 5 mm/¼ in thick and stamp out bells using a 6 cm/2½ in bell-shaped cutter. Re-roll the trimmings and stamp out more bells and place on to the baking sheets. Make a hole at the top of each cookie with a metal skewer (so that you can tie ribbon through the bells when iced).

● Bake the cookies for 10 to 15 minutes or until golden-brown. Transfer to a wire rack and leave to cool. Brush each cookie with warmed apricot jam.

● Add a few drops of yellow colouring to the icing. Knead the icing until soft and smooth. On a surface lightly sprinkled with icing sugar, roll out the icing and stamp out 30 bells using the same bell-shaped cutter, re-rolling as necessary. Press the icing "bell" onto each cookie and re-shape the hole with a metal skewer. Tie ribbon through the holes and pair up the bells.

Golden Ginger Cookies

Preparation time: 25 minutes + chilling ● *Cooking time: 15 minutes* ● *Makes: 16*

These ginger cookies are deliciously moist but crisp around the edges.

INGREDIENTS

125 g/4 oz lightly salted butter, softened

125 g/4 oz light brown sugar

1 egg, beaten

150 g/5 oz plain flour, sifted

2 tsp ground ginger

2 Tbsp crystallized ginger, finely chopped

DECORATION

6 Tbsp icing sugar, sifted

3 tsp lemon juice

In a mixing bowl beat together the butter and sugar until light and fluffy. Beat in the egg. Add the flour, ground ginger and crystallized ginger and bring the mixture together to form a soft ball. Wrap and chill for 30 minutes.

● Pre-heat oven to 350°F/175°C/Gas mark 4. Grease several baking sheets or line with non-stick baking parchment.

● On a lightly floured surface divide the dough into 16 equal-sized pieces. Roll each piece into a ball and place on the baking sheets. Bake only 6 cookies on each sheet as they will spread during baking. Flatten slightly with a wet fork.

● Bake the cookies for 15 minutes, or until lightly golden at the edges. Allow to cool on the baking sheets before transferring to a wire rack.

● To decorate the cookies, mix the icing sugar with the lemon juice and mix to a thin icing. Using a paper piping bag, drizzle the icing randomly over each cookie and allow to set.

Cranberry Cookies

Preparation time: 45 minutes + chilling ● *Cooking time: 30 minutes* ● *Makes: 16*

These stunning ruby-coloured cookies are great for special wedding anniversaries.

INGREDIENTS

75 g/3 oz cranberries

5 Tbsp caster sugar

1 Tbsp water

225 g/8 oz plain flour, sifted

75 g/3 oz icing sugar, sifted

150 g/5 oz slightly salted butter, cut into small pieces

Granulated sugar, for sprinkling

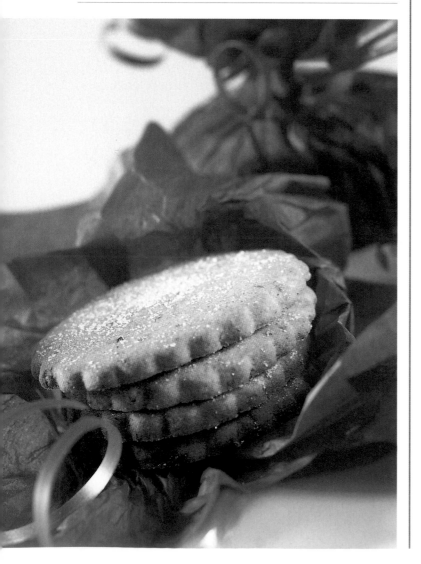

Place the cranberries, sugar and water in a small saucepan and set over a medium heat until the sugar dissolves. Reduce the heat and simmer uncovered for 8 to 10 minutes until the mixture is very thick and jam-like; cool.

● Place the flour and icing sugar in a mixing bowl and blend in the butter using your fingertips until the mixture resembles fine breadcrumbs, add the cooled cranberry sauce mixture and bring all the ingredients together to form a soft ball. Wrap and chill for 30 minutes.

● Pre-heat oven to 350°F/175°C/Gas mark 4. Grease several baking sheets or line with non-stick baking parchment.

● On a lightly floured work surface, roll out the dough to about 5 mm/¼ in thick and stamp out 8-cm/3-in fluted ovals or rounds, re-rolling the dough as necessary; there should be about 16. Transfer to the baking sheets.

● Bake the cookies for 15 minutes or until they are lightly golden at the edges. Transfer to a wire rack to cool. Just before serving sprinkle with granulated sugar.

Lemon Rings

Preparation time: 35 minutes ● *Cooking time:*
10 to 15 minutes ● *Makes: 16*

**These cookies are sandwiched together with a lemon
butter icing to symbolize wedding rings.**

INGREDIENTS

25 g/1 oz butter, softened

120 g/4 oz caster sugar

1 egg, beaten

225 g/8 oz self-raising flour

Grated rind of 1 lemon

2 Tbsp lemon juice

ICING

50 g/2 oz unsalted butter, softened

120 g/4 oz icing sugar

2 tsp lemon juice

1 tsp grated lemon rind

Icing sugar, for dusting

Pre-heat oven to 350°F/175°C/Gas mark 4. Grease several baking sheets.

● In a mixing bowl beat together the butter and sugar until light and fluffy. Beat in the egg. Fold in the flour, lemon rind and lemon juice and mix to a firm dough. On a lightly floured surface roll out the dough to about 5 mm/¼ in thick. Using a 6-cm/2½-in and 2.5-cm/1-in cutter, cut out rings from the dough, carefully removing the central circle, and lift on to the baking sheets. Re-roll the trimmings as necessary. Bake for 10 to 15 minutes. Transfer to a wire rack to cool.

● To decorate the cookies, in a mixing bowl beat together the butter and icing sugar to give a fluffy consistency. Gradually beat in the lemon juice and rind. Sandwich the rings together with the filling and dust with icing sugar before serving.

Pine Nut Biscotti

Preparation time: 30 miniutes ● *Cooking time:*
35 to 40 minutes ● *Makes: 13*

**Pine nuts and ground cinnamon are used to flavour these
crisp cookies. Serve them with black coffee after a meal.**

INGREDIENTS

1 egg

7 Tbsp caster sugar

120 g/4 oz plain flour, sifted

½ tsp baking powder

1 tsp ground cinnamon

50 g/2 oz pine nuts

Icing sugar, for dusting

Pre-heat oven to 350°F/175°C/Gas mark 4. Grease a large baking tray or line with non-stick baking parchment.

● In a mixing bowl whisk together the egg and sugar with an electric hand-held mixer until pale and thick (ribbons of mixture should leave a trail from the whisk as you lift it).

● Fold in the flour, baking powder, cinnamon and pine nuts and mix everything together to form a soft dough. Turn out onto a lightly floured work surface and roll into a 23-cm/9-in long log. Transfer onto the prepared baking sheet and flatten the dough until it is about 5 mm/¾ in thick.

● Bake the dough for about 30 minutes or until golden and firm. Leave to cool for about 5 minutes. Transfer to a cutting board and using a serrated bread knife cut the log on the diagonal into 1-cm/½-in thick slices. Lift onto the baking sheet and cook for a further 10 to 15 minutes or until crisp.

● Transfer to a wire rack to cool. Dust with icing sugar and store in an airtight container for up to one week.

Confetti Cookies

Preparation time: 50 minutes ● *Cooking time: 10 to 12 minutes* ● *Makes: 35 small cookies*

These tiny crisp cookies with a delicate hint of lime are decorated with clear icing to resemble confetti.

INGREDIENTS

120 g/4 oz plain flour, sifted

1 tsp grated lime rind

3 Tbsp icing sugar

70 g/2½ oz butter, cut into small pieces

DECORATION

125 g/4 oz Icing sugar, sifted

1 Tbsp water

Blue, yellow and pink food colouring

Pre-heat oven to 350°F/175°C/Gas mark 4. Grease several baking sheets or line with non-stick baking parchment.

● In a large mixing bowl place the flour, grated lime and icing sugar. Blend in the butter, using your fingertips, until the mixture begins to form together in a soft ball. On a lightly floured surface roll out the dough to 5 mm/ ¼ in thick and using a selection of small cutters, stamp out different shapes. Re-roll the trimmings to make about 35 cookies in all and lift on to the baking sheets. Bake for 10 to 12 minutes or until lightly golden. Transfer the cookies to a wire rack and leave to cool completely.

● To decorate the cookies, mix the icing sugar with sufficient water to form a thin icing and divide into four bowls. Colour the icing blue, yellow and pink, leaving one quarter white. Spread a little icing on each cookie and allow to set. Gift-wrap in coloured cellophane bags to look just like confetti!

Butter Viennese Fingers

Preparation time: 25 minutes ● Cooking time: 10 to 15 minutes ● Makes: 20

These cookies look very impressive, they are crisp on the outside but have a melt-in-the-mouth texture.

INGREDIENTS

175 g/6 oz butter, softened

3 Tbsp icing sugar, sifted

175 g/6 oz plain flour, sifted

DECORATION

50 g/2 oz plain chocolate, broken into pieces

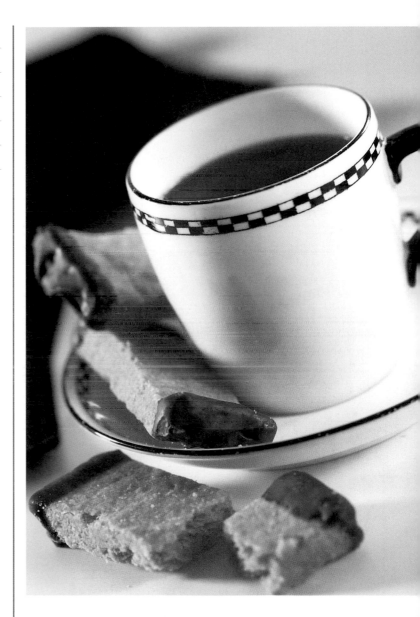

Pre-heat oven to 350°F/175°/Gas mark 4. Grease several baking sheets or line with non-stick baking parchment.

● In a large mixing bowl beat together the butter and icing sugar until very soft (this will take about 5 minutes), then beat in the flour until thoroughly mixed and a soft consistency.

● Using a piping bag fitted with a medium star nozzle, pipe 8-cm/3-in long finger shapes on the baking sheets, spacing them well apart. Bake the cookies for 10 to 15 minutes or until pale golden. Transfer to a wire rack to cool.

● To decorate the cookies, place the chocolate in a small bowl and put this in a double boiler set over a saucepan of simmering water and stir frequently until the chocolate has melted. Dip the ends of each cookie in the chocolate and allow to set on a piece of greaseproof paper or baking parchment.

Two-tone Cookies

Preparation time: 30 minutes + chilling ●
Cooking time: 10 to 12 minutes ● Makes: 32

Once you have mastered the basic technique, have fun creating different cookie patterns.

INGREDIENTS

175 g/6 oz butter, softened

75 g/3 oz icing sugar

150 g/5 oz plain flour, sifted

½ tsp grated lemon rind

2 Tbsp unsweetened cocoa powder, sifted

1 egg white, for glazing

In a mixing bowl, beat together the butter and sugar until light and fluffy. Stir in the flour and lemon rind, then combine the ingredients to form a soft ball. Transfer half the mixture to another bowl and stir in the cocoa powder. Wrap separately and chill for 30 minutes.
● Pre-heat oven to 350°F/175°C/Gas mark 4. Grease several baking sheets or line with non-stick baking parchment.
● On a lightly floured work surface divide each dough in half and roll into four sausage shapes about 30 cm/12 in long and 1 cm/½ in wide. Using the egg white, brush the sausage shapes and stack together alternating the colours. Cut the log shape into 32 slices and lift onto the baking sheets. Bake the cookies for 10 to 12 minutes. Transfer to a wire rack to cool completely. Store the cookies in an airtight container.

Hot Ham and Cheese Triangles

Preparation time: 25minutes + chilling ●
Cooking time: 15 minutes ● Makes: 28

These cookies have a great colour from the red Leicester cheese and the dried red chilli flakes give the taste buds a kick!

INGREDIENTS

120 g/4 oz plain flour, sifted

½ tsp salt

½ tsp dried crushed chillies

75 g/3 oz butter, cut into small pieces

175 g/6 oz grated red Leicester cheese

75 g/3 oz ham, finely chopped

Place the flour, salt and dried chilli flakes in a mixing bowl and using your fingers blend in the butter until the mixture resembles fine breadcrumbs. Stir in the cheese and ham and mix together using your hands to form a dough. Wrap and chill for 30 minutes.
● Pre-heat oven to 375°F/190°C/Gas mark 5. Grease several baking sheets or line with non-stick baking parchment.
● On a lightly floured work surface, roll out the dough about 5 mm/¼ in thick and stamp out squares using a 10-cm/4-in fluted cutter, cut in half to make triangles. Lift onto the baking sheets. Bake the cookies for 15 minutes, or until puffed up and lightly golden-brown. Transfer to a wire rack to cool. Store in an airtight container and eat within one week.

Lime and Coconut Hearts

Preparation time: 35 minutes ● Cooking time: 15 minutes ● Makes: 16

Ideal for any journey, the exotic flavours of coconut and lime are reminiscent of the Caribbean.

INGREDIENTS

225 g/8 oz plain flour, sifted

50 g/2 oz rice flour

175 g/6 oz butter, cut into small pieces

50 g/2 oz caster sugar

75 g/3 oz unsweetened flaked coconut

Grated rind of 1 lime

2 Tbsp milk

DECORATION

7 Tbsp icing sugar, sifted

3 tsp cold water

Grated rind of 1 lime

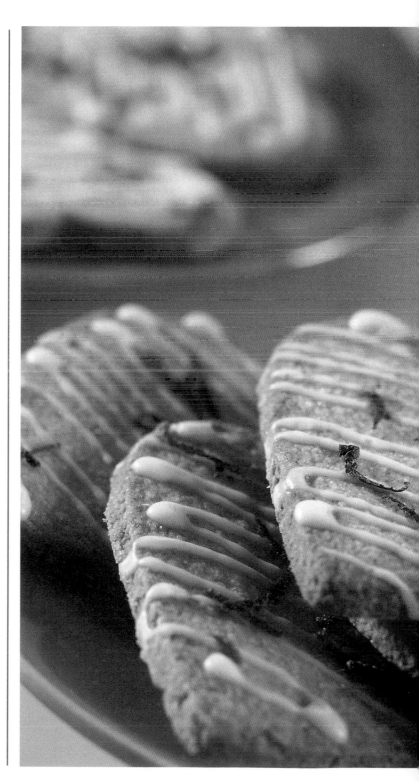

Pre-heat oven to 350°F/175°C/Gas mark 4. Grease several baking sheets or line with non-stick baking parchment.

● Place the flour and rice flour in a mixing bowl and add the butter. Blend in the butter using your fingers until the mixture resembles fine breadcrumbs, add the sugar, coconut, lime rind and milk and mix all the ingredients together to form a soft dough.

● On a lightly floured work surface, roll out the dough to about 5 mm/¼ in thick, stamp out hearts using an 8-cm/3-in heart-shaped cutter and lift onto the baking sheets. Bake the cookies for 15 minutes or until they are lightly golden. Transfer to a wire rack to cool.

● To decorate the cookies, mix the icing sugar with the cold water and mix to a thin icing. Fill a paper pastry bag with icing and drizzle it over the cookies, sprinkle with lime rind and allow the icing to set. Store in an airtight container.

Rosemary and Lime Cookies

Preparation time: 25 minutes ● Cooking time: 15 to 20 minutes ● Makes: 30

The combination of fresh rosemary with lime results in a crisp scented cookie.

INGREDIENTS

50 g/2 oz lightly salted butter, softened
120 g/4 oz light brown sugar
1 egg, separated
Grated rind of 1 lime
200 g/7 oz plain flour, sifted
2 Tbsp lime juice
2 tsp finely chopped fresh rosemary
Granulated sugar, for sprinkling

Pre-heat oven to 350°F/175°C/Gas mark 4. Grease several baking sheets or line with non-stick baking parchment.

● In a mixing bowl beat together the butter and sugar until light and fluffy. Beat in the egg yolk and lime rind. Add the flour and begin to work the mixture into a soft dough. Add the lime juice and rosemary and using your hands bring the dough together in a soft ball.

● On a lightly floured surface, roll out the dough to 5 mm/¼ in thick, stamp out diamond shapes using a 8-cm/3-in cutter. Re-roll the trimmings and stamp out more shapes and place on the baking sheets.

● Lightly whisk the egg white in a small bowl, gently brush over the surface of each cookie, then sprinkle with a little granulated sugar. Bake the cookies for 15 to 20 minutes or until lightly golden. Transfer to a wire rack to cool. Store the cookies in an airtight container for up to one week.

Smiling Faces

Preparation time: 35 minutes ● Cooking time: 15 minutes ● Makes: 16

These coffee-flavoured cookies are great for cheering up a special friend!

INGREDIENTS

1 Tbsp instant coffee powder
1 Tbsp hot water
225 g/8 oz plain flour, sifted
75 g/3 oz icing sugar, sifted
150 g/5 oz butter, cut into small pieces

DECORATION

6 Tbsp icing sugar
3 tsp water

Pre-heat oven to 350°F/175°C/Gas mark 4. Grease several baking sheets or line with non-stick baking parchment.

● Dissolve the coffee in the hot water and leave to cool completely.

● Place the flour and icing sugar in a mixing bowl and blend in the butter using your fingertips until the mixture resembles fine breadcrumbs. Pour in the cooled coffee and bring all the ingredients together to form a soft dough.

● On a lightly floured surface, roll out the dough to about 5 mm/¼ in thick. Using an 8-cm/3-in cutter, stamp out rounds and lift on to the prepared baking sheets, re-rolling the dough as necessary. Prick the cookies with a fork. Bake for about 15 minutes or until crisp. Transfer to a wire rack to cool.

● To decorate, mix the icing sugar with sufficient cold water to make a thin icing. Using a paper pastry bag, pipe smiling faces onto the cookies. Leave to set. Store in an airtight container.

Pecan Pinwheel Cookies

Preparation time: 25 minutes + chilling ● *Cooking time: 20 minutes* ● *Makes: 24*

A cinnamon cookie base is sprinkled with pecan nuts and orange rind then rolled up and cut into pinwheels.

INGREDIENTS

175 g/6 oz plain flour, sifted

1 tsp ground cinnamon

120 g/4 oz sugar

120 g/4 oz lightly salted butter, cut into small pieces

1 Tbsp maple syrup

FILLING

5 Tbsp smooth peanut butter

2 Tbsp maple syrup

Grated rind of 1 orange

50 g/2 oz chopped pecan nuts

2 Tbsp maple syrup, optional

Place the flour, cinnamon and sugar in a mixing bowl and using your fingers blend in the butter until the mixture resembles fine breadcrumbs. Add the maple syrup and mix everything together with your hands to form a soft dough. Wrap and chill for 30 minutes.

● On a lightly floured work surface roll out the dough to a 30 x 8-cm/12 x 7-in rectangle. In a small bowl combine the peanut butter and maple syrup and beat using a wooden spoon until soft enough to spread. Spread this mixture over the rectangle leaving a 2.5-cm/1-in border around the edge of the dough. Sprinkle over the orange rind and pecan nuts. Starting from the long end, roll up the dough tightly into a "sausage" shape. Wrap and chill for 30 minutes.

● Pre-heat oven to 350°F/175°C/Gas mark 4. Grease several baking sheets or line with non-stick baking parchment.

● Using a sharp knife cut the log into 24 equal slices (discarding the first and last slice, which have little filling) and lift onto the baking sheets. Bake the cookies for 20 minutes or until lightly golden. Drizzle with maple syrup to glaze, if liked. Transfer to a wire rack to cool. Store in an airtight container until required.

Fan-tailed Shortbread

Preparation time: 25 minutes ● *Cooking time: 35 to 40 minutes* ● *Makes: 8*

This classic buttery shortbread is very rewarding to make – and a great gift.

INGREDIENTS

120 g/4 oz butter, softened
25 g/1 oz caster sugar
75 g/3 oz plain flour, sifted
2 Tbsp rice flour
Pinch of salt
2 Tbsp finely chopped mixed nuts, to sprinkle

Pre-heat oven to 300°F/150°C/Gas mark 2. Grease a baking sheet or line with non-stick baking parchment.

● In a mixing bowl beat together the butter and sugar until light and fluffy. Add the flour, rice flour and salt and mix everything together to form a soft dough. On a lightly floured surface, roll out the dough to form a neat circle about 20 cm/8 in across and 5 mm/¼ in thick.

● Transfer to the prepared baking sheet, then crimp the edges with your fingertips and mark into 8 even wedges with a sharp knife. Prick with a fork, sprinkle with the chopped nuts and bake for about 35 to 40 minutes until lightly golden.

● Leave to cool slightly on the tray before transferring to a wire rack to cool completely. Cut along the scored lines to divide into 8 wedges.

Sesame Cracker Cookies

Preparation time: 20 minutes ● *Cooking time: 15 minutes* ● *Makes: 15*

Serve these savoury cookies with chunks of Cheddar cheese.

INGREDIENTS

175 g/6 oz wholemeal flour
50 g/2 oz oat bran
½ tsp salt
1 tsp baking powder
15 g/½ oz caster sugar
2 Tbsp sesame seeds
125 g/4 oz butter, cut into small pieces
1 Tbsp water

Pre-heat oven to 375°F/190°C/Gas mark 5. Grease several baking sheets or line with non-stick baking parchment.

● In a mixing bowl place the wholemeal flour, oat bran, salt, baking powder, sugar and sesame seeds and give a good mix. Blend in the butter, using your fingers, until the mixture resembles fine breadcrumbs. Add sufficient cold water (about 1 tablespoon) and work all the ingredients together into a firm dough.

● On a lightly floured work surface, roll out the dough to about 5 mm/¼ in thick and using an 8-cm/3-in round cutter, stamp out 15 circles and lift onto the baking sheets, re-rolling the dough as necessary. Prick the cookies with a fork. Bake for 15 minutes. Transfer to a wire rack to cool, then store these cookies in an airtight container.

Coffee Meringue Snails

Preparation time: 25 minutes ● *Cooking time: 1 hour and 30 minutes* ● *Makes: 15*

The addition of coffee to the meringue makes it quite soft when piping but the taste is delicious. Any gardener should see the funny side of making a snail cookie!

INGREDIENTS

1 Tbsp instant coffee powder

1 Tbsp boiling water

4 egg whites

Pinch of salt

400 g/14 oz caster sugar

DECORATION

3 Tbsp icing sugar

1 tsp water

Black food colouring

Dissolve the coffee in the boiling water in a small jug and leave to go cold. Pre-heat the oven to 250°F/120°C/Gas mark ½. Line several baking sheets with non-stick baking parchment.

● In a large clean bowl, using a balloon whisk or hand-held electric mixer, whisk together the egg whites and salt until they form stiff peaks. Whisk in the sugar a little at a time. The meringue should start to look glossy.

● Continue whisking in the sugar until it has been incorporated and the meringue is thick and shiny and stands in stiff peaks. Fold in the coffee and mix through.

● Fill a piping bag with the meringue, using a 5-mm/¾-in plain nozzle, pipe about 15 "snail" shapes. Bake the meringues for 1 hour and 30 minutes until they are dry and crisp and can be easily lifted off the paper.

● To decorate the snails, mix the icing sugar with the water to form a thin icing. Add a few drops of colouring. Fill a piping bag with the black icing and pipe on eyes and mouths. Store in an airtight container.

Almond Tiles

Preparation time: 45 minutes ● Cooking time: 4 to 5 minutes per batch ● Makes: 30

These are one of the most popular French cookies, "tuiles aux amandes", so called because they resemble the curved roof tiles seen all over France.

INGREDIENTS

50 g/2 oz whole blanched almonds, lightly toasted
225 g/8 oz sugar
3 Tbsp unsalted butter
2 egg whites
½ tsp almond essence
25 g/1 oz flour, sifted
75 g/3 oz flaked almonds

In a food processor fitted with a metal blade, process the toasted almonds with 2 tablespoons of the sugar until finè crumbs form.

● Preheat oven to 400°F/200°C/Gas mark 6. Generously butter 2 baking sheets or line with non-stick baking parchment.

● In a medium bowl beat the butter until creamy, add the sugar and beat until light and fluffy. Gradually beat in the egg whites and almond essence until well blended. Sift over the flour and fold into the butter mixture, then fold in the almond-sugar mixture.

● Begin by working in batches of 4 cookies on each sheet. Drop tablespoonfuls of batter about 15-cm/6-in apart on the baking sheet. With the back of a moistened spoon, spread each mound of batter into very thin 8-cm/3-in rounds. Each round should be transparant. If you make a few holes, the batter will spread and fill them in. Sprinkle tops with flaked almonds.

● Bake, one sheet at a time, until the edges are browned and the centres are just golden, 4 to 5 minutes. Remove baking sheet to a wire rack, working quickly, use a thin-bladed metal spatula to loosen the edge of a hot cookie and transfer to a rolling pin or glass tumbler. Gently press, side down, to shape each cookie. If the cookie becomes too firm to transfer, return to the oven for 30 seconds to soften, the proceed as above. When cool, transfer immediately to airtight containers in single layers. These cookies are very fragile.

Hazelnut and Nutmeg Cookies

Preparation time: 30 minutes + chilling ● *Cooking time: 15 to 18 minutes* ● *Makes: 24*

The crunchy hazelnuts and spicy nutmeg make these a great treat for morning coffee.

INGREDIENTS

225 g/8 oz lightly salted butter, softened

175 g/6 oz caster sugar

2 egg yolks

1 tsp vanilla essence

225 g/8 oz self-raising flour, sifted

½ tsp ground nutmeg

¾ cup chopped hazelnuts

Icing sugar, for dusting, optional

In a mixing bowl cream together the butter and sugar until light and fluffy. Beat in the egg yolks and vanilla essence, add the flour and nutmeg and mix everything together to form a soft dough. Wrap and chill in the refrigerator for 30 minutes.

● Pre-heat oven to 375°F/190°C/Gas mark 5. Grease several baking sheets or line with non-stick baking parchment.

● On a lightly floured work surface, divide the dough into 24 equal-sized pieces, roll each into a ball and flatten slightly. Place the chopped hazelnuts on a large plate, roll the flattened balls in the chopped hazelnuts and then lift onto the baking sheets spaced well apart. Bake the cookies for 15 to 18 minutes or until lightly golden. Transfer to a wire rack to cool. Dust with icing sugar before serving. Store these cookies in an airtight container.

Cardamom Crisps

Preparation time: 25 minutes ● Cooking time: 15 minutes ● Makes: 20

These indulgent cookies flavoured with cardamom and ginger are delicious. They will liven up anyone's nightcap.

INGREDIENTS

275 g/9 oz plain flour, sifted

½ tsp ground cardamom

Pinch of salt

120 g/4 oz lightly salted butter, cut into small pieces

225 g/8 oz soft brown sugar

2 egg yolks

2 Tbsp finely chopped stem ginger or ginger preserves

Granulated sugar, for sprinkling

Pre-heat oven to 350°F/175°C/Gas mark 4. Grease several baking sheets or line with non-stick baking parchment.

● In a mixing bowl, place the flour, ground cardamom and salt. Blend in the butter, using your fingers, until the mixture resembles fine bread crumbs, stir in the sugar. Add the egg yolks and mix all the ingredients together to form a soft dough.

● On a lightly floured surface, roll out the dough to 5-mm/¼-in thick. Cut out the cookies using a 6-cm/2½-in shaped cutter, re-rolling the trimmings to make about 20, place on to the baking sheets.

● Sprinkle a little stem ginger or ginger preserves on the top of each cookie. Bake the cookies for 15 minutes or until lightly golden and crisp. Transfer the cookies to a wire rack and leave to cool. Sprinkle with granulated sugar before serving.

TIP

If using cardamom pods, crack open 7 pods, remove the black seeds and crush with a pestle and mortar.

Double Chocolate Mint Sandwiches

Preparation time: 1 hour + chilling ● *Cooking time: 12 to 16 minutes* ● *Makes: About 24*

A delicious combination of mint-flavoured white chocolate ganache sandwiched between thin cocoa wafers, glazed with dark chocolate. These cookies are time-consuming to make, but make an excellent presentation gift.

INGREDIENTS

120 g/4 oz plain flour

3 Tbsp unsweetened cocoa powder

120 g/4 oz butter

50 g/2 oz caster sugar

1 egg

1 tsp mint essence

FILLING

120 ml/4 fl oz whipping cream

200 g/7 oz fine-quality white chocolate, chopped

GLAZE

150 g/5 oz plain chocolate, chopped

75 g/3 oz butter, cut into pieces

Sift together the flour and cocoa. In a large bowl, beat the butter until creamy, add the sugar and continue beating until light and fluffy. Beat in the egg and mint essence until blended. Stir in the flour-cocoa mixture until a soft dough forms. Place the dough in clingfilm and refrigerate for 1 to 2 hours until firm.

● Preheat oven to 350°F/175°C/Gas mark 4. Grease 2 baking sheets with non-stick baking parchment.

● On a lightly floured work surface, roll out half the dough to about 2.5 cm/⅛ in thick. Using a 5-cm/2½-in cutter, stamp out as many cookies as possible, re-rolling the dough as necessary and lift onto the baking sheets.

● Bake for 6 to 8 minutes or until the edges are set. Allow to cool and then transfer to a wire rack to cool completely. Repeat with the remaining dough.

● In a medium saucepan over a medium heat, bring the cream to a boil. Remove from the heat and add the white chocoate, stirring constantly until melted. Stir in mint essence and strain into a bowl. Cool until firm.

● Slightly beat white chocolate cream to lighten, then spread a little filling onto half of the cookies, pressing together gently. Allow to set for 24 hours.

● In a small saucepan over a low heat, melt the chocolate and butter for the glaze, stirring until smooth. Remove from the heat. Cool until thickened to spreading consistency, 20 to 30 minutes. Spread a small amount of glaze onto the top of each sandwiched cookie, smoothing tops. Refrigerate until set, 30 minutes or so. Store these cookies in an airtight container, refrigerated, with greaseproof paper between the layers.

Strawberry Jam Sandwiches

Preparation time: 25 minutes + chilling ● *Cooking time: 8 to 10 minutes* ● *Makes: About 24*

Children love strawberry jam sandwiches and these are the perfect cookies to take to a family party.

INGREDIENTS

75 g/3 oz blanched almonds
175 g/6 oz plain flour
175 g/6 oz lightly salted butter
225 g/8 oz caster sugar
1 egg, separated
Grated rind of 1 lemon
1 tsp vanilla essence
½ tsp salt
50 g/2 oz flaked almonds, chopped
5 Tbsp strawberry jam
1 Tbsp lemon juice

In a food processor fitted with a metal blade, process the blanched almonds and 15 g/1 oz flour until the mixture becomes very fine. In a separate bowl, beat the butter until creamy, add the sugar and continue beating until light and fluffy. Beat in the egg yolk, lemon rind and vanilla essence until blended. Stir in the almond mixture and add the remaining flour and salt; process until combined. Wrap the dough in clingfilm and refrigerate for 2 hours or overnight, until the dough is firm enough to handle.

● Pre-heat oven to 350°F/175°C/Gas mark 4. Grease or line two baking sheets with non-stick baking parchment.

● On a floured surface, roll half the dough into a 30-cm/12-in square; keep the other half refrigerated. Cut the square crosswise and lengthwise into 6 strips to make 24 squares. Using a 5-mm/¾-in cutter, cut out centres from half the squares.

● Place the squares on baking sheets 1 cm/½ in apart. In a small bowl, whisk the egg white until frothy. Brush the top of cookies only with it and sprinkle with the almonds. Bake until just golden, 8 to 10 minutes. Allow the cookies to cool slightly, then transfer to wire racks to cool completely.

● In a saucepan over a low heat, melt the strawberry jam with the lemon juice. Spoon a little of the glaze over the cookie squares, then top with an almond-topped cookie, pressing the two gently together. Allow the jam to set before serving. These cookies are best eaten as soon as possible after baking as they will begin to go soft if kept for too long.

Real Vanilla Cookies

Preparation time: 30 minutes ● *Cooking time: 8 to 10 minutes* ● *Makes: About 24*

These cookies are a Danish speciality. They use real vanilla seeds from a pod.

INGREDIENTS

225 g/8 oz plain flour

2 Tbsp cornflour

5 Tbsp caster sugar

3 Tbsp finely chopped blanched almonds

½ vanilla pod or 1 tsp vanilla essence

225 g/8 oz unsalted butter, cut into small pieces

1 egg, separated

Sugar, for sprinkling

Icing sugar, for dusting

Pre-heat oven to 400°F/200°C/Gas mark 6. Grease two baking sheets, or line with non-stick baking parchment.

● Sift together the flour and cornflour and stir in the sugar and almonds.

● Using a sharp knife, split the vanilla pod and scrape out the seeds. Add to the flour mixture and mix well. (If using vanilla essence, mix with the egg yolk and add later.) Blend the butter into the flour mixture until it resembles breadcrumbs. In a separate bowl, beat the egg yolk (and vanilla essence) and add to the crumb mixture. Knead until a soft dough forms. (If the dough seems a little wet, add a little more flour.)

● Spoon the dough into a large piping bag fitted with a large plain nozzle and pipe "doughnut" shapes 4 cm/ 1½ in apart on the baking sheets. In a small bowl, beat the egg whites until foamy, then use to brush the shapes. Sprinkle with sugar.

● Bake until lightly golden and set, 8 to 10 minutes. Allow to cool slightly, then, using a metal spatula, transfer to wire racks to cool completely. Dust with icing sugar. Store in an airtight container for up to one week.

Bitter Chocolate Discs

Preparation time: 25 minutes ● Cooking time: 15 minutes ● Makes: 16

These cookies have a crumbly melt-in-the-mouth texture with a rich chocolate flavour.

INGREDIENTS

150 g/5 oz butter, softened

120 g/4 oz caster sugar

225 g/8 oz plain flour, sifted

Pinch of salt

50 g/2 oz unsweetened cocoa powder, sifted

DECORATION

75 g/3 oz white chocolate, melted

Pre-heat oven to 350°F/175°C/Gas mark 4. Grease several baking sheets or line with non-stick baking parchment.

● In a mixing bowl beat together the butter and sugar until light and fluffy. Add the flour, salt and cocoa. Using your hands work these ingredients into the butter and sugar mixture until it comes together in a firm dough.

● On a lightly floured surface, roll out the dough to 5 mm/¼ in thick. Using an 8-cm/3-in fluted round cutter, stamp out 16 cookies, re-rolling as necessary and transfer onto the baking sheets. Prick with a fork and bake the cookies for 15 minutes. Cool on a wire rack.

● Decorate the cookies by drizzling freestyle with melted white chocolate using a paper piping bag. Leave on the wire rack until the chocolate icing becomes firm.

Chocolate Cookies

For many people, this will be their favourite chapter in the book. The appeal of chocolate just cannot be denied, even its Latin name acknowledges this, *Theobroma cacao* means "food of the gods" and who could doubt it. Chocoholics will find reading through these recipes alone will send them on a chocolate high.

When shopping for chocolate, be sure to buy real chocolate and not a synthetic chocolate-flavoured substitute. Different brands of the same type of chocolate can vary in taste, so to avoid disappointment, make sure that the chocolate you cook with tastes the same as the one you most enjoy eating. If you are not sure, then have a nibble before you begin.

The biggest problem will be which recipe to cook first – maybe a purely chocolate cookie, or one with a hint of orange, or perhaps a chocolate cookie with a nutty crunch. One thing is guaranteed, and that is the enjoyment of tasting these rich and sumptuous cookies.

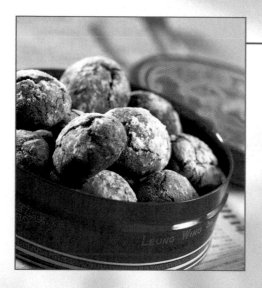

Lunch-box or Picnic Treats

Cookies with Crunch

Afternoon Tea

Special Occasions

After-dinner Cookies

No-cook Peanut Squares

Preparation time: 30 minutes + chilling ● Cooking time: 5 minutes ● Makes: About 24

You do not even have to switch the oven on to make these chocolatey treats.

INGREDIENTS

300 ml/10 fl oz golden syrup
225 g/8 oz peanut butter
250 g/9 oz All-Bran breakfast cereal
225 g/8 oz chopped peanuts
200 g/7 oz milk chocolate

Grease or line a shallow 18 x 28-cm/7 x 11-in tin with non-stick baking parchment.

● Mix the syrup and peanut butter together in a large saucepan and cook over a medium heat stirring until the mixture begins to boil. Remove from the heat and stir in the breakfast cereal and chopped peanuts until well blended. Spread the mixture into the baking tin. Press out evenly and chill for 1 hour in the refrigerator.

● Melt the chocolate in a small bowl set over a saucepan of simmering water and spread over the cookie base using a spatula. When set cut into squares and store in an airtight container.

TIP

All the cookies in this chapter will freeze for up to one month unless otherwise stated.

Lunch-box Crunchies

Preparation time: 20 minutes ● Cooking time: 15 minutes ● Makes: About 24

This is a small crunchy cookie, suitable for a lunch-box or picnic.

INGREDIENTS

175 g/6 oz plain flour
50 g/2 oz slightly salted butter, softened
50 g/2 oz light brown sugar
1 egg
75 g/3 oz plain chocolate, chopped

Pre-heat oven to 350°F/175°C/Gas mark 4. Grease two baking sheets or line with non-stick baking parchment.

● Sift the flour into a bowl. Beat together the butter and sugar in a separate bowl. Beat in the egg. Mix the sifted flour into the butter with the chocolate pieces.

● Mould the mixture into 24 pieces. Place on baking sheets and press the top lightly with a fork. Bake for 15 minutes. Leave to cool on the baking sheet. Store in an airtight container.

Chequerboards

Preparation time: 25 minutes ● *Cooking time: 15 to 20 minutes* ● *Makes: About 26*

These cookies are good fun to make and look great for children's parties.

INGREDIENTS

175 g/6 oz butter, softened

200 g/7 oz caster sugar

½ tsp vanilla essence

2 eggs

600 g/1¼ lb plain flour

2 tsp baking powder

1 tsp milk

1½ Tbsp unsweetened cocoa powder, sifted

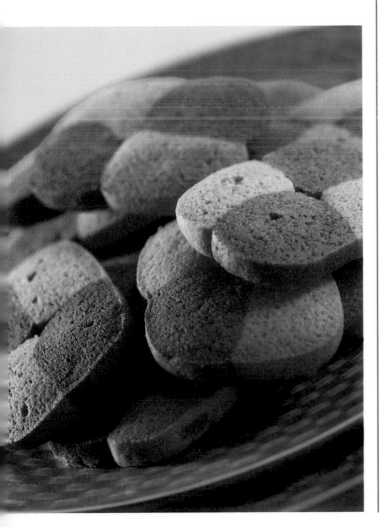

Divide the butter and sugar evenly between 2 bowls. For the vanilla dough, beat butter and sugar until light and fluffy. Beat in the vanilla essence and one egg. Sift half the flour and baking powder into the bowl. Blend in with a spoon and then work by hand to form a smooth dough.

● Make the chocolate dough in the same way with the remaining butter, sugar and egg, adding milk and sifted cocoa along with the remaining flour and baking powder. Divide each portion of dough into 4 equal pieces.

● On a floured surface roll each piece into a rope 30 cm/12 in long. Place a chocolate rope next to a vanilla one. Place a chocolate one on top of the vanilla rope and a vanilla one on top of the chocolate. Press firmly together to form a square. Wrap in clingfilm. Repeat with the remaining dough. Chill for 1 hour in the refrigerator.

● Pre-heat oven to 350°F/175°C/Gas mark 4. Grease two baking sheets or line with non-stick baking parchment.

● Cut dough into 26 slices and place onto the baking sheets. Bake for 15 to 20 minutes until lightly browned. Transfer to a wire rack to cool. Once completely cool, store in an airtight container.

Chocolate Crackle-Tops

Preparation time: 25 minutes + chilling ● *Cooking time: 10 to 15 minutes* ● *Makes: About 48*

A simple chocolate cookie which is easy to make and will become a family favourite.

INGREDIENTS

200 g/7 oz plain chocolate, chopped

50 g/2 oz slightly salted butter, softened

120 g/4 oz caster sugar

3 eggs

1 tsp vanilla essence

175 g/6 oz plain flour

25 g/1 oz unsweetened cocoa powder

½ tsp baking powder

175 g/6 oz icing sugar, for decoration

Heat the chocolate and butter in a saucepan over a low heat, stirring frequently. Remove from the heat and stir in the sugar. Continue stirring for 2 to 3 minutes until the sugar dissolves. Add the eggs one at a time, beating well. Add the vanilla essence.

● Sift the flour, cocoa, and baking powder into a bowl. Gradually stir into the chocolate mixture in batches, until just blended. Cover dough and refrigerate for 1 hour or until cold.

● Pre-heat oven to 325°F/160°C/Gas mark 3. Grease two baking sheets or line with non-stick baking parchment.

● Place the icing sugar in a small bowl. Using a teaspoon, scoop dough into small balls and between palms of hand, roll into 1-cm/½-in balls. Drop balls one at a time into icing sugar and roll until heavily coated. Remove ball with a slotted spoon and tap against the side of the bowl to remove excess sugar.

● Place the cookies on baking sheets spaced well apart. Bake for 10 to 15 minutes. Leave to cool on baking sheet for 3 minutes then remove to wire cooling rack. Eat within 2 days.

Oaty Jacks

Preparation time: 15 minutes ● Cooking time: 25 to 30 minutes ● Makes: 12

A perfect lunch-box treat or a substantial afternoon snack. Try dipping them in white chocolate too.

INGREDIENTS

120 g/4 oz slightly salted butter, softened
120 g/4 oz light brown sugar
200 g/7 oz rolled oats
175 g/6 oz plain chocolate

Pre-heat oven to 325°F/160°C/Gas mark 3. Grease or line a shallow 20 x 20-cm/8 x 8-in tin with non-stick baking parchment.

● Melt the butter over a medium heat in a saucepan, then transfer to a bowl. Stir in the sugar and rolled oats.

● Spoon the mixture into the baking tin and bake for 25 to 30 minutes. Leave to cool in the tin for 5 minutes, then cut into squares.

● Melt the chocolate in a bowl over a saucepan of simmering water. When the oaty jacks are cold, dip each piece into melted chocolate and leave to set on greaseproof paper. Once the chocolate is set, store the cookies in an airtight container.

Amaretti Drops

Preparation time: 25 minutes ● Cooking time: 12 to 15 minutes ● Makes: About 15

This cookie is light and crispy on the outside, chewy on the inside and ideal as after-dinner treat.

INGREDIENTS

50 g/2 oz amaretti cookies, crushed
1 Tbsp unsweetened cocoa powder
50 g/2 oz icing sugar
2 egg whites

Pre-heat oven to 350°F/170°C/Gas mark 4. Grease or line a large baking sheet with non-stick paper.

● Place the cookies in a food processor and process briefly to produce coarse crumbs. Place in a bowl and sift in the unsweetened cocoa powder. Stir to blend.

● In a medium bowl beat the egg whites until stiff peaks form. Gradually beat in the icing sugar a tablespoonful at a time. Then add the cookie mixture to the egg whites and fold the two together gently until just blended.

● Place rounded teaspoonfuls of the cookie mixture well apart on the prepared baking sheet and bake for 12 to 15 minutes. Cool the cookies on the baking sheet for about 10 minutes, then remove to a wire rack to cool completely. When cool, store cookies in an airtight container. Not suitable for freezing.

Apricot and Chocolate Cookies

Preparation time: 20 minutes ● *Cooking time: 12 minutes* ● *Makes: About 25*

A lovely chewy cookie with the unusual but delicious combination of chocolate and apricots.

INGREDIENTS

175 g/6 oz butter

120 g/4 oz light brown sugar

1 egg, beaten

175 g/6 oz plain flour

Pinch of salt

1 tsp baking powder

75 g/3 oz chopped ready-to-eat dried apricots

25 g/1 oz chocolate chips

Pre-heat oven to 350°F/175°C/Gas mark 4. Grease two baking sheets or line with non-stick baking parchment.

● Beat the butter and sugar together until smooth and soft. Beat in the egg until fluffy. Sift the flour with the salt and baking powder into the butter mixture. Mix together until thoroughly blended. Beat in the apricots and chocolate chips.

● Roll the mixture into small balls and place well apart on baking sheets. Flatten with the prongs of a fork. Bake for 12 to 14 minutes until golden-brown. While hot, ease off the baking sheets and cool on a wire rack. Once completely cool, store in an airtight container.

Spiced Rum Chocolate Cookies

Preparation time: 20 minutes ● Cooking time:
10 to 12 minutes ● Makes: About 18

A small, dark and spicy cookie which is strictly for the adults.

INGREDIENTS

50 g/2 oz light brown sugar
2 eggs, separated
175 g/6 oz plain flour
1 Tbsp unsweetened cocoa powder
1 tsp ground cinnamon
1 tsp allspice
225 g/8 oz caster sugar
Grated rind of ½ orange
2 Tbsp dark rum

Pre-heat oven to 375°F/190°C/Gas mark 5. Grease two baking sheets or line with non-stick baking parchment.

● Beat together the brown sugar with the egg yolks until light and fluffy. Sift the flour and spices together, then stir in until the mixture resembles breadcrumbs. Whisk the egg whites until they form stiff peaks and then beat in the caster sugar until glossy. Fold into the mixture with the grated orange rind.

● Roll the mixture into walnut-sized pieces, and place on the baking sheets. Bake for 10 to 15 minutes. Brush with rum while still warm, then use a metal spatula to transfer to a wire cooling rack to cool completely. Store in an airtight container.

Cherry Chocolate Dreams

Preparation time: 15 minutes ● Cooking time:
12 to 15 minutes ● Makes: About 15

A winning combination of cherries and chocolate.

INGREDIENTS

120 g/4 oz slightly salted butter, softened
50 g/2 oz caster sugar
½ tsp vanilla essence
150 g/5 oz plain flour, sifted
2 Tbsp finely chopped glacé cherries
2 Tbsp finely chopped plain chocolate,

Pre-heat oven to 375°F/190°C/Gas mark 5. Grease two baking sheets or line with non-stick baking parchment.

● Beat together the butter, sugar and vanilla essence until light and fluffy. Stir in the flour until well combined. Add the cherries and chocolate and mix until blended. Place teaspoonfuls of the mixture on baking sheets.

● Bake for 12 to 15 minutes until lightly golden. Leave to cool for 2 minutes before transferring onto a wire cooling rack. Once cool, store in an airtight container.

TIP

It is easier to chop glacé cherries if they have first been dipped in flour. Try using floured scissors instead of a knife.

Chocolate Pinwheels

Preparation time: 25 minutes + chilling ● *Cooking time: 8 to 10 minutes* ● *Makes: About 25*

A good, fun cookie, that is great for children's parties.

INGREDIENTS

120 g/4 oz slightly salted butter, softened
50 g/2 oz caster sugar
1 egg, beaten
1 tsp vanilla essence
150 g/5 oz plain flour
Pinch of salt
25 g/1 oz plain chocolate

In a large bowl beat together the butter and sugar until light and fluffy. Beat in the egg and vanilla essence until blended. Sift the flour and salt onto the mixture and beat briefly until combined.

● Divide the dough in half and wrap one half in clingfilm. Refrigerate until firm enough to roll. Melt the chocolate in a small bowl set over a saucepan of simmering water. Allow to cool slightly. Add the melted chocolate to remaining dough and mix until completely blended. Wrap chocolate dough in clingfilm and refrigerate until firm enough to roll.

● On a lightly floured surface or between 2 sheets of clingfilm, roll the vanilla dough to a rectangle. Repeat with the chocolate dough, rolling to the same size. If rolling between sheets of film, remove top sheet and place chocolate dough on top of plain dough. Roll up dough, from one short end as tightly as possible. Wrap tightly and refrigerate until very firm.

● Pre-heat oven to 375°F/190°C/Gas mark 5. Grease two baking sheets or line with non-stick baking parchment.

● Using a sharp knife, cut the dough roll into 5-mm/¼-in slices and place well apart onto the baking sheets. Bake for 7 to 10 minutes, until beginning to change colour at the edges. Transfer to a wire rack and once completely cool, store in an airtight container.

TIP

The initial beating together of the butter and sugar is best done using an electric mixer. Beat for between 1 and 2 minutes, until light and fluffy. Reduce the speed to low to add any dry ingredients.

Orange Chocolate Cookies

Preparation time: 20 minutes ● Cooking time: 20 minutes ● Makes: About 18

Orange and chocolate are such a good combination. Try these with a cup of coffee at any time of day.

INGREDIENTS

175 g/6 oz plain flour
¼ tsp baking powder
Pinch of salt
1 tsp grated orange rind
120 g/4 oz granulated sugar
50 g/2 oz light brown sugar
120 g/4 oz slightly salted butter, softened
1 egg
½ tsp orange liqueur, optional
120 g/4 oz plain chocolate, coarsely chopped

Pre-heat oven to 300°F/150°C/Gas mark 2. Grease two baking sheets or line with non-stick baking parchment.

● Sift the flour, baking powder and salt into a bowl. In a large bowl blend the orange rind, sugars and butter together until light and fluffy. Add the egg and orange liqueur if using and beat until light and well combined. Add the flour mixture and chopped chocolate. Mix together with a spoon to combine.

● Drop rounded tablespoons onto the baking sheet spaced 5 cm/2 in apart. Bake for 20 minutes until golden. Transfer cookies to a flat surface to cool completely. Once completely cool, store in an airtight container.

Mocha Chunk Cookies

Preparation time: 20 minutes ● Cooking time: 20 minutes ● Makes: About 16

A classic chunky style cookie with a rich coffee taste.

INGREDIENTS

150 g/5 oz plain flour
2 Tbsp unsweetened cocoa powder
¼ tsp baking soda
Pinch of salt
2 tsp instant coffee powder
1 tsp coffee liqueur, optional
120 g/4 oz caster sugar
50 g/2 oz dark brown sugar
120 g/4 oz slightly salted butter, softened
1 egg
175 g/6 oz plain chocolate, coarsely chopped

Pre-heat oven to 350°F/175°C/Gas mark 4. Grease 2 baking sheets or line with non-stick baking parchment.

● Into a medium-sized bowl, sift the flour, cocoa, baking soda and salt. In a small bowl dissolve coffee powder in coffee liqueur or hot water and set aside. In a large bowl, mix together the sugars. Add the butter and mix thoroughly until light. Add the eggs and coffee mixture and beat until smooth. Add the flour mixture and the chocolate chunks and mix gently with a spoon until well combined.

● Place rounded tablespoons of the mixture onto the baking sheets spaced 5 cm/2 in apart. Bake for 20 minutes until set. Transfer cookies to a flat surface to cool. Once completely cool, store in an airtight container.

Chocolate Chip and Raisin Cookies

Preparation time: 20 minutes ● Cooking time: 18 to 20 minutes ● Makes: About 18

A classic cookie which is moist, chewy and delicious.

INGREDIENTS

150 g/5 oz plain flour

¼ tsp baking powder

50 g/2 oz light brown sugar

120 g/4 oz caster sugar

120 g/4 oz slightly salted butter, softened

1 egg

1 tsp vanilla essence

150 g/5 oz raisins

120 g/4 oz plain chocolate chips

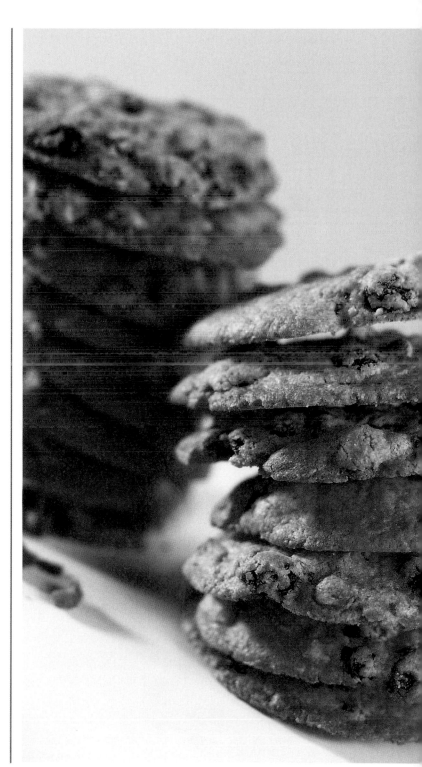

Pre-heat oven to 300°F/150°C/Gas mark 2. Grease two baking sheets or line with non-stick baking parchment.

● Combine the flour and baking powder in a medium-sized bowl. Place the sugars in a separate bowl, add the butter, then beat in the sugar until light and fluffy. Add the egg and vanilla essence and mix well. Add the flour mixture, raisins and chocolate and blend well with a spoon.

● Drop rounded tablespoons of the mixture onto the baking sheet spaced 5 cm/2 in apart. Bake for 18 to 20 minutes until lightly golden. Remove cookies to a cool flat surface to cool completely. Store in an airtight container.

Coconut and Chocolate Crunch

Preparation time: 20 minutes ● Cooking time: 20 minutes ● Makes: About 28

The coconut in these cookies makes them really moist and chewy. This makes a good lunch-box cookie.

INGREDIENTS

120 g/4 oz slightly salted butter, softened

5 Tbsp light brown sugar

1 egg, beaten

1 tsp vanilla essence

120 g/4 oz plain flour

½ tsp baking powder

Pinch of salt

75 g/3 oz shredded coconut

75 g/3 oz plain chocolate chips

200 g/7 oz hazelnuts, finely chopped

Pre-heat oven to 300°F/150°C/Gas mark 2. Grease two baking sheets or line with non-stick baking parchment.

● In a medium bowl beat together the butter and sugar. Beat in the egg and vanilla essence. Mix thoroughly until light and fluffy. Sift in the flour, baking powder and salt. Stir in the coconut, chocolate and chopped nuts. Mix well with a spoon to combine.

● Drop rounded tablespoons of the cookie dough (spaced well apart) onto the baking sheets. Bake the cookies for 20 minutes until lightly golden, then transfer to a wire rack to cool. Once completely cool, store in an airtight container.

White Chocolate Cashew Thins

Preparation time: 20 minutes ● Cooking time: 8 to 10 minutes ● Makes: About 30

These cookies are really thin and crunchy. Try eating them with ice cream.

INGREDIENTS

50 g/2 oz slightly salted butter, softened

50 g/2 oz light brown sugar

3 Tbsp golden syrup

120 g/4 oz finely chopped salted cashews

5 Tbsp plain flour

1 tsp vanilla essence

175 g/6 oz white chocolate, coarsely chopped

Pre-heat oven to 350°F/175°C/Gas mark 4. Grease two baking sheets or line with non-stick baking parchment.

● Melt the butter in a saucepan. Add the brown sugar and golden syrup, then bring to the boil stirring constantly for 3 to 4 minutes until the sugar dissolves. Remove from the heat. Stir in the cashews, flour and vanilla essence.

● Drop half-teaspoon mounds spaced well apart onto the baking sheet. Use the back of a spoon to spread each mound into a circle. Bake for 8 to 10 minutes or until golden-brown. Turn the baking sheet around halfway through cooking. Cool on the baking sheet for 1 minute, then transfer to a wire rack to cool completely.

● Melt the chocolate in a small bowl set over a saucepan of barely simmering water. Dip a fork into the melted chocolate and drizzle over the cookies. Return to cooling rack to set. Once set, store in an airtight container. Not suitable for freezing.

White Chocolate Chunk and Pecan Cookies

Preparation time: 20 minutes ● *Cooking time: 20 minutes* ● *Makes: About 26*

These cookies are really rich and chocolatey.

INGREDIENTS

250 g/9 oz plain flour, sifted

½ tsp baking powder

Pinch of salt

225 g/8 oz light brown sugar

120 g/4 oz caster sugar

175 g/6 oz butter, softened

2 eggs

1 tsp vanilla essence

225 g/8 oz pecan nuts, coarsely chopped

225 g/8 oz white chocolate, coarsely chopped

Pre-heat oven to 300°F/150°C/Gas mark 2. Grease two baking sheets or line with non-stick baking parchment.

● Sift the flour, baking powder and salt into a bowl. In a large bowl mix together the sugars and butter until well blended. Add the eggs and vanilla essence and beat until light and fluffy. Add the flour, pecans and white chocolate and mix together with a spoon until combined.

● Drop rounded tablespoons of the mixture onto the greased or lined baking sheets spaced about 5 cm/2 in apart. Bake the cookies for 20 minutes until golden-brown. Transfer to a flat surface to cool. Once completely cool, store in an airtight container.

Chocolate-dipped Macaroons

*Preparation time: 25 minutes + cooling ●
Cooking time: 12 minutes ● Makes: About 18*

These lovely little mounds of coconut dipped in chocolate make a great addition to a special afternoon tea.

INGREDIENTS

200 g/7 oz shredded coconut, unpacked
200 g/7 oz chopped blanched almonds
150 ml/5 fl oz sweetened condensed milk
1 tsp vanilla essence
2 egg whites
Pinch of salt
175 g/6 oz plain chocolate

Pre-heat oven to 350°F/175°C/Gas mark 4. Line two baking sheets with non-stick baking parchment and brush with oil.

● Place the coconut on one baking sheet and the almonds on another. Toast in the oven for 5 minutes, shaking frequently. Pour onto separate plates to cool.

● Place the condensed milk, vanilla essence, coconut and nuts in a large bowl and mix well to combine. Place the egg whites in a medium bowl and beat until foamy. Add the salt and continue beating until stiff peaks form. Fold egg whites into coconut mixture.

● Drop tablespoonfuls onto the baking sheets. Bake for 12 minutes, or until golden. Place baking sheets on wire racks to cool completely, then peel off the paper.

● Melt the chocolate in a small bowl set in a saucepan of barely simmering water. Dip macaroon bottoms into the melted chocolate then place on greaseproof paper to set. Store in an airtight container. Not suitable for freezing.

Muesli Chocolate Chip Cookies

*Preparation time: 20 minutes ● Cooking time: 15 to
20 minutes ● Makes: About 24*

Choose a muesli that contains your favourite ingredients. These cookies make a substantial lunch-box or picnic treat.

INGREDIENTS

225 g/8 oz plain flour
1 tsp ground cinnamon
2 tsp baking powder
½ tsp bicarbonate of soda
Pinch of salt
120 g/4 oz slightly salted butter, softened
50 g/2 oz caster sugar
50 ml/2 fl oz fresh orange juice
1 egg
150 g/5 oz unsweetened muesli
75 g/3 oz milk chocolate chips

Pre-heat oven to 275°F/140°C/Gas mark 1. Grease two baking sheets or line with non-stick baking parchment.

● Sift the flour, cinnamon, baking powder, bicarbonate and salt into a bowl. In a separate bowl, beat the butter and sugar together until light and fluffy. Gradually beat in the orange juice and egg. Stir in flour mixture and then the muesli and chocolate chips.

● Drop rounded tablespoonfuls spaced 5 cm/2 in apart onto the baking sheets. Flatten a little with the back of a spoon. Bake for 15 to 20 minutes until lightly browned. Cool on the baking sheet for a few minutes, then transfer to a wire rack. Once completely cool, store in an airtight container.

Chocolate Cream-filled Hearts

Preparation time: 40 minutes + chilling ● Cooking time: 12 to 15 minutes Makes: About 18

A special-occasion cookie with a delicious chocolate-fudge filling.

INGREDIENTS

175 g/6 oz slightly salted butter, softened

120 g/4 oz icing sugar

2 tsp vanilla essence

150 g/5 oz plain flour

FILLING

5 Tbsp double cream

50 g/2 oz plain chocolate chips

Beat the butter until soft and fluffy. Add the icing sugar and vanilla essence and beat until smooth. Stir in the flour. Gather dough into 2 balls and flatten into discs. Wrap in clingfilm. Refrigerate for 1 hour until firm.

● Pre-heat oven to 325°F/160°C/Gas mark 3. Grease two baking sheets or line with non-stick baking parchment.

● On a lightly floured surface, roll out the dough to 5 mm/¼ in thick. Cut out 5-cm/2-in hearts with a cutter. Repeat with all of the dough. Place the cookies on baking sheets spaced 2.5 cm/1 in apart. Bake for 12 to 15 minutes until firm. Transfer to a wire rack to cool.

● Place the cream in a small saucepan and warm briefly, add in the chocolate chips and stir until melted. Transfer to a small bowl. Set to one side and allow to cool at room temperature.

● To assemble, spread 1 teaspoon of the chocolate filling on the bottom side of half the cookies. Top with bottom side of another cookie to form a sandwich. Repeat with remaining cookies and cream. These cookies are best eaten soon after filling as they contain fresh cream; however, they may be stored for up to 2 days in an airtight container in the refrigerator.

Ultimate Chocolate Chip Cookies

Preparation time: 20 minutes ● *Cooking time: 18 to 20 minutes* ● *Makes: 10 to 12*

A huge cookie, the ultimate indulgence, packed with 3 types of chocolate. Make them as large as you dare.

INGREDIENTS

175 g/6 oz plain flour
½ tsp baking powder
Pinch of salt
120 g/4 oz slightly salted butter, softened
120 g/4 oz light brown sugar
½ Tbsp honey
1 egg
1 tsp vanilla essence
175 g/6 oz plain chocolate, chopped
75 g/3 oz milk chocolate, chopped
75 g/3 oz white chocolate, chopped

Pre-heat oven to 325°F/160°C/Gas mark 3. Grease two baking sheets or line with non-stick baking parchment.

● Sift the flour, baking powder and salt together into a bowl. Beat together the softened butter and light brown sugar until light and fluffy. Gradually beat in the egg, vanilla essence and honey. Stir in the flour mixture and all of the chocolate. Mix all the ingredients to combine.

● Drop about 2 tablespoonfuls of the dough spaced 5 to 8 cm/2 to 3 in apart on baking sheets. Bake the cookies for 18 to 22 minutes, depending on their size. Transfer them to a wire rack to cool. Once completely cool, store in an airtight container.

Chocolate Ginger Cookies

Preparation time: 25 minutes ● Cooking time: 18 to 20 minutes ● Makes: About 20

Ginger preserves give a lovely flavour without the harshness sometimes associated with ground ginger.

INGREDIENTS

120 g/4 oz dark brown sugar

50 g/2 oz granulated sugar

120 g/4 oz slightly salted butter, softened

1 egg

1 tsp ginger or golden syrup

175 g/6 oz plain flour

½ tsp baking powder

Pinch of salt

50 g/2 oz chocolate chips

3 Tbsp ginger preserves

Pre-heat oven to 300°F/150°C/Gas mark 2. Grease two baking sheets or line with non-stick baking parchment.

● In a large bowl blend the sugars together. Add the butter and beat together until light. Add the egg and ginger or golden syrup and mix well. Sift the flour, baking powder and salt into the mixture. Add the chocolate chips and ginger preserves and mix thoroughly with a spoon.

● Drop rounded tablespoons onto a baking sheet spaced 5 cm/2 in apart. Bake the cookies for 18 to 20 minutes or until golden-brown. Transfer cookies to a flat surface to allow to cool completely. Store in an airtight container.

Red, White and Blue Cookies

Preparation time: 20 minutes ● Cooking time: 8 to 10 minutes ● Makes: About 36

Dried sour cherries and blueberries make a lovely sweet-sour contrast to the sweet white chocolate.

INGREDIENTS

120 g/4 oz plain flour

3 Tbsp unsweetened cocoa powder

1 tsp baking powder

Pinch of salt

120 g/4 oz slightly salted butter, softened

225 g/8 oz granulated sugar

1 egg

½ tsp vanilla essence

120 g/4 oz white chocolate chips

50 g/2 oz chopped dried sour cherries

50 g/2 oz dried blueberries

Pre-heat oven to 350°F/175°C/Gas mark 4. Grease two baking sheets or line with non-stick baking parchment.

● Sift the flour, cocoa, baking powder and salt into a medium bowl. Beat together the butter and sugar in a large bowl until light and fluffy. Beat in the egg and vanilla essence until blended. Beat in the flour mixture at low speed until just combined. Stir in the chocolate chips, sour cherries and blueberries.

● Drop rounded teaspoonfuls of the dough onto the baking sheets. Bake for 8 to 10 minutes, until just firm. Transfer to a wire rack to cool. Once completely cool, store in airtight container.

Chocolate Refrigerator Cookies

Preparation time: 20 minutes + chilling ● *Cooking time: 10 to 12 minutes* ● *Makes: About 45 in all*

This dough enables you to bake fresh cookies whenever you want them.

INGREDIENTS

150 g/5 oz plain flour

1 tsp baking powder

120 g/4 oz slightly salted butter, softened

50 g/2 oz caster sugar

5 Tbsp finely grated plain chocolate

1 tsp vanilla essence

1 egg, beaten

Sift together the flour and baking powder. Blend in the butter using the fingertips until mixture resembles fine breadcrumbs. Add sugar and chocolate. Mix to form a dough with vanilla essence and beaten egg.

● Shape into a sausage. Transfer to a length of clingfilm. Wrap the film around dough and twist ends. Work backwards and forwards to form a roll about 5 cm/2 in in diameter. Refrigerate for one hour.

● When you are ready to make the cookies, pre-heat oven to 375°F/190°C/Gas mark 4. Grease two baking sheets or line with non-stick baking parchment.

● Cut very thin slices from the dough roll and place well apart onto the baking sheets. Bake for 10 to 12 minutes until pale gold. Cool on a wire cooling rack. The remaining roll can be returned to refrigerator and left for up to a week until required. Alternatively, freeze the dough for up to 1 month. Store the baked cookies in an airtight container.

TIP

A food processor can be used to blend the butter into the flour.

Chocolate and Orange Sandwiches

Preparation time: 45 minutes + chilling ● *Cooking time: 8 minutes* ● *Makes: About 25*

Orange cream is sandwiched between wafer cookies topped with melted chocolate.

INGREDIENTS

120 g/4 oz plain flour

5 Tbsp unsweetened cocoa powder

120 g/4 oz slightly salted butter, softened

50 g/2 oz caster sugar

1 egg

FILLING

120 ml/4 fl oz whipping cream

200 g/7 oz white chocolate, chopped

1 tsp orange essence or liqueur

TOPPING

150 g/5 oz plain chocolate

75 g/3 oz unsalted butter, chopped

Sift the flour and cocoa into a bowl. In a separate large bowl, beat the butter and sugar together until light and fluffy. Gradually beat in the egg until well combined; stir in the flour–cocoa mixture. Spoon the dough into a piece of clingfilm and shape into a flat disc. Wrap well and refrigerate for 2 hours or overnight until firm.

● Pre-heat oven to 350°F/175°C/Gas mark 4. Grease two baking sheets or line with non-stick baking parchment.

● On a lightly floured surface roll out half of the cookie dough as thin as possible. Using a 5-cm/2-in heart-shaped cutter, cut out as many cookies as possible. Re-roll and cut out trimmings. Bake the cookies for 6 to 8 minutes until set. Cool on a wire rack and then repeat the process with remaining dough.

● Place the whipping cream in a saucepan over a medium heat and bring to the boil. Remove from the heat and add the white chocolate, stirring constantly until melted and smooth. Stir in orange essence or liqueur and pour into a bowl. Cool until firm but not hard, about 1 hour.

● Beat the orange filling with a wooden spoon until smooth. Spread a little filling onto half the cookies and immediately cover with another cookie, pressing together very gently. Repeat with remaining cookies. Allow to set at room temperature.

● Melt the plain chocolate and butter in a small saucepan until smooth. Remove from the heat and cool until thickened slightly, about 20 to 30 minutes. Using a metal spatula, spread a small amount of chocolate onto the top of each cookie. Refrigerate until set. Once set, store in an airtight container in layers separated by greaseproof paper. These cookies are best eaten soon after filling as they contain fresh cream; however, they may be stored for up to 2 days in the refrigerator.

Chocolate-dipped Orange Shortbread

Preparation time: 30 minutes ● *Cooking time: 10 minutes* ● *Makes: About 35*

These elegant piped cookies make a great addition to a smart afternoon tea.

INGREDIENTS

250 g/9 oz plain flour
Pinch of salt
1 tsp baking powder
225 g/8 oz butter, softened
225 g/8 oz granulated sugar
1 egg
1 tsp grated orange rind
120 g/4 oz plain chocolate, chopped

Pre-heat oven to 350°F/175°C/Gas mark 4. Grease two baking sheets or line with non-stick baking parchment.

● Combine the flour, salt and baking powder in a bowl. Beat the butter and sugar in a large bowl until light and fluffy. Beat in the egg and orange rind. Fold in the flour until just combined.

● Spoon the mixture into a piping bag fitted with a large star nozzle. Pipe 4-cm/1½-in swirls, spaced 5 cm/2 in apart onto the baking sheets. Bake 10 to 12 minutes until just beginning to turn light gold around the edges. Transfer to a wire rack to cool completely.

● Melt the chocolate in a small bowl over a saucepan of barely simmering water. Dip the top of each cookie into the melted chocolate. Place cookies on a wire rack to set. Once cool, store in an airtight container.

Marble Cookies

Preparation time: 20 minutes ● *Cooking time: 18 minutes* ● *Makes: About 26*

A really unusual looking cookie with a rich velvety chocolate taste.

INGREDIENTS

250 g/9 oz plain flour

½ tsp baking powder

Pinch of salt

120 g/4 oz light brown sugar

120 g/4 oz granulated sugar

120 g/4 oz slightly salted butter, softened

1 egg

125 ml/4 fl oz soured cream

1 tsp vanilla essence

120 g/4 oz plain chocolate chips

Pre-heat oven to 300°F/150°C/Gas mark 2. Grease two baking sheets.

● Sift the flour, baking powder and salt into a bowl. Beat together the butter and sugars in a large bowl until well blended. Add the egg, soured cream and vanilla essence and beat until light and fluffy. Add the flour mixture and blend until just combined.

● Melt the chocolate chips in a bowl set over a saucepan of barely simmering water. Cool chocolate for a few minutes, then pour into the cookie mixture. Using a wooden spoon very lightly fold chocolate into the cookie mixture. Do not mix completely.

● Drop rounded tablespoonfuls of the mixture spaced 5 cm/2 in apart onto the baking sheets. Bake for 20 minutes. Transfer to a flat surface to cool. Once completely cool, store in an airtight container.

Sesame Chocolate Chewies

Preparation time: 20 minutes ●
Cooking time: 12 minutes ● Makes: About 12

A thin and crispy cookie great with ice cream.

INGREDIENTS

2 egg whites
175 g/6 oz icing sugar
3 Tbsp unsweetened cocoa powder
2 Tbsp plain flour
50 g/2 oz sesame seeds

Pre-heat oven to 350°F/175°C/Gas mark 4. Line a large baking sheet with non-stick baking parchment.

● Using an electric hand-mixer whisk the egg whites together until frothy. Add the sugar, cocoa and flour to the bowl. Beat slowly firstly to incorporate the ingredients, then increase the speed of the hand mixer and beat until the cookie mixture thickens. Carefully fold in the sesame seeds.

● Place tablespoonfuls of the cookie mixture about 2.5 cm/1 in apart on the baking sheet. Bake the cookies for 12 minutes. Using a spatula, transfer the cookies to a wire rack and leave to cool at room temperature. Once cool, store in an airtight container. Not suitable for freezing.

Chocolate Pistachio Cookies

Preparation time: 20 minutes ● Cooking time: 15 to 20 minutes ● Makes: About 12

Sweet pistachio nuts are lovely when combined with chocolate in this classic-style cookie.

INGREDIENTS

120 g/4 oz slightly salted butter, softened
50 g/2 oz caster sugar
½ tsp vanilla essence
120 g/4 oz plain flour
½ tsp baking powder
120 g/4 oz pistachio nuts, coarsely chopped
25 g/1 oz plain chocolate, chopped

Pre-heat oven to 375°F/190°C/Gas mark 5. Grease two baking sheets or line with non-stick baking parchment.

● Beat together the butter, sugar and vanilla essence until light and creamy. Stir in the flour and baking powder, and then mix well. Add nuts and chocolate and mix to combine.

● Drop rounded teaspoonfuls of the mixture 2.5 cm/1 in apart onto the baking sheets. Bake for 15 to 20 minutes. Leave to cool onto the baking sheet for 2 minutes. Transfer to a wire rack to cool completely. Once completely cool, store in an airtight container.

Chocolate Pockets

Preparation time: 45 minutes + chilling ● *Cooking time: 15 minutes* ● *Makes: About 12*

These little pastry pockets are filled with a melt-in-the-mouth creamy chocolate filling.

INGREDIENTS

175 g/6 oz slightly salted butter, softened
25 g/1 oz icing sugar
3 Tbsp light brown sugar
2 egg yolks
1 tsp vanilla essence
150 g/5 oz plain flour

FILLING

125 ml/4 fl oz double cream
120 g/4 oz plain chocolate chips

In a medium bowl, beat together the butter and sugars until well blended. Add the egg yolks and vanilla essence and beat well until light and fluffy. Add the flour and stir until combined. Gather into a ball and flatten to a disc. Place between 2 sheets of clingfilm and refrigerate for 1 hour.

● Meanwhile, heat the cream until just hot but not boiling. Remove pan from the heat and add the chocolate chips and stir well until melted.

● Pre-heat oven to 325°F/160°C/Gas mark 3. Grease two baking sheets or line with non-stick baking parchment.

● On a lightly floured surface, roll out half of the dough to 5 mm/¼ in thick. Cut out circles using a 5-cm/2-in round cutter. Place on baking sheets spaced 2.5 cm/ 1 in apart.

● Repeat with the remaining dough but set circles aside. Drop 1 teaspoon of the chocolate filling in the centre of each circle onto the baking sheet, and then top with another circle. Use a fork to press down and seal the edges of the pockets. Bake for 15 minutes or until golden-brown on the top. Transfer cookies with a spatula to a wire rack to cool. Once cool, store in an airtight container in a cool place. Not suitable for freezing.

Chocolate-frosted Heart Cookies

Preparation time: 1 hour + chilling ● *Cooking time: 8 to 10 minutes* ● *Makes: About 45*

Decorate these little cookies with sugar strands, sugar crystals, or silver and gold dragées, depending on the occasion.

INGREDIENTS

120 g/4 oz slightly salted butter, softened

50 g/2 oz brown sugar

3 Tbsp treacle

1 tsp ground ginger

1 tsp ground cinnamon

½ tsp ground cloves

1 tsp bicarbonate of soda

1 egg, beaten

450 g/1 lb plain flour

DECORATION

120 g/4 oz icing sugar

2 Tbsp unsweetened cocoa powder

1 egg white

Sugar strands or dragées to decorate

Pre-heat oven to 325°F/160°C/Gas mark 3. Grease two baking sheets or line with non-stick baking parchment.

● Cut the butter into pieces and place in a large bowl. Place the sugar, treacle and spices in a saucepan and bring to the boil. Add the bicarbonate and pour into the bowl with the butter. Stir until butter has melted, then stir in the egg. Sift in the flour and mix until thoroughly combined. Chill the dough until firm enough to roll out.

● Roll out on a lightly floured surface to 5 mm/¼ in thick. Cut into heart shapes with an 8-cm/3-in cutter. Place onto the baking sheets and bake in batches for 8 to 10 minutes. Transfer to a wire rack to cool completely.

● Sift the icing sugar and cocoa into a bowl. Beat in the egg white and continue beating until soft peak consistency is reached. Spoon the icing onto the cookies to cover then decorate with sugar strands or drageés. Return the cookies to wire rack to set. Once set, store in an airtight container.

Monkey Puzzles

Preparation time: 45 minutes ● Cooking time: 10 minutes ● Makes: About 14

The cookies are really rich and chocolatey, great with a cup of coffee.

INGREDIENTS

50 g/2 oz plain flour

1½ Tbsp unsweetened cocoa powder

¼ tsp baking powder

75 g/3 oz slightly salted butter, softened

6 Tbsp golden syrup

25 g/1 oz bran flakes, coarsely crushed

175 g/6 oz plain chocolate, roughly chopped

Pre-heat oven to 350°F/175°C/Gas mark 4. Grease two baking sheets or line with non-stick baking parchment.

● Sift the flour, cocoa and baking powder into a bowl. Beat together the butter and syrup until soft. Stir in the flour mixture until combined. Blend in the bran flakes.

● Place spoonfuls of the mixture spaced apart onto the baking sheets. Bake for 10 minutes. Transfer to a wire rack to cool.

● Melt the chocolate in a bowl set over a saucepan of barely simmering water. When the cookies are completely cold, spread spoonfuls of the melted chocolate over the surface of the cookies then return to the wire rack to allow the chocolate to set. Once set, store in an airtight container.

TIP

Decorate these cookies with white chocolate, if liked. Melt it as above and drizzle over the cookies.

Chocolate-dipped Cinnamon Meringues

Preparation time: 30 minutes + cooling ● Cooking time: 1 hour 15 minutes ● Makes: About 36

These delicate little meringues are easy to make and are great for a special occasion.

INGREDIENTS

2 egg whites
¼ tsp cream of tartar
Pinch of salt
120 g/4 oz caster sugar
½ tsp vanilla essence
3 Tbsp unsweetened cocoa powder
¼ tsp ground cinnamon
120 g/4 oz plain chocolate, roughly chopped

Pre-heat oven to 225°F/110°C/Gas mark ¼. Line two cookie sheets with foil.

● Beat the egg whites in a large mixing bowl with a hand-held electric mixer until foamy. Add the cream of tartar and salt and continue to beat until soft peaks form. Gradually beat in the sugar, 1 tablespoon at a time, then continue to beat until stiff.

● Gently fold in the vanilla essence, cocoa and cinnamon with a large spoon until just blended. Spoon the meringue mixture into a large piping bag fitted with a large star nozzle. Pipe into 8-cm/3-in lengths onto the baking sheets. Bake for 1 hour 15 minutes. Turn off oven and leave meringues in the oven to cool for 1½ hours or preferably overnight.

● Melt the chocolate in a bowl over a saucepan of barely simmering water. Gently peel the meringues away from the foil. Dip the tip of each meringue into the melted chocolate. Transfer the meringues to a wire rack and let stand until chocolate is set. Once set, store the meringues in an airtight container.

Chocolate Wafers

Preparation time: 20 minutes ● *Cooking time: 15 minutes* ● *Makes: About 28*

These nutty thins are great served with ice cream.

INGREDIENTS

120 g/4 oz slightly salted butter, softened

50 g/2 oz caster sugar

125 ml/4 fl oz golden syrup

1 egg

½ tsp vanilla essence

120 g/4 oz plain flour

1 Tbsp unsweetened cocoa powder

¼ tsp bicarbonate of soda

75 g/3 oz chopped mixed nuts

Pre-heat oven to 350°F/175°C/Gas mark 4. Line two baking sheets with non-stick baking parchment.

● Beat the butter, sugar and syrup together until light and fluffy. Thoroughly beat in the egg and vanilla essence. Sift the flour, cocoa and bicarbonate onto the butter mixture. Lightly stir into the mixture with the chopped mixed nuts.

● Place walnut-sized spoonfuls spaced 5 cm/2 in apart onto the baking sheets. Bake for 15 minutes. Lift from the baking sheet with a thin metal spatula and lay over a lightly oiled rolling pin to produce a curved shape. Leave to cool on the rolling pin for a few minutes before transferring to a wire rack to cool completely. Once completely cool, store in an airtight container.

Almond and Chocolate Clusters

Preparation time: 25 minutes ● *Cooking time: 15 minutes* ● *Makes: About 22*

A light nutty cookie which you can either dip in or drizzle with chocolate.

INGREDIENTS

120 g/4 oz slightly salted butter, softened

150 g/5 oz sugar

1 egg

½ tsp almond essence

50 g/2 oz ground almonds

120 g/4 oz flaked almonds

150 g/5 oz plain flour

TOPPING

50 ml/2 fl oz double cream

120 g/4 oz plain chocolate chips

2 tsp golden syrup

Pre-heat oven to 350°F/175°C/Gas mark 4. Grease two baking sheets or line with non-stick baking parchment.

● Beat together the butter and sugar until well blended. Add the egg and almond essence and beat until light and fluffy. Add the ground almonds and flour then stir until just combined. Form dough into walnut-sized balls and roll in the flaked almonds, pressing down slightly to coat each ball thoroughly.

● Place the balls onto the baking sheets spaced 5 cm/2 in apart. Bake for 15 minutes. Transfer cookies to a cool flat surface covered with greaseproof paper.

● Meanwhile, heat the cream, but do not allow to boil. Remove from the heat and stir in the chocolate chips and golden syrup. Cover and allow to stand for 10 minutes. Mix glaze gently with a wooden spoon until smooth.

● When cookies are cool, drizzle patterns on them with the warm chocolate or dip half of each cookie into the chocolate. Return the cookies to the greaseproof paper and place in the refrigerator until set. Once set, store in an airtight container. These cookies are best eaten soon after decorating as they contain fresh cream; however, they may be stored for up to 2 days in the refrigerator.

Hazelnut Chocolate Crescents

Preparation time: 30 minutes + chilling ● *Cooking time: 15 to 20 minutes* ● *Makes: 24*

These delicious nutty shortbread crescents can be dipped in or drizzled with chocolate.

INGREDIENTS

75 g/3 oz hazelnuts, unskinned

50 g/2 oz plain chocolate, coarsely chopped

4 Tbsp granulated sugar

120 g/4 oz plain flour

Pinch of salt

200 g/7 oz slightly salted butter

Pre-heat oven to 350°F/175°C/Gas mark 4. Spread the hazelnuts on a baking sheet. Toast for 12 to 15 minutes until lightly browned. Leave to cool completely.

● Melt half the chocolate in a small bowl over a saucepan of barely simmering water. Remove and set aside to cool.

● Process the nuts and 1 tablespoon of sugar in a food processor until fine, do not overprocess. Transfer to a medium bowl with the flour and salt. Beat the butter and remaining sugar until light and fluffy. Beat in the melted chocolate and the nut mixture and mix well to combine. Cover and refrigerate for 2 hours.

● Pre-heat oven to 350°F/175°C/Gas mark 4. Grease 2 baking sheets or line with non-stick baking parchment.

● Shape teaspoonfuls of the dough into crescents and place onto the baking sheets spaced 5 cm/2 in apart. Bake for 15 to 20 minutes. Transfer to a wire rack to cool completely.

● Melt the remaining chocolate in a bowl set over a saucepan of barely simmering water. Remove from the heat. Dip one end of the cookie into the chocolate or drizzle the surface with a thin stream of chocolate. Return to wire rack and allow chocolate to set. Once set, store the cookies in airtight containers. Not suitable for freezing.

Strawberry Cocoa Sandwich Stars

Preparation time: 1 hour + chilling ● *Cooking time: 8 to 10 minutes* ● *Makes: About 20*

This makes a lovely special-occasion cookie.

INGREDIENTS

200 g/7 oz plain flour

3 Tbsp unsweetened cocoa powder

1½ tsp baking powder

½ tsp ground cinnamon

Pinch of salt

175 g/6 oz lightly salted butter

120 g/4 oz caster sugar

50 g/2 oz light brown sugar

1 egg, beaten

2 tsp vanilla essence

Grated rind of 1 lemon

FILLING

225 g/8 oz strawberry jam

1 Tbsp lemon juice

1 Tbsp caster sugar

Icing sugar, for dusting

Sift the flour, cocoa, baking powder, cinnamon and salt. In a separate bowl, beat together the butter and sugars until light and creamy. Gradually beat in the egg, vanilla essence and lemon rind until well combined. Scrape the dough onto a piece of clingfilm, cover with another sheet and press the dough into a disc. Refrigerate until firm enough to roll.

● Grease two baking sheets or line with non-stick baking parchment.

● On a lightly floured surface roll out half of the dough to 3 mm/⅛ in thick. Refrigerate remaining dough. Using a 9-cm/3½-in star-shaped cutter, cut out an even number of cookies. Using a 2.5-cm/1-in or 4-cm/1½-in star-shaped cutter, cut out the centre of half of the cookies. Arrange cookies on baking sheets spaced 2.5 cm/1 in apart. Cover and refrigerate for 15 minutes.

● Pre-heat oven to 350°F/175°C/Gas mark 4.

● Bake cookies for 8 to 10 minutes. Cool onto the baking sheets for a couple of minutes then transfer to wire rack to cool completely. Repeat with remaining dough.

● Place the strawberry jam, sugar and lemon juice in a small pan. Heat gently until runny. Sieve into a small bowl and allow to cool. Spread about 1 teaspoon of the strawberry mixture on each whole biscuit star to within 1 cm/½ in of the edge. Arrange cut out biscuit stars on a wire cooling rack. Dust liberally with icing sugar. Carefully place cut out tops over whole stars, gently pressing together. Allow cookies to set for 1 hour at room temperature. Once set, store in an airtight container. Not suitable for freezing.

Chocolate and Chilli Cookies

Preparation time: 20 minutes ● Cooking time: 10 to 12 minutes ● Makes: About 20

An unusual but fantastic combination.

INGREDIENTS

120 g/4 oz butter
25 g/1 oz caster sugar
50 g/2 oz dark brown sugar
1 egg, beaten
½ tsp vanilla essence
120 g/4 oz plain flour
½ tsp baking powder
½ to 1 tsp dried chilli flakes
75 g/3 oz plain chocolate chips

Pre-heat oven to 350°F/175°C/Gas mark 4. Grease two baking sheets or line with non-stick baking parchment.

● Beat the butter and sugar together in a medium bowl, until light and fluffy. Gradually add the egg and vanilla essence and beat well. Stir the flour, baking powder and chilli flakes into the butter mixture and mix well to combine. Stir in the chocolate chips.

● Drop teaspoonfuls spaced 2.5 cm/1 in apart onto the baking sheets. Bake for 10 to 12 minutes. Remove with a spatula and place on a flat surface to cool. Once completely cool, store cookies in an airtight container.

Chocolate Viennese Whirls

Preparation time: 25 minutes ● Cooking time: 20 minutes ● Makes: About 20

A rich and attractive cookie, great for a smart afternoon tea party.

INGREDIENTS

175 g/6 oz butter
50 g/2 oz icing sugar
175 g/6 oz plain flour
½ tsp vanilla essence
10 glacé cherries, halved
175 g/6 oz plain chocolate, coarsely chopped

Pre-heat oven to 325°F/160°C/Gas mark 3. Grease two baking sheets or line with non-stick baking parchment.

● Beat together the butter and sugar until light and fluffy. Sift the flour into the bowl, add the vanilla and mix well to combine.

● Spoon the mixture into a piping bag fitted with a large star-shaped nozzle. Pipe flat whirls onto the baking sheets. Put half a cherry on each one. Bake for 20 minutes until just golden. Leave to cool onto the baking sheet for 5 minutes then transfer to a wire rack to cool completely.

● Meanwhile, melt the chocolate in a small bowl set over a saucepan of simmering water. When the cookies are cold, dip into the melted chocolate. Return to the wire rack until the chocolate has completely set, then store in an airtight container.

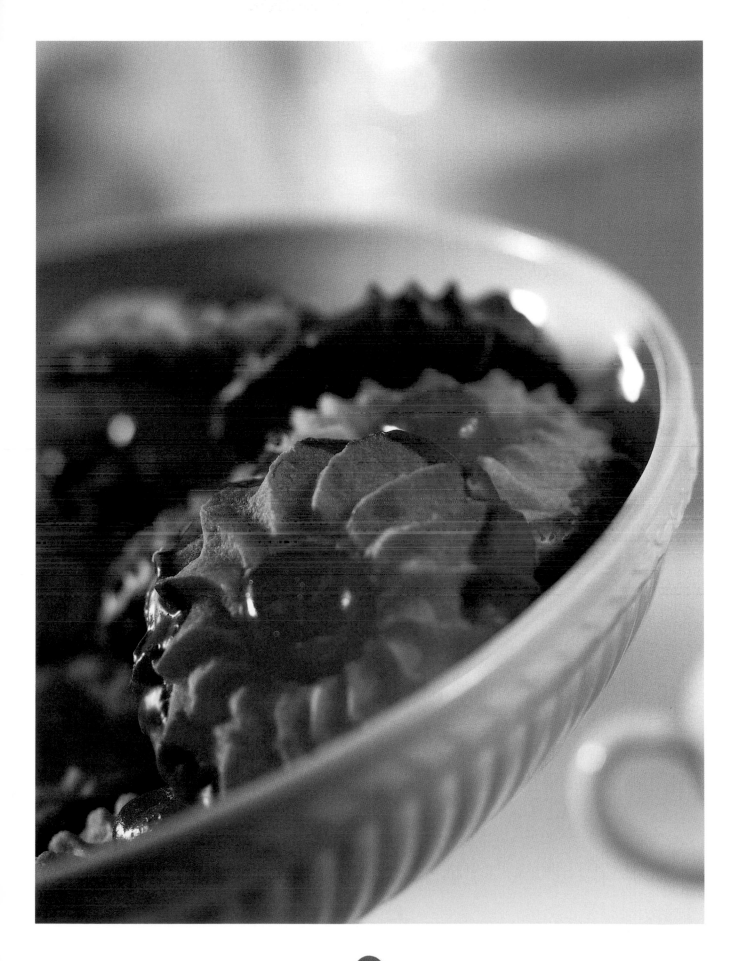

Crunchy Chocolate Chip Cookies

Preparation time: 15 minutes ● Cooking time: 10 to 12 minutes ● Makes: About 20

A cookie jar classic with a twist, crisp on the outside and chewy on the inside.

INGREDIENTS

120 g/4 oz slightly salted butter, softened

50 g/2 oz caster sugar

5 Tbsp dark brown sugar

1 egg, beaten

½ tsp vanilla essence

120 g/4 oz plain flour

½ tsp baking powder

175 g/6 oz chocolate bar containing crisped rice, chopped

Pre-heat oven to 350°F/175°C/Gas mark 4. Grease two baking sheets or line with non-stick baking parchment.

● Beat the butter and sugar together in a medium bowl, until light and fluffy. Gradually add the egg and vanilla essence and beat well. Stir the flour and baking powder into the butter mixture and mix well to combine. Stir in the chocolate chunks.

● Drop teaspoons spaced 2.5 cm/1 in apart onto the baking sheets. Bake for 10 to 12 minutes. Remove with a spatula and place on a flat surface to cool. Once completely cool, store cookies in an airtight container.

TIP

Other flavoured chocolates could be substituted. Dark chocolate orange is particularly good, so is rum and raisin, and mint-flavoured chocolates that contain small pieces of crunchy mint are great too. The chunks should be left quite large to get the maximum effect from their flavours.

Raspberry and White Chocolate Cookies

Preparation time: 20 minutes ● *Cooking time: 20 minutes* ● *Makes: About 16*

A sweet and fruity cookie, great served with vanilla ice cream.

INGREDIENTS

175 g/6 oz plain flour

¼ tsp bicarbonate of soda

Pinch of salt

75 g/3 oz caster sugar

120 g/4 oz slightly salted butter, softened

1 Tbsp beaten egg

5 Tbsp sieved raspberry jam

175 g/6 oz white chocolate, coarsely chopped

Pre-heat oven to 300°F/150°C/Gas mark 2. Grease two baking sheets.

● Sift the flour, baking soda and salt and set aside. Beat together the sugar and butter until light and fluffy. Beat in the egg and then the raspberry jam. Add the flour mixture and white chocolate chunks and mix to combine.

● Drop tablespoonfuls onto the baking sheets spaced 5 cm/2 in apart. Bake for 20 minutes. Transfer to a cool surface. When cold, store in an airtight container.

Chocolate Fudge Cookies

Preparation time: 20 minutes ● *Cooking time: 18 to 20 minutes* ● *Makes: About 28*

These cookies have a pure chocolate taste and a really smooth texture.

INGREDIENTS

175 g/6 oz plain chocolate, finely chopped

175 g/6 oz plain flour

3 Tbsp unsweetened cocoa powder

½ tsp baking powder

Pinch of salt

120 g/4 oz slightly salted butter, softened

225 g/8 oz dark brown sugar

2 eggs

1 tsp vanilla essence

75 g/3 oz white chocolate, coarsely chopped

Pre-heat oven to 300°F/150°C/Gas mark 2. Grease two baking sheets.

● Melt the chocolate in a bowl set over a saucepan of simmering water. Set aside to cool slightly.

● Sift the flour, cocoa, bicarbonate and salt and set aside. In a separate bowl, beat the butter and sugar together until light and fluffy. Beat in the eggs and vanilla essence until well blended. Mix in the cooled chocolate and fold in the flour until just combined.

● Drop rounded tablespoonfuls of the dough spaced 5 cm/2 in apart onto the baking sheet. Bake for 18 to 20 minutes. Cool the cookies on the sheet for one minute then transfer to a wire rack to cool completely.

● Melt the white chocolate as above. Dip a fork into the melted chocolate and drizzle over the cookies. Leave to set and store in an airtight container.

Chocolate Mint Cookies

Preparation time: 20 minutes ● *Cooking time: 20 minutes* ● *Makes: About 18*

A nice cookie to enjoy after dinner.

INGREDIENTS

175 g/6 oz plain flour

¼ tsp baking powder

Pinch of salt

3 Tbsp unsweetened cocoa powder

5 Tbsp light brown sugar

3 Tbsp granulated sugar

120 g/4 oz slightly salted butter, softened

1 egg

1 tsp peppermint essence

⅔ cup semi-sweet chocolate chips

Pre-heat oven to 300°F/150°C/Gas mark 2. Grease two baking sheets or line with non-stick baking parchment.

● Sift the flour, baking powder, salt and cocoa into a bowl and set aside. In a separate bowl, beat together the sugars and butter until light. Beat in the eggs and peppermint essence until thoroughly blended. Add the flour mixture and chocolate chips, mix well to combine. Do not over-mix.

● Drop rounded tablespoonfuls of the mixture onto the baking sheets spaced 4 cm/1½ in apart. Bake 20 minutes apart. Bake 20 minutes until lightly golden. Transfer to a cool flat surface. When completely cool, store in an airtight container.

Chocolate Rugelach

Preparation time: 45 minutes + chilling ● *Cooking time: 20 minutes* ● *Makes: About 60*

A traditional Jewish cookie much loved by children.

INGREDIENTS

225 g/8 oz strong white flour

Pinch of salt

120 g/4 oz slightly salted butter, softened

120 g/4 oz cream cheese

50 ml/2 fl oz soured cream

3 Tbsp caster sugar

1 egg, separated

150 g/5 oz apricot jam

75 g/3 oz plain chocolate, finely chopped

2 Tbsp caster sugar

Sift the flour and salt into a large bowl. Place the flour with the butter, cream cheese, soured cream, sugar and egg yolk in a food processor. Process until a soft dough forms. Shape dough into a ball and flatten into a disc. Wrap in clingfilm and refrigerate for 1 to 2 hours.

● Pre-heat oven to 350°F/175°C/Gas mark 4. Grease two baking sheets or line with non-stick baking parchment.

● On a lightly floured surface roll out one quarter of the dough to 3 mm/⅛ in thick. Using a plate as a guide, cut the dough into a 25- to 28-cm/10- to 11-in round. Spread with 3 tablespoons of apricot jam, leaving a small border around the edge. Sprinkle with the chopped chocolate.

● Cut this round into 12 equal-sized wedges. Starting the widest end, roll up each wedge like a Swiss roll. Place on the baking sheet spaced 2.5 cm/1 in apart. Beat the egg white with 1 tablespoon of water, and brush each roll with a little of the egg and water. Sprinkle each roll with a little sugar. Repeat with remaining dough.

● Bake until puffed and golden-brown. Turn the baking sheet around halfway through cooking. Cool onto the baking sheet for a few minutes then transfer to a wire cooling rack to cool completely.

Chocolate Crescents

Preparation time: 20 minutes ● Cooking time: 15 minutes ● Makes: About 30

Dusted with plenty of sugar, these make a great cookie.

INGREDIENTS

225 g/8 oz plain flour
3 Tbsp unsweetened cocoa powder
120 g/4 oz slightly salted butter, softened
200 g/7 oz caster sugar
1 tsp vanilla essence
1 egg
Icing sugar, for decorating

Pre-heat oven to 325°F/160°C/Gas mark 3. Grease two baking sheets or line with non-stick baking parchment.

● Combine the flour and cocoa in a small bowl. In a medium bowl, beat together the butter and sugar until creamy. Add the vanilla and egg and beat well until light and fluffy. Fold in the flour–cocoa mixture until just blended.

● Shape a tablespoonful of the mixture into an 8-cm/3-in long log. Bend into a crescent shape. Repeat with remaining dough. Place onto the baking sheets, spaced 2.5 cm/1 in apart. Bake for 15 minutes. Cool onto the baking sheet and then transfer to a wire rack. While still warm, roll the cookies in icing sugar to coat. Once completely cool, store in an airtight container. Freeze for up to 1 month without the icing sugar.

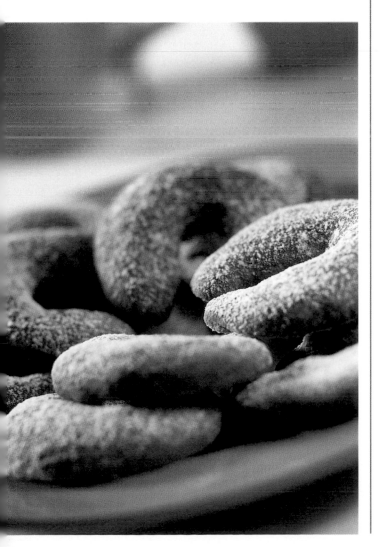

Children's Cookies

This part of the book has some creative ideas to make your snacks a bit more fun and they have all been specially written for children to make. Some of them are ideal to take in lunch boxes, like the cheesy ones, for example. Others are more for parties, such as the Chocolate Octopuses or the Snakes, and some are for when you just feel hungry.

I like making cookies because they are quick and easy, and most people eat them. If I make a batch of cookies on Monday I know that they will be gone by Friday. They are great to share – sometimes I take some Chocolate Chip Cookies to school and give them to my friends. I made cookies for the teachers at Christmas too and put them in pretty china bowls.

If you are quite slow at cooking (like me) or you don't have an electric mixer, then do not pre-heat the oven immediately – wait for a bit! Good Luck.

Katherine Gray, aged 11.

After-school Snacks

Cookies for Special Friends

Birthday Parties

Lunch-Box Favourites

Alphabet Cookies

Preparation time: 30 minutes ●
Cooking time: 20 minutes ● *Makes: 25*

These cookies have a full lemon flavour which melts in the mouth.

INGREDIENTS

50 g/2 oz butter, softened

5 Tbsp caster sugar

1 egg yolk

175 g/6 oz plain flour, sifted

½ tsp baking powder

2 Tbsp lemon juice

Grated rind of ½ lemon

1 Tbsp milk

Icing sugar, for dredging

Pre-heat oven to 325°F/160°C/Gas mark 3. Grease two baking sheets or line with non-stick baking parchment.

● In a mixing bowl, beat together the butter and caster sugar until pale and fluffy, add the egg yolk, flour, baking powder, lemon juice and lemon rind, then blend together.

● Add the milk and mix to a firm dough using your hands so that the dough comes together in a soft ball. Turn the dough out on to a lightly floured work surface and divide into about 25 equal-sized pieces. Roll each piece into a sausage shape with your hands and make letters of the alphabet, twisting the dough and trimming with a small knife if needed.

● Place the cookies on to the baking sheets and bake for 15 to 20 minutes. Lift them on to a wire rack to cool completely before dusting with icing sugar. Store in an airtight container for up to 1 week.

Teddy Bear Cookies

Preparation time: 35 minutes ●
Cooking time: 10 to 12 minutes ● *Makes: 26*

These cookies are made with a spicy dough, you can use any other similar-sized cutter if you like.

INGREDIENTS

175 g/6 oz plain flour, sifted

½ tsp baking powder

1 tsp ground ginger

½ tsp ground cinnamon

120 g/4 oz icing sugar

150 g/5 oz butter, cut into small pieces

½ tsp vanilla essence

1 Tbsp water

DECORATION

120 g/4 oz icing sugar

1 Tbsp water

Pre-heat oven to 375°F/190°C/Gas mark 5. Grease several baking sheets or line with non-stick baking parchment.

● Place the flour, baking powder, ground ginger, ground cinnamon and icing sugar in a bowl and combine. Blend in the butter using your fingertips, add the vanilla essence and 1 Tbsp cold water and, using your hands, bring together in a soft ball.

● Roll out the dough to about 5 mm/¼ in thick. Using an 8-cm/3-in teddy bear cutter, stamp out shapes and lift them on to the baking sheets, spacing well apart. Gather up the remaining dough and roll it out again and cut into more shapes. Bake for 10 to 12 minutes or until evenly golden. Transfer to a wire rack to cool.

● To decorate, mix the icing sugar with sufficient cold water to form a thin icing. Using a piping bag, pipe on the faces and patterns.

Balloon Cookies

Preparation time: 40 minutes + chilling ● Cooking time: 20 minutes ● Makes: 16

These cookies are thick and crunchy, and you can really taste the coconut and orange flavours.

INGREDIENTS

50 g/2 oz butter, softened

120 g/4 oz caster sugar

1 egg, beaten

250 g/9 oz self-raising flour

75 g/3 oz sweetened flaked coconut

Grated rind of 1 orange

DECORATION

120 g/4 oz icing sugar, sifted

1 Tbsp water

Food colourings

Coloured ribbon

In a mixing bowl beat together the butter and sugar until pale and fluffy. Beat in the egg, sift in the flour and add the coconut and orange rind. Mix all the ingredients together with your hands, until they come together in a soft ball. Chill the dough in clingfilm in the refrigerator for 30 minutes.

● Pre-heat oven to 325°F/160°C/Gas mark 3. Grease two baking sheets or line with non-stick baking parchment.

● On a lightly floured working surface, roll out the dough. Keep the dough quite thick when rolling out, if cracks appear gather up the dough, sprinkle more flour on the work surface and try again. Using a 6-cm/2½-in round cutter, cut out the cookies and lift on to the baking sheets. Using a metal skewer, make a hole at the top of each cookie for the ribbon. Bake the cookies for 15 to 20 minutes or until lightly golden. As soon as they come out of the oven re-shape the holes with a skewer. Lift them on to a wire rack to cool.

● To decorate the cookies, mix the icing sugar with sufficient water to form a thin icing. Divide into four bowls and colour each one using a few drops of food colouring. Spread different colours onto each cookie and when the icing has set, tie ribbons through the holes.

Big White Chocolate and Apricot Cookies

Preparation time: 5 minutes ● Cooking time: 12 to 15 minutes ● Makes: 12

These chewy cookies contain pieces of apricot that give a really juicy texture as well as pieces of chocolate.

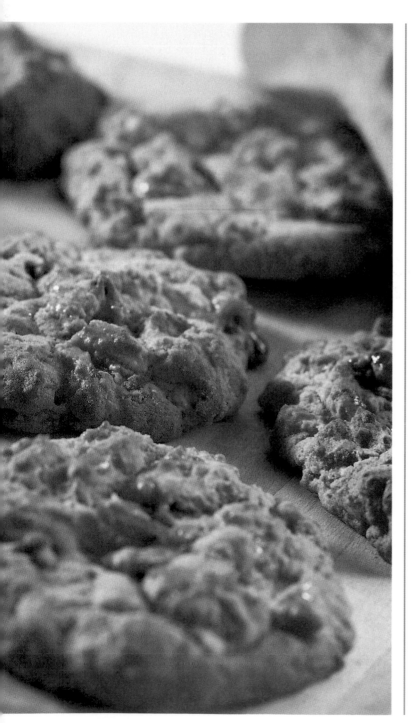

INGREDIENTS

120 g/4 oz butter, softened

120 g/4 oz light brown sugar

1 egg, beaten

200 g/7 oz self-raising flour

75 g/3 oz white chocolate chips, or white chocolate, chopped

50 g/2 oz milk or plain chocolate chips

50 g/2 oz dried apricots, chopped

Pre-heat oven to 375°F/190°C/Gas mark 5. Grease two baking sheets or line with non-stick baking parchment.

● In a mixing bowl, beat together the butter and sugar until light and fluffy. Beat in the egg. Sift in the flour, both types of chocolate chips and apricots, then stir everything together, until evenly mixed.

● Place mounds of the mixture onto the baking sheets, spaced well apart to allow for spreading. Bake the cookies for 12 to 15 minutes or until golden-brown. Lift onto wire racks to cool. These cookies are best eaten on the day they are baked, but once the cookies are completely cold, they may be stored in an airtight container.

Sunflower Cookies

Preparation time: 35 minutes ● *Cooking time: 15 to 20 minutes* ● *Makes: 10*

These happy sunflowers will brighten up your day. The cookies taste great too, with crunchy sunflower seeds mixed into the cookie dough.

INGREDIENTS

75 g/3 oz butter, softened

5 Tbsp caster sugar

120 g/4 oz plain flour, sifted

1 egg, beaten

3 Tbsp sunflower seeds

2 Tbsp lemon juice

DECORATION

6 Tbsp icing sugar, sifted

4 tsp water

Yellow and orange food colourings

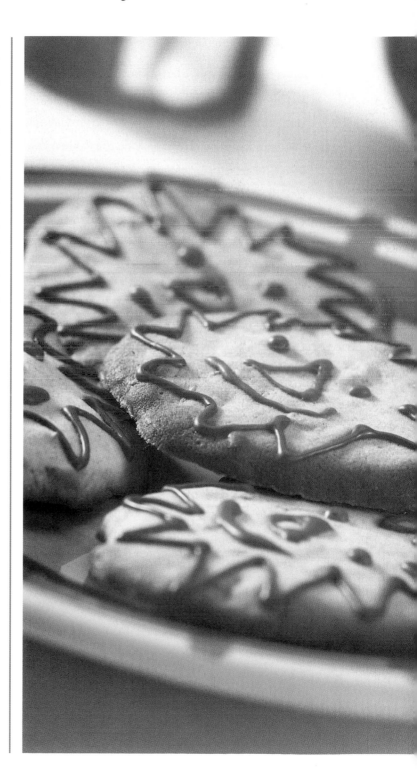

Pre-heat oven to 350°F/175°C/Gas mark 4. Grease several baking sheets or line with non-stick baking parchment.

● In a mixing bowl beat together the butter and sugar until pale and fluffy. Add the flour, then the egg, sunflower seeds and lemon juice and mix everything together to combine.

● Using two teaspoons, place mounds of dough on the baking sheet about 10 cm/4 in apart to allow for the cookies to spread, and flatten slightly with a wet knife. Bake the cookies for 15 to 20 minutes or until lightly golden around the edges. Lift them on to a wire rack to cool. If your rounds are not even after cooking, don't worry, they will still make good faces.

● To decorate the sunflowers, mix the icing sugar with sufficient cold water to form a thin icing, colour half yellow and half orange. Using piping bags, pipe on a happy face and then pipe a pattern around each face.

205

Tutti Frutti Faces

Preparation time: 35 minutes ● *Cooking time: 15 minutes* ● *Makes: 10*

Adding glacé cherries to this recipe makes these cookies really tasty as well as pretty.

INGREDIENTS

50 g/2 oz soft tub margarine

75 g/3 oz caster sugar

1 egg, beaten

200 g/7 oz plain flour, sifted

50 g/2 oz multi-coloured glacé cherries, chopped

DECORATION

5 Tbsp icing sugar, sifted

3–4 tsp water

Food colourings

Pre-heat oven to 350°F/175°C/Gas mark 4. Grease several baking sheets or line with non-stick baking parchment.

● In a mixing bowl beat together the margarine and sugar until pale and fluffy. Beat in the egg. Stir in the flour and chopped cherries and mix everything together. Use your hands to bring the dough together to form a soft ball.

● Turn the dough out onto a lightly floured work surface and roll out to 5 mm/¼ in. Using a large 9-cm/3½-in round cutter, cut out your shapes. Gather up the left-over dough, roll it out again and cut out more shapes and lift the cookies onto the baking sheets. Bake the cookies for 15 minutes or until golden. Lift them onto a wire rack to cool.

● To decorate the faces, mix the icing sugar with 3 to 4 teaspoons of cold water to make a thin icing. Divide the icing into three bowls and colour one blue, one pink and one yellow. Fill piping bags with the icing and pipe carefully onto the cookies to make different faces.

Wholesome Hearts

Preparation time: 25 minutes ● Cooking time: 20 minutes ● Makes: 10 Large cookies

These cookies are full of good things, so no extra icing is needed.

INGREDIENTS

120 g/4 oz butter, softened

120 g/4 oz caster sugar

1 egg, beaten

1 tsp vanilla essence

225 g/8 oz self-raising flour, sifted

150 g/5 oz rolled oats

50 g/2 oz sweetened flaked coconut, plus 2 Tbsp extra for sprinkling

Pre-heat oven to 350°F/175°C/Gas mark 4. Grease several baking sheets or line with non-stick baking parchment.

● In a mixing bowl, beat together the butter and sugar until pale and fluffy. Beat in the egg with the vanilla essence, followed by the flour. Mix well. Stir in the rolled oats and 50 g/2 oz coconut and knead the mixture with your hands to form a soft ball.

● Turn the dough out onto a lightly floured work surface and roll out to 5 mm/¼ in thick. Using a heart cutter, cut out your shapes and lift the cookies onto the baking sheets. Gather up the left-over dough, roll it out again, and cut more shapes. Sprinkle each with the remaining coconut. Bake for 20 minutes or until lightly golden. Lift them on to a wire rack to cool.

Apple Cookies

Preparation time: 35 minutes + chilling ●
Cooking time: 18 to 20 minutes ● *Makes: 10*

**Using apple sauce in these cookies creates a smooth
texture as well as sweetness.**

INGREDIENTS

225 g/8 oz plain all-purpose flour, sifted

75 g/3 oz icing sugar

150 g/5 oz butter, cut into small pieces

3 Tbsp apple sauce

DECORATION

7 Tbsp icing sugar

3 tsp cold water

Green food colouring

Place the flour and icing sugar in a mixing bowl and
blend in the butter using your fingertips until the
mixture resembles fine breadcrumbs. Add the apple
sauce and bring the mixture together in a soft ball. Wrap in
clingfilm and chill in the refrigerator for 30 minutes.

● Pre-heat oven to 350°F/175°C/Gas mark 4. Grease
several baking sheets or line with non-stick baking
parchment.

● On a lightly floured surface, roll out the dough to
about 5 mm/¼ in thick. Using a 9-cm/3½-in cutter,
stamp out rounds and lift onto the baking sheets. Roll
out the remaining dough again and cut out more shapes.
Roll the trimmings into sausage shapes and attach these
to the top of the circles to look like stalks.

● Bake the cookies for about 18 to 20 minutes or until
golden at the edges. Transfer to a wire rack.

● To decorate, mix the icing sugar with water to form a
thin icing, and add a few drops of colouring. Using a
piping bag, decorate each apple with eyes and mouths.

Butterflies

Preparation time: 25 minutes + chilling ●
Cooking time: 15 minutes ● *Makes: 20*

**These cookies are made by mixing melted chocolate
through the dough, creating a marbled effect.**

INGREDIENTS

75 g/3 oz milk chocolate, broken into pieces

120 g/4 oz butter, softened

120 g/4 oz caster sugar

1 egg, beaten

175 g/6 oz plain flour, sifted

Icing sugar, for dusting

Ask an adult to help you place a saucepan of water
to boil on the hob. When the water is simmering,
place the chocolate in a heatproof bowl on top of the
saucepan, gently melt the chocolate, stirring until
smooth. Remove from the heat and allow to cool.

● In a mixing bowl, beat together the butter and sugar
until light and fluffy. Beat in the egg. Stir in the flour
and combine all the ingredients to form a soft ball. Add
the chocolate and gently stir through to give a marbled
effect. Wrap the dough in clingfilm and chill in the
refrigerator for 30 minutes.

● Pre-heat oven to 350°F/175°C/Gas mark 4. Grease
several baking sheets or line with non-stick baking
parchment.

● On a lightly floured surface, roll out the dough to
about 5 mm/¼ in. Using an 8-cm/3-in butterfly cutter,
stamp out shapes and lift onto the baking sheets. Roll
out the remaining dough again and cut out more shapes.

● Bake the cookies for 15 minutes or until evenly
golden-brown. Transfer to a wire rack to cool. Just
before eating dust with icing sugar.

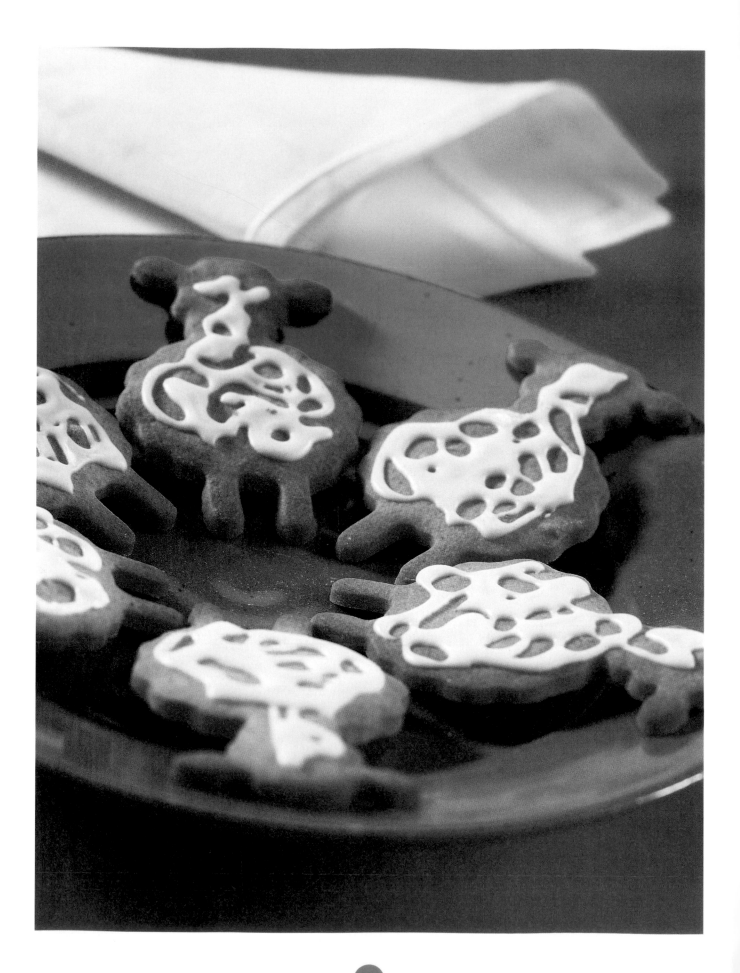

212

Wiggly Sheep

Preparation time: 30 minutes ● Cooking time: 15 minutes ● Makes: 18

This lemon shortbread is delicious, so bake double the quantity!

INGREDIENTS

150 g/5 oz butter, softened

75 g/3 oz icing sugar

225 g/8 oz plain flour, sifted

Grated rind of 1 lemon

1 Tbsp milk

DECORATION

5 Tbsp sugar, sifted

3–4 tsp water

Pre-heat oven to 350°F/175°C/Gas mark 4. Grease several baking sheets or line with non-stick baking parchment.

● In a mixing bowl beat together the butter and icing sugar until pale and fluffy. Stir in the flour, then add the lemon rind and milk. Mix everything together to form a soft dough using your hands.

● On a lightly floured work surface, roll out the dough to 5 mm/¼-in. Using your cutter, cut out your shapes and lift the cookies onto the baking sheets. Gather up the left-over dough, roll it out again and cut out more shapes. Bake the cookies for 15 minutes or until lightly golden. Lift them on to a wire rack to cool.

● To decorate the sheep, mix the icing sugar with sufficient cold water to make a thin icing. Fill a piping bag with the icing and pipe it in a wiggly pattern, onto the body of the sheep.

Ice-cream Cone Cookie

Preparation time: 40 minutes ● Cooking time: 15 minutes ● Makes: 18

Decorate these cookies with your favourite coloured icing to look like real ice-cream cones with different toppings!

INGREDIENTS

175 g/6 oz plain flour, sifted

120 g/4 oz butter, cut into small pieces

120 g/4 oz caster sugar

50 g/2 oz dried apricots, chopped

Grated rind of ½ orange

2 Tbsp orange juice

DECORATION

7 Tbsp icing sugar

About 3 tsp water

Yellow or other food colouring

Pre-heat oven to 350°F/175°C/Gas mark 4. Grease several baking sheets or line with non-stick baking parchment.

● Place the flour in a mixing bowl and blend in the butter using your fingers, until the mixture resembles fine breadcrumbs. Stir in the sugar, apricot, orange rind and orange juice and mix everything together, bring the mixture together in a soft ball using your hands. Then on a lightly floured surface roll out the dough to about 5 mm/¼ in.

● Using a 10-cm/4-in heart cutter, stamp out hearts, gather up the left over dough, roll it out again and cut out more hearts. Cut each heart in half lengthways and lift onto the baking sheets. Using the back of a knife, mark a line halfway across the top of the cookie, then below make criss-cross lines to resemble the cone. Bake the cookies for 15 minutes or until golden-brown. Lift onto a wire rack to cool.

● To decorate the cookies, mix the icing sugar with about 3 teaspoons of cold water to form a thin icing, add a few drops of yellow or other food colouring. Using a piping bag, pipe the icing onto the cookies to decorate. Allow to set.

Cheese Fish Sticks

Preparation time: 30 minutes + chilling ●
Cooking time: 20 minutes ● *Makes: 16*

These crunchy cookies, coated in crushed cornflakes, are cut into bars to look like savoury fish sticks!

INGREDIENTS

150 g/5 oz plain flour, sifted

150 g/5 oz butter, cut into small pieces

150 g/5 oz mature Cheddar cheese, grated

50 g/2 oz tinned sweetcorn, drained and dried on kitchen paper

25 g/1 oz cornflakes, crushed

1 egg, beaten

Place the flour in a mixing bowl and blend in the butter using your fingertips until the mixture resembles fine breadcrumbs. Stir in the cheese and corn and bring the mixture together in a soft ball using your hands. Wrap in clingfilm and chill for 30 minutes.
● Pre-heat oven to 375°F/190°C/Gas mark 5. Grease several baking sheets or line with non-stick baking parchment.
● On a lightly floured surface, roll out the dough to a 23 x 18-cm/9 x 7-in rectangle. Cut in half widthways, then cut each half of dough into 8 equal bars. Place the crushed cornflakes on a large plate. Dip each cookie in beaten egg, then coat well by pressing each bar down on to the crushed cornflakes. Lift onto the prepared baking sheets. Bake the cookies for 15 to 20 minutes, until evenly golden and crisp. Transfer to a wire rack to cool. These cookies are best eaten the day they are made.

Ladybird Cookies

Preparation time: 25 minutes ●
Cooking time: 20 minutes ● *Makes: 8*

These savoury cookies get their colour from tomato purée, which also adds to their flavour.

INGREDIENTS

120 g/4 oz plain flour, sifted

120 g/4 oz butter, cut into small pieces

50 g/2 oz mature Cheddar cheese, grated

1 Tbsp tomato purée

About 50 g/2 oz currants

Pre-heat oven to 375°F/190°C/Gas mark 5. Grease several baking sheets or line with non-stick baking parchment.
● Place the flour in a mixing bowl and blend in the butter using your fingertips until the mixture resembles fine breadcrumbs. Stir in the cheese with the tomato purée and bring the mixture together in a soft ball using your hands. On a lightly floured surface, divide into 8.
● Roll each piece into a ball using the palms of your hands, then flatten to an 8-cm/3-in oval shape and lift onto the baking sheets. Using the back of a knife mark a line down the centre of the oval to make the body of the ladybirds.
● Using 4 currants for each half of one ladybird, press down well into the dough to look like spots and repeat. Bake for 20 minutes or until evenly golden. Transfer to a wire rack to cool. Eat these cookies on the same day.

215

Noughts and Crosses

Preparation time: 30 minutes + chilling ● Cooking time 10 to 15 minutes ● Makes: 24

Have fun with these two coloured cookies and see who can win!

INGREDIENTS

120 g/4 oz butter, softened

120 g/4 oz caster sugar

1 egg, beaten

225 g/8 oz plain flour

¼ tsp baking powder

Grated rind of 1 orange

2 Tbsp unsweetened cocoa powder, sifted

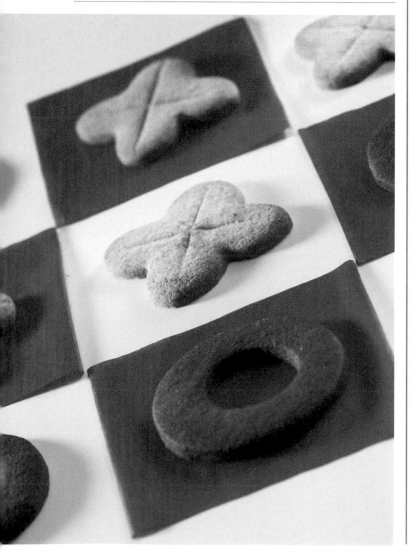

In a mixing bowl, beat the butter and sugar together until pale and fluffy. Beat in the egg. Sift in the flour with the baking powder and stir in the grated orange rind. Mix everything together to form a soft dough.

● Divide the mixture in half, to one half fold in the cocoa powder thoroughly, so you are left with two mixtures. Chill the dough separately in clingfilm in the refrigerator for 30 minutes.

● Pre-heat oven to 375°F/190°C/Gas mark 5. Grease two baking sheets or line with non-stick baking parchment. On a lightly floured surface, roll out the chocolate dough and using a 6-cm/2½-in round cutter, stamp out rounds, then using a 4-cm/1½-in round cutter place in the middle of the cookie to create another circle, this becoming the "zero". Re-roll the dough to make 12 "zeros".

● Roll out the orange dough on a lightly floured surface and, using a cutter or a sharp knife, cut out 12 crosses and lift onto the baking sheets. Bake the cookies for 15 minutes or until lightly golden and crisp. Lift the cookies onto a wire rack to cool. Store in an airtight container for up to 1 week.

Chocolate Chip Cookies

Preparation time: 25 minutes ● Cooking time: 12 minutes ● Makes: 18

These chocolate chip cookies are so easy to make; they are chewy and full of chocolate chunks in every mouth-watering bite.

INGREDIENTS

120 g/4 oz butter, softened

150 g/5 oz light brown sugar

1 egg, beaten

120 g/4 oz plain flour, sifted

½ tsp bicarbonate of soda

1 tsp vanilla essence

50 g/2 oz plain chocolate or white chocolate chips

Pre-heat oven to 375°F/190°C/GAs mark 5. Grease two baking sheets or line with non-stick baking parchment.

● In a mixing bowl, beat together the butter and sugar until light and fluffy. Beat in the egg. Mix together the flour and bicarbonate. Add to the mixture with the vanilla essence and stir together well. Add the chocolate chips and stir them in until evenly spread.

● Spoon mounds of the mixture onto the baking sheets, leaving big spaces between each cookie for spreading. Bake the cookies for 10 to 12 minutes or until golden brown. Lift onto wire racks to cool.

Jewelled Cookie Bars

Preparation time: 25 minutes plus 4 hours to set (up to 24 hours) ● *Makes:16 bars*

**This a really easy recipe for children to use when they start cooking by themselves
as these cookies do not require baking.**

INGREDIENTS

300 g/10 oz milk or plain chocolate

250 g/9 oz digestive biscuits

50 g/2 oz multi-coloured candied cherries, chopped

50 g/2 oz raisins

50 g/2 oz dried apricots, chopped

50 g/2 oz white chocolate chips

50 g/2 oz flaked almonds

Line a 23 x 23-cm/9 x 9-in shallow tin with non-stick baking parchment.

● Under adult supervision, melt the chocolate over a pan of simmering water. Break the chocolate into pieces and place in a heatproof bowl and sit on top of the saucepan. Gently melt the chocolate, stirring until smooth.

● Using your fingers break up the digestives into tiny pieces and place in a large mixing bowl. Keeping some of the remaining ingredients aside for the top of the cookies, add the remaining ingredients to the crushed digestives. Add the melted chocolate and mix well.

● Press the mixture into the tin, level the surface and sprinkle on the remaining ingredients and press gently down to set. Leave the tin in the refrigerator for 4 hours or overnight until it sets hard. Turn out of the tin onto a chopping board and cut into bars.

Mushroom Cookies

Preparation time: 35 minutes ● Cooking time: 20 minutes ● Makes: 16

The stalks of these mushrooms are made from ready-made marzipan, with a chocolate macaroon for the top!

INGREDIENTS

Edible rice paper

75 g/3 oz icing sugar

3 Tbsp ground almonds

2 tsp unsweetened cocoa powder

1 egg white

1½ tsp caster sugar

300 g/10 oz white marzipan

DECORATION

Pink food colouring

3 Tbsp icing sugar

2 tsp water

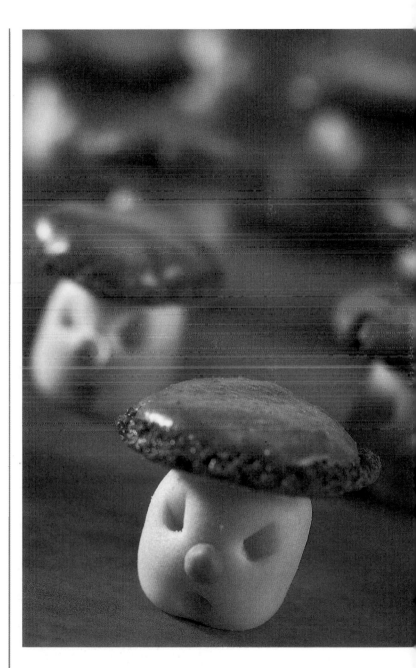

Pre-heat oven to 350°F/175°C/Gas mark 4. Line a baking sheet with a sheet of rice paper.

● Sift the icing sugar, ground almonds and cocoa together in a small bowl. In another mixing bowl, whisk the egg white until it forms soft peaks, then whisk in the caster sugar. Fold in the sifted ingredients until combined.

● Spoon 16 small dots onto the rice paper, spaced well apart. Bake for 20 minutes or until firm and cracking has appeared on the top of each cookie. Leave to go cold on the baking sheet, then neaten the edges of each cookie by trimming away the unwanted rice paper.

● Divide the marzipan into 17 equal-sized pieces. On a lightly floured work surface, roll 16 balls into a pear-shaped stalk. Colour the remaining ball with the pink food colouring to make 16 small noses. To decorate the mushrooms, mix the icing sugar with sufficient cold water to form a thin icing and fill a piping bag. Squeeze a small dot of icing on the underside of each cookie and press on top of the marzipan stalk to complete the mushroom. Eyes and mouths can be pressed into the marzipan using the back of a sharp knife. Pipe a small dot of icing to attach the nose.

Chocolate Button Cookies

Preparation time: 30 minutes + chilling ●
Cooking time: 15 minutes ● *Makes: 13*

These brightly coloured cookies bring enjoyment to any play time!

INGREDIENTS

6 Tbsp soft tub margarine
120 g/4 oz light brown sugar
1 egg, beaten
175 g/6 oz self-raising flour, sifted
1 tsp ground cinnamon
2 packets chocolate milk buttons

In a mixing bowl, beat together the margarine and sugar until pale and fluffy. Beat in the egg and stir in the flour and ground cinnamon. Knead the mixture together with your hands until it comes together in a soft ball. Chill the dough in clingfilm in the refrigerator for 30 minutes.

● Pre-heat oven to 350°F/175°C/Gas mark 4. Grease two baking sheets or line with non-stick baking parchment.

● Roll out the dough on a lightly floured surface, adding more flour if it begins to stick. Using an 8-cm/3-in oval or round cutter, stamp out the cookies. Gather up the left-over dough, roll it out again and cut out more shapes and lift on to baking sheets. Lightly press the chocolate buttons into the dough to decorate the egg shape. Bake the cookies for 15 minutes. Lift the cookies on to a wire rack to cool completely, then store them in an airtight container.

Love Hearts

Preparation time: 40 minutes + chilling ●
Cooking time: 15 minutes ● *Makes: 16*

Choose your favourite colours to decorate these heart-shaped cookies.

INGREDIENTS

75 g/3 oz butter, softened
150 g/5 oz caster sugar
1 egg, beaten
175 g/6 oz plain flour, sifted
Grated rind of 1 lemon

DECORATION

120 g/4 oz icing sugar
1 Tbsp water
Pink, green and yellow food colouring

In a mixing bowl beat together the butter and sugar until light and fluffy. Beat in the egg. Stir in the flour and lemon rind and using your hands bring the mixture together in a soft ball. Wrap the dough in clingfilm and chill in the refrigerator for 30 minutes.

● Pre-heat oven to 350°F/175°C/Gas mark 4. Grease several baking sheets.

● On a lightly floured surface roll out the dough to about 5 mm/¼ in. Using an 8-cm/3-in heart cutter, stamp out hearts and lift onto the baking sheets. Gather up the remaining dough and roll it out again and cut out more shapes. Bake the cookies for 15 minutes or until lightly golden at the edges.

● To decorate the cookies, mix the icing sugar with sufficient water to form a thin icing. Transfer some of the icing to two other bowls and add drops of food colouring to each bowl. Spread each cookie with different coloured icings and allow to set.

Peppermint Rings

Preparation time: 30 minutes + chilling ● *Cooking time: 15 minutes* ● *Makes: 20*

These cookies are for anyone who enjoys mint, they have peppermint essence in the dough with a mint-flavoured boiled sweet in the centre.

INGREDIENTS

175 g/6 oz plain flour, sifted

50 g/2 oz icing sugar

120 g/4 oz lightly salted butter, cut into small pieces

1 tsp peppermint essence

1 Tbsp water

20 sparkling clear mint sweets

Place the flour and icing sugar in a large mixing bowl and blend in the butter until the mixture resembles fine breadcrumbs. Add the peppermint essence and water, using your hands bring the mixture together to form a dough. Wrap the dough in a plastic bag and chill in the refrigerator for 30 minutes or so.

● Line several baking sheets with non-stick baking parchment.

● On a lightly floured work surface, roll out the dough to about 5-mm/¼-inch thick, using a 6-cm/2½-in round cutter, stamp out the middle of each cookie. Unwrap the sweets and place in the gaps. Re-roll the trimmings and cut out more shapes. Chill the cookies in the refrigerator for 15 minutes.

● Pre-heat oven to 350°F/175°C/Gas mark 4. Bake the cookies for 15 minutes or until lightly golden. Allow to cool on the baking sheets and for the sweets to harden, before lifting onto a wire rack to cool. Store in an airtight container.

Flower Cookies

Preparation time: 40 minutes ●
Cooking time: 15 minutes ● *Makes: 20*

The children will love these cookies as they contain little pieces of chocolate buttons in the cooked dough.

INGREDIENTS

175 g/6 oz plain flour, sifted

120 g/4 oz butter, cut into small pieces

120 g/4 oz caster sugar

3 Tbsp chocolate buttons, broken into small pieces

2 Tbsp milk

DECORATION

7 Tbsp icing sugar

About 3 tsp water

Yellow and pink food colourings

Pre-heat oven to 350°F/175°C/Gas mark 4. Grease several baking sheets.

● Place the flour in a mixing bowl and blend in the butter using your fingers until the mixture resembles fine breadcrumbs. Stir in the sugar, chocolate buttons and milk and bring the mixture together in a soft ball using your hands. On a lightly floured surface, roll out the dough to about 5 mm/¼ in.

● Using a 6-cm/2½-in fluted cutter, cut out your shapes and lift the cookies onto the baking sheets. Gather up the left-over dough, roll it out again and cut more shapes. Bake for 15 minutes. Transfer to a wire rack to cool.

● To decorate the flowers, mix the icing sugar with the water and mix to a thin icing. Transfer half the icing to another bowl, add a few drops of yellow colouring to one bowl and pink colouring to the other bowl.

● Using piping bags, pipe it carefully onto the flowers to make patterns. Allow to set.

Golden Circles

Preparation time: 25 minutes + chilling ●
Cooking time: 15 to 20 minutes ● *Makes: 18*

Crisp cookies with a hint of cheese and sesame seed will make the perfect snack.

INGREDIENTS

120 g/4 oz plain flour, sifted

1 tsp dried mixed herbs

75 g/3 oz butter, cut into small pieces

120 g/4 oz mature Cheddar cheese, grated

1 egg, beaten

3 Tbsp sesame seeds

Place the flour in a mixing bowl with the dried mixed herbs and blend in the butter using your fingertips until the mixture resembles fine breadcrumbs. Add the cheese and bring the mixture together in a soft ball using your hands. On a lightly floured surface, shape the dough into a 23 x 2.5-cm/9 x 1-in log shape. Wrap in clingfilm and chill in the refrigerator for 30 minutes.

● Brush the log shaped dough with beaten egg, place the sesame seeds on a large plate and roll the dough in the sesame seeds until they evenly coat the log. Chill in the refrigerator for 15 minutes.

● Pre-heat oven to 375°F/190°C/Gas mark 5. Grease several baking sheets or line with non-stick baking parchment.

● Cut the dough into 18 equal slices and lift onto the baking sheets. Bake the cookies for 15 to 20 minutes or until golden and crisp. Transfer to a wire rack to cool. These cookies are best eaten on the day they are made.

Mouse Cookies

Preparation time: 30 minutes ●
Cooking time: 20 minutes ● Makes: 14

These cheeky little "mice" are flavoured with cinnamon. If you like, you can dust them with extra cinnamon and icing sugar after they have come out of the oven!

INGREDIENTS

175 g/6 oz plain flour, sifted
1 tsp ground cinnamon
120 g/4 oz butter, cut into small pieces
120 g/4 oz caster sugar
2 Tbsp milk

DECORATION

7 currants, halved
Ground cinnamon, for dusting
Icing sugar, for dusting

Pre-heat oven to 350°F/175°C/Gas mark 4. Grease several baking sheets or line with non-stick baking parchment.

● Place the flour and ground cinnamon in a bowl and blend in the butter using your fingertips to form fine breadcrumbs. Add the sugar and milk and using your hands bring together to form a soft dough.

● Divide the dough into 16 equal-sized pieces. Roll 14 pieces into balls using the palms of your hands, then flatten one side to look like the nose of a mouse.

● Divide the remaining 2 balls into 14 little balls and roll each one to a long sausage shape for the tail. Using a little water, attach each tail to the back of the mice. Position the currants to look like eyes then, using a pair of small scissors, snip into the dough to look like ears. Lift the mice onto the baking sheets.

● Bake the cookies for 20 minutes. Lift onto a wire rack to cool. Dust with a little cinnamon and icing sugar.

Chicks

Preparation time: 25 minutes ● Cooking time: 1 hour 30 minutes ● Makes: 30

These cookies are made with meringue. If you do not want to use a piping bag, make small blobs with teaspoons, they will be just as fun.

INGREDIENTS

3 egg whites
Pinch of salt
200 g/7 oz caster sugar

DECORATION

25 g/1 oz marzipan
Yellow food colouring
3 Tbsp icing sugar, sifted
2 tsp water

Pre-heat oven to 250°F/120°C/Gas mark ½. Line several baking sheets with non-stick baking parchment.

● In a mixing bowl, whisk the egg whites with the salt until they form soft peaks. Whisk in the sugar, a little at a time, until the mixture is very thick and glossy. If you are using a piping bag, fit it with a plain nozzle and pipe the meringue into small circles. Lift up and pipe a smaller circle to create a head. Allow a little space in between each chick.

● Bake the chicks for 1 hour and 30 minutes, until crisp and dried out so that the meringue lifts off the paper easily. Meanwhile, in a small bowl, colour the marzipan yellow and shape into 60 small balls for the eyes and 30 bigger balls for the beak shape.

● Mix the icing sugar with sufficient water to form a thin icing and using a piping bag, pipe little dots on each chick and place the eyes and beak in place. These meringues store well in an airtight container, if there are any left over!

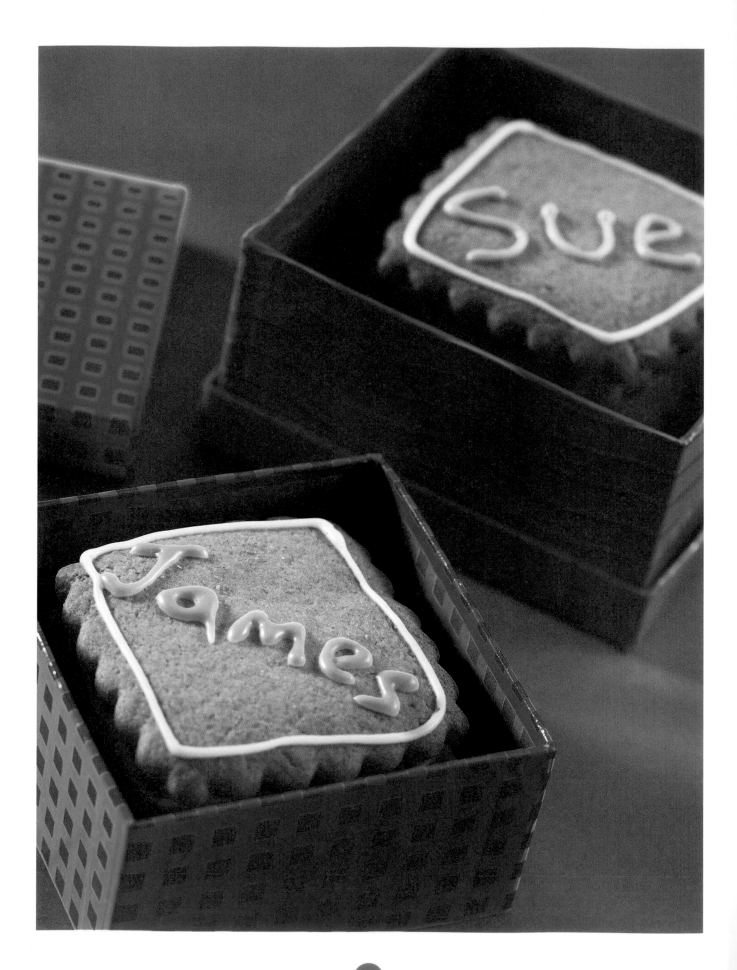

Children's Name Cookies

Preparation time: 40 minutes + chilling ● Cooking time: 15 minutes ● Makes: 15

**Using a banana-flavoured pudding mix in these cookies gives them a real banana boost.
Try using other flavours if you prefer.**

INGREDIENTS

6 Tbsp soft tub margarine

5 Tbsp caster sugar

1 egg, beaten

175 g/6 oz self-raising flour, sifted

¼ cup banana-flavoured pudding mix

DECORATION

150 g/5 oz icing sugar, sifted

2 Tbsp water

Pink and blue food colouring

In a mixing bowl, beat together the margarine and sugar until pale and fluffy. Beat in the egg, add the flour and banana pudding mix. Knead the mixture together with your hands until it comes together in a soft ball. Chill the dough in clingfilm in the refrigerator for 30 minutes.

● Pre-heat oven to 350°F/175°C/Gas mark 4. Grease two baking sheets or line with non-stick baking parchment.

● Sprinkle some flour on the work surface and a rolling pin. Roll out the dough to about 5 mm/¼ in. Using a 6-cm/2½-in square cutter, cut out your cookies and lift onto the baking sheets. Gather up the left-over dough, roll it out again and cut out more shapes. Bake the cookies for 15 minutes or until golden then lift them onto a wire rack to cool.

● To decorate the squares, mix the icing sugar with sufficient water to form a thin icing. Keeping about 3 tablespoons of the icing in the bowl, place the remaining icing in two bowls and colour one pink and one blue. Fill piping bags with the icings, pipe your favourite boys' names with the blue icing on half the cookies and use the pink icing to pipe girls' names onto the cookies. Use the white icing to make a border around the names. Eat on the day iced.

Chocolate Octopus

Preparation time: 35 minutes + chilling ● Cooking time: 20 minutes ● Makes: 2 giant cookies

This recipe makes two giant octopuses, if you prefer you can make lots of little ones!

INGREDIENTS

50 g/2 oz soft tub margarine

120 g/4 oz caster sugar

1 egg, beaten

220 g/7 oz plain flour

2 Tbsp unsweetened cocoa powder

DECORATION

3 Tbsp icing sugar, sifted

2 tsp water

4 chocolate buttons or chocolate chips

In a mixing bowl beat together the margarine and sugar until pale and fluffy. Add the egg. Sift together the flour and cocoa and mix everything together. Using your hands, bring the dough together until it forms a ball. Chill the dough in clingfilm in the refrigerator for 30 minutes.

● Pre-heat oven to 325°F/160°C/Gas mark 3. Grease two baking sheets or line with non-stick baking parchment. Divide the dough roughly in half to make two bodies for the octopus. Shape into a large oval and then cut five or six strips halfway up the oval to make the tentacles, push the dough apart and curl the edges of the strips. Transfer onto a baking sheet and make the second octopus. Bake the cookies for 20 minutes or until crisp, lift the two cookies on to wire racks to cool.

● To decorate mix the icing sugar with sufficient water and mix to a thin icing. Using a piping bag pipe around the body with the icing and pipe eyes on each octopus and top with the candies. Allow the icing to set.

Treasure Coins

Preparation time: 30 minutes ●
Cooking time: 25 minutes ● *Makes: 24*

Small discs of vanilla shortbread are encrusted with glacé cherries, candied citrus peel and nuts to make these delicious edible coins.

INGREDIENTS

175 g/6 oz plain flour, sifted
120 g/4 oz caster sugar
120 g/4 oz butter, cut into small pieces
2 tsp vanilla essence
50 g/2 oz candied citrus peel
12 glacé cherries, halved
24 whole blanched hazelnuts

Pre-heat oven to 350°F/175°C/Gas mark 4. Grease two baking sheets or line with non-stick baking parchment.

● Place the flour and sugar in a mixing bowl. Blend in the butter using your fingertips until the mixture resembles fine breadcrumbs, add the vanilla essence and, using your hands, bring the mixture together in a soft ball.

● On a lightly floured surface, roll out the dough to about 5 mm/¼ in. Using a 5-cm/2-in round cutter, stamp out rounds and lift onto the baking sheets. Gather up the remaining dough and roll it out again and cut out more shapes.

● Press a little bit of candied citrus peel onto each cookie, then add half a cherry to each cookie, followed by a hazelnut. Bake the cookies for 25 minutes or until pale golden at the edges. Transfer to a wire rack to cool. Store these cookies in an airtight container and eat within one week.

Mandarin Flying Saucers

Preparation time: 30 minutes + chilling ●
Cooking time: 15 to 20 minutes ● *Makes: 10*

The tinned mandarins used in these cookies make for a great flavour and colour.

INGREDIENTS

175 g/6 oz plain flour, sifted
120 g/4 oz icing sugar
150 g/5 oz lightly salted butter, cut into small pieces
Grated rind of 1 orange
50 g/2 oz tinned mandarin segments, drained and dried

DECORATION

7 Tbsp icing sugar
About 3 tsp reserved mandarin juice or water
Few mandarin segments, chopped

Place the flour and icing sugar in a bowl, blend in the butter using your fingertips until the mixture resembles fine breadcrumbs. Add the orange rind and mandarin segments, chopped, and, using your hands, bring together in a soft ball. Wrap in clingfilm and chill in the refrigerator for 30 minutes.

● Pre-heat oven to 350°F/175°C/Gas mark 4. Grease several baking sheets or line with non-stick baking parchment. Roll out the dough to about 5 mm/¼ in. Using a 10-cm/4-in round cutter, stamp out rounds and lift onto the baking sheets. Gather up the remaining dough and roll it out again and cut out more rounds.

● Bake the cookies for 15 to 20 minutes or until just golden at the edges. Transfer to a wire rack to cool.

● To decorate, mix the icing sugar with sufficient juice or water to form a thin icing. Place a dollop of icing on each cookie and top with mandarin pieces.

Chocolate Snakes

Preparation time: 30 minutes ● Cooking time: 15 minutes ● Makes: 8

These crunchy chocolate cookies are fun to make. Glazing them with egg white and sugar makes all the difference.

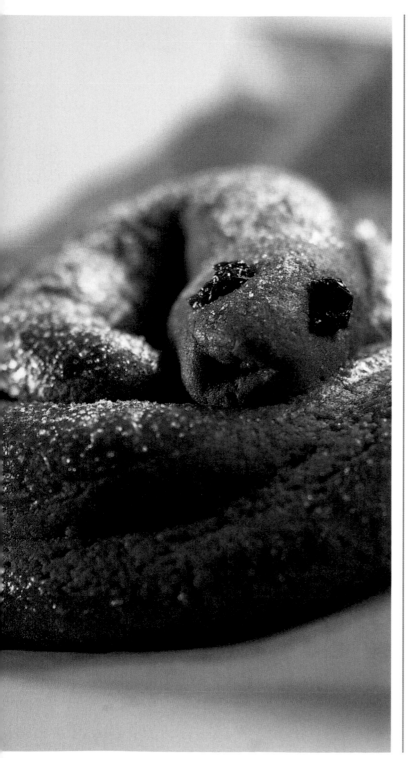

INGREDIENTS

4 Tbsp soft tub margarine

50 g/2 oz caster sugar

1 egg, separated

120 g/4 oz plain flour

¼ tsp baking powder

2 Tbsp unsweetened cocoa powder, sifted

1 Tbsp milk

DECORATION

4 currants, halved

Granulated sugar, for sprinkling

Pre-heat oven to 375°F/190°C/Gas mark 5. Grease two baking sheets or line with non-stick baking parchment.

● In a mixing bowl beat together the margarine and sugar until pale and fluffy. Add the egg yolk. Sift together the flour, baking powder and unsweetened cocoa powder then add with the milk and mix thoroughly. The dough should come together in a soft ball.

● Turn the dough out onto a lightly floured work surface and divide into 8 equal-sized pieces. Roll each piece into a long sausage shape with your hands. Then make a spiral pattern with one piece of dough and overlap as you wind the dough up and around. Add 2 pieces of currants to make the eyes and place onto the baking sheets. Repeat with the remaining shapes.

● In a small bowl lightly beat the egg white and then, using a pastry brush, glaze the snakes all over and sprinkle with sugar. Bake for 15 minutes. Lift onto a wire rack to cool. Store in an airtight container.

Fishies

Preparation time: 25 minutes + chilling ● *Cooking time: 10 to 15 minutes* ● *Makes: 40 small cookies*

Adding candied peel to this creamed mixture gives these cookies a really fruity texture.

INGREDIENTS

75 g/3 oz butter, softened or soft tub margarine

150 g/5 oz caster sugar

1 egg, beaten

175 g/6 oz plain flour, sifted

6 Tbsp candied citrus peel

Grated rind of ½ lemon

In a mixing bowl beat together the butter or margarine and sugar until light and fluffy. Beat in the egg. Stir in the flour, then stir in the candied citrus peel and lemon rind. Using your hands, bring the mixture together to form a soft dough. Wrap in clingfilm and chill in the refrigerator for 20 minutes.

● Pre-heat oven to 350°F/175°C/Gas mark 4. Grease two baking sheets or line with non-stick baking parchment.

● On a lightly floured surface roll out the dough to 5 mm/¼ in. Using a cutter, cut out as many fish shapes as possible (the exact number will depend on the size of your cutter) and lift onto the baking sheets. Gather up the remaining dough and roll it out again and cut out more fish shapes.

● Using the back of a teaspoon, decorate the fish with scales and make an eye with a metal skewer. Bake the cookies for 10 to 12 minutes until golden and crisp. Lift onto a wire rack to cool. Store in an airtight container.

Gingerbread Selection

Preparation time: 40 minutes + chilling ● *Cooking time: 8 to 10 minutes* ● *Makes: 24*

**These cookies are just as good as traditional gingerbread but with currants in the mixture.
You can use any cookie cutter you like.**

INGREDIENTS

50 g/2 oz soft brown sugar

3 Tbsp golden syrup

½ tsp ground cinnamon

½ tsp ground ginger

25 g/1 oz butter

225 g/8 oz plain flour, sifted

1 tsp baking powder

1 egg, beaten

50 g/2 oz currants, chopped

DECORATION

5 Tbsp icing sugar, sifted

About 4 tsp water

Green food colouring

Grease two baking sheets or line with non-stick baking parchment. Ask an adult to help you dissolve the sugar, syrup, spices and butter together in a saucepan. Stir over a low heat until they have melted.

● Sift the flour and baking powder into a mixing bowl add the syrup mixture, beaten egg and currants. Mix everything together, then knead the mixture into a ball using your hands. Chill the dough in clingfilm in the refrigerator for 30 minutes.

● Pre-heat oven to 325°F/160°C/Gas mark 3. Sprinkle some flour on the work surface and rolling pin. Roll out the dough thinly to about 5 mm/¼ in. Using the cutters, cut out your shapes and lift the cookies onto baking sheets. Gather up the left-over dough, roll it out again and cut out more shapes. Bake the cookies for 8 to 10 minutes or until golden-brown then lift them on to a wire rack to cool.

● To decorate the gingerbread selection, mix the icing sugar with sufficient water to make a thin icing and add a few drops of green colouring. Using a piping bag, pipe onto the cookies and decorate.

Jam Heart Cookies

Preparation time: 30 minutes + chilling ● *Cooking time: 20 minutes* ● *Makes: 12*

**Who can resist a crisp cookie base filled with lots of strawberry jam.
Use a different flavoured jam if you prefer.**

INGREDIENTS

175 g/6 oz plain flour, sifted

50 g/2 oz ground almonds

120 g/4 oz butter, softened

50 g/2 oz caster sugar

2 Tbsp milk

1 egg, beaten

4 Tbsp strawberry jam

Place the flour and ground almonds in a mixing bowl, blend in the butter until the mixture resembles fine breadcrumbs. Stir in the sugar and milk and, using your hands, work the mixture together to form a dough. Wrap in clingfilm and chill in the refrigerator for 20 minutes.

● Pre-heat oven to 350°F/175°C/Gas mark 4. Grease two baking sheets or line with non-stick baking parchment.

● On a lightly floured surface, roll out the dough and cut out 8-cm/3-in hearts with a cutter. Place 12 of these heart cookies onto the baking sheets and prick with a fork. Cut out a heart shape from the centre of the remaining hearts, using a 5-cm/2-in heart cutter. Gather up the remaining dough and roll it out again and cut out more 5-cm/2-in hearts so you have 12 "lids" for the cookies.

● Using a pastry brush, apply the beaten egg to the large heart cookies. Top with a heart lid and seal around the edges. Brush the whole cookie with more beaten egg. Bake the cookies for 20 minutes or until golden. Lift onto a wire rack to cool.

● Once the cookies have cooled spoon the jam onto each cookie keeping within the heart shape in the centre.

Orange Carrot Shortbread

Preparation time: 35 minutes ● Cooking time: 15 to 20 minutes ● Makes: 16

**A rich, buttery shortbread flavoured with orange rind, with a drop of food colouring.
See how many people take a second look!**

INGREDIENTS

150 g/5 oz butter, softened

5 Tbsp caster sugar

225 g/8 oz plain flour, sifted

Grated rind of 2 oranges

2 Tbsp orange juice

Few drops orange food colouring, optional

Pre-heat oven to 325°F/160°C/Gas mark 3. Grease two baking sheets or line with non-stick baking parchment.

● In a mixing bowl beat together the butter and sugar until light and fluffy. Add all the remaining ingredients and begin to mix well. Using your hands bring the mixture together to form a soft dough.

● On a lightly floured work surface, divide the dough into 16 equal pieces. Roll each piece of dough into a ball using the palms of your hands. Roll backwards and forwards so that one end begins to get thinner and you produce a carrot shape. Repeat with the remaining dough and lift onto the baking sheets. Using the back of a knife lightly score marks all over the carrots.

● Bake the cookies for 15 to 20 minutes or until lightly golden at the edges. Allow to cool slightly before lifting onto a wire rack.

TIP

If you prefer, cut the shortbread into your favourite shape.

Poppy Seed Pinwheels

Preparation time: 25 minutes + chilling ●
Cooking time: 15 to 20 minutes ● Makes: About 20

These crunchy cookies are sweet and sticky from the jam which oozes out during baking. We've used apricot, but you can use your favourite flavour of jam.

INGREDIENTS

120 g/4 oz butter, softened
50 g/2 oz caster sugar
175 g/6 oz plain flour, sifted
2 Tbsp milk
4 Tbsp apricot jam
1½ Tbsp poppy seeds

In a mixing bowl beat together the butter and sugar until light and fluffy. Stir in the flour and milk. Using your hands, bring the mixture together to form a dough. Wrap in clingfilm and chill for 30 minutes.

● Pre-heat oven to 350°F/175°C/Gas mark 4. Line two baking sheets with non-stick baking parchment.

● On a lightly floured surface, roll out the dough to a 30 x 18-cm/12 x 7-in rectangle. Place the apricot jam in a small bowl and stir well with a wooden spoon so it becomes easier to spread. Spoon onto the dough and spread out evenly, sprinkle with poppy seeds.

● Starting from the longest edge, begin to roll up the dough tightly into a large sausage shape. Very carefully slice the dough so you have 20 even slices, lift onto the baking sheets. Bake the cookies for 15 to 20 minutes or until they are lightly golden. Allow to cool slightly on the sheets before lifting onto a wire rack to cool.

Number Cookies

Preparation time: 25 minutes + chilling ●
Cooking time: 10 to 15 minutes ● Makes: 40

These cookies are made with an orange dough, half of it flavoured with cocoa powder to create these two colours.

INGREDIENTS

175 g/6 oz butter, softened
5 Tbsp caster sugar
250 g/9 oz plain flour, sifted
½ tsp grated orange rind
2 Tbsp unsweetened cocoa powder, sifted

In a mixing bowl beat together the butter and sugar until light and fluffy. Add the flour and orange rind and combine all the ingredients together in a soft ball. Transfer half the mixture to another bowl and fold in the cocoa powder until evenly mixed. Wrap the doughs separately in clingfilm and chill in the refrigerator for 30 minutes.

● Pre-heat oven to 350°F/175°C/Gas mark 4. Grease several baking sheets or line with non-stick baking parchment.

● On a lightly floured surface, roll out the chocolate dough to about 5 mm/¼ in and stamp out numbers. Lift onto the baking sheets. Gather up the remaining dough and roll it out again and cut out more numbers. Repeat with the orange dough.

● Bake the cookies for 10 to 15 minutes or until golden at the edges. Lift onto a wire rack to cool. Store in an airtight container.

Apple Cheese Cookies

Preparation time: 20 minutes ●
Cooking time: 20 minutes ● Makes: 16

These savoury cookies have a hint of sweetness from the chopped apple.

INGREDIENTS

150 g/5 oz self-raising flour

Pinch of salt

120 g/4 oz butter, cut into small pieces

120 g/4 oz mature Cheddar cheese, grated

1 apple, cored and finely chopped

Pre-heat oven to 350°F/175°C/Gas mark 4. Grease and line several baking sheets with non-stick baking parchment.

● Place the flour and salt in a mixing bowl and blend in the butter using your fingertips until the mixture resembles fine breadcrumbs. Stir in the cheese and chopped apple and, using your hands, bring all the ingredients together to form a soft ball.

● On a lightly floured surface divide the dough into 16 equal-sized pieces and roll into balls using the palms of your hands and lift onto the baking sheets. Flatten slightly with the back of a fork.

● Bake the cookies for 20 minutes or until evenly golden-brown. Transfer to a wire rack to cool. These cookies are best eaten on the day they are made.

Clock Cookies

Preparation time: 35 minutes + chilling ●
Cooking time: 15 to 20 minutes ● Makes: 10

These cookies are flavoured with sultanas and cut into circles to make big clock faces. Pipe the icing to show a different time on each cookie!

INGREDIENTS

6 Tbsp soft tub margarine

150 g/5 oz caster sugar

1 egg, beaten

175 g/6 oz plain flour, sifted

50 g/2 oz sultanas

DECORATION

120 g/4 oz icing sugar

About 1 Tbsp cold water

In a mixing bowl beat together the margarine and sugar until light and fluffy. Beat in the egg. Stir in the flour and sultanas and, using your hands, bring all the mixture together in a soft ball. Wrap the dough in clingfilm and chill in the refrigerator for 30 minutes.

● Pre-heat oven to 350°F/175°C/Gas mark 4. Grease several baking sheets.

● On a lightly floured surface roll out the dough to about 5 mm/¼-in. Using a 10-cm/4-in round cutter, stamp out rounds and lift onto the baking sheets. Gather up the remaining dough and roll it again and cut out more shapes. Bake the cookies for 15 to 20 minutes or until evenly golden. Transfer to a wire rack to cool.

● To decorate the "clocks", mix the icing sugar with about 1 tablespoon of cold water to form a thin icing. Using a piping bag, pipe the numbers 12, 3, 6 and 9 on to the circles in the correct clock positions. Then pipe an "hour" hand and "minute" hand to show a different time on each cookie. Leave to set.

Fruit Segments

Preparation time: 25 minutes ● Cooking time: 15 minutes ● Makes: 16

These look just like a segment of fruit and they are full of citrus flavours.

INGREDIENTS

120 g/4 oz butter, softened

5 Tbsp caster sugar

1 egg, separated

200 g/7 oz plain flour, sifted

Grated rind of 1 lemon

Grated rind of 1 orange

2 Tbsp orange juice

Granulated sugar, for sprinkling

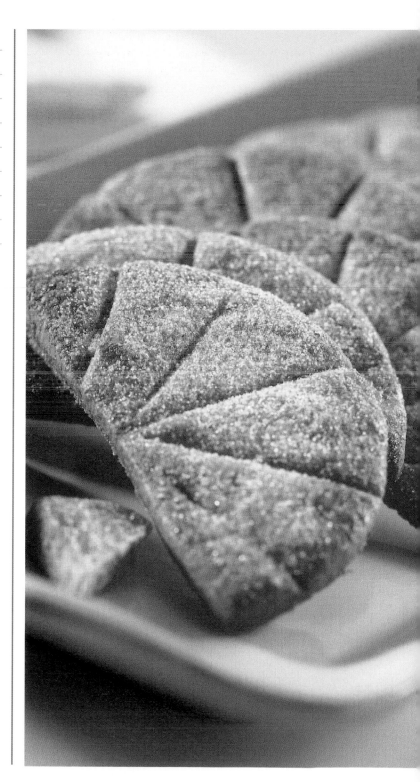

Pre-heat oven to 350°F/175°C/Gas mark 4. Grease two baking sheets or line with non-stick baking parchment.

● In a mixing bowl, beat together the butter and sugar until pale and fluffy. Beat in the egg yolk. Stir in the flour, grated rinds and orange juice and mix everything together. Using your hands bring the dough together to form a ball.

● Turn the dough out on to a lightly floured work surface and roll out to 5 mm/¼ in. Using a 9-cm/3½-in round cutter, cut out rounds, then cut each circle in half to make the segments. Gather up the left-over dough and roll it out again and cut out more circles. Lift the cookies onto the baking sheets and, using the back of a small knife, score marks across each segment.

● In a small bowl, whisk the egg white lightly with a fork and, using a pastry brush, glaze each cookie then sprinkle with a little extra sugar. Bake the cookies for 15 minutes or until lightly golden and crisp. Lift them onto a wire rack to cool. When cold store them in an airtight container.

Cookies for Special Diets

Some people believe that being on a special diet puts an end to treats such as cookies. However, this need not be the case. This chapter is full of recipes specially created for those with specific dietary requirements. These cookies are so delicious that they will become firm favourites with the whole family.

Many of the recipes retain butter as the suggested fat because butter really does give the cookies a richness of flavour. However, margarine can be substituted for the butter, but be aware that the trans fats found in hard margarines are saturated like those in butter. Trans fats behave like saturated fats, increasing the risk of heart disease. Reduced and low-fat spreads have a high water content so cannot be substituted for butter. The butter content is kept as low as possible in these recipes and inventive techniques using prunes and apple sauce are used in some recipes to reduce the need for fat.

High Fibre

Increasing fibre is one of the basic tenets of healthy eating.

Reduced Fat

Being placed on a low-cholesterol diet does not have to mean total denial of cookies as these recipes show.

Gluten-Free/Wheat-Free/Healthy

Coconut Crisps

Preparation time: 10 minutes ● Cooking time: 15 minutes ● Makes: About 20

These deliciously light, crisp cookies are quick and easy to make and simply melt in the mouth.

INGREDIENTS

120 g/4 oz lightly salted butter
1 heaped Tbsp golden syrup
50 g/2 oz demerara sugar
150 g/5 oz rolled oats
75 g/3 oz sweetened flaked coconut
120 g/4 oz plain flour
1 tsp bicarbonate of soda
1 tsp hot water

Pre-heat oven to 350°F/175°C/Gas mark 4. Grease or line two baking sheets with non-stick baking parchment.

● Place the butter, syrup and sugar in a large saucepan. Heat the mixture gently until the butter has melted and the sugar dissolved. Stir in the rolled oats and flour and mix well. Dissolve the bicarbonate in the hot water and stir into the mixture. Allow to cool slightly.

● Roll heaped teaspoonfuls of the mixture into balls the size of a walnut. Then place on the baking sheets allowing plenty of space for the mixture to spread. Bake for 15 minutes or until evenly browned. Leave to cool slightly, then use a thin metal spatula to transfer to a wire rack to cool completely. Store for up to 1 week in an airtight container.

Wholemeal Shortbread

Preparation time: 15 minutes + chilling ● Cooking time: 15 minutes ● Makes: About 15

The fibre content of these shortbread cookies is increased by substituting half the plain flour with wholemeal.

INGREDIENTS

50 g/2 oz plain flour
Pinch of salt
50 g/2 oz plain wholemeal flour
5 Tbsp ground rice
120 g/4 oz lightly salted butter
25 g/1 oz icing sugar

Sift the plain flour and salt together and stir in the wholemeal flour and ground rice.

● Beat the butter and sugar until light and fluffy. Mix in the dry ingredients. When the mixture resembles breadcrumbs, gather the dough together with your hands and turn onto a clean work surface. Knead lightly until it forms a ball then roll into a sausage shape, about 5 cm/2 in in diameter. Wrap in clingfilm and chill in the refrigerator for at least 1 hour or until firm.

● Pre-heat oven to 375°F/190°C/Gas mark 5. Grease or line two baking sheets with non-stick baking parchment.

● Using a sharp knife slice the dough into 8-mm/⅓-in thick slices. Transfer to the baking sheets and bake for 15 minutes. Allow to cool slightly then, using a thin metal spatula, transfer to a wire rack to cool completely. Store in an airtight container for up to 1 week.

Peanut and Raisin Cookies

Preparation time: 15 minutes + cooling ● *Cooking time: 15 minutes* ● *Makes: About 20*

Diets which contain a daily intake of peanuts, peanut butter or peanut oil may help protect against heart disease.

INGREDIENTS

120 g/4 oz lightly salted butter, melted
75 g/3 oz caster sugar
1 egg, beaten
5 tsp baking powder
200 g/7 oz crunchy peanut butter
5 Tbsp plain flour
50 g/2 oz wholemeal flour
150 g/5 oz raisins

Pre-heat oven to 375°F/190°C/Gas mark 5. Grease or line two baking sheets.

● Place all the ingredients except the raisins into a bowl and beat together until well blended. Stir in the raisins. Spoon heaping teaspoonfuls of the mixture onto baking sheets spaced well apart to allow the mixture to spread. Bake for 15 to 20 minutes or until brown around the edges.

● Leave to cool slightly, then using a thin metal spatula, transfer to a wire rack to cool completely. Store for up to 1 week, in an airtight container.

Banana and Date Cookies

Preparation time: 15 minutes ● Cooking time: 15 to 20 minutes ● Makes: About 15

Bananas are an excellent source of fibre and potassium and are rich in vitamin B6.

INGREDIENTS

120 g/4 oz lightly salted butter or margarine
5 Tbsp caster sugar
1 egg, beaten
75 g/3 oz plain flour
1 tsp baking powder
50 g/2 oz plain wholemeal flour
50 g/2 oz roughly chopped dried banana chips
200 g/7 oz roughly chopped dates

Pre-heat oven to 375°F/190°C/Gas mark 5. Grease or line two baking sheets with non-stick baking parchment.

● Beat together the butter and sugar until light and fluffy. Beat in the egg. Sift the plain flour and baking powder into a bowl. Stir in the wholemeal flour, banana chips and dates.

● With floured hands, roll the dough into balls the size of walnuts. Place on baking sheets, allowing enough space for the mixture to spread. Bake for 15 to 20 minutes or until brown around the edges. Allow to cool slightly, then use a thin, metal spatula, to transfer to a wire rack to cool completely. Store for up to 1 week in an airtight container.

Caribbean Lime Cookies

Preparation time: 15 minutes ● Cooking time: 15 to 20 minutes ● Makes: About 15

Dried tropical fruits are readily available and make a good alternative to dried apricots.

INGREDIENTS

120 g/4 oz lightly salted butter
75 g/3 oz caster sugar
1 egg, beaten
75 g/3 oz plain flour
1 level tsp baking powder
50 g/2 oz wholemeal flour
75 g/3 oz chopped dried mango
75 g/3 oz sweetened flaked coconut
Grated rind of 2 limes

Pre-heat oven to 375°F/190°C/Gas mark 5. Grease or line two baking sheets with non-stick baking parchment.

● Beat together the butter and sugar until soft. Beat in the egg. Sift the plain flour and the baking powder into a bowl. Stir in the wholemeal flour, mango, coconut and grated lime rind.

● With floured hands roll the dough into balls the size of walnuts. Place on the baking sheets, allowing enough space for the mixture to spread. Bake in the oven for 15 to 20 minutes or until brown around the edges. Allow to cool slightly, then use a thin metal spatula to transfer to a wire rack to cool completely. Store for up to 1 week in an airtight container.

Apricot and Almond Cookies

Preparation time: 15 minutes + cooling ● *Cooking time: 15 minutes* ● *Makes: 15 to 20*

**Dried apricots provide good amounts of betacarotene, potassium and soluble fibre.
They are also a useful source of iron.**

INGREDIENTS

120 g/4 oz lightly salted butter

5 Tbsp caster sugar

1 egg, beaten

75 g/3 oz plain flour

1 tsp baking powder

75 g/3 oz wholemeal flour

50 g/2 oz roughly chopped ready-to-eat dried apricots

75 g/3 oz flaked almonds

1 tsp almond essence

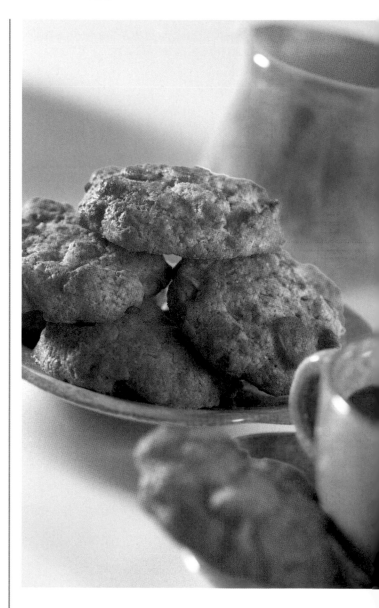

Pre-heat oven to 375°F/190°C/Gas mark 5. Grease or line two baking sheets with non-stick baking parchment.

● Beat together the butter and sugar until soft. Beat in the egg. Sift the plain flour together with the baking powder in a bowl. Stir in the wholemeal flour, apricots, almonds and almond essence.

● With floured hands roll the dough into balls the size of walnuts. Place on the baking sheets, allowing enough space for the mixture to spread. Bake for 15 to 20 minutes or until brown around the edges. Allow to cool slightly, then transfer to a wire rack to cool completely. Store for up to 1 week in an airtight container.

Sesame Oat Crisps

Preparation time: 10 minutes ● *Cooking time: 15 minutes* ● *Makes: About 20*

Sesame seeds are a good source of calcium and vitamin E and add a delicious nutty flavour to these cookies.

INGREDIENTS

120 g/4 oz lightly salted butter

1¼ Tbsp golden syrup

120 g/4 oz demerera sugar

75 g/3 oz rolled oats

5 Tbsp sesame seeds

120 g/4 oz plain flour

1 tsp bicarbonate of soda

1 tsp hot water

Pre-heat oven to 350°F/175°C/Gas mark 4. Grease or line two baking sheets.

● Place butter, syrup and sugar in a large saucepan. Heat the mixture gently until the butter has melted and the sugar dissolved. Stir in rolled oats, sesame seeds and flour and mix well. Dissolve the bicarbonate in the hot water and stir into the mixture. Leave to cool slightly.

● Roll heaped teaspoonfuls of the mixture into balls the size of walnuts. Place on the baking sheets allowing plenty of space for the mixture to spread as it bakes. Bake for 15 minutes or until evenly browned. Remove from the oven and allow to cool slightly, then using a thin metal spatula transfer to a wire rack to cool completely. Store for up to 1 week in an airtight container.

Ginger Thins

Preparation time: 10 minutes ● Cooking time: 7 minutes ● Makes: About 10

These cookies contain just 1.3g fat each. Serve them with frozen yogurt or reduced-fat ice cream.

INGREDIENTS

15 g/½ oz unsalted butter
1 Tbsp icing sugar
3 Tbsp golden syrup
2 Tbsp plain flour
1 level tsp ground ginger
Pinch of salt

Pre-heat oven to 375°F/190°C/Gas mark 5. Grease or line two baking sheets with non-stick baking parchment.

● Place the butter, icing sugar and syrup in a small saucepan and heat gently until the sugar has dissolved. Remove from the heat and leave to cool slightly.

● Sift together the flour, ginger and salt and stir into the butter mixture.

● Place small spoonfuls of the mixture on to the prepared baking sheets, allowing plenty of space for the mixture to spread. Bake for 7 minutes or until golden brown. Allow the cookies to cool on the tray for about 30 seconds. Using a thin, metal spatula carefully lift the cookies off the baking sheet and while they are still warm and pliable, shape them over a rolling pin or tall glass. Once set, transfer to a wire rack to cool completely. Store for up to 1 week in an airtight container.

Treacle Cookies

Preparation time: 10 minutes ● Cooking time: 20 minutes ● Makes: About 15

These cookies contain just 1.7g fat. Oatmeal is rich in soluble fibre, which can help reduce high blood cholesterol levels.

INGREDIENTS

120 g/4 oz self-raising flour
50 g/2 oz fine oatmeal
3 Tbsp caster sugar
3 Tbsp treacle
50 g/2 oz lightly salted butter
2 Tbsp skimmed milk

Pre-heat oven to 375°F/190°C/Gas mark 5. Grease or line two baking sheets with non-stick baking parchment.

● Mix all the dry ingredients in a bowl. Place the butter and treacle in a small saucepan and heat gently until the butter has melted. Pour the treacle mixture onto the dry ingredients, add the milk and mix to make smooth dough.

● Knead the dough on a lightly floured surface then roll out to about 8 mm/⅓ in thick. Using a 5-cm/2-in round cutter, cut out the cookies and transfer to baking sheet. Using a sharp knife make shallow cuts across the surface and bake for 20 minutes or until firm to the touch. Transfer to a wire rack to cool. Store for up to 1 week in an airtight container.

Lemon and Poppy Seed Cookies

Preparation time: 15 minutes ● Cooking time: 15 to 20 minutes ● Makes: About 36

Poppy seeds give these healthy gluten-free cookies an added crunch.

INGREDIENTS

120 g/4 oz lightly salted butter or margarine

120 g/4 oz caster sugar

1 egg, beaten

175 g/6 oz gluten-free flour

Grated rind of 2 lemons

2 Tbsp poppy seeds

Pre-heat oven to 350°F/175°C/Gas mark 4. Grease or line two baking sheets.

● Beat together the butter and sugar until light and fluffy. Gradually beat in the egg. Add in the gluten-free flour, lemon rind and poppy seeds and mix well.

● On a lightly floured surface roll out the dough to 5 mm/¼ in thick. Using a 5-cm/2-in round cutter, cut out the cookies and transfer to the baking sheets and bake for 15 to 20 minutes. Cool slightly on the baking sheets then, using a thin metal spatula carefully transfer to a wire rack to cool completely.

Sour Cherry and Orange Oatmeal Cookies

Preparation time: 15 minutes ● Cooking time: 15 to 20 minutes ● Makes: 15 to 20

Oats are an excellent source of soluble fibre which can help reduce high blood cholesterol levels, thereby lessening the risk of heart disease.

INGREDIENTS

120 g/4 oz plain flour

½ tsp bicarbonate of soda

½ tsp baking powder

½ tsp salt

120 g/4 oz unsalted butter

225 g/8 oz dark brown sugar

1 egg, beaten

1 tsp vanilla essence

1 Tbsp milk

Grated rind of 1 large orange

175 g/6 oz rolled oats

50 g/2 oz roughly chopped sour cherries

Pre-heat oven to 350°F175°C/Gas mark 4. Grease or line two baking sheets.

● Sift together the flour, bicarbonate, baking powder and salt. Beat together the butter and sugar. Gradually add the egg, vanilla essence and milk and beat until smooth. Stir in the sifted ingredients and mix well. Stir in the grated orange rind, oats and sour cherries.

● Scoop up balls of dough with a tablespoon and place them spaced well apart on the baking sheets to allow the mixture to spread. Bake for 15 to 20 minutes or until just brown. Remove from the oven and leave to cool slightly then, using a thin metal spatula, transfer to a wire rack to cool completely. Store for up to 1 week in an airtight container.

Low-Fat Chocolate Brownies

Preparation time: 15 minutes ● Cooking time: 50 to 60 minutes ● Makes: 9

These brownies contain a fraction of the fat used in traditional brownies.

INGREDIENTS

225 g/8 oz ready-to-eat prunes

3 Tbsp water

120 g/4 oz plain chocolate

3 egg whites

225 g/8 oz light brown sugar

1 tsp salt

1 tsp vanilla essence

50 g/2 oz plain flour, sifted

25 g/1 oz pecan nuts, chopped

Pre-heat oven to 350°F/175°C/Gas mark 4. Grease and line the base of an 20 x 20-cm/8 x 8-in shallow cake tin with non-stick baking parchment.

● Using a blender, blend the prunes with the water until they make a smooth purée. Break the chocolate into a bowl and place over a saucepan of simmering water. Stir occasionally until the chocolate has melted. Remove from the heat and set aside to cool slightly.

● In a bowl mix together the prune purée, melted chocolate, egg whites, sugar, salt and vanilla essence. Fold in the sifted flour.

● Spread the mixture into the prepared tin, sprinkle with pecans and bake for about 50 to 60 minutes or until firm to the touch. Leave in the tin to cool completely. Store, covered in the tin, for 3 days.

Muesli Cookies

Preparation time: 10 minutes ● Cooking time: 15 to 20 minutes ● Makes: About 15

Muesli is high in fibre and rich in vitamins.

INGREDIENTS

120 g/4 oz lightly salted butter or margarine

5 Tbsp demerara sugar

1 egg, beaten

120 g/4 oz sugar-free muesli

50 g/2 oz wholemeal flour

1¼ tsp baking powder

Pre-heat oven to 375°F/190°C/Gas mark 5. Grease or line two baking sheets with non-stick baking parchment.

● Beat together the butter and sugar until light and fluffy. Gradually beat in the egg. Stir in the muesli and flour and mix well. Roll into balls the size of a walnut and place on the baking sheets, allowing space for the cookies to spread. Using the palm of your hand flatten the cookies slightly.

● Bake the cookies for 15 to 20 minutes. Allow to cool slightly on the baking sheets then use a thin metal spatula to transfer to a wire rack to cool completely. Store in an airtight container.

Cookies for Festive Occasions

Cookies are treats and treats are for enjoying on special occasions. It is no wonder that there are cookies associated with specific festivities throughout the world. The very best ingredients are always reserved for these special times, so the cookies are packed with dried fruit, nuts and exotic spices. In America and some other countries special cookies are baked for Christmas, Valentine's Day and Easter.

Children love being involved in the preparation for these events, so have them help make the cookies and maybe decorate some too. Their childish cookies will have a special appeal and would make a lovely, personalized gift.

Christmas

The rich scent of warm cinnamon and spice is one of the first smells of Christmas. Some recipes can be cooked in advance and frozen.

Thanksgiving

An important holiday in the American calendar. Try some of these delicious cookies as an autumn treat.

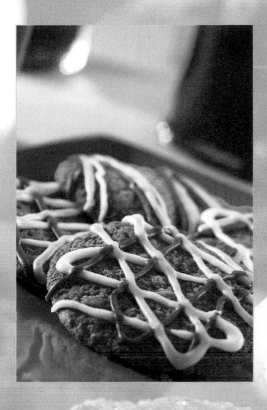

National Holidays

Cookies can be baked to serve as part of National Holiday celebrations. Ice them according to the relevant flag colours!

Passover and Hanukkah

Home-baked treats are an essential part of Jewish holidays.

Valentine's Day

These cookies are perfect gifts for loved ones. They are light and airy, pink and fancy – and fun to make.

Saints' Days and Special Days

Many saints and even some poets have a special day with accompanying customs and traditional foods. The following are just a few.

Cinnamon Jelly Bean Trees

Preparation time: 30 minutes ● Cooking time: 15 minutes ● Makes: About 20

These crisp cinnamon Christmas cookies are decorated with jelly beans.

INGREDIENTS

120 g/4 oz unsalted butter

50 g/2 oz caster sugar

150 g/5 oz plain flour

½ tsp ground cinnamon

5 Tbsp rice flour

ICING

25 g/1 oz icing sugar

1 tsp lemon juice

2 small packets small jelly beans

Pre-heat oven to 350°F/170°C/Gas mark 4. Line two large baking sheets with non-stick baking parchment.

● Beat the butter in a bowl until soft, then gradually mix in the sugar. Stir in the flour, cinnamon and rice flour until well mixed, then knead lightly. Roll out on a lightly floured surface to 5 mm/¼ in. Cut out twenty 8-cm/3-in tree shapes. Lift onto the baking sheets, spacing slightly apart.

● Bake for 15 minutes, until golden. Leave on the baking sheets for a few minutes, then remove and cool on wire racks. Sift the icing sugar into a small bowl and stir in the lemon juice to make a smooth icing. Dip the bases of the jelly beans into the icing and stick onto the trees. Leave to set.

VARIATION

● Substitute 50 g/2 oz unsweetened cocoa powder for the same amount of flour and omit the cinnamon.

Spiced Christmas Cookies

Preparation time: 30 minutes ● Cooking time: 15 minutes ● Makes: About 20

**With their crunchy, sugary topping and warm spicy flavouring, these cookies are
good with mulled wine.**

INGREDIENTS

120 g/4 oz unsalted butter, softened

5 Tbsp light brown sugar

1 egg, separated

150 g/5 oz plain flour, sifted

1 tsp ground cinnamon

½ tsp ground ginger

¼ tsp freshly grated nutmeg

¼ tsp ground cloves

2 Tbsp granulated sugar

Pre-heat oven to 350°F/170°C/Gas mark 4. Line two baking sheets with non-stick baking parchment.
● Beat the butter and sugar together until light and fluffy. Reserve 2 teaspoons egg white. Add the remaining white and yolk to the mixture and mix well. Stir in the flour and spices to make a soft dough. Wrap in clingfilm and chill in the refrigerator for 1 hour.

● Roll out the dough to about 5 mm/¼ in on a lightly floured surface. Cut into Christmas shapes with floured 6-cm/2½-in cutters.

● Transfer the cookies to baking sheets. Brush with the reserved egg white and sprinkle with sugar. Bake for 10 to 12 minutes. Leave for 1 or 2 minutes before lifting off the baking sheets and cooling on wire racks.

TIP

If you want to hang the cookies on the Christmas tree, make a small hole in each with a skewer before baking to allow a ribbon to be threaded through.

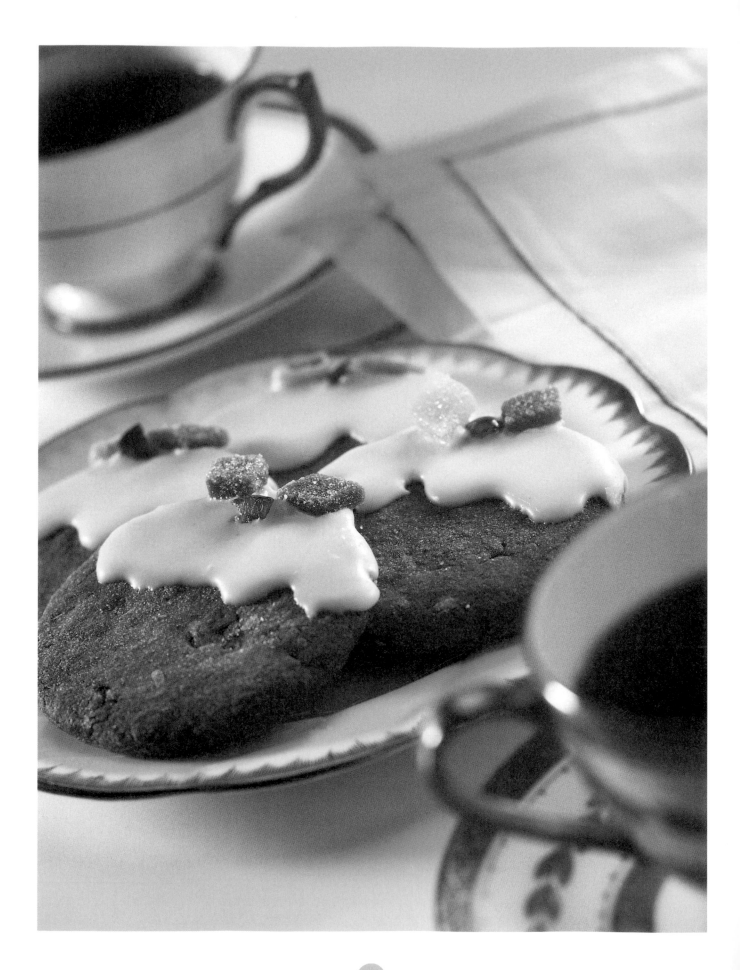

Tipsy Christmas Puddings

Preparation time: 30 minutes ●
Cooking time: 15 minutes ● *Makes: About 20*

These spice and fruit cookies are half-coated in a rich rum icing to look like Christmas puddings.

INGREDIENTS

120 g/4 oz lightly salted butter

120 g/4 oz dark brown sugar

2 egg yolks

225 g/8 oz plain flour

½ tsp ground mixed spice

25 g/1 oz glacé cherries, chopped

50 g/2 oz dried mixed fruit

ICING

120 g/4 oz icing sugar

2 tsp white rum or lemon juice

1–2 tsp hot water

Glacé cherries and angelica, to decorate

Pre-heat oven to 350°F/175°C/Gas mark 4. Lightly grease two baking sheets.

● Beat the butter and sugar until light and fluffy. Add the egg yolks and mix. Work in the flour with the mixed spice, cherries and mixed fruit to make a firm dough. Lightly knead, then roll out on a lightly floured surface to 5 mm/¼ in. Cut into rounds, using a plain 6-cm/2¾-in cutter. Transfer to baking sheets.

● Bake for about 15 minutes, until lightly browned. Then transfer to wire racks to cool.

● Sift the icing sugar into a bowl. Stir in enough rum or lemon juice to make a thick icing. Ice the top half of each cookie and decorate with a piece of glacé cherry and angelica.

Stained-glass Windows

Preparation time: 45 minutes ●
Cooking time: 8 to 10 minutes ● *Makes: About 20*

These cookies look wonderful hanging on the Christmas tree with light shining through.

INGREDIENTS

225 g/8 oz plain flour

150 g/5 oz lightly salted butter

200 g/7 oz caster sugar

Grated rind of 1 orange

1 egg yolk

Boiled sweets, preferably clear with bright colours

Pre-heat oven to 375°F/190°C/Gas mark 5. Line two large baking sheets with non-stick baking parchment.

● Sift the flour into a bowl. Blend in the butter until the mixture resembles breadcrumbs. Stir in the sugar and orange rind. Add the egg yolk and mix to a dough.

● Knead on a lightly floured surface for a few seconds, then roll out to 3mm/⅛ in. With floured cutters, cut out various Christmas shapes. Cut out the centres leaving a border at least 5 mm/¼ in all round. Cut a hole in each to hold a ribbon. Transfer to the baking sheets.

● Put the boiled sweets into plastic bags and coarsely crush with a rolling pin. Sprinkle the crushed sweets into the cut-out centres of the cookies. Bake for 8 to 10 minutes, until the cookies are golden and the sweets have melted. Leave to cool completely on the baking sheets. Thread ribbon through the holes in the top of the cookies. Eat within 10 days.

Snowballs

Preparation time: 35 minutes ● *Cooking time: 18 minutes* ● *Makes: About 12*

These little coconut cookies are sandwiched together in pairs, then coated in more coconut to look like snowballs.

INGREDIENTS

175 g/6 oz lightly salted butter

225 g/8 oz caster sugar

2 egg yolks

375 g/12 oz plain flour

½ tsp bicarbonate of soda

75 g/3 oz sweetened flaked coconut

2 Tbsp milk

DECORATION

120 g/4 oz white chocolate

225 g/8 oz apricot jam

250 g/9 oz sweetened flaked coconut

Icing sugar, to dust (optional)

Pre-heat oven to 375°F/190°C/Gas mark 5. Lightly grease two baking sheets or line with non-stick baking parchment.

● Beat the butter and sugar together until light and fluffy. Add the egg yolks and beat well. Sift the flour and bicarbonate together, then work into the butter mixture, with the sweetened flaked coconut and milk. Divide the mixture into 24 pieces and shape into balls. Place on the baking sheets, allowing 4 cm/1½ in for them to spread. Bake for 18 to 20 minutes, or until golden-brown. Remove from the baking sheets and cool on a wire rack.

● Break the white chocolate into squares and put in a small bowl over a pan of near-boiling water. Stir occasionally until melted. Dip one cookie into the chocolate and sandwich together with a second cookie to make 12 pairs. Leave to set for 20 minutes.

● Heat the apricot jam in a small pan until melted, then sift. Brush over the cookies, then roll in the sweetened flaked coconut to coat. If desired, pile up the snowballs on a plate and lightly dust with icing sugar before serving.

White Chocolate Slices

Preparation time: 30 minutes ● *Cook time: 40 minutes* ● *Makes: 14*

These slices are covered in coconut that looks like snow, to give them a really festive feel.

INGREDIENTS

50 g/2 oz dates, stoned

Grated rind and juice of 2 oranges

50 g/2 oz lightly salted butter

120 g/4 oz light brown sugar

1 egg, beaten

50 mg/2 oz self-raising flour

120 g/4 oz plain flour

TOPPING

5 Tbsp clear runny honey

175 g/6 oz sweetened flaked coconut

2 eggs, beaten

2 Tbsp sweetened flaked coconut, for sprinkling

Pre-heat oven to 350°F/175°C/Gas mark 4. Grease and line an 18 x 28-cm/7 x 11-in shallow tin with non-stick parchment.

● Put the dates, orange rind and orange juice into a small pan and heat gently for about 15 minutes, until soft and pulpy. Leave to cool.

● Beat the butter and sugar together until mixed. Gradually add the egg, beating between each addition. Sift the flours together and stir into the mixture. Spread over the base of the prepared tin.

● Spread the date mixture over the base. For the topping, combine the honey, coconut and eggs. Spread evenly over the date mixture. Bake for 40 minutes until pale golden. Leave to cool in the tin then cut into slices. Sprinkle with the coconut flakes and serve.

Cherry Garlands

Preparation time: 40 minutes ●
Cooking time: 15 to 20 minutes ● *Makes: About 20*

These pretty piped cookies are decorated with glacé cherries and angelica.

INGREDIENTS

50 g/2 oz icing sugar

225 g/8 oz soft tub margarine

225 g/8 oz plain flour

50 g/2 oz cornflour

½ tsp almond essence

25 g/1 oz glacé cherries, very finely chopped

Glacé cherries and angelica, for decorating

1 Tbsp icing sugar, for dredging

Pre-heat oven to 375°F. Lightly grease two baking sheets or line with non-stick baking parchment.
● Sift the icing sugar into a bowl. Add the margarine and cream together until light and fluffy. Sift the flour and cornflour together and beat into the mixture with the almond essence and the chopped glacé cherries.
● Spoon half the mixture into a piping bag fitted with a 5-mm/½-in star nozzle. Pipe 5-cm/2-in rings onto the baking sheet, spacing apart. Decorate each cookie with quartered glacé cherries and pieces of angelica. Bake for 15 to 20 minutes until pale golden. Leave on the baking sheets for a few minutes, then transfer to a wire rack and allow to cool. Dredge with icing sugar before serving. Store cooled cookies in an airtight container with greaseproof paper between the layers.

Walnut Macaroons

Preparation time: 20 minutes ● *Cooking time: 15 to 20 minutes* ● *Makes: About 20*

Classic macaroons are made with ground almonds, but here walnuts are used instead. Lightly toasting the nuts before grinding intensifies their flavour. Try a batch using hazelnuts or a mixture of almonds and walnuts.

INGREDIENTS

120 g/4 oz walnut pieces

120 g/4 oz caster sugar

1 egg white

Edible rice paper

1 Tbsp caster sugar, for sprinkling

Pre-heat oven to 350°F/175°C/Gas mark 4. Put the walnuts on a baking sheet and toast for 10 minutes, until lightly browned. Leave to cool then put in a food processor and process until finely ground.
● Mix the ground walnuts with the sugar and enough egg white to make a fairly stiff paste. Spoon into a piping bag fitted with a 5-mm/½-in plain nozzle and pipe small rounds onto a baking sheet lined with rice paper, spacing slightly apart.
● Lightly sprinkle the cookies with caster sugar. Bake for 15 to 20 minutes, until lightly browned. Transfer to a wire rack and carefully remove excess rice paper when the cookies are completely cool. Store in an airtight container.

Rum-glazed Wreaths

Preparation time: 35 minutes ● *Cooking time: 15 minutes* ● *Makes: About 16*

These cookies look impressive, but are very simple to make.

INGREDIENTS

75 g/3 oz lightly salted butter
5 Tbsp light brown sugar
175 g/6 oz plain flour
½ tsp vanilla essence
1 Tbsp milk

RUM GLAZE

120 g/4 oz icing sugar
4 tsp dark rum, orange-flavoured liqueur or lemon juice

Pre-heat oven to 375°F/190°C/Gas mark 5. Lightly grease the base of two baking sheets or line them with non-stick baking parchment.

● Beat the butter and sugar until light and fluffy. Sift the flour and work into the mixture along with the vanilla essence and milk. On a floured surface, lightly knead the dough for a few seconds.

● Divide the dough into 16 pieces, then divide each piece into 8, and roll into balls. Arrange the balls in rings on the baking sheets, touching each other. Bake for 15 minutes until golden. Leave the balls to cool on the baking sheets.

● For the glaze, sift the icing sugar into a bowl and stir in the rum, orange liqueur or lemon juice. Brush over the cookies and leave to set on a wire rack before serving.

Sugar and Spice Stars

Preparation time: 10 minutes ●
Cooking time: 12 to 15 minutes ● Makes: About 12

These crisp spicy cookies are given a festive finish with a dusting of icing sugar and cinnamon.

INGREDIENTS

50 g/2 oz unsalted butter
50 g/2 oz caster sugar
Grated rind of ½ lemon
½ egg, beaten
5 Tbsp ground almonds
120 g/4 oz plain flour
½ tsp mixed spice
3 Tbsp raspberry jam
2 Tbsp icing sugar, for dusting
½ tsp ground cinnamon, for dusting

Pre-heat oven to 350°F/175°C/Gas mark 4. Lightly grease two baking sheets or line with non-stick baking parchment.

● Beat the butter, sugar and lemon rind together until light and fluffy. Add the egg, a little at a time, beating well after each addition. Stir in the ground almonds, then sift in the flour and spice and mix to a dough. Lightly knead for a few seconds, then wrap in clingfilm and chill in the refrigerator for 30 minutes.

● Roll out the dough to about 3 mm/⅛ in on a lightly floured surface. Using a floured 8-cm/3-in star-shaped cutter, cut out 20 cookies and transfer to the baking sheets.

● Bake for 10 minutes, or until golden. Transfer to a wire rack to cool. Warm the raspberry jam and use to sandwich the cookies together in pairs. Dust with icing sugar, then with ground cinnamon before serving.

Winter Logs

Preparation time: 35 minutes ●
Cooking time: 12 minutes ● Makes: About 35

Dipping these meltingly light chocolate cookies in chocolate makes them twice as nice.

INGREDIENTS

175 g/6 oz unsalted butter, softened
5 Tbsp icing sugar
½ tsp vanilla essence
150 g/5 oz plain flour
25 g/1 oz unsweetened cocoa powder
5 Tbsp cornflour
125 g/4 oz plain chocolate
1 Tbsp icing sugar, for dusting

Pre-heat oven to 350°F/175 °C/Gas mark 4. Line two baking sheets with non-stick baking parchment.

● Beat the butter, sugar and vanilla essence together until light and fluffy. Sift the flour, cocoa powder and cornflour together and fold in.

● Spoon the mixture into a piping bag fitted with a 1-cm/½-in star nozzle. Pipe 6-cm/2½-in lengths onto the baking sheets, spacing well apart. Bake the logs for 12 minutes, then remove from the baking sheets and transfer to wire racks to cool.

● Melt the chocolate in a bowl over a pan of near-boiling water. Dip both ends of the logs into the chocolate and leave to set on non-stick baking parchment. Dust with icing sugar before serving.

Maple Moons

Preparation time: 25 minutes + chilling ● Cooking time: 10 minutes ● Makes: 40

Use real maple syrup in these cookies; its taste is vastly superior to synthetic flavourings.

INGREDIENTS

75 g/3 oz lightly salted butter

3 Tbsp light brown sugar

3 Tbsp maple syrup

1 egg yolk

120 g/4 oz plain flour

50 g/2 oz self-raising flour

Lightly grease two baking sheets or line with non-stick baking parchment.

● Beat together the butter and sugar until light and fluffy. Beat in the maple syrup and egg yolk. Sift the flours together and work into the mixture to make a soft dough. Wrap the dough in clingfilm and then chill for 2 hours until firm.

● Pre-heat oven to 350°F/175°C/Gas mark 4.

● Roll out the dough on a lightly floured surface to 3 mm/⅛ in. Cut out moon shapes using a 6-cm/2½-in cutter and place on the baking sheets. Bake for 10 minutes, until golden-brown. Leave on the baking sheets for a few minutes to harden, then transfer to a wire rack and leave to cool.

VARIATION

● Sandwich the moons together in pairs with coffee buttercream. Dissolve 2 teaspoons instant coffee powder in 2 teaspoons near-boiling water. Cream with 120 g/4 oz unsalted butter and 4 tablespoons sifted icing sugar until light and fluffy. Chill in the refrigerator for 15 minutes to firm slightly before serving.

Catherine Wheels

Preparation time: 40 minutes + chilling ● *Cooking time: 10 to 12 minutes* ● *Makes: 40*

Whirls of orange and chocolate dough make these cookies doubly delicious.

INGREDIENTS

120 g/4 oz lightly salted butter

120 g/4 oz caster sugar

2 eggs, beaten

Grated rind of 1 orange

375 g/12 oz plain flour

25 g/1 oz unsweetened cocoa powder

Lightly grease two baking sheets or line with non-stick baking parchment.

● Beat the butter and sugar until very light and fluffy. Divide the butter mixture in two. Work 200 g/7 oz flour and the orange rind into one half of the butter mixture and the remaining flour and the unsweetened cocoa powder into the other. Lightly knead each piece of dough for a few minutes.

● Roll out on a lightly floured surface to a rectangle measuring 25 x 15 cm/10 x 6 in. Lift the sheet of chocolate dough on top of the orange, then roll up like a Swiss roll. Wrap in clingfilm and chill for 2 hours.

● Pre-heat oven to 400°F/200°C/Gas mark 6.

● Cut the roll into 5-mm/¼-in slices and put on the baking sheets. Bake for 10 to 12 minutes, until darkened. Leave to cool on the baking sheets for a few minutes, then remove and cool on a wire rack.

VARIATION

● For liquorice and vanilla wheels, omit the orange rind and add 1 teaspoon vanilla essence to one half of the dough and omit the unsweetened cocoa powder and add an extra 25 g/1 oz plain flour and 1 teaspoon black liquorice flavouring and colouring to the other half.

Praline Sparklers

Preparation time: 50 minutes ● *Cooking time: 20 minutes* ● *Makes: 14*

Sandwich these short almond cookies together in pairs with a creamy coffee filling, then sprinkle with crushed praline, for the ultimate cookie.

INGREDIENTS

150 g/5 oz plain flour

75 g/3 oz ground almonds

120 g/4 oz lightly salted butter

1 Tbsp icing sugar

1 egg yolk

FILLING AND TOPPING

2 Tbsp plain flour

2 Tbsp caster sugar

1 egg yolk

3 Tbsp milk

3 Tbsp icing sugar

50 g/2 oz unsalted butter

1 tsp coffee essence

PRALINE

120 g/4 oz granulated sugar

5 Tbsp flaked almonds

Pre-heat oven to 350°F/175°C/Gas mark 4. Lightly grease two baking sheets or line with non-stick baking parchment.

● Sift the flour into a bowl. Stir in the ground almonds, then blend in the butter until the mixture resembles breadcrumbs. Sift the icing sugar and stir in. Add the egg yolk and mix to a dough.

● Lightly knead for a few seconds, then roll out on a lightly floured surface to 3 mm/⅛ in. Cut into rounds using a 6-cm/2½-in plain or fluted cutter. Place on the baking sheets. Bake for 10 minutes, until lightly browned. Transfer to a wire rack to cool.

● For the filling, put the flour and sugar in a small saucepan. Gradually blend in the egg yolk and milk to make a smooth paste. Bring to the boil and cook for 1 to 2 minutes until thick, stirring all the time. Leave to cool. Sift the icing sugar into a bowl. Add the butter and beat until light. Add the coffee essence and mix well. Beat in the cooled custard, a little at a time. Chill in the refrigerator for 30 minutes.

● For the praline, put the sugar and 2 tablespoons water in a heavy-bottomed saucepan and heat gently until the sugar has completely dissolved. Bring to the boil and cook until a rich golden-brown. Add the nuts and pour onto an oiled baking sheet. Leave until cold, then crush the praline coarsely.

● Sandwich pairs of cookies together with the coffee cream. Spread the top cookie with coffee cream and sprinkle with crushed praline.

Vanilla Fudge Crumbles

Preparation time: 30 minutes + chilling ● *Cooking time: 12 minutes* ● *Makes: About 20*

Chunks of creamy fudge contrast beautifully with the crunchy texture of these substantial cookies.

INGREDIENTS

75 g/3 oz vanilla fudge
225 g/8 oz plain flour
½ tsp bicarbonate of soda
120 g/4 oz unsalted butter
120 g/4 oz light brown sugar
1 egg
1 tsp vanilla essence
Icing sugar, for dusting

Pre-heat oven to 375°F/190°C/Gas mark 5. Lightly grease two baking sheets or line with non-stick baking parchment.

● Finely chop the fudge. Sift the flour and bicarbonate into a bowl. Blend in the butter until the mixture resembles fine breadcrumbs. Stir in the sugar. Mix the egg and vanilla essence together and add to the dry ingredients with the chopped fudge. Mix to a firm dough.

● Turn out onto a lightly floured surface and shape into a cylinder 23 cm/9 in long. Wrap and chill in the refrigerator for 30 minutes. Cut into 20 slices and put the slices on the baking sheets, spaced slightly apart.

● Bake for 12 minutes, until golden-brown. Leave on the baking sheets for 5 minutes, then transfer to a wire rack to cool. Lightly dust with icing sugar before serving.

VARIATIONS

● Try different flavoured fudges in the cookies for a change; chocolate, coffee or rum and raisin fudge all taste delicious.

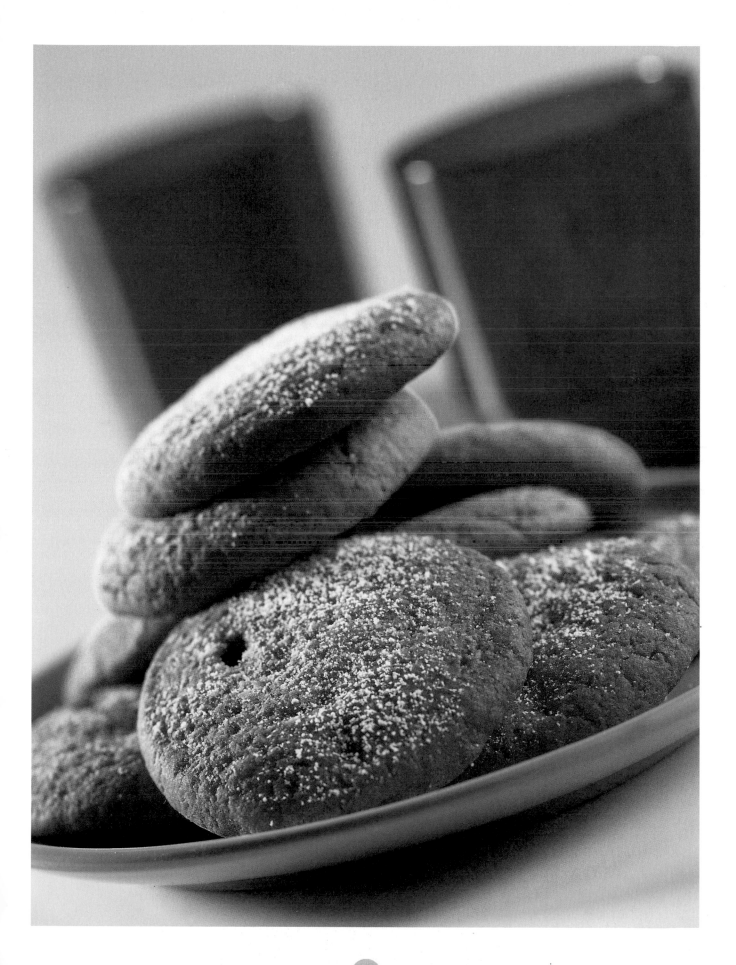

Triple Ginger Cookies

Preparation time: 30 minutes + chilling ●
Cooking time: 10 minutes ● *Makes: About 36*

These festive cookies are packed with ginger – ground, crystallized and fresh – not for the faint-hearted.

INGREDIENTS

250 g/9 oz plain flour
1 Tbsp ground ginger
2 Tbsp bicarbonate of soda
½ tsp salt
175 g/6 oz unsalted butter, softened
200 g/7 oz dark brown sugar
6 Tbsp treacle
1 egg
2 Tbsp finely chopped root ginger
50 g/2 oz chopped crystallized ginger, plus extra for decoration

Into a medium bowl, sift together the flour, ground ginger, bicarbonate and salt.

● In a large bowl, beat the butter until soft, beat in the sugar until the mixture is light and fluffy. Beat in the treacle and egg until combined. Stir in the flour-spice mixture followed by the fresh and crystallized ginger.

● Form the dough into a ball, wrap in clingfilm and refrigerate for 2 to 3 hours, or overnight until chilled.

● Pre-heat oven to 350°F/175°C/Gas mark 4. Grease or line two baking sheets.

● Using a tablespoon to scoop up the mixture, form into 5-mm/½-in balls. Place 5 cm/2 in apart on baking sheets and press a few pieces of crystallized ginger into each. Bake until golden-brown, about 10 minutes. Leave the cookies to cool for 2 minutes, then transfer to wire racks to cool completely. Store in an airtight container.

Kourambiedes

Preparation time: 25 minutes + chilling ●
Cooking time: 15 to 20 minutes ● *Makes: About 30*

These rich, tender almond cookies are served at all festive occasions in Greece. At Christmas a whole clove is often buried in the cookies to symbolize the gifts the three wise men brought to the Christ child.

INGREDIENTS

50 g/2 oz blanched almonds, lightly toasted and cooled
225 g/8 oz unsalted butter
2 Tbsp icing sugar
¼ tsp salt
1 small egg yolk
1 Tbsp brandy or orange-flavoured liqueur
225 g/8 oz plain flour
Icing sugar, for dusting

In a food processor fitted with a metal blade, process the cooled toasted almonds until very fine crumbs are formed.

● In a medium bowl, beat the butter until soft, beat in the sugar until the mixture becomes light and fluffy. Beat in the salt, egg yolk and brandy until combined. Stir in the flour and ground almonds until a soft dough forms. Refrigerate, covered, until firm, about 1 hour.

● Pre-heat oven to 450°F/230°C/Gas mark 8.

● Use a tablespoon to scoop out dough, and form into 2.5-cm/1-in balls. Place on ungreased baking sheets, and bake until set and just golden, about 15 to 20 minutes. Allow to cool slightly, then transfer the cookies onto wire racks to cool completely. Dust with icing sugar. Store in an airtight container.

Cookie Canes

Preparation time: 20 minutes + chilling ●
Cooking time: 15 to 17 minutes ● *Makes: About 24*

**This dough can be shaped into canes or Christmas
wreaths, then tinted whatever colour you like.**

INGREDIENTS

225 g/8 oz unsalted butter, softened

175 g/6 oz icing sugar

½ tsp vanilla essence

¼ tsp peppermint essence

300 g/10 oz plain flour, sifted

¼ tsp salt

¼ tsp red food colouring, optional

50 g/2 oz crushed peppermint sweets

In a large bowl, beat the butter until soft, beat in the
sugar until the mixture becomes light and fluffy. Beat
in the egg, vanilla and peppermint essences until
combined. Stir in the flour and salt until well-blended.
● Place half the dough in clingfilm and seal. Add food
colouring and crushed peppermint sweets to the
remaining dough and beat until mixed. Wrap in
clingfilm and refrigerate both doughs for 1 hour.
● Pre-heat oven to 350°F/175°C/Gas mark 4. Grease two
baking sheets or line with non-stick baking parchment.
● To form canes, use a teaspoon to scoop out a piece of
plain dough then roll into a 10-cm/4-in long log shape.
Repeat with the red-coloured dough. Twist the two logs
together, and bend the top end to form into a cane
shape. Set canes 5 cm/2 in apart on baking sheets.
● Bake until firm, about 8 to 10 minutes; do not allow
to brown. Cool for a few minutes then place on wire
racks to cool completely. Store in an airtight container.

Brandied Shortbread

Preparation time: 25 minutes ●
Cooking time: 25 minutes ● *Makes: 8 wedges*

**This buttery brandy-flavoured shortbread is enhanced
by the addition of rice flour, giving it a lighter and
crunchier texture.**

INGREDIENTS

120 g/4 oz unsalted butter, softened

120 g/4 oz caster sugar

1 Tbsp brandy

Few drops brandy essence

120 g/4 oz plain flour

5 Tbsp fine rice flour

4 Tbsp glacé cherries

Few pieces angelica

1 Tbsp caster sugar, for sprinkling

Pre-heat oven to 350°F/175°C/Gas mark 4. Beat the
butter in a mixing bowl, then gradually add the
sugar, brandy and brandy essence. Add the flour and rice
flour and stir with a thin metal spatula until blended.
● Press the mixture into an 18-cm/7-in round shallow
tin with a removable base and level the top. Prick all
over with a fork. Mark into eight equal wedges and
decorate each with glacé cherries and angelica. Sprinkle
the wedges with caster sugar and bake for 25 minutes,
or until pale golden.
● While the shortbread is still hot, carefully remove
from the tin, but leave on the base. Cut into eight
wedges, as marked, but do not separate the pieces, or
they will dry out. Transfer to a wire rack to cool. Stored
in an airtight tin or wrapped in foil, the shortbread will
keep for up to a week.

Cranberry and Orange Clusters

Preparation time: 20 minutes ●
Cooking time: 15 minutes ● *Makes: 20*

The tartness of dried cranberries adds a certain bite to these soft-textured drop cookies.

INGREDIENTS

120 g/4 oz unsalted butter
120 g/4 oz caster sugar
Grated rind of 1 orange
1 egg
120 g/4 oz rolled oats
50 g/2 oz dried cranberries
150 g/5 oz plain flour
½ tsp baking powder

Pre-heat oven to 350°F/175°C/Gas mark 4. Lightly grease two baking sheets or line with non-stick baking parchment.

● Beat the butter, sugar and orange rind in a bowl until creamy. Gradually add the egg, beating well between each addition. Stir in the oats and cranberries. Sift the flour and baking powder into the bowl and mix until evenly combined.

● Place small tablespoons of the mixture on the prepared baking sheets, spacing them well apart. Flatten slightly with the back of a fork. Bake for 15 minutes until risen and light golden-brown. Leave on the baking sheets for 5 minutes, then transfer to a wire rack to cool. The cookies will still be soft when you take them out of the oven, but will become firm as they cool.

Pumpkin Fingers

Preparation time: 30 minutes ●
Cooking time: 50 minutes ● *Makes: 18*

These buttery shortbread fingers with a pumpkin topping could be served for a Thanksgiving or Halloween party.

INGREDIENTS

120 g/4 oz plain flour
50 g/2 oz icing sugar
50 g/2 oz unsalted butter
1 egg yolk

TOPPING

120 g/4 oz cooked pumpkin
225 ml/8 fl oz single cream
2 eggs, beaten
225 g/8 oz light brown sugar
1 tsp ground cinnamon
1 Tbsp icing sugar, for dusting

Pre-heat oven to 350°F/175°C/Gas mark 4. Grease a shallow 18 x 28-cm/7 x 11-in tin and line with non-stick baking parchment.

● Sift the flour and icing sugar into a bowl. Blend in the butter until the mixture resembles fine breadcrumbs. Add the egg yolk and mix to a dough. Lightly knead on a floured surface until smooth, then press into the base of the tin. Prick all over with a fork, then bake for 10 minutes, until golden.

● For the filling, sieve the cooked pumpkin to make a smooth purée. Stir in the cream, eggs, sugar and cinnamon. Pour over the base and bake for 40 to 45 minutes more, or until a skewer inserted into the middle comes out clean.

● Leave to cool in the tin, then cut into 18 fingers. Remove from the tin and lightly dust with icing sugar before serving.

Sticky Toffee Apple Treats

Preparation time: 25 minutes ● Cooking time: 10 minutes ● Makes: 20

These autumn cookies are packed with chunks of apple and drizzled with toffee icing.

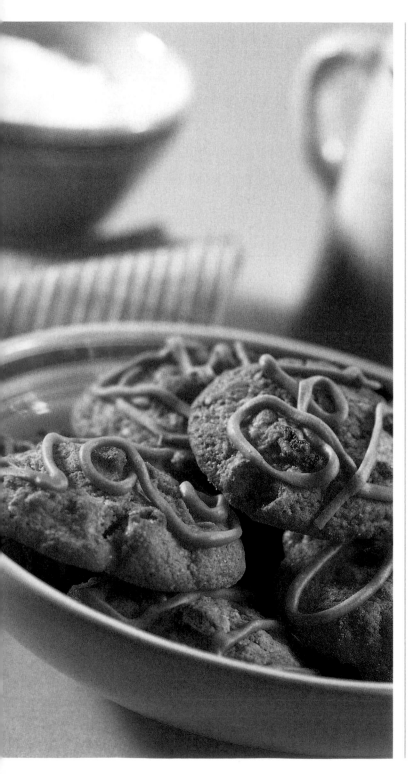

INGREDIENTS

120 g/4 oz lightly salted butter

120 g/4 oz light brown sugar

1 egg, beaten

200 g/7 oz self-raising flour

Pinch of salt

120 g/4 oz dried apples, chopped

ICING

50 g/2 oz butter

5 Tbsp light brown sugar

3 Tbsp milk

75 g/3 oz icing sugar

Pre-heat oven to 375°F/190°C/Gas mark 5. Lightly grease two baking sheets or line with non-stick baking parchment.

● Beat the butter and sugar until light and fluffy. Gradually add the egg, beating well each time. Sift the flour and salt into the mixture and mix in the apples.

● Place heaped teaspoonfuls of the mixture onto the prepared baking sheets, spacing well apart to allow the cookies to spread. Bake for 10 minutes or until just golden-brown. Leave on the baking sheets for 3 minutes, then remove and cool on a wire rack.

● For the toffee icing, melt the butter over a gentle heat. Add the brown sugar and milk and stir gently until dissolved. Boil for 1 minute. Remove from the heat, then sift the icing sugar and beat in. Spoon into a piping bag while still warm, snip off the end and drizzle over the cookies. Ice the cookies quickly before the icing cools and starts to harden. Leave the icing to set.

Shooting Stars

Preparation time: 40 minutes ● *Cooking time: 10 to 12 minutes* ● *Makes: 30*

Cut these cookies into stars of several sizes and sprinkle with coloured sugar crystals before baking, for a sparkling effect.

INGREDIENTS

120 g/4 oz lightly salted butter
120 g/4 oz caster sugar
Grated rind of 1 lemon
1 egg, beaten
250 g/9 oz plain flour
25 g/1 oz cornflour
½ tsp vanilla essence
3 Tbsp coloured sugar crystals

Pre-heat oven to 350°F/175°C/Gas mark 4. Lightly grease two baking sheets or line with non-stick baking parchment.

● Beat the butter, sugar and lemon rind until pale and fluffy. Gradually add the egg, beating after each addition.

● Sift the flour and cornflour together and blend into the butter mixture with the vanilla essence. Lightly knead for a few seconds until smooth. Roll out on a floured surface to 1 cm/¼ in thick, then cut into large and small star shapes using 6-cm/2½-in, 4-cm/1½-in and 2.5-cm/1-in floured cutters. Place on the prepared baking sheets, separating the largest stars.

● Sprinkle with sugar crystals, then press them down gently. Bake the smaller cookies for 10 minutes and the larger ones for 12 minutes. Cool on the baking sheets for 3 minutes, then transfer to a wire rack to cool.

Celebration Cookies

Preparation time: 35 minutes ● *Cooking time: 15 minutes* ● *Makes: 8*

These traditional all-American giant cookies are drizzled with icing in the colours of the flag – red, white, and blue. Vary the icing colours to suit your own flag.

INGREDIENTS

50 g/2 oz lightly salted butter

120 g/4 oz white vegetable fat

5 Tbsp light brown sugar

1 egg, beaten

½ tsp vanilla essence

150 g/5 oz self-raising flour

ICING

120 g/4 oz icing sugar

1 Tbsp hot water

Red and blue food colouring

Pre-heat oven to 375°F/190°C/Gas mark 5. Lightly grease two baking sheets or line with non-stick baking parchment.

● Beat the butter, white vegetable fat and sugar together until light and fluffy. Gradually add the egg and vanilla essence, beating well between each addition. Sift the flour and stir into the mixture.

● Drop tablespoonfuls of the mixture onto the baking sheets, spacing well apart. Flatten to about 2 cm/¾ in thick. Bake for 15 minutes until golden. Leave on the baking sheets for 2 to 3 minutes, then remove and cool on a wire rack.

● Sift the icing sugar into a bowl and stir in enough water to make a thick piping consistency. Divide the icing into three. Leave one white, colour one red, and one blue. Spoon into separate piping bags, snip off the ends and drizzle over the cookies. Leave to set before serving.

TIP

Unbaked, the cookie mixture will keep in a sealed container in the refrigerator for up to a week. The cookies are best eaten on the day they are iced.

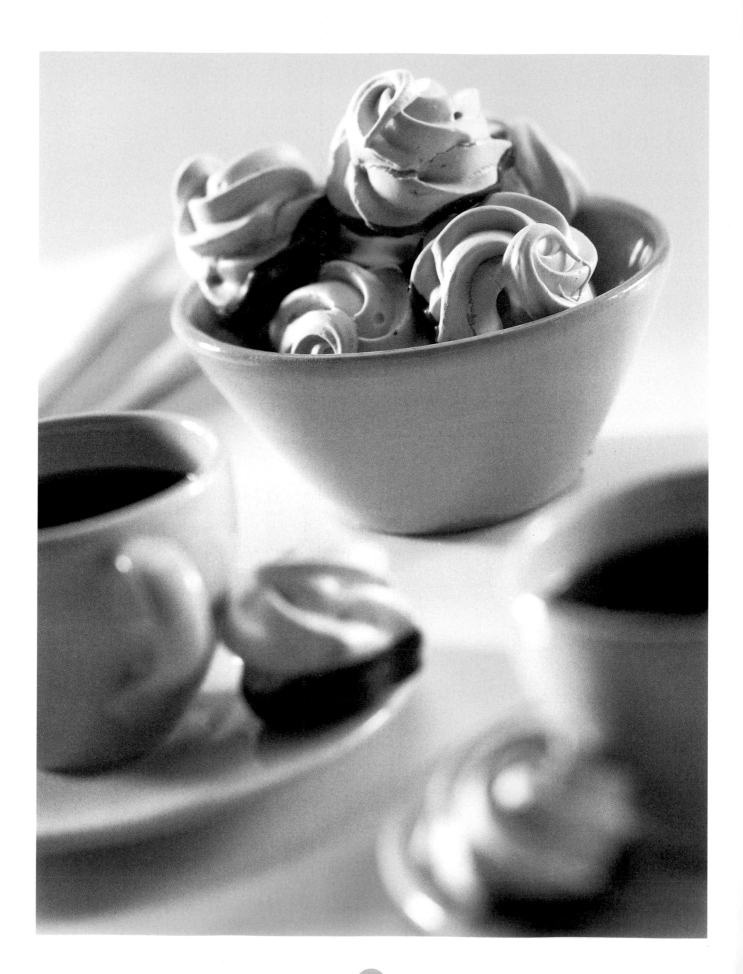

Coffee Meringues

Preparation time: 20 minutes ●
Cooking time: 2 hours ● *Makes: 50*

Light as air crisp meringues with just a hint of coffee, are dipped in smooth chocolate for bite-sized treats.

INGREDIENTS

4 egg whites
225 g/8 oz caster sugar
1 tsp coffee essence
225 g/8 oz plain chocolate

Pre-heat oven to 275°F/140°C/Gas mark 1. Lightly grease two baking sheets or line with non-stick baking parchment.

● Put the egg whites and sugar into a large bowl over a pan of very hot water and whisk until stiff and shiny, making sure that the water does not boil, or the mixture will get too hot. Remove the bowl from the heat, add the coffee essence and continue whisking until the mixture will hold stiff peaks.

● Spoon the mixture into a piping bag fitted with a large star nozzle and pipe swirls of meringue on the baking sheets. Bake for 2 hours or until completely dried out, switching the baking sheets around halfway through cooking. Allow the meringues to cool on the baking sheets.

● Melt the chocolate in a bowl over very hot water. Dip the base of the meringues into the chocolate and leave to set on greaseproof paper before serving, or if prefered, sandwich the meringues together in pairs.

Cinnamon Balls

Preparation time: 20 minutes ●
Cooking time: 25 to 30 minutes ● *Makes: About 20*

These are very popular Passover cookies, as they contain no flour.

INGREDIENTS

225 g/8 oz blanched and ground almonds, walnuts, or pecan nuts
250 g/7 oz caster sugar
2 Tbsp ground cinnamon
2 egg whites
¼ tsp cream of tartar
200 g/7 oz icing sugar

Pre-heat oven to 325°F/160°C/Gas mark 3. Grease or line two baking sheets with non-stick baking parchment.

● In a medium bowl, combine the nuts, half the sugar, and half the cinnamon. In a separate bowl, beat the egg whites until foamy. Add the cream of tartar, and continue beating until soft peaks form. Gradually add the remaining sugar, a tablespoon at a time, beating well after each addition, until the whites are stiff and glossy. Gently fold in the nut mixture.

● With moistened hands, shape mixture into walnut-size balls. Place on baking sheets 2.5 cm/1 in apart. Bake until set and golden, 25 to 30 minutes, turning baking sheets halfway through cooking. Allow the cookies to cool slightly.

● Combine the icing sugar and remaining cinnamon. Roll each warm cinnamon ball in the mixture to coat completely, then set on a wire rack to cool. Roll balls in the cinnamon-sugar again when cold. Store in an airtight container.

Hanukkah Sugar Cookies

Preparation time: 45 minutes + chilling ● Cooking time: 20 to 24 minutes ● Makes: About 40

**Search out some unusual cutters for this special joyous holiday, or make your own
Jewish star template from a piece of cardboard.**

INGREDIENTS

250 g/9 oz plain flour

½ tsp baking powder

½ tsp salt

175 g/6 oz unsalted butter, softened

200 g/7 oz caster sugar

1 egg, beaten

Grated rind of 1 lemon

1 Tbsp lemon juice

1 tsp vanilla essence

½ tsp lemon essence

ICING

450 g/1 lb icing sugar

2–3 Tbsp milk

1 Tbsp lemon juice

Blue food colouring

Into a medium bowl, sift together the flour, baking powder and salt. In a large bowl beat the butter, until creamy, then add the sugar and beat until light and fluffy. Gradually beat in the egg, lemon rind and juice, vanilla and lemon essences until well blended. Little by little add the flour mixture until a soft dough forms.

Wrap in clingfilm and refrigerate for several hours or overnight until firm enough to roll (the dough can be made up to 2 days ahead).

● Pre-heat oven to 350°F/175°C/Gas mark 4. Grease or line two baking sheets with non-stick baking parchment.

● On a lightly floured surface, roll out half the dough to 5 mm/¼ in thick (keep the remaining dough refrigerated). Using a floured cutter or template, cut out as many shapes as possible. Place 2.5 cm/1 in apart on the baking sheets. Bake until golden, 10 to 12 minutes. Allow the cookies to cool slightly, then transfer to wire racks to cool completely. Repeat with remaining dough.

● In a medium bowl, sift the icing sugar. Stir in 2 tablespoons of milk and the lemon juice, adding a little more milk if the mixture is too thick. Spoon half of the icing into a separate bowl and add a few drops of food colouring mixing to the desired shade. Spoon the icings into two piping bags and pipe designs or decorations onto each cookie shape. Leave icing to set for 2 hours. Store in an airtight container with a layer of greaseproof paper between each of the cookie layers.

Sweethearts

Preparation time: 45 minutes ● *Cooking time: 10 minutes* ● *Makes: 20*

Use gingerbread men and women cutters to make these cute cookies with tiny hearts.

INGREDIENTS

1 Tbsp golden syrup	1 egg yolk
50 g/2 oz butter	50 g/2 oz pink or red boiled sweets
50 g/2 oz caster sugar	ICING
225 g/8 oz plain flour	225 g/8 oz icing sugar
½ tsp bicarbonate of soda	1 egg white
3 Tbsp milk	¼ tsp lemon juice

Pre-heat oven to 350°F/175°C/Gas mark 4. Line two baking sheets with non-stick baking parchment.

● Put the syrup, butter and sugar in a small saucepan and heat gently until melted, stirring occasionally. Remove from the heat and leave to cool for 2 to 3 minutes. Sift the flour and bicarbonate into a mixing bowl and make a well in the middle. Pour in the syrup mixture, milk and egg yolk. Mix to form a soft smooth dough.

● Roll out the warm dough between two sheets of non-stick baking parchment or clingfilm until 3 mm/⅛ in thick. Cut into men and women using 8-cm/3-in cutters. Transfer to the baking sheets. Cut a small heart shape from the centre of each.

● Roughly crush the boiled sweets and sprinkle about a quarter of a candy in each cutout section. Bake for 10 minutes, until lightly browned and firm. Leave to cool on the baking sheets.

● Sift the icing sugar twice. Put the egg white in a bowl and whisk lightly. Gradually beat in enough icing sugar until the mixture stands in soft peaks and is a pipeable consistency. Spoon into a piping bag fitted with a very fine nozzle and pipe faces, buttons and bows on the people. Leave to set.

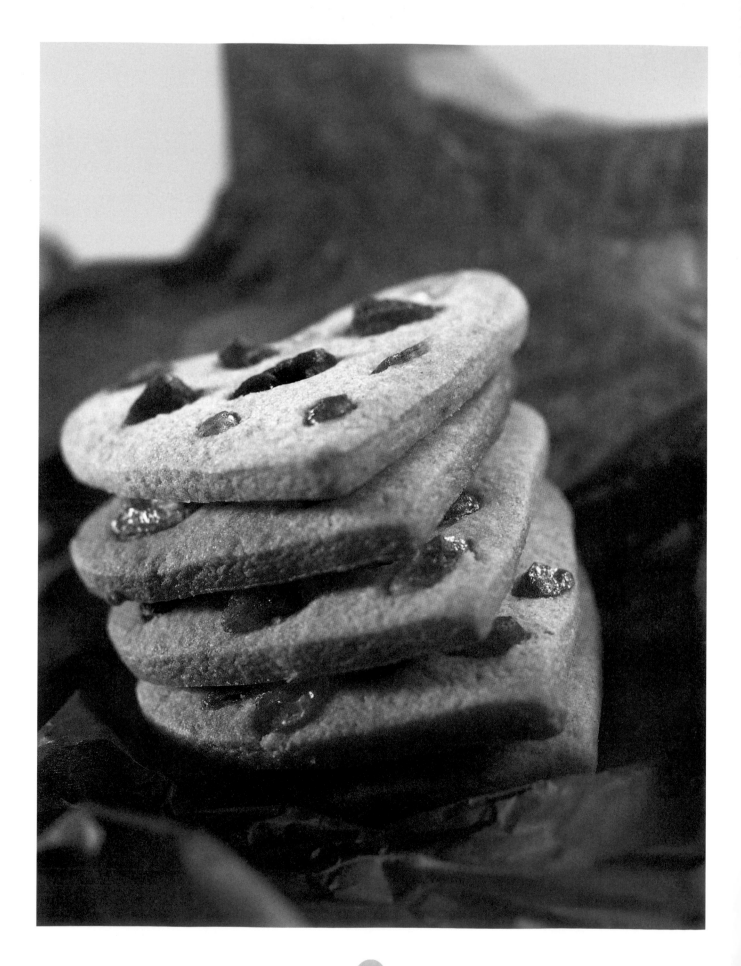

Honeyed Hearts

Preparation time: 20 minutes + chilling ●
Cooking time: 15 minutes ● *Makes: 30*

These honey cookies with a crunchy sugar topping will melt even the hardest heart.

INGREDIENTS

75 g/3 oz lightly salted butter
120 g/4 oz caster sugar
1 Tbsp set honey
1 egg, beaten
175 g/6 oz plain flour
2 Tbsp cornflour
1 Tbsp egg white
2 Tbsp brown sugar crystals

Pre-heat oven to 350°F/175°C/Gas mark 4. Lightly grease two baking sheets or line with non-stick baking parchment.

● Beat the butter, sugar and honey until very soft, light and fluffy. Gradually add the egg. Sift the flour and cornflour together and work into the butter mixture to make a soft dough. Lightly knead on a floured surface for a few seconds until smooth, then wrap in clingfilm and chill in the refrigerator for 30 minutes.

● Roll out on a lightly floured surface to a thickness of 5 mm/¼ in. Cut into heart shapes using a floured 5-cm/2-in cutter. Place on the baking sheets, spacing slightly apart. Brush the cookies with egg white and sprinkle each with a few sugar crystals. Bake for 15 minutes, or until lightly browned. Leave the cookies on the baking sheets for 2 to 3 minutes, then remove and cool on a wire rack.

Rose Petal Cookies

Preparation time: 25 minutes + chilling ●
Cooking time: 10 minutes ● *Makes: 16*

Make these fragrant cookies using red or yellow perfumed rose petals.

INGREDIENTS

250 g/9 oz plain flour
120 g/4 oz icing sugar
200 g/7 oz unsalted butter
Petals of 2 roses

Lightly grease two baking sheets or line with non-stick baking parchment. Sift the flour and icing sugar into a bowl. Blend in the butter until the mixture resembles fine breadcrumbs.

● Snip the rose petals into small pieces with scissors and stir into the mixture. Continue to blend with your fingers until a dough forms. Lightly knead for a few seconds on a floured surface until smooth. Roll the dough into a cylinder about 20 cm/8 in long. Wrap in clingfilm and chill in the refrigerator for 1 hour.

● Pre-heat oven to 325°F/160°C/Gas mark 3. Cut the dough into 1-cm/½-in slices and arrange on the baking sheets, spacing slightly apart. Bake for 8 to 10 minutes until light golden-brown. Leave on the baking sheets for 2 minutes, then remove and cool on a wire rack.

TIP

Make sure you use unsprayed freshly picked roses for these cookies.

Lovers' Knots

Preparation time: 45 minutes + chilling ●
Cooking time: 10 minutes ● *Makes: 20*

Rich, dark and handsome, chocolate dough is twisted into knots, then dipped into yet more chocolate.

INGREDIENTS

50 g/2 oz unsweetened cocoa powder
2 Tbsp boiling water
1 tsp vanilla essence
120 g/4 oz lightly salted butter
120 g/4 oz icing sugar
1 egg, beaten
225 g/8 oz plain flour
375 g/12 oz plain chocolate

Lightly grease two baking sheets or line with non-stick baking parchment. Sift the unsweetened cocoa powder into a small bowl and pour on the boiling water. Stir to form a smooth paste, then stir in the vanilla essence.

● Beat the butter and sugar until light and fluffy. Gradually add the egg, beating well after each addition. Beat in the cocoa mixture until well mixed. Sift the flour and work into the mixture to make a soft dough. Wrap in clingfilm and chill for 1 hour.

● Pre-heat oven to 325°F/160°C/Gas mark 3. Divide the dough into 20 pieces. Roll each piece into a sausage shape about 15 cm/6 in long, then tie in a loose knot, tucking the ends under. Arrange on the prepared baking sheets and bake for 10 minutes until firm. Allow to cool on the sheets.

● Break the chocolate into pieces and melt, stirring, in a double boiler. Coat the knots, one at a time, with the chocolate. Leave to set on a wire rack.

Soft Centres

Preparation time: 25 minutes + chilling ●
Cooking time: 10 minutes ● *Makes: 20*

A crisp coffee case conceals a melted chocolate centre. Serve these cookies freshly baked while still warm.

INGREDIENTS

150 g/5 oz unsalted butter
200 g/7 oz caster sugar
2 tsp coffee essence
1 egg yolk
300 g/10 oz self-raising flour
50 g/2 oz plain chocolate
50 g/2 oz white chocolate
1 Tbsp unsweetened cocoa powder, for dusting

Lightly grease a large baking sheet or line with non-stick baking parchment. Beat the butter and sugar until light and fluffy. Beat in the coffee essence and egg yolk. Sift the flour into the bowl and mix to a firm dough. Wrap and chill in the refrigerator for 20 minutes.

● Pre-heat oven to 350°F/175°C/Gas mark 4.

● Roll out about a third of the dough on a lightly floured surface to 3 mm/⅛ in thick and cut out 20 circles with a 5-cm/2-in cutter. Transfer to the prepared baking sheet. Place a square of chocolate in the middle of each circle. Roll out the remaining dough and cut out 20 circles with a 6-cm/2½-in cutter. Lay these over the chocolate-topped bases, pressing the edges together to seal and enclose the filling.

● Bake for 10 minutes, until darkened and risen. Leave on the baking sheets for 5 minutes, then remove and cool on a wire rack. Dust with cocoa powder before serving.

Shamrocks

Preparation time: 25 minutes + chilling ● Cooking time: 15 minutes ● Makes: 20

The shamrock is the emblem of Ireland is and these cookies are ideal to serve on St Patrick's day.

INGREDIENTS

50 g/2 oz mint-flavoured chocolate sticks

175 g/6 oz butter

225 g/8 oz caster sugar

1 egg

375 g/12 oz plain flour

ICING

225 g/8 oz icing sugar

¼ tsp peppermint essence

2 Tbsp hot water

Green food colouring

Lightly grease two baking sheets or line with non-stick baking parchment. Finely chop the mint-flavoured chocolate sticks. Beat the butter and sugar until light and fluffy. Gradually add the egg, beating well after each addition. Sift the flour into the bowl, add the chocolate pieces, and mix to a soft dough. Lightly knead for a few seconds until smooth, then wrap in clingfilm and chill in the refrigerator for 30 minutes.

● Pre-heat oven to 350°F/175°C/Gas mark 4. Roll out the dough on a lightly floured surface until 5 mm/¼ in thick and cut into shamrock shapes with a 6-cm/2½-in cutter. Transfer to the baking sheets. Bake for 15 minutes, until light golden-brown. Leave on the baking sheets for 2 to 3 minutes, then remove and cool on a wire rack.

● Sift the icing sugar into a bowl. Add the peppermint essence and enough water to make a thick icing. Stir in a drop of green food colouring. Use to ice the cookies. Leave the icing to set before serving.

Sedgemoor Easter Biscuits

Preparation time: 15 minutes ● Cooking time: 20 minutes ● Makes: 16

Legend has it that when the Duke of Monmouth was fleeing the Battle of Sedgemoor, he fell into a ditch. A local woman thought he was an unfortunate peasant down on his luck and baked him these cookies.

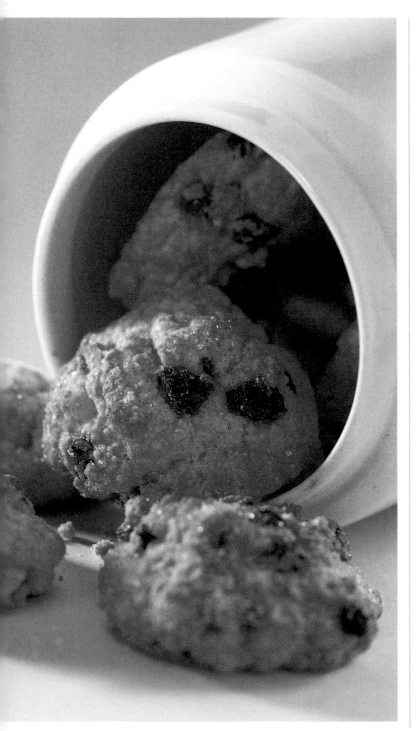

INGREDIENTS

225 g/8 oz plain flour

1 tsp ground cinnamon

120 g/4 oz lightly salted butter

120 g/4 oz caster sugar

50 g/2 oz currants

1 egg, beaten

2 Tbsp brandy

1 Tbsp milk

1 Tbsp granulated sugar, for sprinkling

Pre-heat oven to 350°F/175 °C/Gas mark 4. Lightly grease two baking sheets or line with non-stick baking parchment.

● Sift the flour and cinnamon into a bowl and blend in the butter until the mixture resembles breadcrumbs. Stir in the sugar and currants. Mix the egg, brandy and milk together and stir into the dry mixture to produce a soft dropping consistency.

● Drop tablespoonfuls of the mixture onto the baking sheet and sprinkle with granulated sugar. Bake for 20 minutes, until lightly browned and firm. Leave on the baking sheets for a few minutes, then remove and cool on a wire rack.

VARIATION

Mixed dried fruit or quartered glacé cherries can be added to the mixture instead of currants.

Iced Easter Ovals

Preparation time: 25 minutes ● Cooking time: 15 minutes ● Makes: 20

These chocolate chip cookies with pastel ribbon and bow icing make great Easter treats.

INGREDIENTS

50 g/2 oz butter
225 g/8 oz caster sugar
1 egg, beaten
375 g/12 oz plain flour
2 Tbsp cornflour
5 Tbsp plain chocolate chips

ICING

225 g/8 oz icing sugar
2 Tbsp hot water
Pink, green and yellow food colouring

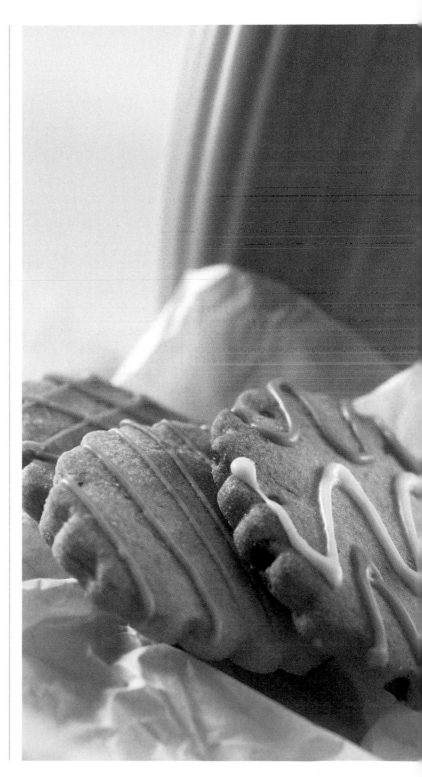

Pre-heat oven to 350°F/175°C/Gas mark 4. Lightly grease two baking sheets or line with non-stick baking parchment.

● Beat the butter and sugar until light and fluffy. Gradually add the egg. Sift the flour with the cornflour and work into the butter mixture with the chocolate chips to make a stiff dough. Lightly knead the dough for a few seconds until smooth.

● Roll out on a floured surface to a thickness of 5 mm/¼ in. Cut into 20 ovals with a plain or fluted 8-cm/3-in oval cutter. Bake in the oven for 15 minutes, until light golden-brown. Leave to cool on the baking sheets for a few minutes, then cool on a wire rack.

● For the icing, sift the icing sugar into a bowl and stir in enough hot water to make a smooth frosting. Divide the icing into three and colour one pale pink, one pale green and one yellow. Spoon into piping bags, snip off the ends and pipe a ribbon and bow design on each cookie. Leave to set before serving.

Maypole Twists

Preparation time: 40 minutes + chilling ● Cooking time: 10 minutes ● Makes: 12

Strands of dough, one coated in coloured sugar crystals are twisted together to make these cookies.

INGREDIENTS

225 g/8 oz plain flour
1 tsp baking powder
120 g/4 oz unsalted butter
120 g/4 oz caster sugar
Grated rind of 1 lemon
1 Tbsp lemon juice
1 egg, beaten
2 Tbsp yellow and orange sugar crystals

Line two baking sheets with non-stick baking parchment. Sift the flour and baking powder into a bowl. Blend in the butter until the mixture resembles fine breadcrumbs. Stir in the sugar and lemon rind. Add the lemon juice and beaten egg and mix to a soft dough. Lightly knead for a few seconds until smooth. Wrap in clingfilm and chill in the refrigerator for 30 minutes.

● Pre-heat oven to 350°F/175°C/Gas mark 4. Divide the dough into 24 pieces. Roll each into a 10-cm/4-in length, then roll 12 of the lengths in the sugar crystals. Place 2 lengths side by side, one sugar-coated and one plain, and press the top ends together. Twist the two lengths together, pressing the ends to join again at the finish and trimming.

● Place on the prepared baking sheets, spacing slightly apart, and bake for 10 minutes until light golden-brown. Leave on the baking sheets for 2 minutes, then remove and cool on a wire rack.

VARIATION

● If preferred the twists can be glazed with a lemon icing instead of using the sugar crystals. Sift 120 g/4 oz icing sugar into a bowl. Stir in 5 teaspoons lemon juice to make a thin icing. Lightly brush over the twists while still warm. Leave the cookies to cool and the icing to set before serving.

COOKIES FOR FESTIVE OCCASIONS

Cattern Cakes

Preparation time: 25 minutes ●
Cooking time: 10 minutes ● *Makes: 15*

These cookies were served on November 25 in honour of St Catherine, martyred in AD 310, who gave her name to the Catherine Wheel firework. She became the protector of unmarried girls who would crown her statue with a wreath of greenery in the hope of finding a husband.

INGREDIENTS

120 g/4 oz lightly salted butter
120 g/4 oz caster sugar
1 egg, beaten
225 g/8 oz plain flour
¼ tsp baking powder
½ tsp ground cinnamon
½ cup ground almonds
2 Tbsp currants
1 Tbsp caraway seeds
4 Tbsp seedless raspberry jam

Pre-heat oven to 350°F/175°C/Gas mark 4. Lightly grease two baking sheets or line with non-stick baking parchment.

● Beat the butter and sugar together, then gradually add the egg, beating between each addition. Sift the flour, baking powder and cinnamon into the bowl and stir into the mixture with the ground almonds, currants and caraway seeds to make a dough. Lightly knead on a floured surface until smooth. Roll out the dough into a 25 x 30-cm/10 x 12-in rectangle.

● Warm the jam in a small pan until runny and thinly brush over the dough. Roll up from one of the long sides like a Swiss roll and cut into 5-mm/¾-in thick slices. Arrange on the baking sheets, spacing slightly apart and bake for 10 minutes. Leave on the baking sheets for 5 minutes, then transfer to a wire rack to cool.

Honey and Oat Bites

Preparation time: 20 minutes ●
Cooking time: 20 minutes ● *Makes: 30*

Use the thicker whole rolled oats for these substantial cookies with their crisp edges and slightly chewy centres.

INGREDIENTS

2 Tbsp set honey
175 g/6 oz lightly salted butter
120 g/4 oz caster sugar
150 g/5 oz rolled oats
75 g/3 oz sweetened flaked coconut
150 g/5 oz plain flour
1 tsp bicarbonate of soda
1 Tbsp hot water

Pre-heat oven to 325°F/160°C/Gas mark 3. Lightly grease two baking sheets or line with non-stick baking parchment.

● Put the honey, butter and sugar in a small pan and heat gently until the butter has melted and the sugar dissolved. Remove from the heat and stir in the oats, coconut and flour. Blend the bicarbonate with the water, add to the mixture, and stir well.

● Shape the mixture into 30 balls and place on the baking sheets, spacing well apart. Bake for 20 minutes until golden-brown. Leave on the trays for 10 minutes, then transfer to a wire rack to cool.

Whisky and Ginger Shortbreads

Preparation time: 30 minutes ● Cooking time: 40 minutes ● Makes: 16

Join the celebrations with these special shortbread fingers.

INGREDIENTS

225 g/8 oz unsalted butter

120 g/4 oz caster sugar

2 egg yolks

1 Tbsp golden syrup

1 Tbsp whisky

375 g/12 oz plain flour

½ tsp baking powder

50 g/2 oz finely chopped stem ginger

2 Tbsp milk

25 g/1 oz flaked almonds

2 Tbsp caster sugar, for sprinkling

Pre-heat oven to 325°F/160°C/Gas mark 3. Then lightly grease an 18 x 28-cm/7 x 11 x ¾-in tin. Put the butter, sugar, egg yolks, golden syrup and whisky into a mixing bowl and beat together until light and creamy. Sift the flour and baking powder into the bowl and mix together to make a soft dough.

● Lightly knead for a few seconds on a floured surface until smooth, then divide into 2 equal pieces. Roll out each piece to the size of the tin. Transfer one piece to the tin, pressing it firmly into the edges. Sprinkle the chopped stem ginger over, then cover with the second piece of shortbread and press down firmly. Brush the top with milk, then sprinkle with flaked almonds and caster sugar.

● Bake for 40 minutes or until light golden. Leave for 5 minutes, then score into 16 fingers. Cool in the tin and cut into fingers to serve.

Fruit Cookies

This chapter is full of unusual cookies using the wide range of fruit now on the market. Everyday fruit, such as apples, oranges and bananas, make an appearance along with exotic star fruits and papayas. Some recipes use fresh fruit, but many more exploit the rich, intense flavours of dried fruit. A number of cookies contrast the sharp flavour of fruit with the sweetness of the cookie with stunning effect.

There are several bar cookies in this section that would be excellent in lunch boxes and many of the chunky fruit cookies would travel well. Next time you plan a hike or take a trip to the beach, make up a batch of cookies to nibble when hunger pangs strike.

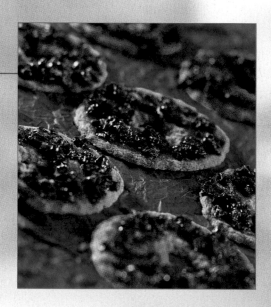

Quick Bites

Combined Flavours

Fruity Treats

Fresh and Dried Fruits

Date and Cinnamon Cookies

Preparation time: 15 minutes + chilling ●
Cooking time: 15 to 18 minutes ● *Makes: About 30*

Dates are soft and chewy and keep these cookies really moist.

INGREDIENTS

225 g/8 oz butter, softened
200 g/7 oz light brown sugar
3 Tbsp golden syrup
2 eggs, beaten
375 g/12 oz plain flour
1 tsp ground cinnamon
225 g/8 oz chopped dates

Put butter, sugar and golden syrup in a bowl. Beat until light and fluffy. Gradually add the eggs; mix well between additions. Sift in the flour and cinnamon; mix well. Stir in the dates. Chill for 2 hours.

● Pre-heat oven to 350°F/175°C/Gas mark 4. Grease two baking sheets or line with non-stick baking parchment.

● Roll teaspoons of the mixture into balls and flatten slightly. Arrange on the baking sheets at least 5 cm/2 in apart and bake for 15 to 18 minutes. Leave to cool for 5 minutes then transfer to wire racks to cool completely. Store in an airtight container.

Orange and Cardamom Thins

Preparation time: 40 minutes + chilling ●
Cooking time: 12 minutes ● *Makes: About 20 filled cookies*

These are delicate sandwich cookies, but they are also great fun for kids to make.

INGREDIENTS

120 g/4 oz butter, softened
200 g/7 oz caster sugar
2 medium eggs, beaten
Grated rind of 1 large orange
120 g/4 oz plain flour
2 tsp ground cardamom

FILLING

150 g/5 oz icing sugar
50 g/2 oz butter, softened
1 Tbsp orange juice

Put the butter and sugar in a bowl and beat until light and fluffy. Gradually beat in the eggs and orange rind. Sift in the flour and ground cardamom and mix well. Form into a ball and chill for 30 minutes.

● Meanwhile, beat together the filling ingredients, adding the orange juice gradually.

● Pre-heat oven to 375°F/190°C/Gas mark 5. Grease two baking sheets or line with non-stick baking parchment.

● Roll out the dough thinly and stamp out 5-cm/2-in rounds using a straight-edged cutter. Place the cookies on the baking sheets spaced about 2.5 cm/1 in apart. Bake for about 12 minutes until golden. Cool for 5 minutes on the sheet then transfer to wire racks to cool completely.

● Sandwich the cookies with a little filling and serve.

Cherry Rings

Preparation time: 40 minutes + chilling ● *Cooking time: 20 minutes* ● *Makes: About 30*

These are crisp cookies with a soft cherry topping.

INGREDIENTS

200 g/7 oz butter, softened

120 g/4 oz caster sugar

200 g/7 oz light brown sugar

1 tsp vanilla essence

300g/10 oz plain flour

120 g/4 oz dried cherries, roughly chopped

GLAZE

1 small egg, beaten

3 tsp milk

2 tsp caster sugar

Put the butter, sugars and vanilla essence in a mixing bowl and beat with an electric mixer until light and fluffy. Sift in the flour, mix well, form into a soft dough and chill for 30 minutes in the refrigerator.

● Pre-heat oven to 325°F/160°C/Gas mark 3. Grease two large baking sheets or line with non-stick baking parchment.

● Mix the glaze ingredients together.

● Dust work surface with flour and roll out dough to 1 cm/½ in. Stamp out 6-cm/2½-in rounds with a fluted cutter. Then, cut out the centre with a 1-cm/½-in cutter. Transfer to the baking sheets and brush with the glaze. Decorate with the cherries, covering the entire surface.

● Bake for about 20 minutes until light brown. Cool for 5 minutes then transfer to wire racks to cool completely. Store in an airtight container.

VARIATION

● Substitute 125 g/4 oz of dried blueberries for the cherries.

The Ultimate Banana Cookies

Preparation time: 15 minutes + chilling ● Cooking time: 18 to 20 minutes ● Makes: About 35

You simply can't fit any more bananas into these banana-coconut cookies!

INGREDIENTS

175 g/6 oz butter, softened
120 g/4 oz caster sugar
120 g/4 oz soft brown sugar
1 egg, beaten
3 medium bananas, mashed
1 tsp vanilla essence
250 g/9 oz plain flour
1 tsp baking powder
175 g/6 oz dried banana chips, broken up
50 g/2 oz desiccated coconut

Put the butter and sugars in a bowl and beat until light and fluffy. Gradually beat in the egg ensuring each addition is well incorporated. Stir in the mashed bananas and vanilla essence. Sift in the flour and baking powder. Then stir in the banana chips and coconut. Chill for at least 2 hours in the refrigerator.

● Pre-heat oven to 375°F/190°C/Gas mark 5. Grease two baking sheets or line with non-stick baking parchment.

● Take tablespoons of the mixture and roll into balls. Flatten slightly then place on the baking sheets at least 5 cm/2 in apart. Bake for 18 to 20 minutes until golden. Chill for 5 minutes then transfer to wire cooling racks. Store in an airtight container.

Spicy Mixed Fruit Bars

Preparation time: 30 minutes ● *Cooking time: 40 minutes* ● *Makes: 12 bars*

These are substantial bars of moist fruit and coconut, well worth the effort.

INGREDIENTS

TOPPING

75 g/3 oz finely chopped dried apricots

40 g/1½ oz sultanas

75 g/3 oz finely chopped dried peaches

75 g/3 oz dried blueberries

3 Tbsp brandy

3 eggs, beaten

120 g/4 oz light brown sugar

50 g/2 oz plain flour

1 tsp baking powder

50 g/2 oz desiccated coconut

BASE

120 g/4 oz butter, softened

5 Tbsp caster sugar

150 g/5 oz plain flour

1 tsp ground ginger

1 tsp ground cinnamon

Put the apricots, sultanas, peaches and blueberries in a bowl and add the brandy. Leave to soak for 20 minutes.

● Pre-heat oven to 350°F/1175°C/Gas mark 4. Grease and line the base of a 32.5 x 23-cm/13 x 9-in tin with non-stick baking parchment.

● Prepare the base. Place the butter and sugar in a bowl and beat until light and fluffy. Sift in the flour, ginger and cinnamon and mix to a dough. Spread over the base of the tin and bake for 8 to 10 minutes.

● While the base is cooking, finish making the topping. Beat the eggs and sugar together for about 5 minutes until thick and creamy. Sift in the flour and baking powder. Stir in the coconut and soaked fruit. Pour over the baked base and bake for a further 30 to 35 minutes until firm to the touch. Cool in the tin before cutting into 12 bars. Store in an airtight container.

Cranberry and Orange Cookies

Preparation time: 20 minutes + chilling ● Cooking time: 15 to 17 minutes ● Makes: About 35

Use dried blueberries if cranberries are unavailable.

INGREDIENTS

225 g/8 oz butter, softened

200 g/7 oz caster sugar

200 g/7 oz light brown sugar

2 eggs, beaten

Grated rind of 1 orange

250 g/9 oz plain flour

1 tsp salt

1 tsp baking powder

150 g/5 oz whole dried cranberries

Beat butter and sugars together until soft and creamy. Gradually beat in the eggs and orange rind. The mixture may look as if it is curdling, but it will be fine when cooked. Sift in flour, salt and baking powder and mix to combine. Add the cranberries and mix well. Chill the mixture for at least one hour in the refrigerator.

● Pre-heat oven to 350°F/175°C/Gas mark 4. Grease two large baking sheets or line with non-stick baking parchment.

● Roll tablespoons of the mixture into balls and place on the baking sheets at least 8 cm/3 in apart. Flatten slightly with the back of a spoon. Bake for 15 to 17 minutes until golden. Leave to cool for 5 minutes then transfer to wire racks to cool completely. Store in an airtight container.

TIP

Dried apricots, papayas, mangoes or peaches also work well in these cookies.

Lemon and Lime Thins

Preparation time: 15 minutes + chilling ● *Cooking time: 15 to 18 minutes* ● *Makes: About 20*

The frosted lemon rind garnish is an effective way to decorate simple cookies.

INGREDIENTS

2 lemons
1 lime
120 g/4 oz butter, softened
5 Tbsp caster sugar
150 g/5 oz plain flour
1 egg white
Icing sugar, for decorating

Pare the rind from one lemon and place in a bowl. Grate the rind from the lime and other lemon into a separate bowl and squeeze 2 tablespoons of juice from the lemon.

● Put butter, 3 tablespoons of the sugar and grated rinds in a bowl and beat until light and fluffy. Add lemon juice gradually. Sift in the flour and mix to a soft dough. Place on a piece of greaseproof paper and form into a log. Chill for one hour.

● Meanwhile, place the lemon rind in a pan of boiling water for one minute. Drain and pat dry. Lightly beat the egg white until frothy. Dip the rind into the egg white then into the remaining sugar to frost. Leave to dry on greaseproof paper.

● Pre-heat oven to 350°F/175°C/Gas mark 4. Grease two baking sheets or line with non-stick baking parchment.

● Slice the dough log into 1-cm/½-in slices and place on the baking sheets. Bake for 15 to 18 minutes. Leave to cool for 5 minutes then transfer to wire cooling racks. Top with the frosted rind and dust lightly with icing sugar to serve, if liked.

Strawberry Pinwheels

Preparation time: 35 minutes + chilling ● *Cooking time: 11 to 13 minutes* ● *Makes: About 16*

Adults and children alike will have great fun making these festive cookies.

INGREDIENTS

120 g/4 oz butter, softened

1 Tbsp caster sugar

1 tsp vanilla essence

200 g/7 oz plain flour

3 Tbsp strawberry jam

Put butter, sugar and vanilla in a bowl and beat until light and creamy. Sift in the flour. Mix to a dough by hand then chill for 30 minutes.

● Pre-heat oven to 350°F/175°C/Gas mark 4. Grease two baking sheets or line with non-stick baking parchment.

● Roll out half the dough on a piece of floured greaseproof paper to a 25-cm/10-in square. Trim to these dimensions. Cut into 16 equal-sized squares with a blunt knife or fluted pastry cutter. Cut a 2.5-cm/1-in slice from each corner towards the centre. If the dough sticks to the knife dip it in flour.

● Put half a teaspoon of jam into the centre of each cookie. Fold over every other corner to the centre to form a pinwheel, lightly sticking the dough to the jam. Transfer to the baking sheets and bake for 11 to 13 minutes.

● Cool for 5 minutes on the baking sheets then transfer to wire cooling racks. Store in an airtight container.

Tropical Papaya Drops

Preparation time: 20 minutes + cooling ● *Cooking time: 15 to 18 minutes* ● *Makes: About 30 drops*

Dried papaya has a more intense flavour than fresh, so a little gives a strong flavour.

INGREDIENTS

200 g/7 oz plain flour
1 tsp baking powder
1 Tbsp caster sugar
120 g/4 oz finely chopped dried papaya
120 g/4 oz butter
6 Tbsp golden syrup
1 tsp vanilla essence

Pre-heat oven to 350°F/175°C/Gas mark 4. Grease two baking sheets or line with non-stick baking parchment.

● Sift the flour and baking powder into a large bowl. Stir in the sugar and chopped papaya and make a well in the centre. Put the butter, golden syrup and vanilla essence in a small saucepan and stir over a gentle heat until the butter has melted. Pour into the dry ingredients and mix to a soft dough. Cool for 10 minutes.

● Take teaspoons of the mixture and roll into balls. Place on the baking sheets at least 5 cm/2 in apart and flatten slightly with the back of a spoon. Bake for 15 to 18 minutes. Cool for 5 minutes, then transfer to wire cooling racks. Store in an airtight container.

VARIATION

Try using a combination of mango and papaya for truly tropical cookie treats.

Cherry and Vanilla Squares

Preparation time: 20 minutes ●
Cooking time: 30 to 35 minutes ● Makes: 16

Use dried Morello or sour cherries, rather than glacé cherries for these moist squares.

INGREDIENTS

150 g/5 oz plain flour
5 Tbsp icing sugar
200 g/7 oz cold butter
2 tsp vanilla essence
120 g/4 oz dried cherries

Pre-heat oven to 350°F/175°C/Gas mark 4. Grease or line a 20 x 20-cm/8 x 8-in tin with non-stick baking parchment.

● Sift flour and icing sugar together into a bowl. Add the butter and vanilla essence and blend in with your fingertips until the mixture resembles coarse breadcrumbs. Stir in the cherries and form into a soft dough.

● Transfer to the tin and press to fit. Bake for 30 to 35 minutes. Leave to cool then cut into 16 bars. Store, covered, in the tin or in an airtight container.

TIP

For extra flavour and glaze, brush the cooked dough with cherry or strawberry jam when it comes out of the oven.

Banana and Cointreau Temptations

Preparation time: 20 minutes + chilling ●
Cooking time: 15 to18 minutes ● Makes: About 30

Cointreau is delicately flavoured with orange, which is the perfect partner for bananas.

INGREDIENTS

200 g/7 oz dried banana chips
225 g/8 oz butter, softened
200 g/7 oz caster sugar
200 g/7 oz light brown sugar
2 eggs, beaten
2 Tbsp Cointreau
250 g/9 oz plain flour
1 tsp salt
1 tsp baking powder

Place the banana chips in a bag and crush with a rolling pin or wooden spoon to break them up.

● Beat together butter and sugars until soft and creamy. Gradually beat in eggs and Cointreau. Sift in flour, salt and baking powder and mix to combine. Add bananas and mix well. Chill for one hour in the refrigerator.

● Pre-heat oven to 350°F/175°C/Gas mark 4. Grease two large baking sheets or line with non-stick baking parchment.

● Roll tablespoons of the mixture into balls and place on the baking sheets at least 8 cm/3 in apart. Flatten slightly with the back of a spoon. Bake for 15 to 18 minutes until golden.

● Leave to cool for 5 minutes then transfer to wire racks to cool completely. Store in an airtight container.

Carrot and Date Drops

Preparation time: 15 minutes + chilling ● *Cooking time: 10 to 12 minutes* ● *Makes: About 25*

These are unusual, delicious, and moist – maybe more like a cake than a cookie.

INGREDIENTS

120 g/4 oz butter, softened
125 g/4 oz light brown sugar
1 egg, beaten
75 g/3 oz plain flour
1 tsp baking powder
1 tsp salt
1 tsp ground nutmeg
½ tsp ground ginger
75 g/3 oz grated carrot
120 g/4 oz chopped dates

Put butter and sugar in a bowl and beat until light and fluffy. Gradually beat in the egg. Sift in the flour, baking powder, salt, nutmeg and ginger and stir until combined. Then stir in the carrots and dates. Chill for at least 2 hours.

● Pre-heat oven to 375°F/190°C/Gas mark 4. Grease two baking sheets or line with non-stick baking parchment.

● Take small tablespoons of the mixture and roll into balls, then flatten slightly. Place at least 5 cm/2 in apart on the baking sheets and bake for 10 to 12 minutes. Cool for 5 minutes on the baking sheets then transfer to wire racks to cool completely. Store the drops in an airtight container.

Passionfruit Shortbread

Preparation time: 25 minutes + chilling ● *Cooking time: 20 minutes* ● *Makes: About 20*

Passion fruit pulp contains masses of small seeds that are left in the dough for an added crunch.

INGREDIENTS

175 g/6 oz butter, softened

50 g/2 oz caster sugar

175 g/6 oz plain flour

50 g/2 oz cornflour

Pulp of 3 passion fruit

Icing sugar, for decorating, optional

Put butter and sugar in a bowl and beat until light and fluffy. Sift in the flour and cornflour and mix to a dough by hand. Stir in the passion fruit pulp.

● Transfer to a piece of greaseproof paper and form the dough into a log shape. Chill for at least one hour in the refrigerator.

● Pre-heat oven to 350°F/175°C/Gas mark 4. Grease two baking sheets or line with non-stick baking parchment.

● Cut 5-mm/½-in slices from the log and place on the baking sheets. Bake for about 20 minutes until golden-brown. Cool for 5 minutes on the baking sheets then transfer to wire racks to cool completely. Dust with icing sugar to serve, if liked. Store in an airtight container and eat within 4 days.

Pineapple Drops

Preparation time: 20 minutes + chilling ●
Cooking time: 15 minutes ● Makes: About 30

These are very sweet cookies.

INGREDIENTS

225 g/8 oz butter, softened
200 g/7 oz caster sugar
200 g/7 oz light brown sugar
2 eggs, beaten
2 Tbsp honey
250 g/9 oz plain flour
1 tsp salt
1 tsp baking powder
120 g/4 oz chopped dried pineapple

Beat together butter and sugars until light and fluffy. Gradually beat in the egg and honey. The mixture may look as if it is curdling, but it will be fine when cooked. Sift in flour, salt and baking powder and mix to combine. Add pineapple and mix well. Chill the mixture for at least one hour in the refrigerator.

● Pre-heat oven to 350°F/175°C/Gas mark 4. Grease two large baking sheets or line with non-stick baking parchment.

● Roll heaped teaspoons of the mixture into balls and place on the baking sheets at least 8 cm/3 in apart. Flatten slightly with the back of a spoon. Bake for 15 minutes until golden. Leave to cool for 5 minutes on the sheets then transfer the cookies to wire racks to cool completely. Store in an airtight container.

Dried Mango and Ginger Delights

Preparation time: 20 minutes ●
Cooking time: 15 minutes ● Makes: About 40

Using cream cheese makes this cookie dough really soft and pliable.

INGREDIENTS

75 g/3 oz butter, softened
100 g/3½ oz full-fat soft cheese, softened
200 g/7 oz caster sugar
1 tsp baking powder
1 egg, beaten
1 Tbsp ginger preserve or stem ginger syrup
(from the stem ginger jar)
250 g/9 oz plain flour
120 g/4 oz finely chopped dried mango
2 tsp finely chopped stem ginger

Put butter and cream cheese in a bowl and beat for 30 seconds. Add sugar and beat until light and fluffy. Add the baking powder, egg and ginger preserve or syrup and beat again. Sift in the flour and beat for 30 seconds.

● Stir in the mango and ginger and form the mixture into a soft dough. Form into a ball, wrap in clingfilm and chill for 30 minutes in the refrigerator.

● Pre-heat oven to 350°F/175°C/Gas mark 4. Grease two baking sheets or line with non-stick baking parchment.

● Roll out dough to about 8 mm/⅓ in thick and stamp out shapes with cutters. Re-roll as necessary. Transfer to the baking sheets and bake for about 15 minutes until lightly golden. Chill for 5 minutes on the baking sheets then transfer to wire cooling racks to cool completely. Store the cookies in an airtight container.

Honeyed Apricot Cookies

Preparation time: 15 minutes + chilling ●
Cooking time: 15 minutes ● *Makes: About 30*

If you can find honeyed apricots, use these and omit the honey from this recipe.

INGREDIENTS

225 g/8 oz butter, softened

200 g/7 oz caster sugar

200 g/7 oz light brown sugar

2 eggs, beaten

2 Tbsp honey

1 tsp ground ginger

250 g/9 oz plain flour

1 tsp salt

1 tsp baking powder

225 g/8 oz chopped apricots

Beat together butter and sugars until soft and creamy. Gradually beat in the eggs and honey. The mixture may look as if it is curdling, but it will be fine when cooked. Sift in ginger, flour, salt and baking powder and mix to combine. Add the diced apricots and mix well. Chill the mixture for at least one hour in the refrigerator.

● Pre-heat oven to 350°F/175°C/Gas mark 4. Grease two large baking sheets or line with non-stick baking parchment.

● Roll tablespoons of the mixture into balls and place on the baking sheets at least 8 cm/3 in apart. Flatten slightly with the back of a spoon. Bake for 15 minutes until golden. Leave to cool on the sheets for 5 minutes on the sheets then transfer to wire racks to cool completely. Store in an airtight container.

Prune and Grapefruit Marmalade Drops

Preparation time: 15 minutes + chilling ●
Cooking time: 15 to 17 minutes ● *Makes: About 30*

These are quite dry, chunky cookies.

INGREDIENTS

225 g/8 oz butter, softened

200 g/7 oz light brown sugar

2 Tbsp golden syrup

2 eggs, beaten

4 Tbsp grapefruit marmalade

300 g/10 oz plain flour

1 tsp salt

1 tsp baking powder

125 g/4 oz chopped, stoned prunes

Icing sugar, optional

Put the butter, sugar and syrup in a bowl and beat until light and fluffy. Gradually beat in eggs and grapefruit marmalade. It may look as if it is curdling, but it will be fine when cooked. Sift in flour, salt and baking powder and mix to combine. Add prunes and mix well. Chill for one hour in the refrigerator.

● Pre-heat oven to 350°F/175°C/Gas mark 4. Grease two large baking sheets or line with non-stick baking parchment.

● Roll tablespoons of the mixture into balls, then flatten between your palms. Place on the baking sheets at least 2.5 cm/1 in apart. Bake for 15 to 17 minutes until golden. Leave to cool for 5 minutes then transfer to wire racks to cool completely.

● Dust lightly with icing sugar to serve, if liked. Store in an airtight container.

Cherry Chocolate Cookies

Preparation time: 20 minutes + chilling ●
Cooking time: 15 to 18 minutes ● *Makes: About 18*

Cherries and chocolate are a classic combination.

INGREDIENTS

150 g/5 oz butter
200 g/7 oz caster sugar
1 egg yolk
200 g/7 oz plain flour
120 g/4 oz coarsely chopped glacé cherries
75 g/3 oz plain chocolate chips

Put butter and sugar in a bowl and mix well until light and fluffy. Add the egg yolk and beat. Sift in flour and mix well then stir in the cherries and chocolate chips. Chill for at least 2 hours.

● Pre-heat oven to 375°F/190°C/Gas mark 5. Grease two baking sheets or line with non-stick baking parchment.

● Take tablespoons of the mixture and roll into balls, then flatten slightly. Place onto the baking sheets at least 2.5 cm/1 in apart. Bake for 15 to 18 minutes. Cool for 5 minutes on the baking sheets then transfer to wire racks to cool completely. Store in an airtight container.

Dried Fruit and Brazil Nut Cookies

Preparation time: 20 minutes + chilling ●
Cooking time: 17 minutes ● *Makes: About 35*

Soft fruit and crunchy nuts give you everything you desire from a cookie.

INGREDIENTS

225 g/8 oz butter, softened
200 g/7 oz caster sugar
200 g/7 oz light brown sugar
2 eggs, beaten
250 g/9 oz plain flour
1 tsp salt
1 tsp baking powder
75 g/3 oz chopped dried fruit salad
75 g/3 oz chopped Brazil nuts

Beat together the butter and sugars until soft and creamy. Gradually beat in the eggs. The mixture may look as if it is curdling, but it will be fine when cooked. Sift in flour, salt and baking powder and mix to combine. Add the fruit salad and Brazil nuts and mix together well. Chill the mixture for at least one hour in the refrigerator.

● Pre-heat oven to 350°F/175°C/Gas mark 4. Grease two large baking sheets or line with non-stick baking parchment.

● Roll tablespoons of the mixture into balls and place on the baking sheets at least 8 cm/3 in apart. Flatten slightly with the back of a spoon. Bake for 15 to 17 minutes until golden. Leave to cool for 5 minutes then transfer to wire racks to cool completely. Store in an airtight container.

Exotic Fruit and Coconut Treats

Preparation time: 20 minutes + chilling ● *Cooking time: 15 to 18 minutes* ● *Makes: About 30*

Look for packets of assorted tropical fruits, or experiment with your own combinations.

INGREDIENTS

225 g/8 oz butter, softened

200 g/7 oz caster sugar

200 g/7 oz light brown sugar

2 eggs, beaten

Grated rind of 1 orange

250 g/9 oz plain flour

1 tsp salt

1 tsp baking powder

120 g/4 oz chopped mixed tropical dried fruit or fruit salad

225 g/8 oz desiccated coconut

Beat together butter and sugars until soft and creamy. Gradually beat in the eggs and orange rind. The mixture may look as if it is curdling, but it will be fine when cooked. Sift in flour, salt and baking powder and mix to combine. Add tropical fruits and coconut and mix well. Chill the mixture for at least one hour in the refrigerator.

● Pre-heat oven to 350°F/175°C/Gas mark 4. Grease two large baking sheets or line with non-stick baking parchment.

● Roll tablespoons of the mixture into balls and place on the baking sheets at least 8 cm/3 in apart. Flatten slightly with the back of a spoon. Bake for 15 to 18 minutes until golden. Leave to cool for 5 minutes then cool on wire racks. Store in an airtight container.

Tangerine Fingers

Preparation time: 30 minutes + chilling ● *Cooking time: 40 to 45 minutes* ● *Makes: About 30*

Scrumptious shortbread with a tangy tangerine orange topping.

INGREDIENTS

BASE

225 g/8 oz butter

5 Tbsp caster sugar

Grated rind of 1 tangerine

225 g/8 oz plain flour

50 g/2 oz cornflour

TOPPING

Grated rind of 2 tangerines

3 Tbsp freshly squeezed tangerine juice

225 g/8 oz caster sugar

3 eggs, beaten

75 g/3 oz plain flour

½ tsp baking powder

Grease a 23 x 32.5-cm/9 x 13-in tin or line with non-stick baking parchment.

● Put butter, sugar and tangerine rind in a bowl and beat together until light and fluffy. Sift in flour and cornflour; mix well then form into a soft dough. Press into the prepared tin and smooth with a knife. Chill for 30 minutes in the refrigerator.

● Pre-heat oven to 350°F/175°C/Gas mark 4.

● Bake for 15 to 20 minutes until lightly golden. Remove from the oven, leaving the oven switched on.

● Beat together the tangerine rind, sugar and eggs until creamy. Sift in the flour and baking powder and fold in. Beat in the tangerine juice. Pour over the shortbread and bake for a further 25 minutes. Cool in the tin. Cut into 30 bars. Dust with icing sugar to serve, if liked.

Banana Chocolate Squares

Preparation time: 30 minutes ● Cooking time: 25 to 30 minutes ● Makes: 18

These delicious cookies are like shortbread with a dark and white chocolate topping.

INGREDIENTS

200 g/7 oz plain flour

Pinch salt

8 tsp cornflour

50 g/2 oz caster sugar

175 g/6 oz cold butter, chopped

75 g/3 oz dried banana chips, roughly chopped

75 g/3 oz plain chocolate chips

75 g/3 oz white chocolate chips

Pre-heat oven to 350°F/175°C/Gas mark 4. Grease and line a shallow 28 x 18-cm/11 x 7-in tin with non-stick baking parchment.

● Sift flour, salt and cornflour into a bowl then stir in the sugar. Add the butter and blend in with your fingertips until it resembles coarse breadcrumbs. Stir in the banana chips and form into a soft dough.

● Roll out to just under the size of the tin. Transfer to the tin and press to fit. Bake for 25 to 30 minutes until lightly browned. Leave to cool for a few minutes then mark out 18 squares (3 rows of 6 squares across). Cool in the tin.

● Cut the squares out of the tin and place on a sheet of greaseproof paper. Melt the dark and white chocolate in 2 separate bowls in the microwave or in a bowl over a saucepan of simmering water. Pipe lines of plain and white chocolate over each square. Leave to set before serving. Store in an airtight container.

TIP

If you do not have a piping bag, place the chocolate into one corner of a small plastic bag, snip off the end and drizzle lines over each cookie.

Cranberry and White Chocolate Cookies

Preparation time: 30 minutes + chilling ● *Cooking time: 15 to 20 minutes* ● *Makes: About 30*

Dried cranberries are not as tart as fresh ones and these cookies are made even sweeter by the addition of chocolate.

INGREDIENTS

225 g/8 oz butter, softened

200 g/7 oz caster sugar

200 g/7 oz light brown sugar

2 eggs, beaten

250 g/9 oz plain flour

1 tsp salt

1 tsp baking powder

120 g/4 oz dried cranberries

175 g/6 oz white chocolate chips, or white chocolate, chopped

Beat together butter and sugars until soft and creamy. Gradually beat in the eggs. The mixture may look as if it is curdling, but it will be fine when cooked. Sift in flour, salt and baking powder and mix to combine. Add cranberries and 75 g/3 oz of the white chocolate chips and mix well. Chill the mixture for at least one hour in the refrigerator.

● Pre-heat oven to 350°F/175°C/Gas mark 4. Grease two large baking sheets or line with non-stick baking parchment.

● Roll tablespoons of the mixture into balls and place on the baking sheets at least 8 cm/3 in apart. Flatten slightly with the back of a spoon. Bake for 15 to 20 minutes until golden.

● Leave to cool for 5 minutes then transfer to wire racks to cool completely. Melt the white chocolate and drizzle it over the cookies. Leave to cool before serving. Store in an airtight container.

Mixed Fruit Squares

Preparation time: 20 minutes ● *Cooking time: 60 to 70 minutes* ● *Makes: 16*

These are moist, spongy squares baked just like a cake. Each square is packed with fruit.

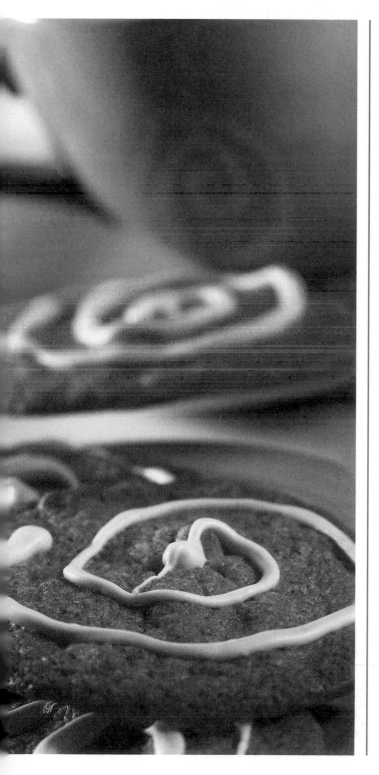

INGREDIENTS

120 g/4 oz butter, softened

200 g/7 oz caster sugar

1 tsp vanilla essence

2 medium eggs, beaten

125 ml/4 fl oz milk

175 g/6 oz plain flour

600 g/1¼ lb dried and fresh mixed fruit (see Tip)

2 Tbsp raw sugar

Pre-heat oven to 350°F/175°C/Gas mark 4. Grease and line an 18 x 18-cm/7 x 7-in square tin with non-stick baking parchment.

● Put butter, sugar, vanilla essence and eggs in a bowl and beat together for 2 minutes. Beat in the milk, then sift in the flour and mix until smooth.

● Pour half the batter into the prepared tin then scatter over half the mixed fruit. Spoon over the remaining mixture, smooth with a blunt knife and scatter over the remaining fruit and the raw sugar.

● Bake for 60 to 70 minutes until the cake is cooked through. To test if the cake is cooked, insert a skewer into the centre of the cake and leave it for 5 seconds. When the skewer is removed it should be dry with no soggy cake mixture attached. Cool in the tin for 10 minutes, then cut into 16 squares.

TIP

Just about any mixed fruit can be used in this recipe. Try apricots, blueberries, dried banana chips, pineapple, or mango, depending on seasonal availability.

Truly Blueberry Cookies

Preparation time: 20 minutes + chilling ● *Cooking time: 15 to 18 minutes* ● *Makes: About 30*

Macerating (soaking) the blueberries in orange and brandy makes the cookies even moister and more delicious. Omit the brandy and increase the orange juice if you want to make these cookies for children.

INGREDIENTS

120 g/4 oz dried blueberries
4 Tbsp orange juice
2 Tbsp brandy
225 g/8 oz butter, softened
200 g/7 oz caster sugar
200 g/7 oz light brown sugar
2 eggs, beaten
250 g/9 oz plain flour
1 tsp baking powder

Place blueberries, orange juice and brandy in a small pan and simmer for 5 minutes. Remove from the heat and leave to cool. Beat together butter and sugars until soft and creamy. Gradually beat in eggs. The mixture may look as if it is curdling, but it will be fine when cooked.

● Sift in flour and baking powder and mix to combine. Strain the blueberries, discarding any liquid, and add to cookie mixture. Mix well. Chill the mixture for at least one hour in the refrigerator.

● Pre-heat oven to 350°F/175°C/Gas mark 4. Grease two large baking sheets or line with non-stick baking parchment.

● Roll tablespoons of the mixture into balls and place on the baking sheets at least 8 cm/3 in apart. Flatten slightly with the back of a spoon. Bake for 15 to 18 minutes until golden. Leave to cool for 5 minutes then transfer to wire racks to cool completely.

● Store in an airtight container.

Pear Flapjacks

Preparation time: 15 minutes ● Cooking time: 20 to 25 minutes ● Makes: About 16

Dried pears make these flapjacks deliciously moist.

INGREDIENTS

120 g/4 oz butter

200 g/7 oz soft brown sugar

2 Tbsp golden syrup

425 g/15 oz rolled oats

120 g/4 oz chopped dried pears

75 g/3 oz currants

Pre-heat oven to 375°F/190°C/Gas mark 5. Lightly grease a shallow 28 x 18-cm/11 x 7-in tin.

● Put butter, sugar and golden syrup in a pan and cook over a gentle heat until the butter has melted. Combine the dry ingredients and add to the pan; stir well.

● Spoon into the prepared tin and press down with the back of a spoon. Bake for 20 to 25 minutes until lightly golden. Cool for 5 minutes in the tin then mark into 6 bars; leave to cool completely in the tin. Store in an airtight container.

Glacé Cherry Florentines

Preparation time: 20 minutes ● *Cooking time: 8 to 10 minutes* ● *Makes: About 12*

This is the best recipe to use when you want a quick, but impressive cookie.

INGREDIENTS

50 g/2 oz lightly salted butter

2 Tbsp golden syrup

50 g/2 oz caster sugar

75 g/3 oz plain flour

75 g/3 oz finely chopped glacé cherries

Grated rind of 1 orange

Pre-heat oven to 350°F/175°C/Gas mark 4. Grease two large baking sheets or line with non-stick baking parchment.

● Put the butter, golden syrup and sugar in a saucepan over a medium heat and stir until the sugar dissolves. Remove from the heat and cool for 5 minutes, stirring. Sift in the flour, then mix in the cherries and orange rind.

● Drop heaped teaspoons onto the baking sheets, at least 8 cm/3 in apart. Shape into neat rounds. Bake for 8 to 10 minutes. Re-shape into rounds while hot, if necessary. Cool for 5 minutes, then transfer to wire racks to cool completely. Store in an airtight container.

Candied Peel and Dark Chocolate Squares

Preparation time: 45 minutes ● Cooking time: 30 to 35 minutes ● Makes: 24

For a special occasion these bitter treats are perfect. Make up a batch and place in a gift box to take to a dinner party.

INGREDIENTS

250 g/9 oz plain flour

50 g/2 oz caster sugar

175 g/6 oz cold butter, diced

75 g/3 oz chopped candied peel

4 squares (25 g/1 oz each) good-quality plain chocolate

Pre-heat oven to 350°F/175°C/Gas mark 4. Grease and line the base of a shallow 28 x 18-cm/11 x 7-in pan.

● Sift flour into a bowl and stir in the sugar. Add the butter and blend in with your fingertips until the mixture resembles coarse breadcrumbs. Stir in 50 g/2 oz of the mixed peel and form into a soft dough.

● Roll out to just under the size of the tin. Transfer to the tin and press to fit. Prick all over with a fork. Bake for 25 to 30 minutes until lightly browned. Cool for 5 minutes then mark into 24 bars. Cool in the tin.

● Melt chocolate in a microwave or in a glass bowl over a saucepan of simmering water. Cut dough into the squares and remove from the tin. Dip each bar into the chocolate to coat the top and sides and place on greaseproof paper. While the chocolate is still warm, sprinkle over a few pieces of candied peel. Leave to harden before serving. Store in an airtight container between layers of greaseproof paper.

Apricot Wheels

Preparation time: 40 minutes + chilling ● *Cooking time: 10 to 12 minutes* ● *Makes: About 40*

These wheels are cut from a log of dough filled with a sweet apricot filling.

INGREDIENTS

FILLING

150 g/5 oz dried apricots, finely chopped (see Tip)

120 g/4 oz caster sugar

1 tsp ground nutmeg

125 ml/4 fl oz orange juice

DOUGH

175 g/6 oz butter, softened

200 g/7 oz light brown sugar

1 medium egg, beaten

1 tsp almond essence

375 g/12 oz plain flour

1 tsp baking powder

Place all the filling ingredients in a small saucepan and bring to the boil. Simmer for 3 minutes until most of the orange juice has evaporated and the mixture is thick. Set aside and cool.

● Put the butter and sugar in a bowl and mix until light and fluffy. Gradually add the egg; mixing well between each addition. Stir in the almond essence. Sift in the flour and baking powder and form into a dough. Wrap in clingfilm and chill for at least 30 minutes.

● Divide the dough in half, then place one half on a piece of floured greaseproof paper. Roll out the dough on the paper to a 20 x 25-cm/8 x 10-in rectangle. Slide a thin, metal spatula between the paper and the dough so that it does not stick to the paper when rolled up. Cover dough with half the filling and roll up from a long side using the paper to help you roll. Rewrap in clingfilm and chill for about 20 minutes. Repeat with remaining dough and filling.

● Pre-heat oven to 350°F/175°C/Gas mark 4. Grease two baking sheets or line with non-stick baking parchment.

● Cut 1-cm/½-in slices from the log and place on the baking sheets. Bake for 10 to 12 minutes. Cool on baking sheets for 5 minutes then transfer to wire cooling racks. Store in an airtight container.

TIP

It's important to chop the apricots finely, otherwise it will be difficult to roll up the dough.

Rum and Raisin Cookies

Preparation time: 20 minutes + chilling ●
Cooking time: 15 to 17 minutes ● *Makes: About 35*

The traditional combination of rum and raisins is perfect for cookies as it makes them moist and chewy.

INGREDIENTS

225 g/8 oz butter, softened

200 g/7 oz caster sugar

200 g/7 oz light brown sugar

1 egg, beaten

3 Tbsp rum

250 g/9 oz plain flour

1 tsp salt

1 tsp baking powder

150 g/5 oz seedless raisins

Beat together the butter and sugars until soft and creamy. Gradually beat in the egg and rum. The mixture may look as if it is curdling, but it will be fine when cooked. Sift in the flour, salt and baking powder and mix to combine. Add the raisins and mix well. Chill for at least one hour in the refrigerator.

● Pre-heat oven to 350°F/175°C/Gas mark 4. Grease two large baking sheets or line with non-stick baking parchment.

● Roll tablespoons of the mixture into balls and place on the baking sheets at least 8 cm/3 in apart. Flatten slightly with the back of a spoon. Bake for 15 to 17 minutes until golden. Leave to cool for 5 minutes then transfer to wire racks to cool completely. Store in an airtight container.

Brandy and Fresh Apple Cookies

Preparation time: 20 minutes ●
Cooking time: 15 minutes ● *Makes: About 10 to 12*

Fresh apples add texture and a sweet flavour.

INGREDIENTS

75 g/3 oz grated apple

1 Tbsp lemon juice

50 g/2 oz butter

2 Tbsp golden syrup

50 g/2 oz caster sugar

2 Tbsp brandy

50 g/2 oz plain flour

50 g/2 oz chopped almonds

Pre-heat oven to 350°F/175°C/Gas mark 4. Grease two large baking sheets or line with non-stick baking parchment.

● Squeeze the grated apples in your hand to essence the juice. Discard the juice then toss the apple in the lemon juice to coat.

● Put butter, golden syrup, sugar and brandy in a saucepan over a medium heat and stir until the sugar dissolves. Remove from the heat and cool for 5 minutes, stirring frequently. Sift in the flour, then stir in the almonds and apple. Mix well.

● Drop heaped teaspoons onto the baking sheets, at least 8 cm/3 in apart. Shape them into neat rounds. Bake for about 15 minutes. Cool for 5 minutes, then transfer to wire racks to cool completely. Store in an airtight container.

Pineapple Crumble Cookies

Preparation time: 30 minutes + chilling ● *Cooking time: 20 to 25 minutes* ● *Makes: About 24*

These cookies are different as they have a pineapple crumble on top of sweet cookie bases.

INGREDIENTS

120 g/4 oz butter

3 Tbsp caster sugar

1 tsp vanilla essence

150 g/5 oz plain flour

75 g/3 oz ground almonds

1 egg yolk

CRUMBLE TOPPING

120 g/4 oz plain flour

50 g/2 oz caster sugar

50 g/2 oz cold butter, chopped

120 g/4 oz dried pineapple, finely chopped

Grease two large baking sheets or line with non-stick baking parchment.

● Put the butter and sugar in a bowl and beat until light and fluffy. Stir in the vanilla essence. Sift in flour then stir in the ground almonds. Mix to a soft dough. Chill for 30 minutes in the refrigerator.

● Dust the work surface with a little flour, then roll out the dough to about 8 mm/⅓-in thick. Stamp out 3-inch rounds with a cutter, re-rolling and stamping out the trimmings. Place the cookies on the baking sheets and chill for at least 30 minutes in the refrigerator.

● Meanwhile, combine the flour and sugar for the topping. Add the butter and mix with your fingertips to the consistency of coarse breadcrumbs. Stir in the chopped pineapple.

● Pre-heat oven to 325°F/160°C/Gas mark 3.

● Brush the cookies with the egg yolk then sprinkle a little crumble onto each. Bake cookies for 20 to 25 minutes until lightly golden. Leave to cool slightly, then transfer to wire racks to cool completely. Store in an airtight container.

Star Fruit Cookies

Preparation time: 20 minutes + chilling ●
Cooking time: 15 to 17 minutes ● *Makes: About 35*

Dried star fruit has a slightly perfumed flavour and make these most unusual cookies really special.

INGREDIENTS

225 g/8 oz butter, softened

200 g/7 oz caster sugar

200 g/7 oz light brown sugar

2 eggs, beaten

Grated rind of 1 lemon

250 g/9 oz plain flour

1 tsp salt

1 tsp baking powder

375 g/12 oz dried star fruit, roughly chopped

Beat together the butter and sugars until soft and creamy. Gradually beat in the eggs and lemon rind. The mixture may look as if it is curdling, but it will be fine when cooked. Sift in the flour, salt and baking powder and mix to combine. Stir in the chopped star fruit and mix well. Chill the mixture for at least one hour in the refrigerator.

● Pre-heat oven to 350°F/175°C/Gas mark 4. Grease two large baking sheets or line with non-stick paper.

● Roll tablespoons of the mixture into balls and place on the baking sheets at least 8 cm/3 in apart. Flatten slightly with the back of a spoon. Bake for 15 to 17 minutes until golden. Leave to cool for 5 minutes then transfer to wire racks to cool completely. Store in an airtight container.

TIP

Dried star fruit is quite difficult to find. Look for it in health shops and good-quality specialized shops.

Peach and Cherry Thins

Preparation time: 15 minutes ●
Cooking time: 10 minutes ● *Makes: About 10*

These cookies are packed full of fruit with just a little dough to hold them together.

INGREDIENTS

50 g/2 oz butter

2 Tbsp golden syrup

50 g/2 oz caster sugar

75 g/3 oz plain flour

50 g/2 oz chopped dried peaches

75 g/3 oz dried Morello or sour cherries

Pre-heat oven to 350°F/175°C/Gas mark 4. Grease two large baking sheets or line with non-stick baking parchment.

● Put butter, golden syrup and sugar in a saucepan over a medium heat and stir until the sugar dissolves. Remove from the heat and cool for 5 minutes, stirring frequently. Stir in the flour, followed by the dried peaches and cherries. Mix well.

● Drop heaped teaspoons onto the baking sheets, at least 4 cm/1½ in apart. Shape them into neat rounds. Bake for about 10 minutes. Re-shape into rounds while hot, if necessary. Cool for 5 minutes, then transfer to wire racks to cool. Store in an airtight container.

Pineapple and Ginger Cookies

Preparation time: 15 minutes + chilling ● *Cooking time: 15 to 17 minutes* ● *Makes: About 25*

Chewy cookies with a hint of ginger.

INGREDIENTS

225 g/8 oz butter, softened

200 g/7 oz light brown sugar

200 g/7 oz caster sugar

2 eggs, beaten

1 Tbsp finely chopped stem ginger or ginger preserve

3 tsp stem ginger syrup (from the stem ginger jar) or golden syrup

250 g/9 oz plain flour

1 tsp baking powder

1 tsp salt

120 g/4 oz diced dried pineapple

Put the butter and sugars in a bowl and beat together until pale and creamy. Gradually beat in the eggs, stem ginger and ginger syrup. Do not worry if the mixture looks as if it is curdling, it will be fine when cooked. Sift in the flour, baking powder and salt and mix. Stir in the pineapple and mix well. Chill for at least one hour in the refrigerator.

● Pre-heat oven to 350°F/175°C/Gas mark 4. Grease two baking sheets or line with non-stick baking parchment.

● Roll tablespoons of the mixture into balls and place onto the baking sheets, at least 8 cm/3 in apart. Flatten with the back of a spoon. Bake for 15 to 17 minutes until golden, but still soft. Cool for 5 minutes on the baking sheets then transfer to wire cooling racks. Store in an airtight container.

Winter Fruit Cookies

Preparation time: 20 minutes + chilling ●
Cooking time: 15 to 17 minutes ● Makes: About 30

These cookies are full of the flavour of Christmas as they are packed with the dried fruit associated with the festive season.

INGREDIENTS

225 g/8 oz butter, softened

200 g/7 oz caster sugar

200 g/7 oz light brown sugar

2 eggs, beaten

250 g/9 oz plain flour

1 tsp salt

1 tsp baking powder

75 g/3 oz chopped dates

75 g/3 oz dried cherries

75 g/3 oz diced candied citrus peel

12 whole glacé cherries, halved

Put the butter and sugars in a bowl and beat until light and fluffy. Gradually beat in the eggs. The mixture may look as if it is curdling but it will be fine when cooked. Sift in the flour, salt and baking powder and mix. Add dates, cherries and candied peel and mix well. Chill for 1 hour in the refrigerator.

● Pre-heat oven to 350°F/175°C/Gas mark 4. Grease two large baking sheets or line with non-stick baking paper.

● Roll tablespoons of the mixture into balls and place on the baking sheets at least 8 cm/3 in apart. Flatten slightly between your palms and push half a cherry into the centre of each cookie. Bake for 15 to 17 minutes until golden. Leave to cool for 5 minutes then transfer to wire racks to cool completely. Store in an airtight container.

Dried Pear and Walnut Wheaties

Preparation time: 15 minutes + chilling ●
Cooking time: 15 to 17 minutes ● Makes: About 30

The wholemeal flour gives the cookies a really rich flavour.

INGREDIENTS

225 g/8 oz butter, softened

200 g/7 oz light brown sugar

200 g/7 oz caster sugar

2 eggs, beaten

1 tsp vanilla essence

250 g/9 oz wholemeal flour

1 tsp baking powder

1 tsp salt

120 g/4 oz finely chopped dried pears

120 g/4 oz chopped walnut pieces

Put the butter and sugars in a bowl and beat together until pale and creamy. Gradually beat in the eggs and vanilla essence. Do not worry if the mixture looks as if it is curdling, it will be fine when cooked. Sift in the flour, baking powder and salt and mix. Stir in the pears and walnuts and mix well. Chill for at least one hour in the refrigerator.

● Pre-heat oven to 350°F/175°C/Gas mark 4. Grease two baking sheets or line with non-stick baking parchment.

● Roll tablespoons of the mixture into balls and place onto the baking sheets, at least 8 cm/3 in apart. Flatten with the back of a spoon. Bake for 15 to 17 minutes until golden, but still soft. Cool for 5 minutes on the baking sheets then transfer to wire cooling racks. Store in an airtight container.

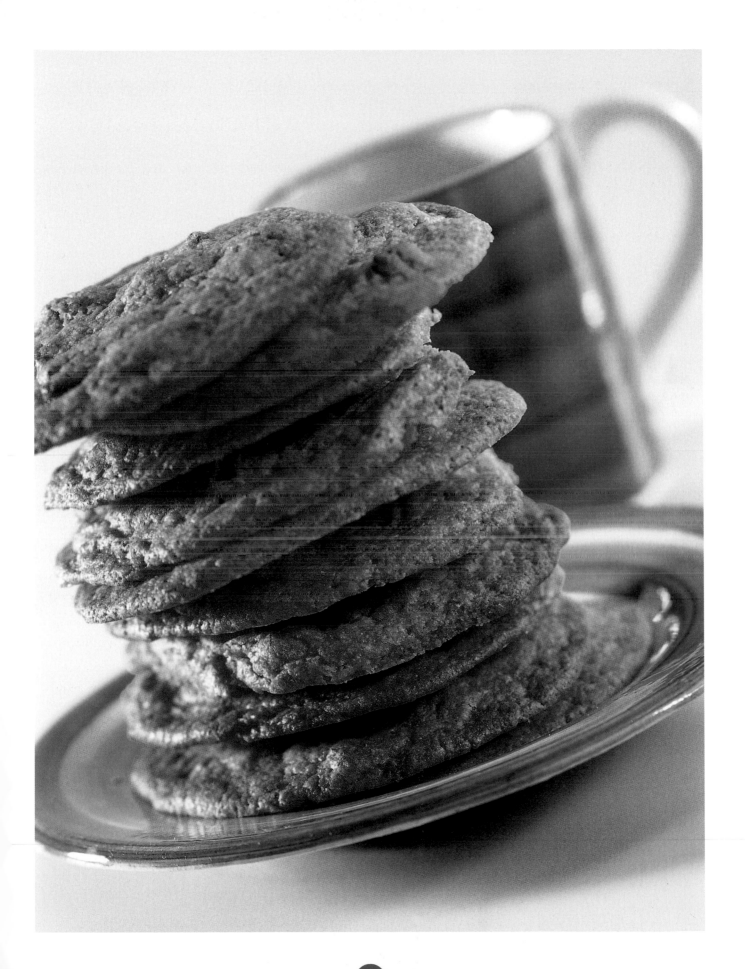

Nut Cookies

Nuts are a central feature in many of the most successful cookies. They add an additional crunch to already crunchy cookies or a contrasting bite to soft, chewy cookies. Some cookies substitute ground nuts for flour, giving the resulting cookies a rich, dense flavour. The subtle flavours and textures of almonds, macadamia, pecan and cashew nuts, for instance, can be used on their own or in clever combinations that enhance each to best advantage. Combined with fragrant spices or delectable chocolate, nut-based cookies are simply wonderful.

Anyone who loves nutty cookies will be pleased to learn that the latest health findings are in favour of nuts. Nuts are high in proteins, monounsaturated fats, (the same fats found in olive oil), and polyunsaturated fats (which help lower cholesterol levels), and masses of micronutrients including vitamin E and folic acid. Of course, these cookies still contain butter and sugar so it's not all good news, but eaten in moderation they make a truly satisfying treat.

Traditional Classics

Family Favourites

Clever Combinations

Exotic Delights

Almond Brittle Cookies

Preparation time: 25 minutes + chilling ●
Cooking time: 15 to 20 minutes ● *Makes: About 20*

Almond brittle is unusual, yet simple to make.

INGREDIENTS

ALMOND BRITTLE

150 g/5 oz blanched almonds

50 g/2 oz caster sugar

COOKIE DOUGH

225 g/8 oz butter, softened

225 g/8 oz caster sugar

2 eggs, beaten

225 g/8 oz plain flour

1 tsp baking powder

1 tsp salt

For the almond brittle, pre-heat oven to 425°F/220°C/Gas mark 7. Place almonds on a baking sheet and toast for 3 to 4 minutes. Melt sugar in a small saucepan over a medium heat without stirring. Add the almonds, mix, then remove from the heat. Quickly spread onto a baking sheet and cool. Chop.

● To make the cookies, put the butter and sugars in a bowl and beat until pale and creamy. Gradually beat in the eggs. Sift in flour, baking powder and salt; mix well. Stir in the almond brittle and mix. Chill for 1 hour.

● Pre-heat oven to 350°F/175°C/Gas mark 4. Grease or line two baking sheets.

● Drop teaspoons of the mixture onto the baking sheets, at least 8 cm/3 in apart. Flatten with the back of a spoon. Bake for 15 to 18 minutes until golden. Cool for 5 minutes then transfer to wire racks. Store in an airtight container.

PistachioDrops

Preparation time: 20 minutes + chilling ●
Cooking time: 15 to 18 minutes ● *Makes: About 25*

The green of the pistachios gives these cookies an exotic appeal.

INGREDIENTS

225 g/8 oz butter, softened

175 g/6 oz caster sugar

175 g/6 oz light brown sugar

2 eggs, beaten

250 g/9 oz plain flour

1 tsp salt

1 tsp baking powder

175 g/6 oz chopped unsalted, pistachios

1 tsp vanilla essence

Beat together butter and sugars until soft and creamy. Gradually beat in eggs. The mixture may look as if it is curdling, but it will be fine when cooked. Sift in flour, salt and baking powder; mix to combine. Stir in pistachios and vanilla essence. Chill mixture for at least 1 hour in the refrigerator.

● Pre-heat oven to 350°F/175°C/Gas mark 4. Grease two baking sheets or line with non-stick baking parchment.

● Roll tablespoons of the mixture into balls and place on the sheets at least 8 cm/3 in apart. Flatten slightly with the back of a spoon. Bake for 15 to 18 minutes until golden. Leave to cool for 5 minutes then transfer to wire racks to cool. Store in an airtight container for up to 1 week.

Almond and Ginger Hearts

Preparation time: 30 minutes + chilling ● *Cooking time: 20 to 25 minutes* ● *Makes: About 24*

These delicate hearts are perfect for afternoon tea.

INGREDIENTS

120 g/4 oz butter

3 Tbsp caster sugar

150 g/5 oz plain flour, plus extra for rolling

75 g/3 oz ground almonds

2 tsp finely chopped stem ginger or ginger preserve

2 tsp stem ginger syrup (from the stem ginger jar) or golden syrup

Icing sugar, for serving, optional

Grease two baking sheets or line with non-stick baking parchment.

● Put the butter and sugar in a bowl and beat until light and fluffy. Sift in flour then stir in almonds, stem ginger or ginger preserve and syrup. Mix to a soft dough. Chill for 30 minutes.

● Roll out dough on a floured surface to a thickness of about 8 mm/⅓ in. Stamp out heart shapes with a pastry cutter, re-rolling and stamping out the trimmings. Transfer to the baking sheets and chill for at least 30 minutes in the refrigerator.

● Pre-heat oven to 325°F/160°C/Gas mark 3. Bake cookies for 20 to 25 minutes until lightly golden. Transfer to wire racks to cool. Dust with icing sugar to serve, if liked. Store in an airtight container for up to 1 week.

Peanut Butter Cookies

Preparation time: 30 minutes + chilling ●
Cooking time: 15 to 20 minutes ● *Makes: About 20*

These are really chunky, perfect for lunch boxes and picnics.

INGREDIENTS

75 g/3 oz butter, softened
5 Tbsp crunchy peanut butter
5 Tbsp dark brown sugar
120 g/4 oz caster sugar
1 egg, beaten
150 g/5 oz plain flour
1 tsp baking powder

Put the butter, peanut butter and sugars in a bowl and beat until light and fluffy. Gradually beat in the egg. Don't worry if it looks as if it is curdling, it will be fine once cooked. Sift in the flour and baking powder. Chill mixture for 1 hour.

● Pre-heat oven to 350°F/175°C/Gas mark 4. Grease two baking sheets or line with non-stick baking parchment.

● Place spoonfuls of the dough onto the baking sheets at least 8 cm/3 in apart. Flatten slightly with the back of a spoon. Bake for 15 to 20 minutes until golden. Cool for 5 minutes on the baking sheet then transfer to wire racks to cool. Store in an airtight container for up to 1 week.

Pecan and Cinnamon Cookies

Preparation time: 20 minutes + chilling ●
Cooking time: 12 to 15 minutes ● *Makes: 25*

Pecans and cinnamon are an excellent combination.

INGREDIENTS

225 g/8 oz butter, softened
200 g/7 oz caster sugar
200 g/7 oz light brown sugar
2 eggs, beaten
250 g/9 oz plain flour
1 tsp salt
2 tsp ground cinnamon
1 tsp baking powder
225 g/8 oz chopped pecan nuts

Beat together butter and sugars in a bowl until soft and creamy. Gradually beat in eggs. The mixture may look as if it is curdling, but it will be fine when cooked. Sift in flour, salt, ground cinnamon and baking powder and mix to combine. Stir in pecans and ground cinnamon. Chill mixture for at least 1 hour in the refrigerator.

● Pre-heat oven to 350°F/175°C/Gas mark 4. Grease two baking sheets or line with non-stick baking parchment.

● Roll tablespoons of the mixture into balls and place on the sheets at least 8 cm/3 in apart. Flatten slightly with the back of a spoon. Bake for 12 to 15 minutes until golden. Leave to cool for 5 minutes then transfer to wire racks to cool. Store in an airtight container for up to 1 week.

White Chocolate and Macadamia Nut Treats

Preparation time: 15 minutes + chilling • *Cooking time: 10 to 15 minutes* • *Makes: About 20*

You can really get your teeth into these chunky cookies.

INGREDIENTS

225 g/8 oz butter, softened
200 g/7 oz caster sugar
200 g/7 oz light brown sugar
2 eggs, beaten
250 g/9 oz plain flour
1 tsp salt
1 tsp baking powder
120 g/4 oz chopped macadamia nuts
125 g/4 oz white chocolate chips

Beat together butter and sugars until soft and creamy. Gradually beat in eggs. The mixture may look as if it is curdling, but it will be fine when cooked. Sift in flour, salt and baking powder; mix to combine. Add macadamia nuts and white chocolate chips and mix together well. Chill mixture for at least 1 hour in the refrigerator.

● Pre-heat oven to 350°F/175°C/Gas mark 4. Grease two baking sheets or line with non-stick baking parchment.

● Roll tablespoons of the mixture into balls and place on the sheets at least 8 cm/3 in apart. Flatten slightly with the back of a spoon. Bake for 10 to 15 minutes until golden. Leave to cool for 5 minutes then transfer to wire racks to cool. Store in an airtight container for up to 1 week.

Walnut Crescents

Preparation time: 30 minutes + chilling ● *Cooking time: 20 to 25 minutes* ● *Makes: About 25*

These cookies are light, crumbly and nutty.

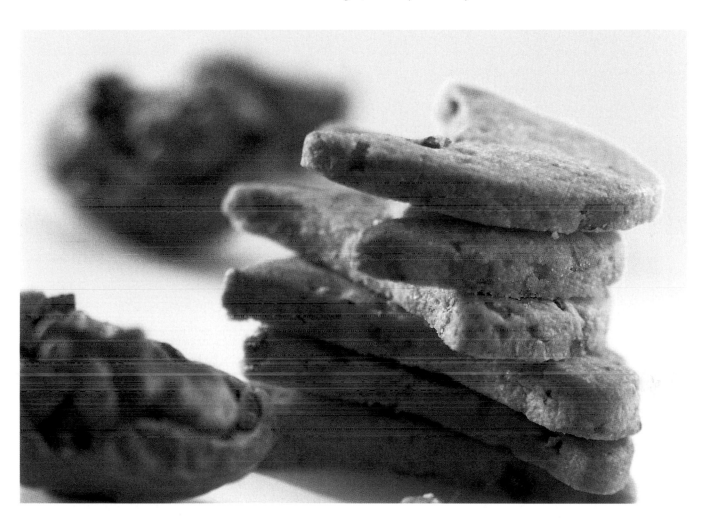

INGREDIENTS

120 g/4 oz butter
3 Tbsp caster sugar
150 g/5 oz plain flour
50 g/2 oz finely chopped walnuts

Put the butter and sugar in a bowl and beat until light and fluffy. Sift in the flour then stir in the walnuts. Mix to form a soft dough. Chill the dough for 30 minutes in the refrigerator.

● Grease two baking sheets or line with non-stick baking parchment. Dust work surface with a little flour, then roll out dough to a thickness of about 8 mm/⅓ in. Stamp out crescent shapes with a cutter, re-rolling and stamping out the trimmings. Transfer to the baking sheets and chill for a further 30 minutes.

● Pre-heat oven to 325°F/160°C/Gas mark 3. Bake cookies for 20 to 25 minutes until lightly golden. Transfer to wire racks to cool. Store in an airtight container for up to 1 week.

Hazelnut and Orange Cookies

Preparation time: 20 minutes + chilling ●
Cooking time: 18 to 20 minutes ● *Makes: 40*

The combination of hazelnut and orange works really well in these cut-out cookies. Use Christmas cutters and serve over the festive season.

INGREDIENTS

225 g/8 oz butter, softened

120 g/4 oz caster sugar

120 g/4 oz light brown sugar

300 g/10 oz plain flour, plus extra for rolling

150 g/5 oz chopped hazelnuts

Grated rind of 1 orange

Put the butter and sugars in a mixing bowl and beat with an electric beater until light and fluffy. Sift in the flour and mix to a dough. Stir in the chopped hazelnuts and orange rind. Mix well. Chill for 30 minutes.

● Pre-heat oven to 325°F/160°C/Gas mark 3. Grease two baking sheets or line with non-stick baking parchment.

● Dust work surface with flour and roll out dough to 5 mm/½ in thick. Stamp out 5-cm/2-in rounds with a cutter. Transfer to the baking sheets. Bake for 18 to 20 minutes until golden. Cool for 5 minutes then transfer to wire racks to cool. Store in an airtight container.

Pine Nut and Peach Chews

Preparation time: 20 minutes + chilling ●
Cooking time: 12 to 15 minutes ● *Makes: About 25*

The crystallized peaches in these cookies give them a great chewy texture.

INGREDIENTS

225 g/8 oz butter, softened

200 g/7 oz light brown sugar

200 g/7 oz caster sugar

2 eggs, beaten

225 g/8 oz plain flour

1 tsp baking powder

1 tsp salt

150 g/5 oz pine nuts

75 g/3 oz crystallized peaches, roughly chopped

Put the butter and sugars in a bowl and beat together until pale and creamy. Gradually beat in the eggs. Don't worry if the mixture looks as if it is curdling, it will be fine when cooked. Sift in flour, baking powder and salt; stir to combine. Stir in the pine nuts and glacé peaches and mix well. Chill for 1 hour.

● Pre-heat oven to 350°F/175°C/Gas mark 4. Grease two baking sheets or line with non-stick baking parchment.

● Roll tablespoons of the mixture into balls and place onto the baking sheets, at least 8 cm/3 in apart. Flatten with the back of a spoon. Bake for 12 to 15 minutes until golden, but still soft. Cool for 5 minutes on the baking sheets then transfer to wire racks. Store in an airtight container for up to 1 week.

Pecan and Chocolate Pebbles

Preparation time: 30 minutes ● *Cooking time: 10 to 12 minutes* ● *Makes: 15*

**These are very rich meringue-style cookies that look just like beach pebbles!
They are filled with a delicious chocolate ganache.**

INGREDIENTS

175 g/6 oz pecan nuts

250 g/9 oz caster sugar

3 egg whites

1 tsp vanilla essence

GANACHE FILLING

200 g/7 oz good-quality plain chocolate, broken up

25 g/1 oz unsalted butter

50 ml/2 fl oz double cream

Pre-heat oven to 325°F/160°C/Gas mark 3. Grease two baking sheets or line with non-stick baking parchment.

● Place pecans in a food processor and grind until finely chopped but not into a paste. Add 225 g/8 oz of the sugar and grind for 10 seconds more.

● Beat the egg whites until stiff peaks form. Beat in the remaining sugar a little at a time, beating well after each addition. Beat in the vanilla essence. Gradually beat in the pecan mixture a little at a time until it is all incorporated.

● Fit a piping bag with a 5-mm/½-in nozzle and fill with the mixture. Pipe 5-cm/2-in fingers about 2.5 cm/ 1 in apart on the baking sheets. Bake for 10 to 12 minutes until pale golden. Leave to cool completely on the baking sheets before adding the ganache.

● To make the ganache, melt the chocolate in a bowl in the microwave or in a double boiler over simmering water. Heat the butter and cream in a small saucepan, add to the chocolate and stir until smooth and glossy. Cool, stirring occasionally, until a spreadable consistency is reached. Carefully spread half the fingers with the ganache and sandwich with another finger. Because these cookies contain fresh cream they should be eaten on the day they are made.

Coconut and Chocolate Swirls

Preparation time: 40 minutes + chilling ● *Cooking time: 10 to 15 minutes* ● *Makes: About 25*

These are very delicate pinwheel cookies, ideal for a child's party.

INGREDIENTS

120 g/4 oz butter, softened

150 g/5 oz light brown sugar

120 g/4 oz plain flour

50 g/2 oz unsweetened cocoa powder

½ tsp salt

½ tsp baking powder

COCONUT FILLING

2 heaped Tbsp apricot jam

75 g/3 oz sweetened flaked coconut

Beat butter and sugar together in a bowl until light and fluffy. Sift in flour, cocoa powder, salt and baking powder. Gradually mix to a soft dough using your fingertips. Roll out on a piece of greaseproof paper to a 23 x 25-cm/9 x 10-in rectangle, cutting the dough to shape. Do not flour the greaseproof paper as it will change the colour of the dough. Carefully slide a thin metal spatula under the dough to release it from the paper, but leave it on the paper.

● Gently warm the jam then brush all over the cookie dough. Sprinkle over the coconut, patting it into the jam. Roll up the dough from a long side using the paper to help, but ensuring that it does not go inside the rolled dough. Do not allow the dough to crack. If it does, gently warm a knife and seal the crack. Roll up in the paper and chill for at least 30 minutes.

● Pre-heat oven to 350°F/175°C/Gas mark 4. Grease or line a baking sheet with non-stick baking parchment.

● Allow the rolled dough to sit at room temperature for 5 minutes then, using a thin-bladed knife, cut the log into 5-mm/½-in slices and place on the baking sheet. Bake for 10 to 15 minutes. Cool for 5 minutes then transfer to wire racks to cool. Store in an airtight container for up to 1 week.

Toasted Cashew and Raisin Cookies

Preparation time: 20 minutes + chilling ●
Cooking time: 12 to 15 minutes ● *Makes: About 20*

Toasting the cashews makes them crisper, so the cookies are crunchier.

INGREDIENTS

150 g/5 oz cashew nuts

120 g/4 oz butter, softened

150 g/5 oz light brown sugar

1 egg, beaten

2 tsp almond essence

120 g/4 oz plain flour

2 tsp baking powder

1 tsp salt

175 g/6 oz raisins

Pre-heat oven to 375°F/190°C/Gas mark 5. Place cashew nuts on a baking sheet and toast for 5 minutes. Cool then roughly chop.

● Put butter and sugars in a bowl and beat until light and fluffy. Beat in the egg and almond essence. Sift in the flour, baking powder and salt; mix well. Add the chopped cashew nuts and raisins. Mix to a dough. Chill for 30 minutes if the dough is really soft.

● Pre-heat oven to 350°F/175°C/Gas mark 4. Grease two baking sheets or line with non-stick baking parchment.

● Drop heaped teaspoons of the mixture onto the sheets at least 5 cm/2 in apart and flatten slightly. Bake for 12 to 15 minutes until lightly golden. Cool for 5 minutes on the baking sheets then transfer to wire racks. Store in an airtight container for up to 1 week.

Orange and Macadamia Half Moons

Preparation time: 30 minutes + chilling ●
Cooking time: 20 to 25 minutes ● *Makes: 25*

Orange flower-water gives the cookies a subtle orange flavour.

INGREDIENTS

120 g/4 oz butter, softened

3 Tbsp caster sugar

175 g/6 oz plain flour, plus extra for rolling

75 g/3 oz chopped macadamia nuts

1 Tbsp orange flower-water

75 g/3 oz good-quality plain chocolate, broken up

Grease two baking sheets or line with non-stick baking parchment.

● Put the butter and sugar in a bowl and beat until light and fluffy. Sift in flour, then stir in macadamia nuts and orange flower-water. Mix to a soft dough. Chill for 30 minutes.

● Dust work surface with a little flour, then roll out dough to about 8 mm/⅓ in thick. Stamp out half-moon shapes with a cutter, re-rolling and stamping out the trimmings. Transfer to the baking sheets and chill for at least 30 minutes in the refrigerator.

● Pre-heat oven to 325°F/160°C/Gas mark 3. Bake cookies for 20 to 25 minutes until golden. Cool on wire racks.

● Meanwhile, melt the chocolate in a bowl in the microwave or in a double boiler over simmering water. Once the cookies have cooled, dip one half into the melted chocolate. Place on greaseproof paper to set. Store in an airtight container, but eat within a day or two.

Banoffee Squares

Preparation time: 35 minutes + chilling ● *Cooking time: 35 minutes* ● *Makes: 24*

**These cookies are packed with dried banana chips and topped with a rich
toffee and pecan sauce – truly scrumptious!**

INGREDIENTS

BANANA BASE

120 g/4 oz butter, softened

120 g/4 oz caster sugar

1 medium egg, beaten

175 g/6 oz plain flour

½ tsp baking powder

75 g/3 oz dried banana chips

PECAN TOPPING

50 g/2 oz unsalted butter

200 g/7 oz light brown sugar

50 ml/2 fl oz double cream

125 ml/4 fl oz golden syrup

150 g/5 oz roughly chopped pecan nuts

Grease and line the base and sides of a 28 x 20-cm/11 x 8-in baking tin with non-stick baking parchment.

● Put the butter and sugar in a bowl and beat until light and fluffy. Beat in the egg. Sift in the flour and baking powder and mix well. Stir the banana chips into the mixture. Spoon the mixture into the tin, spreading it evenly. This takes a little time and is easiest with a small spatula or round-bladed knife. Chill for 30 minutes.

● Pre-heat oven to 375°F/190°C/Gas mark 5. Cover dough with a piece of greaseproof paper and bake for 5 minutes. Remove paper and bake for a further 5 minutes. Cool while making the topping. (Leave the oven turned on.)

● To make the topping, put the butter, sugar, cream and golden syrup in a saucepan and melt gently over a low heat until the sugar dissolves, stirring frequently. Boil hard for 1 minute. Remove from the heat and stir in the pecans. Pour over the baked crust and bake for a further 10 minutes until the top is bubbling. Leave to cool completely in the tin on a wire rack.

● Run a knife around the edges, between the tin and the paper and lift out onto a board. Cut into 24 pieces, 6 across and 4 down. Store in an airtight container for up to 1 week.

Walnut and Banana Cookies

Preparation time: 20 minutes + chilling ● *Cooking time: 10 to 15 minutes* ● *Makes: 25*

These cookies are quite sweet, with a soft consistency.

INGREDIENTS

175 g/6 oz butter, softened

200 g/7 oz light brown sugar

200 g/7 oz caster sugar

2 large ripe bananas, mashed

300 g/10 oz plain flour

1 tsp salt

1 tsp baking powder

120 g/4 oz chopped walnuts

Put the butter and sugars in a bowl and beat until light and fluffy. Mix in the bananas. Sift in the flour, salt and baking powder and mix well. Stir in the walnuts. Chill for about 2 hours.

● Pre-heat oven to 350°F/175°C/Gas mark 4. Grease two baking sheets or line with non-stick baking parchment.

● Drop heaped teaspoons of the mixture onto the baking sheets and flatten with the back of a spoon. Bake for 10 to 15 minutes until golden. Cool for 5 minutes on the baking sheets then transfer to wire racks. Store in an airtight container for up to 1 week.

Pistachio and Orange Thins

Preparation time: 30 minutes + chilling ● *Cooking time: 15 minutes* ● *Makes: About 25*

Look out for shelled pistachios which will save you lots of time shelling them!

INGREDIENTS

120 g/4 oz butter, softened

3 Tbsp caster sugar

3 Tbsp light brown sugar

3 Tbsp Grand Marnier

175 g/6 oz plain flour

50 g/2 oz shelled, unsalted pistachios

Put butter and sugars in a mixing bowl and beat until pale and creamy. Beat in Grand Marnier. Sift in the flour and mix to a firm dough. Transfer to a piece of greaseproof paper and roll into a log 5 cm/2 in in diameter. Chill for 30 minutes.

● Meanwhile, grind or finely chop the pistachios and transfer to a sheet of greaseproof paper. Roll log in the pistachios several times, ensuring the whole log is covered in nuts. Rewrap in the greaseproof paper and chill for a further 30 minutes.

● Pre-heat oven to 325°F/160°C/Gas mark 3. Grease two baking sheets or line with non-stick baking parchment.

● Cut the log into 8-mm/⅓-in thick slices and place on the baking sheets 5 cm/2 in apart. Bake for 15 minutes. Cool for 5 minutes then transfer to wire racks to cool. Store in an airtight container for up to 1 week.

Chunky Pine Nut and Lemon Cookies

Preparation time: 15 minutes + chilling ● *Cooking time: 10 to 15 minutes* ● *Makes: 20*

Toasting pine nuts brings out their flavour and gives them a slightly smoky taste.

INGREDIENTS

COOKIES

200 g/7 oz pine nuts

120 g/4 oz butter, softened

200 g/7 oz light brown sugar

200 g/7 oz caster sugar

2 eggs, beaten

Grated rind of 1 lemon

250 g/9 oz plain flour

1 tsp baking powder

1 tsp salt

GLAZE (OPTIONAL)

5 Tbsp granulated sugar

2 Tbsp water

1 Tbsp lemon juice

Grated rind of 1 lemon

Pre-heat oven to 375°F/190°C/Gas mark 5. Place pine nuts on a baking sheet and toast for 5 minutes. Cool.

● Put the butter and sugars in a bowl and beat together until pale and creamy. Gradually beat in the eggs. Don't worry if the mixture looks as if it is curdling, it will be fine when cooked. Stir in the lemon rind. Sift in flour, baking powder and salt and mix. Stir in the nuts and mix well. Chill for 1 hour.

● Pre-heat oven to 350°F/175°C/Gas mark 4. Line two baking sheets with non-stick baking parchment.

● Roll tablespoons of the mixture into balls and place onto the baking sheets at least 8 cm/3 in apart. Flatten with the back of a spoon. Bake for 10 to 15 minutes until golden, but still soft. Cool for 5 minutes on the baking sheets then transfer to wire racks.

● If making the glaze, gently dissolve the sugar in the water and lemon juice. Boil for 5 minutes. Remove from the heat and stir in the lemon rind. Cool then drizzle a little over each cookie. Eat within a day or two, otherwise the cookies will go soft due to the glaze.

TIP

For a special occasion, omit 1 tablespoon of the water and stir in 1 tablespoon of liqueur into the glaze once it has cooled.

Coffee Brazil Cookies

Preparation time: 30 minutes + chilling ●
Cooking time: 15 to 20 minutes ● *Makes: About 25*

These elegant cookies are subtly flavoured with coffee.

INGREDIENTS

1 Tbsp strong instant coffee granules

2 Tbsp boiling water

50 g/2 oz Brazil nuts

120 g/4 oz butter, softened

50 g/2 oz light brown sugar

175 g/6 oz plain flour, plus extra for dusting

Dissolve the coffee in the boiling water and cool. Put the Brazil nuts in a food processor and finely grind, but take care not to grind to a paste.

● Place butter and sugar in a mixing bowl and beat together until light and fluffy. Beat in the coffee, then sift in the flour. Stir in the ground Brazil nuts and mix to a stiff dough. Chill for at least 30 minutes.

● Grease two baking sheets or line with non-stick baking parchment. Dust work surface with flour and roll out the dough to 8 mm/⅓ in thick. Stamp out shapes using cookie cutters, re-rolling and stamping out the trimmings. Transfer to the baking sheets and chill for about 15 minutes.

● Pre-heat oven to 350°F/175°C/Gas mark 4. Bake for 15 to 20 minutes. Cool for 5 minutes then transfer to wire racks. Store in an airtight container for up to 1 week.

Coconut and Walnut Cookies

Preparation time: 15 minutes + chilling ●
Cooking time: 12 minutes ● *Makes: About 40*

The coconut gives these cookies a delicious chewy texture.

INGREDIENTS

225 g/8 oz butter, softened

225 g/8 oz granulated sugar

2 eggs, beaten

1 tsp vanilla essence

225 g/8 oz plain flour

1 tsp baking powder

1 tsp salt

120 g/4 oz sweetened flaked coconut

About 75 g/3 oz walnut halves

Put butter and sugar in a bowl and beat until pale and creamy. Gradually add the eggs and vanilla essence. Sift in the flour, baking powder and salt and stir in the sweetened flaked coconut. Divide the dough into two pieces, transfer to two pieces of greaseproof paper and form each piece into a log about 5 cm/2 in in diameter. Chill for at least 2 hours and preferably overnight.

● Pre-heat oven to 350°F/175°C/Gas mark 4. Grease two baking sheets or line with non-stick baking parchment.

● Unwrap one log and slice into 5-mm/½ in slices. Transfer to the baking sheets and press a walnut half into the centre of each cookie. Bake for about 12 minutes until lightly golden around the edges. Cool for 5 minutes then transfer to wire cooling racks. Repeat with the second log. Store in an airtight container for up to 1 week.

Hazelnut and Cinnamon Rounds with Vanilla Glaze

Preparation time: 25 minutes + chilling ●
Cooking time: 15 minutes ● *Makes: About 40*

Have fun with these cookies stamping out all different shapes and sizes.

INGREDIENTS

120 g/4 oz butter, softened

3 Tbsp caster sugar

120 g/4 oz plain flour

2 tsp ground cinnamon

175 g/6 oz ground hazelnuts

GLAZE

75 g/3 oz icing sugar, sifted

1 tsp vanilla essence

2–3 tsp water

Put butter and sugar in a bowl and beat until light and creamy. Sift in the flour and cinnamon, then stir in the ground hazelnuts. Mix to a dough. Transfer to non-stick baking parchment and roll into a log about 5 cm/2 in in diameter. Chill for 2 hours.

● Grease two baking sheets or line with non-stick baking parchment. Cut 8-mm/⅓-in slices from the log. Transfer to the baking sheets.

● Pre-heat oven to 350°F/175°C/Gas mark 4. Bake cookies for 15 minutes until lightly browned. Cool for 5 minutes on the sheets then transfer to wire racks.

● To make the glaze, place the icing sugar and vanilla essence in a small bowl and add sufficient water to make a pourable icing. Drizzle over the cookies. Allow glaze to set before serving.

Double Almond Cookies

Preparation time: 15 minutes + chilling ●
Cooking time: 15 to 17 minutes ● *Makes: About 30*

If you like almonds, you'll love these cookies! You simply couldn't fit any more almonds in the batter.

INGREDIENTS

225 g/8 oz butter, softened

200 g/7 oz caster sugar

200 g/7 oz light brown sugar

2 large eggs, beaten

225 g/8 oz plain flour

1 tsp salt

1 tsp baking powder

175 g/6 oz chopped blanched almonds

125 g/4 oz flaked almonds

Beat together butter and sugars until soft and creamy. Gradually beat in the eggs. The mixture may look as if it is curdling, but it will be fine when cooked. Sift in flour, salt and baking powder and mix to combine. Add all the almonds and mix well. Chill mixture for at least 1 hour in the refrigerator.

● Pre-heat oven to 350°F/175°C/Gas mark 4. Line two large baking sheets with non-stick baking parchment.

● Roll tablespoons of the mixture into balls and place on the baking sheets at least 8 cm/3 in apart. Flatten slightly with the back of a spoon. Bake for about 15 to 17 minutes until golden. Leave to cool for five minutes then transfer to wire racks to cool. Store in an airtight container.

Drizzled Chocolate and Brazil Nut Cookies

Preparation time: 35 minutes + chilling ● *Cooking time: 10 to 15 minutes* ● *Makes: About 25*

The swirled chocolate makes these cookies a bit special.

INGREDIENTS

225 g/8 oz butter, softened

200 g/4 oz light brown sugar

200 g/7 oz caster sugar

2 eggs, beaten

250 g/9 oz plain flour

1 tsp baking powder

1 tsp salt

120 g/4 oz finely chopped Brazil nuts

50 g/2 oz plain chocolate, chopped

Put the butter and sugars in a bowl and beat together until pale and creamy. Gradually beat in the eggs. Don't worry if the mixture looks as if it is curdling, it will be fine when cooked. Sift in flour, baking powder and salt and mix. Stir in the Brazil nuts and mix well. Chill for 1 hour.

● Pre-heat oven to 350°F/175°C/Gas mark 4. Grease two baking sheets or line with non-stick baking parchment.

● Roll tablespoons of the mixture into balls and place onto the baking sheets, at least 8 cm/3 in apart to allow for speading. Flatten with the back of a spoon. Bake for 10 to 15 minutes until golden, but still soft. Cool for 5 minutes on the baking sheets then transfer to wire cooling racks.

● Melt the chocolate in a microwave or in a bowl over a pan of simmering water. Using a teaspoon, drizzle the chocolate over the cookies. Allow to set before serving. Best eaten on the day they are made, but may be stored in an airtight container.

Pistachio and Apricot Cookies

Preparation time: 25 minutes + chilling ● *Cooking time: 15 to 20 minutes* ● *Makes: 20*

These are very buttery cookies and need a little care in cooking.

INGREDIENTS

175 g/6 oz butter, softened

150 g/5 oz caster sugar

2 medium egg yolks

Grated rind of 1 orange

1 tsp vanilla essence

175 g/6 oz plain flour

3 Tbsp shelled pistachios, finely chopped

3 Tbsp apricot jam

Place butter and sugar in a bowl and beat until pale and fluffy. Beat in the egg yolks, orange rind and vanilla essence. Sift in the flour and mix to a soft dough. Chill for at least 1 hour.

● Pre-heat oven to 350°F/175°C/Gas mark 4. Grease two baking sheets or line with non-stick baking parchment.

● Roll tablespoons of the dough into balls then flatten between your palms. Place on the baking sheets, at least 2.5 cm/1 in apart. Bake for 15 to 20 minutes.

● Meanwhile, place the pistachios in a food processor and finely grind. Take care not to over-grind them, otherwise a paste will form. Warm the jam or preserve over low heat until melted. As soon as the cookies come out of the oven, brush with the melted jam and sprinkle with the nuts. Cool for 5 minutes then transfer to wire racks. Store in airtight containers.

TIP

If you don't have a food processor, chop the nuts finely by hand or buy them ready-chopped.

Flaky Chocolate and Peanut Cookies

Preparation time: 15 minutes + chilling ●
Cooking time: 10 to 15 minutes ● *Makes: 25*

Chocolate flakes in the dough give these cookies a crazy speckled appearance.

INGREDIENTS

75 g/3 oz blanched, unsalted peanuts, finely chopped
225 g/8 oz butter, softened
200 g/7 oz light brown sugar
200 g/7 oz caster sugar
2 eggs, beaten
250 g/9 oz plain flour
1 tsp baking powder
1 tsp salt
50 g/2 oz chocolate flakes

Pre-heat oven to 375°F/190°C/Gas mark 5. Place peanuts on a baking sheet and toast for 5 to 8 minutes. Cool.

● Put the butter and sugars in a bowl and beat together until pale and creamy. Gradually beat in the eggs. Don't worry if the mixture looks as if it is curdling, it will be fine when cooked. Sift in flour, baking powder and salt and mix. Stir in the peanuts and chocolate flakes and mix well. Chill for 1 hour.

● Pre-heat oven to 350°F/175°C/Gas mark 4. Grease two baking sheets or line with non-stick baking parchment.

● Roll tablespoons of the mixture into balls and place onto the baking sheets, at least 8 cm/3 in apart. Flatten with the back of a spoon. Bake for 10 to 15 minutes until golden, but still soft. Cool for 5 minutes on the baking sheets then transfer to wire racks.

Coffee and Walnut Cookies

Preparation time: 20 minutes + chilling ●
Cooking time: 15 to 18 minutes ● *Makes: 35*

Chocolate-covered coffee beans give you the best of both worlds with their combination of flavours.

INGREDIENTS

225 g/8 oz butter, softened
200 g/4 oz light brown sugar
200 g/7 oz caster sugar
2 eggs, beaten
250 g/9 oz plain flour
1 tsp baking powder
125 g/4 oz finely chopped walnuts
75 g/3 oz chocolate-covered coffee beans, finely chopped (see tip)

Put the butter and sugar in a bowl and beat until light and fluffy. Gradually beat in the eggs. Don't worry if the mixture looks as if it is curdling, it will be fine when cooked. Sift in flour and baking powder and mix. Stir in the walnuts and chocolate-covered coffee beans and mix well. Chill for 1 hour.

● Pre-heat oven to 350°F/175°C/Gas mark 4. Grease two baking sheets or line with non-stick baking parchment.

● Roll tablespoons of the mixture into balls and place onto the baking sheets, at least 8 cm/3 in apart. Flatten with the back of a spoon. Bake for 15 to 18 minutes until golden, but still soft. Cool for 5 minutes on the baking sheets then transfer to wire racks. Store in an airtight container for up to 1 week.

TIP

You can find chocolate-covered coffee beans in good supermarkets or gourmet food shops.

Almond and Orange Sandwich Cookies

Preparation time: 35 to 40 minutes ● *Cooking time: 10 minutes* ● *Makes: About 15*

Crunchy almond cookies sandwiched together with an orange buttercream filling.

INGREDIENTS

150 g/5 oz plain flour

1 tsp baking powder

1 Tbsp caster sugar

75 g/3 oz ground almonds

120 g/4 oz butter

125 ml/4 fl oz golden syrup

FILLING

50 g/2 oz unsalted butter, softened

120 g/4 oz icing sugar

Grated rind of 1 orange

1 Tbsp orange juice

Pre-heat oven to 375°F/190°C/Gas mark 5. Grease two baking sheets or line with non-stick baking parchment.

● Sift the flour and baking powder into a large bowl. Stir in the sugar and ground almonds and make a well in the centre. Put the butter and golden syrup in a small saucepan and stir over a gentle heat until the butter has melted. Pour into the dry ingredients and mix to a soft dough. Cool slightly.

● Take teaspoons of the mixture and roll into balls. Place on the baking sheets at least 5 cm/2 in apart and flatten slightly with the back of a spoon. Bake for 10 minutes. Cool for 5 minutes then transfer to wire racks.

● To make the filling, beat the butter until very soft and creamy, then gradually beat in the icing sugar. Slowly beat in the orange rind and juice. Leave it to harden slightly, then use to sandwich the cookies together. These cookies are best eaten soon after filling but may be stored in an airtight container.

Coconut and Lime Crunchies

Preparation time: 20 minutes + chilling ●
Cooking time: 7 minutes ● *Makes: About 12*

These are light and crispy cookies with a hint of tangy lime.

INGREDIENTS

75 g/3 oz sweetened flaked coconut

120 g/4 oz butter, softened

50 g/2 oz caster sugar

Pinch of salt

Grated rind of 1 lime

1 Tbsp fresh lime juice

Heat a frying pan over a medium to high heat. Add sweetened flaked coconut a little at a time and dry fry for about 30 seconds, stirring continuously until lightly golden. Transfer to a mixing bowl.

● In a separate bowl beat the butter and sugar together until pale and fluffy. Beat in salt, lime rind and lime juice. Stir in toasted coconut and form a soft dough. Cover and chill for at least 2 hours.

● Pre-heat oven to 375°F/190°C/Gas mark 5. Grease two baking sheets or line with non-stick baking parchment.

● Take teaspoons of the mixture, roll into balls then squash flat. Place on baking sheets at least 2.5 cm/1 in apart. Bake for about 7 minutes. Cool on the baking sheets. Store in an airtight container for up to 1 week.

TIP

Toasting coconut before using it really improves the flavour and gives it a chewy texture.

Crunchy Nut Cookies

Preparation time: 15 minutes + chilling ●
Cooking time: 10 to 15 minutes ● *Makes: 30*

Crunchy nut cereals are great for adding to cookie dough because they already contain nuts and the cereal makes the cookies really crunchy.

INGREDIENTS

225 g/8 oz butter, softened

200 g/7 oz light brown sugar

200 g/7 oz caster sugar

2 eggs, beaten

250 g/9 oz plain flour

1 tsp baking powder

1 tsp salt

70 g/2½ oz crunchy nut cereal

Put the butter and sugars in a bowl and beat together until pale and creamy. Gradually beat in the eggs. Don't worry if the mixture looks as if it is curdling it will be fine when cooked. Sift in flour, baking powder and salt; fold into the mixture. Stir in the crunchy nut cereal and mix well. Chill for 1 hour.

● Pre-heat oven to 350°F/175°C/Gas mark 4. Grease two baking sheets or line with non-stick baking parchment.

● Roll tablespoons of the mixture into balls and place onto the baking sheets, at least 8 cm/3 in apart. Flatten with the back of a spoon. Bake for 10 to 15 minutes until golden, but still soft. Cool for 5 minutes on the baking sheets then transfer to wire racks. Store in an airtight container for up to 1 week.

Double Ginger Pecan Cookies

Preparation time: 20 minutes ● *Cooking time: 12 minutes* ● *Makes: 25*

These cookies are for real ginger lovers. They contain both ground ginger and stem or preserved ginger.

INGREDIENTS

200 g/7 oz plain flour

1 tsp baking powder

2 tsp ground ginger

1 Tbsp caster sugar

75 g/3 oz chopped pecan nuts

120 g/4 oz butter

125 ml/4 fl oz golden syrup

1 Tbsp finely chopped stem ginger or ginger preserve

2 tsp stem ginger syrup (from the stem ginger jar)

or additional golden syrup

Pre-heat oven to 375°F/190°C/Gas mark 5. Grease two baking sheets or line with non-stick baking parchment.

● Sift the flour, baking powder and ground ginger into a large bowl. Stir in the sugar and pecans and make a well in the centre.

● Put butter, syrup, stem ginger and stem ginger syrup, if using, in a small saucepan and stir over a gentle heat until the butter has melted. Pour into the dry ingredients and mix to a soft dough. Cool for 10 minutes.

● Take teaspoons of the mixture and roll into balls. Place on the baking sheets at least 5 cm/2 in apart and flatten slightly with the back of a spoon. Bake for 15 to 20 minutes until golden. Cool for 5 minutes then transfer to wire racks. Store in an airtight container for up to 1 week.

Pistachio and Mint Creams

Preparation time: 30 minutes + chilling ● *Cooking time: 10 to 15 minutes* ● *Makes: About 20*

Delicate pistachio cookies sandwiched together with a rich, dark chocolate and mint ganache

INGREDIENTS

75 g/3 oz pistachios

120 g/4 oz butter, softened

3 Tbsp caster sugar

150 g/5 oz plain flour

MINT GANACHE

25 g/1 oz butter

125 g/4 oz plain chocolate

1 tsp peppermint essence

2 Tbsp whipping cream, at room temperature

Put pistachios in a food processor and finely grind. Put butter and sugar in a bowl and beat until light and fluffy. Sift in the flour, add the ground pistachios, and mix to a dough. Scrape onto a piece of greaseproof paper and form into a log 5 cm/2 in in diameter. Chill for 1 hour.

● Pre-heat oven to 350°F/175°C/Gas mark 4. Grease two baking sheets or line with non-stick baking parchment.

● Slice 5-mm/½-in thick cookies from the dough and put on baking sheets 2.5 cm/1 in apart. Bake for 10 to 15 minutes. Cool, then transfer to wire racks.

● To make the ganache, place the butter, chocolate and peppermint essence and cream in a double boiler over simmering water. Stir until melted and smooth. Remove from the heat and cool for 5 minutes. Then stir until thick. Spread over the base of half the cookies and gently stick to the base of the remaining cookies. These are best eaten on the day they are made.

Chocolate and Hazelnut Treats

Preparation time: 25 minutes ●
Cooking time: 10 to 15 minutes ●
Makes: 30 double cookies

These are deliciously crumbly and you get twice the amount of cookie!

INGREDIENTS

225 g/8 oz butter, softened

200 g/7 oz light brown sugar

200 g/7 oz caster sugar

2 eggs, beaten

250 g/9 oz plain flour

1 tsp baking powder

1 tsp salt

175 g/6 oz chopped hazelnuts

175 g/6 oz chocolate and hazelnut spread

Put the butter and sugars in a bowl and beat together until pale and creamy. Gradually beat in the eggs. Don't worry if the mixture looks as if it is curdling, it will be fine when cooked. Sift in flour, baking powder and salt and mix. Stir in the hazelnuts and mix well. Chill for 1 hour.

● Pre-heat oven to 350°F/175°C/Gas mark 4. Grease two baking sheets or line with non-stick baking parchment.

● Roll level teaspoons of the mixture into balls and place onto the baking sheets, at least 5 cm/2 in apart. Flatten with the back of a spoon. Bake for 10 to 15 minutes until golden, but still soft. Cool for 5 minutes on the sheets then transfer to wire cooling racks. Once cooled, sandwich together with the chocolate spread. Best eaten soon after filling but may be stored in an airtight container.

Mixed Nut and Cherry Cookies

Preparation time: 30 minutes + chilling ●
Cooking time: 13 to 15 minutes ● *Makes: About 30*

Any combination of nuts can be used, or buy a packet of ready-mixed nuts.

INGREDIENTS

225 g/8 oz butter, softened

120 g/4 oz light brown sugar

200 g/7 oz caster sugar

2 eggs, beaten

250 g/9 oz plain flour

1 tsp baking powder

1 tsp salt

120 g/4 oz finely chopped mixed nuts

125 g/4 oz dried Morello or sour cherries

Put the butter and sugars in a bowl and beat together until pale and creamy. Gradually beat in the eggs. Don't worry if the mixture looks as if it is curdling, it will be fine when cooked. Sift in flour and baking powder and mix. Stir in the chopped nuts and dried cherries mix well. Chill for 1 hour.

● Pre-heat oven to 350°F/175°C/Gas mark 4. Grease two baking sheets or line with non-stick baking parchment.

● Roll tablespoons of the mixture into balls and place onto the baking sheets, at least 8 cm/3 in apart. Flatten with the back of a spoon. Bake for 13 to 15 minutes until golden, but still soft. Cool for 5 minutes on the sheets then transfer to wire cooling racks.

● These cookies are best eaten on the day they are made, but may be stored in an airtight container.

Pecan and Marshmallow Munchies

Preparation time: 15 minutes + chilling ●
Cooking time: 12 to 15 minutes ● *Makes: About 25*

These chewy cookies are simply irresistible! The marshmallows melt in little patches of each cookie giving an unexpected change of flavour.

INGREDIENTS

175 g/6 oz butter, softened

50 g/2 oz light brown sugar

200 g/7 oz caster sugar

2 eggs, beaten

3 Tbsp clear runny honey

250 g/9 oz plain flour

1 tsp baking powder

1 tsp salt

120 g/4 oz finely chopped pecan nuts

120 g/4 oz mini marshmallows

Put the butter and sugars in a bowl and beat together until pale and creamy. Gradually beat in the eggs and honey. Sift in flour, baking powder and salt; mix well. Stir in the pecans and marshmallows until well combined. Chill for at least 1 hour.

● Pre-heat oven to 350°F/175°C/Gas mark 4. Grease two baking sheets or line with non-stick baking parchment.

● Roll tablespoons of the mixture into balls and place onto the baking sheets, at least 8 cm/3 in apart. Flatten with the back of a spoon. Bake for 12 to 15 minutes until golden, but still soft. Cool for 5 minutes on the baking sheets then transfer to wire racks. Store in an airtight container for up to 1 week.

Walnut and Marmalade Cookies

Preparation time: 15 minutes + chilling ●
Cooking time: 15 to 18 minutes ● *Makes: About 30*

Adding marmalade to cookies gives them a toffee-like flavour and texture.

INGREDIENTS

225 g/8 oz butter, softened

200 g/7 oz light brown sugar

200 g/7 oz caster sugar

2 eggs, beaten

3 Tbsp orange marmalade

250 g/9 oz plain flour

1 tsp baking powder

1 tsp salt

120 g/4 oz finely chopped walnuts

Put the butter and sugars in a bowl and beat together until pale and creamy. Gradually beat in the eggs and marmalade. Don't worry if the mixture looks as if it is curdling, it will be fine when cooked. Sift in flour, baking powder and salt and mix. Stir in the walnuts and mix well. Chill for 1 hour.

● Pre-heat oven to 350F/175°C/Gas mark 4. Grease two baking sheets or line with non-stick baking parchment.

● Roll tablespoons of the mixture into balls and place onto the baking sheets, at least 8 cm/3 in apart. Flatten with the back of a spoon. Bake for 15 to 18 minutes until golden, but still soft. Cool for 5 minutes on the baking sheets then transfer to wire racks. Store in an airtight container for up to 1 week.

Walnut and Carrot Cookies

Preparation time: 30 minutes + chilling ●
Cooking time: 10 to 12 minutes ● *Makes: About 20*

Carrots have a sweet flavour and make the perfect match for walnuts.

INGREDIENTS

175 g/6 oz butter, softened
250 g/9 oz caster sugar
2 eggs, beaten
150 g/5 oz chopped walnuts
50 g/2 oz grated carrot
400 g/14 oz plain flour
1 tsp baking powder

Put butter and sugar in a mixing bowl and beat until pale and fluffy. Gradually beat in the eggs. Don't worry if the mixture looks as if it is curdling, it will be fine once cooked. Stir in the walnuts and grated carrot. Sift in the flour and baking powder and form into a dough. Chill for 1 hour.

● Pre-heat oven to 350°F/175°C/Gas mark 4. Grease two baking sheets or line with non-stick baking parchment.

● Take tablespoonfuls of the dough and form into balls. Place on the baking sheets at least 2.5 cm/1 in apart and flatten with the back of a spoon. Bake for 10 to 12 minutes. Cool on the baking sheets. Store the cookies in an airtight container.

Syrupy Macadamia Nut Cookies

Preparation time: 30 minutes + chilling ●
Cooking time: 20 minutes ● *Makes: About 16*

Macadamia nuts are very rich so not many are required to give a strong, nutty flavour.

INGREDIENTS

120 g/4 oz butter, softened
150 g/5 oz light brown sugar
4 tsp golden syrup
1 medium egg yolk
1 Tbsp orange juice
175 g/6 oz plain flour
½ tsp baking powder
120 g/4 oz macadamia nuts, roughly chopped
50 g/2 oz white chocolate chips

Put butter and sugar in a bowl and beat until pale and fluffy. Beat in the golden syrup, egg yolk and orange juice. Sift in the flour and baking powder; mix well. Stir in the macadamia nuts and mix to a soft dough.

● Press into a greased 20-cm/8-in square tin and chill for 30 minutes.

● Pre-heat oven to 350°F/175°C/Gas mark 4. Bake the mixture for about 20 minutes until cooked through.

● Meanwhile, melt the chocolate in a microwave or in a double boiler over simmering water. Drizzle the baked dough with the chocolate. Allow to harden before slicing into 16 squares. Store in an airtight container for up to 1 week.

Macadamia Chocolate Bars

Preparation time: 35 minutes ●
Cooking time: 25 minutes ● *Makes: 21*

The easy way to make a chocolate topping – just use whole bars of chocolate and let them melt over the warm cookie dough!

INGREDIENTS

175 g/6 oz butter, softened

120 g/4 oz caster sugar

3 Tbsp milk

1 tsp almond essence

175 g/6 oz plain flour

Pinch of salt

120 g/4 oz macadamia nuts, roughly chopped

300 g/10 oz good-quality milk or plain chocolate bars

Pre-heat oven to 350°F/175°C/Gas mark 4. Grease and base line a 32.5 x 23-cm/13 x 9-in baking tin.
● Put the butter and sugar in a bowl and beat until light and fluffy. Beat in the milk and almond essence. Sift in the flour and salt and form into a dough. Add half the nuts and mix well. Spread into the prepared tin and bake for 20 to 25 minutes until lightly browned around the edges.
● As soon as it is out of the oven, cover with the chocolate bars, then return to the oven for 2 minutes. Once out of the oven leave for 1 minute to let the chocolate melt. Once melted spread the chocolate evenly over the baked dough. Scatter over the remaining nuts and leave to cool completely. Cut into 21 bars, 7 across and 3 down. Store in an airtight container for up to 1 week.

Hazelnut and Treacle Cookies

Preparation time: 15 minutes + chilling ●
Cooking time: 15 minutes ● *Makes: About 25*

Some of the sugar is replaced by treacle in this drop cookie. It makes the cookies rich, rather than intensely sweet.

INGREDIENTS

175 g/6 oz butter, softened

200 g/7 oz light brown sugar

3 Tbsp treacle

1 egg, beaten

250 g/9 oz plain flour

1 tsp baking powder

1 tsp grated nutmeg

1 tsp salt

120 g/4 oz chopped hazelnuts

Put the butter and sugar in a bowl and beat until light and fluffy. Gradually beat in the treacle and egg. Sift in the flour, baking powder, nutmeg and salt; then mix. Stir in the nuts and form into a dough. Chill for at least 1 hour or overnight.
● Pre-heat oven to 350°F/175°C/Gas mark 4. Grease two baking sheets or line with non-stick baking parchment.
● Take heaped teaspoons of the dough, form into balls and flatten slightly between your palms. Place on the baking sheets at least 5 cm/2 in apart and bake for 15 minutes. Cool for 5 minutes and then transfer to wire racks.

Coconut Macaroons

Preparation time: 10 minutes ● *Cooking time: 20 minutes* ● *Makes: 20*

These are so simple to make, you'll never buy shop-bought macaroons again!

INGREDIENTS

4 egg whites

4 tsp cornflour

225 g/8 oz caster sugar

225 g/8 oz sweetened flaked coconut

20 whole blanched almonds

Edible rice paper, optional

Pre-heat oven to 350°F/175°C/Gas mark 4. Grease two baking sheets or line with rice paper or non-stick baking parchment.

● Beat the egg whites until foamy but not holding their shape. Stir in the remaining ingredients and mix well. Place 2 teaspoons of the mixture on the baking sheets about 5 cm/2 in in diameter, spaced well apart. Flatten slightly and place an almond in the centre of each.

● Bake for 20 minutes until just turning golden. Cool on the baking sheets. If using rice paper, tear from around each macaroon once cooled.

Coconut and Rum Cookies

Preparation time: 30 minutes + chilling ● Cooking time: 15 to 20 minutes ● Makes: About 20

These are delicate, crisp and crumbly cookies.

INGREDIENTS

120 g/4 oz sweetened flaked coconut

225 g/8 oz butter, softened

200 g/7 oz light brown sugar

2 Tbsp dark rum

200 g/7 oz plain flour

Pinch of salt

50 g/2 oz chopped flaked almonds

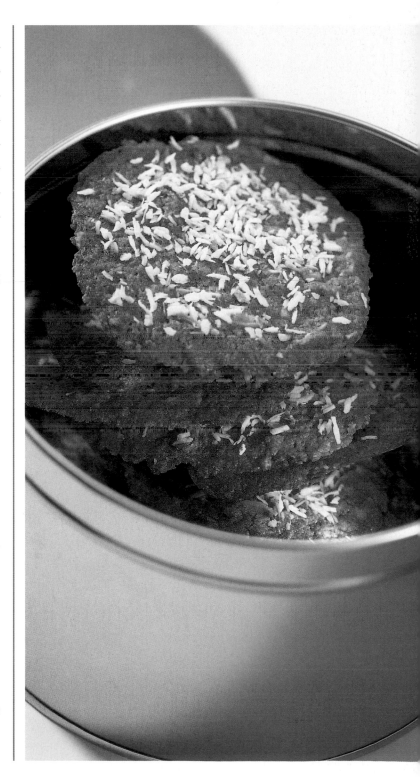

Heat a frying pan over high heat. Add half the coconut and dry-fry for about 30 seconds, stirring continuously until lightly golden. Place in a bowl and repeat with remaining coconut.

● Place the butter and sugar in a separate bowl and beat until light and fluffy. Beat in the rum. Sift in the flour and salt and mix well. Stir in the almonds and half the toasted coconut; mix well. Lightly flour the work surface and knead dough until soft.

● Divide mixture in two. Place each piece in a piece of greaseproof paper and shape each into a log about 5 cm/2 in in diameter and wrap each piece in greaseproof paper. Chill for at least 2 hours or overnight.

● Pre-heat oven to 350°F/175°C/Gas mark 4. Grease two baking sheets or line with non-stick baking parchment.

● Cut dough into 5-mm/½-in slices and arrange on the baking sheets at least 5 cm/2 in apart. Cook for 15 to 20 minutes until very lightly browned. As soon as the cookies are out of the oven, sprinkle over the remaining toasted coconut. Cool for 5 minutes on the baking sheets then transfer to wire racks. Store in an airtight container for up to 1 week.

Mocha Mixed Nut Drops

Preparation time: 30 minutes + chilling ●
Cooking time: 15 minutes ● Makes: About 25

Nuts, coffee and chocolate – there is something for everyone in these delicate cookies.

INGREDIENTS

1 Tbsp strong instant coffee granules
2 Tbsp boiling water
120 g/4 oz butter
3 Tbsp caster sugar
150 g/5 oz plain flour
50 g/2 oz mixed nuts

Dissolve the coffee granules in the boiling water and leave to cool.

● Put the butter and sugar in a bowl and beat until light and fluffy. Add the cooled coffee. Sift in the flour, then stir in the mixed nuts. Mix to a soft dough, then transfer to greaseproof paper and roll into a fat log, about 5 cm/2 in in diameter. Chill for 1 hour.

● Pre-heat oven to 325°F/175°C/Gas mark 2. Grease two baking sheets or line with non-stick baking parchment.

● Using a sharp knife, cut 2-cm/¾-in slices off the log and transfer to the baking sheets. If you have time, chill for a further 30 minutes in the refrigerator. Bake for about 15 minutes until lightly golden. Cool for 5 minutes then transfer to wire racks. Store in an airtight container for up to 1 week.

Brazil and Orange Chocolate Treats

Preparation time: 15 minutes + chilling ●
Cooking time: 10 to 15 minutes ● Makes: About 30

This is the best type of cookie for a quick, scrumptious snack – rich and chewy.

INGREDIENTS

225 g/8 oz butter, softened
200 g/7 oz caster sugar
200 g/7 oz light brown sugar
2 eggs, beaten
250 g/9 oz plain flour
1 tsp salt
1 tsp baking powder
150 g/5 oz chopped Brazil nuts
150 g/5 oz orange-flavoured chocolate, chopped

Beat together butter and sugars until soft and creamy. Gradually beat in the eggs. The mixture may look as if it is curdling, but it will be fine when cooked. Sift in flour, salt and baking powder and mix to combine. Stir in Brazil nuts and chocolate until combined. Chill mixture for at least 1 hour in the refrigerator.

● Pre-heat oven to 350°F/175°C/Gas mark 4. Line two large baking sheets with non-stick baking parchment.

● Roll tablespoons of the mixture into balls and place on the baking sheets at least 8 cm/3 in apart. Flatten slightly with the back of a spoon. Bake for 10 to 15 minutes until golden. Leave to cool for 5 minutes then transfer to wire racks to cool. Store in an airtight container.

Almond and Ginger Florentines

Preparation time: 20 minutes ●
Cooking time: 10 minutes ● *Makes: About 10*

Delicious tangy nut cookies are ideal as a gift.

INGREDIENTS

50 g/2 oz butter
2 Tbsp golden syrup
50 g/2 oz caster sugar
3 Tbsp plain flour
½ tsp ground ginger
50 g/2 oz chopped almonds
5 Tbsp flaked almonds
5 Tbsp chopped crystallized ginger
Grated rind of 1 lemon
50 g/2 oz good-quality plain chocolate
50 g/2 oz good-quality white chocolate

Pre-heat oven to 350°F/175°C/Gas mark 4. Grease two baking sheets.

● Put butter, golden syrup and sugar in a saucepan over medium heat and stir until the sugar dissolves. Remove from the heat and cool for 5 minutes, stirring. Sift in the flour and ground ginger, then stir in the almonds, crystallized ginger and lemon rind. Drop heaped teaspoons onto the baking sheets at least 8 cm/3 in apart. Shape into neat rounds. Bake for about 10 minutes. Cool for 5 minutes, then transfer to wire racks to cool.

● Melt the dark and white chocolates in two separate bowls in a microwave or over pans of simmering water. Spread the base of each Florentine with either dark or white chocolate then run a fork over the chocolate. Leave upside down to cool.

Cheddar and Peanut Cookies

Preparation time: 20 minutes + chilling ●
Cooking time: 15 to 17 minutes ● *Makes: About 30*

This savory cookie is great for lunch boxes or a quick snack.

INGREDIENTS

250 g/9 oz grated Cheddar cheese
175 g/6 oz butter, diced
125 ml/4 fl oz milk
150 g/5 oz plain flour
Pinch of salt
1 tsp baking powder
125 g/4 oz salted peanuts, chopped
About 20 whole salted peanuts

Combine all the ingredients, except the whole peanuts in a large bowl and mix with your fingers until a dough is formed. Chill for 30 minutes.

● Pre-heat oven to 350°F/175°C/Gas mark 4. Grease two baking sheets or line with non-stick baking parchment.

● Take heaped teaspoons of the mixture, roll into balls then flatten slightly. Place on the sheets at least 5 cm/ 2 in apart and press a whole peanut into each cookie. Bake for about 15 to 17 minutes until golden-brown. Cool on the baking sheets and serve warm or cold.

Bar Cookies

A cross between a cookie and a cake, bar cookies make a satisfying treat. This selection includes some old favourites as well as some new ideas that draw on the new ingredients on the market. There is even a short-cut recipe for making delicious brownies in the microwave. So whether you're making bar cookies as a dessert, or to pack in a lunch box, whether you want them crispy or crunchy, healthy or indulgent, you'll find plenty of inspiration in this chapter.

Old Favourites

Special Treats

Quick Bites

Portable Snacks

Grasmere Gingerbread

Preparation time: 20 minutes ●
Cooking time: 30 minutes ● Makes: 16 pieces

Grasmere, one of the prettiest lakes in the English Lake District, is famous for a ginger shortbread. The gingerbread shop in Grasmere jealously guards its recipe but this family recipe is as good, if not better!

INGREDIENTS

225 g/8 oz plain flour

1½ teaspoons ground ginger

120 g/4 oz lightly salted butter

200 g/7 oz light brown sugar

1 Tbsp golden syrup

1 Tbsp chopped candied orange peel or candied citrus peel

1 Tbsp chopped crystallized ginger

Pre-heat oven to 350°F/175°C/Gas mark 4. Grease and base-line an 18 x 28-cm/7 x 11-in shallow tin and line with waxed paper or nonstick baking parchment.

● Beat the butter, sugar and golden syrup until light and well blended. Beat in the remaining ingredients and press into the prepared tin.

● Bake for 25 to 30 minutes or until pale golden. Cut into 16 pieces while still hot but leave in the tin to cool. Store in an airtight container.

TIP

Try to find candied orange peel rather than candied citrus peel as the flavour and texture is superior.

Coconut and Prune Triangles

Preparation time: 30 minutes ●
Cooking time: 35 to 40 minutes ● Makes: 18 triangles

This recipe is a delicious mixture of basic store cupboard ingredients.

INGREDIENTS

50 g/2 oz stoned prunes

Juice and rind of 1 lemon

4 Tbsp water

1 Tbsp sugar

50 g/2 oz wholemeal flour

¾ tsp baking powder

120 g/4 oz plain flour

6 Tbsp soft tub margarine

200 g/7 oz soft brown sugar

1 egg, beaten

TOPPING

225 g/8 oz sweetened flaked coconut

4 Tbsp clear/runny honey

2 eggs

Pre-heat oven to 350°F/175°C/Gas mark 4. Grease and base line an 18 x 28-cm/7 x 11-in shallow tin.

● Chop the prunes and place in a pan with the lemon rind and juice, water and sugar. Cook until soft.

● Sift the two flours and baking powder, retaining the bran. Beat the margarine and sugar and beat in the egg. Work in the flours to form a dough and press into the pan. Spread the prune mixture over the dough.

● Beat the remaining 2 eggs, then beat in the honey and stir in the coconut. Spread over the prune mixture.

● Bake for 30 to 35 minutes or until golden-brown. Cool in the tin, then cut into squares and across into triangles.

Double Pear Treats

Preparation time: 1 hour ● Cooking time: 40 to 45 minutes ● Makes: 15 pieces

Double Pear Treats are delicious served hot with cream or yoghurt as a dessert. Or store them in an airlight container and eat cold whenever you feel like spoiling yourself.

INGREDIENTS

BASIC SHORTBREAD

75 g/3 oz plain flour

50 g/2 oz lightly salted butter

25 g/1 oz caster sugar

BASIC TOPPING

50 g/2 oz lightly salted butter or margarine

50 g/2 oz soft brown sugar

1 egg, beaten

50 g/2 oz wholewheat flour

1½ tsp baking powder

¼ tsp mixed spice

¼ tsp nutmeg

Grated rind of ½ orange

1 Tbsp milk

FILLING

3 pear halves from a tin of pears in natural juice

4 dried pear halves

2 Tbsp plain chocolate chips

To make the shortbread, pre-heat oven to 350°F/175°C/Gas mark 4. Grease a 20-cm/8-in square tin and line with non-stick baking parchment, so it stands 2.5-cm/1-in above the sides.

● Sift the flour into a bowl and blend in the butter until it resembles breadcrumbs, then stir in the sugar. Press the crumb mixture into the tin, making sure it is smooth and level.

● Bake for 10 to 15 minutes or until the centre is pale golden. Remove from the oven and cool while you make the filling.

● For the topping, beat the butter and sugar until light and fluffy. Gradually beat in the egg. Sift the spices and flour and fold into the mixture, together with the bran left in the sifter, the orange rind and the milk.

● Thoroughly drain the pear halves and chop. Scatter over the shortbread. Dice the dried pears and mix into a bowl of basic topping together with the chocolate chips. Pour over the chopped pears and level.

● Bake for 40 to 45 minutes or until the centres are firm. Cool in the tin for 15 minutes. Turn onto a cooling rack and when cool, cut into portions. Store in an airtight container, or freeze for up to 3 months.

Simnel Bars

Preparation time: 1 hour ● Cooking time: 40 to 45 minutes ● Makes: 15 pieces

You can make Simnel Bars less seasonal by leaving out the marzipan topping and instead, when cooked and cold, the top can be coated with a thin layer of icing.

INGREDIENTS

BASIC SHORTBREAD

75 g/3 oz plain flour

50 g/2 oz lightly salted butter

25 g/1 oz caster sugar

BASIC TOPPING

50 g/2 oz lightly salted butter or margarine

50 g/2 oz soft brown sugar

1 egg, beaten

50 g/2 oz wholewheat flour

1½ tsp baking powder

¼ tsp mixed spice

¼ tsp nutmeg

Grated rind of ½ orange

1 Tbsp milk

FILLING

120 g/4 oz mixed dried fruit

6 glacé cherries

2 tsp brandy

175 g/6 oz marzipan

1 Tbsp apricot jam

Prepare the basic shortbread and basic topping in the same way as for Double Pear Treats on the previous page.

● Chop the cherries and lightly mix into a bowl of basic topping together with the brandy and mixed dried fruit. Pour over the shortbread and level the surface.

● Bake for 40 to 45 minutes or until the centres are firm and the sides coming away from the edge of the tin. Cool in the pan for 15 minutes.

● Meanwhile, roll out the marzipan to fit half the sheet, using icing sugar to prevent it sticking to the work surface. Pre-heat the grill for 5 minutes.

● Warm the apricot jam and brush over the bake. Carefully lift the marzipan over and press lightly to fit. Using a sharp knife, mark diagonal lines across the top, making diamonds.

● Place under the grill and turn the heat down to medium. Leave until the marzipan has started to brown, checking constantly. Then gently turn onto a cooling rack covered with a folded teatowel.

● Slip onto a board and cut into portions with a sharp knife. Cool completely before storing or freezing for up to 3 months.

Coconut and Sesame Crunch

Preparation time: 15 minutes ●
Cooking time: 20 minutes ● *Makes: 12 pieces*

A delicious crunch bar with a distinctive nutty flavour. It is a great favourite, with a quick and easy method.

INGREDIENTS

120 g/4 oz margarine or butter
50 g/2 oz caster sugar
½ Tbsp golden syrup
75 g/3 oz self-raising flour
50 g/2 oz rolled oats
75 g/3 oz sweetened flaked coconut
2 Tbsp sesame seeds

Pre-heat oven to 350°F/175°C/Gas mark 4. Grease and base-line a 20 x 20-cm/8 x 8-in shallow tin.
● Melt the fat, sugar and syrup over a low heat in a large saucepan. Remove from the heat and stir in the remaining ingredients. Press into the tin. Do not worry if it looks very greasy at this stage, it is dry when cooked. Bake for 15 to 20 minutes until golden. Leave to cool for 10 minutes then cut into 12 pieces but leave to cool completely in the tin. Store in an airtight container for up to 1 week.

Boston Brownies

Preparation time: 20 minutes ●
Cooking time: 30 to 35 minutes ●
Makes: 9 large squares

Brownies are quite irresistible gooey squares of chocolate heaven and crunchy nuts. This recipe uses only cocoa which gives it a rich, full flavour – and is useful when the chocolate has disappeared from the cupboard.

INGREDIENTS

50 g/2 oz unsweetened cocoa powder
5 Tbsp water
¾ stick lightly salted butter
2 eggs
225 g/8 oz granulated sugar
75 g/3 oz plain flour
75 g/3 oz coarsely chopped pecan nuts

Pre-heat oven to 350°F/175°C/Gas mark 4. Grease and base-line a 20 x 20-cm/8 x 8-in tin.
● Place the cocoa in a small saucepan and gradually blend in the water. Briefly stir over a low heat to make a smooth paste. Add the butter or margarine and heat until it has melted.
● Beat the eggs and sugar until light and fluffy, then beat in the cocoa mixture.
● Sift the flour and fold in, then stir in the nuts. Spread into the tin.
● Bake for 25 to 30 minutes until risen and firm in the center. It is normal for the mixture to sink a little in the centre on cooling. Cool for 15 minutes, then cut into squares. Store in an airtight container.

Sweet Pizza

Preparation time: 40 minutes ● *Cooking time: 20 minutes + 10 minutes* ● *Makes: 8 wedges*

The rocky road cookie appears in many guises. In this version, a traditional, lemon-flavoured mixture is used to make the base.

INGREDIENTS

LEMON BASE

225 g/8 oz plain flour

120 g/4 oz lightly salted butter or margarine

120 g/4 oz caster sugar

Grated rind of 1 lemon

1 egg

Milk, if required

TOPPING

50 g/2 oz mixed chopped nuts

75 g/3 oz mini marshmallows

50 g/2 oz milk or plain chocolate chips

2 Tbsp caramel topping

Pre-heat oven to 350°F/175°C/Gas mark 4. Grease or line a baking sheet with non-stick baking parchment.

● Prepare the base. Sift the flour into a bowl and blend in the butter or margarine to make fine breadcrumbs. Stir in the sugar and lemon rind. Beat the egg and use it, together with milk if needed, to make a firm but soft dough. It must not be sticky.

● To make a 20-cm/8-in base, take three-quarters of the dough and roll out in a circle. Lift onto the baking sheet and use a flan ring or plate as a guide to the correct shape.

● Bake for about 20 minutes until pale golden and cooked in the centre. Five minutes before the end of the cooking time, place the mixed chopped nuts on a baking sheet and slip into the oven to toast. Leave there for about 10 minutes, until just starting to colour.

● Leave the "pizza" base to cool slightly, then scatter the marshmallows over the surface, followed by the nuts and the chocolate chips. Drizzle the caramel topping over and return to the oven for about 10 minutes until the pizza edges are a deeper colour and the marshmallows are just starting to melt. Serve hot or cold.

Brazil Nut Blondies

Preparation time: 15 minutes ● Cooking time: 20 minutes ● Makes: 12 pieces

Blondies are brownies without chocolate. To make up for the disappointment, there are plenty of nuts in this sweet, chewy mixture and the colour is quite dark due to the dark sugar.

INGREDIENTS

1 egg

375 g/12 oz dark brown sugar

1 tsp vanilla essence

75 g/3 oz plain flour

¼ tsp bicarbonate of soda

1 cup chopped Brazil nuts

2 tsp milk

Pre-heat oven to 350°F/175°C/Gas mark 4. Grease and base-line a 20 x 20-cm/8 x 8-in tin.

● Beat the egg and stir in the sugar and vanilla essence. Sift the flour and bicarbonate into the mixture and stir in, together with the nuts and milk. The mixture will be very stiff.

● Spread into the tin and bake for 15 to 20 minutes. Mark into squares before completely cold and leave to cool in the tin. Store in an airtight container.

Chocolate and Raspberry Macaroon Bars

Preparation time: 25 minutes ● Cooking time: 20 to 25 minutes ● Makes: 25

These are small, rich bars with an intense chocolate flavour. Use homemade raspberry jam if possible as the flavour mingles deliciously with the chocolate.

INGREDIENTS

CHOCOLATE SHORTBREAD

75 g/3 oz plain flour

5 Tbsp unsweetened cocoa powder

75 g/3 oz lightly salted butter

2 egg yolks

3 Tbsp caster sugar

4-5 Tbsp good quality raspberry jam or preserve

MACAROON MIXTURE

75 g/3 oz ground almonds

1½ Tbsp ground rice

2 egg whites

3 drops almond essence

1½ tsp unsweetened cocoa powder

Pre-heat oven to 350°F/175°C/Gas mark 4. Grease and base-line an 18 x 18-cm/7 x 11-in tin.

● Sift the flour and cocoa, blend in the butter, stir in the egg yolks and sugar. Work together to form a dough and press into the tin. Lightly spread the raspberry jam over the shortbread.

● Place the sugar, ground almonds and ground rice in a bowl and gently mix. Whisk the egg whites and almond essence until stiff peaks form. Gradually fold in the dry ingredients to a stiff mixture. Spoon over the jam and spread roughly with a fork dipped in water.

● Bake for 25 to 35 minutes until dry but not coloured. Mark into pieces while still warm and leave in the tin until cold. Lightly dust with sifted cocoa powder. Store in an airtight container.

Cherry and Cinnamon Bars

Preparation time: 45 minutes ● *Cooking time: 25 minutes* ● *Makes: 10 bars*

These ever-popular caramel fingers are combined with powdered cinnamon and dried cherries to give a new slant to a favourite recipe.

INGREDIENTS

SHORTBREAD BASE

75 g/3 oz butter or margarine

2 Tbsp granulated sugar

1 tsp ground cinnamon

120 g/4 oz plain flour

FILLING

120 g/4 oz lightly salted butter

50 g/2 oz caster sugar

2 Tbsp golden syrup

225 ml/8 fl oz condensed milk

½ tsp almond essence

1 tsp ground cinnamon

50 g/2 oz dried cherries, halved

TOPPING

75 g/3 oz plain chocolate

15 g/½ oz unsalted butter

Pre-heat oven to 350°F/175°C/Gas mark 4. Grease and base-line a 20 x 20-cm/8 x 8-in tin.

● Prepare the base first by beating together the butter and sugar. Sift the flour and cinnamon and work into the mixture. Press evenly into the tin. Prick well and bake for about 20 to 25 minutes until golden. Allow to cool.

● To make the filling, place the butter, sugar, syrup and condensed milk in a heavy-bottomed saucepan and stir over a gentle heat to dissolve. Slowly bring to the boil and cook, stirring constantly, for about 7 minutes until thick and a pale toffee colour. Remove from the heat and beat in the almond essence and cinnamon. Pour half the mixture over the shortbread, sprinkle over the cherries, then the remaining filling. Leave to cool to room temperature and then place in the refrigerator.

● When this layer is cold, melt the chocolate and butter together, either over a bowl of hot water or in the microwave for 1 to 2 minutes. Stir gently and pour over the cherry caramel. Spread evenly over and leave to set. Cut into bars when cold and then store in an airtight container.

Chocolate Chip and Pecan Shortbread

Preparation time: 25 minutes ● Cooking time: 50 to 60 minutes ● Makes: 8 pieces

**This pale, traditional shortbread is made even more tempting by the addition of nuts and chocolate.
It would make a welcome gift at any time of year but especially for Christmas.**

INGREDIENTS

5 Tbsp chocolate chips

225 g/8 oz plain flour

50 g/2 oz ground rice

120 g/4 oz caster sugar

Pinch of salt

225 g/8 oz lightly salted butter

75 g/3 oz chopped pecan nuts

Grease a 20-cm/8-in tart tin with a removable base. Place the chocolate chips in the freezer for at least 30 minutes.

● Sift the flour and ground rice into a large bowl, mix in the sugar and salt, then blend in the butter. Stir in the nuts and the chilled chocolate and bring together to form a crumbly dough. Transfer this to the prepared tin and press down firmly using a knife. Prick the surface evenly with a skewer and mark a pattern round the edge using the flat point of a vegetable peeler. Chill for one hour. Mark into 8 portions.

● Pre-heat oven to 300°F/150°C/Gas mark 2. Bake for 50 to 60 minutes. The shortbread must look pale but be cooked in the centre. Return to the oven if necessary for up to 10 minutes longer. Score into portions again and leave to cool in the tin.

Chocolate and Orange Slices

Preparation time: 30 minutes •
Cooking time: 20 minutes • *Makes: 12 slices*

These easy slices are another example of the versatility of rolled oats. The orange flavour is only in the icing, so make sure it tastes strong enough before you pour it on.

INGREDIENTS

120 g/4 oz margarine

120 g/4 oz self-raising flour

1 Tbsp unsweetened cocoa powder

150 g/2 oz rolled oats

50 g/2 oz superfine sugar

TOPPING

3 Tbsp icing sugar

1 tsp unsweetened cocoa powder

Grated rind and juice of ½ orange

Candied orange pieces, to decorate

Pre-heat oven to 350°F/175°C/Gas mark 4. Grease and base-line a 20 x 20-cm/8 x 8-in tin.

• Melt the margarine gently in a large saucepan. Sift the flour and cocoa and stir into the margarine with the oats and sugar.

• Press into the tin and level the surface. Bake for 15 to 20 minutes until shrinking from the sides of the tin. Leave to cool while preparing the topping.

• Sift the icing sugar and cocoa together and mix with sufficient orange juice to make a thin icing. Stir in the orange rind and pour over the cookies while still warm.

• It will look more like a glaze than a thick icing. Cut each one into slices and decorate with a small piece of candied orange.

Date and Oat Crumb Squares

Preparation time: 30 minutes •
Cooking time: 25 to 30 minutes • *Makes: 18*

This recipe can be utilized to use up dates left over after Christmas and provide snacks in the dark weeks of the New Year. The sharpness of lemon contrasts well with the dates but orange could be used instead.

INGREDIENTS

375 g/12 oz rolled oats

120 g/4 oz wholemeal flour

175 g/6 oz margarine

50 g/2 oz soft brown sugar

500 g/1 lb stoned dates

8 Tbsp water

2 Tbsp lemon juice

2 tsp grated lemon rind

Pre-heat oven to 375°F/190°C/Gas mark 5. Grease and base-line an 18 x 28-cm/7 x 11-in shallow tin.

• Mix the oats and flour in a large bowl and blend in the margarine. Stir in the sugar.

• Chop the dates and place in a saucepan with the remaining ingredients. Heat gently until they form a pulp.

• Press half the crumble mixture firmly into the base of the tin. Gently spread the date mixture over, then the remaining crumb mixture. Press and level the mixture. Bake for about 25 minutes until golden and the mixture is starting to shrink from the sides of the tin.

• Cool in the tin but cut into squares while still warm. Store in an airtight container.

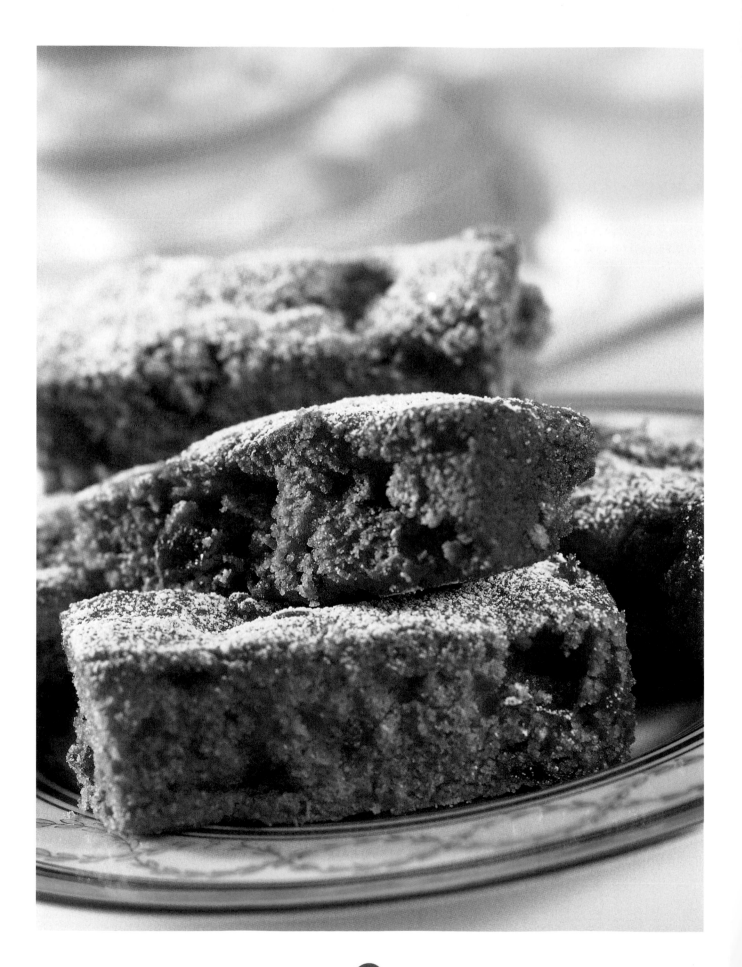

Cranberry and Sultana Bars

Preparation time: 20 minutes ●
Cooking time: 25 to 30 minutes ● *Makes: 16 pieces*

Cranberries give a vivid colour and sharp flavour in contrast to the sweet base mixture. They are most widely available in the autumn, in the run-up to Christmas and freeze well. In this recipe they can be used from frozen if they are free-flowing.

INGREDIENTS

120 g/4 oz margarine or butter

125 g/4 oz soft brown sugar

2 eggs, beaten

120 g/4 oz self-raising flour

50 g/2 oz ground almonds

120 g/4 oz cranberries

75 g/3 oz sultanas

Pre-heat oven to 350°F/175°C/Gas mark 4. Grease and base-line a 20 x 20-cm/8 x 8-in tin.

● Beat the margarine and sugar until light and fluffy. Beat the eggs in gradually. Sift the flour and gently fold in, together with the ground almonds, whole cranberries and sultanas.

● Pour into the tin and bake for 25 to 35 minutes until well risen, firm in the centre and shrinking slightly from the sides of the tin. Turn out onto a wire sheet to cool, then cut into slices. These bars are best stored in the refrigerator.

Easy Apricot Squares

Preparation time: 15 minutes ●
Cooking time: 20 to 30 minutes ● *Makes: 9 pieces*

These are easy as only five ingredients are quickly combined into a soft, succulent bar. Do leave the apricots in large pieces to make the squares more unusual.

INGREDIENTS

50 g/2 oz lightly salted butter

3 Tbsp set honey

3 Tbsp golden syrup

¾ cup ready to eat dried apricots, halved

2⅔ cups muesli

Pre-heat oven to 325°F/160°C/Gas mark 3. Grease and base-line a 20 x 20-cm/8 x 8-in tin.

● Soften the butter, beat until light, then beat in the honey and syrup. Stir in the remaining ingredients thoroughly and press into the tin. Bake for 20 to 30 minutes. Cool for 5 minutes, then cut into 9 squares. Leave to cool completely before removing from the tin. Store in an airtight container.

Double Chocolate and Mango Brownies

Preparation time: 30 minutes ●
Cooking time: 30 minutes ● Makes: 12 pieces

A luscious brownie with white chocolate pieces inside. The mango contrasts well with the traditional rich chocolate and pecan mixture. This version is firmer than the other brownie recipes, to hold up all these exciting textures.

INGREDIENTS

120 g/4 oz plain chocolate
50 g/2 oz lightly salted butter
2 eggs
120 g/4 oz soft brown sugar
120 g/4 oz self-raising flour
50 g/2 oz chopped crystallized mango
50 g/2 oz chopped pecan nuts
5 Tbsp white chocolate chips
5 Tbsp plain chocolate chips

Pre-heat oven to 375°F/190°C/Gas mark 5. Grease and base-line a 20 x 20-cm/8 x 8-in tin.

● Melt the chocolate over a bowl of hot water or in the microwave for 1½ to 2 minutes. Slice the butter into the chocolate and stir to melt, reheating briefly if necessary.

● Beat the eggs and sugar until thick and stir into the chocolate mixture. Beat again, then gently fold in the flour, nuts, mango and the chocolate chips. Pour the mixture into the tin. Bake for 25 to 30 minutes or until the centre appears stable. Cool in the tin and cut into 12 pieces.

Fig and Oat Slices

Preparation time: 20 minutes ●
Cooking time: 30 to 35 minutes ● Makes: 12 pieces

This is a useful and economical recipe. It freezes well for up to three months, it is a welcome addition to lunch boxes and may be served warm with yoghurt for a winter dessert.

INGREDIENTS

120 g/4 oz figs
5 Tbsp water
Grated rind of ½ orange
175 g/6 oz wholemeal flour
300 g/10 oz rolled oats
5 Tbsp packed soft brown sugar
175 g/6 oz margarine

Pre-heat oven to 350°F/175°C/Gas mark 4. Meanwhile, grease and base-line a 20 x 20-cm/8 x 8-in tin.

● Chop the figs, discarding the stalks, and place in a pan with the water and orange rind. Bring to the boil and simmer for 5 minutes until very soft.

● Mix the flour and oats in a large bowl. Melt the sugar and margarine gently and stir into the oat mixture. Thoroughly combine and press half into the tin. Level the top and press well in.

● Spread the fig mixture on top and cover with the remaining oat mixture, levelling and pressing it as much as possible. Bake for 30 to 35 minutes until golden and is shrinking from the sides of the tin. Cool, cut into pieces and store in an airtight container.

TIP

● Try to find unwaxed lemons, oranges and limes for grating, as even a good wash does not remove all the waxes from the skins.

Exotic Fruit and Almond Slices

Preparation time: 45 minutes ● Cooking time: 35 minutes ● Makes: 16 slices

This is another opportunity to use up small quantities of fruit and nuts including some of the more recent additions to the dried fruit range.

INGREDIENTS

BASE

75 g/3 oz lightly salted butter or margarine

5 Tbsp caster sugar

75 g/3 oz wholemeal flour

1 tsp baking powder

75 g/3 oz ground rice or semolina

3 Tbsp caster sugar

TOPPING

5 Tbsp raisins

5 Tbsp glacé cherries

5 Tbsp dried mango pieces

5 Tbsp crystallized pineapple

75 g/3 oz ready-to-eat dried apricots

5 Tbsp chopped walnuts

120 g/4 oz lightly salted butter or margarine

225 g/8 oz caster sugar

1 egg, beaten

50 g/2 oz ground almonds

50 g/2 oz ground rice or semolina

2 Tbsp flaked almonds

Pre-heat oven to 350°F/175°C/Gas mark 4. Grease and base-line an 18 x 28-cm/7 x 11-in shallow tin.
● Make the base by beating the sugar and butter together until light and stirring in the flour, ground rice or semolina and sugar. Press firmly into the tin.
● Coarsely chop the fruit and nuts.
● Beat the remaining butter and sugar, then beat in the egg. Fold in the ground almonds and ground rice. Stir in the chopped fruit and nuts and pour over the base. Sprinkle with the flaked almonds. Bake for about 35 minutes until the mixture and the almonds are golden-brown. Leave in the tin to cool and cut in slices. Store in an airtight container.

Dried Cranberry Flapjacks

Preparation time: 15 minutes ● *Cooking time: 25 to 35 minutes* ● *Makes: 24*

This recipe has a high percentage of fat, but it is worth using butter for the flavour and reserving the flapjacks for special occasions.

INGREDIENTS

175 g/6 oz butter

200 g/7 oz soft brown sugar

2 Tbsp golden syrup

400 g/14 oz rolled oats

75 g/3 oz dried cranberries

Pre-heat oven to 325°F/160°C/Gas mark 3. Grease and base-line an 18 x 28-cm/7 x 11-in shallow tin.

● Melt the butter, sugar and syrup until the sugar is dissolved. Stir in the oats and cranberries and press into the tin.

● Bake for 25 to 35 minutes until set. Cool in the tin and cut into pieces while still warm. Store in an airtight container.

Fruit and Brandy Sticks

Preparation time: 30 minutes ● *Cooking time: none* ● *Makes: 25 small sticks*

This recipe is an excellent way of preserving left-over fruit cake. If much of it is still left in the tin after New Year, use some of it in this recipe, freeze and use to accompany vanilla ice cream.

INGREDIENTS

120 g/4 oz left-over fruit cake

50 g/2 oz lightly salted butter

2 Tbsp golden syrup

50 g/2 oz plain chocolate

1 Tbsp brandy

ICING

6 Tbsp icing sugar

Rose flower-water or water

Pink food colouring

Grease a 20 x 20-cm/8 x 8-in tin and then line the base of the pan as well.

● Crumble the cake into a bowl and chop any large pieces of fruit or nuts. Melt the butter, syrup and chocolate very gently and combine with the cake crumbs and brandy.

● Press into the tin. Level and firm the mixture and chill for at least a day before completing. The cookies may be frozen at this stage.

● Remove the mixture from the tin and place on a board. To make the icing, sift the icing sugar and mix to a thick consistency with sufficient water and/or rose flower-water to make a thin icing. However, add the rose flower-water cautiously and taste for strength before use, mixing it with water if it is too strong. Add a drop or two of pink food colouring, beat well and add a few drops more of water if the icing is too stiff. Pour evenly over the cake.

● Before the icing sets completely, cut into pieces with a sharp knife dipped into hot water. Leave to dry before storing the pieces in an airtight container.

Flapjacks

Preparation time: 15 minutes ●
Cooking time: 30 minutes ● *Makes: 18*

This is a delicious, basic recipe for flapjacks, suitable for everyday packed lunches and snacks. They are so easy to make, young members of the family will soon be making them for you.

INGREDIENTS

120 g/4 oz margarine or lightly salted butter

3 Tbsp golden syrup

5 Tbsp soft brown sugar

400 g/14 oz rolled oats

Pre-heat oven to 325°F/160°C/Gas mark 3. Grease and base line an 18 x 28-cm/7 x 11-in shallow tin. ● Place margarine, syrup, and sugar in a large pan and heat gently, stirring from time to time until the sugar has melted. Stir in the oats and press into the tin. Bake for about 30 minutes until golden. Cool slightly before cutting into 18 pieces. Leave to cool completely before removing from the tin. Store in an airtight container for up to 1 week.

Hazelnut Flapjacks

Preparation time: 15 minutes ●
Cooking time: 25 to 30 minutes ● *Makes: 18*

Cooks sometimes avoid hazelnuts because they need roasting and rubbing to remove their skins. In this recipe that is not necessary, all you do is chop them.

INGREDIENTS

120 g/4 oz margarine or lightly salted butter

8 Tbsp honey

5 Tbsp light brown sugar

375 g/12 oz rolled oats

120 g/4 oz chopped hazelnuts

Pre-heat oven to 350°F/175°C/Gas mark 4. Grease and base-line an 18 x 28-cm/7 x 11-in shallow tin. ● Melt the margarine or butter, honey and sugar in a large heavy-bottomed saucepan. Stir in the oats and nuts. Press into the tin and level the top. Bake for 25 to 30 minutes. Cool in the tin and cut into bars when still slightly warm. Store in an airtight container.

Lemon Cheesecake Fingers

Preparation time: 50 minutes ● Cooking time: 40 minutes ● Makes: 12 fingers

These fingers would be excellent taken on a summer picnic to round off a sumptuous meal with friends. The cream cheese makes them a little more substantial to withstand any knocks en route.

INGREDIENTS

PASTRY BASE

175 g/6 oz plain flour

75 g/3 oz margarine or lightly salted butter

1 egg, separated

1 Tbsp water

CHEESECAKE MIXTURE

250 g/9 oz full-fat soft cheese

1 egg, separated

120 g/4 oz caster sugar

Grated rind and juice of 1 lemon

1 Tbsp plain flour

5 Tbsp sultanas

1 Tbsp rum, optional

Pre-heat oven to 375°F/190°C/Gas mark 4. Grease, base- and side-line an 18 x 28-cm/7 x 11-in shallow tin.

● Make the pastry by lightly blending the margarine or butter into the flour. Beat together the egg yolk (reserve the white for later) and water, add to the mixture to make a soft dough. Use a little more water if necessary as the dough must be pliable. Reserve one-quarter of the pastry.

● Roll out the remaining pastry and line the base of the tin. Press a piece of foil on top of the pastry. Bake for about 20 minutes. Remove the foil and cool. Increase oven temperature to 400°F/200°C/Gas mark 6.

● Beat the cream cheese, egg yolk, sugar, lemon rind and juice to thoroughly combine and stir in flour, sultanas and rum, if using.

● Beat the 2 egg whites to a firm peak and beat 2 tablespoons into the cheese mixture, then fold in the rest. Pour over the cooled pastry base and level gently.

● Roll out the remaining pastry and either cut strips to make a lattice or cut leaves to decorate the top. Bake for 15 minutes, then reduce temperature to 350°F/190°C/Gas mark 5 and bake for 15 minutes longer. Cool in the tin and cut into fingers. Store in an airtight container in the refrigerator for 2 to 3 days.

Fruit and Nut Bars

Preparation time: 45 minutes ● Cooking time: 30 minutes ● Makes: 24 bars

The name of this recipe could be "spring-cleaning bars" because the topping is excellent for using up ends of packets of nuts and dried fruit you come across when sorting out cupboards.

INGREDIENTS

SHORTBREAD BASE

225 g/8 oz plain flour

2 Tbsp cornflour

50 g/2 oz icing sugar

300 g/10 oz butter

TOPPING

175 g/6 oz nuts to include at least half the volume in almonds

120 g/4 oz chopped dried fruit, at least half to be glacé cherries

25 g/1 oz lightly salted butter

3 Tbsp caster sugar

1 Tbsp milk

2 tsp vanilla essence

Pre-heat oven to 400°F/200°C/Gas mark 6. Grease and base-line an 18 x 28-cm/7 x 11-in shallow tin.
● Prepare the base by sifting the flour, cornflour and icing sugar into a bowl and blending in the butter to look like breadcrumbs. Press the crumbs into the tin. Level and firm down, then bake for 15 to 20 minutes. Leave in the tin to cool.
● Prepare and chop the nuts, leaving them in large pieces. Whole almonds should first be blanched, then halved. Cut the cherries into quarters and other fruit to a similar size.
● Place the topping in a heavy-bottomed saucepan and heat gently to dissolve. Try to avoid stirring too much. Add the nuts and leave to cool.
● Stir in the fruit and pour over the base. Return to the oven and bake at the same temperature for about 15 minutes or until the nuts are browning. Cool in the tin and cut into bars when cold. Store in an airtight container.

TIP

Suitable fruits to use in this recipe include crystallized pineapple, ginger, angelica, ready-to-eat prunes and apricots, raisins and sultanas.

Lemon and Hazelnut Fingers

Preparation time: 20 minutes ●
Cooking time: 25 minutes ● *Makes: 16 fingers*

These are truly heavenly. They are also incredibly easy to make and are perfect for a celebration picnic.

INGREDIENTS

PASTRY

120 g/4 oz plain flour

75 g/3 oz lightly salted butter

3 tsp icing sugar

LEMON CURD FILLING

2 eggs, beaten

120 g/4 oz icing sugar

2 small lemons

50 g/2 oz unsalted butter

75 g/3 oz ground hazelnuts

Pre-heat oven to 375°F/190°C/Gas mark 5. Grease, base- and side-line an 18 x 28-cm/7 x 11-in shallow tin.

● Place all the ingredients for the pastry in a food processor and process until they resemble fine breadcrumbs. Tip the pastry mixture into the tin and press into the base. Bake for 5 minutes.

● Meanwhile, make the filling. Soften the butter to the consistency of tub margarine and place in a large bowl with the remaining ingredients. Whisk well to combine. Pour the filling over the pastry and return to the oven for 15 to 20 minutes until golden and set. Leave to get cold in the tin before cutting into pieces. Best eaten when freshly made.

Melting Almond Shortbread

Preparation time: 10 minutes ● *Cooking time: 45 to 50 minutes* ● *Makes: 16 bars*

This is called "melting" for two reasons. Firstly, because it melts in the mouth. Secondly, because the butter (and it must be butter) is melted and the other ingredients are simply stirred in.

INGREDIENTS

225 g/8 oz butter

175 g/6 oz self-raising flour

50 g/2 oz plain flour

2 Tbsp cornflour

50 g/2 oz caster sugar

4 drops almond essence

50 g/2 oz flaked almonds

Pre-heat oven to 350°F/175°C/Gas mark 4. Grease and base-line a 18 x 28-cm/7 x 11-in shallow tin.

● Gently melt the butter. Meanwhile, sift the flour and cornflour together into a bowl and stir in the caster sugar. Add all but 2 tablespoons of the flaked almonds.

● Make a well in the centre and stir in the melted butter.

● Turn into the tin, press in place, and sprinkle over the remaining flaked almonds. Do not worry if the mixture seems rather sparse in the tin as it will increase in volume while cooking. Bake for 45 to 50 minutes until very pale golden but the centre looks cooked and the shortbread is beginning to shrink away from the sides of the tin. Leave in the tin to cool, then cut up into pieces.

Linzer Bake

Preparation time: 40 minutes ● *Cooking time: 30 to 35 minutes* ● *Makes: 9 dessert portions*

**A cross between a cake and a pastry, Linzer Torte is a traditional Austrian dessert of raspberries
and a light, spiced pastry.**

INGREDIENTS

175 g/6 oz self-raising flour

½ tsp ground cloves

½ tsp mixed spice

75 g/3 oz lightly salted butter

120 g/4 oz caster sugar

5 Tbsp ground almonds or hazelnuts

Grated rind of ½ lemon

½ tsp vanilla essence

1 egg

1–2 Tbsp milk

300 g/10 oz raspberry jam

Pre-heat oven to 350°F/175°C/Gas mark 4. Grease and base-line a 20 x 20-cm/8 x 8-in tin.

● Sift the flour and spices and blend in the butter. Stir in the sugar, ground almonds and lemon rind. Beat together the egg and vanilla essence and stir in, followed by sufficient milk to make up to a firm but slightly soft dough. Gently knead to remove any cracks, wrap in clingfilm and chill for 30 minutes.

● Roll out the pastry and use to line the tin. Trim the pastry level with the top of the tin. Fill the centre with raspberry jam.

● Roll out the trimmings and cut into lattice strips. Place two or three in each direction over the jam to make an even lattice. Do not try weaving the strips as this pastry is too fragile.

● Bake in the oven for 25 to 30 minutes until the pastry is barely coloured.

Mango and Pistachio Slices

Preparation time: 20 minutes ● *Cooking time: 30 minutes* ● *Makes: 16 slices*

Lightly spiced and slightly chewy, these slices look and taste glorious, with the golden mango contrasting beautifully with the green colour of the nuts.

INGREDIENTS

120 g/4 oz lightly salted butter
120 g/4 oz caster sugar
1 egg
½ tsp vanilla essence
125 g/4 oz self-raising flour
½ tsp grated nutmeg
50 g/2 oz dried mango pieces
75 g/3 oz pistachio nuts
1 Tbsp sherry
4 Tbsp icing sugar

Pre-heat oven to 350°F/175°C/Gas mark 4. Grease and base-line an 18 x 28-cm/7 x 11-in shallow tin.

● Check the dried mango packet for directions and, if necessary, soak in boiling water for 10 minutes. Drain and dry on kitchen paper and rough chop.

● Grind half the pistachio nuts to a powder and roughly chop the rest.

● Beat the butter and sugar until light and beat in the egg, vanilla essence and mango pieces.

● Stir in the nuts, flour and sherry. The mixture should be quite stiff. Spread in the tin and bake 30 minutes. Leave to cool in the tin.

● Sift the icing sugar and mix with a little water until sufficiently runny to drizzle over the bars. When set cut into pieces with a sharp knife. Store in an airtight container.

Microwave Brownies

Preparation time: 10 minutes ● *Cooking time: 7 minutes* ● *Makes: 8 wedges*

**These microwaved Brownies are amazingly good and well worth trying. Eat them fresh from the
microwave or at least the same day they are baked.**

INGREDIENTS

50 g/2 oz plain chocolate, chopped

75 g/3 oz butter or margarine

75 g/3 oz dark brown sugar

2 eggs

120 g/4 oz plain flour

3 Tbsp unsweetened cocoa powder

¼ tsp baking powder

1 tsp vanilla essence

5 Tbsp chopped walnuts

2 Tbsp milk

Cook in a 25 x 15 x 5-cm/10 x 6 x 2-in heatproof
glass or pottery dish lined with lightly greased
greaseproof paper.

● Melt the chocolate and butter or margarine in the
microwave on high for 2 minutes. Beat in the sugar and
egg until smooth. Stir in the remaining ingredients to
form a smooth batter. Spread in the prepared dish.

● Microwave on high for about 7 minutes until the
mixture is slightly risen and a few broken bubbles break
the surface. The centre will probably look damp but will
set during standing time. Cool the brownies in the dish
for 10 minutes then cut into 16 wedges.

TIP

Check the brownies after 5½ minutes then check every
30 seconds until cooked, to prevent over-cooking.

Prune and Two-Chocolate Pieces

Preparation time: 40 minutes ●
Cooking time: 15 minutes ● *Makes: 25*

These delectable pieces can be served with after-dinner coffee or arranged in an attractive box as a gift. Choose the ready-to-eat type of prune to avoid having to soak them.

INGREDIENTS

120 g/4 oz ready-to-eat prunes
1 Tbsp sweet sherry or orange juice
2 Tbsp water
50 g/2 oz self-raising flour
1 tsp ground cinnamon
150 g/5 oz rolled oats
75 g/3 oz lightly salted butter
50 g/2 oz soft brown sugar
5 Tbsp white chocolate chips
50 g/2 oz milk or plain chocolate

Pre-heat oven to 375°F/190°C/Gas mark 5. Grease and base-line a 20 x 20-cm/8 x 8-in tin.

● Chop the prunes and place in a saucepan with the sherry or orange juice and water. Bring to the boil and cook for 2 minutes, stirring all the time. Leave to cool.

● Mix the flour, cinnamon and oats, blend in the butter and stir in the sugar.

● Stir in the white chocolate chips and the prune mixture. Press into the tin and bake for 12 to 15 minutes or until just starting to turn golden. Leave in the tin to cool.

● Melt the remaining chocolate and pour over the bake. Using a sharp knife, cut into squares while still warm. Drizzle with more melted chocolate, if liked. Store in an airtight container.

Orange and Raisin Shortbread

Preparation time: 30 minutes + chilling ●
Cooking time: 30 to 40 minutes ● *Makes: 8 pieces*

This is a delicious alternative to traditional shortbread.

INGREDIENTS

75 g/3 oz plain flour
50 g/2 oz cornflour
120 g/4 oz lightly salted butter
50 g/2 oz caster sugar
25 g/1 oz ground almonds
Grated rind of 1 small orange
25 g/1 oz raisins
1 tsp caster sugar

Start by lightly greasing the base and sides of a 20 x 20-cm/8-in tart tin with a removable base.

● Sift the flour and cornflour and blend in the butter. Stir in the sugar, ground almonds and orange rind. Press the mixture together and incorporate the raisins before the dough is fully formed. Knead lightly to evenly distribute the ingredients and ensure the dough is free from cracks.

● Lift onto the base of the tin. Leave the ring in place and smooth the surface to fill the base. Half-cut through to mark 8 portions and prick evenly with a fork. Chill for 1 hour.

● Pre-heat oven to 325°F/160°C/Gas mark 3 and bake for 30 to 40 minutes or until very pale apricot-coloured. Dust with the remaining caster sugar. Remove the ring from the tin and cut into portions. Leave on the sheet to cool and harden. Store in an airtight container.

Spanish Date Meringue Slices

Preparation time: 45 minutes ●
Cooking time: 40 minutes ● *Makes: 16 slices*

This traditional recipe uses a delicious combination of dates and oranges.

INGREDIENTS

PASTRY BASE

50 g/2 oz lightly salted butter or margarine

2 Tbsp caster sugar

1 Tbsp beaten egg

Grated rind of ½ orange

120 g/4 oz plain flour

FILLING

225 g/8 oz stoned dates

1 Tbsp rum or orange juice

3 egg whites

50 g/2 oz ground almonds

2 Tbsp cornflour

5 Tbsp caster sugar

Pre-heat oven to 350°F/175°C/Gas mark 4. Grease and base-line an 18 x 28-cm/7 x 11-in shallow tin.
● Make the pastry base. Beat the butter or margarine and sugar together until light and fluffy. Beat in the egg and orange rind, then work in the flour. Press into the base of the tin.
● Chop the dates and pour over the rum or orange juice. Mix the ground almonds, cornflour and sugar.
● Beat the egg whites to a stiff peak, fold in the soaked dates and the dry ingredients. Spread over the pastry. Bake for about 40 minutes or until the centre is firm. Leave to cool in the tin, then cut into slices. Store in an airtight container.

Munch

Preparation time: 15 minutes ●
Cooking time: 20 to 30 minutes ● *Makes: 12 pieces*

A simple, traditional American recipe. Munch used to be prepared during the morning, ready to slip into the hot oven when lunch came out.

INGREDIENTS

225 g/8 oz margarine

225 g/8 oz soft brown sugar

375 g/12 oz rolled oats

Pre-heat oven to 350°F/175°C/Gas mark 4. Grease and base-line a 20 x 20-cm/ 8 x 8-in tin.
● Beat the butter until soft and gradually beat in the sugar until light and fluffy. Stir in the oats. Press into the tin and bake for 25 to 30 minutes or until golden. Cut into pieces. Store in an airtight container.

Stollen Bars

Preparation time: 1 hour + rising time ● *Cooking time: 25 to 30 minutes* ● *Makes: 30 bars*

**Here, Stollen, the traditional flat, oval German Christmas cake, is converted into bars.
Try them warmed for a special Christmas breakfast.**

INGREDIENTS

225 g/8 oz strong white flour
2 tsp easy-blend dried yeast
1 Tbsp lukewarm water
2 Tbsp sugar
50 g/2 oz lightly salted butter
1 egg
5 Tbsp lukewarm milk
Grated rind of ½ lemon
1 Tbsp chopped almonds
75 g/3 oz chopped candied citrus peel
50 g/2 oz glacé cherries
50 g/2 oz sultanas
175 g/6 oz marzipan
1 Tbsp melted butter
2 Tbsp icing sugar

Grease the base of an 18 x 28-cm/7 x 11-in shallow tin and then line it.

● Take 1 teaspoon of flour from the measured amount and place in a small bowl with the yeast, warm water and a pinch of the measured sugar. Blend and leave about 10 minutes in a warm place until the mixture froths.

● Meanwhile, blend the butter into the remaining flour and stir in the sugar.

● Beat the egg. Slightly warm the milk.

● Make a well in the centre of the flour and work in the yeast mixture, egg and milk to make a pliable dough which is slightly stiffer than bread dough. Add a little more milk or flour as necessary. Turn out and knead for about 10 minutes until silky. Place in a lightly greased bowl, cover the bowl with a teatowel or clingfilm and leave in a warm, draught-free place until doubled in size.

● Punch back the dough, then knead lightly. Knead in the lemon rind, candied citrus peel, chopped glacé cherries and sultanas.

● Divide the dough in half and roll a piece to fit the base of the tin. Slice the marzipan thinly in an even layer over the top. Roll the second piece of dough to fit over.

● Cover with lightly greased clingfilm and leave in a warm draught-free place for about 20 minutes until risen and slightly puffy.

● Pre-heat oven to 450°F/230°C/Gas mark 8 and bake for about 20 minutes until golden-brown and firm in the centre. Immediately brush with melted butter. When cold dredge heavily with icing sugar and cut into 30 pieces. Store in an airtight container.

Toffee Bars

Preparation time: 45 minutes ●
Cooking time: 20 minutes ● *Makes: 16*

These bars hide under a multitude of recipe names but the three layers of shortbread, caramel and chocolate are universally popular with people of all ages.

INGREDIENTS

SHORTBREAD BASE

175 g/6 oz plain flour

50 g/2 oz caster sugar

120 g/4 oz lightly salted butter

FILLING

120 g/4 oz lightly salted butter

225 g/8 oz caster sugar

225 ml/8 fl oz evaporated milk

Few drops vanilla essence

TOPPING

75 g/3 oz plain chocolate

25 g/1 oz unsalted butter

Pre-heat oven to 350°F/175°C/Gas mark 4. Grease and base-line an 18 x 28-cm/7 x 11-in shallow tin.
● Make the base by beating the butter and sugar together until light, then working in the flour. Press the dough into the tin and bake for 20 minutes or until firm in the centre and lightly golden. Cool in the tin.
● Put the butter, sugar and evaporated milk into a heavy-bottomed saucepan and stir over a gentle heat until the sugar has dissolved. Bring to the boil and, stirring constantly, cook for about 15 minutes until thick. Remove from the heat and beat in the vanilla essence and pour over the shortbread. Allow to cool.
● Gently melt the butter and chocolate together. Pour over the caramel and cut into pieces when set. Store in an airtight container.

Double Ginger Flapjacks

Preparation time: 20 minutes ●
Cooking time: 20 to 25 minutes ● *Makes: 8 to 16 slices*

This flapjack has a strong gingery taste with succulent pieces of crystallized ginger hidden in the sweet, chewy cookie base.

INGREDIENTS

50 g/2 oz butter

1½ Tbsp treacle

50 g/2 oz dark brown sugar

1 tsp ground ginger

300 g/10 oz rolled oats

75 g/3 oz chopped crystallized ginger

50 g/2 oz chopped pecan nuts

¼ tsp salt

Pre-heat oven to 350°F/175°C/Gas mark 4. Line a 20 x 20-cm/8 x 8-in baking tin with non-stick parchment.
● In a medium saucepan, cook the butter, syrup, sugar and ground ginger over a medium heat until well-blended. Remove from the heat and stir in the oats, crystallized ginger, pecans and salt. Pour into the prepared tin and level.
● Bake until crisp and golden-brown, 20 to 25 minutes. Transfer the tin to a wire rack to cool slightly, 5 to 10 minutes. Invert onto a board and peel off the paper. While still warm, cut into 8 or 16 slices. Return to the wire rack to cool completely. Store in an airtight container.

Chocolate Orange Dream Bars

Preparation time: 30 minutes ● Cooking time: 35 to 40 minutes ● Makes: 18

These bars are made with the magical combination of chocolate and orange. They are really rich – a little goes a long way.

INGREDIENTS

BASE

120 g/4 oz plain flour

3 Tbsp unsweetened cocoa powder

¼ tsp salt

175 g/6 oz unsalted butter, softened

5 Tbsp caster sugar

50 g/2 oz icing sugar

ORANGE TOPPING

Grated rind of 1 orange

125 ml/4 fl oz fresh orange juice

3 Tbsp water

4 tsp cornflour

1 tsp lemon juice

25 g/1 oz butter

3 Tbsp orange marmalade

CHOCOLATE GLAZE

3 Tbsp double cream

½ tsp golden syrup

75 g/3 oz plain chocolate, chopped

Pre-heat oven to 325°F/160°C/Gas mark 3. Grease and line a 20 x 20-cm/8 x 8-in baking tin.

● Sift together the flour, cocoa and salt. In a separate bowl beat the butter until creamy, add the sugars and continue beating until light and fluffy. Beat in the flour mixture in 2 or 3 batches until a dough forms. If necessary, turn the dough out onto a lightly floured surface and knead until blended.

● Pat down the dough into the base of the baking tin in an even layer. Prick the dough bottom all over with a fork. Bake until set and golden, 30 to 35 minutes. Transfer to a wire rack while preparing topping.

● In a medium saucepan, whisk together the orange rind, juice, water, cornflour and lemon juice. Over a medium heat, bring to the boil whisking constantly until mixture thickens, about 1 minute. Remove from the heat and whisk in butter and marmalade until melted and smooth. Pour over the warm pastry base and return to the oven. Bake for 5 minutes more. Transfer to a wire cooling rack to cool completely, then refrigerate until the topping is set, about 1 hour.

● In a small saucepan, bring the cream and golden syrup to the boil. Remove from the heat and all at once, stir in the chocolate until melted and smooth. Cool the chocolate slightly until thickened, stirring occasionally.

● Using the paper to help, remove the cookies from the tin. Peel off the paper and cut into bars. Spoon the cooled, thickened chocolate into a piping bag and drizzle the chocolate over the bars. Refrigerate until set, about 30 minutes. Store in the refrigerator in an airtight container.

Savoury Cookies

Some of these cookies are served fresh from the oven, others are eaten cold. Either way this fabulous selection of savoury cookies will liven up any occasion. Unless otherwise stated, most of the cookies can be prepared in advance and frozen for up to three months.

Cheese Cookies

Cheese cookies make a wonderful addition to any lunch box, picnic, buffet or even formal meal. Once you start producing home-baked cheese cookies, you will never want to buy them again.

Meat and Fish

A selection of tangy cookies that would be perfect for brunch or cocktail parties. Most would be good served with soft cheeses or pâtés.

Nuts and Seeds

Vegetable Cookies

*A bright and tasty selection of vegetable-based cookies that are great to
serve with drinks as an informal appetizer and wonderful to take to
ball games and other outdoor events. They are so delicious that the
kids won't object to eating vegetables.*

Quattro Formaggi

*Preparation time: 20 minutes ● Cooking time:
25 minutes ● Makes: 15*

**Just like the familiar pizza topping, these cookies are
flavoured with 4 different cheeses.**

INGREDIENTS

1 Tbsp freshly grated Parmesan cheese

1 Tbsp crumbled blue cheese such as Roquefort, Danish or Stilton

1 Tbsp grated Gruyère cheese

1 Tbsp grated mature Cheddar cheese

120 g/4 oz plain flour

Pinch of salt

120 g/4 oz lightly salted butter or margarine, softened

1 tsp dried oregano

Pre-heat oven to 350°F/175°C/Gas mark 4. Grease
or line two baking sheets with non-stick baking
parchment.

● Mix all the cheeses together and sift in the flour and
salt. Make a well in the centre and add the butter or
margarine and oregano. Using a round-bladed knife, or
fingertips blend the mixture together, and shape it into
a soft dough.

● Divide into 15 walnut-sized balls and place on baking
sheets, spaced about 5 cm/2 in apart. Flatten slightly
with a fork, and bake for 20 to 25 minutes until lightly
golden and firm to the touch. Cool on the sheets. Best
served slightly warmed. Store in an airtight container
for 3 to 4 days, or freeze for up to 3 months.

Parmesan Paprika Crisps

*Preparation time: 15 minutes ● Cooking time:
10 minutes ● Makes: 18*

**These thin, nutty cheese morsels are delicious served as a
snack on their own or to accompany a fine wine.**

INGREDIENTS

75 g/3 oz lightly salted butter or margarine

75 g/3 oz flaked almonds

50 g/2 oz ground almonds

225 g/8 oz freshly grated Parmesan cheese

¼ tsp cayenne pepper

1 tsp paprika

Pre-heat oven to 350°F/175°C/Gas mark 4. Line
three baking sheets with non-stick baking
parchment.

● Melt the butter or margarine in a small saucepan.
Remove from the heat and stir in the slivered and
ground almonds. Stir in the Parmesan cheese, cayenne
and paprika.

● Drop the mixture, spaced well apart, in 18 small, well-
rounded heaps onto the baking sheets. Bake in the oven
for 10 minutes until golden-brown. Remove from the
oven and push around the edges of the cookies with the
blade of a knife to neaten the shape. Leave on the sheets
to cool completely. Carefully lift off using a thin, metal
spatula. Store between sheets of greaseproof paper in an
airtight container for 3 to 4 days, or freeze in the same
way for up to 3 months.

Feta, Olive and Sun-dried Tomato Bites

Preparation time: 20 minutes ● Cooking time: 25 minutes ● Makes: 15

Using feta cheese gives these cookies a creamy, sharp flavour. Try a different goat's or sheep's milk cheese if preferred.

INGREDIENTS

120 g/4 oz feta cheese
120 g/4 oz plain flour
2 Tbsp finely chopped sun-dried tomatoes in oil, drained
6 large black olives, stoned and chopped
120 g/4 oz lightly salted butter or margarine, softened

Pre-heat oven to 350°F/175°C/Gas mark 4. Grease or line two baking sheets with non-stick baking parchment. Cut the cheese into very small cubes and set aside.

● Sift the flour into a bowl and mix in the chopped tomatoes and olives, then blend in the butter using a round-bladed knife. Carefully stir in the cubed cheese. Bring together the mixture with your hands to form a firm dough.

● Divide the dough into 15 walnut-sized balls and place on baking sheets, spaced about 5 cm/2 in apart. Flatten them slightly with a fork, and then bake for 20 to 25 minutes until lightly golden and firm to the touch. Leave to cool on the sheets. These cookies are best served slightly warmed. Store in an airtight container for 3 to 4 days.

Blue Cheese Shortbread

Preparation time: 15 minutes ● Cooking time: 40 minutes ● Serves: 8

This shortbread version combines with the rich flavour of blue cheese and the mild onion tang of fresh chives. Excellent served with port.

INGREDIENTS

150 g/5 oz plain flour
3 Tbsp rice flour
120 g/4 oz lightly salted butter
50 g/2 oz crumbled blue cheese
3 Tbsp freshly snipped chives

Pre-heat oven to 325°F/160°C/Gas mark 3. Lightly grease an 18-cm/7-in round baking tin.

● Sift the flours into a bowl. Work in the butter using your fingertips, keep it in one piece and gradually work in the dry ingredients. Stir in the blue cheese and chives and knead well.

● Pack the dough into the prepared tin, prick well with a fork and pinch the edges decoratively using your finger and thumb.

● Bake for about 35 to 40 minutes, until firm and pale golden in colour. Score into 8 triangles while still hot. Cool for 10 minutes and then transfer to a wire rack to cool completely.

● Serve split into triangles. Store in an airtight container for up to 5 days.

Cheese and Relish Puffs

Preparation time: 20 minutes + chilling ● Cooking time: 25 minutes ● Makes: 25

Serve these cheesy fingers for cocktail nibbles during the Christmas season, or at a party with a hot punch.

INGREDIENTS

150 g/5 oz grated Gruyère cheese
4 Tbsp tomato relish
Freshly ground black pepper
1 egg, beaten
350 g/12 oz puff pastry, thawed if frozen

Pre-heat oven to 400°F/200°C/Gas mark 6. Meanwhile, in a bowl, mix together the cheese, relish, pepper and all but 2 teaspoons of the egg. Set aside.

● Roll out the pastry on a lightly floured surface to a 30 x 40-cm/12 x 16-in rectangle. Divide the pastry evenly down the centre of the rectangle, and then divide each half into 5 equal width portions.

● Lay 5 pieces on a large ungreased baking sheet and divide the filling equally between them, spreading it out evenly, almost to the edge. Brush the edges with water and cover with remaining pastry, lightly pressing the edges to seal. Cover and chill for 30 minutes.

● Mark each pastry strip into 5 fingers and brush with the reserved egg. Bake for about 20 to 25 minutes until risen and golden-brown. Cut the pastry through into fingers, allow to cool for 10 minutes and then serve while still hot.

Smoked Cheese Twists

Preparation time: 25 minutes + chilling ●
Cooking time: 20 minutes ● *Makes: 30*

**Long, thin twisting pastries are just the thing for parties.
Serve on their own or with a dip.**

INGREDIENTS

75 g/3 oz lightly salted butter or margarine, softened

3 Tbsp full-fat soft cheese

1 egg yolk

175 g/6 oz plain flour

Pinch of salt

2 cloves garlic, crushed

120 g/4 oz finely grated smoked cheese

2 Tbsp cold water

In a bowl, beat the butter or margarine with the soft cheese and egg yolk. Sift in the flour and salt. Add the garlic, half the grated cheese and 2 tablespoons cold water. Stir the mixture to bring the mixture together. Turn on to a lightly floured surface and knead lightly to form a smooth dough. Wrap and chill for 30 minutes.

● Pre-heat oven to 350°F/175°C/Gas mark 4. Line two baking sheets with non-stick baking parchment.

● Roll out the dough to 5 mm/¼-in thick, and cut into ½-inch wide strips, about 15 cm/6 in long. Twist the strips and place on baking sheets, pressing down the edges well to prevent them untwisting. Sprinkle lightly with the remaining cheese. Bake for about 20 minutes until lightly golden. Transfer to wire racks and cool for about 15 minutes before serving. Cool completely and place in an airtight container for up to 10 days.

Hot Cheese Melts

Preparation time: 20 minutes + chilling ●
Cooking time: 15 minutes ● *Makes: 16*

**For easy eating, spear each hot cookie on a cocktail stick
or small skewer before arranging them on a serving platter.**

INGREDIENTS

120 g/4 oz finely grated mature Cheddar cheese

50 g/2 oz plain flour

1 tsp mustard powder

Pinch of salt

50 g/2 oz lightly salted butter or margarine, softened

1 Tbsp wholegrain mustard

1 tsp black mustard seeds

Place all the ingredients together in a large bowl and work the mixture until a firm dough is formed.

● Divide the mixture into 16 equal portions, and shape it into balls. Arrange the balls on a large ungreased baking sheet. Cover and chill for 1 hour until they become firm.

● Pre-heat oven to 375°F/190°C/Gas mark 5. Just prior to serving, uncover and bake in the oven for about 10 to 15 minutes until golden. Cool for 10 minutes and then serve hot.

Cream Cheese and Chive Cornbread Cakes

Preparation time: 20 minutes ● Cooking time: 20 minutes ● Makes: 20

A cross between biscuit and a cookie, these cakes can be served with soups and stews, or as part of a lunch box.

INGREDIENTS

120 g/4 oz cornmeal

50 g/2 oz plain flour

2 tsp baking powder

50 g/2 oz lightly salted butter or margarine

1 egg, beaten

3 Tbsp freshly snipped chives

6 to 7 Tbsp milk

Full-fat soft cheese

Pre-heat oven to 375°F/190°C/Gas mark 5. Grease or line two baking sheets.

● Sift the cornmeal, flour, baking powder, and salt into a mixing bowl and blend in the butter or margarine until well mixed. Make a well in the centre and gradually mix in the egg, 2 tablespoons of the chives and milk, to form a thick batter.

● Using a teaspoon, spoon 20 small mounds of the mixture, about 5 cm/2 in apart, on baking sheets, and bake for 15 to 20 minutes until lightly golden and firm to the touch. Transfer to wire racks to cool completely.

● Beat the soft cheese to soften and spread gently on the cookies then top with the remaining chives to serve. Best eaten on same day as topped. Store, before topping with soft cheese and chives, in an airtight container for up to 1 week.

Red Leicester and Fruit Relish Palmiers

Preparation time: 20 minutes • Cooking time: 12 minutes • Makes: 16

Small, heart-shaped pastry puffs filled with red cheese and tangy relish make attractive canapés.

INGREDIENTS

175 g/6 oz puff pastry, thawed if frozen

3 Tbsp savoury fruit relish, finely chopped

50 g/2 oz fine grated Red Leicester cheese

Freshly ground black pepper

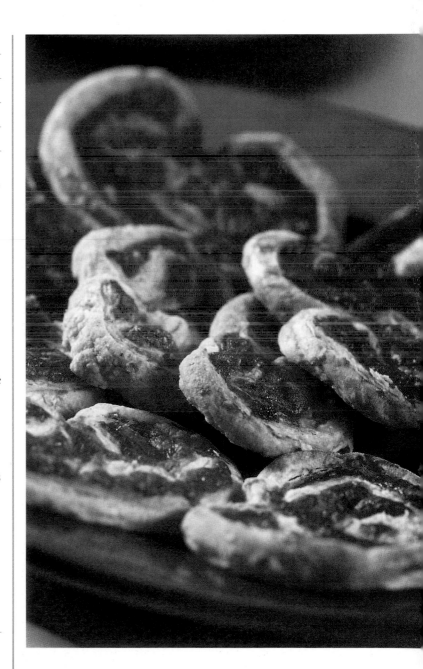

Pre-heat oven to 425°F/220°C/Gas mark 7. Grease or line a large baking sheet with non-stick baking parchment.

● Roll out the pastry to a 40 x 20-cm/16 x 8-in rectangle. Spread thinly with 2 tablespoons of the relish and then sprinkle with two thirds of the cheese. Season with plenty of black pepper.

● Fold the pastry two ends up and over the filling, equally from each side, to meet in the middle. Spread the pastry top with the remaining relish and sprinkle with the cheese. Season with pepper. Fold the pastry ends as before, turn over and press together firmly.

● Using a sharp knife, cut the folded pastry into 16 slices and transfer to the baking sheet, leaving a small space between each. Bake for 10 to 12 minutes until lightly golden. Cool for 10 minutes then transfer to a wire rack to cool. Best served warm.

TIP

These can be made 24 hours in advance. Store in an airtight container and re-crisp them in a hot oven for a few minutes just before serving.

Hot Pizza Snacks

Preparation time: 25 minutes ● Cooking time:
20 minutes ● Makes: 12

Best served warm, these tomato snacks contain the
familiar ingredients you would find on a pizza, and have
a soft Mozzarella cheese centre.

INGREDIENTS

1 Tbsp plain flour
Pinch of salt
1 tsp dried oregano
125 g/4 oz lightly salted butter or margarine, softened
2 Tbsp freshly grated Parmesan cheese
2 Tbsp tomato purée
25-g/1-oz piece block Mozzarella cheese, cut into 12 small cubes
6 black olives, stoned and halved

Pre-heat oven to 375°F/190°C/Gas mark 5. Grease or line a baking sheet with non-stick baking parchment.

● Sift the flour and salt into a bowl and stir in the oregano, butter or margarine, Parmesan and tomato purée using a round-bladed knife, and bring together with your hands to form a firm dough. Divide the mixture into 12 portions, and form into balls. Press a piece of cheese into the centre of each and reform the dough over it to enclose the cheese.

● Place on the baking sheet and lightly press an olive half on top of each. Sprinkle with a little Parmesan cheese and bake for 20 minutes until lightly golden and firm. Cool for 10 minutes before serving.

Oaty Clusters with Cheese Crumble Top

Preparation time: 20 minutes ● Cooking time:
20 minutes ● Makes: 18

Easy to make and delicious, these crackers have a crisp
and chewy texture, with a lightly spiced, topping.

INGREDIENTS

175 g/6 oz lightly salted butter or margarine
200 g/7 oz rolled oats
50 g/2 oz wholemeal flour
1 tsp salt

TOPPING

1 Tbsp freshly grated Parmesan cheese
6 Tbsp wholemeal flour
25 g/1 oz lightly salted butter or margarine
1 tsp cumin seeds, crushed
1 tsp dried thyme

Pre-heat oven to 375°F/190°C/Gas mark 5. Grease or line two baking sheets.

● Melt the butter or margarine for the cookies in a saucepan. Remove from the heat and stir in the oats, flour and salt. Set aside.

● Now make the crumble. Mix the cheese and flour together and blend in the butter or margarine until well mixed, and it resembles large fresh breadcrumbs.

● Drop the oat mixture onto baking sheets to form 18 walnut-sized mounds. Space them about 2.5 cm/1 in apart. Press them down lightly with a fork and then sprinkle each with a little of the crumble topping, a few cumin seeds and some thyme. Bake in the oven for 20 minutes until a rich golden-brown. Leave to cool on the baking sheets. Store in airtight containers between sheets of greaseproof paper for up to 1 week.

429

Smoked Ham Rings

Preparation time: 20 minutes ● Cooking time: 20 minutes ● Makes: 24

These cookies are good to serve with dips, or try sandwiching them together with cream cheese.

INGREDIENTS

175 g/6 oz butter or margarine, softened
50 g/2 oz lean smoked ham, very finely chopped
50 g/2 oz finely grated smoked cheese
120 g/4 oz plain flour
50 g/2 oz cornflour
Pinch of salt
½ tsp mustard powder

Pre-heat oven to 350°F/175°C/Gas mark 4. Line two baking sheets with non-stick baking parchment.

● In a bowl, beat the butter or margarine, ham and cheese together until well mixed.

● Sift the remaining ingredients into the bowl, mix well.

● Place the dough in a piping bag fitted with a 1-cm/½-in all-purpose nozzle. Pipe 24 6-cm/2½-in rings, spaced well apart, on the baking sheets. Bake in the oven for 20 minutes until lightly golden. Cool for 5 minutes then transfer to a wire rack to cool completely. Store in an airtight container for up to 4 days or freeze for up to 3 months.

Halloumi Cookies

Preparation time: 15 minutes ● Cooking time: 25 minutes ● Makes: 14

Halloumi cheese is mild tasting, slightly salty, and perfect for baking as it holds its shape well.

INGREDIENTS

120 g/4 oz plain flour
75 g/3 oz Halloumi cheese, cut into small pieces
2 Tbsp black olives, drained, stoned and chopped
2 Tbsp freshly chopped coriander
5 Tbsp good-quality olive oil

Pre-heat oven to 350°F/175°C/Gas mark 4. Grease or line a large baking sheet with non-stick baking parchment.

● Sift the flour into a bowl and mix in the cheese, olives and coriander. Bind together with the olive oil to form a dough. Turn on to a lightly floured surface and knead gently until smooth.

● Using a teaspoon, pile 14 small mounds onto the baking sheet, and press down lightly using a fork. Bake in the oven for 20 to 25 minutes until lightly golden and firm. Cool for 10 minutes, then transfer to a wire rack. Best served slightly warmed.

Ham Pineapple Corn Cakes

Preparation time: 15 minutes ● Cooking time: 20 minutes ● Makes: 15

Serve these soft cookies to accompany soups, stews and casseroles.

INGREDIENTS

120 g/4 oz cornmeal
50 g/2 oz plain flour
2 tsp baking powder
50 g/2 oz lightly salted butter or margarine
50 g/2 oz lean ham, finely chopped
50 g/2 oz finely chopped fresh or tinned pineapple
2 Tbsp freshly chopped parsley
1 egg, beaten
6 Tbsp milk

Pre-heat oven to 375°F/190°C/Gas mark 5. Line two baking sheets with non-stick baking parchment.

● Sift the cornmeal, flour, baking powder and salt into a bowl. Blend in the butter or margarine. Stir in the ham and pineapple. Make a well in the centre and add the egg, then gradually pour in the milk, stirring to form a thick batter.

● Using a teaspoon, drop 15 mounds, spaced well apart on the baking sheets. Bake for 15 to 20 minutes until lightly golden and firm. Cool for 10 minutes, then transfer to a wire rack. Store in an airtight container for up to 5 days or freeze for up to 3 months.

Thai Prawn Crackers

Preparation time: 30 minutes + chilling ● Cooking time: 25 minutes ● Makes: 16

These light and flaky cookies are flavoured with Oriental ingredients. Serve with satay sauce.

INGREDIENTS

225 g/8 oz self-raising flour
1 tsp salt
½ tsp ground white pepper
½ tsp hot chilli powder
50 g/2 oz lightly salted butter or margarine
2 Tbsp crunchy peanut butter
7 to 8 Tbsp cold water
4 spring onions, trimmed and finely chopped
50 g/2 oz peeled prawns, thawed if frozen, ground or finely chopped

Sift the flour, salt, pepper and chilli powder into a bowl. Blend in the butter or margarine until well mixed, and stir in the peanut butter. Mix in sufficient cold water to form a firm dough. Turn on to a lightly floured surface and knead until smooth.

● Roll out to a 38 x 15-cm/15 x 6-in rectangle. Score into three. Mix the spring onions and prawns and place one-third in the middle section. Fold up the bottom third, bring the top third over it, seal the edges and give the pastry a half-turn. Repeat twice more, sprinkling the spring onion and prawn mixture each time. Re-roll and fold again. Wrap and chill for 30 minutes.

● Pre-heat oven to 350°F/175°C/Gas mark 4. Grease and flour a baking sheet. Roll the dough out on a floured surface to form a 30-cm/12-in square and divide into 16 squares. Transfer to baking sheet, prick all over and bake for 20 to 25 minutes until golden. Cool on wire racks.

Smoked Salmon Snacks

Preparation time: 25 minutes + chilling ● Cooking time: 15 minutes ● Makes: 15

Try these luxurious cookies for a buffet lunch.

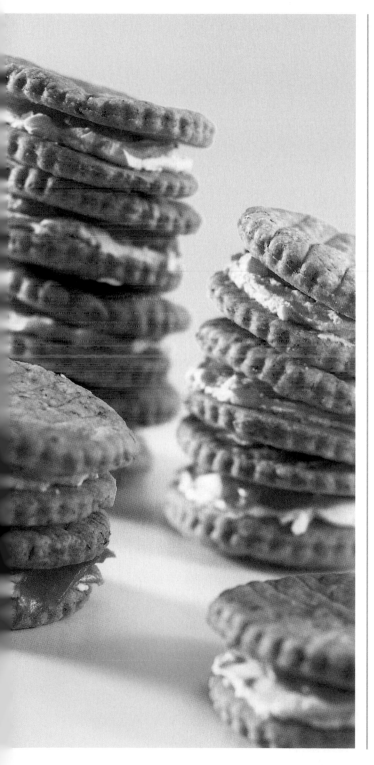

INGREDIENTS

75 g/3 oz lightly salted butter or margarine, softened

3 Tbsp full-fat soft cheese

1 egg yolk

175 g/6 oz plain flour

Pinch salt

4 Tbsp freshly chopped dill

2 Tbsp cold water

FILLING

225 g/8 oz full-fat soft cheese

125 g/4 oz smoked salmon pieces, shredded fine

In a bowl, beat the butter or margarine with the soft cheese and egg yolk. Sift in the flour and salt and add the dill, then stir until evenly mixed. Stir in sufficient cold water to form a dough.

● Turn onto a floured surface and knead until smooth; place in clingfilm and chill for 30 minutes.

● Pre-heat oven to 350°F/175°C/Gas mark 4. Line two baking sheets with non-stick baking parchment.

● Roll out the pastry thinly and stamp out 30 circles using a 6-cm/2½-in cutter, re-rolling as necessary. Place on the prepared baking sheets, score lightly with a knife in diagonal lines, and then bake in the oven for about 15 minutes until lightly golden. Leave to cool on the sheets.

● To serve, beat the soft cheese until smooth and spread over half the cookies. Sprinkle with a few strips of smoked salmon and then top with the remaining cookies. Serve immediately.

● Store, unfilled, in an airtight container for up to 1 week, or freeze unfilled for up to 3 months.

Crispy Bacon and Blue Cheese Melts

Preparation time: 25 minutes ● Cooking time: 30 minutes ● Makes: 15

Basic cookie dough is transformed into a melting mixture by adding cheese. Serve these tasty snacks as an accompaniment to other cheeses or with fruit, soups and salads.

INGREDIENTS

6 rashers rindless bacon

50 g/2 oz crumbled blue cheese

120 g/4 oz plain flour

120 g/4 oz lightly salted butter or margarine, softened

Pinch of cayenne pepper

Pre-heat oven to 350°F/175°C/Gas mark 4. Grease or line two baking sheets with non-stick baking parchment.

● Pre-heat the grill to a hot setting and cook the bacon for 2 to 3 minutes on each side until golden and crispy. Drain on kitchen paper and cool. Then finely chop.

● Mix all the ingredients and the chopped bacon together using a round-bladed knife, and bring together with your hands to form a dough.

● Divide the dough into 15 portions and shape each one into a small disc. Prick the surfaces with a fork and bake in the oven for 20 to 25 minutes until lightly golden and firm to the touch. Leave to cool for 15 minutes and then serve warm. Store in an airtight container for up to 4 days.

Pepperoni and Peppercorn Shortbreads

Preparation time: 15 minutes + chilling ● *Cooking time: 25 minutes* ● *Makes: 14*

You can make and freeze these tasty pre-dinner nibbles ahead of time, and you may want to double the recipe as they will be very popular.

INGREDIENTS

120 g/4 oz plain flour

Pinch of salt

75 g/3 oz unsalted butter

50 g/2 oz sliced pepperoni sausage, finely chopped

1 Tbsp pickled green peppercorns, drained

1 egg, beaten

Freshly ground black pepper

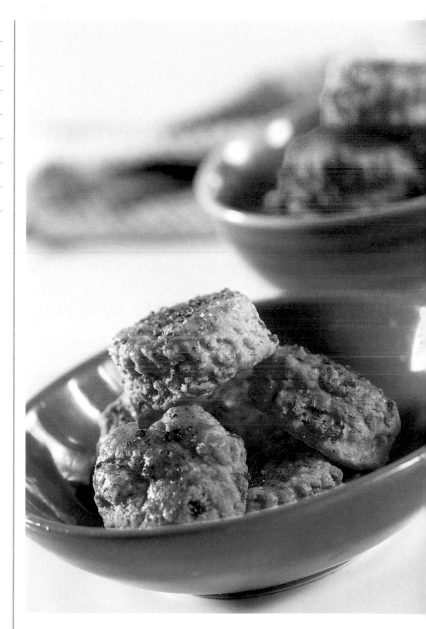

Sift the flour and salt into a bowl, then blend in the butter until you have fine crumbs. Stir in the pepperoni and peppercorns and add enough egg to bring together to form a dough; reserve the rest for glazing.

● Turn onto a lightly floured surface and knead until smooth. Wrap and chill for 20 minutes.

● Pre-heat oven to 325°F/160°C/Gas mark 3. Line two baking sheets with non-stick baking parchment.

● Roll out to 1 cm/½ in thick. Using a 4-cm/1½-in round cutter, stamp out 14 rounds, re-rolling as necessary. Transfer to the baking sheet, brush with reserved egg and then dust with ground black pepper. Bake in the oven for 20 to 25 minutes until firm to the touch and golden. Cool for 5 minutes and then transfer to a wire rack to cool completely. To make ahead, pack into an airtight container and freeze for up to 3 months.

Anchovy, Olive and Basil Spirals

Preparation time: 20 minutes ● *Cooking time: 12 minutes* ● *Makes: 24*

A sophisticated puff pastry snack with a deliciously fishy flavour. They are best eaten on the day they are made, and served slightly warm.

INGREDIENTS

175 g/6 oz puff pastry, thawed if frozen
1 egg, beaten
50 g/2 oz anchovy fillets, drained
2 Tbsp black olives, drained, stoned and finely chopped
2 Tbsp pimiento-stuffed green olives, finely chopped
Handful fresh basil leaves

Pre-heat oven to 425°F/220°C/Gas mark 7. Line two baking sheets with non-stick baking parchment.

● Roll out the pastry on a lightly floured surface to a 30 x 20-cm/12 x 8-in rectangle. Brush the pastry with beaten egg and lay the anchovy fillets, lengthways, over the pastry. Sprinkle with the olives and lay the basil leaves on top. Starting from the long side, roll up the pastry tightly, like a Swiss roll. Press lightly to seal the end, and then slice into 24 pieces.

● Lay the pastry pieces, spaced a little apart, on the baking sheets, and brush with more egg. Bake for 10 to 12 minutes until golden and crisp. Cool for 10 minutes before serving. These are best eaten on the day they are made, and served slightly warm.

Curried Prawn Diamond Oatcakes

Preparation time: 20 minutes ● *Cooking time: 15 minutes* ● *Makes: 18*

These crisp oatcakes are flavoured with Chinese curry spices and chopped prawns. Good with fish pâté.

INGREDIENTS

25 g/1 oz plain flour
175 g/6 oz medium oatmeal
½ tsp baking powder
½ tsp salt
1½ tsp Chinese curry powder
75 g/3 oz white vegetable fat
50 g/2 oz peeled prawns, thawed if frozen, very finely chopped
1–2 tsp cold water
1 egg, beaten
2 Tbsp sesame seeds

Pre-heat oven to 400°F/200°C/Gas mark 6. Grease or line a baking sheet with non-stick baking parchment.

● Sift the flour, oatmeal, baking powder, salt and curry powder into a bowl. Blend in the white vegetable fat with your fingertips until the mixture is crumbly, then stir in the prawns and mix with sufficient water to form a firm dough.

● Roll out the dough to 5 mm/¼ in thick on a lightly floured surface. Slice the dough into 4-cm/1½-in strips, then cut each strip on the diagonal into diamond shapes (you should make about 18).

● Transfer to the baking sheet. Brush with egg and sprinkle with sesame seeds. Bake for about 15 minutes until firm and lightly golden. Leave to cool.

Smoked Salmon and Lemon Kisses

Preparation time: 20 minutes ● *Cooking time: 25 minutes* ● *Makes: 12*

**These delicately flavoured melt-in-the-mouth soft-bake cookies are good served with cream cheese.
Substitute ham for the salmon if preferred.**

INGREDIENTS

120 g/4 oz plain flour

Pinch of salt

2 Tbsp freshly chopped parsley

120 g/4 oz smoked salmon, finely chopped

½ tsp finely grated lemon rind

120 g/4 oz lightly salted butter or margarine, softened

Pre-heat oven to 350°F/175°C/Gas mark 4. Grease or line two baking sheets with non-stick baking parchment.

● Sift the flour and salt into a bowl. Stir in the parsley, smoked salmon, lemon rind and butter or margarine using a round-bladed knife. Bring together with your hands to form a dough.

● Divide the dough into 12 pieces and form them into walnut-sized balls. Place on baking sheets, spaced about 5 cm/2 in apart. Flatten slightly and bake for 20 to 25 minutes until lightly golden and firm to the touch. Leave to cool for 15 minutes. These cookies are best served slightly warm, and on the same day as baking. They can be frozen, once baked, for up to 3 months.

Honeyed Ham and Onion Cookies

Preparation time: 25 minutes + chilling ● Cooking time: 30 minutes ● Makes: 16

With a little advance preparation, these cookies make truly delicious snacks. They also make an interesting accompaniment to salads or soups.

INGREDIENTS

75 g/3 oz lightly salted butter or margarine

1 medium onion, finely sliced

2 tsp honey

120 g/4 oz plain flour

Pinch of salt

1 Tbsp freshly chopped sage or 1 tsp dried sage

75 g/3 oz lean honey roast ham, finely chopped

2–3 tsp cold water

1 small egg, beaten

Bunch small sage leaves, optional

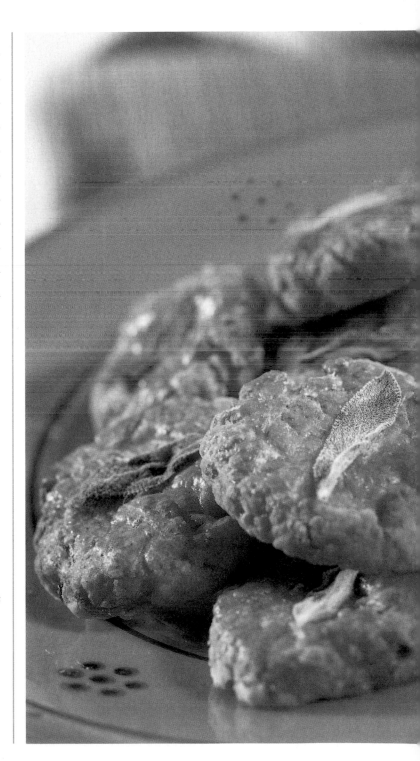

Melt 25 g/1 oz of butter in a small frying pan and gently fry the onion for 5 minutes, stirring, until just softened. Add the honey, raise the heat and cook for a further 2 to 3 minutes until lightly golden. Set the mixture aside to cool.

● Sift the flour, salt and sage together into a bowl. Blend in the remaining butter and stir in the ham and prepared onion. Bind together with sufficient cold water to form a soft dough. Turn onto a lightly floured surface and knead until smooth. Wrap and chill the dough for 30 minutes.

● Pre-heat oven to 350°F/175°C/Gas mark 4. Line a large baking sheet with non-stick baking parchment.

● Divide the dough into 16 and form into small round discs. Place on the baking sheet, brush with beaten egg and press a sage leaf onto each, if using. Bake for 20 to 25 minutes until lightly golden and firm. Cool for 10 minutes and then serve warm.

Peanut, Sesame, Carrot and Raisin Pinwheels

Preparation time: 25 minutes + chilling ● *Cooking time: 20 minutes* ● *Makes: 24*

A healthy combination of ingredients makes these cookies an excellent addition to the lunch box – the peanut flavour will make them popular with children.

INGREDIENTS

75 g/3 oz lightly salted butter or margarine, softened

3 Tbsp full-fat soft cheese

1 egg yolk

200 g/7 oz wholemeal flour

Pinch of salt

2 Tbsp cold water

4 Tbsp crunchy peanut butter

50 g/2 oz finely grated carrot

3 Tbsp raisins, finely chopped

1 Tbsp toasted sesame seeds

In a bowl, beat together the butter, soft cheese and egg yolk. Sift the flour and salt into the bowl, adding any husks which remain in the strainer, then stir in the water until evenly mixed. Stir in to form a dough. Turn on to a lightly floured surface and knead lightly until smooth. Wrap and chill for 30 minutes.

● Pre-heat oven to 350°F/175°C/Gas mark 4. Line two baking sheets with non-stick baking parchment.

● Roll out the dough to a 30 x 23-cm/12 x 9-in rectangle. Soften the peanut butter by heating it gently and then thinly spread over the dough. Sprinkle with the carrot, raisins and sesame seeds.

● Starting at the longest side, roll up the dough tightly, like a Swiss roll, and press gently to seal the edge. Slice the roll into 24 pieces and place the pinwheels on the lined baking sheets. Bake in the oven for about 20 minutes until firm and lightly golden. Cool for 10 minutes then transfer to a wire rack to cool completely. Store in an airtight container for up to 3 days. Not suitable for freezing.

Mixed Nut Clusters with Cajun Spices

Preparation time: 20 minutes ●
Cooking time: 25 minutes ● *Makes: 15*

These cookies are for the real nut lover. You can use any combination of nuts for this recipe, but choose a good spread of flavours, and use unsalted varieties.

INGREDIENTS

3 Tbsp walnut pieces
3 Tbsp flaked whole almonds
3 Tbsp macadamia nuts, lightly crushed
3 Tbsp shelled unsalted pistachios, lightly crushed
120 g/4 oz plain flour
Pinch of celery salt
Pinch of onion salt
1 tsp paprika
¼ tsp cayenne pepper
1 tsp dried thyme
120 g/4 oz lightly salted butter or margarine, softened

Pre-heat oven to 350°F/175°C/Gas mark 4. Grease or line two baking sheets with non-stick baking parchment.

● Mix all the nuts together and place in a bowl. Sift in the flour, salts, paprika and cayenne. Add the thyme and butter or margarine and mix together with a round-bladed knife. Bring together with your hands to form a dough.

● Divide into 15 and form into walnut-sized balls. Place on baking sheets, spaced about 5 cm/2 in apart. Flatten slightly, and bake in the oven for 20 to 25 minutes until lightly golden and firm to the touch. Leave to cool on the baking sheets. Excellent served slightly warm. Store in an airtight container for up to 1 week, or freeze for up to 3 months.

Pine Tree Shillings

Preparation time: 15 minutes ●
Cooking time: 25 minutes ● *Makes: 14*

Pine nuts have a fragrant, resinous flavour which goes very well with the woodiness of rosemary and olives. A very Mediterranean cocktail nibble.

INGREDIENTS

120 g/4 oz plain flour
1 tsp salt
1 Tbsp freshly chopped rosemary or 1 tsp dried
120 g/4 oz pine nuts
3 Tbsp black olives, drained, stoned and chopped
5 Tbsp good-quality olive oil

Pre-heat oven to 350°F/175°C/Gas mark 4. Line two baking sheets with non-stick baking parchment.

● Sift the flour and salt into a bowl and stir in the rosemary, pine nuts and olives. Add the olive oil and stir to mix into a dough.

● Drop 14 teaspoonfuls of the mixture on to baking sheets and bake for 20 to 25 minutes. Cool for 10 minutes and then transfer to a rack to cool completely.

● Store in an airtight container for up to 1 week, or freeze for up to 3 months.

Poppy Seed Spirals

Preparation time: 25 minutes ● *Cooking time: 27 minutes* ● *Makes: 16*

The small black seeds in these crisp pastry rolls have a nutty flavour and crunchy texture. Substitute with sesame seeds or crushed pumpkin seeds if preferred.

INGREDIENTS

150 g/5 oz lightly salted butter or margarine

1 medium red onion, finely sliced

1 Tbsp lemon juice

1 tsp coriander seeds, crushed

2 tsp honey

9 large sheets of filo pastry (45 x 30 cm/18 x 12 in)

6 Tbsp poppy seeds

4 Tbsp freshly chopped coriander

Pre-heat oven to 400°F/200°C/Gas mark 6. Line a baking sheet with non-stick baking parchment.

● Melt 25 g/1 oz lightly salted butter or margarine in a small frying pan and gently fry the onion with the lemon juice and coriander seeds for 5 minutes until softened. Add the honey and cook, stirring, over a high heat for a further 2 minutes. Set aside to cool.

● In a small saucepan, gently melt the remaining butter or margarine.

● To assemble the spirals, lay a sheet of filo pastry on the work surface and brush with melted fat. Lay two more sheets on top, brushing with fat as you go. Sprinkle over 2 tablespoons poppy seeds and 1 tablespoon chopped coriander.

● Prepare three more sheets of filo as before and place on top of the seeds. Sprinkle with 2 tablespoons poppy seeds and another 1 tablespoon coriander. Spread over the cooked onion mixture. Finally, prepare the remaining three sheets of filo as before and lay over the onion layer. Sprinkle with remaining seeds and coriander. From the shortest side, carefully roll up the pastry like a Swiss roll, pressing the roll gently to seal the edge.

● Slice into 16 pieces and arrange on the baking sheet. Brush with the remaining melted fat and bake in the oven for 15 to 20 minutes until richly golden. Cool for 10 minutes and then serve. These pastries can be made up to 24 hours in advance of baking, and stored in the fridge until ready for use.

Toasted Pecan Snacks

Preparation time: 30 minutes + chilling ● Cooking time: 25 minutes ● Makes: 24

Use ready-roasted pecan halves in this recipe for a more intense flavour. Alternatively try honey-roasted pecans, available from good whole food stores.

INGREDIENTS

225 g/8 oz self-raising flour

1 tsp salt

50 g/2 oz lightly salted butter or margarine

7–8 Tbsp cold water

75 g/3 oz toasted pecan nuts, finely chopped

Sift the flour and salt into a bowl and blend in the fat. Add sufficient water to form a pliable dough. Turn on to a lightly floured surface and knead until smooth.

● Roll into a 38 x 15-cm/15 x 6-in rectangle. Mark lightly into three equal portions, and sprinkle the middle portion with one third of the nuts. Fold up the bottom third, bring the top third over it, seal the edges and give the pastry a half turn. Repeat this rolling and folding twice more, sprinkling with the nuts each time. Re-roll and fold once more. Wrap and chill.

● Pre-heat oven to 350°F175°C/Gas mark 4. Grease and flour a baking sheet.

● Roll out the pastry thinly and evenly to form a square slightly bigger than 30 cm/12 in. Trim away the edges to neaten, and then cut into 2.5 x 15-cm/1 x 6-in thin fingers. Transfer to the baking sheet, prick all over with a fork and baken for 20 to 25 minutes until lightly golden and puffed up. Transfer to a wire rack to cool. Store in an airtight container for up to 1 week.

Mixed Seed Crunchies

Preparation time: 10 minutes + standing ●
Cooking time: 15 minutes ● *Makes: 18*

Use small seeds in this recipe to give a very crisp texture. The oats in this recipe add a healthy touch, making them an ideal wholesome snack.

INGREDIENTS

175 g/6 oz rolled oats
75 g/3 oz medium oatmeal
2 Tbsp poppy seeds
2 Tbsp sesame seeds
1 tsp celery seeds
1 tsp fennel seeds, lightly crushed
125 ml/4 fl oz sunflower oil
1 tsp salt
1 egg, beaten

Place the oats, oatmeal and seeds in a bowl, and mix in the oil. Leave to stand for 1 hour.

● Pre-heat oven to 325°F/160°C/Gas mark 3. Line a baking sheet with non-stick baking parchment.

● Add the salt and egg to the oat mixture and beat together thoroughly. Place 18 teaspoonfuls of the mixture, spaced a little apart on the baking sheet and press flat with a wetted fork. Bake in the oven for about 15 minutes until golden-brown. Leave to cool on the sheets. Store in an airtight container for up to 1 week.

Wholemeal Pumpkin Shorties

Preparation time: 15 minutes + chilling ●
Cooking time: 20 to 25 minutes ● *Makes: 14*

Green pumpkin seeds have a nutty flavour, and they add texture to a rich, crumbly wholemeal shortbread mixture. Use white plain flour if preferred.

INGREDIENTS

120 g/4 oz wholemeal flour
Pinch of salt
50 g/2 oz unsalted butter
7 Tbsp pumpkin seeds, lightly crushed
1 egg yolk
2 Tbsp milk

Pre-heat oven to 325°F/160°C/Gas mark 3. Line two baking sheets with non-stick baking parchment.

● Sift the flour and salt into a bowl and blend in the butter until you have fine crumbs. Stir in the pumpkin seeds and egg yolk. Bring together with your hands to form a dough. Turn onto a lightly floured surface and knead lightly until smooth. Wrap and chill for 20 minutes.

● Roll out to 5 cm/½ in thick and cut into 14 5-cm/½-in squares, re-rolling as necessary. Place on the baking sheets and score the tops lightly with a knife. Brush lightly with the milk and bake for 20 to 25 minutes until firm and golden. Cool on the baking sheets for 5 minutes and then transfer to a wire rack to cool completely. Store in an airtight container for up to 1 week.

Apricot and Pecan Rye Cookies

Preparation time: 20 minutes ● Cooking time: 20 minutes ● Makes: 18

Rye flour has a distinctive nutty flavour and makes an interesting cookie. The addition of dried apricots gives a delicate sweetness; chopped dates or raisins could also be used.

INGREDIENTS

120 g/4 oz dark rye flour

Pinch of salt

50 g/2 oz pecan nuts, lightly crushed

3 Tbsp finely chopped dried apricots

120 g/4 oz lightly salted butter or margarine, softened

2 Tbsp freshly chopped parsley

Pre-heat oven to 350°F/175°C/Gas mark 4. Grease or line two baking sheets.

● Mix all the ingredients together with a round-bladed knife to form into a dough.

● Divide into 18 portions and form into small balls. Place about 2 cm/1 in apart on the baking sheets and flatten slightly with a fork. Bake for 20 minutes until golden and firm to the touch. Cool on the baking sheets. Store in an airtight container for 3 to 4 days.

Buttery Hazelnut Hoops

Preparation time: 20 minutes ● *Cooking time: 15 minutes* ● *Makes: 24*

Toasted hazelnuts have a rich flavour and are perfect for baking. These piped cookies look good on a platter of canapés, and taste excellent with blue cheese and grapes.

INGREDIENTS

175 g/6 oz lightly salted butter or margarine, softened
50 g/2 oz ground toasted hazelnuts
120 g/4 oz plain flour
50 g/2 oz cornflour
Pinch of salt
3 Tbsp lightly crushed hazelnuts

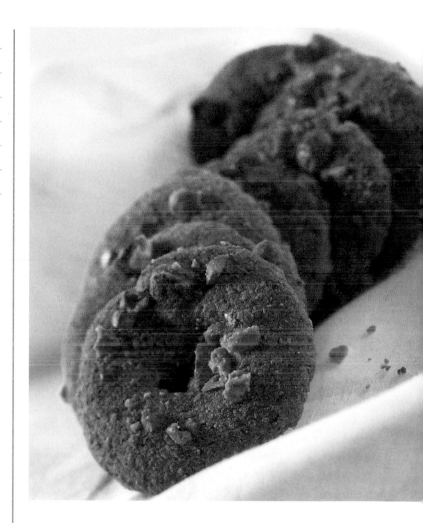

Pre-heat oven to 350°F/175°C/Gas mark 4. Line two baking sheets with non-stick baking parchment.

● Beat the butter or margarine and ground hazelnuts together. Sift in the flour, cornflour and salt, and beat well. Place in a piping bag fitted with an all-purpose 1-cm/½-in round nozzle, and pipe 24 6-cm/2½-in rings, spaced well apart, onto the baking sheets. Sprinkle the rings with the crushed hazelnuts.

● Bake in the oven for 15 minutes until golden. Cool for 5 minutes and then transfer to wire rack to cool completely. Store between layers of greaseproof paper in an airtight container for up to 5 days.

447

Middle Eastern Almond Rolls

Preparation time: 30 minutes + chilling ● Cooking time: 25 minutes ● Makes: 18

Mild tasting buttery almonds combine well with sweet Middle Eastern spices and sweet red onion in this filling.

INGREDIENTS

75 g/3 oz lightly salted butter or margarine, softened

3 Tbsp full-fat soft cheese

1 egg yolk

120 g/4 oz plain flour

50 g/2 oz ground almonds

Pinch of salt

2 Tbsp cold water

FILLING

50 g/2 oz lightly salted butter or margarine

1 small red onion, finely chopped

1 Tbsp lemon juice

50 g/2 oz finely chopped blanched almonds

1 tsp ground coriander

1 tsp ground cumin

3 Tbsp sultanas

2 Tbsp freshly chopped coriander

1 egg, beaten

In a bowl, beat the butter or margarine, soft cheese, and egg yolk. Sift the flour and add the ground almonds and salt. Stir until evenly mixed. Add sufficient water to form a dough. Turn on to a lightly floured surface and knead lightly until smooth. Wrap and chill for 30 minutes.

● Meanwhile, make the filling. Melt the butter or margarine and gently fry the onion with the lemon juice, chopped almonds and spices, stirring, for 5 minutes until the onion is softened. Remove from the heat and add the sultanas and coriander. Set the filling aside to cool.

● Pre-heat oven to 350°F/175°C/Gas mark 4. Line a baking sheet with non-stick baking parchment.

● Roll out the dough thinly to an approximate 26-cm/ 10½-in square. Trim away the edges to neaten and divide into 9 smaller squares. Divide the mixture between each square, and form a mound down the centre of each. Brush the edges with beaten egg and carefully roll each square up. Press the edge gently to seal. Cut each roll in half.

● Transfer the rolls to the baking sheet. Score the tops lightly with a sharp knife, then brush with beaten egg to glaze and bake in the oven for 20 minutes until golden. Leave to cool on the baking sheet. Store in an airtight container for up to 1 week.

Hot Cashew Crumbles

Preparation time: 10 minutes + chilling • Cooking time: 15 minutes • Makes: 16

Cashews have a nutty sweetness, and are delicious flavoured with Indian spices. Serve these crumbly cookies while still warm. Replace the chickpea flour with plain flour if preferred.

INGREDIENTS

50 g/2 oz ground unsalted cashew nuts

25 g/1 oz lightly chopped, roasted cashew nuts

50 g/2 oz chickpea flour

1 tsp mild curry powder

120 g/4 oz lightly salted butter or margarine, softened

2 Tbsp freshly chopped coriander

16 unsalted cashew halves

Place the ground and chopped cashews together in a a large mixing bowl and sift in the chickpea flour and curry powder. Add the butter or margarine and chopped coriander and mix all the ingredients together to form a firm dough.

● Use your hands to roll the dough out into 16 balls and arrange on a large ungreased baking sheet. Press a cashew half on to the top of each. Cover and chill for 1 hour until firm.

● Pre-heat oven to 375°F/190°C/Gas mark 5. To serve, uncover the cookies and bake in the oven for about 15 minutes until golden. Leave to stand for 10 minutes and then carefully lift the cookies off the sheets and serve them while they are still warm.

● The uncooked dough will keep covered in the refrigerator for 24 hours.

449

Brazil Nut Bakes

Preparation time: 15 minutes ●
Cooking time: 10 minutes ● *Makes: 18*

Here chips of smooth-tasting Brazil nuts combine with cheese to make crisp and slightly chewy cookies. Serve as cocktail nibbles.

INGREDIENTS

120 g/4 oz lightly salted butter or margarine

50 g/2 oz Brazil nuts, chipped or flaked

50 g/2 oz ground Brazil nuts

225 g/8 oz freshly grated Parmesan cheese

Salt and pepper

2 Tbsp freshly chopped parsley

Pre-heat oven to 350°F/175°C/Gas mark 4. Line a baking sheet with non-stick baking parchment.
● Melt the butter or margarine in a saucepan. Remove from the heat and stir in the remaining ingredients.
● Drop spoonfuls of the cookie mixture, spaced well apart, in 18 small mounds on the baking sheets. Flatten with a fork and bake in the oven for 10 minutes until golden-brown. Remove from the oven and push in the edges using a knife, to neaten. Cool for 5 minutes on the sheets, and then transfer to a wire rack to cool completely. Store in an airtight container between layers of greaseproof paper for 3 to 4 days.

Roast Pepper Cookies

Preparation time: 25 minutes ●
Cooking time: 25 minutes ● *Makes: 12*

These colourful cookies use three different coloured peppers, but you can use just one or two varieties if you prefer.

INGREDIENTS

½ small red pepper, seeded

½ small orange pepper, seeded

½ small green pepper, seeded

120 g/4 oz plain flour

Pinch of salt

½ tsp hot chilli powder

120 g/4 oz lightly salted butter or margarine, softened

2 tsp dried chilli flakes, optional

Pre-heat the grill to a high setting and place the peppers on the rack. Cook the peppers for 5 minutes on each side until softened and lightly charred. Cool for 10 minutes. Skin if preferred, and then finely chop the flesh. Leave to cool completely.
● Pre-heat oven to 350°F/175°C/Gas mark 4. Grease or line two baking sheets with non-stick baking parchment.
● Sift the flour, salt and chilli powder into a bowl. Stir in the peppers and butter or margarine. Using a round-bladed knife, mix to form a dough. Divide into 12, and form into walnut-sized balls. Place on the baking sheets, spaced about 5 cm/2 in apart. Flatten slightly and sprinkle each with a few chilli flakes, if using. Bake in the oven for 20 minutes until lightly golden and firm. Cool on the sheets. Best served slightly warm. Store in an airtight container for 3 to 4 days.

Herb Crackers

Preparation time: 25 minutes + chilling ●
Cooking time: 25 minutes ● *Makes: 16*

These crisp cookies can be made in any shape. They are ideal for serving with cheese, or could be crumbled into small pieces and used as croûtons for soups and salads.

INGREDIENTS

225 g/8 oz self-raising cake flour

1 tsp salt

½ tsp ground white pepper

25 g/1 oz white vegetable fat

50 g/2 oz grated hard cheese such as Cheddar or Gruyère

3 Tbsp freshly chopped parsley

3 Tbsp freshly snipped chives

Sift the flour, salt and pepper into a bowl and blend in the white vegetable fat. Mix to form a pliable dough by adding 7 to 8 tablespoons cold water.

● On a lightly floured surface, roll the dough into a 38 x 15-cm/15 x 6-in rectangle. Mark lightly into three equal segments. Mix the cheese and herbs together and sprinkle the middle section of pastry with one third of the herbed cheese. Fold up the bottom third, bring the top third down over it, seal the edges and give the pastry a half-turn. Repeat the rolling and folding twice more, to use up the herbed cheese. Re-roll and fold once more, then wrap and chill for 30 minutes.

● Pre-heat oven to 350°F/175°C/Gas mark 4. Lightly grease and flour a baking sheet.

● Roll out the pastry to a square slightly larger than 30 cm/12 in. Trim the edge to neaten and then divide into 16 equal square portions. Transfer to the prepared baking sheet and prick all over with a fork. Bake for 20 to 25 minutes until lightly golden and puffed up. Transfer to a wire rack to cool. Store in an airtight container for up to 1 week.

Fried Onion and Thyme Crackers

Preparation time: 30 minutes + chilling ● *Cooking time: 33 minutes* ● *Makes: 16*

These puffed wheat crackers are interlaced with a rich mixture of buttery fried onion and fresh thyme.

INGREDIENTS

120 g/4 oz lightly salted butter or margarine

1 large onion, finely chopped

1 Tbsp freshly chopped thyme or 1 tsp dried thyme

225 g/8 oz self-raising flour

1 tsp salt

7–8 Tbsp cold water

Melt half of the fat in a small frying pan and gently cook the onion and thyme, stirring occasionally, for 7 to 8 minutes until lightly golden. Set aside to cool.

● Sift the flour and salt into a bowl. Blend in the remaining butter or margarine, and mix in sufficient water to form a firm dough. Turn onto a lightly floured surface and knead until smooth.

● Roll out to a 38 x 15-cm/15 x 6-in rectangle. Mark lightly into three equal portions. Place one-third of the cooked onion mixture in the middle section and fold up the bottom third. Bring the top third down over it, seal the edges and give the pastry a half-turn. Repeat this rolling and folding twice, adding the onion mixture each time. Re-roll and fold once more. Wrap and chill for 30 minutes.

● Pre-heat oven to 350°F/175°C/Gas mark 4. Grease and flour a baking sheet.

● Roll the dough out thinly on a lightly floured surface to form a square slightly bigger than 30 cm/12 in. Using a 6-cm/2½-in round cutter, stamp out 16 circles; do not re-roll trimmings. Transfer to the baking sheet. Prick all over with a fork and bake for 20 to 25 minutes until lightly golden and puffed up. Transfer to wire racks to cool. Best eaten on day of baking.

Hot Herbed Mushroom Bites

Preparation time: 20 minutes + chilling ●
Cooking time: 21 minutes ● Makes: 16

**Serve these cookies straight from the oven for their
melt-in-the-mouth texture.**

INGREDIENTS

120 g/4 oz lightly salted butter or margarine, softened

50 g/2 oz finely chopped button mushrooms

2 cloves garlic, crushed

1 tsp dried mixed herbs

120 g/4 oz plain flour

½ tsp salt

2 Tbsp freshly snipped chives

Melt half the fat in a frying pan and stir-fry the mushrooms, garlic and mixed herbs over a high heat for 1 minute until softened. Leave to cool.

● Sift the flour and salt into a bowl. Blend the remaining fat into the flour and stir in the chives and mushroom mixture. Mix together to form a dough. Wrap and chill for 1 hour.

● Pre-heat oven to 375°F/190°C/Gas mark 5. Line a large baking sheet with non-stick baking parchment.

● Form into 16 balls and place on the baking sheet. Bake in the oven for about 15 to 20 minutes until lightly golden. Cool for 10 minutes and then serve. The uncooked dough will keep covered in the refrigerator for 24 hours and so this recipe can be prepared in advance.

Courgette Flapjacks

Preparation time: 15 minutes ●
Cooking time: 32 minutes ● Makes: 18

**An unusual version of this popular cookie.
Here grated courgettes are added to an oat-based
mixture and baked.**

INGREDIENTS

120 g/4 oz lightly salted butter or margarine

175 g/6 oz grated courgettes

200 g/7 oz rolled oats

2 heaped Tbsp sesame seeds

150 g/5 oz wholemeal flour

1 tsp salt

Pre-heat oven to 375°F/190°C/Gas mark 5. Grease and base-line an 18-cm/7-in square baking tin.

● Place the butter or margarine in a saucepan to melt. Add the courgettes and gently cook in the fat, stirring, for 4 to 5 minutes until softened. Remove from the heat and carefully stir in the rolled oats, 2 tablespoons sesame seeds, flour and salt. Mix well.

● Transfer the mixture to the tin, and press down evenly. Sprinkle the surface with the remaining sesame seeds. Bake for 30 minutes until golden and firm to the touch. Cut into 9 squares and then cut these in half diagonally to make 18 small triangles. Leave to cool in the tin. Best eaten on day of baking.

Soft-Bake Artichoke and Olive Fingers

Preparation time: 15 minutes ●
Cooking time: 45 minutes ● *Makes: 12*

These luxuriously moist fingers will impress guests at a party or as pre-dinner drinks are served. If preferred, replace the blue cheese with grated hard cheese such as Cheddar.

INGREDIENTS

120 g/4 oz plain flour

Pinch of salt

75 g/3 oz unsalted butter

75 g/3 oz crumbled blue cheese

75 g/3 oz tinned artichoke hearts, drained and finely chopped

2 Tbsp black olives, drained, stoned and finely chopped

1 egg, beaten

½ tsp paprika

Pre-heat oven to 325°F/160°C/Gas mark 3. Grease and base-line an 18-cm/7-in square baking tin.
● Sift the flour and salt into a bowl, then blend in the butter until you have fine crumbs. Stir in the cheese, artichokes and olives. Add sufficient egg to bring together to form a dough; reserve the rest of the egg for glazing. Turn on to a lightly floured surface and knead until smooth.
● Press the mixture into the prepared tin. Prick all over with a fork, brush lightly with the remaining egg and dust with paprika. Bake in the oven on the middle shelf for 40 to 45 minutes. Slice in half and then into 12 fingers. Leave to cool in the tin. Store in an airtight container for 3 to 4 days.

Carrot, Cumin and Orange Filo Crisps

Preparation time: 25 minutes ●
Cooking time: 25 minutes ● *Makes: 16*

Crisp, buttery filo pastry is best eaten warm.

INGREDIENTS

175 g/6 oz butter or margarine

50 g/2 oz grated carrots

1 Tbsp freshly squeezed orange juice

1 tsp cumin seeds, crushed

½ tsp finely grated orange rind

½ tsp salt

Fresh ground black pepper

9 large sheets filo pastry, (45 x 30 cm/18 x 12 in)

Pre-heat oven to 400°F/200°C/Gas mark 6. Line two baking sheets with non-stick baking parchment
● Melt ¼ stick of butter or margarine in a frying pan and gently cook the carrot with the orange juice and cumin seeds for 5 minutes until softened. Season and leave to cool.
● In a saucepan, melt the remaining butter or margarine.
● To assemble the filo crisps, brush a sheet of pastry with melted butter. Lay 2 more sheets on top, brushing with fat as you go. Spread over one-third of the carrot mixture. Prepare 3 more sheets of filo as before and place on top of the carrot. Spread with another third of carrot mixture. Prepare the remaining sheets of pastry, place on top and spread with carrot.
● From the shortest side, carefully roll up the pastry like a Swiss roll, pressing gently to seal the edge. Slice into 16 pieces and arrange on the baking sheets. Brush with the remaining fat and bake in the oven for 20 minutes until golden-brown. Cool for 10 minutes and serve.

Soft-Bake Buckwheat Beetroot Snacks

Preparation time: 20 minutes ● Cooking time: 20 minutes ● Makes: 15

For this recipe, use cooked beetroot that has not been soaked in vinegar. Buckwheat is a gluten-free grain with a deliciously nutty flavour.

INGREDIENTS

200 g/7 oz buckwheat flour

Pinch of salt

50 g/2 oz grated cooked, peeled beetroot

120 g/4 oz freshly grated Parmesan cheese

1 tsp caraway seeds

120 g/4 oz lightly salted butter or margarine, softened

Pre-heat oven to 350°F/175°C/Gas mark 4. Grease or line two baking sheets with non-stick baking parchment.

● Sift the flour and salt together into a bowl, adding any husks which remain in the sieve. Stir in the beetroot, cheese and caraway seeds. Using a round-bladed knife, stir in the butter or margarine, to form the mixture into a dough.

● Divide into 15 and form into walnut-sized balls. Place on baking sheets, spaced about 5 cm/2 in apart. Flatten slightly with a fork and bake for 15 to 20 minutes until golden and firm to the touch. Cool for 10 minutes and then transfer to a wire rack to cool. Best served slightly warm. Store in an airtight container for up to 4 days.

Mexican Potato and Chilli Bean Corn Cakes

Preparation time: 10 minutes ● *Cooking time: 15 minutes* ● *Makes: 14*

Little mounds of golden yellow corn with diced potato and kidney beans make these cookies a substantial snack and ideal lunch-box filler or tea-time treat.

INGREDIENTS

120 g/4 oz cornmeal

50 g/2 oz plain flour

2 tsp baking powder

50 g/2 oz lightly salted butter or margarine

1 large cooked potato, cubed

5 Tbsp tinned kidney beans, drained

1 clove garlic, crushed

½ tsp chilli powder

2 Tbsp freshly chopped coriander

1 egg, beaten

6 Tbsp milk

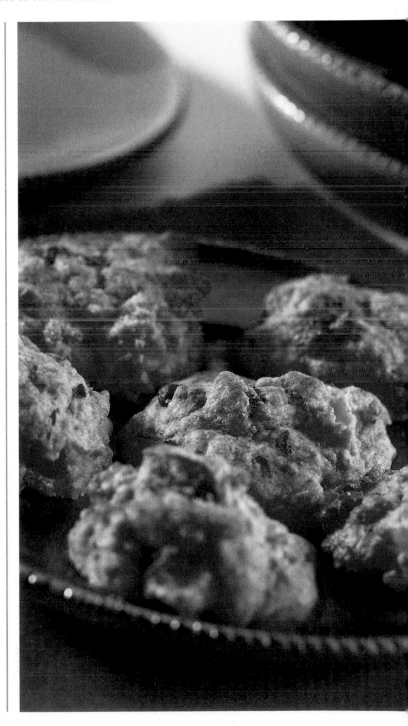

Pre-heat oven to 375°F/190°C/Gas mark 4. Grease or line two baking sheets with non-stick baking parchment.

● Sift the cornmeal, flour, baking powder and salt into a bowl. Blend the butter or margarine into the dry ingredients until well mixed. Stir in the potato, beans, garlic and coriander. Make a well in the centre and add the egg. Gradually pour in the milk, stirring until the mixture forms a thick batter.

● Using a teaspoon, drop 14 mounds, spaced about 5 cm/2 in apart on baking sheets. Bake in the oven for about 15 minutes until lightly golden and firm to the touch. Cool for 10 minutes, then transfer to a wire rack to cool completely. Store in an airtight container for up to 5 days. Not suitable for freezing.

Index